# FORBIDDEN BONDS OF AUSCHWITZ

*Book 1*

CURT O'RILEY

# CONTENTS

*" Through the veils of history, we hear the voices of those who refused to be silenced, etching a testament of resilience that echoes across the pages of time. "*

# 1

## TRANSITION

I casted an anxious look at my father, who was standing next to me. We stood on the ramp after the awful train ride, where we had been squished uncomfortably close, the stench of overheating human flesh overpowering, not to mention the human feces from persons who hadn't been able to wait until the conclusion of the trip, which had lasted several hours.

Coming from the small town of Ajka in the Hungarian mountains to the Auschwitz camp, the letters scratched onto the sides of the train carriages informed us of our location which I assumed to be Germany based on the accents.

It felt great to stretch my legs when we arrived; despite knowing this wasn't somewhere I wanted to be under any circumstances.

But I didn't have a choice.

The SS officers had ransacked the area, pointing guns at everyone who had even stepped out of place. Terrified and barely in control of my movements, I'd climbed aboard the train like a zombie, clutching my father for dear life in an effort to maintain my sanity.

We were now squeezed into an unimaginably long queue of Jewish men, women, and children, including myself. From the train we'd gotten off over an hour ago, I could barely see the two men seated at a desk for perhaps half a mile in the other direction.

Many officers surrounded us, all armed with firearms in case there were any troublemakers. I saw folks practically collapsing, whether from weariness or thirst, I wasn't sure, but it wasn't a pretty sight.

They must have been among those who had already boarded the train when it arrived at Ajka, having endured considerably more agony.

Our community was not especially large, and the people who lived there couldn't afford the nice residences seen in some of the larger cities.

We weren't exactly a mud-hut tribe, but the dwellings weren't very large or well-furnished. We typically avoided touch with the outside world since we were so high up in the mountains, but today seemed to be an exception.

There was barely any talking as a deathly stillness was over the gathering, only broken by the odd scream when someone dropped to the floor - unconscious or dead, I didn't care.

I saw a pattern in what transpired as we moved closer to the two males. There were two more lines behind them, and it was obvious who ended up where.

In the first line was a group of males and girls ranging in age from seventeen to twenty-five. In the second line were youngsters, the elderly, pregnant women, and a variety of other persons who had not been placed in the first line.

I was perplexed as to why there were two lines, and judging by the expressions on everyone's faces, neither was positive.

I held my father's arm even harder, knowing there was a good chance I'd be separated from him. He did not fit into the first group at the age of fifty-four, although I did. However, many people my age might be recognized in the second line as well. If I'm fortunate, I could be chosen for that line as well. I simply wanted to be with my father since he was the only person I had left.

I never had any other relatives. Because my mother died after delivery, I was raised entirely by my father. She had no other children before me, and my father never remarried. I could tell he was madly in love with my mother by the way he spoke about her, his voice filled with amazement as he remembered. I always wished I had met her, even if just briefly since she had to be an extraordinary person for my father to love her so much.

I had friends in the hamlet, but when we crowded into the train, we were separated, and I'd now lost contact with them.

I knew it would take a long time to find them based on the scale of the foreboding structure in front of me.

I was eventually introduced to the two men behind the desk after another half-hour of quiet.

There was no documentation or anything like that, which surprised me. Instead, there was an ashtray and several glasses of scotch on the table, since practically everyone smoked. Even though I didn't drink alcohol, I could understand what it would be like to have any form of liquid satiate my unquenchable thirst.

The men were dressed well in army uniforms, with headgears and their emblems on their coats. As he stared at me, the first seemed pompous and arrogant. He leaned forward and across the desk slightly to gaze at me closer, forcing me to naturally inch backward.

I knew I wasn't unattractive since numerous local males had courted me back in the hamlet.

But I'd never been interested. I didn't want to be married since I was just 17 years old. I still had a life left to live, or so I believed. Maybe I should have married so that I could have become pregnant and ensured a seat in the same line as my father.

The first officer rasped with a thick German accent, "She's a pretty one."

His voice was filthy, and it made me want to back up even more. But I kept my posture because I didn't want to seem weak in front of these men. My stubbornness was one of my biggest issues, and I had the feeling it wasn't going to help me in this place, based on how they had handled us so far.

The second soldier responded to the first with a small grunt.

His hat was somewhat awry, revealing some dark hair trimmed in an unusual way. The majority of the males in the hamlet grew their hair long and tied it back to keep it out of their way. This man's, on the other hand, was short and brushed over the side of his face to hide his forehead.

It fell just beyond his ears, and I had to admit that it looked great on his young face. He had to be about twenty years old and seemed extremely awkward when the first officer, who was much older, possibly in his mid-thirties, addressed him.

The second officer's gaze swept over me, igniting a distinct emotion inside me. It was still obviously unsettling; I'd never had a man gaze at me that way before in this type of scenario; nevertheless, it also created a feeling of fascination. The way this man looked at me was not the same as the previous official's; it lacked the same sleazy character as if he intended to hurt me if he could get his hands on me.

My father was still standing next to me, and when I went closer to him for the comfort, I knew his presence would provide, they began to notice him.

"In that line," the shady soldier said, pointing to the queue I knew my father would be joining.

But they still hadn't instructed me to go, so I didn't. I didn't want to become any worse than I was already.

I felt hollow without my father beside me, and the confident façade I was portraying started to disintegrate beneath their scrutinizing gazes. They started talking in German, which I couldn't even begin to interpret. I knew Hungarian since it was my first language, but I didn't understand German. I had the impression that English was our sole common language.

When they parted ways, both with blank expressions on their faces, the second officer with the gentler eyes gestured to the other line different from my father's.

I nearly objected, unable to believe I was being taken from my own family. I saw the warning glares and remained silent as I trudged towards the shorter queue. This was not before I casted one final glance at my father. He flashed me a kind grin, but I didn't see the tear that rolled down his cheek or that which rolled down mine.

I got to the rear of the line that headed inside one-half of the industrial-looking structure. I knew it wasn't just a single building complex, but it was the only thing I could see at the time, apart from the barbed wire fences and masonry walls that prevented any type of escape individuals who would have been crazy enough to try.

It was everything so gloomy and man-made that it gave me a feeling of doom. I didn't want to go under any circumstances, but it wasn't my choice. I also didn't want to get my head blown off by the terrifying firearms the troops carried.

I looked at the folks around me. They all looked frightened and were either facing straight ahead, unwilling to give onlookers the pleasure of seeing them so alone and afraid, or peeking back at their loved ones in the other line, tears pouring down their cheeks, apparent misery on their faces.

I could see one or two persons conversing with acquaintances or family they seemed to already know.

One demonstrated how many fewer persons were in one queue than in the other.

When I glanced back out of curiosity, I recognized practically everyone in the queue with my father. And when I let my eyes wander along the line, I only saw one individual who seemed remotely familiar.

I couldn't decide whether it was a good or terrible thing. All I knew was that I really wanted to be in the other line, with my father.

This line was going quickly, and I soon found myself being pushed forward by the man behind me since I was too focused on taking in my surroundings and being unresponsive with shock.

When we arrived at the front, there were two more soldiers there, handing out torn clothing for us to put on. What I didn't realize was where we were supposed to change.

I watched in dread as the people in front of me stripped naked and changed into the new clothing given.

I was virtually frozen solid when it was my time. Even though I knew everyone else had done it and felt the same embarrassment I did, it was still horrifying. I tried to persuade myself that I had to do this as I grasped the thin outfit that reminded me of a curtain or a potato sack.

It was either this or death, I determined as I observed the pistols on the officer's belts within a moment's movement.

As everyone else did, I attempted to be as fast as possible.

After witnessing the last group, I realized there would be no underpants, which made it much more uncomfortable.

It seemed like everyone's eyes were on me for the few seconds I was entirely nude. I knew no one was really paying attention to me, yet it seemed like everyone was staring at me. It just accelerated my tug on the material. It reached my knee and slightly over my breasts. They were droopy and unpleasant without any type of underwear, making me quite self-conscious. I knew I didn't have the tiniest breasts, and I felt as if everyone was just interested in my looks.

I ran onward, my feet now bare against the uneven earth, and followed the swarm of individuals with whom I had formed a group. The next station I saw we were approaching was where arms were being tattooed.

I had never considered getting a tattoo since it was deemed unfeminine, and I doubted I would have wanted one even if I were a male.

I knew it wasn't voluntary, and when I saw a series of numbers being blasted onto the skin with permanent ink, I realized it was a kind of identification.

I had been perplexed as to why there was no documentation in the first place, but I now understood. There was no need for names when a far easier method of cataloging was available.

I was curious as to whether it hurt. The victims of the tattooists made no screams of anguish, but from the looks on their faces, I could tell it wasn't pleasant - they were probably simply too terrified to convey their suffering publicly.

I took a nervous seat in front of a man clothed in the same outfit I'd seen on all the officers. The only difference this time was that he had a sharp needle with which to permanently brand me. I had my doubts about him being a professional and predicted that he didn't care if he wounded me or not.

I tried not to squirm in anticipation, and when I finally felt the cold metal on my flesh, I had to stifle a surprised scream. It felt like I'd been zapped with a hot piece of metal. I was astonished they didn't just cauterize me. It became somewhat more bearable as he walked about, but I couldn't imagine enduring seven digits. It was still hurting incessantly.

My arm was numb when he was done. I had scarcely felt the final couple of fingers since my arm had been anesthetized, unintentionally.

I examined the seven numbers that had been imprinted on my flesh.

*"0173315"*

Did it imply I was the one hundred and seventy-third thousandth prisoner in this facility? I took another glance around the frigid building, wondering how far it truly reached.

It seemed to be large enough to accommodate that many people. But why someone would want to was a more difficult question to address.

At the following stage, I was rushed through, without having to do anything except see what other people were dealing with. The lads' heads were being shaved, but I was happy to preserve mine. My naturally wavy dark brown hair, which fell down to the middle of my back, had always been a favorite of mine. Even if the rationale was that "the officers found women with long hair a commodity," I was relieved that I didn't have to shave. Some of the females with short hair had theirs cut off.

The next phase in this horrible journey was being shown our lodging. We eventually made it to the end of the building and stepped outside into the fresh air. In front of us stood a series of little huts, each with individuals who looked just like our group, except thinner and worse, resting outdoors. The cottages themselves seemed ill and frail, and disintegrating, as if a little blow of wind might entirely obliterate them.

I could see an almost sympathetic expression in the other inmate's eyes as they quietly watched us pass. I took in their skeleton appearances and begged God not to let me face the same fate.

I wanted to be back in that other line now more than ever; to have been rejected by the two officermen as a fit candidate for this group of people and to be secure in my father's arms.

Our party of roughly sixteen ladies was then taken to our own cabin; we had been segregated from the males, who would presumably have their own quarters on the opposite side of this. It seemed to be about the size of my bedroom back home, which wasn't especially enormous and was crammed full of bunk beds from head to toe along each wall. There was hardly enough space to walk around the room, but if I did get that malnourished, moving around my new refuge would become less of a burden.

I stood outside the hut when the SS officers departed and we were left alone, with the strong command not to go too far since we'd be put straight to work as soon as tonight was over.

The blazing sun pounded down on me, heating up my light skin and turning it an odd hue of pink.

I'd always burned easily and being out in the German summer heat wasn't going to be good for my skin. I was content to enjoy it while it lasted, knowing that I wouldn't be seeing it again.

I found myself blinking back tears as I watched the clouds glide across the sky, wondering how on earth I had gotten myself into this predicament. I already missed my father and worried whether I'd ever see him again. He'd been the one constant in my life, and the thought of him being gone had made me sob.

Then I heard my name called, and I had to restore my composure.

"Kamilla!"

# 2

## SOLACE

My head shot up as a loud voice traveled to my ears. I could recognize that tongue anywhere, and it gave me a thrill to know I wasn't wholly alone.

"Veronika?" I screamed, looking in astonishment as she raced over and smothered me.

"I can't believe you're here as well!"

Knowing I wasn't entirely alone in this hell hole and had at least one person to talk to had made my dreadful day just a little bit more tolerable. I still missed my father, but I was hoping to see him again soon. He'd been placed in a different line, but he had to be held someplace in this massive building.

Keeping that concept in mind provided me some motivation to

maintain my cool, if only for a little bit longer.

"I thought I'd lost you when the officers raided the village; I'm so glad I finally get to see you!" She shouted, finally releasing me from the bone-chilling grip she'd wrapped around me.

"What is your number?" She queried, making me recall that my arm still ached badly from where the needle had punctured it.

I didn't have a sleeve in the thin potato sack dress we'd been given, so I twisted and showed Veronika the seven little numerals decorated in a band around the top of my arm.

She didn't seem bothered by the fact that we'd be identified by a series of numbers rather than our birth names, however, I was enraged. Whatever made them believe they could modify how we were recognized and erase our identities was plainly incorrect. This was the name my mother and father had chosen before I was born; it was the one thing I had that was linked to my mother, and no German official, no matter how great they thought they were, was going to get away for it.

"We're only a few numbers apart," Veronika said, breaking off my mental rant.

That made me realize that almost no one in our hamlet had been assigned to this area of work. There had previously been others on the train when we were herded aboard, but if Veronika and I were thus close in number, only a select few must have been picked to enter this side of the camp.

If it hadn't been for the fact that I could have been with my father on the other side, I would have felt honored.

"That's odd," I remarked.

"So, do you know what this place is yet?"" I queried, knowing it was time to do some research.

We were under strict monitoring, and I knew better than getting on the wrong side of the guards, but that didn't stop my curiosity to figure out what I was doing here.

This was plainly not a nice place to be, and we hadn't chosen to be here, so why were we here?

I was definitely aware of the battle that was occurring around us. It had been going on for three years, since 1939, but since we were a little community, we'd escaped any direct fighting.

Hungary was an Axis power, and we were associated with Germany, Austria, and Italy, which contributed to my perplexity. We seemed to be some sort of war prisoners, yet Germany was supposed to be on our side. I could readily see that the detainees were Jewish, with the exception of a few in my vision, and this proved to be some type of explanation.

One of the primary reasons we lived in such a remote location was because Hungary's administration was filled with anti-Semites.

Being anti-Jewish had led to higher-ranking authorities labeling us as outsiders, which had an impact on our way of life.

"I'm not sure, but I've met some really nice people so far. My roommates are really nice; come talk to them with me," she said.

I let out a sigh.

Veronika had always struck me as being too hopeful. Whereas I saw the drawbacks in almost every circumstance and had to cast a gloomy eye on everything, Veronika could be optimistic, imagine the best-case scenario, and then persuade herself that was how it would turn out. I wanted to be like that occasionally, but I knew I'd be setting myself up for perpetual unhappiness if I ever got that idealistic.

"Okay, sure." I realized that turning her down wasn't the way to go about things, and I should be grateful that she maintained her upbeat demeanor, despite my developing misgivings about how we'd do throughout our stay.

Of course, I had expected us to be taken someplace terrible in the first place, but never to this level. I hadn't expected to see a happy ending as we were crammed aboard the already congested train.

Then we arrived at the camp, and my original suspicions were confirmed, and merely by the ominous mood the facility exuded, I knew this location was terrible news. But I was beginning to realize that it was considerably much worse than that.

The pictures of the skeleton folks we had seen on the way here stayed with me, continually reminding me that I would end up like them.

They were very malnourished and plainly on the verge of death. However, if I ended up like that, dying may become a tempting option.

Their clothing was much worse than the shabby ones we were wearing; it was evident we wouldn't receive a replacement, therefore I wanted to preserve this one in the best shape I could.

Their bare feet were another thing that caught my attention. I had anticipated we'd be given new shoes, or at least replacement shoes, but that had never occurred, and I now suspect it won't.

My feet were already hurting from walking on the dry, uneven ground that the camp seemed to be constructed on, and if the task we were supposed to perform entailed a lot of walking, I would be in a lot of pain.

I followed Veronika to her hut, which was two down from mine. Surveying the location, I assumed I'd be calling home for the foreseeable future, I pondered whether the broader picture matched the same as my eyes could see.

Despite the range of colors, I found everything to be drab. The continuous rows of ridiculously tiny cottages for the amount of people who were meant to live in them extended as far as I could see.

I was accustomed to cramped sleeping quarters, but this was pushing it.

Even I couldn't comprehend why there were sixteen individuals in such a little place when there was so much land around.

When we arrived at Veronika's hut, many other females were seated about, all looking dismal and miserable. When we walked in, they glanced up, and the one closest to the entrance whispered a hello in Hungarian.

Because there were so many various ethnicities here, it was easy to stick to English. I'd been fluent in it my whole life, so it was no issue for me.

I sat on the bottom level of a bunk bed near the entrance. They'd all arrived on the same train as me and Veronika, so they were as clueless as I was. I was glad for the rest, but I couldn't help but think that I wouldn't have many chances to do it after tonight.

"Where are you all from?" I inquired, breaking the stillness that was creating the mood of melancholy."

There was a chorus of deviant nations, ranging from Germany to the Netherlands to Hungary. It made me wonder how long some people had truly spent on that train, and I considered myself fortunate to have arrived at the last stop before being pushed into this desolate camp.

After determining that no one here was prepared to speak about anything other than antisocial grunts, I went to Veronika and inquired about her family's fate.

Unlike me, she had a large family that included her mother, father, elder brother, and two younger twin sisters.

They'd always been close, and I knew she'd be hurting just as much as I was, despite her outward look.

"Do you remember what happened to your family when you approached the desk with the two officers behind it?"

She made a shaky motion with her head.

"My brother was assigned to the same line as me, but they separated us from the boys, and I have no idea where he is now. My parents were transferred to the other line, but something strange happened to my sisters," she added.

I looked at her, perplexed. Everything else she told made sense, but what happened to her sisters?

Because they were so much younger, at the age of twelve, I believed they'd be placed in the same line as her parents.

"When one of the men saw them, he went wild." They summoned new troops and carried them away."

My scowl widened. What were the soldier's plans for the twins?

Who wouldn't find it amazing that Veronika's sisters were identical?

But I didn't anticipate it would make them an outlier when it came to line selection on the ramp.

I didn't want to irritate Veronika any more than I already had, so I didn't push it.

"Did your father work in the same industry as my parents?" She double-checked, knowing the answer.

The idea of my father and what he would be doing now aggravated the tightening agony in my chest. Would he be under the same suffocating conditions?

Is he missing me as well? Would he have found someone from the community as I did? Perhaps he'd located Veronika's parents, and they'd be having a talk identical to the one we were having now.

"Yeah," I said simply, not feeling the need to clarify or bring up such a sensitive subject.

I knew Veronika would be experiencing the same agony, but she was more open and eager to communicate her sentiments than I was, while I would bottle them up within and hope they would simply go away.

Veronika gave me a compassionate glance, clearly knowing the inner struggle that was brewing inside my head. I wanted to be a rebel. Losing my father made me want to yell and wail. I hadn't been apart from him for more than a day in practically my entire life, and the prospect of not seeing him anytime soon wounded deeper and was much more worrisome than the tattoo.

I wanted to get out of this horrible environment.

Even though I knew I hadn't seen half of it yet or felt even a quarter of the fear I knew I was in for, it was already the worst experience I'd ever experienced.

It was worse than when my ten-year best buddy died of typhoid when I was fifteen. Adrian had been the one person with whom I had shared everything, and his diagnosis with the horrible disease had crushed me. But that was nothing compared to the agonizing sadness I had felt following his death.

We were supposed to marry when I turned sixteen, and he was the only one I was prepared to commit to.

I had turned down any other offers following his death because I felt I owed it to him.

I hadn't loved him in the way that I'd read about. Famous authors constantly portrayed love with such intensity that I felt it was inconceivable, but if it was true, I never experienced it with Adrian. We had exchanged numerous covert kisses, but the fireworks I had fantasized about had never materialized.

I had appreciated them, as well as being with Adrian; he had listened to me and comprehended all of my concerns. When he died, I vowed that I would not give myself away to somebody I cared less about than Adrian. He was the model for all of my dream man's characteristics. I wouldn't allow anybody to take his place. No one could replace the void Adrian's death had left.

I felt it was time to get some rest, weighed down by my sad thoughts and terrible recollections. It was still early in the morning, but I had gotten used to getting up early to help my father with some chores. His back was becoming an issue for him, and he depended on me more and more.

I didn't mind since I wanted him to live as long as possible in excellent health.

I had an unexpected notion. If we were required to work in the morning, would the individuals in the other line be forced to work as well? Maybe that's why they'd separated us.

Because we were the only ones who were physically capable, the others would be employed for more mental work such as arithmetic or writing.

I exhaled deeply and rose up, extending my arms over my head, only to realize that my incredibly short dress-like garment was riding up to an even more improper area. Despite the fact that no one was looking at me, I blushed slightly and immediately dropped my arms.

"I'm going to sleep in my bed," I told Veronika, who agreed and laid down in her bed.

She'd had an equally difficult trip today, if not a more difficult one, having been separated from all of her family members. rather than the one I was missing, and I could understand how she felt.

I made my way back to my shelter, feeling the setting light on my exhausted face as it warmed my already hot body even more. I was missing my hometown and hoped to wake up soon to realize this was all a dream and reality was completely another story.

All I knew was that if this was a dream, I'd cherish what I had in Ajka much more when I awoke.

# 3

## SILENCE

The following morning, at dawn, I was woken up by a lot of yelling and an incredibly high-pitched whistle. The sun had only just begun to rise in the sky and seeing without the help of lights was difficult.

I'd slept in the dress because I didn't want to be completely nude under the thin cover we'd been given. Despite the fact that it was warm during the day, it was much colder at night, and even though I'd kept my clothing on, I was shivering, and goose bumps covered my skin.

Despite my internal complaints and desire to shut my eyes and fall off into another deep slumber, I raced along like everyone else, anxious not to stand out.

Another factor which influenced my hasty action was the presence of two SS officers at the door, one armed with a rifle and the other with an unceasing whistle.

I realized I didn't have any shoes after hastily looking around for them. That lowered my nil enthusiasm even further, and the frown on my face became even deeper.

I nonetheless raced out the door with the other females in my dorm and soon found myself in a chaotic queue with many other hut prisoners.

I noticed Veronika behind me, but I was too afraid of the authorities who were already inspecting the queue and attempting to arrange it to go back to her, so I opted for a wave instead. That wasn't too difficult with the prospect of getting shot hanging over everyone's heads.

Veronika, on the other hand, didn't seem to mind and started forcing her way through the diminishing throng, making her way towards me. She was halted in her tracks, however, when a general purposefully stepped in front of her.

I could watch every gruesome detail of what transpired as he questioned where she thought she was heading from my vantage point.

I was frozen in place as she pointed to me and smiled sweetly at the man, apparently unaware of the terrible predicament she was in. Disobeying any of these men's commands was a horrible idea, and Veronika was a fool to believe otherwise.

The hulking man who had stopped her from going any farther turned around till his horrible face met mine. Before returning to Veronika, he offered me a sleazy smirk. He had smacked her across the face in one swift stroke. "You don't do anything unless you're told to," he said harshly, before returning to his spot on the line.

Veronika staggered and then rose erect after being struck sideways. She didn't dare to glance up and meet my gaze, but the drop of water that trickled from her face and onto the ground didn't escape my notice.

I had realized that this environment was nasty, but not so horrible that I would face violence if I stepped out of line - literally. That concept frightened me even more.

What would happen if someone did anything substantially wrong if such a simple act resulted in such severe treatment?

I'd assumed the weapons were just a show of power, designed to intimidate us, but I now realized they were for much more, and I wouldn't be shocked if I saw them used.

I trudged along in the now-organized line of people, wondering where we were going.

Perhaps we'd be working on the section of the camp where my

father was stationed. Even catching a glance at him would be enough to reassure me that he was safe. I knew I wouldn't be that fortunate, so I didn't get my hopes up.

We were stopped after approximately five minutes of walking, and an officer in front of us started ordering us about and dividing us into groups. We approached a desk and were advised to walk one of two ways, just as when we initially came.

I recognized a pattern in who was going where and assumed Veronika would be in my group. The second line was mostly made up of males or powerful women.

People with physical strength were picked, while the rest of us were sent to the front lines.

While I was completely healthy, my small physique didn't carry much muscle, therefore I was passed over for the second line. But I wasn't disappointed since I was dreading the prospect of physical labor.

When we arrived at our destination, a small but broad gray structure, we were directed to congregate around the chief officer who was issuing orders. He was wearing glasses and was holding them in his hand.

"You will be separating the glass from the metal. It might hurt your hands, but you won't complain," he said as he led us into another room.

The scene in front of me took me completely by surprise. A big mound of different sorts of glasses was against the wall, with something like troughs arranged in pairs around the perimeter. I recognized them as the locations for the rims and lenses. However, there were no chairs, and I doubted we'd be permitted to sit. I was curious how long we would be working for since I wasn't sure how long I could stand.

My thoughts immediately turned to my father. He'd been wearing an outdated pair of spectacles and was as blind as a bat without them.

How would he be coping if they had taken it away from him?

I suppose there was no use in removing them from someone who couldn't see without them, for what good was a virtually blind person to these men? I also noticed that no one in our company wore glasses.

He exited the room after assigning each of us a station. That didn't mean we were alone; there were still a few additional officers scattered throughout the room, standing against different parts of the wall.

As I surveyed them all, I noticed a variety of looks. From the small and plump-looking males to the tall and powerful ones. Even when everyone was wearing the same uniform, it was simple to tell who had particular attributes.

I'd only seen a few troops up close enough to recognize their faces, but one of those present today stood out.

It was the same soldier who had greeted us when we originally arrived.

He was standing against the wall with his back straight and his arms folded behind him. I could see his revolver holstered at his side and the way his hat was slightly askew on his head, displaying a smidgeon of his brown hair that I found weirdly appealing.

Despite his tight stance, I could see his eyes darting across the room. They didn't simply pass by when they got to me, and our gazes met in an intense look. He didn't simply survey my physique and smile appreciatively; his stare didn't even leave my face.

Just like the previous time, it piqued my interest, and I wondered why he was staring at me in a manner that none of the other troops seemed to be capable of. His gleaming gray eyes penetrated me, yet they were not harsh like the others'. He didn't give me a sleazy or sinister expression, in fact, just the reverse. His expression was almost empathetic.

I averted my gaze when I realized I had to be working. Slacking off would almost certainly result in some type of punishment, and I wasn't as prepared to be backhanded as Veronika looked to be.

So, I got to work on the time-consuming task at hand. I took up a pair of glasses and thought about how I should approach the work at hand. After much deliberation, I chose to proceed in the most traditional manner. I tried to get the glass out of the rims.

To my absolute amazement, it just came out and landed with an almost unintelligible thud on the floor. I picked it up and shrugged before dumping it into the proper trough, then repeated the process with the second lens. It was equally effective, and despite the gloomy circumstances, I found myself smiling. At the very least, doing the assignment without too much difficulty will make it a lot less of a strain.

My legs were starting to hurt after what had to be a couple of hours.

I also realized that my strategy wasn't nearly as flawless as I'd assumed. I now had many tiny lacerations on both hands and one on my arm.

I'd gotten it when one of the lenses I'd been trying to remove fractured and splattered everywhere, including my arm.

It wouldn't have been so bad if I'd stopped working and just rested my bloodied hands, but that wasn't an option. Instead, I'd continued, worsening the gashes, and widening them while also producing new ones.

I wasn't sure how long we'd be working, but I hoped we would be done soon.

My first problem was, of course, the dull pain in my hands. The second issue was the concern for my legs; about having to hold my weight for such an extended period of time. I wouldn't have been so upset if we could have done this sitting down, or even on the floor.

That wouldn't have remedied my third issue, which was an increasingly full bladder. Only one individual had requested to use the restroom in the last half hour. She'd been cautious and shy while inquiring about.

It was obvious no one was going to the restroom after suffering verbal abuse and having a set of glasses hurled in their face.

The men who had been assigned to work in this area had just urinated on the floor, with no objections from the authorities. It had proven to be far more difficult for females, who made up the bulk of us. To my chagrin, I had seen a couple of people kneeling on the floor and satisfying their demands.

After another hour, I was relieved when the general who had given us orders returned to the room.

My stomach was growling uncomfortably loudly, and I was

certain that everyone could hear it. Going by the malnutrition of the emaciated bodies, which hadn't entirely been erased from my consciousness, I was only anticipating inadequate meals, if any at all.

I found myself in yet another queue when I arrived at the long-awaited restroom. Everyone seemed to need to use the restroom, and I'd be fortunate if I even had a chance before we were forced to decapitate some more spectacles.

I almost retched in disgust when I finally made it to the restroom. Unlike at home, this was unmistakably a public restroom. There was waste all around the seat and no paper to be found. I watched it in horror and was tempted to just urinate where I was working since it seemed more hygienic.

I crouched about an inch over the seat and relieved myself, deciding not to embarrass myself so openly. I was itching to sit on the seat, just to give my legs a break, but I would rather collapse from the pains than sit on that sickening, awful excuse for a seat.

I departed the little cabin it was in, feeling embarrassed and horrified that others could believe I'd contributed to the filth in the toilet. There were still a lot of people in line, and I felt sorry for the ones who wouldn't be able to utilize it.

I was ecstatic when I saw the other primary attraction that

everyone had flocked to. The sight of water being dispersed around the workers made my dry throat even drier. I dashed over to where it was being distributed.

The precious liquid was being served by the same soldier who had caught my attention earlier, and I patiently joined queue.

I assumed everyone had taken water and then ran off to the toilet, but I would rather be thirsty than humiliate myself by going to there in full view of everyone else, particularly the young officer.

When I got to the head of the line, the young officer's eyes assessed me before pouring some water.

"There you go," he said, his strong German accent wrapping around me as he spoke with unexpected kindness.

He had also seen my wounded hands and had given me a worried look. It made something warm develop within me simply knowing he didn't look at me with disdain as many others would.

"Thank you," I said, giving him one more look before turning around and allowing the next person their turn.

When they turned back, I observed that they had much less than I had.

I immediately drank some, allowing the cold liquid to trickle down my throat as I sighed in happiness. I needed that drink, and despite my still rumbling stomach, I was feeling a little better.

I returned the bottle that had been containing the water to the now-unoccupied soldier after I had finished the last of it. I offered it to him fairly nervously and was taken aback when he gave me a stunning grin.

"Danke Schön," he said in German, the words I dimly recognized as "thank you."

I returned his cautious grin and ran back to my workstation. We barely had approximately five minutes to relax before being hustled back to our allocated positions and pressed to finish removing the pairs of glasses.

We'd been granted another five-minute break by the time it became dark, this time with the extra advantage of a moldy slice of bread to feed our starving tummies. I was now dead on my feet and yearned for the uncomfortable bed I was presently occupying.

I tripped a number of times as we walked back to our lodging. I would surely be sleeping comfortably tonight, perhaps without interruptions. Working a ten-hour, nonstop day had taken its toll on me, and I wasn't sure whether I'd be able to handle it for much longer.

As soon as I returned, I sank into my bunk, listening to the other females grumble about their miserable day. However, we had a unique instance in our hut. One of the females had been identified as a physically capable one and had been sent to the second line, which had not assisted us in disassembling glasses all day.

As a result, the other females were grilling her viciously about what she had done all day, figuring she had it easier than the rest of us.

When she finally revealed what she had been up to, we were all startled into silence.

# 4

## SHADOWS

When we arrived at our destination, an officer explained to us what we were expected to do," she shivered at the recollection, and I anticipated she would reveal something horrible.

"He told us; we'd be carrying...dead bodies."

I couldn't help but let out a startled cry as I stared at her incredulously. I had anticipated some torturous physical labor, such as shifting bricks or dragging large materials, but I had no clue the heavy stuff would be human flesh.

She shuddered in disgust as she relived the events of the day in her imagination, disgusting pictures no doubt occupying her mind.

"We had to carry them to the crematorium, where they were

thrown into a furnace," she stopped, sobbing.

"There were children," she said, shivering as one of the girls drew her into a kind embrace.

As she shared that information, I found myself stunned. Sure, I knew this place was awful, but murdering children was going too far. To begin with, I was perplexed as to why there were so many dead corpses in the first place.

When we initially arrived, I saw the malnourished convicts, but that wasn't enough to result in so many dead, and they weren't children. My thoughts immediately switched to the other camp. Were they treated the same as we were over there? Being fed in small quantities and confined in tight quarters. I trembled as I pictured my father in the same condition.

Despite his age, he was a strong man who would be alright for a few weeks, but I didn't want him to suffer. If it came down to it, I'd prefer he died than go through such a debilitating condition.

The girl was still weeping into another person's shoulder when I figured it was time for me to sleep. I didn't need to stay up all night knowing that there would be more arduous work for me to complete in the morning.

I needed all the rest I could get here, and I knew it.

Nonetheless, despite my knowledge and logic, I found myself lying awake while everyone else slept. I watched as everyone gradually made their way to their bunks and settled in. Everyone was now dead asleep and completely ignorant of their surroundings. But I couldn't shake the uneasy sensation that something was really wrong.

So, I stood up nearly hitting my head on the terribly low ceiling and crept down the shaky ladder without awakening the girl sleeping below me. Apart from a little creak when I eventually reached the floor, I tiptoed out to the entryway after what felt like the most perilous voyage I'd ever had.

It hadn't been completely closed, so I could peek out without risking anybody waking up and scolding me.

When my legs started to hurt, I pushed the door open, disregarding the excruciating shriek it produced for a short second. I looked around the room cautiously, looking for any disruptions but finding none.

I felt myself hugged by the outer world after slipping through the little crack I had created. The weather wasn't ideal, but it was warm enough for me to go outdoors in my light dress. The moon had risen high in the sky, lighting the surrounding region, and enabling me to view the enormous stretch of industrial-looking structures on each side of me.

I could almost make out a mountain rising over the complex in the distance if I strained my eyes. It was enough to tell me that we weren't on another planet and that we weren't in a bad version of Earth. It also served to remind me how small I was in all of this, as well as how secluded we were here. If the closest recognized element of the natural world was that far away from me, I was in a horrific other reality.

Back in the hamlet, we'd been surrounded by nature.

Because we were so high in the mountains, we were surrounded by trees and tiny plants and frequently depended on them to sustain our way of life. We lacked some of the most advanced technologies since we were so far away from any major civilizations. As a result, little things like rivers and plants became necessary for survival and a decent quality of life.

It felt weirdly unnerving to be apart from any genuine nature. I'd often gone to climb a tree on the outskirts of Ajka. I'd always liked climbing trees and the exhilaration of being so far up. This tree had been extremely difficult to climb, with limbs extending so far out that I didn't know which ones to trust, and which would send me tumbling.

I'd taken it on since I was always up for a challenge and was keen to go near the top. I'd finally done it, excluding the occasional scrape and gash.

I'd struck home and grabbed the top branch, allowing a sensation of accomplishment to wash over me.

It had been a shelter for me after Adrian's death, and I used to climb it when I wanted to be alone, knowing that no one else would have a chance in hell of reaching me at the summit. I could use a tree like that around here. The only difference here is that anybody underneath me would get a clear view of my womanly bits.

I sighed, but it was quickly followed by a yawn as I covered my mouth out of habit. There was no one present to witness my manners, so it didn't really matter. My assertion was proven inaccurate, however, when I saw someone approaching me.

I figured he was another prisoner like me until I saw the cap on his head. I attempted to escape back inside my tent, hoping that the officer hadn't seen me. I didn't need an SS officer determining that I deserved to be punished in some terrible way because I'd been outside my hut when I was meant to be in bed. But I was never so lucky, and his loud German accent cut me off.

"Wait!" He didn't really command but requested.

His voice wasn't forceful, but it seemed as if he was asking me not to move.

I remained still, regardless of whether he was kind or not. In any case, I was scared that if I moved, a pistol would be drawn on me. I didn't have faith in anybody, particularly a German officer. I held my breath, waiting till he informed me I could leave since he didn't remove any kind of firearm from his person. He simply kept approaching me without saying anything. I was astonished as recognized him while he approached.

It was the same young officer who had given me additional water earlier in the day. When he arrived within talking distance, near but not too close, he gave me a little grin that appeared to lift my spirits despite the darkness. Apart from Veronika, who was generally much too cheerful, I hadn't seen a single smiling face since I arrived. That wasn't including the wonderful grin this same man had given me only this morning, which had brightened my day tremendously, and even though it was just a modest smile, it was enough to elicit a comparable one from me.

It was only now that I realized how much taller he was than me.

He towered over me, making my little body seem inconsequential. He had to be about six feet tall, yet that didn't disturb me. Indeed, it appeared to enhance his appeal, as did his physique.

"What brings you out here so late?"" He enquired rather than scold me, as I had anticipated.

He appeared really interested, and I imagine he didn't see many offenders loitering outside their accommodations when they might be sleeping peacefully.

I shook my head. "I couldn't fall asleep. This is a lot to take in," I stated, hoping not to offend anybody and wind myself in even more trouble than I was already in by being here.

This man seemed to be kind, but I wasn't expecting much.

He let out a sigh. "I know. I can't believe they're doing this at all. It's horrifying," he said, leaving me gaping at him, stunned.

"But..." I mumbled, unable to make a coherent phrase.

Someone who worked here, someone who was meant to be protecting the law, agreed that what was going on here was horrible.

If he believed that, why would he work here?

"However, you work here!" I eventually spoke, unable to conceal my astonishment and interest.

"Not by choice," he said.

I lifted an inquisitive brow at him. However, before answering, he gestured to the step I was previously sitting on, implying that I should sit down. I sat down as he had asked and smoothed out the sack slung around me.

"My father worked against Hitler," he said as he sat down next to me.

"He didn't believe in his rule or the way he judged individuals. He was a member of the Abwehr and was involved in one of the assassination plots against Hitler. He was apprehended, taken prisoner, and subjected to what I can only guess was excruciating torment. As his son, I was immediately labeled a traitor. However, I was permitted to demonstrate my patriotism by enlisting as a soldier. If I had refused, I would have met the same end as my father," he added, glancing away from my eyes and lowering them.

My first instinct was to dismiss him, to label him a coward for even being a part of this and refusing to experience the pain in order to demonstrate his devotion to his father.

"I know was a wimp. I couldn't do it, I couldn't put myself through that torture," he grumbled as if he could read my thoughts.

He sounded almost as if he was speaking to himself rather than to me. When it came down to reality, and I attempted to put myself in his place, I pondered how I would have handled the scenario.

I loved my father more than anybody else in the world, but could I consign myself to death, and suffer such horrible agony as a result of it? Or would I also do the cowardly thing? Refuse the suffering but join something I loathe and betray the person who was my sole family.

"I know why you did it," I finally said after some thought. "I'd do the same," I admitted.

His head shot up and he glanced at me with interest.

"Why? What I did was inexcusable," he said.

He clearly felt bad about what he'd done, but he made no move to make amends now. If he really wanted to, he could simply approach the troops, tell them he couldn't handle it any longer, and even prevent the torture by shooting himself with the pistol in his belt. The fact was that he hadn't convinced me that he was as terrified of death as he claimed, no matter how dire the implications of remaining alive were.

"Well, accepting your own death would be difficult, especially given the agony that would undoubtedly accompany it. I don't think I could make that decision knowing what was going to happen," I stated.

I was still trying not to say too much. This soldier may seem to be giving me the truth, yet whatever he said might have been a lie. Apart from Veronika, I didn't trust a single soul in this place, and this officer was no exception.

He just shook his head.

"You're too understanding," he said,

"And I almost wish you'd tell me how much of a coward I am. I should immediately grab this gun and point it toward my head. I feel like I've earned it."

I glanced across at him, and our eyes met. I could see the regret in his eyes, and I believed him at the time. I believed what he'd just stated without even thinking about it. The look of shame on his face couldn't be manufactured, and if it could, he should be an actress instead of a soldier.

I paused before addressing the question that had been bothering me since I'd attempted to sleep.

"May I ask you a question?"

He glanced up at me, trying to figure out what kind of inquiry I was going to ask. He probably thought it was about his father, but it wasn't.

"Sure."

"This girl in our hut," I said, motioning to the structure behind me, "she says she spent the day carrying...dead people."

An uncontrollable chill ran up my spine at the notion of doing something so heinous.

I saw the officer's face blanch, and he averted his gaze once again. He confessed, "She's telling the truth."

That wasn't exactly what I was looking for, but I'd already determined that she wasn't lying. What I was most curious about was who they were and why there were so many of them.

He was plainly attempting to dodge the issue, and although I knew I shouldn't push my luck, I couldn't help but try.

"Who exactly are they?" I queried hesitantly, my sentences longer than usual as I feared a negative response.

"I don't think you'll want to know that" he said solemnly.

I cocked my brow. "What's the harm? Isn't it horrible enough that they're dead?"

"It's dreadful and so much worse than that," he shook his head.

"I...I don't want to tell you," he said.

I locked my gaze on him. "What's the harm?" I demanded, scowling, and entirely forgetting my position.

"Don't I have a right to know?"

It was now his turn to sneer at me.

"Don't you think you should control your tongue?" He snapped, which startled me for a few seconds.

As he yelled the order, his voice was rough and icy. It made me realize that he'd probably been working here for a long and was more accustomed to dealing with the convicts harshly than I'd thought.

"Anyone but me would have abused you in some form for simply being outside this late."

I kept my mouth shut but couldn't get the frown off my face. I knew I shouldn't have said anything; to be honest, I had become much too comfortable in his presence.

If I had been that dumb in front of any of the other officers, I would have gotten a red mark on my face, and maybe more.

I had to keep my mouth shut and remember that I was not in a welcoming environment.

He gave me a more compassionate glance.

"I don't want you to get hurt and being too comfortable around the Schutzstaffel is not something you should become."

I recognized the full German term for SS, but it was seldom uttered since it could be condensed to two letters so simply.

"If you do, it will end up being bad for you and I don't want you to get hurt."

That comment, spoken with such earnestness that it made my heart throb, was not something I expected to hear from a German anytime soon. To be fair, anyone's mouth. I'd already decided that I wasn't going to visit my father anytime soon, and I was too afraid to talk with Veronika again without risking harming her or myself.

"Can you tell me your name?" I questioned, abruptly shifting the tone of our talk to something much more conversational and lighter. I was tired of feeling tense all the time. Aside from that, I was quite anxious to learn what his name was.

"Lukas," he said, gently smiling as he caught my gaze. "You?"

I'd anticipated him to know my name for some reason, but I wasn't sure why. My number was the only kind of identity I had here. I carelessly stroked my arm, where the tattoo stood out against my pure white skin.

"Kamilla," I said, my Hungarian accent becoming stronger as I stated my name fluently.

He said softly, "It's a nice name."

Before we could say anything further, another shadow could be seen in the distance. I knew it was an officer, so I got up immediately, Lukas followed suit.

"I'd better go, and you should go inside," he said quickly.

"I hope to speak with you again, Kamilla."

The way my name slid off his mouth in his thick accent made my pulse beat rise slightly, and I wished he'd repeat it again.

Then he dashed away, no doubt to go back to work on the task he was meant to be performing when he noticed me.

I obeyed his instructions and entered the hut, not caring whether the squeaky door awakened my roommates; all I wanted was to get away from whatever was coming.

Thankfully, I was safe, and no one so much as stirred in their bunks. I raced up to my bunk quickly and fell asleep almost instantaneously.

Speaking with Lukas had been enlightening in more ways than one.

# 5

## GRATITUDE

I spent the entire day going over everything Lukas had said to me the night before, understanding his choice more and more each time we spoke. While this was a lot more fun than popping the glasses out of the frames, it did result in a lot more scrapes and gashes than yesterday.

Unfortunately, I didn't see Lukas while I was working and was only given a small amount of water compared to what I was given yesterday. I knew it was terrible for me to want to see him, but I couldn't stop myself. In some ways, I understood it was only fair and that I shouldn't be treated any differently than everyone else, but it didn't stop me from wishing I had more.

A few mouthfuls were insufficient to carry me through the day, particularly in the oppressive heat that appeared to have blanketed the camp.

My thoughts returned to the girl who had detailed her harrowing day lugging corpses.

Was she going to do it again today? If she was, it made me worry about where they were obtaining the corpses from once again. Maybe yesterday was an exception, and it was simply corpses that had accumulated over a few weeks. That would still be horrifying, but it would be marginally less so. She hadn't said anything about them being rotten or anything, so I can't suppose it's true. In any case, it was horrible, and I prayed she wouldn't be compelled to do it again.

By the time we finished working, I was completely out of breath and stumbled a number of times on the way back to our hut. There was no way I could live if this continued. I would not only degenerate psychologically but also physically.

I still longed for my father. I hadn't gone more than a night without him in almost 10 years, and I couldn't picture not seeing him again anytime soon. I questioned why someone would be so nasty as to divide towns, even families, and put us in such deplorable circumstances.

I knew it was an anti-Semitic institution, but even with such prejudiced ideas against Jews, I couldn't understand why we should be kept in this hell hole. We were subjected to forced labor, which was most likely the major reason we were imprisoned in the first place.

My father's cell was packed with less physically competent prisoners, which I viewed as a positive indication since they didn't have to participate in the strenuous tasks, giving them a better chance of survival. They weren't being pushed to exhaustion before being released, so I had high expectations for my father's survival. If one of was to die, I would choose myself above him.

Despite my exhaustion, Veronika approached me and asked me to join her back to her hut so we could catch up on what had transpired thus far.

She still seemed joyful, which astonished me given my sour expression. Veronika has always been a cheerful girl, but I don't see how anybody could retain their cool in this situation.

She had gotten a bottom bunk bed, but I had gotten a top bunk, and so I could sit on it comfortably while Veronika sat next to me. Even though it was still little, we fitted just fine with our legs crossed.

"Did you have a good time popping glasses out of specs today?" She asked cynically, beginning a discussion.

As a response, I extended my hands for her to see the multiple gashes that covered them.

They were really uncomfortable, but I was able to bear them to some extent. I realized I'd have to grow accustomed to the discomfort.

"I think it's pretty self-explanatory that I hate glasses."

She laughed, and if I had the energy or considered it hilarious, I would have joined in. I didn't, and so I sat there looking gloomy.

"So, what have you been doing at night? Is there anything noteworthy? The people in here are actually really nice," she said, gesturing around to the few other individuals who hadn't left the hut to go someplace else and were conversing in small groups.

I shook my head, but then remembered the night before, how I had spent most of it chatting with Lukas. Given the circumstances, it was both educational and fun. I almost wished I could speak to him tonight, but I knew that wasn't going to happen. I should have been satisfied with just one talk with someone who wasn't Veronika, not that I despised her company. I should not have been attempting to converse with an SS officer who had the ability to aim a pistol at my head if he so desired.

"No, I've mostly slept and worked since I arrived. That's the life," I said cynically.

It was pointless to pretend to be pleased when I plainly wasn't. She let out a sigh.

"I know this place is horrible and disgusting, and I miss my family, but if I get too depressed about it, I'll lose it."

"I'll give up hope of ever seeing them again, and I won't even try to survive in this place," she added.

"I see what you're saying. I do, but I can't do it. I can't act as if I'm pleased when I'm not. I wish I could, but..." I trailed off, unable to fully express what I was trying to say.

I wanted to pretend to be clueless and that everything was good, but I couldn't. I was too realistic to do that. I hadn't allowed any of the pain or agony that was crawling around inside of me to overwhelm me yet, but I couldn't promise that it wouldn't happen soon.

"Well, I guess we all cope with things differently." That's what she said.

I agreed by nodding. "Yeah, you cope with them better than me."

She laughed, but I couldn't force myself to laugh along with her.

"So, have you seen any attractive officers?" She was curious.

I gazed at her incredulously, but my thoughts kept returning to Lukas. He looked stunning, even down to his hat, which was worn askew on his head.

"Are you sure, Veronika?" I asked.

"They're keeping us imprisoned in here, and you're wondering if I've checked them out?"

"Yesterday morning you were smacked, plus, they're all sleazy," I snarled, remembering the numerous officers' eyes roving over my small figure.

She seemed surprised by the venom in my voice as I remembered the soldiers who were keeping us captive.

"I understand," she conceded.

"Besides, I've only ever seen one worth looking at. He's approximately twenty years old and has dark hair."

I realized she was talking about Lukas right away and tried not to show it. It wasn't that I didn't trust Veronika; it was just that she was notorious for talking about anything to anybody, and if I recapped our late-night conversation, it would no likely have spread across the camp by tomorrow. I didn't want to bring him into trouble, so I kept that information to myself.

"You mean the one who chose which line we took on the first day?"

"I guess he was okay, but he's still carrying a gun and is probably perfectly willing to point it at our heads," I said.

She gave a nod. "I know, but you've got to admit that he's

handsome."

For the first time since I'd come, I smiled. It was pointless to denying it.

"He's quite attractive," I agreed.

We both laughed to ourselves, which reminded me of how we used to be. We'd been extremely close friends in the village, often chatting about weird things and overall having a nice time. We'd spend our days spying on boys in Ajka and giggling hysterically as we narrowly dodged them. It was shocking to imagine how childish we'd been only a few months before.

But I'd grown up a lot since then, and I knew that if we got out of here alive, nothing would be the same as it was before.

"Hey, I heard that someone in your hut was assigned to a line that wasn't dismantling glasses; I'm curious about what she's been up to." "I hope it wasn't something simpler than us," she grumbled.

I opened my lips, ready to tell her what they'd been up to, how difficult it was, but then shut it again. Veronika had managed to maintain a cheerful demeanor, avoiding the dread and gloom that had already started to consume me. Should I destroy it by telling her what was actually going on here?

I didn't know all the specifics, including who the dead were, but I knew enough to know that this location was worse than I could have imagined. I didn't want to drag her spirit down by bringing this to her attention.

"I'm not sure. She hasn't spoken much about it. She has really kept to herself." I lied.

I didn't enjoy lying to people I cared about, but it was for the best. I knew she would find out eventually, but I was content for her to have her innocence for the time being.

She seemed dissatisfied. "That's unfortunate. Around here, I could use some gossip."

I rolled my eyes at her folly but couldn't say anything further because the door burst open and two officers stormed in, one of whom I immediately recognized as Lukas. He wasn't as forthright as the other, and he retained the same awkward aspect that he appeared to have whenever he did something aggressive.

"The curfew is on! Back to your own huts, immediately," the haughty officer said, staring around the room.

Uncomfortably, I rose up and moved closer to the entrance, where the two guards stood. I realized I was the only one who had relocated and was unsure of what to do.

They were blocking the exit, and I couldn't go by without asking them to move. I was much too apprehensive to do so, and I was terrified of the repercussions, so I merely stood in the center of the tight room, uncertain of where I should position myself.

Unfortunately, it drew some attention, and the officer, whose name I didn't know, leered at me. "What are you doing there? Will you return to your tent or not?"

He ordered, his voice icy as he swept his gaze over my body, pausing on my legs and breasts.

I didn't dare to speak, so I nodded instead, moving ahead and fully expecting them to just let me pass so that I could return to my own hut.

I hadn't gone far when the officer grabbed my arm and stopped me dead in my tracks.

I winced as I tried not to fight his vice-like hold. His nails dug into me, no doubt drawing blood, and I shuddered but did not attempt to flee. I didn't want to further irritate him. He hissed, "You didn't answer my question."

I moaned, "Yes."

He pushed his claws further into my skin, and I squealed in agony against my will.

"Look at me when I'm speaking to you."

I turned my head, so it was now facing him. As I took in his animal-like features, his face was a picture of rage. As he retained his grip on my arm, his eyes were filled with wrath. He'd thrown me backward before I could react, sending me flying into Lukas.

He immediately assisted me up, and I moved away from him. I thought it heartwarming that he hadn't even considered the repercussions before reaching out to aid me. The officer didn't appear to enjoy Lukas's display of devotion though. He told him to punish him.

As he stared at the commanding officer, Lukas's expression was filled with terror.

"What? How?" He inquired, still a little taken aback.

I deduced that he hadn't dealt with the detainees in a violent manner before and that this was something he had particularly wanted to avoid.

"I'm not sure!" he said, frustrated.

"Slap her or something. Just let her know she has to know her place around here."

My eyes widened as I looked up at Lukas. My arm was numb with anguish as I waited for Lukas to hands on my face. He caught my gaze and lifted his hand to slap me in the face.

I closed my eyes and braced myself for the agony.

But it never did. Lukas lifted his other hand at the last second and smacked it instead of the vulnerable skin on my face. The sound of striking palms echoed across the room, and I thought I heard Veronika gasp.

The officer apparently hadn't noticed that he never really hit me, for which I was thankful. I forced tears to fall from the corners of my eyes and immediately brought my hands to my face, attempting to conceal the fact that there was no red mark there. But I didn't leave without saying a quiet 'thank you' to Lukas. I had to at least attempt to express my gratitude to him for not hitting me.

I kept my head down and fled the room, clutching my cheek and making sure the officer didn't see my uninjured face.

Lukas had just taken a huge risk by not hurting me. If the general had seen his evasion, he would have been punished. He just had to smack me, nothing serious, and I wouldn't have cared if he had carried it out to protect himself.

It wouldn't have hurt that much, and I didn't want to endanger Lukas by treating me too nicely.

As it was, I was immensely thankful to him for sparing me from additional pain that night.

# 6

## REBEL

I struggled back to my hut after another hard day at labor. I wasn't prepared for the danger of going to visit Veronika. I'd put Lukas and myself at risk by doing so, and it wasn't something I wanted to repeat.

Veronika was apparently foolish enough to risk her safety; after a few minutes of lying on the bottom bunk next to mine, she walked over and sat beside me.

"Are you okay?" She inquired hastily.

She hadn't seen me all day, and I could tell she'd been dying to ask that question since last night. All of her pent-up anxiety was building up.

I reassured her, "I'm fine."

"But he slapped you really hard!" she wept, making me flinch, hoping that she would take my wince as me recalling a traumatic memory rather than the genuine cause.

Lukas hadn't really struck me, but he'd been convincing enough that Veronika believed him.

She reminded me, "And there was blood running down your arm."

Whereas there was no evidence of Lukas's phony slap, I had a clear cut on my arm from the older soldier's gouged nails. It had bled for a long time, but I'd wrapped it in the thin blanket we had to sleep with until the blood flow stopped. It was starting to scab up and wasn't as painful anymore, luckily.

I shook my head. "It wasn't so bad." I noticed a little red mark on my arm before going to bed, but that was all. "I think it sounded harder than it was."

I tried to be reasonable, but I also didn't want to cast Lukas in an unfavorable light.

"I didn't think that young officer was all that bad, but that has definitely convinced me otherwise. Everyone in this place is evil," she shouted, letting her rage show.

The harshness in her voice made me grimace. It hurt to hear her speak about Lukas in that way when he'd done nothing wrong. He'd shielded me despite knowing it was a bad idea.

It made me feel awful that I was making Veronika dislike him by protecting her from the truth.

As I tried to defend him, I tried not to seem too kind; appearing like I was on his side would only create additional suspicions.

"He didn't really have a choice, I know he wouldn't want to disobey that man," I reminded her, holding out my arm.

"I know what happens when you don't do exactly what he commands."

Veronika shuddered as she took in another terrible slice. "I guess so. But he wouldn't have chosen this job in the first place if he wasn't willing to obey directions," she pointed out.

I tried not to grimace since it would reveal how irritated I was that she was guessing how he was.

"Having said that, I will assume that every other soldier in this camp is a war criminal unless proven otherwise. In this instance, instead of being innocent until proven guilty, it is guilty until proven innocent."

"Good point," I acknowledged, my jaws clenched. Even though I should have, I wasn't going to reveal how I felt about it or how much more I knew than she. It would be a betrayal of the faith Lukas had evidently placed in me if I revealed his secrets to the loudest-voiced prisoner here.

"Have you figured out what the other line is up to yet?" She queried, abruptly shifting the topic.

"I'll still be jealous if they're doing something less strenuous than dismantling glasses."

I grimaced and shook my head. I'd been concealing more and more secrets recently, and it wasn't a habit I enjoyed. I'd never been good at lying to others, but I could do it when it came to protecting others.

This was one of those times.

"When are we going to see the other side of the camp again?" She then inquired, utterly perplexing me.

I honestly felt she had realized by now that we weren't going to see them again - ever. That was something I was still coming to grips with. That time I saw my father may have been the final time I saw him.

It also came with the realization that he would suffer alone. I knew it had been difficult for him when Mom died, and he'd only barely managed to raise me.

But now he was alone again, and he was going through the anguish of losing two people, something I wasn't sure I could bear. This was difficult enough.

Hopefully, he'd run across someone he knew from the hamlet. Ajka may be a little town, but if I'd discovered Veronika, I couldn't see why he couldn't find someone he knew as well.

Having said that, more individuals were being picked to go into his side of the camp, which meant it would be much more congested and he would have a much lower chance of recognizing anybody.

"Veronika..." I stumbled, wondering how to approach the matter. Despite the awful circumstances we'd been put in, she nevertheless seemed optimistic and full of life.

"I..." I had no clue how to break it to her in a way that made it seem better than it was.

"I don't think there's a nice way to tell you that you'd never see your family again."

Veronika averted her gaze from mine. "I know," she mumbled.

"I realize I'm being silly. Everyone here is aware of the truth. I will never see them again. They'll work us up until we look like the skeleton creatures we saw coming in, but I have to try. Knowing I'll never see them again is killing me, Kamilla."

I drew her into a warm embrace. Veronika, with her numerous family members, was losing so much more than I was, and yet she was so upbeat. I was still perplexed about what had happened to her two younger sisters, but I knew I'd never find out.

If the officers here were interested in twins, they had the ability and authority to ask questions about it.

I, on the other hand, had no one to pose my inquiries to. Even Lukas had refused to answer my questions.

I saw tears streaming down her cheeks as we leaned back again. I hadn't shed another tear since I'd spoken my goodbyes to my father or rather mouthed them.

It wasn't that I didn't have something to weep about; I could certainly break into tears right now at the horrifying predicament I was in. It was because I didn't want to waste my tears. There was no use in allowing myself to get even more angry by expressing how I felt. I was able to maintain some kind of calm by sealing them up and keeping everything contained. It seemed like a darker version of what Veronika was doing.

We didn't say anything since there was no need to. My embrace demonstrated how much I cared about her. I didn't mind being her shoulder to cry on when she couldn't stand it any longer since I appreciated the comfort just as much.

I then realized that a few individuals returned to our cabin. It must have gotten to the time when the officers started gathering us up and sending us back to our huts.

I didn't want Veronika to face the same fate as me, so I hurried her to rise.

"You should go back, people are starting to move," I said, gesturing around the hut at the large crowd that had gathered.

Veronika made the same sweeping motion that I did. "You're right, I don't want any injuries by tomorrow." She nodded her head.

"I'll see you soon," she promised before exiting and returning to her own hut.

I sighed as she hurriedly left the hut, avoiding every other person. Our cabin was now packed, although there wasn't much conversation. Everyone was seated on their assigned beds and looked to be as deep in contemplation, as I was. And there was a lot to consider.

Everyone else seemed to have concluded that we were locked up here till it came to the worst possible end as well. They realized there was no way out, that we were stuck here till we died.

That had exacerbated the mood even more if that was possible, and I knew I would be watching the breakdowns soon, even after just a few days.

The door burst open like it had done the day before, and I automatically cowered down in my top bed, where I had retreated. I peeked over the side and saw the same two officers. Lukas, as well as the hostile older man.

"Officer Elias, make sure that every varmint here is in their proper hut," he said, motioning to Lukas, whom he must have been referring to as "Officer Elias."

He took a tentative step forward inside the small room, moving from bunk to bunk, simply gazing at everyone.

He had a good view of the tattoo imprinted onto their flesh since most folks were still on the bottom bunks. Because that was our sole form of identification, it was evident that was what he was looking for.

I was on the final bunk, being the farthest away from the entrance and hence the last on his journey.

When he got near me, he looked up and appeared to realize I was there just then.

He'd kept his eyes downcast at the front, avoiding staring at anybody, particularly his commanding officer.

I was taken aback as he reached out and gently touched my arm, drawing it down so he could see the seven little numerals engraved on my arm.

His touch on my arm was gentle, almost caressing. He didn't treat me aggressively, as his supervisor had, and it seemed almost relaxing. It also caused goosebumps to appear on my skin as I attempted to battle the blush that was about to appear on my cheeks. I didn't want to come out as a stupid young girl who found a gentle touch on the arm appealing.

He let go after barely a split second. I didn’t miss his turning away from the easily angered soldier in front of me and whispering three simple words to me.

"Are you okay?"

The earnestness in his words forced me to smother a grin.

Aside from Veronika, he was the only one who had shown even a smidgeon of sympathy for me, and I was moved by that.

I gave him a modest nod of the head, telling him that I was as good as he expected me to be given the circumstances. He gave me the biggest grin he could muster before turning around and heading back towards his supervisor.

He didn't dare to look back at me, but I could tell by the simple question he'd asked me that he cared significantly since he hadn't given anybody else such preferential treatment - and I'd been watching him very carefully while he'd been approaching me.

But it wasn't the only thing he'd been doing for me. When we were given rations at work and he was the one distributing them, I was usually given a little larger share.

Whereas everyone else got two mouthfuls of water, I got five. Whereas everyone else would receive a half-slice of bread, I'd get a whole one, with somewhat less mold than everyone else's green crumbs.

It was the simple things that made me realize he cared, at least a little. For all I knew, he might be doing be same thing for other individuals when he handed them their rations, but I wasn't going to question it while I was still unaware.

In addition, I saw that he was often staring at me. When we were working, the soldiers positioned themselves against the wall so that they could see all of the workers.

One would sometimes approach, getting closer and hitting individuals if they didn't seem to be deconstructing quickly enough.

But Lukas never did anything like that. Not that I was expecting him to. He appeared more passive than everyone else, which I assumed was because, unlike the others, he didn't want to be there.

All I could hope for was that they didn't finally convert him; by making him think that what they were doing was correct.

# 7

## DESOLATION

As each shard of glass bore through my delicate fingers, I could see drops of blood falling to the ground. With displeasure, I murmured a Hungarian swear word under my breath. If I continued being negligent, my hands would be inadequate for removing these glasses, I thought to myself. The only challenge was that we had to be fast to avoid being penalized, which was difficult to do while still avoiding harm.

When I looked around at the officers lined up against the wall, I immediately recognized Lukas. His pupils were dilated as he gazed straight ahead, ignoring those of us who were working in front of him.

I couldn't blame him for not wanting to upset his eyes with our slowly wilting frames. We were not a pleasant sight to see.

A loud cough jolted me out of my reverie, and I focused my attention on the little girl beside me. She seemed to be sixteen years old and much frailer than I was. Obviously, owing to Lukas's additional meals, I was in somewhat better physical condition than the others, but this girl looked to have suffered much.

She let out another harsh bark, and I sympathized with her wholeheartedly, particularly as a soldier approached.

I immediately found myself getting distracted with the most recent of spectacles. If I was found slacking off, I would be severely reprimanded along with the other few I had observed avoiding their responsibilities. I did watch the conversation from the corner of my eye, unable to suppress my interest.

The gruff soldier said sternly, "Stop coughing, girl."

He was short, but his girth compensated for his lack of height, his stomach bulging from his waistband in an unflattering manner. His expression was harsh, and it was clear he was one of the officers who wasn't hesitant to use his authority over us detainees.

"Yes, sir," the girl groaned before bursting into yet another bout of intense coughing and sputtering.

When she was done, a horrified expression crossed her face, and she fidgeted anxiously, knowing that something terrible was going to happen. And she wasn't wrong.

The officer had stretched his hand and smacked the vulnerable girl in less than a second. Not the type of slap Veronika had received, which, although hard enough to hurt and bruise, had not been delivered with full force. This hit knocked the fragile girl off her feet and left her sprawled over the floor.

I halted, raising my head from the glasses I was meant to be dismantling, and waited for her to get up and move. But she never did.

She simply laid there, motionless. Her face lay on the dusty floor, her lips slightly parted. A red mark was plainly apparent where the soldier had inflicted his palm on it, and as I looked up, I realized that he seemed content - almost proud of himself. I felt like throwing up. He motioned for all of the authorities to come around him and see.

When I saw Lukas, he gave the sense that he didn't want to go look, that he knew what was going to happen and was hesitant to watch it.

When he finally made his way forward, he opted to stand as near to me as he could. He gave me a reassuring look, but he didn't seem overjoyed. In fact, he seemed pallid from realization. I maneuvered slightly to have a better view of what was going to happen, not daring to get any closer to the scene for fear of being wounded myself. I realized it was probably a stupid move on my part, that I didn't want to see what was going on, but my curiosity got the best of me, and I couldn't stop myself.

I watched as the man who smacked her stepped forward, putting her arm up and looking for a pulse. My heart sank as I saw his disappointed expression. She could be dead.

"She's alive," he said, his tone indicating his displeasure. Why would he want to murder the poor girl? She was still a baby! That in itself demonstrated the kind of monstrosities operating here, individuals who want to murder.

"What should we do now?" One of the officers gathered around queried.

"Should we return her to her hut and send her back to work tomorrow?" He proposed.

The officer who had started it all shook his head with an evil smile returning to his face as he moved around the girl's drooping figure. He smirked and waved his hand dismissively in response to the officer's advice.

"This girl is far too sick to continue working," he said, motioning to her gaunt frame.

"She's useless now."

"So, what are we going to do with her?" The same officer

inquired.

In an instant, the man withdrew his revolver from his belt and shot the girl in the head.

"Sorted," he said, dismissing the group and returning to his position on the wall, letting the other troops follow.

But I couldn't take my gaze away. I was wide-eyed and terrified as I witnessed the blood that streamed from her now-disfigured skull. Because I was so near, the wound was a disaster, gushing significantly more blood than I had anticipated.

I sat beside the puddle of blood around her, and tears welled up in my eyes. He'd taken her life in an instant. He had no regrets, no regard for what he'd done, no remorse. He didn't mind that she was someone's daughter or even a sister. He'd just killed her. She was murdered.

And now that I'd seen, I couldn't take my gaze away. My gaze was fixed on her, and I realized I was in shock. The terror, as well as the dread, I was feeling were unimaginable. Even though I realized I was putting myself in danger by continuing to look, I couldn't stop myself.

With one look away from the now-dead girl, I saw Lukas was the only other officer still standing away from the wall. His look revealed that he, too, was as surprised as I was, yet was dealing with the same issue. He couldn't take his gaze away from her.

When he performed the same thing as me, we both looked shocked. It informed me even more about how he felt about how people were treated here than I already knew. I got the idea that he'd never seen something so heinous, so terrible before, and he was as astonished as I was.

Then he seemed to gain his grasp of reality and the circumstances we were in. He made a subtle motion to the glasses in my hand, reminding me of what I was doing. When I looked around at the other convicts, I saw that everyone was doing exactly what they were supposed to be doing, dismantling glasses at breakneck speed. Of course, most of them were pale, shivering, and crying profusely, but they persisted. Not like me.

In anxiety, I attempted to resume my task, tearing my focus away from the mutilated corpse in front of me and returning it to the glasses in my hand. Lukas, who had been the one to remind me of my responsibility in the first place, appeared to have remembered his, as he returned to his position on the wall.

His complexion was a much darker tint now, and I realized that this girl's murder had touched more than just myself and the other convicts.

What made matters worse was that I could only address her by the number plainly visible on her pale and motionless arm.

* * *

Veronika shuddered at the news I'd just delivered.

"And he just killed her?" She asked.

I shook my head. "No, she was already on the ground. He just finished the job," I said coldly.

Veronika had been in another hut today, performing the same task, but at a different location. That merely demonstrated to me that there were more deaths here than I had previously assumed. The sheer quantity of eyeglasses in my own building had terrified me, but another one full of them? That was incredible. Who was to say there wasn't anymore? Rows of buildings might be filled with the same number of glasses, symbolizing an increased number of fatalities.

"I can't believe it," Veronika said at least three times since the start of the discussion.

"And you happened to be right next to her when it happened?" She reiterated what I had already told her.

I fought the immediate impulse to roll my eyes at her infantile behavior, but then I realized it wasn't the right circumstance for such a careless gesture. This was a dangerous situation. More than serious, in fact. I knew this would haunt me and stick with me for the rest of my life. It was one of those experiences that one could never forget.

"Yes," I said quietly, having recovered from the shock and panic that had held me when it occurred. "I was right next to her."

"This might sound selfish but I'm glad I wasn't there," she said.

I nodded. "I wish I wasn't there too, but in a way, it's definitely taught me a lesson," I told her.

"It reminded me how much I really don't want to be here, that's for certain."

I wasn't going to convey the several realizations I'd had earlier since I wasn't very good at expressing myself. I was able to manage my own thoughts and emotions without having to share them with Veronika, who was the polar opposite. She had always told me how she felt, and always confided in me, but I kept everything to myself.

Veronika nodded in agreement. "And for that reason, I almost wish I had been there."

It struck me as odd to see Veronika so solemn. Back in the hamlet, she'd always been the cheerful one, the one with the bright personality who made everyone happy. Despite my evident melancholy to everyone around me, Adrian managed to bring some brightness into my life even after his death. But now I could see how this was affecting her.

I was certain that this was wearing her down, and the melancholy expression in her eyes had just appeared since we'd come. I could read the painful glances she cast periodically, examining the neighborhood with paranoia. She was hurting, no matter how hard she tried not to show it.

She departed as people started to leave, knowing it wasn't a smart idea to push her appearance tonight. Not after the happenings of the day so far.

I figured it would be best if I went to bed immediately to get rid of the horrible sensation I'd acquired and got some much-needed sleep. As I climbed into my bunk, I let myself drift off to sleep.

* * *

I awoke from sleep, startled. My mind had evidently decided that sleep would not be an option for me tonight, as pictures of the weak girl's dead corpse scattered over the floor and gushing blood haunted me. As I had suspected before, this was not going to leave me immediately. This would disrupt my sleep for a long time.

I got down quietly, unable to lay in my bed any longer, suffocating myself with the low ceiling that was barely inches from my head and the little blanket that still seemed to limit my movements. I snuck out to the rickety stairs that I'd visited just a few nights before, away from the sleeping folks.

However, I would be more cautious this time. I wouldn't let an officer see me; instead, I'd go inside and appear to sleep, so that if anybody came to check, they'd never know it was me. My strategy, I believed, was infallible.

I let my mind wander, to my father, to the atrocities perpetrated today, and even to Adrian. But none of them could lift my spirits. In fact, they caused it to fall even further. No doubt, my father would be suffering in the other camp as well. What had occurred today couldn't be made any better, which was evident even before I started thinking about it.

Adrian was another. When I needed a short pick-me-up, the memories I had with him always made me happy. But today, I couldn't even conjure up the happy recollections. All I could think of was the awful anguish I had felt upon his death. When I compared it to my current sadness, I discovered that it was a close second. I wasn't sure which one affected me the most, and I was already certain that things couldn't get much worse for me here.

I'd been so preoccupied with my thoughts that I hadn't even spotted the approaching figure, a fatal oversight. Alarmed, I sprang up and tried to flee back inside. The soldier beat me to it, grabbing my arm and spinning me around, just as I was ready to grasp the door and open it.

The grip was neither possessive nor unpleasant or furious. As a result, I assumed Lukas had tracked me down.

When he turned me around, I found myself considerably closer to him than I had anticipated. He was towering over me, but not in an unpleasant manner; rather, I felt secure with him, which was dumb in my opinion. But I couldn't help myself.

My nose was virtually brushing his chest, so when I raised my head and glanced up timidly, I was much closer to his face than I'd imagined, but I wasn't complaining. His beautiful eyes reminded me of the girl being shot today, and how he looked just as repulsed as I did.

And, for the first time since the morning's events, I shed a tear. I'd been too startled to cry for this girl whose identity I didn't even know, but now I could, hopefully to an understanding Lukas.

He lifted a hesitant hand and wiped away a stray tear from my face, leaving tingles where he'd touched my skin. It had the opposite effect of what he had meant, since I erupted into full-fledged sobbing now.

As an involuntary response, I took a step closer and buried my face in his chest, wrapping my arms around his body to stifle the cries from my lips for fear of being caught. He stopped for a second, evidently taken aback by my daring gestures, but then he appeared to realize what he was intended to do and returned my embrace, his hands firmly resting on my waist.

I sought his consolation and after what seemed like an eternity, I managed to clumsily draw back. That was absolutely wrong of me, but I couldn't stop myself in the heat of the moment. I wanted him to reassure me, even if it was only by holding me gently as he had.

"Sorry," I said, mortified.

With a tiny grin on his face, he shook his head. "It's ok. I think I needed it as well," he said. It was only then that I saw his still disturbed expression. He, too, couldn't get the picture of the girl out of his thoughts.

He took a step away from me, but only to take a seat on the steps we'd shared a few nights before. I took my spot next to him without even looking at him. We sat in comfortable silence for some minutes, simply mulling over our ideas.

"I'm sorry you had to see that this morning," he apologized as if it were his fault that I'd seen the atrocity.

"There was nothing you could do about it, besides, you didn't want to see it as much as I also didn't, so I could be saying the same to you," I said.

"Well, that's fine." A little tilt of his lips indicated that he was pleased by my explanation. His posture was more relaxed now, and he sat somewhat forward, as opposed to how he sat throughout the day, with his back straight and trained to attention. His hat, on the other hand, was still slightly awry in his typical stance, displaying a wisp of brown hair from behind it.

"How do you believe my father is doing?" I inquired abruptly. My mind had been on him for most of the day, and this may be my last chance to receive some form of truth from someone.

Lukas's expression became uneasy and guilty, and I understood what it meant.

"Kamilla..." He trailed off, briefly taking my focus away from the objective at hand. Something about the way he pronounced my name made me feel warm inside. His German accent, which I should have despised, just added to how wonderful my name sounded in his mouth. "I don't know if I can tell you the truth," he said.

I took a breather, knowing that I needed to persuade him that he could.

"Why?" I encouraged him to continue, to at least provide a tidbit of knowledge to me.

"Because I don't want to hurt you."

As much as it moved me, it wasn't a satisfactory response. "I'm hurting because I don't know the truth, because I worry about him every minute of every day. Just tell me, please." I implored, hoping he'd realize how important this was to me.

He murmured something beneath his breath in his native language that I couldn't understand. He suddenly grabbed my hand.

"Kamilla," he called out again. You are right, you do deserve the truth," he said.

"But you can't tell anyone else," he said with his eyes fixed on me.

I opened my mouth to ask whether I might inform Veronika, but he interrupted me, saying, "No one. If people found out, I'll be killed for having told you."

That put things into perspective for me, and I blanched. Under any circumstances, I didn't want to be held accountable for Lukas's death.

"I'm not going to tell anyone," I promised firmly. This seemed to be additional knowledge I had to keep to myself.

"Your father is dead," he replied flatly, his eyes showing how much he despised saying it.

The shock of this knowledge hit me hard, and if I had been standing, I would have stumbled backward as if he had punched me.

Dead? No. Never. It was impossible for me to believe. I'd been fooling myself that I wanted to know the truth, but this had entirely altered my mind. I'd rather live in blissful ignorance than be aware of the fact that my father was no longer among the living.

Lukas extended his hand in genuine support, but I fixed him with an icy stare. "Don't touch me," I said as I drew away from him.

It wasn't that I blamed Lukas; it was only that I needed to keep my cool and resist falling into his comfort. I would keep my cool and ask him what I truly wanted to know. However, the expression on his face made me feel somewhat bad.

"How did he pass away?" I gasped out, trying to ignore his bleeding face as much as I could.

Lukas groaned and turned away. "He was gassed, along with everyone else who went into the same line as he did." He clarified.

My surprise became stronger when I considered the wider picture. This wasn't only my father; hundreds, if not thousands, of people, were killed because of some strong racial belief. "Everyone?" I said again. And to think I wanted to work there as well.

In some ways, I still wanted to. I wouldn't have to deal with all of this then. I wouldn't have had to face the fact that my father had died. I wouldn't have had to suffer through starvation and thirst, see the atrocities committed here, just to perish in the end. It would have been a lot simpler.

"I'm sorry," Lukas said, his eyes indicating how serious he was. But I couldn't accept it yet; I had to keep pushing.

"Would it have been easy? Or would he have had to suffer?" I pleaded with him to tell me more.

This was the key question I was looking for an answer to. I could accept it if it hadn't been painful, and he hadn't suffered. I tried to accept that it was all for the best. That if he had lived, he would have suffered, while a painless death would have been better for him - he wouldn't have even noticed.

I noticed Lukas's uncertainty at the time, and I knew the answer before he spoke it. He'd been debating whether or not to lie in order to save my emotions, but in the end, he did what I asked and told me the truth.

"It would have been unbearable," he said sadly.

"It took about twenty minutes for them to die in the chambers, as their skin turned different colors. Many patients were foaming at the lips and bleeding from their ears. I can't even imagine-" He paused, unwilling to continue.

I couldn't stop the sorrowful cries from leaving this time. My facade had entirely crumbled, and I was nearly motionless on the floor. Lukas hesitantly rubbed my back, but it didn't help.

I was filled with anguish, which only became more when I realized what had happened to Veronika's parents, and to everyone else's family who had survived this long. It was heinous.

"I'm so sorry," Lukas said quietly.

I just barely managed to keep my cool enough to convince him that it wasn't his fault, because it wasn't. He was just the messenger, and he couldn't change that. "Thank you for telling me the truth" I said.

He stared at me as if I were insane. "What made you want to know that?" He inquired, perplexed.

"Because I wanted to know." Sure, it may have dimmed my view on life even more, but I now know for certain.

"There will be no more deliberation," I reasoned.

Lukas's expression softened with comprehension. "I was the same way with my father. I was appalled when I discovered what they'd done to him, but at least I knew. It had me guessing what he'd gone through for hours."

It was weird how we had experienced similar events. Lukas could relate to me since he'd lost his father to the atrocities that occurred here as well; hearing that was probably much worse since Lukas's father had been tortured and suffered far more than mine had.

I wiped my eyes hurriedly, attempting to remove the tear that had formed on my cheeks.

"I'm sorry about what happened to your father," I said solemnly.

Nobody deserved that fate, particularly for doing nothing wrong except standing up for what was right.

When I die, I would want it to be for a noble cause as well, but trapped in this hell hole, I know it would be a useless death.

# 8

## UNVEILED

Trying not to seem excessively guilty while denying any knowledge to Veronika's questioning was becoming more difficult.

"I just want to know what happened to my parents," she murmured a faint trace of desperation in her voice.

I understood exactly how she felt, down to the last emotion. She was terrified, sad, and enraged. I'd been there and knew what it was like to wonder where your family was and what was going on with them, but I'd found out now.

Like when I withheld knowledge of what the girl transporting corpses was up to, I was withholding this information for a cause other than the fact that Lukas had made me swear not to tell anybody.

Veronika, despite her flaws that were suddenly visible, was doing a far better job of keeping cheerful than I was. She remained hopeful, attempting to make the most of a bad situation.

This realization would be the last straw for her. Knowing she'd lost her parents, permanently, would cause her to lose the upbeat attitude she'd developed, and I didn't want that for her.

As well as the obvious reason that I didn't want her to suffer any longer than she already had since I was her friend, and I wouldn't want that for her - or anybody else.

No, I had selfish reasons for wanting her to be psychologically stable.

Veronika was one of just two people who kept me sane here. Having someone to speak to and trust kept me almost balanced. She was there when I wanted to gripe, when I needed to voice my disdain for the numerous individuals here. Without it, I'd let even more hatred fester within me until it drove me over the line. I knew I wouldn't be able to survive without Veronika's assistance.

Sure, Lukas was assisting me, but it wasn't enough. I only saw him on rare occasions, and even then, it was a significant risk. I couldn't bring myself to be entirely honest with him since, although I trusted him, I couldn't promise anything in this situation, which was reasonable.

No, I needed Veronika to keep me standing.

"I wish I knew," I said, trying to be as nostalgic as possible. I also attempted to hide the agony that was building up inside of me. I was aware of my father's whereabouts. He was a mound of ashes, like hundreds of others, dispersed in some forgotten area. He was one of countless people who had been slain needlessly, for no reason at all.

"And I'm still curious about what happened to the twins, that was really strange," she said, her expression contemplative but still irritated.

I didn't have to disguise my expertise in responding to the question since I didn't have any knowledge. However, I could absolutely agree that it was unusual. I had my doubts that anybody would be treated like a president here, but that looked to be the case.

"I've no idea."

I couldn't conceive of any reason why the twins needed to be separated if they were going to be slaughtered regardless. If such was the case, they would have been placed in the line to be gassed.

No, even I could see that there was something strange going on. These officers had strong feelings either for or against twins. It was something I'd have to discuss with Lukas. If there was anybody I could acquire information from around here, it would be him.

I wasn't sure I wanted to know what was going on with them; I was sure it would be just as horrible as what had happened to my father, if not worse if that was even possible.

"Did anything unusual happen while you were at work today?" She abruptly shifted the topic of the discussion. It had been two days since the girl was cruelly gunned down, yet nothing noteworthy had occurred since then.

It had been precisely the same as usual. Lukas was once again overseeing us and giving out meals today. I assumed he was compelled to do this rather than having a choice like the others since he didn't have as high a ranking as the others.

He'd given me a far larger piece of everything, which I had to keep hidden from everyone else.

While everyone else was starting to deteriorate, I was still just slightly malnourished than when I came.

"Nope, everything was as it should be today," I said to Veronika sadly. Even though I would never wish anyone's death, it seemed awful to declare that this was as things should be. Nothing like this should ever happen. Everything was off.

The scuffling of individuals scurrying back to their own shelters drew my attention, and I gave Veronika a worried expression. "Come on, you need to go back," I said hurriedly. I gestured towards the door, almost expecting someone to burst through it and chastise us when Lukas carefully opened the door.

My expectations were not far off. He was alone today, which was unusual, so there was no animosity in his look or behavior.

We locked eyes in a second, generating a shudder up my spine from something I couldn't quite describe. He moved his gaze away from me after giving me an almost unmistakable grin, so as not to draw attention to myself.

"Has everyone returned to their huts?" he checked, his German accent enveloping me and coloring his words. It was something I found curiously appealing. It enhanced his deep, almost gruff voice.

I pulled Veronika, who was visibly scared, up and motioned for her to return to her own quarters.

However, I could understand Veronika's fear. The last time this occurred, I got a ' slap' from Lukas, so Veronika assumed he wasn't scared to hurt any of us.

I, on the other hand, knew differently, and thus I wasn't frightened to make Veronika move. She just wanted to go back before anybody else came in and harmed her.

Lukas took in her weak shape as she moved towards him and then she scurried out the door. I didn't blame her for not even looking back. I would have been sprinting as quickly as I could as well.

I thought it humorous that when Veronika emerged unscathed, many more individuals had the confidence to move and return to their own huts. A wry grin emerged on my face, and I found myself fighting back a tiny giggle.

Lukas captured my attention, as well as my delight, with a little grin on his own face. "I just came around to inspect the bunks," he said before proceeding.

He rapidly reached my bunk after peering over every top and bottom bunk. Unlike everyone else, he came considerably closer to me and had a lot more attentive stare at me, not the bed.

"Are you alright?" He nearly mumbled incoherently.

I managed a modest nod, not wanting to draw attention to myself by speaking too loudly.

"Good," Lukas said, just loud enough for me to hear. "Well, sweet dreams, Kamilla."

I felt the same goosebumps as he shouted my name, but I tried not to speak but responded by giving him a nice smile and assuring him that he should really be going by now, having already spent at least twice as much time here as anywhere else.

We exchanged one more little twist of the lips before he was gone, leaving the hut and most probably going on to the next.

I sighed and returned to my bed. All I had to do now was follow his advice and sleep well.

But in this hell hole, I didn't believe it was going to be easy.

* * *

"May I ask you a question?" As we sat next to each other in front of my hut, I asked Lukas my query. These late-night meetings had become something of a habit for us, as well as one of the few respites from the horrors of the day.

Lukas was apprehensive once again, which I could understand. "I guess," he said grudgingly.

I knew he was anticipating me to ask him a question to which he wasn't meant to respond, or to which he didn't feel comfortable responding. And he was right, since I wasn't making a normal inquiry.

"What is it about twins that fascinate people here?" I ventured to ask.

In some ways, I wasn't anticipating a response. He'd been reluctant to tell me about my father at first but had ultimately caved in since it was directly tied to me. This, on the other hand, was not about me. It was all about Veronika. I owed it to her to find out, even if I hadn't told her the whole truth to begin with.

He hesitated, but unlike the knowing, but hesitant look he gave me the last time, this one was filled with sheer bemusement.

"I have no idea," he said, and I could tell he was saying the truth.

I cocked my brow slightly. "No hints at all?" I double-checked. He'd have to know something. Even if he just understood a few specifics, he couldn't be wholly unaware of what was going on here.

He thought about it, then shook his head in disbelief. He repeated, "No. The senior officials, the men in charge, they always tell us to keep an eye out for twins. That if we find a pair, we will be rewarded. But they've never fully articulated why they were obsessed with twins.

Obviously, no one dared to be curious, since one is more likely to be punished than rewarded in here."

I exhaled and delicately tapped my fingertips across my cheek. Something really unusual was happening there.

"That's not right," I thought out loud. "There's something really not right about that, considering where we are."

Lukas gave a nod. "You know, I've never actually considered it before.

"That only makes me feel worse. It occurred just once, witnessing twins, two females, maybe twelve, thirteen?"

I frowned when I realized who they were. "Twelve," I said glumly. So Lukas was the one who had sent Veronika's sisters into the unknown, as was the case with twins.

Lukas cocked his brow. "Did you know them?" He queried, looking even more guilty.

I explained simply, "Veronika's sisters."

"I'm sorry," he seemed to be saying this to me a lot recently. I wasn't sure how I felt about it. I didn't want his apologies or pity since, although I understood he was partially at fault for everything that was going on here, he was also a victim. He didn't have to be here tormenting people psychologically and physically, but I knew he was in pain as well.

I tried to keep my cool and waved him off.

"What became of them?" I inquired, asking him to continue the story he was telling.

"My colleague, whose name I can't remember, went to fetch someone, and then the twins were taken away. I didn't see where they were taken, but it wasn't into either the concentration or extermination camps."

Although I had never heard the terminology used properly, I could surmise that this side was concentration and my father's side was elimination; after all, it was the best way to characterize his death. It wasn't a compassionate killing, and there was no justification for the manner he was slain. It was total annihilation.

"So there's no way of finding out about them then," I deduced, mildly disappointed. But at the very least, I could claim I tried. I'd done all I could, no matter how little. That helped me feel a little better.

Lukas nodded, his face contorted, as if the guilt was being directed internally. "Unless I can snoop around and see what I can find. There are a lot of rooms I've never been in before, and I'm sure I could plan an expedition around them." He offered gallantly.

But I quickly shook my head. "No, you can't risk it," I said. "You've already put yourself in danger for me, so that's going too far. I wouldn't be able to forgive myself if you got in trouble because of me." I said openly.

Lukas fixed his gaze on me. "You shouldn't even care what happens to me," he pointed out, still staring at me with interest.

I averted my gaze, unable to maintain eye contact and hesitant to confront the reality that was developing inside me.

"You've risked so much for me," I told him.

"You've helped me so much since I've been here, I couldn't possibly want anything to happen to you now."

I felt the heat rise to my cheeks as I spoke something I'd only ever thought about. Despite the fact that I didn't even describe half of my feelings, it was more than I had intended to express. Lukas, on the other hand, had been a tremendous help to me, and it was only right that I should have feelings for him now. It's impossible to get such affection from someone and then expect to detest them; it simply doesn't work that way.

When I looked back up at Lukas, his gaze was no longer questioning; it had taken on a tender tone, as his eyes shone with something I couldn't quite name.

"I don't want to get hurt, but for a good cause like this or you, I'd definitely be more willing," he said, a little grin showing how sincere his comment was.

I was still perplexed as to why Lukas had shown such an interest in me in the first place, but I couldn't say I was complaining. Anyone would be blessed to have him looking out for them here, and he and Veronika were the only things that could possibly make my day brighter.

The level of honesty in our chat was somewhat unsettling, but I couldn't take my stare away from his. It was so full of emotion that I wasn't sure I'd ever seen something so genuine.

The only other time I'd seen a countenance full of real emotions was when Adrian was dying.

He laid down, clearly in his last moments, and then grasped my hand. We were absolutely alone, and he simply stared at me, his face slightly distorted with anguish.

Then he broke the stillness with three words I hadn't anticipated from him.

"I love you," he said almost incoherently, before coughing violently and grimacing in what I can only imagine was excruciating pain.

I'd plainly never heard the words uttered to me before, save by my father, who definitely meant it in a different manner than Adrian, who was certainly intending it in a different way.

He wheezed again, jolting me back to the fact that these were his dying minutes. Of course, he'd chose to confess to me now. When I didn't have time to consider a sensible reaction.

I was at a loss for words, but as he laid there, staring at me with such hope, I simply smiled and tried to seem as passionate as he did.

"I love you, too," I lied, tears streaming down my cheeks.

It wasn't that I didn't love him; I did. As my best buddy, I adored him since he was always there for me. But I wasn't in love with him the way he was with me. But I couldn't tell him that since he was going to lose his life at such a young age.

No, it was preferable to lie in order to make him feel better, at least while he was still alive. Although lying to him made me feel bad, telling him I didn't love him would have killed me. I couldn't live with myself knowing I'd crushed him like that only minutes before he died.

When I spoke the words back to him, his whole face brightened, gaining such a relief and happy expression that it reaffirmed my choice.

Then his expression darkened once more, and he sank backward into another sputtering fit. Only after this one was over did he grasp my hand to let me know he was ok. He didn't give me a modest grin that was both painful and happy at the same time. There was nothing there. Only his serene face, which didn't move in the least. He was gone.

As I returned to reality, I saw the dampness around my eyes. I avoided recalling that memory for the simple reason that it made me weep every time.

I missed Adrian all the time, but I'm happy he's not still here to suffer through this environment. His strength and youth would have guaranteed him a spot on this side of the camp, which meant he'd still be alive today, but instead of deconstructing glasses like me, he'd be dragging dead corpses. Not something I would wish on anybody, save maybe the heinous individuals who were imposing it on us.

A smooth hand resting on my shoulder jolted me out of my present state of mind. It was difficult for me to stop thinking about Adrian once I got started. He was such a sensitive subject for me.

"Are you all right?" Lukas queried softly, extending his arm a step farther and wiping the tears from my most likely scarlet, eyes with his thumb.

"I was just thinking about someone I used to know," I said, trying not to let my voice tremble as much as it wanted. I didn't enjoy displaying my weaknesses in public, and Adrian was certainly one of them.

"Would you like to talk about it?" He wasn't interrogating, simply providing assistance. He had no idea how to assist me until I told him what I was thinking.

Our statements of emotions were long gone, but I realized that I really wanted to tell him. Considering the perilous circumstances, it wasn't conceivable that I would be around for much longer. When I was gone, who would I tell about Adrian? No one would know how much I admired him; I should simply tell Lukas so that I'd have told someone.

"His name was Adrian," I said, still trying to keep my voice quiet so it didn't reveal how angry I was thinking about him.

"We've been best friends since we were really little, we were engaged and everything," I said with a little grin. Adrian had whispered those three simple words to me, and I knew he was overjoyed with our marriage arrangement.

"When I was fifteen, he got typhoid and died," I concluded simply.

Lukas's expression softened even more, and he gave me a compassionate glance. He didn't apologize to me, as he had when I described those who had been hurt inside the gates of this prison, since he felt he had nothing to do with it; it was just a bad fate.

Instead, his grip on my shoulder tightened, as if he was extending his support by the slightest touch.

He said almost softly, "I hate how you've had to go through so much. You don't deserve any of it."

I couldn't stop the little grin that formed on my face. Nobody had ever empathized with me so much before since he'd endured the same loss as me and hurt every day.

"You don't deserve all of this misery either," I said honestly.

"I do. I'm a wimp."

I sighed; if he can't forgive himself for working here, I'm not sure how he'll ever go on.

"You can't keep feeling guilty," I exasperatedly told him.

"I already said I would have done the same, so doesn't that mean I deserve all of this?" I pointed out, hoping to make him picture what I was trying to say.

He then hesitated, apparently considering a counterargument to my well-argued claim.

"But..." he started, before pausing again, perplexed.

"But nothing," I responded.

"It's not your fault about what happened to your father, and none of this...." I indicated, pointing at the surrounding structures, "is your fault either. You aren't to fault for any of this devastation."

"I don't know how you worked that out." He told me in disbelief. "Don't you hold me responsible for any of this? Don't forget that I placed you in this situation. Shouldn't you be cursing me and yearning for something bad to happen to me right now?"

He just didn't understand what I was saying. I couldn't hold it against him.

"If you were truly evil, you wouldn't be sitting here with me right now, having a normal conversation and commiserating with me because my best friend died two years ago. You wouldn't be sneaking me more rations. And you would have smacked me if I had commanded you to." The final one really sank home, and I knew he couldn't avoid saying what he'd done was excellent, not terrible.

Lukas took off his hat, which was skewed on his head, showing short brown hair, which he swiftly ran his fingers over. It was odd how different he appeared without the hat, and how gorgeous he was both ways.

"I suppose." He acknowledged, drawing my focus back to him from his indisputable beautiful looks.

I grinned broadly. "Good, well at least you know that I don't blame you for all of this."

"You don't realize how much it means to hear you say that." He said this with a slight grin on his own face."

"Also, I'd appreciate it if you didn't tell anyone that I give you more food and water than everyone else."

I gazed at him as if he were insane. "Of course not. I'm sure you'd be in a lot of trouble for it."

He shook his head. "I wouldn't get into trouble for it." He stated, confounding me considerably.

"What's the harm? I thought the entire idea of this institution was that you worked us until we died." There was no point in trying to soften up the truth. That was what they were doing.

"Why would you be let off for keeping me more alive than everyone else?"

"Because nearly all the officers do it." He replied, perplexing me more. These officer all appeared like brutes, why would they be striving to save someone's life?

"It's not that I would get punished for this, it's what I'd have to claim I was doing."

My eyebrows knitted together. I knew that Lukas was delaying spilling it to me, but I was going to get it out of him, so he may as well get it over and done with.

"The soldiers, they all have their favourites." He continued, his face turning black with wrath.

"They keep them alive, but it's not out of kindness, it's because they like to have the same one every time."

I was still a little bewildered, but I grasped the broad notion. Lukas knew that I wasn't entirely aware of it, however, and so he simply said it frankly. "They rape them."

I couldn't stop myself from gasping. I shouldn't have been astonished given how many other atrocities had occurred around here; it's only that I hadn't really considered the idea. Rape? It was unprecedented in my experience. It was almost a fable, a myth since it could never have occurred in Ajka.

"I can't believe it," I said, almost incoherently.

"If someone found out, you'd have to say you were raping me?"

Lukas averted his gaze while nodding. "And I'm not sure I could do that. When one person is known to be targeted, the other officers begin to target her as well.

"I couldn't let that happen to you," he stated.

I shook my head, not fully understanding what he was saying to me since I was still struggling to understand the scenario in the first place.

"Do you know of anyone who is currently being targeted?" I couldn't help but enquire. It might have been someone in my hut, and I wouldn't have given it a second thought.

"No," he confessed. "No one near here, but you can normally pick them out anyway, just because they've not lost enough weight."

"Who was still looking rather brawny?" I thought.

"Is that the girl you were sitting with earlier, Veronika?" She seems to be in good health, given how long you've all been going without adequate nourishment."

My respiration came to a total halt. "Do you believe Veronika is being raped?" I shivered at the notion of someone using such a nice child. Veronika didn't deserve it, there was no doubt about that.

Then I remembered her upbeat demeanour. No one could be doing such a horrible thing to her when she was still so amazingly cheerful. It had to be a coincidence that she didn't seem as emaciated as she should have by now.

"No, she's not. Veronika couldn't keep going if she was being mistreated like that."

I knew I was insuring myself more than him, but I couldn't believe that something so heinous was occurring and I was doing nothing to stop it.

When I dismissed his remarks, Lukas shook his head. "I agree, it must just be that she hasn't been affected by the lack of food quite yet."

I gave a firm nod. Nothing could possibly be happening to Veronika.

# 9

## EMBERS

The sound of yelling, shooting, and agonizing cries woke me up that night. I'd only just drifted asleep after absorbing the alarming news that Lukas had given me, implying that Veronika was being exploited in this manner.

When the door burst open, that flew right out of my thoughts.

Looking around, most people had already been awakened by the mysterious ruckus, but the few who had been sleeping quietly were suddenly completely awake and sat up.

I believed some slept with an eye open at this point, which was acceptable given the circumstances.

Lukas, ironically, was now standing in the doorway, his attitude substantially more hostile than usual.

That surprised me so much that the hairs on the back of my neck sprang up. If anything was serious enough to get Lukas so worked up, it had to be something worth worrying about.

"Everyone up now," he said, his commanding voice echoing throughout the room.

People hurried about manically, coming down from their upper bunks and scrabbling around, seeking to keep order for fear of being chastised by the shockingly bellicose-looking Lukas at the doorway.

I couldn't help but admire his body from the rear of the sudden single line wait, despite knowing the danger that surrounded my thoughts. Everything had gone quiet while we awaited further instructions, but this only gave me more time to admire his appearance.

His imposing stature exuded a sense of danger that I found strangely intriguing. It made him seem much more macho than usual, and the fierce gleam in his eyes made my insides feel strangely heated and my chest tighten.

Averting my gaze, I listened as he screamed out a few more commands, his German accent becoming more prominent in his annoyance. "Follow me."

Some folks were trembling with fear, evidently expecting something horrible to happen. I was already prepared if anything heinous was going to happen. I'd been anticipating something terrible to happen to me since I went through this door.

It had only become worse as I acquired more and more information. Others seemed to be having the same thoughts as mine, maintaining a straight face but hiding their terror behind their eyes. These thoughts immediately turned to Veronika, wondering how she was doing. Because, based on the amount of commotion I could now hear, it wasn't only our cabin that had been invaded.

Walking outside, I was welcomed by a sea of people, yet they weren't milling around as you'd expect from such a huge throng. Instead, they were all organized into hut-mates, exactly as we were, with an officer in charge of their line.

Then we were brought around the several shelters line by line. The longer we travelled, the more raucous the yelling grew, and the sound of gunshots became louder and more stunning. I was nervously looking about, not knowing what to anticipate.

Apart from the fact that the Germans were firing and, no doubt, shooting at the Jews, I had no idea why they were being shot at or what the repercussions would be.

But I had a feeling that was where we were going. Had they suddenly chosen to slaughter us all? Had we completed our mission? Had we become too frail? Or were they giving us a heads-up? Showing us what would happen if we weren't cautious and killing those who had already stayed too long. I didn't know, and to be honest, I don't believe I cared.

The image that unfolded in front of me once we turned took the next curve left me dumbfounded. There were people everywhere. All the men were half-dressed in pristine uniforms with the SS emblem, the others in torn shorts and t-shirts that barely covered them.

The gunfire could now be seen as well as heard as the German forces fired round after round into the crowd of Jewish men our age. I wasn't sure why, but I knew it was unjust and harsh without an explanation.

I resisted the want to rush to the front and ask Lukas questions. I didn't want to be the one with a bullet in my head.

I attempted to comprehend the issue by paying attention to the ruckus in front of me once again. Unlike what I originally saw and assumed that the officers were just shooting into the crowd, it was quite the contrary.

The men were fighting for their lives, hurling themselves at officers, choking them, and attempting to suffocate them while sheltering their bodies, with some even attempting to break necks. The troops were stopping them, firing numerous rounds at their aggressive postures, but missing many times due to a combination of their poor aim and how quickly their targets moved.

We were lined up so that we could readily observe the tragedy. Because we were one of the closest huts to the disturbance, we were lined up at the front, giving us front-row seats to the carnage. Lukas opted to stand right in front of me, despite the fact that he was still at the front of our hut's group.

He made eye contact with me, and even though he tried to be soothing, I could see the wrath in his eyes; the same rage he had shown when barging into our room earlier. I wasn't sure what was causing that rage, but I was going to attempt to put it together until I had more knowledge about the scenario.

I could tell he was attempting to spare me from the anguish of seeing such crimes by standing so close to me that his back hid much of the view. However, it wasn't that effective as I could still see blood washing over the grey floor.

Instead of being horrified by the dead corpses and limbs sprawled over the ground, I was astounded by the sheer number of deaths; how many individuals, both SS and Jewish, had been slain. I couldn't bring myself to sympathize with the troops, but that didn't mean I would ever wish for their deaths. It still made me nervous to think that so many people had died in such a short amount of time.

Looking to either side and searching among the throng for Veronika, I was unable to see her. She must be lost in the sea of other girls crammed together to see the butchery. Hopefully, she'd be farther back, with no clear view of what was going on. If she saw the totality of this, it could be enough to ruin her hopeful view.

A man's voice called me back from my quest through the throng to the spectacle in front of me. There were just a few men remaining, and they were all lined up facing us.

With two officers for every man, they had little hope of escape, no matter how hard they tried. They were anticipating death if not punishment, so I could understand their furious opposition to the people holding them back.

One man suddenly stood in front, pacing up and down, smugly spinning a revolver around his finger. I was disgusted by the way he stood so triumphantly. No one should be able to take delight in carrying out all of that slaughter.

He glared at the crowd in front of him, especially a few of the females closer to the front. At that moment, I recognized him as the same man who had hit Veronika the day we arrived. His hefty physique, with the same evil gleam in his eyes, was unmistakable, and I wasn't shocked he'd been the one in charge of such heinous occurrences.

"These people...." he said, motioning to the line of nervous men behind him and then to the dead on the floor. His voice travelled all the way to the back of the audience, far louder than I had anticipated.

".... thought it would be a good idea to hold a rebellion and commit mutiny." he said, his quotation marks surrounded by a smile and a few brief, humourless chuckles from the men behind him. He made a point of taunting them even on their deathbeds.

"And we've pulled you out here, so you can see why we wouldn't recommend it."

He had turned around in a hurry, shooting one of the men in the skull, causing him to drop to the ground, with his blood creating an increasingly enormous pool around him. The two soldiers who had been detaining him took a step back, but their expressions were stern with delight rather than disdain.

As he inspected the now-lifeless corpse, the officer revealed a glimmer of frenzied joy.

"All these men are going to die," he said, with no pity or care in his voice, just anticipation of the cold murder he was about to perpetrate.

Another gunshot rang out, and I heard a man moan in agony. I observed a man gripping his arm in anguish as I peered past Lukas's shoulder, which was still partly obstructing my vision. The two officers who had been detaining him had also taken a step back, allowing the man to be fired on at any time.

"Only some will have a much more painful death," snarled the officer in front of him before firing two more rounds, striking the man in one foot and the leg. Both areas would not kill him instantaneously but would let him suffer for a considerably longer amount of time while he bled to death slowly.

As if the killing wasn't horrible enough, torturing someone on purpose was absurd and wicked - pure evil.

The man slumped, still writhing, and screaming in pain, and I heard a crash. His sobs burnt my ears, but I fought the irresistible temptation to block them with my fingers.

He didn't deserve to be silenced; it would be insulting, exacerbating his terrible death, and rewarding me with a guilty conscience.

I anticipated that within half an hour, every single one of the soldiers would be dead. Some were straightforward murders, with shootings to the heart, head, or neck, or anywhere else that would kill them instantaneously. Others had been dragged out, suffering many bullets to the leg, arm, foot, and even the stomach before being slowly drained of their life.

When he was done, I saw the wicked smirk on his face as his eyes surveyed the crowd once again. He came to a halt in front of one individual, allowing his face to distort with a sinister look, his eye twitching in what might almost be mistaken for a wink. I instantly felt awful for whomever the gesture was intended for.

"Well, I think you all got the message I was trying to get across," he chuckled at himself, smirking as he looked back at the damaged carcasses.

"But...." he said as he fired a random bullet, ".....let that be your final warning."

A terrifyingly near-stifled gasp spun my head around as I saw a girl drop dead. Lukas's head jerked just as swiftly as mine had, but he was filled with fear when he met my gaze instead of even looking at the deceased female.

I could tell he was worried because of his face. For a brief minute, he had feared I might have been the one shot, which had made him nervous. Our gazes locked, and I immediately saw his relaxation as he let out a loud sigh.

Then he appeared to recall where we were and jerked his head forward, breaking our look in case someone was watching.

When he turned around, I could still sense the fury in the backdrop of his emotions, so I attempted to figure out what was wrong with him.

My first assumption was that he was upset at being awakened. Yes, it was childish and absolutely impractical, but when I considered the many options, I thought it might have been a factor.

My next thought was that it had something to do with forcing us to see this. As far as I knew, Lukas was as opposed to everything that occurred here as I was; he wouldn't necessarily want us to see such heinous slaughter. That was a lot more reasonable estimate, and I realized it was more than likely the source of his rage.

However, another notion that occurred to me was not so

favourable. Perhaps he was irritated by these men's attempts to rebel, to break free. Was he upset with them for attempting to flee such a horrible place? I'm guessing the detainees knew their destiny before they attempted to revolt against the officers, but might Lukas be furious with them for trying? If that was the response, it drastically diminished my view of him.

I sighed, waiting for something else to happen. I was anticipating more death, or at the very least more fire from that hellish rifle, which he'd already had to replace numerous times due to running out of ammo.

But nothing happened. We were just dismissed and escorted back to our huts by the same officer who had taken us there in the first place.

I was in front on the way back because I had been at the rear when we arrived. I noticed the horrified expressions on the faces of the many other girls who were now being returned to their respective huts as I looked around. They were as white as a sheet, scared by what had just transpired, and using it to scare others away from following the dead men in their tracks had clearly worked.

We were one of the first groups to arrive at our destination, but we were also one of the final groups to leave. As we arrived, Lukas held the door open for us, he was too near as I went through.

He had his reasons, as I soon discovered when I heard him

speak into to my ear. "Come outside after everyone has gone to bed," he whispered softly.

I nodded in response before entering the room and returning to my bunk.

It took a lot of effort not to fall asleep, since after being up earlier chatting with Lukas, and then waking up again to see the dreadful exhibition, I was going to be much more weary than usual when it came to working time.

Still, I made it since I was eager to speak with Lukas. I was curious as to why he'd kept me and him awake.

Although I often lamented about being forced to work such long hours and experience the difficulties that came with it, Lukas was typically awake when I was. He must have worked comparable hours to us, as well as his late-night meetings with me. As a result, I assumed he was tired as well.

The only difference was that he would have enough food to work such long days. He wouldn't be battling to subsist on mouldy bread, the rare chunk of cheese, and minuscule quantities of water. Lukas had more than enough stuff to consume, judging by his toned and muscly frame.

I crept up to the door, opened it a bit, and slid out. Lukas was sitting on the steps, his face buried in his hands, which were supported up by his elbows on his knees.

He was so immersed in contemplation that he didn't even

notice the door creaking. That was reassuring since it meant no one inside the shack would hear it either.

As I took my usual seat next to him, he jumped out of his reverie, flashing me a little grin that did wonders to make me feel better.

"Guten abend," he said in his own language, which I assumed was a welcome.

"Jó éjszakát," I responded in Hungarian, a language I hadn't spoken in what seemed like an eternity. My accent was stronger than I had anticipated, and I enjoyed how the words felt on my tongue.

I'd forgotten how natural it was to me because it had been so long since I'd spoken my first language.

Lukas's lips quirked, and he gave me a considerably larger grin this time. "You should speak Hungarian more often," he said, echoing my earlier thoughts. "It sounds nice."

"Köszönöm," I said, a smile spreading over my face as I thanked him. Then, when I reflected on the events of the night so far, my look became solemn once again. "How are you?" I questioned, figuring that the best way to find answers was to plunge in and ask questions.

He shook his head, indicating that he wasn't quite sure what to say. Instead of answering, he just laid his head back in his hands and closed his eyes, his face contorted with uncertainty. But I couldn't help but notice that the fury was gone, which made me happy.

I realized what distinct need I was experiencing as my palm twitched. It was the want to console him. My hand, off its own back, wanted to reach out and provide some type of assistance, whether it was as simple as soothingly rubbing his back or removing his hat and running my fingers over his groomed hair. However, I restrained myself since I believed such activities would elicit a reaction from Lukas and were more likely to distract him.

After a few minutes, he raised his head again, this time looking me straight in the eyes.

After a little pause, he reached out and took my hands in his own, diverting his gaze to stare down at them instead.

The warmth that ran through me from barely that little touch was incredible, and I felt my mouth become dry as I tried not to allow my breathing to become erratic. His hands were warm and calloused as they stroked mine, which I mistook for his fear.

"Kamilla," he said, his voice softened with passion.

His apprehensive demeanour made me nervous as well. What was it that took him so long to say? In any case, it was causing me concern.

"Kamilla," he said again, raising his gaze to meet mine. "When that shot went off earlier, I really thought he'd shot you." The look of despondency in his eyes made my chest tighten. Was he truly that scared of my being shot? He must have seen people die every day. What made me so unique?

"In that small moment, thinking that you were dead for a small instant, made me realize that I cared for you a lot more than I'd been admitting to myself."

My breathing became laboured, and my heart rate increased alarmingly rapidly. I fought the urge to let my mouth drop, so I simply stared at Lukas, wide-eyed, wondering how to digest such a statement. Inside, I was ecstatic, unable to believe that Lukas might possibly have emotions for me, but I couldn't quite bring myself to convert it to my exterior.

Lukas withdrew his gaze once again after my lack of answer.

"Of course, I understand if you're uninterested in me. I'm working in this place, inflicting so much anguish on so many people, and I believe I would despise myself if I were in your shoes."

He started rambling, which eventually jolted me out of my stunned daze. I took my hands away from his, causing his face to droop even more with the idea that I was horrified by his contact, as I softly touched the side of his face.

I could see him suppressing the impulse to arch his brow as he returned his gaze to mine. "I do care about you, Lukas," I informed him, my eyes conveying my sincerity.

The way his face lit up proved that I had succeeded, and his genuine happiness made my heart skip a beat. I'd never seen him appear so genuinely happy in all my time with him. He'd shown signs of happiness before, but never like this.

"Really?" He checked, trying not to grin as he considered the possibility of a negative response.

I burst out laughing. "Really," I said confidently.

As he stared unwaveringly into my eyes, the smile that stretched over his face made him appear even more stunningly gorgeous than usual.

His hands, which were still lying in his lap from where I had let them go, lifted and he softly clasped my waist.

He drew me closer to him so that we were just centimetres apart. My hands, which were still softly gripping his cheeks, slid away so I could wrap them around his neck instead, understanding what his goal was. He tentatively kissed my lips as he leaned closer.

My cheeks burned an unusual shade of crimson, but it wasn't from shame; it was from the sentiments provoked by his kiss. Even though it was just a short kiss that he soon drew back from, it made my lips thirst, and my senses go crazy for him.

Never before had I received such a kiss, and I was astounded that something so basic could be so potent. Then I caught him looking at my face as if he'd done something wrong. I drew his lips back to mine for a somewhat longer kiss, one that had left me breathless by the end.

This time, we drew back and rested our brows on each other's.

"We shouldn't have done that," Lukas said quietly, causing my heart to fall.

"But I don't regret it."

I couldn't help but agree while laughing.

Even in our dire condition, anything as raw as that could never be excused.

**To be continued....**

## Author Note

Thank you for reading one of my books.. Please leave a review/suggestion for me to read.. I would love to make improvements in subsequent books based on your opinion, to make my works more appreciable to you and others.

## About The Author

I am a storyteller with a knack for finding the extraordinary in everyday life. Hailing from a small town, I bring a down-to-earth charm to the world of fiction, where relatable characters navigate the twists and turns of life in compelling and authentic ways.

I draw inspiration from the simplicity of my small-town living and the complexity of human relationships, I try to make my stories resonate with readers who appreciate the beauty found in the ordinary. With a writing style that is approachable and engaging, I have crafted narratives that capture the essence of the human experience.

Whether exploring the dynamics of family, delving into the challenges of modern relationships, or simply observing the quirks of daily life, my stories are grounded in a realism that makes them both accessible and compelling.

# HIGH CURIOUS

## A REFORMING RAT-RACER'S JOURNEY TO WELLNESS

Lauren Mundell
Jennifer Giacalone

Cataloguing in publication information is available from Library and Archives U.S.

ISBN 978-1-956257-10-6 (paperback)
Formatting, publishing, cover design by Pierucci Publishing
Edited by Jonathan Grant
Co-written by Jennifer Giacalone

Jacket design by Stephanie Pierucci at Pierucci Publishing
Interior design by Sophie Hanks
Cover Photo by Karen Jacot
Interior Photography by Karen Jacot
Printed and Bound by Amazon.com and Disk.com

Dear
Victor,
Stay high vibes!
xo
Auntie
Lauren

# Dedication

For myself. Finally.

# Contents

If the New York rat race is inside you, there's the fear that if you stop racing, even for a second, you will be lost forever. The game never stops.

# Prologue

It was on a vacation in the summer of 2018 that I heard my own voice for the first time in a long time. I hadn't heard it for at least twelve years, not since I moved "back home" to New York as a newly divorced thirty-something with a five-year-old, a one-year-old, and a clean slate that I'd gone and muddied.

Looking out from that beach on that vacation in Clearwater, Florida, out into the clear blue waters of the Gulf of Mexico, I reminisced on what I'd become since becoming a PR executive and rejoining the New York rat race. Initially, it had all felt good: making money and living in the fast lane. But I'd been wearing a million hats and they had, over time, become a mask. I no longer knew who I was.

I looked out into the Gulf and took a couple hits from the cannabis pen in my hand.

This deep sense of knowing swept over me, a wave at once both profound and calming: "I am more than what I have been doing," my inner voice told me. "I am more than a cog in a revenue machine. I am more than a leash to a cell phone, more than a tether to emails, more than a hamster on a wheel going round and round."

I felt the cannabis flow through my body, through my mind, and into my soul. I was a human being, and it was time to start feeling like one again.

Since moving back to New York after my divorce, I had built, to the outsider looking in, what may have looked like the perfect life. I had the high-powered career. I was working with some of the best leaders in my field and had built a heck of a portfolio. I was a recognized name in "influencer relations." I was making the agency a lot of money and they were paying me well for it.

But, after those years as a serf to corporate America, my life came to feel unsustainable. I was unfulfilled. I was unhappy.

For a decade and a half, I'd been paid by the machine to worry about its parts, to scenario-plan for any and every outcome that may arise, to advise and hand-hold my clients on how to protect and promote their brands, to scrutinize projections and balance budgets, to game-plan on "what can go wrong and how to fix it before it does."

The game, once exciting and even a little fun, had come to consume me.

So, I went to Clearwater on this vacation so I may find some perspective. And it was on that beach that I realized the fire inside was no longer roaring, that the once roaring flame now nothing more than simmering coals that were cooling fast. New York wasn't me anymore—the fake smiles, the stress of it all, the everyday frustrations and anger.

The wave of knowing that washed over me on the beach told me to leave my job. My heart knew it. My soul knew it. But my ego was still trapped by the trappings of my life. I'd built exactly the life I wanted—the money, the house, the neighbors, the things—and once I had it, I couldn't stand it.

It had all become too much, like some house of cards where,

I knew, if just one card was pulled the whole thing would come crashing down. My life was a façade, and if I stayed in it, I would lose myself beyond repair.

I needed something new. I needed something better. I needed something more rewarding. I needed something more in flow.

If the New York rat race is inside you (wherever you may live), there's the fear that if you stop racing, even for a second, you will be lost forever. The game never stops.

The benefit of intuition, of the inner voice, is that once you start listening to it, you begin to trust it.

That day on the beach, I decided to start listening to this inner voice. And cannabis helped me do it.

I took another hit of my cannabis pen and held the vapor in before exhaling. I looked out at the teal waters of the gulf. The clouds were painted in their pastels and the waters glistened with what looked like a million diamonds of rippling sunlight.

"I need a change," I said.

I looked at the cannabis pen in my hand and I had an idea.

See, at forty-three, I'd found weed—or maybe it found me. And the plant, with all its wisdom-giving perspectives, had begun to unlock parts of me, parts of me that'd been buried deep below the *corporate me*. Parts of me I'd been afraid to look at.

I'd take a puff of the stuff, this ancient medicine that humans have been using for vision for so long, and I'd feel an instant elevation. It wasn't just "getting high," it was these lessons in perspective that were getting me high. And once I discovered cannabis, the medicine began to help me overcome my self-limiting beliefs, my social anxieties, my depressions, and my emotional pains. Those had been unwanted companions my entire life and cannabis helped me feel more centered, calmer, more creative. More me.

The meaning of life was not an endless pursuit for more money to fill an empty soul. It wasn't about more control. It was about doing things I loved with people I loved, for purposes that moved me. On that beach in Florida, I had a vision of my life, a new life built upon a new foundation. A strong foundation.

I came to see what I wanted to build and how I wanted to build it.

This book will detail events and feelings from my life both before and after this awakening moment on that beach in Clearwater. On these pages, you will read of a human being, of a person rechartering her life to find new direction.

My hope is that through my message, you may discover your own message, your own understanding of what can make you feel more whole, more in flow.

The words in this book are a journey to a clearer vision. The words in this book are my awakening, in middle age, to a new world through the healing smoke of cannabis. The words in this book are a pathway to using the herb as a wellness supplement to "live your best life."

This book is a celebration of the opening of the minds of humanity to the ancient truth that cannabis is a symbiotic—and even necessary—wellness supplement.

Because the truth has been pushed under the rug for too long—and it doesn't have to be anymore.

XOXO

Lauren

Dear Reader,

This book will take you on a journey through the healing one woman experienced when she discovered the power of cannabis as a healing plant for herself and her family.

Among stories that will bring you both laughter and maybe even tears.

You will learn about how in order to save her health, Lauren Mundell was faced with the choice to sacrifice her reputation, and even relationships with some people she loved most.

You may feel compelled to explore cannabis as a healing plant for your mind and body.

We encourage you to speak to your doctor and use responsibly with respect to any applicable local laws.

We accept no responsibility for irresponsible cannabis use, as this book is designed as a memoir, not as a medical recommendation.

Lauren's stories are designed solely to share one woman's journey.

If you're curious about how cannabis may be right for you, please join our community by scanning the QR code below.

Our community is eager to support your journey to learn more about cannabis for wellness.

With love and respect,

Lauren Mundell and the Hi-Curious Team

September 2021

In 2018, I was ahead of the wave. Today I still am. What I didn't understand then was that I was already becoming a pioneer in unchartered territories. I thought it would be easy to bring people around to believe in the power of the plant; I had 'seen it around' my whole life, and I thought people already using it would speak up for it. I was wrong.

# One

# *Motherly Intuition*

He was writhing on top of the blankets on his bed, his face buried in the pillow, his body tight. My son. His sobbing uncontrollable. His legs kicking, wildly.

I sat down next to him on the queen bed, his emotions, his energy seemingly taking up the whole mattress. I was pressed between Ethan and the wall, and I placed my hand on his back. His skin was hot. I tried to soothe him like I had when he was a baby, my baby boy who never wanted me to leave the room until he was sound asleep. But he wasn't a baby anymore and his breathing did not slow. His skin on fire. He was being stabbed by the swords of anxiety, and they were pulling him deeper and further away from me.

It wasn't the first time I'd seen Ethan in the throes of an anxiety attack, but it was the worst one yet. He hadn't left his room for days. He'd been reeling, living and reliving a nightmare. Crying and trembling and worrying his teenage mind that this was the end. See, in May of his junior year, Ethan had been kicked out of high school.

How we handled this event, together, would change his life—and my life—forever.

Ethan struggled socially in public school. By middle school, he'd gotten lost in the struggle to stay organized and while he did find some joy in soccer, he wasn't fitting in with his teammates. In hindsight, he'd always been a little anxious. But because I didn't yet understand my own anxiety, I didn't see it. Adults loved him, but he didn't make friends easily with his peers. He'd been bullied badly in sixth grade. I could see he was miserable. My son.

He needed change, so I tried my best to provide that for him. When he returned from sleepaway camp just before seventh grade, I made plans for him to transfer to a private school.

Thanks to some great kids and their wonderful stay-at-home moms, good communication between school and parent, and a godsend advisor named Jane, Ethan was doing well, becoming himself.

But when he needed their support the most, the school turned its back on him.

In a sick turn of events, the kid who'd been Ethan's biggest bully in public school enrolled in the same private school. What?! And the boy hadn't done a lot of changing.

The bullying slowly resumed, spiking to a peak in eleventh grade.

Ethan had tried to earn some cred, maybe get him to back off a little, by talking about having acquired a marijuana vape pen. Well, the bully took this as fodder and pressured Ethan to bring it along on a field trip to Adventure Island.

He did.

"Mom," the conversation began when Ethan called me from the field trip, "I got caught with a pen."

I was sitting at the common table in the lobby of my New York

City office with six of my colleagues. “What kind of pen?” I asked getting up from the table and finishing my bite of salad.

“You know what kind, Mom.”

Ugh.

“I didn’t smoke it Mom,” Ethan insisted. “I just left it in the bathroom for Dave, Keith, and Robert like they asked me to.”

“Really?”

“Why would I want to be high on a ropes course?” he almost whispered into the line. “That’s dumb and scary.”

I know kids lie to their moms about getting in trouble to avoid getting in more trouble. I know I did, but I also believed Ethan. And the video from outside the bathroom *did* show that Ethan went into the bathroom, by himself, and immediately exited while three other boys walked in and lingered long enough to have the dean enter and smell the residual odor.

Could Ethan have used it by himself in the bathroom? Sure. But knowing my son, his heart was pounding a million miles an hour and he wanted to do what he said he’d do for the boys and get out.

Or, maybe I think my son is an angel and he isn’t—you decide.

“Mrs. Mundell?” said a new voice over the phone. It was the dean, the same dean from the bathroom.

“Yes?”

“Hello and good day. Regarding this unfortunate circumstance, we have a zero-tolerance policy for drugs and there will be a board meeting to decide Ethan’s future here at our school.”

“Um,” I said, stalling. “Okay, I’ll be there.”

“No, Mrs. Mundell. Just Ethan, just he and the three other boys.”

The hours until the board meeting dripped by like molasses. Ethan wrote an essay in his defense and prepared in every way he could. When the time came, Ethan got dressed and I drove him to campus and watched him walk into the hall to defend his right to stay in school.

He tried. I know he did.

The next day, my phone rang. It was the headmaster. (I'll call him Mr. McBritishy.) "We have decided Ethan's fate," he orated from the other end of the line, no doubt wearing that black bowtie of his, "that since it is May, we will simply call Ethan's current grades final and that he will not be invited back in the fall."

I was stunned. Ashamed. I couldn't believe it. We spoke a bit more, and I hung up the phone.

"Zero tolerance," I said aloud—only to learn that "zero tolerance" meant different things for different people. Two of the other boys, whose parents held enough power, enough sway to speak out and "encourage" the school to allow their sons to stay, were *not* kicked out.

Yep.

A harsh lesson in elitism and privilege—and without getting too mired in the entangled issues of class and culture, suffice to say, the other boys didn't get kicked out but my Ethan did!!!

I could see how this experience would heighten his already problematic anxieties and insecurities.

The school was well aware of the reasons I chose to send Ethan there in the first place. He needed a place to grow. And the choice they made to push him out instead of supporting him in an hour of need was telling about their goals as a school. Donation money, it seemed, was higher on their priorities than helping one of their students through a tough time.

And it also painted a larger picture of the misunderstood nature of cannabis.

That is why I've chosen to begin this book with this story. That school's thinking, like the rest of mass America's stance on cannabis (calling it a zero-tolerance drug), was antiquated. Despite the plant's growing acceptance and legalization—despite the evidence of its benefits across a range of mental, physical, and emotional ailments—it was still so very misunderstood.

Misunderstood? Hmm, that's a good word. Because that's what I was, toward cannabis, for the first forty-three years of my life.

Until I actually took the leap of faith and tried the medicine for myself.

A year prior to that school kicking Ethan out, I'd had my discovery season with cannabis. I was starting to understand that, when I used it correctly, it helped me. A lot. It reduced my anxiety. It improved my capacity for mindfulness. It was an awakening.

I kept thinking, "Does everyone feel this good when they use cannabis? Can this illegal drug actually be helpful?"

I was finding, every day, that it was.

I started to ask my "stoner friends" why they never told anyone how much cannabis helps them.

"No one would believe me anyway, so why bother?" they'd respond. "I just keep it to myself and figure my secret to happiness doesn't have to be public knowledge."

At a Long Island Bar Mitzvah, I joined the "joint circle" with some Wall Street guys (who I also rode the train with). For years, I had seen them at these parties smoking weed after tying on their cocktails.

"What do you guys think of the idea of cannabis as a wellness supplement—like that it is actually *good* for you?"

"If I could use cannabis at work," one quipped back, "I'd be unstoppable."

"Yeah, but you'd also be *fired*," said one of his friends.

When I was out with the girls, I started telling them, "I'm not really into drinking Rosé anymore. It gives me a headache, and weed doesn't—it just makes me feel. . . good."

They sipped their sweet pink liquid and giggled that their crazy friend was "just on another kick." A kick just like my fitness obsession, the time I got to 9% body fat, the no-carb diet, my passion for knitting, the million other things I'd fallen in love with before they were cool.

"It's the best wellness supplement I've ever used," I'd tell to anyone I could. My words though, I was finding, were being met with skepticism—or worse.

"Why isn't anyone in my circle willing to talk about this?" I asked myself. What I didn't understand then was that I was already becoming a pioneer in unchartered territories. I thought it would be easy to bring people around to believe in the power of the plant; I had seen it around my whole life, and I thought people already using it would speak up for it. I was wrong. In 2018, I was ahead of the wave. Today I still am. And, as a society, I thought we'd be a lot further along these years later. And while it *is* a business opportunity that we aren't taking advantage of, as an advocate it's frustrating to know something that others can't yet see.

I came to the conclusion that most people in my mainstream world weren't ready to see what I was seeing. Their vision was still blinded by the decades-long mistruths about the plant and its health benefits. (And with my job working brand marketing with wellness brands, I was supposedly *in* the wellness world. Wow.)

That night I came into Ethan's room to find the anxiety coiled around him like a snake, a lightbulb went on inside me. It was definitely an outside-the-box lightbulb, outside what I'd been programmed to believe. But it was my instinct talking, I knew, and I had to follow my motherly intuition.

I slipped out of the room and grabbed a cannabis vaporizer pen from my drawer. I walked into the living room and told my husband about my idea to help Ethan.

He thought a moment. "Absolutely," he said finally, "we have to help him."

Without a second thought, I trusted my instincts and went back into Ethan's room. He was still writhing about. So much agony.

"Honey," I said, the cannabis dispenser in my open palm, "do you think this may help you feel better?"

He looked at the pen and he looked in my eye. "Yes," he said, a sound of relief in his voice.

I gave him the medicine and he put it to his lips and inhaled slowly.

The tension drained from his body like a frozen pond turning to liquid in the spring. His heaving chest turned into calm breathing. His wet t-shirt began to dry and his skin came to cool.

There was an immediate shift in his energy. He began to talk. For the first time in weeks, he spoke beyond mere utterances and formed actual, thoughtful sentences. He opened up.

"Mom," he said, "I haven't been able to stop thinking about what happened—did I ruin my life?"

"No, honey, I know it feels like that now, but someday this will just be 'something that happened to you.' Today it just really sucks."

He proceeded to apologize for taking the pen to school, telling me about the pressure he was feeling from the boys. How he wanted to fit in. How he'd made the wrong decision. How he knew school was not a place for marijuana. "I've only had it for a couple weeks and I've just been using it every once in a while to ease my anxiety," he told me. "The Lexapro makes me feel like I'm looking at myself through a mirror. This stuff helps. I've just been so anxious."

My child had been in pain.

Any parent knows the feeling of wanting to take that pain away. He was sixteen and had been living the nightmare of believing he'd just messed up the rest of his life. He needed help. He needed medicine. And he needed to not have to hide that fact anymore. When I saw him inhale the cannabis, I saw the plant working its magic.

That was the night my child started healing—through proper use of an eons-old medicine from the earth. It had worked for me and I saw it work for my son. I was on board to become an advocate for cannabis, in a big way.

That night with my son was the beginning of the understanding that medicines need not be prescribed by doctors or accepted by the status quo—the understanding that I could take power over my health, and the health of those I loved. Cannabis, from then forward, would be an integral part of my overall wellness approach.

And something I began openly talking about with doctors—and anyone else who'd listen.

# Two
## *Into the Rat Race*

My whole life, I'd been the "good girl." Marijuana was not a part of what I did or who I was.

When I tried it in college, that one time at Cornell, I had no idea how much to have. So I did a bong hit. Bad idea for a first-time user. Bad experience. I judged it. Badly. I decided that my parents and Nancy Reagan were right: *Just Say No to Drugs*.

What I didn't understand is that cannabis can heighten whatever state you happen to be in. If you're in a positive mindset, it'll heighten that. If you're seething with unaddressed self-doubt and feelings of pent-up otherness and tomb-like anxiety, it may heighten those feelings—and after a bong hit in a fraternity bedroom in Ithaca, every anxiety I had ever felt about not fitting in, about my fear of not belonging at this Ivy League school, about my fear of saying the wrong thing, of looking stupid, of making a fool of myself, of being an out-of-control mess in front of other people, started rushing at me at a million miles an hour. My mind feasted on bad thoughts.

When they say cannabis causes anxiety, I would edit that to say: cannabis breaks down the dam that anxiety lives behind, which is

good—great even—but when you use too much too soon it can feel like an eruption.

(If you ever find yourself in this situation, try to tell yourself it will end, because it will, even if you don't believe yourself.)

I'd had no parameters or guidance for this first use, and I had a bad experience because of it. When I started taking Lexapro for anxiety at forty-three, the doctor told me to "start slow and work up to 10mgs over a month."That's how we should all be introduced to this cannabis, too. Slowly. A frat house bong rip wasn't—and still is not—the ideal introduction.

The first time we drink alcohol, we should probably start with a glass of wine or one or two beers. It's the same for weed. Well, I smoked too much and the cannabis smoke yanked off an emotional band-aid that I was wholly unprepared to have yanked.

I judged that experience, and for almost three decades didn't give cannabis a fair shot.

Though I didn't really like drinking, it was way more socially accepted—and so that's what I did in social situations. I didn't realize until much later that all of this was related to social anxiety and the fear of messing up in public. If my brain needed numbing, I chose alcohol. It was legal, and that made it safe, right? No matter that alcohol causes so many chronic problems in society, within families, and within the minds of habitual users that we have about five different AA options in our culture.

I know this because my first husband came from a long line of men who lived unevolved lives and were never able to admit their depression: men who, instead, medicated with alcohol. I saw booze kill his father and brother (something that is literally impossible to do with marijuana.)

But, back in 1991 when I was a freshman at Cornell, we didn't talk about any of this. I never connected substances like caffeine and alcohol with mental or physical health.

As I grew up, I rarely over-indulged in drinking—except for the

year I was twenty-one and worked at a bar in Tucson called Dirtbag's. *And* the time I worked at Club Med and the wine flowed like water. *And* after the divorce to get through the bad dates and be more open to the good ones.

And sometimes in the PR industry, at those networking events where I was expected to "be myself." I overdrank once or twice before settling into the routine of 2-5 drinks. If I hadn't been drinking, it wouldn't have looked right to the industry types. Other than that, after I became a parent, I really didn't drink much at all; it made me too tired.

I am telling you this because I want you to know that I didn't start cannabis because I had to quit drinking or anything like that. It wasn't a replacement. I wasn't someone who had a glass of wine in the middle of the day and four cocktails a night. I didn't start my Sundays with Bloody Marys.

Drinking didn't play an important role in my life at all, especially after I learned more and more about wellness, learning that everything you put into your body affects its performance—and I wanted to be in peak performance. So I stopped all alcohol intake.

Still, if you would have told me even seven years ago that I would be a cannabis advocate, living in Colorado and helping people build businesses in the cannabis industry, I'd have told you that *you* were high. I was a mainstreamer for sure.

And the striving to find success the "right way" permeated pretty much every decision I made about my life. I did what people expected of me. I became what I thought I "should" be. For a long time.

When my boys were babies, I divorced from my husband Bobby and moved from Connecticut back home to Port Washington, NY—a wealthy community on Long Island with a waterfront dotted by sailboats, charming Cape Cod-style homes with their rolling green

lawns, and Sands Point, the actual "East Egg" in F. Scott Fitzgerald's *The Great Gatsby*.

That's where I returned to feeling like a failure.

The "inexpensive homes" in Port Washington start around $700K—not a place you can afford to live if you don't have a very well-paying job. It's a New York place with a *New York State of Mind*.

A mindset I can see—now that I'm living a mile above it and 1700 miles from it—that places money on a par with God. An artificial place with an artificial way of living. And I grew up there. So when I got a divorce, it's where I went back to. Because that was what I knew and what I thought was "right."

I returned to Port Washington with a mission: to be able to support my children in the lifestyle in which I was raised—or better. Through my own means. Any child support that came in would be "gravy"; I'd never have to rely on it.

"He's not always going to be able to help," I told my mother one night. "And, I want to be in control. I need to have the financial freedom to take care of myself and my children."

So I decided to work my ass off. I would get into the corporate world and climb the ladder as high as I could and make as much money as possible.

I would prove myself—I would get the home in the wealthy suburb, get my kids into the expensive prep school, be part of the temple where the upper crust of Challah hung out. I would have the cars, the clothes, the body, and all the trappings.

I was also looking for a man who fit into this fantasy. It was tough being a single mother. So I dated. I put myself out there. I met a few good candidates, one who even worked at Lehman Brothers and had all the things I thought I wanted. All the things I thought I needed. When that bottom fell out, I was so proud of myself for building my own career.

As a kid, for years, I thought I was "keeping up with the Joneses," not realizing that, in fact, we *were* the Joneses. Or the Cohens, rather.

Now I was lost in a race to be better than my parents were, making more, doing more, having more. But even when I achieved—when I hit the target goal or passed one finish line on the way to another—I was left feeling empty. If we were the Cohens, then I had to strive higher.

I didn't really know what I wanted. I felt a deep sense of wanting, craving more, and I made a lot of money. I did. But it came at the cost of my freedom.

Sure, I enjoyed this lifestyle. At least thought I did. I'd have my days when I felt powerful, felt "in control" when I'd look at my body or my bank account. But it never lasted. The moment was fleeting, the hungry LACK monster never satisfied for long. More. More. More.

If this seems incongruous with the mountain-town cannabis-lifestyle I live in now, you're right. Ultimately, my lifestyle would have to change, change so *I* could. But before I realized that, I fully embraced what I was doing. I dove into mainstream life blindly because I felt like it was the only way. *The* way. The one way to live.

I returned to New York and returned to striving to live the life my father lived.

I was living how other upper-class New York Jews lived. Corporate, strait-laced, fancy things. That was me. My dad had built and sold two public relations firms at a time when the big guys were paying big bucks for a small agency with blue-chip clients like Burger King, Revlon, Frito Lay, and Chiquita Banana. He was the one who "placed" me on my career track in PR, giving me my first break into the industry. And I took it. It didn't give me a lot of pride to take it, but I saw that a little nepotism would enable me to support the image of the lifestyle that had become so important to me. Money, I came to think, would get me where I wanted to go. I had gotten into debt and felt so much shame about it during my marriage. So money became my motivating force. I never wanted to feel that way again. Money equaled security, so I strove to get it—only to have it open up a bottle of problems I thought I'd left behind.

I convinced myself I'd left that bottle back in Ithaca when I did so poorly at Cornell that I was "not invited back." Or, maybe I'd at least left it at the Club Med in Eleuthera when I was a GO (yeah, that job that meant drinking way too much, performing in shows on stage, staying up late, having sex, and making friends with other people who needed a break from real life).

I told myself that I'd moved beyond those experiences. I'd been married, divorced, and now re-married. I had a highly successful career; I should be okay, right? I shouldn't have anything to worry about anymore. I'd grown out of my bad habits and a bad marriage and surely I couldn't still be carrying that bottle of anxiety around. I couldn't possibly be actually killing myself by adding *more* daily stress to my life.

Yeah, I was shaking the bottle of anxiety around like some sort of weaponized soda bottle.

The thing is, just like the old saying goes, "wherever you go, there you are."

I've been saying this for years, but only recently have I come to understand it. For me, now, it means that: until you start to work on your demons and shadows and nightmares, they stay in the bottle ready to erupt. And living a life without dealing with them only allows them to fester, to shake up their bottle and give them power. The pressure builds over time until they simply become too strong to remain dormant.

Also, being the boss' daughter really messed with me. It did for a long time. Feelings of inadequacy were pervasive.

"Do my colleagues like me or are they just being nice because they *have* to?" I'd ask myself, all the time. "Am I good at this, or are people just saying 'yes' to me?"

Working at a company with my maiden name on the door built a nagging sense of constantly needing to be better than everyone. But I

also wanted to make sure everyone liked me for *me*, not just because they had to pretend to like me because I was "the boss' daughter." I also wanted them to respect me for my work, so I worked harder than everyone even though I never quite knew exactly what I was supposed to be proving. I mean, we all have our "things," I know, and I'm not trying to sound ungrateful or anything, but it was hard. Sure, my early life came with its privileges, but therapy is teaching me that no one gets out of childhood unscathed.

What I didn't realize is that I already had it all. My mindset was the only thing holding me back. And cannabis began to help me shift that mindset. Cannabis gifted me the perspective to shift my being from one of this 'lack' to one of 'abundance.

# Three
## *In the Room*

To earn me a place on the team, my dad invited me to the 2006 pitch for a new Frito-Lay chip called Flat Earth. Yeah, they don't exist anymore but at the time they were a big deal: the first chips to be made with fruit, way ahead of their time. I suppose my dad and the team felt I represented the "mom target" the chips were created for.

I got the job to give the big pitch and was served up as the "account director." I got in the room, and I did what they told me to do. I don't know if I was good, if I came across as a rookie or if I was awesome. But, we won, and I do know this—it felt awesome. The whole thing was intoxicating: the room, the pitch, the theater, and the magic of what it takes to "be successful at business."

I can't say that I didn't like the feeling.

The pitch room made my competitive juices flow. Eventually, people saw I was good at it. And that was the start of my career of going "in the room" to make the play that won us the game. It was an intoxicant—competitive as hell and it afforded me the lifestyle I thought I wanted.

I also loved talking to my dad about it. It was something we connected on, something he could be proud of me for; me, the little girl who always wanted to feel seen by him, felt very visible when we spoke about my success at work.

I got to work with companies like NutriSystem (during the Tori Spelling and Joey Fatone days). I got to pitch. I got to learn business. I got to feel successful.

I soaked it up like a sponge. In my ambition to keep up with the Joneses, it started to come naturally to me. I became great at engineering a meeting, at delivering the pitch, at fostering relationships. I had signed up for the gig, and I was going to be the best I could be at it. Every relationship started with an objective, every meeting closing with "next steps." I turned into a machine; it came naturally, the wins fueling me and the losses spurring me.

Everything in this corporate world, I came to learn, had an end goal—and that end goal was money. We weren't so much creators as movers. We were movers of money. We were movers of ideas that led to clients spending more money. Money. Money. Money.

Notorious B.I.G. may have been right when he said, "Mo Money, Mo Problems."

I took the stresses on as my own. Relentlessly trying to rise above being the boss' daughter and prove myself (prove what, I still didn't know). I got so good that I kept getting promoted. In 2008, I left the comfort/stigma of having my name on the door for the global agency Ogilvy—*MadMen* is said to have been loosely based on the genius David Ogilvy. That's the stuff I was doing.

There, I worked on and eventually came to run the Unilever Foods account (Bertolli, Lipton, Knorr, & Slim Fast at the time) with a team of ten working under and with me. We did breakthrough work, elevating mainstream brands into award shows and pioneering new types of celebrity endorsements for CPG brands. I was good. I made what most would consider lots of money, but it never felt like enough.

In 2011, I left Ogilvy for Ketchum Communications. One big New York agency for another. To my mind, Ketchum was the pinnacle of the agency world for consumer products. They held (and still do) the epically fun-seeming Frito-Lay account. They had Mattel, worked on Barbie and Hot Wheels, Wendy's, Chase, all the big brands, and fancy budgets.

I had interviewed there when I wanted to leave my dad's agency in 2008 but did not get the job. In January of 2011, Ketchum offered the lead role on the Pfizer account running Advil, Centrum, Thermacare, and a few others. It was the "dream job" I'd been looking for.

My ego told me it was satisfied. (For about one minute).

I was pitching, winning, and earning the support of some of the biggest clients in the world. In my first six months, my team won the Weight Watchers account. I was "in the room" with CEOs and advising them how to spend their money.

It all seemed so powerful.

Except, really, I was powerless. I was just a cog in the wheel and I was replaceable, fireable, and I spent plenty of time under the bus while I was supposed to be sitting in my boss' front rows.

I can see, now, that all of that time trying to stay on the bus turned me into someone I didn't like that much. And, public relations is, at its core, professional anxiety. You're entirely defined by the ability to imagine anything and everything that could possibly go wrong before it happens. The more and more I got paid, the more I was responsible for worrying about what may, might, would, or could get fucked up and to game-plan various strategies to un-fuck them up: I was paid to be a professional anxiety machine.

So, this was literally both the best and worst field I could have chosen. The best because, unfortunately, it suited the professional worrier I was—and the worst because it suited the professional worrier I was. It made me even better at worrying, and I was already too good at that.

Because when you become a slave to your worries, to your fears, that equates to giving up your freedom. And living without freedom is living without power.

Why do I tell you all this boring stuff about PR, New York, big brands, and money? Well, to establish who I was; this was what my life was like before I really began to break things down and start my awakening with the aid of cannabis. Many of us have a "before and after" in our lives. Maybe even, like me, a "before and after" with cannabis. And to show you how it changed my life, I want to show you what my life was like before.

I also want to show how a wellness approach that includes cannabis isn't just for "stoner culture" (whatever *that* is) but for anyone looking for a natural augmentation to living. I was about as corporate as it gets, and cannabis benefited me.

Cannabis can be of benefit for all of us—no matter our backgrounds—because it helps humans. It helps humanity. It helps with the universal struggles of the human condition.

Me? Yeah, I was on the hamster wheel of the career track, pursuing more and more "success." I was a product of mainstream society's belief in "attaining." Always *more*. And it was coming at the price of my mental, physical, emotional, and familial health.

I started working so hard and so much that I was killing myself to provide a "lifestyle" for my kids. And, because of my devotion to the corporation and always on for my clients, I barely got to see them or live the lifestyle I was supposedly creating. So, what was I really providing? What lifestyle was I showing them? Not a good one. Not a natural one.

I was exhausted when I was with my kids. I was secretly happy they wanted to play video games on the weekends instead of play with me. I needed a break. Because I never took one. In hindsight, I was more absent like my dad than the mother I once dreamed of being. I shut off my heart, the part that hurt when they got on the

kindergarten bus, I told myself I had to work harder, for them. But, was it?

So many of us do this—the rat race is practically woven into the fabric of America: we're expected to work ourselves to death to provide the things we "need" in life. And that doesn't make sense.

That moment in Ethan's room when I reached out to him and offered the cannabis was the beginning of a year-long journey that culminated on the beach in Florida. The journey showed me how unhealthy the life I'd built had become.

I was calling myself "a wellness and fitness advocate and expert" for Pete's sake, but I was anything but "well." All I was doing was perpetuating everything that was wrong with the New York rat race.

"Lauren," people would tell me, "you're a winner. You are in it to win it—and you do!"

Sure didn't feel like a winner. I was simply playing a game I was told to play. I was living my life from the mindset that I was lacking something; for, if all we seek is more, that innately means we don't believe we have enough. That "lack" was what drove me.

What I didn't realize is that I already had it all. My mindset was the only thing holding me back. And cannabis began to help me shift that mindset. Cannabis gifted me the perspective to shift my being from one of this "lack" to one of "abundance."

To sum up this chapter before it gets away from me: there is historical evidence that cannabis is the "burning bush" of the Bible. There is testimony that the "third eye" of Eastern thought stems, historically, from cannabis use. Whether that is ultimately true or not, it *was* for me. Cannabis showed me a new way to view my world.

And a new way to view our world is the power to shift our own reality.

It just makes everything feel better, he'd say. Sex, love, even the hard stuff like being a stepdad to kids who don't think they need one.

# Four
## *It Felt Good*

When I met and married a buttoned-up navy commander, I would never have predicted *he'd* be the one to help me learn about Mary Jane.

As the months leading up to his retirement after twenty years of service ticked by, Barry began talking about what it'd be like to no longer be tethered to monthly fit reps and drug tests. "I'm looking forward to smoking weed again," he said flippantly one night at dinner. He had mentioned it before, but if I am being honest, I didn't think he would go through with it—I thought it was just something he said. As the days grew closer to his retirement, the conversation got more real.

"You're really going to smoke weed?" I asked him, shocked. "Here? In our house? With the children home?"

"I'll make sure they don't know," said Barry, calmly. "*You* don't even have to know if you don't want to."

"You talking, like, a one-time thing?"

"No, probably more like a few times a week thing. You can try it if you want—"

"I don't think so."

To understand why I thought my husband was merely fantasizing about his teenage years on the beach back in Cali, you need to understand a few things about Barry. First off, he was the chief of interrogations at Guantanamo Bay. Yep. Under the Obama administration. He was the guy that the other guys reported to.

Barry is, by all accounts, what one would call a "serious person." He was about as far removed from what I thought a pot smoker could be. I thought only "stoners" smoked marijuana, society dropouts who played video games or threw frisbees all day.

When he told me he was going to start using cannabis recreationally, I immediately pictured my clean-shaven husband devolving into some Cheeto-eating, wifebeater-wearing gamer. (Well, the gamer part was already a thing. I hear he's pretty good at video games for an old dude.)

But I was more than a little scared. I didn't want him to change. I loved him. I loved Barry. He was my "forever husband."

Yet there he was. When his retirement became official, Barry bought a pipe and started smoking weed in the evenings.

I started getting curious.

"It just makes everything *feel* better," he'd say. "Sex, love, even the hard stuff like being a stepdad to kids who don't think they need one."

I'd watch him take his few hits of cannabis and I would see a change. Not anything drastic—he was still Barry—but he seemed almost like a better Barry. More relaxed and more engaged at the same time. Like he had more chill and less angst or something. More zest, more curiosity. It took the edge off from the day and helped him unwind, helped him seem more free.

He seemed better, and I wanted that too.

In fact, though I hadn't quite yet realized it, I *needed* that. I had become "hi-curious."

The motto came to me later, but that's what I was then. I saw what Barry was receiving from the plant and wondered, "Could I get that too?"

"Partaking" represented a state of being that had always seemed out of reach for me. So much so, in fact, that until seeing my husband's response to the plant I had not once (since that time in college) entertained the idea it was even a possibility.

"Maybe I *will* like it," I said to him one night in the living room. "Maybe I am different than I was twenty-five years ago? Maybe . . ."

The curiosity became too much to control. And the next evening, I did it. I took one incy-wincy-tiny-little-baby hit of cannabis.

I felt good.

The next night, I took a little less of an incy-wincy-tiny-little-baby hit of cannabis.

I felt good again.

Because it's me, my mind, I documented every little feeling I had. Took notes. And by the third or fourth week, I took a proper draw on the pipe, held my breath for a bit, and then exhaled.

I was dipping my foot into the pool, one toe at a time. And I liked the waters.

Giving ourselves the freedom to transform is the greatest kindness we can give. When we begin to change, it might make others uncomfortable. Especially the people who've known the 1.0 version for a long time.

# Five

## *The Freedom to Transform*

Is cannabis for everyone? No. Nothing is for *everyone*. But is it for a lot more people than we've been led to believe? I think so.

It might be for hippies with long hair, who don't wear shoes, dance at Phish shows on the weekends, and carpool to the office during the week. It might be for twenty-somethings who live on pizza and suffer from social anxiety because they were raised in the digital age and are now expected to make eye contact. It might be for a CEO who has always battled stage fright or flight anxiety but is "nails at numbers" and "the next thing."

It can also be for stay-at-home moms who want to be more present with their kids. It can also be for baristas-creatives, construction workers with PTSD, or academics with insomnia. Cannabis can "be" for a large percentage of our society who may have wondered about its benefits but who've never tried it because of the stigma still attached to it.

And for those pot smokers who keep it in the closet (literally), I say that it's time to come out and learn about *why* this plant has helped

you behind the scenes most every evening for the past two decades. And, together, we'll let the next generation in on Mother Nature's secret: Mary Jane and her uncanny ability to calm the turbulence of what it is to be human in the twenty-second century.

Unfortunately, there's no book out yet that can teach you everything about how to use cannabis; there's just not enough research and modern medicine is extremely far behind. It'll be years before doctors can precisely prescribe cannabis like they do with pharmaceuticals, so it's up to each of us to learn the "hows and whys" of this natural medicine.

You picked up this book, which means you want to learn. Which makes me happy. Because my experience with cannabis has told me that it's exactly that: a medicine, a tool, an herb from Eden's garden put here to help us.

And I'll tell you this. Real quick. Almost secret-like: our body has something called the endocannabinoid system, a receptor-system within our body, evolved within our body, made precisely to absorb marijuana.

A bit intriguing?

Benjamin Franklin once said that "beer is proof that God loves us and wants us to be happy." Well, it makes more sense to me, ol' Ben, to replace the word "beer" with "weed."

Use it to overcome anxiety. Use it to replace "Mommy's five o'clock wine." Use it instead of Advil for muscle pain. Use it to replace those two cocktails or those 6-12 beers every night. Use it to laugh a little easier. Use it to feel more during sex. Use it to be more patient. Use it however it helps you.

Get to know the plant. Because user experience differs greatly from person to person.

Yeah, there are some overarching effects, but most of the people I know and work with feel benefits in unique ways. For, I feel (and science is proving through endocannabinoid system research), that the plant works with us, works with our unique brain and body chemistries, to give us what we most need in that moment. Think

about it like food. It's fuel. Some people eat before they workout, some people prefer a shake after. But if you don't eat, you get depleted.

Similarly, some people get super energized and smoke *before* they go exercise. Others take a hit and it gives them the peace to just veg out. For some artists, it spurs creativity. For some athletes, it gives them a better feel for the ball.

And life's a game, one that—according to Simon Sinek, one of my "virtual mentors" (meaning he has no idea he's my teacher)—is an *Infinite Game*. The way to win is by having the most fun while you play. We only have a short time to make an impact, and mine (yours too; heck, everyone's) is now.

That's why I've chosen to share my story, my journey of discovery. Because I know, in my bones, that there are so many people living like I was—crushed under stresses both internal and external—who cannabis can help.

And I want to put this incredible wellness tool into the hands of those who need it.

I've gotten out of the corporate world and into the helping world. And maybe for the first time in my life, I have a mission I feel good about. It's not a mission about helping companies get richer or one that centers on acquiring more things; it's a mission about giving people something that can do them good. My work no longer detracts from my life. My work with cannabis, through cannabis, fills me up—by helping fill others up.

That's why I left the New York rat race for a career in the cannabis industry; to build a wellness brand and a tech platform that will help people make a sustainable income sharing their cannabis lifestyles and inspiring others.

The move was a radical one for sure. And a lot of people gave me a lot of shit for it. I suppose choosing wellness and self-care first, and the bottom line second, can seem radical to some people. To much of our culture, it's downright blasphemous. To me it felt natural. To me it felt good. And, yeah, allowing ourselves to heal from a scrambling life of one stressor to the next in pursuit of the almighty

buck *is* a revolutionary act. A revolutionary act of compassion. For ourselves.

Giving ourselves the freedom to transform is the greatest kindness we can give. When we begin to change, it might make others uncomfortable. Especially the people who've known the 1.0 version for a long time.

But we gotta do it.

As I evolve and grow, the idea of healing my inner child still makes me uncomfortable—still feels like this "woo woo" thing to say. But the further I go on my journey, the more truth I see in it. See, we are all grown-up versions of our child-selves. And, for a lot of us, a lot of pain has been building up for a long time.

The pain of our inner childhood isn't something we always talk about with our friends. I know it's something I'm still working on—understanding the pain of the eight-year-old who's sitting on the couch hearing that "Daddy is moving out" or connecting to the sixteen-year-old who feels trapped by "tight ass rules."

Without cannabis, I don't know if I'd ever been able to look at those little girls within and tell them it's going to be okay. I needed the gift of perspective that the medicine gives me. Now I talk with little Lauren a lot.

I also talk a lot with my husband.

For months, in the beginning of my cannabis journey, Barry and I would sit in his home office on our blue Smurf couch and heal. We would talk. We would listen.

Well, mostly I talked and he listened.

I opened up about my fears, and he helped me play them out. We strategized our lives; he learned about me and I learned to trust someone else with my heart, for real. Cannabis gave me the patience to open up and connect with myself and my husband—and to start living instead of existing in a constant state of worry.

Friends would ask me all the time: "Really? It makes you feel better? It has helped you . . . *change?*"

"Yes," I'd answered, time and again. "It has."

And, time and again I remind myself how lucky I am to have found this medicine that I believe gives me a leg up on those who haven't had the chance to yet face their shadows.

Cannabis has opened that third eye for me, allowing a rediscovery into myself and the nature of the life I wish to live. It has given me an all-natural door-opening away from what was ingrained in me by the family and culture in which I grew up. It has allowed me to live more in the present, eliminating the unnecessary need to overthink and over-plan and over-worry about each and everything that might go wrong.

Through cannabis, I came to see how anxiety was robbing me of my life. There's a Mark Twain quote out there that goes something like, "I've been through a lot of shit in my life. *Some* of it actually happened." And that was me. So much of my shit was in my head. I was so busy planning and figuring out solutions to things that could go wrong that I failed to see the good things right in front of me. I became blind to the fact that I was working so much and so hard that I barely saw my kids. I had become inured to the quest to keep up with the Joneses or the Cohens or the whoevers.

I was like that fly who keeps beating his head against the window trying to get out—when all that fly needs to do is back up, gain some new perspective, and fly two feet to the right where the window is wide open.

And that's a good image to linger on as we close out this chapter. For so long, I *was* that fly. (Though I prefer butterfly, the meaning remains.) It is only through backing off the pedal and utilizing a natural and ancient medicine that I've found my wings to fly in open air. I've rediscovered how to breathe. And I'm finding out I can soar, that I *am* soaring. On wings illuminated by cannabis.

So, let's see what this humble and awesome plant may be able to do for your life. What wings it may give you.

Any chance I got, I was working out: I'd skip out of work and literally run over to my trainer to get a 45-minute session in, grab an ultra-quick shower, and dial into the conference call before I was even back at the office.

Balance always feels like pressure to keep two sides of some imaginary scale from falling over to one side. Flow lets me live my life the best I can, learning from both my good days and my not so good days in a continuous path toward where I know I am going.

# Six
## *Stress and Flow*

I keep this photo of me that was taken during my high-pressure, high-power, executive years. It's over on the opposite page. Give it a glance. Pretty hot, right?

Yeah, well it took a lot of work. The lighting, the pose, the Batman tank top pushed up just so to show off the abs. (You could bounce a quarter off those things.) The boobs weren't cheap either.

The shoot took place seventy-five days before my fortieth birthday, back in March of 2013. I'd been working my ass off (literally) for four years and had committed the past sixteen weeks to what I called "perfectly clean eating."

I wanted to document what I looked like, flaunt it almost. A little narcissistic perhaps, but for the next seven years I used the photos (not Bat Girl) for headshots and social media photos and they did the job. And, on a deeper level, I'm glad I captured the version of me that was: the ripped, money-making, fitness-obsessed, business-winning, team-leading animal who ran a 1:53 half marathon and was

hard as a nail. Which, in all honesty, was what I thought I should be. What I thought people thought I should be.

To be the person I am now, I truly believe, I had to be the person I was then.

I had to make the money to support the lifestyle to give my kids more than my parents had given me. The body and the drive were by-products of the time, end-results of the anxiety machine.

I had the photos taken as proof that "I was here." Where "here" was I know I didn't really know. But, from the outside looking in—at my job titles and my income and those abs—someone could have looked at that picture and seen what a female executive should look like.

Thing is, I didn't feel like a female executive, not on the inside. It felt like it was all an act, like someone was going to catch me, call me out as not worthy of my role.

I turned to fitness as a release, as an escape. My body became something I could control. It became an obsession.

What started in 2009 with a borrowed set of *BeachBody* workout DVDs to tone up before my then-boyfriend's son's Bar Mitzvah, turned into, three years later, 7-10 grueling workouts a week. I held three or four gym memberships at any given time; spin classes; boxing; Barry's bootcamp classes; a personal trainer twice a week; three Tough Mudders; more than a few fitness-themed "vacations"; a Peloton; six half-marathons and uncountable shorter races; 30/60/90; becoming a *BeachBody* coach.

I loved everything fitness except CrossFit (those around me were not safe from my lack of balance and hand-eye coordination). Oh, and though I gave it a fair shot, Pilates too: my lower abs, the ones below the belt, the ones that create the "eight pack," never got as strong as the other six (blame it on the C-sections) and so Pilates made me feel weak. I couldn't have that. Not in my state of mind. No weakness!

Any chance I got, I was working out: I'd skip out of work and

literally run over to my trainer to get a forty-five-minute session in, grab an ultra-quick shower, and dial into the conference call before I was even back at the office.

Obsessed. I packed protein and veggie lunches, my only carbs the sweet potato. Yeah, I got made fun of more than once for pulling out my snacks at client offsites, but I wore it like a badge; I was better than you.

I was in, deep—a high-performance machine running on ambition, protein bars, and sweat. Climbing the corporate ladder *and* the rope ladder (okay, not true—not enough arm-strength—but I do like the phrase). I ate like a machine and I worked out like a machine. I was frazzling mightily between the ears and I felt like working out and having abs were keeping me together. A house of cards, I tell you.

And, remember, I was also *working* like a machine too. From 2013-2015 I doubled, and then redoubled, my revenue numbers for the agency. In 2011, I managed one million dollars; by 2017 it was the closest to my goal of ten million dollars we ever got.

I was good, yeah, but in my mind, I could always be better. Ah, the hamster wheel.

This stamina and the ability to work harder, longer, to push mind and body to the limit did help me "succeed" in the corporate world. My mind and muscles were like tacks. Like cogs in the wheel of some corporate machine. More, more, more, faster. Faster, faster! Except, I was not a machine. No one is.

We're human beings.

At the time, I had little to zero awareness of my mental health issue—the *Underlying Fear of Everything* that drove my career and life choices.

Professionals generally call this "anxiety," and I was a textbook case. A lot of people drown it out with alcohol or Xanax; fitness was simply *my* coping mechanism of choice. When my heart rate was above 160, I could finally clear my mind. So I went there all the time.

I'd get my hour of hard-core workout in, and it was the lone hour of the day not spent worrying about something (everything).

Now, if you aren't aware of what anxiety can do to the human body, it's not a pretty picture. Long-term, persistent anxiety is a pervasive little demon that nibbles away at your body's inner workings—leading to shortness of breath, skin rashes, heart problems, and a host of other pesky impediments to your body's systems.

For me, anxiety fits would send my mind to this place where I'd convince myself there was something terribly wrong with me, that I was going to die, was going to leave my family all alone while I looked at them like Patrick Swayze does Demi in the first two-thirds of *Ghost*. Helpless.

And, when I got this scary anxiety (or when I occasionally still do) I did not like myself. It sucked.

Perhaps you've experienced something like this yourself. Most Americans do. If you haven't, count your lucky stars.

Now onto Cortisol: Hand in hand with prolonged anxiety comes increased cortisol levels. Cortisol is often referred to as the "stress hormone." Like most chemicals your body produces, it *can* serve a benevolent purpose, that of regulating blood pressure and helping metabolize glucose to reduce inflammation. But, also like most chemicals that your body produces, it needs to exist in a particular balance in order to do its good work. When it's not in balance, it can raise your insulin levels so much so that it causes you to overeat (especially craving sugary foods, and the feedback loop continues). Imbalanced cortisol can also: suppress thyroid function, lower your bone and muscle density, and increase belly fat. And increased belly fat isn't just some cosmetic problem—it leads to an increased chance of heart attacks, strokes, and other not-so-fun cholesterol-related problems.

So, stress = not good. It's not cortisol's fault; you need it, it's vital. It's just that when you're stressed out, you get way too much of it. Stress! That's the root cause of cortisol imbalance.

And that leads me to the word "balance." While I do respect the word, I've never liked it that much—because I never could measure it.

"Am I balanced?"

I never knew. Did I spend enough time with my kids today? This week? This year? Did I give one hundred percent at work today? (Is one hundred percent even on the balance chart?)

That's why I prefer the word "flow." Flow is, for me, *the permission to trust that it will all come out in the wash as long as I live with integrity.*

Flow means: "Hey, Lauren, today you may not have been the world's greatest mom, but tomorrow you can watch a whole movie with your son and (try) not to fall asleep before the credits roll." Flow means, "hey, today I scarfed some fast food, but tomorrow I'll take that hike and eat a shit ton of leafy things."

Balance always feels like pressure to keep two sides of some imaginary scale from falling over to one side. *Flow* lets me live my life the best I can, learning from both my good days and my not-so-good days in a continuous path toward where I know I am going.

I'll probably return to flow a fair amount in this book because I like the word and it's my book, yeah, but mostly because it's been huge in my wellness and maybe it can help you too. And that's really what this book is about. Helping.

Flow has helped me keep my body, heart, and mind going—and I think the essence behind the term can help people.

Say it with me, F L O W.

And my understanding and dedication to flow have been completely elevated by discoveries made through cannabis. In a very self-sustaining way, my intentional use of cannabis has helped me find and increase my capacities for flow—in a lot of different areas of my life.

And getting "in the flow" starts with seeing what *isn't* in flow. Like all that fitness stuff during the corporate big-whig time of my life. It wasn't a flow but that coping mechanism I've spoken of, a way of escaping deep-seated anxiety. It wasn't about the process (which is what flow is), but about results. Goal-oriented results. It was about control, about crazy if-then statements like, "*If* I eat healthy and work out like a maniac, *then* I will be perfect."

I wasn't working out to work out. I was working out to escape and I was working out to attain. Not super Zen.

I could control my life through working out—that was my thinking. That was the thinking of being the product of the New York rat race. And while those abs did look gooood, they were a façade. The lifestyle wasn't sustainable and it would eventually burn me out.

And burnout is not a good thing. I'll say this about mental and physical health: they are inextricably linked. Our culture tends to treat them as separate entities when—by any spiritual *or* scientific measure—they are not.

We are whole beings, nothing within our system is acting in a vacuum. The knee bone is connected to the hip bone, which is connected to your gut health, which is connected to your brain function. Each part of our existence affects the health of the other parts of our existence; emotional and spiritual unwellness can, and will, tank our physical health. Loss of physical health can (and will) trigger depression or chip away at our trust in the universe or cause us to eat an entire pizza and drink a bottle of wine in an hour while mindlessly scrolling Instagram.

On some level, it's a little hard for me to talk about my fitness because, well, I was blessed with good physical genetics; a lot of people won't ever get the anxiety I've had to endure, but I've never really struggled with my weight—I gained and lost, but never more than fifteen pounds. My type of anxiety actually makes me not hungry, sometimes nauseous at even the thought of food. I never

"stress ate." Sorry. We all get dealt different cards. No one's got a royal flush.

Yet even with the physically genetic hand I was dealt, my body *still* became a source of stress. A constant source of stress. It was never good enough. And the harder I worked, the more distant the goals seemed. Once I got the six-pack, I wanted the eight-pack. My body mass index could always "be better." My butt was never firm enough.

I could never touch the rainbow; it was always only glimpsed on some unattainable horizon. Fitness became an obsession largely because my body image became an obsession.

Ironic to say (and almost silly as I look back at it with my new perspective) but the better I looked the better I felt I *could* look. It was a never-ending loop of more—just like the corporate world and its money.

My abs became almost like my brand. People took note. And once I got them, the pressure to never not have them was a whole new source of stress.

It was as if my mind-body system was saying, "Congratulations, Lauren, you've discovered an entirely new form of anxiety!!"

(The ego is a crazy thing. Try not to feed it.)

Outward expressions of fitness—the six-pack, the toned arms, and legs—look good in a photograph. But they're not always good indications of what's going on under the hood. The machine may look shiny, but down where it counts the gears may be grinding. You could be overexerting and over-exercising yourself, to death.

In fact, that's not an entirely uncommon problem in our country; injuries related to overexertion account for millions of emergency room visits each year.

That will tell you a bit about the rat race culture right there. Yeah, turns out less *can* be more. It took me a long time—and a few puffs—to realize the obviousness of that one.

But not before my machine decided to turn on its check engine light.

I'm not here to advocate cannabis as a replacement for a good therapist, a good psychiatrist, diet, exercise, meditation, or even the right 'meds.' One of the things I am here to do is to advocate for: the measured, informed, and thoughtful use of cannabis; use of a plant from the earth with a long relationship with humanity as a means to mitigate the effects of long-term anxiety.

# Seven

## *Machine(s)*

My role in the cog of the corporate America machine was revenue. That's like saying my role in keeping the Nile flowing was providing water. If money was God, the Messiah was revenue. And I was *"director"* of it.

The parent company dictated down to us just how much money we were supposed to bring in in a certain amount of time—how much, when—and it fell to me and the few others at my level to make it happen. Hell or high water. Gain clients, change clients, conjure clients out of thin air. Projections were unrealistic and deadlines came fast. It was big-money, big-America, high-stakes, high-pressure, win-or-go-home type shit.

Our jobs—and the jobs of those on our teams we cared about—rode on unrealistic target projections that were nearly impossible to meet. One of the reasons why is that the numbers were inflated. Yeah. Welcome to the ethos of corporate America.

We were told to "make sure to take your numbers up." This was, we were told, to validate new hires and make sure we didn't have to

lay off our friends. We were betting on big deals before they came home to roost, to assume, to inflate the fish before you told the story. The bigger the story the bigger the sell; the bigger our sell the bigger our image.

It really was a fake currency.

So, we started adding on more and more bullshit. They gave us mile-markers that could not be achieved, and so we did what we had to do to survive. They asked us for higher and higher projections and so we gave them to them. When we met them, we were asked, "Why didn't you shoot higher?" And when you didn't meet them, you didn't get invited to the next pitch and soon there were new holes to fill.

We all killed ourselves to reach the unattainable mountain top. We truly were hamsters.

Every new business pitch, then, came with the grinding weight of: "if we lose it, we're not succeeding. If we lose it, it was a 'bad idea.' If we lose it, we will have to let someone on our team go." No matter how good your idea was, how many hours you put in or how killer of a pitch you just nailed in front of a room of wowed executives to come away with the vibes that you were 'already working together.'

No dice. Someone else "came in lower." That other company had "the angle they wanted." So many things were out of our control, out of my control—and I tried to control them anyway. When I couldn't, I tried harder. I had to succeed at my primary function in life: bringing in revenue to a never-satiated corporate behemoth that had my total devotion.

And I told my friends it was "my dream job." Wow. I'm just sorry it took me so long to pick up that vape pen.

Here's a little scene for you:

It's the summer of 2016 and I'm working on a pitch for a very large piece of the wellness biz's pie. I was the relationship holder of the account. I knew it was a good deal. If we got it, it would make our year—and go a long way to digging me out of the hole from

losing a big client fourteen months prior. Every day was "ER rather than PR." I was all work.

The deal lingered and even when I followed through on my word to meet my family in Cape Cod over the fourth of July, my body was there but I wasn't. I spent the whole time on my computer or on the phone arguing and colluding with colleagues about the proposal—all while schmoosing another new client on the side who was issuing me a huge RFP (request for proposal).

Plus, time with that part of my family is stressful enough under ideal circumstances. (Lotsa different energies there.) Add in being hip-deep in the middle of the deal of the decade and you have a quagmire.

A really stressful and chaotic quagmire.

I couldn't get enough work done because I was expected to actually interact with my family. (I know, right?) And I couldn't ever get in the flow of just being with my family because of the emails and day-and-night calls.

Yet, if I'm being honest, I thrived on being busy, on being busy in front of everyone. It was our culture. Dad always worked on our vacations. And he was eating it all up, the business, his daughter's pitches, and the big companies and their ideas.

Facádes.

Everyone was getting short shrift. It sucked. A really tough few days. I was angry. I felt both like I was getting cheated and that I was cheating everyone else. I was on high alert. I was puffed up—and then came the pin prick.

We were driving along the road between Truro and Provincetown. The sun was setting and the dunes were warm-hued in their red. I looked to the ocean, the reason I was there in the first place, to somehow connect with it. I hadn't touched the water all day because of work. We're driving along, the blue waters of the ocean like something from Tantalus, and next, this shooting, electric pain starts jolting down my leg. It came out of nowhere. It was just there. And

it hurt. And it wasn't stopping. I couldn't explain it.

"Is it a reaction to something?" my sister asked from the front seat.

"I don't think so," I said, rubbing my leg. Being the professional anxiety-haver I am, the next words that came out of my mouth were, "I think it must be multiple sclerosis."

My family half-laughed, but I was scared. An intense pain was shooting down my leg. I had no idea what was causing it. It wasn't cool.

I reached for my phone and consulted WebMD. I performed an extensive Google search and ran down more than a few threads.

Time elapsed. We got where we were going, and after a few drinks, the pain seemed to fade. But on the way home from the Cape, it came back. I was in the car with Barry talking about the weekend we'd just had. Same as before; it came on fast then slowly subsided. When I got back to work a few days later, it resurfaced again.

I eventually forgot about the pain—it would come and it would go and maybe I just learned to live with it—but other things in my life started getting worse too. I lost patience with my kids, with my team, and my clients. I lost patience with a lot of people in my life. I lost patience with Life.

I had no idea then, but those electric pains from the summer would return, on again off again, for a long time to come—and their name was anxiety. I used to only feel my anxiety in my chest and now it had become a full-blown, full-body thing. Some weeks even the most delicious food, my favorite meals, smelled terrible. There were days I was sure I had the flu, some sort of virus, only to realize later that my brain had orchestrated the whole thing.

My commitment to fitness too was killing me. I was working out 6-7 days a week. I was using it to escape instead of to heal. If I skipped a day, I feared I'd lose my gains. I was always going at one hundred and fifty percent. And then my back just started hurting.

Miserable, shooting, constant back pain. Again, a mystery. No idea how or what caused it.

Only later, with the green clarity of cannabinoid hindsight, do I understand why those jarring ailments showed up: It was my mind and my body pleading with me to stop abusing them. The exterior still looked shiny, but the gears were not happy. I needed to slow down. Physically, emotionally, and mentally.

It's important to understand here that the pressures I was under were very, very real. And that for most people who suffer from anxiety, their external circumstances very much influence—trigger—their internal mindset. Anxiety is not a made-up thing, not something your boyfriend or girlfriend is making up to garner attention or to get out of doing the dishes. To exist with perennial and pervasive anxiety is not a normal, healthy state of existence. Left unaddressed and untreated, anxiety takes its toll, deteriorating one's quality of life in a ton of possible ways.

In my case, my body finally cried out, "Please stop. You're killing me."

I needed to remove myself from the hamster wheel or else I was going to die going round and round in place.

"Well, that's fascinating and all, Lauren," you may be asking, "but what does all this have to do with weed?" Well—cannabis was my gateway to mindfulness, and the stillness and perspective it gave me finally allowed me to take the step back and see what was going on.

I'm not here to advocate cannabis as a replacement for a good therapist, a good psychiatrist, diet, exercise, meditation, or even the right "meds." One of the things I *am* here to do is to advocate for: the *measured, informed, and thoughtful use of cannabis*; use of a plant from the earth with a long relationship with humanity as a means to mitigate the effects of long-term anxiety.

What I'm also here to say is that everything is connected. Anxiety,

mind, body, joy, relaxation, pain, pain-freeness—and that cannabis can help the flow and health of the entire wholeness of the system.

When my machine decided to rebel against my routine, I began exploring cannabis more seriously. I was still only smoking rarely, only with Barry, and not in anything but super low amounts. But, even in my limited use, I was discovering that it was possible to feel good again—to get a natural reprieve, to enjoy my husband, my children and breathe a little bit.

A little cannabis in the evenings, I found, helped me keep the Jenga pieces of my life from crashing down.

"It's nice to see you relaxed," my husband told me in so many words. "It's nice to see you smile."

And for the first time I could remember, I came to know relaxation. I came to have a relationship with it, to get to know a side of life that was not perpetual flexing. Until I met cannabis, I had either forgotten or never known what true relaxation was.

I learned to uncurl what was so wound-up inside me. Some of my friends got this through Savasana at the end of our yoga classes. I'd look at them during Savasana, see this sense of tranquility on their faces as they lay still as statues and explored the infinite—all while my mind raced 1.27 million miles per hour above a body that was all twitchy and itchy.

Maybe I'm just not equipped like other people. Maybe I'm not as good at yoga as other people. See, the feeling of relaxation, for me, was akin to the feeling of falling, of giving up, akin to failing.

Relaxation felt like dying. Until cannabis said, "here is a way through the pain, Lauren—here is a way through the fear."

I discovered that I could find some of that Zen. Some flow through cannabis. And I knew other people could too.

Maybe I did absorb some of Thoreau's lessons as a flailing American Lit major–perhaps those Robert Frost poems my mom read have finally gotten through. "I took the path less traveled, and that–that has made all the difference." In these woods, I have finally found my voice.

# Eight

## *Mountain High*

Now, I've gotta be honest—I'm no longer the ripped-bronze statue with abs worthy of the Greek wing of the Met. And that's alright. Better than alright even. I'm happy. What I have now is better. I have a six-pack soul.

I love my body, as it is, for where I am in this "Auntie Lauren" time of my life. Auntie Lauren, that's me at Hi-Curious, my persona. A loving, caring, silver-haired soul.

I do still have the boobs I paid for during that corporate image-building. Those are (thankfully) here to stay, but the rest of me is a little bit softer. Inside and out. The grey hairs that "magically" appeared when I stopped dying them after eighteen years? That's fine too. I guess the follicles simply gave up, and I love the gray. I really do. Maybe people think I'm a little wiser when they see my silver hair. Who knows? I also wear wigs on the regular, as you can see from the pics in the book. It pushes me outside my comfort zone and makes the inside and the outside match.

I also stopped getting Restylane and other enhancements. I am happy trying to love all of me, forever, as I age.

(Feel free to call me out on that sentence when I am repping Botox in 2035.)

And all those stoner stereotypes everyone worried I'd become as I incorporated cannabis into my daily lifestyle?? They didn't happen. Sure, I slowed down from a pace that was killing me. But that was necessary. That was, is, a positive. But I still get shit done. I'm still as motivated as I was before the "puff," just in different ways. I'm not lazy, and I don't eat pizza five times a week. I just needed to stop beating on my body and mind. I needed to feel good.

My other virtual mentor, Gabby Bernstein, reminds us in her book, *Super Attractor*, that "it's good to feel good!" Such a simple sentence that can mean so little or so much depending on how we read it, how we hear it.

In my drive to achieve at all costs, I'd deprived myself of feeling good. Now I make feeling good a priority. Some days it's a little cannabis and some days it's a lot. And it's always a shortcut to feeling better, to help me work through things more quickly and without the fight or flight.

In the choice between heart attacks or hypertension and a little cannabis, I'll take the green weed every time.

And I'm a whole lot kinder to my body now. I'm kinder to my mind. I'm kinder to my family. I'm more in the flow. And that is key.

I no longer live in New York. Had to get out of there! I reside now where the Rocky Mountains meet the Great Plains, in beautiful Boulder, Colorado. To the west lie the Flatirons, their peaks tipped white with snow in the winter months—and I can see them from my back porch. The air is crisp. The sky is huge. And the wilds of nature are at my fingertips anytime I want their taste.

Is Boulder a "hippie town?" Well, kind of. Yes, I suppose it is, and I love it. But, if you think that hippie town means everyone on the street is smoking weed, you're wrong.

One thing you could say is that it's a place where everyone loves the outdoors—a place of competitive athletes and noncompetitive athletes, a place where life moves at a gentler pace than I ever knew before. Boulder is wildlife, conservation, universities, and a vibrant arts and music scene. And that wild nature? I spend at least six hours a week out in it, challenging myself with big hikes and often simply sitting on my back deck with my dogs, working in the out of doors as I listen to the birds chirp and watch the seasons change.

I've been carving out new ways to combine work and wellness, and I live a life of my own design. Not everyone wants to live this way—some people like fast-paced—but for me, at this stage of my life, the mountain vibe is the right choice. The healthy choice.

Building my cannabis company here allows me to live my lifestyle out loud and legal. And that feels good. It also means that when the stress of being an entrepreneur has me so angry that I lose my cool on a Friday conference call (yeah, the stress can still rear its head), I can drive twenty gorgeous minutes to a steep mountain trail that gets the heart rate up and clears my mind.

Just like the old days at the gym, but better, more on my terms. More birds too.

I'll find a sunny rock blocked from the wind, stare at the mountains and sky, and meditate. (Never could do *that* in NY.) My pulse calms. My body releases. My perspective shifts, a life balanced by the ebb and flow of my breath.

And then I'll turn around and come back down the mountain towards town, the descent often filled with my favorite music or me recording some silly video of myself that I send to friends or post on Instagram.

Though I've put on a couple pounds, I just feel lighter these days.

Maybe I did absorb some of Thoreau's lessons as a flailing American Lit major—perhaps those Robert Frost poems my mom read have finally gotten through. "I took the (path) less traveled by, and that has made all the difference." In these woods, I have finally found my voice.

I went through a lot of shit inside my mind. And I feel better now.

And so, yeah, I live in hippie-techy Boulder town, and I smoke and ingest my cannabis and I run my new business ventures, ventures so much more aligned with *who I really am*. My life is more "whole." And in many ways, I'm more active now than I was back then. Active in healthier, more vibrant ways, partaking in activities that are good for both body and mind.

I'm not obsessed with keeping that externally perfect physique anymore. I came to understand was that it was coming at too steep a price. It was coming at the price of just about everything else under the hood. I don't look like an elite athlete anymore and thank God for that. It was killing me.

Being active and fit, now, means doing things that make me feel good rather than things that make me look good. I've come to fully process the idea that my body and my mind are not here for the consumption of others; I'm here to live my greatest potential, period.

So, yeah, Boulder has been a big part of this total life transformation. And a big part of getting here has been the choice to live authentically, and out loud, about how cannabis has helped me do that. I can do this in Boulder, Colorado.

Recently, I drove my newly sixteen-year-old to the Denver airport so he could visit my mom and stepdad in New York for the week. Chase and I were talking about someone in the cannabis industry he knows who recently stopped using weed.

"When are you going to do that, Mom?" he asked with that sixteen-year-old challenge voice.

I took it as non-judgmentally as I could. "You think I should stop smoking weed?"

"No way," he said with a big laugh. "I was just kidding. You are

so much more 'nice mommy' now. You used to be 'mean mommy' a lot."

He's sixteen but we can all talk like toddlers sometimes. And that's good; it's good to connect to our inner child. Even in motherhood. When I heard those words from my youngest son, I knew I was—I knew that I have been—walking the right path.

See, cannabis and Colorado have helped me restore the body-mind connection that we all inherently have. The combination has helped me to be more mindful and enjoy living in my own skin. It's been a good journey, and we all go on journeys. Maybe cannabis—and some time in the mountains—can help you on yours.

I didn't realize that my anger was, really, anxiety. (They do always say that anger is a secondary emotion, right?) And let me tell you, I was angry!

All. The. Time.

# Nine
## *Type-A, Much?*

My sisters found their way to therapy well before I did. Good for them. But when they spoke their "therapy language" to me it might as well have been Portuguese. Or Cantonese. I could never understand their feelings in the ways they tried to explain them.

"My sisters both are deeper than I am," I'd rationalize. "I don't need therapy. I'm fine."

"Fine," though, as every woman knows, is not a good word.

In my perspective now, through these Auntie Lauren eyes, I understand that (1) sometimes there just aren't the words to describe depression and (2) anxiety isn't a "feeling" but a disease that attacks you from your state of mind outward.

I should have been in therapy as a young girl back when my parents got divorced. Because that word "divorce," that experience of divorce, is a seismic shift for a child. It was for me. And it should be supported and assisted whenever possible.

But not me, no, I was always "fine."

I just wanted to be normal. I decided I didn't need any of that therapy shit and tried to move on with my life.

But the truth is, I never truly dealt with how betrayed I felt by my dad after the divorce. It made me feel like *everything* in the world was more important than I was. To be clear (with hindsight I can say this in all honesty) my dad did turn himself inside-out to be a "good dad" after the divorce; he'd drive back and forth all the time between the city and Long Island just to see us. And he eventually even moved out to Long Island to be closer. He did the best he could, and if I didn't know that then, I do now. He didn't have it easy either. None of us did. Our family dynamic was a tough "first-world problem," for sure; yeah, we had money, but we didn't have a lot of the other stuff that happy families do.

I just always wanted more from my father. I wanted him to choose me and my sister and my mom over his new life. I was a kid, and I wanted my dad around more. Maybe no matter what he did, I wouldn't have been happy. I listened to Cat Stevens' *Cats in the Cradle* on repeat, over and over and over, and cried for what might have been.

And that song? I learned recently that it's a true story. It's hard to be a good parent *and* earn real money doing something important to you—whether your name is Cat Stevens, Yusef Islam, Lauren Mundell, or Shakira. I know this now, but I didn't back then.

Maybe I put all my blame on my dad. I know my mom was at least half responsible, but she always seemed like she just wanted him (or maybe just our life) back—and that's what I osmosed. So I blamed Dad. I felt sad. I felt alone. I felt abandoned. No one else I knew had divorced parents—this was way back in the early eighties. I felt lonely and abandoned and dirty. I felt "other," because my parents no longer lived together.

Like a lot of people, my disinterest in therapy was probably due to a few different factors. But honestly, I was just scared that people would find out there was something really wrong with me. When I

finally did go to therapy, I did so to prove to myself (and the therapist) that I was okay. I didn't go there to work on myself. I went to make sure I wasn't crazy.

So, all of my therapy experiences always felt like the pitch room. I was trying to win, and winning—to me, Ms. Female Executive, how I saw it—looked like convincing myself and the therapist that "everyone else in my life is crazy, not me . . . they're the one who needs therapy!"

Thank you very much, here's a check, see you next week.

I had no interest in feeling better. I didn't know that there was a *better* to feel. I just wanted to be normal. Now I have a therapist who really helps me make changes and do hard stuff with more grace. Now I am actually honest about what is going on with me, how I feel, and what I want to work on. And? Turns out, I'm waaaay too hard on myself. I wish I had a therapist call me on my bullshit of normalcy a long time ago—though I am sure I wouldn't have heard a word they said.

Plus, in New York no good therapists take insurance and most of them charge $250 per hour. My justification, for years, was that I "couldn't afford it." Couldn't afford it?! My personal trainer ran $80 an hour and I saw him twice a week. I spent more than $250 on my haircuts for crying out loud. My excuses were bullshit.

"Oh, but Lauren," I'd tell myself, "you can't afford the time."

I couldn't spare one hour a week? *Everyone* can do that. The human being who says these words is the human being who really needs to carve out the time. I was a classic case.

Maybe somewhere in my reticence to therapy were the echoes of that very first, very unpleasant cannabis experience where I had been given way too much way too soon: The paranoia-fit and accidentally kicking over the rock in my subconscious to reveal a bunch of creepy-crawly things I wasn't ready to see. My mind told me those bugs were some remnant artifacts from my parents' divorce and the abandonment issues that came with it. (I guess I could at least psychoanalyze *myself*.)

It's not far-fetched to think that I had no interest in kicking over that rock again, even in the controlled environment of therapy. And when I did finally go to therapy a few times, I never gave it a serious shot. Never put the work in on myself.

I was looking for a co-conspirator out of my therapist, and I never had any doctor call my bluff on it. I just kept psychoanalyzing the analyzer.

I was not going to do therapy—not until proper, well-dosed, thoughtful cannabis use allowed me the insights I needed: I came to see that the anxiety was attacking my body, to a very detrimental degree, and I made the decision to cross that threshold and deal with the damage it was doing.

So, now I go to therapy. And therapy helps me process some things. And one of those things was understanding what my sisters went through with their mental health, understanding why it always felt like a different language and I felt helpless to connect with them.

Looking back now, I understand that my inability to connect with my sisters when they talked about their depressions was because my own struggles weren't manifesting as depression; mine manifested as anger. Mine manifested as frustrated. Mine manifested as having been cheated. Type-A, much?

I was annoyed by everyone and everything. I was annoyed with my work for constantly forcing me to struggle with things beyond my control. I was annoyed with my family for "needing" me. I was annoyed with my friends for inviting me to functions they knew I was "too busy to attend, goddammit!"

In my own head, I was still identifying these negative feelings as "situational stress" rather than the long-term problem they had become. I was always on edge, always just one missed LIRR train away from a rant about whoever happened to be closest to my last nerve.

The final straw, the one that sent me to the doctor and come out with the Lexapro was when I burst into fuming tears with a

particularly difficult colleague. It was an unreasonable response and I felt embarrassed, so I went to my regular MD with complaints of feeling on edge.

Before I got into the exam room, I was asked to take a test: "How many times in the past week have you [insert anxiety-related behavior of your choosing]?"

My responses were telling. To each question, I'd think to myself, "In the last week? How about in the last twenty-four hours?"

Up until that minute, I didn't realize that my anger was, really, anxiety. (They do always say that anger is a secondary emotion, right?) And let me tell you, I was angry!

All. The. Time.

Next question on the exam: "How many times in the past week have you decided not to do something you used to love?" That one stopped me in my tracks. Suddenly made to reckon with the harsh fact that, outside of work, I simply had no energy for anything. Not my family, not my friends; all I was doing was working, working out, and being angry.

I thought everyone else was putting something on me. I didn't see that all of it was me!

I had been an avid knitter for most of my life; I found the act therapeutic in itself, me and the yarn and the needle. It connected me to memories of my grandmother—and to older, gentler parts of myself. When the doc asked me about hobbies that I love, I realized I hadn't "had time" to knit for God knew how long.

"I'm trying to get through life," I admitted, "instead of *living* it. I don't knit anymore. My weekends consist solely of 'recovering' from the pressure of the previous week and preparing for the battles to come."

"Do you allow yourself the entire weekend?"

"Well, the electronic haranguing starts up again with the Sunday-evening emails."

The therapist looked at me and nodded and wrote something down in her notebook. I started Lexapro that coming week. It helped.

And had I not just begun my personal research with cannabis use, gained those first few steps on the path of perspective, I'm not sure I'd have allowed myself to go on the stuff. I had always been so anti-medication. But, like Barry had told me, "weed is kinda like a medicine." And I had been slowly incorporating *it* into my life. Without that, I don't think I would have tried Lexapro.

I found that they worked well together. Combination of the hippie and the pharmaceutical—modern living.

Lexapro helped me not freak out as much, and a few puffs of the pen or the pipe helped me to actually feel good. I was more in the flow for sure, maybe even more balanced. I don't know, still can't measure that one. But I came to experience a life that was a little less wound-up. Before successful therapy and the weed/Lexapro combo, I had no benchmark for what it was that I needed. I hadn't even realized that "living all tightly wound" isn't normal; most people *don't* wake up *and* go to sleep that way.

My inner workings had not been in flow, and I had been feeling that way for so long that it had become invisible. It had become, like I'd say, "just how it *is*."

And in some ways, Lexapro helped me enjoy cannabis even more. There was a clear symbiotic relationship between the two substances, and for the first time in my life, I was beginning to get a handle on what it felt like to not exist in a state of constant anxiety and frustration.

Cannabis enabled me to see the anxiety in the first place, to identify the problem (which is the *first* step)—and Lexapro helped me manage that problem. They were a tag team prescription. One just happened to be illegal where I was living.

Society, man.

But with the measurable results I was receiving in my day-to-day living, I no longer felt any guilt about making space for cannabis in my life. Slowly but surely, I was coming out of the closet.

I knew I had to make a move, and Like John Muir said,
"The mountains were calling..."

# Ten
## *Satiation*

Living in New York and being the daughter of my father, working in the industry that I did, I had a certain meaning associated with the word "strength." I don't think it was an accurate or healthy definition. After some cannabinoid and traditional therapy, I started reading a lot—and started to define the word differently.

I found an author who spoke a new language, another virtual mentor you may have heard of but who probably hasn't heard of me (yet)—Brené Brown. Brené is a vulnerability and shame researcher and author. She taught me to see that where I had been raised to see vulnerability as a weakness or a "soft spot," it was actually a strength. Brené also introduced me to a concept she calls "the lonely feeling." Lonely. This was how I was feeling. Lonely, estranged, not connected, un-whole. I look back now through my "Auntie Lauren lens" to literally see whole stretches of my life where I felt lonely the entire time. I was trying to be my father's version of strong (invulnerable, impenetrable) and it was leaving me empty.

Enter cannabis: it helped me to relax, yes, but it was also giving me this new awareness of the emotional minefield I'd been blindly

navigating for so long. It helped me understand that I had normalized a lifestyle and an attitude that was deeply anormal and "a-healthy."

I was round-pegging the square box, and that is the antithesis of flow. I was trying to fit into what others told me "strong" was.

Sure, we can talk about how common it is in our society for women to turn themselves into sex objects. I mean, yeah, I did get the boob job. ("Sex sells! Sex sells!") But I had also turned myself into a "success object," defining my value as a human being by my occupational wins and external accomplishments. Frankly, as a woman in the business I was in, the two went hand in hand. Part of the game. And I was coming to realize that I didn't want to play it anymore.

The thing is this: we all get to decide what success is for ourselves. I have to, you have to, we all have to.

For me, success came not to be measured by how much money I have in the bank or how highly others regard me. It wasn't about fancy diamonds necklaces or expensive new toys. Success, cannabis helped me see, was simply about: how happy I felt and how much I *felt* like I had. Seems simple, right? I didn't get it, not for a long time.

I'm still on my journey. I don't have it all figured out. Sure, the ways in which I have changed my life have helped moved me into a more healthy lifestyle, a more in-the-flow lifestyle, but sometimes I still hustle too hard, still test my stamina for work. And I know I can continue to improve: I still love to shop and strive to have nice things. I tell myself it stems from a desire for freedom, comfort, and a growing confidence that I am already a "success," but so was Mother Theresa. And she didn't feel the need to shoulder designer purses.

I may never be perfect, but I'm working on it.

Case in point: the Friday conference call with the client who hasn't been doing what she needs to do on her end to get the most out of your work. You may lose it. I did, just the other day. I yelled at the client and then when we hung up, I yelled at myself. I yelled at myself for not listening to my gut. I knew it wasn't a good fit with

this client; I knew the timing was off and I knew I didn't listen to what I knew. I made a decision to go through with the Friday call from my mind and not from my gut. And I got pissed at myself for doing it. I wished I had made a different decision, wished I could go back in time and "do it over." We all get these feelings at times, even the most enlightened among us. Well, maybe the Dalai Lama doesn't, but most of us do.

I know my dad still does.

"I've never felt satisfied," he told me during one of our last face-to-face conversations. "I've bought and sold a few agencies and I've made a lot of money. I've lived in nice homes and I get to play my three hours of tennis every day in Cape Cod . . . I have four children, three grandkids, and a wife who loves me. But I've never been satisfied. I don't know why."

It blew my mind to hear this.

"I figured if *I* could do all that," he continued, "it must not be *that* hard."

Damn, Dad. I guess the perspective of old age had realized him a few things. Or maybe I caught him in a moment where he was just feeling sorry for himself. I don't know. I do know that he never felt "present" to me. He was rarely around the home, always working on a project or doing something that wasn't social with us.

Even when he'd land a big deal, it was always about how he could make it better. If there were ever any roses around, he never stopped to sniff them.

"That's so sad," I thought, and I still can't shake his words. His admission was fuel for me. Fuel to further change how I see Life. My life. All of life.

I decided: "I don't want to be seventy-five years old and telling my sons I've never felt satisfied. That would suck."

With the vision that cannabis has lent me, I've come to see that always seeking more is a recipe for always seeking more. And if you're always seeking more, you're innately unsatisfied.

I can see now that I have all I need. Probably even still too much.

Most of us do, we just don't see it. The happiness quotient tells us that if we make between 70-80 thousand dollars a year, we are happier than if we make a million. And in some places of the country—and definitely the world—you don't even need $70K a year to make it work. I know people who live on communes. I know people who barter for most of the things they need. Jesus didn't seem to need much. Gandhi owned three things: his eyeglasses, his robe, his begging bowl. And that dude seemed okay.

"Yeah," I told myself in the last few months of my life in New York, "I can feel satisfied by enjoying what I have. External markers, shmexternal markers!"

I gave away all of my boutique-bought and always-dry-cleaned clothes to former team members. I even gave away the Jimmy Choos I wore to my wedding.

True happiness lay in what and how I prioritized—and my soul had to come first. I had to stop worrying about "running out of money," which really was the deep-seated fear that drove me. It took moving to Colorado and almost two whole years away from corporate America before I started to truly prioritize my mental, emotional, spiritual, and familial health. And, if I am being honest, workaholism is not something I am "over," maybe never will be over, but it's something I'm actively trying to change in my leadership style at Hi-Curious. Once I stopped to look around at the New York rat race all around me, the traffic, the constant hum of striving energy, the constantly interrupting noise, I started redefining what the word "success" means. And that is good.

If I could have simply quit my job right after that day on Clearwater Beach in 2017, I would have. Instead, I controlled what I could; *transition* is what I needed. I began to shift the pieces of my life to allow me to move out to Colorado and begin a business focused around a cannabis-rich wellness plan. I knew I had to make a move, and like John Muir said, "The mountains were calling . . . "

Plus, with marijuana still illegal in New York, it didn't feel good. It *wasn't* good.

I knew the benefits, and I saw the plant's acceptance growing in other parts of the country in election after election. I didn't want to have to continue to go through a drug dealer to get my medication. (Plus, your local drug dealer isn't exactly a purveyor of wellness products; you don't generally know what you're getting, what's in it, how it's been treated, or how to control the experience you have with it. More on that later.) I wanted to be able to walk into a store and ask knowledgeable people about the product and get what I wanted. Legally and with all the information I could get. I wanted to get the most out of the medicine that I could.

And that meant Colorado.

In the course of my move, I decided to go off Lexapro. I was still clinging to the feeling of wanting to achieve and change without "enhancements" from pharmaceuticals. But you really have to look at hard things in your psyche if you're going to do that. I wasn't prepared yet to do so.

I went off the med cold turkey without talking to my doctor and it affected me. My house in New York wasn't selling. It gave me stress. Obtaining a home in Colorado wasn't going as well as planned. That gave me stress. The tectonic plates of my life were shifting and I struggled to find good footing. I started feeling out of control, and I went back on Lexapro. It felt like some admission of failure, but going off of it for a little bit gave me some more of that valuable perspective I keep talking about. I realized that my chemistry wasn't working like it should and that I needed some help to stay on an even keel. I came to fully understand that there is a place for dosed medications. Weed was showing me that. I had to quiet my ego a bit to admit that, but I did. Finally.

And with medication, it's all about the dose. I could have taken a higher dose of Lexapro to be "more even" but that wasn't what I was looking for. I needed to retain my humanity. (It helps you not feel the bad things, but I decided that some bad things are part of life.) There's a difference between facing stressful situations with

a level head and not responding appropriately when high-stakes circumstances demand you to be fully present.

The same holds true for cannabis. The boogeyman of overuse has some justification insofar as, yes, if you overuse it, you *will* feel it; some people can get way too "into their head." Paranoia can be a real thing. And those images we have of the stereotypical stoner did come from somewhere. So, just like with Lexapro, I kept a strict eye on my dosages with cannabis.

There's an idiom out there that "nothing happens in a vacuum," and it's certainly true for mental health. It took a lot of reading and a lot of thinking and a lot of meditating (another personal activity aided by cannabis) to arrive at the conclusion that I needed to do things differently—and that proper cannabis use was a necessary step on that path. It was all about the ability to see things differently.

I learned through literature, through research, and through my own forays that cannabis has a definitive role to play in mental health and emotional wellness. It can, as it did for me, relax and ease "situational anxiety." It can offer a degree of internal focus that may have been previously lacking—leading to more informed and introspective decision making. In the case of those with ADHD (while I'm not diagnosed, I bear many of the markers) it can simply slow you down enough to allow you to be in the moment, to be mindful, to live in your own skin for a while.

New areas of research are also opening up to explore cannabis as a means of helping those who live with PTSD and in those who cannot rely on pharmaceutical options due to some of their side effects.

It's an exciting time for weed.

The more we come to understand what this plant is and what it can do, the more we are seeing that we are only just beginning to understand its potential as a wellness supplement.

I had to go through some trials to find the balance of supplements that was right for me, and when I did, I was better able to show my best self. I live with an authenticity and confidence now that I simply

wasn't able to do before. Even when I was kicking ass in the pitch rooms and earning all that money, it was an act.

So, am I "all better?"

Good grief, no. Anxiety doesn't work like that. Few things in life do. Becoming your best self is not an endpoint but a journey. Happiness, as they say, is a byproduct of the journey. There really is no "destination."

But am I better now than I was a year ago, two years ago, ten years ago? Absolutely. I'm better in the sense that I'm not afraid of introspection the way I used to be. Introspection used to scare the heck out of me. *To look inward?* Yikes.

Not anymore.

I'm better in the sense that I have given myself the space to create a life that brings me joy and not just more stress. I'm better in the sense that I can strive for more if I want to, but I am also okay to sit back and take delight in what I have: my friends, my work, my home, my family.

In other words, the now.

If you take one thing from this book, take this: There is no shame in living in the present. We've been told by the machine for all of our lives that we must keep looking to the future, that tomorrow must be better than today, that more is always better. It's not. Appreciating what we have is the best bank account.

And there's no reason to feel ashamed of your emotions—we're human beings, we have them. Own them, understand them. And we all have struggles, it's okay to ask for help.

Everyone's personal flow is different, and our is a culture filled with people desperately in need of a method to reconnect with themselves. Cannabis probably isn't the *only* way to do that, but my experience shows that it can be an effective one.

For a lot of people out there, cannabis wellness is worth a try.

For the first time in my life, I understood why they wanted it to be quiet. It was so moving when I finally allowed myself to become part of it. The whole thing. The Rabbi, his voice, the clothes, the sad songs; standing up and sitting back down in those high-heel shoes; singing the prayers that flowed out of me from years of practice; the choir, the cantor's soprano, the different people all around me who shared a common history.

# Eleven
## *Cannabis & Spirituality*

Here's a fun activity if you're ever bored with a group of friends. Ask them what the word "spirituality" means. You'll get something like this:

"Uh, spirituality? You know, God and stuff."

"Yoga and ice cream."

"Understanding the oneness of nature."

"I saw a shooting start once."

"I mean, spirituality . . . it's like when you're 'spiritual.'"

"Sex."

Yeah, it's a loaded word and most of us have our own definitions of it; we're deeply personal with the intensity of our own definitions. Spirituality *can* mean religion, but it doesn't have to. Spirituality *can* mean meditation, but it doesn't have to. Spirituality *can* mean a connection to a higher power, but it doesn't necessarily have to.

But any way we slice it, most of us have a sense of the ineffable, of something that exists outside of our rational minds and outside of

our physical bodies that somehow binds the universe together. And, as "spiritual beings having a human experience," the care we give to that ineffable thing—whatever it may be—is no less important than getting your daily vitamins or step count.

Spirituality, while perhaps somewhat distinct from our emotional wellness, is highly interconnected to it. It's first cousins to our intellect. But spirituality and a connection to Spirit aren't just "woo woo" hippie things. They're not. They're real. They're ancient. And they're even tangible.

It can be a tricky thing to talk about spirituality, so I'm not going to go on and on about it. I'm just going to say this about talking about spirituality: it is possible to do it.

And we can all get to the center of the wheel of truth through different spokes. Just like with me and meditation—at one point in my life I thought it was impossible, and then, over time, I came to see that I could actually do it. If we never try to talk about spirituality, never try to understand it, or listen to others talk about it, it'll remain a foreign concept. Something too "elsewhere" to grasp.

But it doesn't have to be.

And, on that note, I'm going to tell you a little bit about my own experiences with Judaism. And if you're atheist or agnostic, that's okay. I am not going to try to convert you.

Judaism has been called the religion of ritual, and that's because ritual is a large part of the faith. We Jews have things to do at specific times in specific orders. Maybe it helps keep us grounded, maybe it just makes us good at making unleavened bread. I don't know. What I do know is that the first time I went to synagogue with Barry, it felt *right*.

We started dating about six months before our first Rosh Hashana together. Rosh Hashana and Yom Kippur make up the High Holidays. This has no relation to cannabis, at least none that have been made public; they're called this because they are the most important holidays of the year.

As I mentioned before, my first husband was not Jewish and while he did make an effort, it was nothing like the easy connection to religion and tradition I found with Barry. That first Rosh Hashana, sitting in the synagogue with his arm around me, we were able to "be together in synagogue" like I had seen all the Jewish couples do at the High Holidays when I was younger. I'd always been jealous of the romantic love and common love that seemed to exist between Jewish couples together at synagogue, leaning into each other, the husband wrapping his tallit around his wife's shoulders—and I'd longed for that feeling of communion.

With Barry that day, I felt the ritual and the tradition. I felt all those who had come before. I felt connected to the infinite. I felt, for lack of a better word, spiritual.

The younger, stubborn me could never understand why my mom was always preaching at me about, "Lauren, Lau-ren . . . marry a nice Jewish boy, will you? And, make sure he's a mensch!"

Sorry mom, maybe I should've listened to you on that one. I don't think my first marriage ended because of gentile-ness or anything, but maybe it didn't help. It's good to connect to things you know, and with Bobby, there was no connection in a place I very much longed to connect. Spirituality was intangible enough for me at that time. Having a partner who was in the same starting place as me felt different. Felt good.

Before Barry, I never felt comfortable in synagogue. I barely went and when I did, I felt like some sort of imposter. I'm all for inter-religious, inter-race, inter-sex, same-sex, polyamorous, and old-school marriages—find someone who floats your boat and go for a ride—but there is *something* to being able to speak a common language. For Barry and I, we just happened to find a fluency through our Long Island Jewish roots.

With Barry, Jewish practices were normalized for me; they came naturally, to both of us. His parents were from Brooklyn and lived on Long Island, and they kept to their traditions. That's how he was raised. And it *was* nice, Mom, "to marry a good Jewish boy."

At its most effective, ritual is what codifies a route to connect us to our spirituality. Just like we count down from ten before hypnosis, ritual brings us into the present moment, connects us to the past, and gives us the path to see something more. In Judaism, ritual includes prayers and customs that give a sense of order and framework within which to understand life. In meditation, this sense of order is as simple (as challenging?) as focusing on the breath. From one faith to another, the routes to our spiritual core differ, yet the basic intent is the same: ritual is the steps we take to help us transcend beyond our human limitations and into the infinite.

Catholics use incense and Eucharists. Muslims have the call to prayer. Hoodoo religion has mojo sacks and ring shouts. Dervishes whirl. Firedancers spin their flames. And each serve to get us out of ourselves and into the possibility of something bigger.

I was raised, what most people call, "culturally Jewish"—that is to say, I grew up learning the rituals and taking the rites of passage one takes in order to be a member of the tribe. I didn't, however, use these rituals and rites of passage as a spiritual practice as much as I did a cultural practice. I did it to be part of the family, to be part of the temple, the community, the culture. I did it because it was important to my mother. And, as a woman in my family, I feel a sense of responsibility to hand the Jewish faith to the next generation. Our people have fought to keep our religion alive, and if you've ever read a history book you know we've faced some tough shit. I'm not a fan of "the one big umbrella"; we are all unique and whether it is an indigenous practice being kept alive, remembering the Holocaust, or celebrating Passover with matzah, I am all for it. Uniqueness is good. Flavor is a spice.

Maybe that's why I've always sought solace in the rituals of the Jewish faith. They're comforting, like a blanket or something. Yet, it's only been since my time in Colorado and my overall expansion of Life that I have come to use these rituals as part of my *spiritual*

practice. They're another tool in my wellness quiver to still my mind and feel deeply connected to the universe.

I can't say that cannabis didn't help.

It's almost getting old to keep repeating in this manuscript, but cannabis opened me up to new possibilities. It broadened my breadth. It allowed me to see possibilities where I didn't see them before.

And for one group of people on this earth, cannabis has done that for a long time: the Rastafarians.

(And, yes, listen to Bob Marley.)

It may surprise you to learn that Rastas are against drug use. No lines or needles or pills for these inventors of reggae, and many of them don't even drink. They see drugs—no matter if some societies have long embraced them as legal—as poisons to the body.

Spoiler: they're not wrong. What alcohol does to us is criminal. As Elon Musk said on the Joe Rogan Experience about booze, "Wow, that one really got grandfathered in." He's right. And cannabis got grandfathered out, classified right up there with heroin and cocaine back in the *Reefer Madness* propaganda days of the 1940s. One reason why is because reefer was often found in the "colored" parts of town. (Lot to go into there.)

And for those beautiful, mysterious Rastafarians, they see cannabis not as a drug but as a gift, a gift from their divine—a meditative tool meant to bring awareness and understanding, meant to bring connection between oneself and the godly realm.

I think they've been onto something for a long time. Again, the "burning bush" metaphor from scripture may, indeed, be some coded reference to cannabis; same with the third eye of the East. The more I study the Rastafarians, the more I want to learn.

What Rastafarians—and potentially other religions—have been saying about cannabis for a long, long time is that at the core of the plant is spirituality. That it is a gift from the divine to help us connect to the infinite. And, if you simply believe in Mother Cannabis and all

her gifts, last time I checked, it grows straight from the soil (almost like a weed).

The introspection and calm space that cannabis has made possible for me have been at the heart of how I've reopened myself to spirituality. The "ahh" after that first puff five years ago was the most spiritual thing I'd felt in forever.

It did give me a third eye. It almost allowed me to suspend reality, if I wanted to, to try on other thoughts the way I love to try on different outfits. The world even sort of seemed to claymate itself, like I could see the things between the things. I could grasp at hidden meanings, see other worlds. I could slow myself down.

Maybe religion is some sort of simulation and cannabis helps you see the moving pieces more deeply, because, at its best, religion is trying to open a door for us to have a transcendent experience. Religion asks us to suspend reality all the time. (Ever read the Torah? Seen Charleston Heston in *Exodus*?) Religion asks us to believe that in the heat of the moment, a giant sea parted and the good people were able to walk through to a new homeland. Seems crazy far-fetched if you ask me. But what I have learned is that if you want something badly enough, you can make it happen. Call it prayer, call it manifesting, call it hard work or miracles, we all know there are times when it's hard to believe that any of this—this world, the synchronicity, the moments of awe—are "real."

It's these moments of pure joy and knowing that lead us to the understanding there has to be something more, something bigger than train schedules and blue jeans.

So, yeah, religion is asking us to suspend reality, at least to suspend the reality that we have come to accept as reality. The more physics learns about subatomic particles, the more crazy things get. You know an electron can be in two places at once? Can split itself up to occupy two matters at the same time and then join back up. If that doesn't hint at alternate realities, I don't know what does.

So do yourself a favor, take a deep bong rip and listen to universal theorist Neil DeGrasse Tyson break it down in simple terms, or

watch an episode of Sesame Street if you're as much a science-novice as I am. It's good to get our minds blown every once in a while. If we humans never thought outside the box, we'd never have sliced bread. The wheel would never have been invented. No one would have ever eaten an artichoke. (Aren't artichokes just deliciously weird?)

Ask your friends about spirituality. Learn about different religions. Smoke some weed like a good Rastafarian.

# Twelve
## *High Holiday*

One of the reasons I'd fallen off attending synagogue regularly was that I'd come to feel it was—and maybe that it always had been—a show. I felt like I was watching someone "do Judaism." Like some magician or something. Instead of a congregation, it felt like an audience. The Rabbi Show and a roomful of critics.

"Why would I battle my social anxieties to come out of my home on a Saturday for that?" I once asked a friend.

She didn't give me a good enough answer to change my thinking.

I was looking for an experience of inclusion, for some participation, maybe even some immersion. I wasn't getting that. Prayer as a process eluded me.

As a kid, my mom would always point out stuff in the prayer book for me to read, but it didn't *mean* anything to me. She'd been trying to teach me Judaism my whole life. She might as well have been trying to feed salad to a tiger. I wasn't ready for it. Sorry Ma.

But what my mother did do was give me a bedrock upon which to return when I was ready to see it in a different light. She gave

me those rituals. It just took discovering cannabis to figure out how to use them in a way that helped me connect and have a more personal experience.

Then there's this: In 2018, I got high for synagogue. At Rosh Hashana.

"You did what?!" a friend lambasted me after the fact.

"I mean," I said, "they *are* called the High Holidays."

I'd just left my big agency job and was jumping into the unknown abyss of entrepreneurialism. I had traded in one stressor for a different one. I needed grounding. After a nice holiday dinner at my mom's, Barry took the kids home and dropped me off at synagogue.

At dinner, I'd opted to forego the wine in lieu of a ten milligram packet of water-soluble THC. I was starting to get the body-high on the car ride over. I was excited to go to synagogue with a different viewpoint, a different lens. And, while being high for synagogue might sound crazy to a lot of people I know, it was one of the best decisions I'd made to date.

All my previous experiences at synagogue for the High Holidays involved going early with my mom so we could get a seat right up front, as close to the Rabbi, to the Cantor—to God's message—as we could. I didn't like being close to the "stage" when I was a kid; it meant you had to sit still and be quiet because you were right up front where all the super-serious people were. And everyone else could see you the whole time. It always stressed me out.

Not this time. Not with those ten milligrams of THC medicine in me.

For the first time in my life, I understood why they wanted it to be quiet. It was so moving when I finally allowed myself to become part of it. The whole thing. The Rabbi, his voice, the clothes, the sad songs; standing up and sitting back down in those high-heel shoes; singing the prayers that flowed out of me from years of practice; the choir, the cantor's soprano, the different people all around me who shared a common history.

The communal nature of it all was what struck me. Getting to experience transcendence with other human beings.

I was so much more in tune with the message than I had ever been. I wasn't "watching a show," I was having my own experience with the book; I was singing, I was listening, I was feeling. I was finally "in the moment" of it all. I didn't have to think about the rituals because I'd been doing them forever—and it was like all of it was practice done for this one moment. It clicked. It worked. Not only was I able to pay attention to the sermon, it struck home. I was more open to the message and I received it.

Spirituality found, in an instant—for an instant—just like that moment in meditation to feel the void and embrace it.

And, at least for a day, I was the Rasta Jew.

Joy, I've found, is about falling in love with the person you've been trying to fix all these years, in realizing our Higher Self is that inner voice who got told to "shut up" too many times by the neighborhood bully—the inner child who got called "flat-chested" by that little imp in front of the whole class in the 7th grade.

# Thirteen
## *And Now We Meditate*

My brain constantly buzzes with activity, synapses firing on any cylinder they can find. If anyone ever looked in there it would probably look like the Vegas strip. One of the favors that cannabis has done for me is slow down the light show, dim the perpetual parade of ideas and energies. Until it's just me, existing in the moment.

As someone who spent decades running both literal and metaphorical races, the idea of meditating—of stopping the noise to simply exist—was about as foreign as it got.

"What do you mean I'm just supposed to sit here and not think about everything in the entire world?"

Not only did sitting on a cushion with my eyes closed sound foreign; it scared me. And that came from experience; every time I ever tried to "be still" it would backfire. My mind would rev up, my ego clamoring for attention. I would think, "I'm terrible at this," and I would stop.

Now, when people tell me they aren't "wired to meditate," I tell them "that's why you should try it."

I know from experience. I do because that was me. And now I'm committed to my practice; ten minutes a day and some actual stillness.

Yet to this day, my best ideas still come when I am in active meditation: on a hike, on a walk, in the shower, skiing, gardening. Even doing the dishes. And their clarity is augmented by my time on the cushion. It's like a backcountry skier walking up the hill before her run down; the higher she goes, the more steps up the mountain she puts in, the more joy becomes attainable in her swoosh on down (I am not that backcountry skier).

Committing to the traditional, cushion-sitting meditation has given me a lot of discipline, and opened up a lot of doors. It used to be that I could only find stillness when my heart rate was above 160. And my body put its foot down on that one. I'm a forty-eight-year-old woman and I look forward to being able to clear my mind for fifty more years to come—not through heart-pounding bootcamp, but through meditation.

It took some time, but slowly and surely, I was coming to learn to still my mind on that cushion. And cannabis was definitely a big part of doing it. It made me more excited to meditate, more ready.

I had read about weed helping other people like me in their meditative practices, and I was on board. It worked. It was like this shortcut, this pathway. When I incorporated a proper dose of cannabis into my meditation routine, into my mediation *ritual*, everything started to make a bit more sense.

"It smooths out my brain," I told a friend of mine, one who I'd been urging to try mediation for a few months. "I am finding that calm, that peace the gurus are always talking about."

And, hey, if you can meditate without cannabis, more power to you; for me, it helps me get to where you guys can go all on your own. It aids my ability to focus on my breath. It augments my capacity to still the brain.

(Some MRI studies have shown what I'm talking about here. The activities of the brain in individuals with and without THC-

activation; the findings with meditative benefits are fascinating.)

To make sure to not get dependent upon the supplement, I will meditate without a puff or an edible beforehand, a baseline of sorts, which I do advocate as well; while I'm getting better at doing it, as of today, I still get more out of my meditative practice with a little help from my friend Mary.

The real value of meditation isn't simply a one-shot thing but in the consistency of your practice. A session here and there will do some good, but when we incorporate daily meditation for a few weeks straight, the calmness has a way of staying with us, a way of having mindfulness become a true companion, something that walks with us in our journey.

Mindfulness? Yeah, that's the buzzword that gets thrown around a lot, but for me, what I feel, is the opposite of something "full." My mind doesn't feel full but almost empty—not empty in a bad way, just in an uncluttered way. A feeling of light even in darkness, a calm ship on calm waters.

I know I'm in a good meditation routine when I don't lose my cool in situations I would have in the past. I know my meditation practice is working when I choose to step back and consider the situation instead of letting the anger take control.

When I realize I have a choice—when I can control my emotions rather than having them control me—I know my meditative practice is working. When I have the power to "not take my own bait," I know I am in the flow.

That's what mindfulness is to me: the ability to *choose* to go in a different direction, to take a different avenue than what has been preprogrammed.

"In between fight and flight," a wise person once told me, "there must be another option."

And for me, it is taking a breath.

All the breaths I have taken and all the time I have spent on the cushion have taught me to be a kinder and more forgiving person to myself. To not give into the temptation of thought.

I also discovered Gabby Bernstein's *The Universe Has Your Back*. For some reason, I really related to Gabby; the way she talked about spirituality was comfortable for me, relatable. When I picked up her book, I was still frightened by "woo" stuff, scared to "believe."

And, I was definitely not comfortable talking about it. But what I got from Gabby was to just stop worrying and start living. She told me that I was in control of my life and that there was only a positive flow of energy—to be tapped into or to be at friction with. The book challenged me to actually give meditation a chance. I stopped telling myself it was something I could never do.

Why couldn't I?

I started off with a whole lot of chanting, and I wasn't quiet about it. My family later told them it drove them a little batty, but I settled into my voice. I settled into tapping into that positive energy, to positivity, the law of attraction, and to mantras. I started to understand the vibration of the universe and how to tap into a higher vibe. Into my higher self.

I also went digital. In April of 2019, I started using The Calm App, and six months later I was at a conference proudly (but with a dearth of ego) telling the CEO, "I've had 235 meditations so far!"

I like Calm because I can measure my progress. (My mind still likes measuring.) And I love getting on a good streak. I also enjoy the badges. But at its core, the daily ten-minute meditations are a great grounding to start the day. Download it if you want and try it for the free one-week subscription. That's what I did, and I think I'll be on there forever. They're not paying me to say this or anything, I just believe it can help those of us who like to track our progress.

Because, let's be honest, we need all the help we can get to achieve some stillness. We live in a world whose volume is "turned up to eleven." Our cultural religion is workaholism. Our reverence

is to "god money." Meditation can tune all of this shit out, clearing away the distractions to remind us what matters most. Joy.

And joy, for me, comes through my family. It comes through mental and physical health. It comes through the desire to take pride in work that serves me and others. Money, I have finally come to realize, is not everything. I wish I would have learned that back in grammar school, but I didn't.

And so those markers of external success were always big for me. It's how I was raised. It's what I wanted, what I needed. I have come to realize they simply don't matter as much as I was telling myself they did.

And, finally, an aspect of what matters most to me is a connection to the infinite, to the ineffable, to that something greater than myself. It doesn't need to be an old man with a white beard or a dude with a lightsaber. You don't have to call it heaven or even "the universe, man." Sometimes I just call it gratitude. Other times I call it forgiveness. Or, even, hope.

Let's talk about hope for a bit. Hope is what allows us to keep going when we're feeling low and the world is looking bleak. All of us have leaned on hope at one time or another. Hope is what allows us to get out of bed in the morning when we're afraid of what awaits outside. Hope is the countermeasure to the fears—named and unnamed—that hinder us from being our best.

Hope is the feeling that good things can and will happen.

Hope is rad. And one of my hopes is that the healing and life-enhancing qualities of cannabis continue to gain universal acceptance as a genuine wellness tool. It works. It's a gift from the infinite, and we mortals need to see that.

Hope helped me get out of my fitness obsession. While I definitely took my fitness goals over the edge, that path did teach me a lot. I learned a lot about nutrition, about diet and which foods do what, about how to activate certain muscle groups, how to climb a hill on a bike.

Knowing that you can go breathless for thirty seconds running at a "12" on an incline lets you know you can do anything. And though I sometimes have to fight my ego so I don't go back to that over-the-top phase, I'm proud of how I have learned to care for my body.

Except for those few days a year (during Covid it was every month) I still find solace in a Whopper—heavy pickle, with onion rings and a large Dr. Pepper.

But that's all part of it too. I've arrived at a "holistic wellness approach," and I'm still discovering the path to healing, falling in love with myself, and constantly becoming exactly who I am.

Joy, I've found, is about falling in love with the person you've been trying to fix all these years, in realizing our higher self is that inner voice who got told to "shut up" too many times by the neighborhood bully—the inner child who got called "flat-chested" by that little imp in front of the whole class in the seventh grade.

And this self-love goes back to forgiveness. I'm still a work in progress on this one, and we could all use a bit more of it. For, when you forgive, you become grateful, because you're allowing yourself to see a bigger picture, the bigger picture that no matter really what's going on around you, the one thing you can count on is change. And, since nothing stays the same for too long, we may as well live in the present.

Oh, and then there's this: When you start or continue your journey with your cannabis path, you will get these great ideas. They might whisper in your ear; they might run through you like a freight train. Go with them. Allow them to flow. Write them down. Post them on Hi-Curious. Don't judge them, simply recognize them—and allow them to spur more ideas. With the aid of cannabis, you are connecting dots that your mind would very much struggle to do without what you've just given it. See what comes out.

Some "high ideas" will be brilliant. Others, when looking back upon your notes the next morning, will not. That's okay. Babe Ruth struck out 1,330 times. He also hit 714 home runs.

Another truth about cannabis is, that for some people, it spurs creativity. If you've ever listened to a classic rock radio station for more than six minutes, you've heard a song that was written with the influence of cannabis. And the last dance with Mary Jane has not happened yet.

As an augmentation to creative pursuits—not an over-reliant but a *supplement*—I encourage artists and non-artists alike to partake within proximity to instruments, pens and paper, paints, balls, and toys. It's amazing what gets created.

If you think that the only creativity in the world comes in the form of art and music, try writing while using cannabis. Try brainstorming a creative solution to a business problem. Give yourself permission to use cannabis to see the world differently and see if you can change the game instead of just playing it between the lines.

Cannabis has the unique ability to help you "flip the script" of a situation and become curious about the "other side." Heck, even a tertiary side. This is true creativity, and I hope you use it for purpose, turning your "work" into a pursuit of knowledge and change.

Furthermore, while it can spur creativity, spur synaptic connection, cannabis can also help—in my opinion—slow them down, quiet down the voice inside. I'm talking about quieting that mean voice in your head that sounds a lot like the worst version of your mom: "Your room is a mess!" with a point of the finger. "You're a mess. You're not enough."

Yeah, where pharmaceuticals couldn't do it for me, cannabis comes down on that voice like the house upon the Wicked Witch of the East.

And then we get Glinda the Good Witch, that kind and loving spirit-talk voice. It's the soothing voice inside of us that life pushes down, and it gets to come back out and play.

We are all children at heart; the older we get, I think, the more we come to understand that.

Alas, I *am* a Gemini, so maybe I'm just looking at the two sides thing a little too hard.

But one side that's hard to ignore is how we've co-adapted with cannabis. In his book, *The Botany of Desire*, Michael Pollan tells us how cannabis has co-evolved with humans. The plant wanted to spread far and wide, and it found someone to do it for them: humans. Cannabis nurtures us and so we, in turn, nurture cannabis. It makes us happy and we plant it; we each help each other. (Watch the Netflix adaption, it's pretty fascinating.)

Our fore-mothers have shepherded the knowledge of how to cultivate and use the plant for much longer than even the pyramids have been around. And here's a fact that blows my mind (or maybe it makes it really still?): the shape of the marijuana leaf—its beautiful green leaves—are said to match, perfectly, to the endocannabinoid receptors in our brain. Like a lock and key.

Call it providence. Call it order to the universe. Call it a miracle up Gaia's sleeve. I call it really cool. Because it is.

And the more I learn about the universe, the more I don't think it works in coincidences.

I learned something that night. I learned that it was not my job to 'out' other adults to normalize my own use of cannabis. It is each person's plight, unique to how they want to go about their business. I'd overstepped my bounds and I knew it. I was still learning a lot about how to walk in my new world.

# Fourteen
## *Cannabis & My Kids*

In my home, the cannabis rests, unlocked, in the weed room, neatly laid out in a 1930s era bar—the same bar that Barry's great-grandpa Harry kept his booze in during prohibition. As a family, we think this is pretty cool. We're pretty open, okay with our weird selves being weird ourselves.

One way we do this is by living our definition of what it means to have a healthy relationship: *how safe it is to bring your whole self to the arena.*

In our nuclear family—Barry, Ethan, Chase, and I—we've been working on a concept we call "family harmony." It may be a corny name, but I like it. Family harmony means (1) everyone has work to do (2) everyone deserves to have time for themselves as well as time with the family (3) everyone respects each other and (4) do what you can to make other people's lives better. Chase finally strung together a full month of remembering to take the trash out without being asked. (Even brought the cans back up.) Ethan took Chase on a road trip and they didn't kill each other. Barry and I continue to talk about what's on our minds, being super honest with each other.

And we all apologize when we make mistakes.

Call us a modern family.

We have a couple of divorces, kids with hyphenated last names, a few new partners here and there, and we just all do the best we can. We adapt and we forgive. We try to see the best in each other. "Benefits of the doubt" are encouraged.

My harmony got a lot better when Barry came into my life. And when he did, he brought three very important things with him:

1) *The Five Love Languages* by Dr. Gary Chapman (read this book!)

2) A master's degree in Organizational Development

3) Twenty years in the United States military

Over time, this trifecta has built a safe (and, yes, efficient) environment for love to grow and for learning and change to happen. And for my two momma's boys to get some masculine structure. I call it our safety bubble.

We bounce around the house like the ramen-loving taco-freaks that we are, ordering Door Dash and being a little family cocoon of laughs and giggles. But we also live in a world where the kids are adjusting to new schools, where hormones are at their height, where mom is building a company with no road map, and where everyone is human. If you haven't read *Love Languages* (or otherwise couldn't tell) my love language is "quality time"; I love nothing better than the gift of a tech-free few hours with my husband to, as Dr. Chapman says, "refill my tank."

Everyone in our family feels safe bringing themselves to the arena. It wasn't always like that for me growing up, and so Barry and I strive pretty hard to give it to our children.

And it's all about communication—communication and trust and how much we're able to lean on one another. Conceptually, familial wellness is how your family functions (or doesn't) as a unit.

A family should be able to share in each other's successes and be a shoulder for the hard times. A healthy family may not always be harmonious, but at its base full of love, caring, and attentive to one's feelings. A healthy family (not necessarily what I grew up with) is where everyone does their best to be there for the next person because you know that the next person is doing their best to be there for you.

When Barry and I chose our Ketubah—the Jewish marriage contract—we had a few choices. Most of the egalitarian ones were still about "undying devotion to the other," almost to become one. (Not necessarily for us; we like our uniqueness too much.) So the contract we opted for simply asks us to support the other in being the best version of themself. We come back to our Ketubah often. We try to never attempt to change each other, rather endeavor to encourage the better versions of ourselves. And that means, in our family, when we have to, we give tough love; that's why it's so important to feel the safeness of the space.

We haven't achieved Nirvana yet, so there's still a fair share of anger, but we've come to the understanding that even a good yell can even have a place in a healthy family. As long as you know it's safe.

And no one is ever "out"; everyone is welcome, even on their bad days. As long as you want to be in, you're in. You will never be abandoned.

By this metric, my family's familial health had been subpar for much of my time in New York, when I was commuting into the city to work like a dog and workout like a monkey only to come back home with an empty tank. I wasn't giving much, so I wasn't receiving much. My kids were keeping things from me. I knew they were, and I didn't have the energy to be present enough for them to stop them keeping things from me. I was trying (with great difficulty) to mitigate the tension between Barry and Ethan, who was in a constant state of struggle to accept Barry's authority in his life. I was often angry, easily frustrated. At times, I was resentful that I wasn't present for my family the way I knew I should be.

My work was paying me a lot of money to support the lifestyle I had created. We had a big home. We had nice things.

I was resentful of my work for taking so much of my energy, and I was resentful of myself for giving it to them.

"Wanna watch a movie, Mom?" Ethan would ask.

"Ah, not tonight, honey," I'd say, thinking of all the things I had to do that two hours in front of some CGI-drenched movie wasn't going to cure. "How 'bout tomorrow?"

"But, Mom . . ."

And my phone would buzz in my pocket and my mind was transported right back into the office. Work never stopped. To get ahead meant that you were always available. Except that I was never really anywhere. My body would be in one place and my mind in a completely different one.

I must have muttered, "Same shit, different day," six-million three-hundred and forty-two times.

The idea that cannabis can help improve your family relationships is going to be a little controversial, but it is an important thing to address. And rather than sugarcoat it, I'm going to lay out both the positives *and* the drawbacks I've experienced with it and let you decide for yourself how to maneuver the inclusion of cannabis in your family life.

Ethan's incident at school with the vape pen was the start of a change in our relationship. Why? Because it actually forced us to start talking about it.

"What are you using it for, Ethan?"

"It makes me feel good, relaxed . . ."

It came out that Ethan had tried weed for the first time at a party back in tenth grade. Sophomores. This was back in 2015 mind you, a little over a year before I tried it for myself.

"I liked it, Mom," he told me. "I was able to talk more and be more social with people at a party instead of feeling nervous, out of place."

He told me he'd also been using it at night once or twice a week when he couldn't fall asleep. Sometimes he used it recreationally when he played video games. He said it made them "more fun."

"And it helps me feel less anxious," something he was loath to admit at the time. "And Lexapro—sometimes that shit makes me feel like I'm living my life through a window. Weed does the opposite—it makes me feel more . . . more 'me.'"

It became a special year. Ethan came clean with his cannabis use, and I had started my forays with Barry. We were learning together. And with our familial strength growing, we found a safe place in which we could simply talk, lay the cards out on the table and stop hiding things from each other. The year that started so poorly for Ethan turned into a great one. We learned a lot about mental and physical wellness together. A seventeen-year-old son and his forty-four-year-old mom, out in the garage smoking weed together and opening up about life. It was better than therapy. It *was* therapy but without the feeling of pulling teeth. Cannabis, I can say with all honesty, helped my family.

Even with having to change schools at such a crucial time, Ethan got into the University of Colorado—his (and my) dream school. Late in high school, he got his first job, working at a marine shop and then one at a Japanese grocery store where he was the only white kid. He loved Japanese culture: anime, the food, samurais, and he has dreams of traveling to Japan. He participated in the synagogue's Twelfth Grade Confirmation program and even got to go to the fancy private school's prom. (Yes, the one that kicked him out, and Mr. McBritishy, headmaster, even said some kind words about Ethan.)

I like to think that some of this was Ethan growing into a young man, and some of it was already in him and I just hadn't noticed. And some of it was because cannabis offered him a way out of the sometimes-crippling anxiety he was suffering. Also, his senior year

of high school was my first year of entrepreneurship—no more commuting! no more office!—so I was actually home to be with him and watch the transformation.

When Ethan initially got kicked out of that private school, it had "crises" painted all over it. It was a shock, a watershed moment. But the more time that passed, the more silver linings appeared. Ethan saw how the two kids who had money were allowed to stay when he was forced to leave, and the bloom was off the rose for him about the school that had "saved him." He didn't need it anymore.

And saving that $30K tuition didn't hurt me, neither did being able to leave that stifling agency job and get my family out to the fresh airs of Colorado.

As we planned the transition, the move, we talked. A lot. Ethan, a teenager who spoke in monosyllables and few words, began to open up. I could see the cracks in his exterior, the light from within shining through. Sometimes when he smiled, I even saw his teeth. I hadn't seen them since he was a child. We became besties again that year. Just like we'd been when he was young. Just like we'd been before I hopped onto the hamster wheel.

We started to understand one another, to accept one another. We listened. And you can guess what great medicine was helping to fuel this improvement in our relationship. If alcohol is the country's "social lubricant," I can say that cannabis became the emotional lubricant for the Mundell-Krauss House.

And the most profound change, the most enlightened improvement, was the relationship between Ethan and Barry. The thick, icy barrier of tension that hung between them started to melt. Tangibly so. They were no longer locking themselves in separate chambers of the house to silently brood about how ungrateful the other was. The undercurrent of animosity was giving way to a feeling of mutual respect, of mutual expectations—that were being met. And, now, three years later, it's still improving. There have been many ups and downs, and cannabis helps us heal and move forward.

"I can't believe how happy it makes me to see them," I told my

friend over the phone one night a while back. "I mean, they just went for a drive together—for fun!"

Even now, when Ethan comes home from one of his adventures, often the first thing we do together is smoke a bowl. I pack it for him or he packs for me. His quiet exterior opens up a bit. He talks and shares. He asks me how I am and truly listens. It's pretty cool.

In return for his respect and dedication to his schoolwork—his trustworthiness—Ethan earned our trust, and we allowed him to continue his cannabis use even when we weren't around. Ethan earned our trust with the plant and, yes, I am that mom who supplies her son with cannabis. Ethan is the friend who turns on others to the plant. Of course, they're college kids and so they're over-do it every once in a while, but I know Ethan understands and (mostly) practices responsible use.

I'm not here trying to say that cannabis is some magic wand, but it can help human beings open their hearts, quiet their egos and put a lid on insecurities while allowing the inner child to reawaken. Once we incorporated it into our family (in a similar vein to many European cultures allowing their children a glass of wine at dinner time) our family began to heal our rifts. We were able to move on from past hurts and live in the moment together, having authentic experiences and genuinely enjoying being around one another.

With all this positive beta, I made the decision to deal with my younger son honestly about the topic. Again, these are very personal decisions, but for me, it wasn't a hard choice. Since cannabis first became a part of our lives when Chase was just a tween, I felt like we were leaving him out of a secret club. I wanted him to be mature enough for it to be responsible for him to use our family medicine, but I never wanted him to feel left out. I wanted him to understand how I felt about it, how it made me feel so that he could form his own opinions about it.

One night when he was thirteen, the mood felt right, and I led out with: "Chase, what is your experience with marijuana?"

He looked at me like I was crazy. Maybe he thought he was in

trouble. Finally, he sputtered out, "I don't know mom . . . I've never smoked it if that's what you're asking me. . . ."

And we went on to have a calm conversation in which I told him about how I had been using it, about how it is something to be respected and not overused, about how, when he was a little bit older, he could make the decision to use it—or not—for himself. It was like "the birds and the bees" but for weed.

I was glad we had that little talk because a few months later at summer camp, Chase was offered a weed pen by one of his friends. He could have gone in blind that day or he could have been at least a little bit prepared. He decided to accept his friend's offer, and he took a couple puffs at the pen. When he got back from camp, he told me about his experience. I felt good that we had the type of family dynamic in which he felt safe to do so. I'm not judging here at all—to each their own—but I doubt the friend who offered him the pen went home and told his mother all about *his* time at camp.

Kids have pretty good bullshit detectors. They know you're lying to them even if they can't pinpoint why or about what exactly. As someone who was making the choice to live out loud about cannabis in my adult life outside the family, there didn't seem to be much point trying to shield Chase from the truth. Plus, kids are smart; they're good at assimilating new information. Better than we are, I feel.

Chase is now a young man who sees me using cannabis daily. Our family is far from "normal" about cannabis, even by legal Colorado standards. As we've settled into Colorado living, I've been a little shocked to see that the "behind closed doors" attitude among parents and their children still largely prevails.

Before Covid shut down my usual type of anecdotal research (aka making friends in new places) I met some cool people and invited them over to the house. They were of the very professional Boulder stoner type. They made a good living, got after it in the out-of-doors, and smoked cannabis as part of their routine.

We were having a great time just talking and laughing in the

living room when Chase came downstairs to say hello. These friends of mine became visibly uncomfortable, trying to hide the pipe, not exhale and shit like that.

"Oh, it's okay," said Chase. "This is normal for me."

My friends looked at me. "All good," I said.

And I had this aha moment. These "liberated" friends of mine had not opened up to their own children about their cannabis use—despite their kids being nearly eighteen and living in a state where it was legal. They were wide-eyed with near-shock when they learned how I'd opened up the conversation in my home. Yep, my friends were still laboring under the internalized stigma that is associated with cannabis and those who use it.

Chase is now sixteen and is not (outwardly) interested in cannabis. We respect his decision, and he respects ours.

Sometimes I have to keep reminding myself that we are making history. In my family we are learning, every day, how to teach and build a healthy relationship with the cannabis plant. Do I have all of the answers? Hell, no.

In fact, I really screwed up back in New York, screwed up because I didn't realize that most parents don't open up about their "drug" use to their kids.

At a fancy Bar Mitzvah for one of Chase's friends, I was enjoying my night, keeping a sane buzz and getting down to the beats of a very good DJ and some killer dancers they'd hired for the party. (I was grooving.)

Then, the mom of one of Chase's close friends came up to me and started doing the "dance-talk" thing to me. You know the one—when you can't hear what the person's screaming into your ear but they keep talking anyway?

The mom kept screaming awkwardly and I finally deduced what she was trying to say: "Yeah, your son, Chase? He told *my* son that my husband and I smoke marijuana! Not good. You outed me to my son . . ."

That woman had previously told me, in a candid moment, that she and her husband used cannabis. I cringe now as I write this but, yeah, in an open moment with Chase, I told him basically what she told me. Chase had told their son. She was livid. It was an awkward moment. I felt awful and the whole thing really killed my buzz. Which sucked, because that DJ was damn good.

But I learned something that night. I learned that it was not my job to "out" other adults to normalize my own use of cannabis. It is each person's plight, unique to how they want to go about their business. I'd overstepped my bounds and I knew it. I was still learning a lot about how to walk in my new world.

Still, I did think that through my cannabis journey I would start to find more people who looked like me. While I've found many role models and colleagues on a shared scrape to normalize cannabis, I have never found the "me"—a white Jewish girl from NY who fell in love with the cannabis plant at forty-three and wanted to help people use it to heal from the stress that crushes them. On one level, it's hard. I'd like to meet another "me." But on another level, it's kinda cool. I know I am unique. Just like everyone else on their journey.

But normalization was still my aim. For all journeys. I wasn't going to tell anyone how to raise their kids, but for Barry and I, it felt like time to talk with Chase. He was part of the family and I didn't want him left on the sidelines. He'd become older, wiser, his brain more developed. We needed to treat him like the young man he'd become.

I wanted to keep his education going, keep him informed if and when he was offered again.

Initially, we were only smoking after he had gone to bed—and often outside. But the winters in New York can make hanging out outside at night fairly impossible. (That's why we moved the patio furniture into the garage.) One day, Ethan invited Chase to come and hang out with us while we smoked. It was initially weird to sit there and smoke in front of him, but the kite flies highest against the wind, right? It would have been easier to keep hiding it from Chase, but it had ceased to feel right.

Ethan and I partook. Chase played darts nearby and observed, watched, and asked questions. He looked curious. Responsible and curious. And, from that night forward there was a different energy about the house. The family dynamic shifted for the better. There were no more secrets.

When I moved back to Long Island as a divorcee with two kids and no job, I felt like a failure. A failure to my children, to myself, and definitely to my father. And I may sound like a cry baby, but when he 'gave me' that job in the agency, subconsciously I felt like even more of a failure and fraud. Even though I was more than qualified, it felt like I didn't do it on my own. Like I couldn't do it on my own. Like my maiden name was the only thing pulling me along.

# Fifteen
## *Cannabis & My Parents*

Yeah, so as I may have implied in previous chapters, cannabis has shed some light, some really bright light, on my relationship with my father. Remember all that about cannabis and its uncanny ability to rip the band-aid off your trauma? Sometimes before you're ready? It can. It does. It has, for me.

And when it did it for me back in college and then again as an adult, I was not yet prepared to see the gore under the bandage. Not with the divorce stuff, the pressure, the stiffness of our relationship. It kept getting peeled back, pulled off then put back on, and when I finally opened up to share my excitement about cannabis with dad, that band-aid got completely ripped off. For good.

I always wanted my father to be there for me. Always thought he would. And, oftentimes, he would be there, supporting me and being a great dad. It's just that sometimes he wouldn't show up, sometimes through physical distance and sometimes through emotional distance.

I always felt this pressure to live up to his idea of success, and his success mounted throughout my life. I've always felt like I needed his

approval. I ascribed him so much power, power that I internalized to believe that he was right about almost everything. If I ever disagreed with him about something, I figured he knew better and I was just "being stubborn." I put him on a pretty tall and pretty overarching pedestal. Much of which he never asked for.

It was just that every time I made a mistake, I felt his "I told you so" lurking, ever so near and pervasively, in the air.

When I moved back to Long Island as a divorcee with two kids and no job, I felt like a failure. A failure to my children, to myself, and definitely to my father. And I may sound like a cry baby, but when he gave me that job in the agency, subconsciously I felt like even more of a failure and fraud. Even though I was more than qualified, it felt like I didn't do it on my own. Like I couldn't do it on my own. Like my maiden name was the only thing pulling me along.

So, like any good ambitious New York Jew, I spent the next fifteen years toiling away to prove to him—and thereby myself—that I could still succeed at life.

When I woke up to cannabis, I woke up to the fact there is a version of the world where my father can actually be wrong. I realized this world existed. I never had before. I realized I could disagree with him and, in doing so, that *I* could actually be right. He was not God. Just my father. Albeit a super successful 'my father,' but just my father.

Most of us probably have some 'dad issues.' Most of us also moved beyond them before age forty-three.

So when I came out about cannabis in 2018, I didn't come out directly to my parents. No face-to-face in the living room. Nope, I came out to Instagram. Maybe it's the era in which we live or maybe I just didn't want to look in their eyes as I spoke the words (and I was forty-three!). But still, in my heart, I felt that Mom and Dad would be one hundred percent fine with it. They would *have* to see how much better I was doing. How much more me I was. How much more happiness I was exuding.

The plant was helping me. Just like some pharmaceutical may have. They would have to see that for what it was. I was wrong.

They heard of my post. Mom absorbed it better than Dad, for sure, but somewhere in the back of her mind, I could tell she was wishing I'd snap out of it. Just some fad by her daughter who had gone through fads before. But at least she didn't lambast me.

For my father, the fact that his daughter had become some "pot-smoking hippie" was not going to fly. Just wasn't. He began a campaign with me nothing short of intervention. He rallied the siblings to his cause. He told me how "irresponsible this is as a parent, Lauren!"

He told me I was an addict, addicted to cannabis. He stacked the deck against me at a therapy session (a story I'm still hesitant to tell but may just come out in a few pages). He told me I was wrong. My whole life I'd believed him when he'd said this. But not now, not on this one. I was right. Cannabis was making my life better. Why—why?!—could he not accept this? Why could he not expand his paternal lens to embrace his daughter's decisions?

The dynamic between my siblings has been, is, tricky at times. There are big age differences. My brother and youngest sister share my stepmom as their mom, they are fourteen and sixteen years my junior. I was regularly their babysitter and caretaker. And all of us have tricky relationships with our parents. I suppose, at the core of it all, is the approval we crave from our father. We love him. We want to be in his favor. I don't think it's so much a conscious decision as something ingrained from childhood. Perhaps even before that.

In short, we never want to be in the doghouse with him—that place where you are not talked to, but talked about.

That's why when I was leaving my corporate job, I felt like I needed his blessing. But confronting him about it meant risking going into that doghouse.

One fateful day, we found ourselves, Dad and I, father and daughter, sitting in his big, cold den out back of his house. It felt like sitting in one of the offices we'd been having "talks" in for years.

"I'm done at the agency," I said, not really having a plan for what else to do, not knowing how quickly my idea to "freelance and start my own business" would turn into Hi-Curious.

To my surprise, my father—the ultra-competitive PR extraordinaire—was on board. He supported my decision to leave the agency, gave me the green light. "Trust yourself," he told me.

It wasn't until I heard his words, received his approval, that I finally went and got out of that rat race. That's how much power I was still giving him in my forties. Ugh.

He could give me approval to trust my instincts in business matters. Just not on my instincts to seek aid from an ancient herb. I suppose we are all products of our environment.

Right around the time I told the world that I was smoking pot and quitting my job (what a teenage-sounding phrase!), I started making some real changes in my life. I wrote down an intention every morning, how I was going to show up for that day.

*I am Courageous . . . I am Learning . . . I am Listening*, I would write. It felt good. And to keep myself accountable to my daily creeds, it was at this time that I started recording videos, around the theme of the day, videos I would share on social media. Mostly Instagram.

Most of the world knows that when you post on Insta, you can see who's viewed what. So I know my dad never watched a single video directly (more adept on Facebook that one). But my step-mom did. I know that. Saw her view.

And I'm glad she did; I wasn't trying to hide anything from them. On the contrary, that was my way of coming out. To my parents through the world. My hope was that they'd see the posts, feel how happy and healthy I was becoming, and drop the judgment.

Not what went down.

I can only surmise that much of what my dad heard was filtered through my stepmom. Problem is, though, my stepmom is a bit of a reality television fan and a great storyteller; she craves a little bit of drama and has been known to exaggerate the facts to get the effect she desires. And she was the one filtering to my father what I was broadcasting to the world daily.

So, while I'm sure he judged what he heard, I like to think he was not so much judging *me* as judging some fictionalized, selectively edited, dramatic persona his wife was dripping stories about.

Or I am wrong, and he was watching the videos with her. Maybe someday I'll actually ask him.

Anyway, I liked doing the videos. They both held me accountable and gave me momentum. And now, today in my cannabis ventures in Colorado, I continue this daily tradition I started way back when.

Only difference is, these days, I don't just post to Instagram but also host a daily show on Hi-Curious—the mobile app I built, launched, and grew to help digital cannabis entrepreneurs reach their personal and financial dreams. My posts go out to my subscribers, to our community, to help them (us) live more intentional lives. I share my stories with cannabis, how I use the plant to live with intention and personal and financial freedom.

On my Monday AM show, *Becoming Intentional*, for instance, I interact with my community to set intentions and stay accountable. I feel that when we put things out there to people we respect, the power is greater. We have a whole bunch of awesome live shows, and I am not the only star—get the app and come say hi sometime.

Back to my family. Why? Because, well, Hi-Curious is all about community—and the community in which I grew up is called "my family."

And because I'm finally ready to tell that story about going to therapy with my father.

It starts with my sister, Amy. Amy and I are different. She's a lawyer and a mediator, and she fancies herself some kind of balancing agent. I love her to death, but we are, just, different. Maybe that's why we get along so well.

Still, she'd had a couple negative experiences with cannabis and when she heard I'd incorporated the substance into my practice, it was a hard thing for her to accept. She'd heard a lot from Dad about the path I was walking.

After a few months, though, she was coming around to accepting me and my decisions regarding cannabis use. She was not worried about me, simply upset about what the rift in our extended family was doing to everyone. I was really sad about this too, but I didn't see a way around it given how incredibly closed-minded my dad had been acting.

Amy asked me if I would be open to going to therapy with my dad. Perhaps she suggested it to him, too, because a few days later, I received a text from him asking if I would go.

I was skeptical, and the reason was that I didn't know if my dad had ever been to therapy before. It felt like some sort of trap. I knew that my dad was looking to prove that there was something wrong with me. I wished that wasn't the case. I wanted to believe that he really wanted to find a way forward to some kind of relationship. But I knew him too well and had seen him manipulate too many outcomes.

When he sent me the original text, he said that he'd spoken to someone in NYC who he thought "would be great." I was nervous, concerned he was stacking the deck. I suggested that I be the one to choose the therapist. He agreed, but upon beginning my research, I realized that he would never believe or trust someone that I found. So, I decided to go with his person.

He told me that the NYC therapist had an appointment available at her office in Westchester, an hour from Port Washington where Dad and I both lived. I thought it was strange to go so far for therapy, but I agreed.

On the way there, I listened to some Brené Brown, and I was open to the vulnerability she speaks about. I pulled into a parking spot and ingested ten milligrams of Go—a product with a small amount of cannabis plus a small amount of plant-based caffeine. It was the medicine I was using most days at that time, and I felt like I needed to stay true to myself in the session, to keep me both calm *and* on my toes.

"Alright," I said as I locked my door, "therapy with Dad, here we go."

He was waiting for me out front of the office. This caught me a little off guard, but I walked over to him anyway.

"You know," he said as we were walking into the house at the end of a cul de sac, "this therapist was a really good friend of Fran's—*and* she's a former student of Milt's."

Just like ol' dad to pull something at the last minute. Fran was a student of Milt, my stepmother's late father, an incredibly accomplished psychologist as well as a professor and author. Milt was also the family's self-appointed psychologist, and I had heard my stepmom on the phone with him many times dropping diagnoses on people in the family. He had this creepy ability to look right into your soul when you made eye contact with him, so as a teenager I always made sure to avoid him at family gatherings and holidays and such. I know he was an incredible man, extremely smart and kind. He was also a POW and a pioneer in his field. But to me, he was "the creepy grandpa." My father had a lot of respect for Milt and had become friendly with many of his students.

I knew all this, and I knew my dad as the persuasive and strategic person he was. So having this therapist be the one we were going to see felt a little—what's the word?—orchestrated.

No doubt my dad had already told the therapist of his daughter's terrible decline into "potheadery." Fair and balanced, this assessment would not be.

My guard was up. Immediately and firm. My father had promised

multiple times via text message that he was "not stacking the deck." Fortunately, I had prepared for ambush.

The night before, Barry and I talked about how the therapy session could go.

"I'm hoping it is actual therapy," I said, "where we both talk about how we feel and genuinely open a path to some sort of resolution.

"Just be prepared in case you feel the need to protect yourself."

Barry had seen how hurt I had been for months by that point, how hard I was working on my own mental health and how I'd been feeling better. He also knew this thing with my dad was the biggest barrier to me feeling free and in the flow. I wanted to allow myself to be vulnerable, but in case it was an ambush, we came up with a way for me to take control of the situation.

Back to the day of therapy: my dad and I entered the office and sat down on furniture that felt like something from *The Brady Bunch*. Dated. Super seventies. It was weird, made me feel like I was a little kid.

"Thank you both for being here," the therapist said in her honed, soothing voice. "I hope I can help you. Let's talk about what brings you here today."

Dad, always the gentleman, suggested that I go first.

"Okay," I began hopefully, "I guess I have a question to start. Dad, is this *your* therapy that I am joining, or are we here to talk about me?" I hoped that at least if he was stacking the deck, he was also getting some help from this person.

The therapist answered. "No," she said, "this is your father's first time here too. We spoke on the phone and he shared his concerns about you."

My turn again: "Then, Dad, why *are* we here?"

He cleared his throat. "Well, first, I am very concerned about you and I want you to change your behavior." He spoke sternly, fatherly. "And second, I would like to work on our relationship."

The therapist took this one: "You might want to start with number two," she stated rather than suggested.

Angry. That's what I was. I went into complete business-meeting mode. Armor up. This wasn't therapy, this was war—the war I'd been preparing for my whole life. Do or die time.

I went for it. I spoke from my heart and I spoke with logic from my brain. I made clear, connectable points. My father and the therapist listened. I kept talking. More points. More examples of how good I was finally doing being "me."

The therapist—despite whatever picture my dad had painted of me—spoke calmy and lucidly that, in her professional opinion, she believed I was "fine and healthy." She told my dad that "Lauren has done her research and seems to hold a responsible mindset about her life choices."

It felt so dang good to hear those words come out of her mouth. Vindication, in the presence of my father. It gave me the guts to say, "Dad, if I don't stop using cannabis, decide not to change, do you still want to have a relationship with me?"

He looked me in the eye. He waited a count, thinking thoughts I do not know. "I'm not sure," he said.

I took it for what it was: a challenge.

We talked on.

When the molten-heated session ended, the therapist asked us if we wanted to come back and continue the work.

I took that one, saying, "I don't think there's a point to me coming back unless my father figures out if he wants a relationship with me—because I am not planning to change who I am."

She agreed, and I suggested they figure the rest out without me.

I got up from the strange carpet-covered bench I'd been uncomfortably sitting on and walked out of the office. Out of the session, out of therapy with Dad, and I stepped into the April sunshine with this sort of exhilarating sickness that I had just "won"

therapy, that I had outplayed my father. I'd checkmated him, turned the meeting around to make *him* the one who needed help. I knew how much his pride was hurt, him sitting back in the office with the therapist talking about whatever they were talking about.

I'd won at therapy. Exhilarated, yes, a little nauseous, too, because I knew how sad that sentiment was.

The sixteen-year-old who'd been so angry so many times, who felt like her father never heard her or saw her, who felt like she always wanted to do it her way but was never out from the umbrella of her dad's shadow, felt like she was talking to the adult me. Or maybe the forty-three-year-old Lauren was talking to her?

Exhilaration and sickness. Then and even now as I recount the tale. I didn't even cry after the appointment. Which sucked. But I might now. I wish my fear of an ambush had been wrong. But the universe works in mysterious ways.

It was a shift, the confrontation with the male figure, father, god. Because the whole thing was some sort of proof that I didn't need to become my father. I didn't need to walk that path any longer. My life lay ahead of me. My life would include cannabis until the day I die. Take it or leave it, Pop.

I had lived "his way" for a long time. It was time, like that one Sinatra song, to do it "my way."

Coming out of the closet is a brave thing to do. It is standing up for what you believe in. I was coming to a strong belief in cannabis and when I came out, I was judged–extremely harshly and by unwarranted prejudices. And not only by my parents. You probably will be too. Not by everyone, but by many.

# Sixteen
## *Living Out of the Closet*

When I came out of the closet and started experiencing the stigma of being "out," I asked some of my gay friends if it would be appropriate to talk about it in the same manner as what most of them had had to go through. I was given the green light. And while I'm not comparing what it's like to come out of the cannabis closet to your parents to what it's like to come out of the sexuality closet to them, it's still no easy task. If you grew up like most of us, in the mainstream, then weed was not part of your parents' life. Just like if you came from a Mennonite family and started having a couple beers in the evening, it probably just wouldn't jive.

Coming out of the closet is a brave thing to do. It is standing up for what you believe in. I was coming to a strong belief in cannabis and when I came out, I was judged—extremely harshly and by unwarranted prejudices. And not only by my parents. You probably will be too. Not by everyone, but by many.

"What are you doing to your life?" they'll ask.

"Fine," they may say, "but why can't you just do it privately. Why do you have to celebrate it so much?"

But some people will find inspiration in your decision to consume. The stigma around weed in this country is still very strong. The perception of the "stoner" is still very vivid. New ways of seeing have always been disruptive, and disruptive people have always been met with fear. Those in power want to keep their power. Anything that endangers the status quo will be met with resistance.

"Drugs are for losers," your family, friend or coworker may tell you (even if they booze every night).

These people might be coming from a good place, a place of wanting to protect you, but people also thought Noah was crazy for building his ark. Things that ride the forefront of humanity's mind-wave are met with questioning. The sheep follow their shepherd. And being the black sheep isn't easy—but we need black sheep or else the entire flock does the same damn thing on repeat.

My blood family's layers of distrust and expectation were brought to the forefront through the third eye of the skunky smoke. I came to see things I had always known but could never quite put a name to. And I started to break them down.

Time and distance have a way of healing; I went West, in geography and mind-frame, and it has made all the difference.

Still, coping with it all is very much in-progress work for me. I continue to seek a place of clarity about whether my dad's expectations for me were ever reasonable to begin with—whether I ever could or would've really met them, or if, like the man himself, satiation may have proven impossible. That's the mindset of the hamster wheel, something like, "wherever you go, you are not there yet." Into perpetuity.

My dad is now in his mid-seventies; he's probably not going to change his mind very much from here on out (if he was *ever* capable), and that's something I'm going to have to live with. I, on the other hand, have a little more time. We can't go back and change

the things that have happened, but any one of us, from here on, can play with the future like it is silly putty. Seriously, we can.

I can offer you a hundred check-mate arguments to counter the perceptions and biases you may be met with by family and friends as you open up about the role of cannabis in your life, but the best one I can give you is the argument that you are living your best life—so show them this. Don't simply tell this, *show* it.

Show up and show off. Be present. Be open. Create. Smile. Radiate the vibes of the plant and people will see the light. Good vibrations aren't just for surfers. When you use cannabis, you can elevate to another place.

Rise above and shine your light.

Because we all want things to be good with our family. We all want harmony with our friends. It's a wonderful thing. And, to get there, sometimes that wonder lies on the other side of an uncomfortable talk. The way to find buried treasure on the bottom of the ocean is to rile up the seafloor.

I'd be lying if I said that I've driven out all the darkness in the relationship with my dad. But, two years after that fateful therapy, my light is getting brighter and the chasm between us feels less weighty. I would be lying if I said I wasn't afraid about his reaction to this book. All of this was hard to write and important.

I no longer fear the doghouse. I no longer need permission to be myself.

To learn to be kinder to myself, I needed to leave corporate America. Corporate America was always hungry, never satisfied, and I needed to take a break to see that it was killing me.

# Seventeen
## *Authenticity, Morality, and Purple Hair*

I like to say that self-care, true self-care, is not a manicure. Self-care is a radical gift that only you can give yourself. No one can give it to you; it's something you have to take.

And our self-care encompasses every overlapping thing in our life. All the little things that add up to the big thing. Kind of like a pinecone does to the seed of the tree—all those interconnected pieces forming an intertwined whole. With a center, the seed, the heart, right there surrounded by it all. That middle? That's our higher self. The thing that gets us into living our best life possible.

Total self-care is caring for yourself in multiple ways, in knowing that you can become something more, when you're ready. And cannabis can help it grow.

As the years wore on in my corporate job, I felt so disconnected from the heart of my pinecone.

The way I dressed. The way I wore my hair. Those abs. They came to feel like a burden. I'd look in the mirror and it didn't feel like "me" was looking back at me. It didn't feel like I was looking at myself, like I didn't even know myself anymore, that I needed to find my way back to me.

A few weeks before Donald Trump was elected president, I decided to dye my hair purple. I was very much still working at Ketchum at the time and we had just won a very big piece of business. I was running it. The client was based in Indiana, super conservative, and the CEO probably golfs with Pence. I had to go meet him. As me. It was the first step in finding myself again, both a thrill and a challenge to go to a meeting in Indianapolis with the CEO and my purple head held high.

See, when the Obamas were living in the White House, I had some hope that the American Dream still existed—that if you worked hard and had drive and vision, you'd be okay. But now I saw a malignancy living at 1600 Pennsylvania Avenue, a petulance, a blowhard. And, at everything other than demagoguery, he was mediocre. He was even a mediocre businessman for crying out loud. And the things he said and the things he had done were just too much for me. As far as I was concerned, it was a different America, a different world, and I had to make a choice about how I was going to live in it.

This meeting with the big bad CEO was going to be a test to see if I could do it. I styled my purple hair in the hotel bathroom that morning, said a good, "who fucking cares" into the mirror and walked into the room.

He looked at me. I looked at him. The meeting began.

And I did it.

The meeting went great. The CEO either didn't care about my look or just didn't say anything because the logic and vision that was coming out of my mouth was too sound. He gave us reign to do what we wanted with the project. I gotta give him some props for that.

And I gotta give me some props too.

I was damn good at my job, integral to many of our biggest clients. The company was trying to allow the culture to change a bit, make it less like the medieval days of the eighties and nineties. They'd finally started letting people show their tattoos—and apparently, purple hair wasn't a deal-breaker either.

I'd have never known I could pull off bringing my true self into the room unless I actually went and did it. I pushed the envelope a little. It enabled me to feel like *me*. And the company knew that a confident Lauren could make them a lot of money.

Yeah, I'm sure some people spoke about me behind closed doors. But I made the decision to show up to one of the biggest business meetings of my life—as myself. No uniform. Just me. Just me and my purple hair.

It was a small victory. The first of many to come.

When I finally left Ketchum, I had time for my hobbies. I was more interested in participating in life because I wasn't so drained by my job. I wish I could say that I practiced self-care while I worked there, but I didn't. I thought self-care was a weekly mani-pedi.

To learn to be kinder to myself, I needed to leave corporate America. Corporate America was always hungry, never satisfied, and I needed to take a break to see that it was killing me.

The victories in life, for me, started rolling in when I started becoming intentional with my life and living as one person instead of trying to be someone different for everyone else.

The victories came when I began to get super authentic.

The word "authenticity," I was feeling, had come to lose a lot of its intended meaning. It used to mean real, honest, trustworthy—sharing your truth even when you knew others would disagree, and then having a dialogue about it. And the only way to get to this definition of authenticity is through vulnerability. Authenticity means telling the truth, even (especially) when your back is against

the wall and you feel like the other walls are closing in on you. It means sticking to your guns (pinecone) and finding a way forward.

Authenticity means being a leader, and being a leader sometimes takes being the black sheep.

Becoming a leader can manifest in seemingly small ways, like getting professional glam shots taken when the rest of the agency rolls out their Sears-Roebuck headshots. It can manifest in firmer ways, like refusing to work on a piece of business that doesn't align with your core beliefs. (I wish I did that more often.) It can even mean letting someone on your team go when you know the rest of the team will be better off without them.

Being a leader is hard because you are literally out in front—the first one to take the hit. But to lead, you must *lead*.

And it takes a lot of energy. When we're younger, we have so much energy and we can spread it around, spending it freely, almost carelessly. As we get older, our capacity for energy wanes. (See: puppy vs. fourteen-year-old porch-dog.) The nature of the body is that it's built with an expiration date. The day of our birth, to paraphrase a human who came before me, is the day the corpse is slowly borne.

That's not as bleak as it sounds.

From the time of Greek mythology and long before, immortal beings have held some envy for us mortals. At the end of *The Odyssey*, Athena comes down from Olympus to congratulate Odysseus on finally making it back home, and she basically says, all is well that ends well—but Odysseus basically tells her she's wrong. "I've missed twenty years of time with my wife. My infant son is now a man!"

And we kinda see that Athena can never value time as much as a mortal. *She* will live forever. We won't—not even the sly and cunning Odysseus—and so each day is inherently more special.

The motif continues on in endless works of today's popular fiction, the image of some immortal being slogging along in an empty life just waiting for death. The god or vampire or superhero

seemingly "has it all"—*as well as immortality*—but is trapped in an eternal state of ennui. There is no end, and thus there is nothing to look forward to. Life, for the immortal, lacks zest.

That's why there is no gift, for the human being, like the present. We all know we will die, unlike the gods, and not too far off in the future. Especially once we hit forty, most of us are halfway there. If we're lucky. It's precisely the limited supply of mental, physical, and spiritual energy that makes it so important, and fun, how we spend it. It's the briefness and fragility of life that lends it meaning. Therefore our life force *is* currency, the ultimate currency, and whether we squander it or make a gift of it to both ourselves and the world, is how our legacy will be judged by the weights of the sand.

As we age, that currency is in shorter supply. Many a midlife crisis has erupted at this understanding. The sand is running through the hourglass and it's not slowing down.

Maybe that's where that old saying, "Life begins at forty comes from." We realize we've had a lot of good practice years and now we better show up or ship out.

With a diminishing amount of life force, sometimes the best thing we can do is identify the things that aren't serving us and let them go. And it's tough as hell; we might be going there for all we know, so maybe we should stop worrying so much what the boss thinks and just be ourselves. Live our lives, what remains of them.

And the incredibly daunting practice of giving zero fucks, I find, really helps in this arena.

It took a long time for me, but I now know that my value isn't based on what I perceive other people's perceptions of me to be. More stuff doesn't make us richer people. I am not necessarily "better" than the homeless guy on the street. We are all just passengers on the same earth-ship cruising through space.

Oh, and in Greek mythology, Zeus and his crew often came down from their digs on Mount Olympus disguised as beggars and street urchins to mingle with the human folk. Just to hang out and

see how they were treated. If you thought yourself "too cool for school" and weren't nice to them, it didn't go well for you. It paid to be nice to them, to offer what you could. It paid to not give a fuck that they didn't have a shiny chariot and just offer them an apple or something.

So, how should I end this little chapter? How 'bout here: there has never been a human being who got out of life alive. Don't take it so seriously. Dye your hair purple if you want to—and lead, lead by giving your life force to good things.

Cannabis didn't change who I was; it allowed me to see who I was. And I really didn't like a lot of what I saw

# Eighteen
## *Measure for Measure*

To be good at my job in corporate America, I had to become a pretty good chameleon—which, unless you're a chameleon, is not the most authentic thing to be. I went into brand marketing because, at its core, it is a person-to-person business. You and the client. You and the person you are trying to get money from. It's relationship-building with a purpose. And that purpose is money. I was always pretty good at that.

Being good at getting people to part with their money is not about being grandiose or full of bravado. At least for me, it wasn't. It was about reading people. About perceiving the shifts of mood and tone in who I was talking to—picking up their body language, their ticks, the flick of their hair or their look to the ground; the way they leaned back in their chair or onto their elbows on the table; if they brought to the meeting with them a pen or a pencil. I got very good (not unlike my husband, the Guantanamo Bay interrogator) at reading people. I got very good at being hypersensitive to the human being I was talking to and altering what I did to fit what they needed me to be: someone they liked and could relate to.

My therapist told me that while most people on this planet walk around with ears or antennae, I was walking around with a giant satellite dish. I picked up anything and everything and all those things in between.

My satellite dish is both a blessing and a curse.

When it's your job to "be on," it's hard not to internalize the behavior of becoming other people. Which makes it not hard to lose track of yourself.

Which makes it hard to know who, exactly, you are. And when you don't know who you are, it makes it pretty hard to be authentic and give yourself total self-care.

So I turned to Shakespeare. "Go to your bosom," wrote the bard, "and knock there (to) ask your heart what it doth know."

"Alright, cool," I told myself. "I mean, my bosom is augmented at this point, so I'll have to knock pretty deep—but that's where the heart is, right?"

I went deep. And with the new arrow in my quiver, I could go deeper than I had ever known possible. With aid from cannabinoids, Barry and I would do what we called "talk therapy," which was basically us sitting on his blue couch in his office and me actually talking about things that mattered to me without fear of judgement. I started journaling at a pace that even ol' Bill Shakespeare may have shown envy at. I got out the paints, brushes, colored pencils, and watercolors and "did art." I wasn't that good, but it didn't matter; it was an outlet and I was letting my heart express itself upon a canvas. I started with a white sheet of paper, and by the end, it was full of "me."

Yoga became less of a grind and more full of flow, as did meditation. My sessions on the cushion were getting both longer and more frequent. My mind was stilling, allowing for the best introspection I'd ever known, the ability to ask my heart what it knows, and being patient enough to listen as it answers. I was relearning life, not unlike how we learn to play music: one measure at a time.

It was flow.

This feeling of relaxation, of supreme comfort with myself, within myself, was new to me. Perhaps—and sorry fam—but perhaps new to everyone in my lineage since we'd become engrained in the "great American rat race" a few generations ago. I don't know. Maybe not, but it felt revolutionary—what I was able to achieve when I got in tune with my heart, with all those seeds on the core of the pinecone.

And my abilities and those feelings kept building on each other. A little bit of cannabis and some time spent with "heart" perpetuated itself. My third eye was coming to see for the first time. Through a beneficial act of self-compassion. A path I'd chosen, and a path I was following through on.

Before I started my discoveries with cannabis, I hadn't realized how much of my energy was going to "work." Human beings are not meant to toil; I was toiling. And when I stopped giving so much damn time to my j-o-b, I found great abundance within the M-to-the-E. Me, myself, and I were becoming some of my best friends.

Yet I'm no Buddha. I know so many people who can do a lot more with these practices than I, but I have committed to walking the path. Because, as I was letting go of all the performative stuff in my life, what I was left with was Lauren.

Cannabis didn't change who I was; it allowed me to see *who* I was. And I really didn't like a lot of what I saw.

One night I was in the kitchen with Barry. I found half a box of Oreos and just started going at them.

"The pure me wants snacks," I said to my husband.

He laughed and said something like, "I see that."

The "pure me" (yeah, and "the munchies" sometimes *are* a real thing) wanted to eat Oreos. The pure me was honoring the part of me that has always loved Oreos. The pure me was celebrating the fact that a to-die-for set of perfect six-pack abs was, really, not worth killing myself for.

New rule: a couple nights a week, I could eat all the Oreos I wanted.

Talk about not giving a fuck. I used to limit myself to half an Oreo on every fourth blue moon. I mean, not really, but that's what it felt like.

So I eat Oreos. Am I still ambitious and intellectually aspiring, a girl with a desire to do and prove and excel? Hell yeah. Those are traits of my "pure me" too. And with the help of talk therapy, art therapy, yoga therapy, mediation therapy, and Oreo therapy, now I'm using those traits to build something of my own. I'm building Hi-Curious—building a safe place where human beings can come together to share and grow—rather than wasting all my energy on a company to whom I'm ultimately disposable.

And, nowadays, the only person I feel I have to prove anything to is myself. No CEOs. No colleagues. No clients. Not Dad. Just me. And that is empowering. I look at it as competition, a healthy competition where I challenge myself on my own terms rather than striving through toxicity for the approval of others that may or may not come.

I'm still the intelligent and motivated badass from the corporate days in New York. I just happen to be a silver-haired hippie who runs a business on living cannabis life out loud in Colorado.

And I still got a great ass.

Little tip: Conquering the desire for external validation means conquering a lot of the internal fears that have been preventing us from living our best life. "Our doubts," to again quote the bard, "are traitors." They keep us from doing good in the world due only to the fear they breed in us.

My family wanted me to "be the best." I never knew what that meant. Mom and Dad, if it meant being the best me, I'm finally doing it. Thanks.

And cannabis has helped me get here. I no longer hold back or obsessively over-craft sentences before they come out of my

mouth. My inhibitions are lowered and that allows me to say what I really think, what I really feel, without editing it. And it turns out that I'm still smart. I can extemporize and flow and be intelligent. Because I am. And with the inhibitors lowered, I've said words in combinations that have astounded people. Seriously, I can even rap now. The synapses in my brain are firing. And they are firing fast, utilizing connections in the pathways that simply were not there when I was twenty-five or thirty-five.

I was raised on doubt; I was taught to think before I speak and parse every word that came out of my mouth. That's what my dad does. And, hey, maybe it works for him, but it didn't always for me. Yeah, I could memorize a script with the best of them; I did that a lot in the pitch room. But the best art comes from spontaneity. Living is an art form. And my life feels a lot more spontaneous these days.

I'm writing my own song.

I had just found the best thing since sliced bread and I needed someone to eat it with me. I needed support. I needed to know I was not alone. I knew I wasn't; I knew other middle-aged woman with a husband and kids and jobs partook, but where the heck were they?

That's why I choose not to thread the impossible needle of "what's recreational and what's medicinal?" All cannabis is medicinal. All cannabis helps flow. Marijuana is medicinal by nature. That's why I call it a wellness tool—in the same category as vitamins and supplements, fitness, and other health measures.

# Nineteen
## *"Burning" Questions*

Even though I'm this silver-haired Auntie Lauren Colorado version of myself these days, PR is still in my blood. I can't help but promote the things I believe in. It's as natural as breathing. And unless you magically just arrived on this page, you know that I believe in dancing with Mary Jane. So I'm a cannabis advocate—out loud n' proud.

But my goal is not to evangelize. No Joel Olsteen here. Nah, I'm just here to own my experiences in the totality of me as a human and see if anyone else picks up the vibe. And people are. It's been a cool mission getting Hi-Curious to the place it is now. Community is a good thing. Fun too.

When I first started talking about cannabis on social media, I didn't think it would be a big deal. But it definitely was a big deal. It's been eighteen months since the first live on Instagram. With over five hundred live shows under my belt, putting my message of advocacy out into the world, I know there's no going back. I burned the boats on the beach. It is time to storm the castle.

Word of mouth and the history of the plant is the best knowledge we have right now. And for those of you who aren't ready, Hi-Curious will be here for you when you are. The only requirement for our tribe is that you want to be in it and show up for it; if you do that, we've got your back. No hazing. I promise.

And we're all about being bold and unapologetic. Because that means being yourself. Out loud. Because that's how, if you feel the way I do about cannabis, we should act about the plant. Getting it out of the peripheries and into "normal" conversations.

Normalizing is kind of a weird word, I guess; but normalizing it is important. Because if it is a part of us, we need to feel accepted. If you're LGBTQ, you want to feel accepted. If you're a person of color, you want to feel accepted. We Jews want to feel accepted. And people who smoke marijuana should be able to feel accepted too.

Yeah, I want cannabis to be normal for my life—but I am also an open advocate because I want it to be normalized for everyone. People drink coffee. People drink beer. And in this country, and throughout the world, people smoke pot.

When I first started using cannabis, I figured everyone had to be way ahead of me. I mean, I was a fully-formed grownup. Maybe people had, like, twenty years of experience with this stuff? I started looking for other women who looked like me. I looked high, I looked low, and I looked in-between. Couldn't find anyone. I seemed to be a unicorn. And I'm not talking about billion-dollar businesses (yet). There seemed to be no one to talk with about my experience except Barry.

I had just found the best thing since sliced bread and I needed someone to eat it with me. I needed support. I needed to know I was not alone. I knew I wasn't; I knew other middle-aged women with a husband, kids and jobs partook, but where the heck were they?

This difficulty in finding other people to share and open up to

was why I started to do what I do now. If I was looking for "cannabis people," I knew other people were looking too. A wise person once told me, "if you want to go somewhere and there is not a road yet, blaze one." So I did. I am.

And my experience has only shown me that there is a yearning, a craving, in this world to feel normality in sharing and living the lifestyle out of the closet.

So, at this point, let me give you some answers to burning (haha) questions from Auntie Lauren.

## What if I don't Live in a Legal State?

People who follow me on Instagram always want to know where they can get "hooked up" in non-legal states. My best and most frequent type of advice for people that live in a state where marijuana is still illegal is to simply travel to a legal state and try it there.

Treat yourself to an immersion trip; get outside and experience a cannabis vacation. Go to Colorado, California, or Washington State and do everything you'd do on your normal vacations, simply intentionally dose with cannabis throughout your time and see how you like it. Don't start out with cannabis by trying to find a local "guy"; it can make you feel dirty—and breaking the law isn't fun when you're an adult trying it for the first time.

Another reason I don't recommend buying on the black market is that illegal cannabis has no oversight. When we lived in New York, our guy must have somehow got pounds of weed delivered to his home, and he'd then package it up with a FoodSaver into eighths that he'd sell for fifty dollars. He'd put a sticker on the wrapping with the type of strain (probably total bullshit).

He'd also bring half-grams of oil (for vape pens) that he sold for one hundred dollars. Total rip-off. But when you live in a non-legal state, what you get is what you get.

Back in New York when I was first learning about the plant, we'd get our bags from our guy and then go to Leafly.com to learn more about the strains we'd just purchased—what effects we were to expect with different kinds, etc. But back in New York we never knew if the label on the package was accurate. It was like thinking you were buying a six-pack of IPAs when you were never quite sure if it wasn't really a pilsner. But with weed, our taste buds weren't honed enough to taste the difference.

When you buy in a legal state, everything you buy is tracked—all the way back to the seed. Everything is government regulated and you can do research on the companies and the growers who produced your flower. In Colorado, each plant has a sticker and number that stays with the plant. Edibles and other ingestibles are tested and retested, held to a super high standard of consistency. It's another pro to the legalization of the plant; I see a lot of similarities to the alcohol prohibition and folks taking chances on the type of bathtub gin they were putting in their bodies. Same with weed. The cannabis you buy legally will be, on average, better than what you get from "the guy."

We should be able to know exactly where the herb came from, who handled it, and what the effects will be. It's the same with every other medicine we put into our body, and it should be for cannabis as well.

Can I just do it myself?

There's also the grow-it-yourself option. In states where marijuana is legal, you can usually grow up to 5-6 plants per person in the privacy of your home or property. A lot of friends of mine have started doing this, growing their cannabis just like they do their tomatoes and kale.

"I just like knowing where *all* my produce comes from," they tell me. "It makes me feel good to know the source."

If you're the horticultural type, I'd recommend giving it a try. Just know that there are a lot of upfront costs and your first crop will most likely not be a roaring success. Mine sure wasn't. There's a lot of things to learn—weed, ironically, doesn't "grow like a weed"—and those that do it well are not unlike artists. They love the process, love the plants, and can "feel" the plants to a certain level—knowing what nutrients to give when; how to control the humidity and temperature (if growing inside); pH water balance; and a bunch of other things.

Just before I started writing this book, I actually planted an outdoor crop here in Colorado. It's a labor of love for sure, and I am learning a ton in the process. If you're reading this sentence, shoot me an email at lauren@hi-curious.com and ask me how it's going. Maybe I can share a tip or two from what I've learned.

So, back to the question at hand. *Can you use the plant as a wellness supplement in states where it's still illegal?* Yes, you can. It's just a lot harder and carries a level of risk. One way to eliminate that risk is to apply for a medical card. A lot of conditions can get you one, especially if you see the right doctor. Chronic pain, glaucoma, anxiety, and about two dozen other conditions have been proven to be treated with marijuana.

My advice, if you are unfortunate enough to live in a state where our lovely little plant is still not recreational, is to get your card. Don't fly home from legal states with weed and don't mail it back to yourself from a place you vacation. Just don't. My card only cost me $125. Yeah, the medical dispensaries didn't have the selection or knowledgeable staff that I'm used to now in Colorado, but it was a step in the right direction. It eliminated the dirty feelings I had, and just gave me some overall peace of mind. A clear conscience, they say, is the best pillow.

Dispensaries?

If you've never been to a dispensary in a legal state, I'd encourage you to hop in your car or on a plane and go to one. They're pretty cool—many are starting to feel like boutiques, almost like going into an Apple Store or something. They are clean, well-lit, inviting places. You'll typically walk into some sort of front room where a person at a front desk checks your ID. They'll sometimes quiz you about your personal details. Then, they scan your ID into a computer (and yes, the state has it on record that you were in a dispensary.) Depending on the location, you'll then either be ushered past the ID check counter or into a separate room to do your shopping.

In most dispensaries, everything is behind the counter, and you talk with the sales consultant (budtender) to help you. Most of these people are super knowledgeable about everything weed. Most love their jobs and they are happy to answer all range of questions without the slightest hint of judgment. They're like Santa's elves or something, just way happy to come to work and package up gifts for people.

With the level of dedication and know-how they bring behind the counter, some are almost like pharmacists. Not all of them; some people are just at a job to make some tips and get good discounts on weed but a lot are super knowledgeable. And, just like if you get good service at a restaurant, throw these guys and gals a couple bucks in the tip jar. Gratitude—it's a central tenant of the weed world.

When your budtender asks you what you want—"Concentrate? Flower? Some edibles?"—if your first (and maybe only) reply is "huh?" that's cool too. Most of the time you'll find a dispensary and a budtender who'll get you something that makes you feel good.

But even me, with a few years and a ton of trips to these places, some visits are less perfect than others. Cannabinoid products help all sorts of functions with the human body, some fairly discreet;

it's one thing to buy tampons at Walgreens from a guy with tattoos on his fingers, but asking a twenty-something dude about vaginal cannabis suppositories for menstrual pain can be a bit much.

And a lot of dispensaries have a lot of different products. There are like thirty-one flavors or something. A little like Willy Wonka's Chocolate Factory. And you'll find the "snozberries" really do taste like "snozberries." Buy some seeds or a clone to get your grow room growing. Dabble with the lotions and creams, a pre-rolled joint, or various tinctures; chocolates, mints, cookies, gummies, lollypops, vape pens, concentrate sauces, even beverages, and, yes, vaginal suppositories.

But, seriously, to sum up on dispensaries: One of the best things about legalized weed is buying well-crafted, consistent products from knowledgeable people without having to look behind your back. Try one out sometime.

## What about Medical vs. Recreational?

The main difference between recreational dispensaries and medical dispensaries is the products themselves. Medical products are allowed to have higher THC content than recreational. In the case of edibles, the allowed medical dosage in Colorado is double the recreational dose. To get your hands on these, you need to get that med card, which can be a barrier; not everyone qualifies. Yet.

But these higher doses are not necessarily the best thing for people new to the plant anyway. Eating an edible with too much THC can give a bad trip. "Low and slow" is what I teach in my dosage workshops.

For people using marijuana for severe issues like seizures, PTSD, and cancer, oils and tinctures are often prescribed; these products come with the highest doses allowed by the powers that be. And for good reason. The challenge for patients seeking this "alternative

medicine" is that medical schools, as of yet, don't teach cannabis medicine to their students—and many doctors don't feel equipped to provide enough scientific research to back up the claims made about cannabis. Therefore, even doctors who help people get a med card aren't necessarily able to help prescribe, let alone steer, patients toward precise cannabinoid medicines.

Unfortunately, as of the writing of this sentence, research is usually left up to the patient.

That's why I choose not to thread the impossible needle of "what's recreational and what's medicinal?" All cannabis is medicinal. All cannabis helps flow. Marijuana is medicinal by nature. That's why I call it a wellness tool—in the same category as vitamins and supplements, fitness, and other health measures. And taking your health into your own hands, being able to take care of yourself without a doctor or a trainer or a supplement-specialist is a good step to take. We can all be our own doctors, and the same is true with pot.

Maybe in ten years a doctor might be able to tell you "this type of cannabis works best for back pain," for instance, or "this will help for sleep," but for the foreseeable future, you will just have to seek the best information out there, talk to the most knowledgeable people you can find, and perform your own research.

You're taking a good step in reading this book.

Do your research, challenge marketing, push for science, try to know where your cannabis is grown–and go for it.

# Twenty
## *From Sea to Shining Sea*

We're coming to a tipping point in this country, the teeter-totter of public sentiment slowly shifting toward universal legalization. People and politicians have been looking at the states that have already legalized as guineapigs; to mass America's old and stagnant mind, disaster has, shockingly, not befallen them. As cannabis becomes more visible, its truth becomes more visible as well. Broad public acceptance is something that takes time, but the veil is being lifted, and along with it, so is the stigma. Albeit slowly.

As of the publication of this book, thirty-four states in the union have implemented either an active recreational or medical cannabis program. It may not be moving as fast as we'd like, but close to seventy percent of the states allow our plant in some form or another. The movement is happening.

Still, there are setbacks. Especially in the justice realm. Since I started writing this book, the state of Illinois has completely gone back on its word to support social equity applicants (people who have been impacted directly by the war on drugs). And, if dispensaries

look like Apple stores, it's time to free all people who are in jail for non-violent cannabis offenses. It makes no sense that some can profit from the plant and others are still incarcerated.

That's a big bite to chew, and maybe I'll go more into it in my next book. If you're interested, *The New Jim Crow* by Michelle Alexander does good work on the subject.

My life has become one of advocacy because I believe it's important. And the thing is, there are a lot of ways to "do advocacy." You obviously don't need to uproot your life and move to a cannabis-friendly state and build your life and business around it as I've chosen to do. You don't need to become a budtender, a grower, a high priest or priestess of the Church of Weed either.

If you're new to cannabis you might be thinking that maybe you don't want to get involved with something that has a stigma and that you don't want to deal with worrying what people will think. You might be worrying that you have to "get political" about it right away. I promise, you don't.

Discovering cannabis is a process. All I encourage you to do right now is start learning. Read some articles and experiment with the plant. Discover how it makes you feel. Start slow, ask lots of questions, follow as many cannabis advocates as you can.

Do your research, challenge marketing, push for science, try to know where your cannabis is grown—and go for it. You may find, as it starts to make a real difference in your life, that you want to become someone who actively advocates, someone who lives the lifestyle out loud. But you don't have to.

Stay in the closet if that is where you are more comfortable.

Whether you're in or you're out, there are people like me and entities like Hi-Curious trying to change one mind at a time, to get our country to see the plant differently based upon who we are and what our experiences have been, to show others how cannabis has enriched and improved our lives.

Simply by living my cannabis life out loud, by living my best life, I am working to influence the sea of change.

And it's working. The tides are coming in.

The way I use cannabis, I can, and do, produce in my daily life. I get shit done. And, for me, a regulated amount of cannabis helps me do it. And then I sleep well and do it all again the next day. As a result of my cannabis practice, I have actually become more productive, more organized, and more mindful. And, of course, more happy—the greatest gift of all.

# Twenty-One

## *Cannabis. Is. Medicine. Period.*

So we've talked about the idea that legal cannabis means not only safer cannabis for the user but that by being regulated it is also being properly measured and treated just like any other medicine. With legal cannabis you can both control your dosage and regulate the type of experience that you have; you can tailor your intake to treat specific needs rather than the "puff and pray" experience of getting whatever you get from a dealer and hoping for the best.

Now we're going to take a second and synthesize a lot of what we've been discussing—not just the question of whether cannabis has medicinal properties but whether it actually *is* a medicine. I say it is. And many others do too.

I encourage those with whom I work to think about cannabis as an actual medicine—just like Tylenol or Zoloft—because it helps people approach usage in a more thorough and thoughtful manner,

exploring the plant in a more considered way. This leads, to great benefit, to what I call "intentional use."

Intentional use means learning the properties of the product you're using, and what they mean for you. It means learning how you respond to different strains and methods of partaking: how to ingest if you're struggling with mindfulness, what to try if you can't sleep. Intentional means using different products, responsibly, and taking note of their effects on you—then discussing it with your budtender to see how you might alter your approach to get closer to your desired result. It is, in fact, having a desired result in the first place. And then honing in on your aim.

When you set your intention, you are better able to articulate what you ask for. "I want to take the edge off my anxiety," you may say, or "I have neck cramps and want to ease the stiffness."

Figure out what you want your cannabis use to accomplish and you'll be better positioned to get there. If you simply go in expecting a cure-all, you may ultimately be disappointed because that isn't how this works.

Cannabis works as a wellness supplement, yes, and each supplement you take—whatever it may be—should have a desired outcome. If it doesn't, you're simply taking things for the sake of taking things and it doesn't "supplement" anything.

"But," I've heard from a few people, "I'm a generally well-person and I just like to smoke some weed every once in a while to zone out on the couch."

If that's your intended goal, I applaud you for that. Life's tough, and "zoning out" without alcohol or Xanax is a good thing, an improvement to do it more naturally. However, if that's the only way you use cannabis and you believe it's making you unproductive, you're probably using it too frequently or in too great of a dose.

The way I use cannabis, I can, and do, *produce* in my daily life. I get shit done. And, for me, a regulated amount of cannabis helps me do it. And then I sleep well and do it all again the next day.

As a result of my cannabis practice, I have actually become *more* productive, *more* organized, and *more* mindful. And, of course, *more* happy—the greatest gift of all.

My usage varies from day to day depending on the intentions I set and how I need to show up that day. I'm fortunate enough that I don't have to drive my car most days, but if I do, I'll wait until I get back to use it, starting my routine later in the day. I don't skip days. Just like I wouldn't skip a day of my Lexapro.

I tend to do best when I begin my wellness-medicating in the morning. Some people drink a pot of coffee; I don't. I'll opt for a variety of green medicine that has a more stimulating effect; the morning sets the tone for the day, and I usually like to set a tone that is energetic and productive. It might seem counterintuitive that I'd reach for a stimulant with my anxiety condition, but the truth is that the right product helps me convert that anxious energy into creative energy. (Same principle behind prescribed ADHD medicine.) My racing mind, with the right product at the right dosage, is better equipped to direct the mass of sparking neurons and skittering brain cells to what I desire to dig into.

For me, this means getting in tune with a solitary frame of mind—where I do my best thinking and strategizing. I'll go to my home office or my patio and work for usually about three hours. I maximize the experience, and when the effect has ebbed I'll transition into the next part of my day, the middle of the day, a time when I am ready to begin to be more social.

This is typically when I have meetings with my team or make content for social media. At 4:30 p.m. each day, I go live on the Hi-Curious mobile app, holding a "sesh" with my community. Much of the sessions are centered around me consuming cannabis and talking about it with people who drop in. While I may go into my live streams with a general notion of what I want to talk about, they're by no means scripted. I speak off the cuff, responding to the

inquiries of my followers and spouting from my general knowledge on the subject. This extemporaneous style takes a fairly high degree of confidence, a lack of fear, and a disabling of internal filters. Talking for an hour to a bunch of strangers who can only message you in the comments section is a challenge. And I use my medicine to get me in the mindset to go there. I have come to love this challenge, and especially during Covid, these daily shows became my social outlet. Some of the people who showed up daily became part of my family.

During the middle of the day is when I use the highest doses of cannabis. I see a lot of similarities to this dose and Spanish culture's lunch meal, which is its biggest of the day. We've been up for a while and we will be up for a while; it makes sense to *Espana* and it makes sense to me.

Also, my community seems to love seeing me consume cannabis; I get lots of hearts and other emojis when I hold in a big bong hit and don't cough. (We cannabis people find interesting things amusing.)

And, while it is fun, I also feel that the willingness to experiment in front of other people is valuable, important, because there's just not a lot of hard science that my community can turn to. Science is still way behind the times with cannabis (plus, much of the published science is funded by companies or organizations with agendas), and it is vital to get a real-time perspective. The serious study of cannabis is actually fairly recent.

It was only in the nineties, in fact, that scientists discovered the human endocannabinoid system (ECS) that we touched upon earlier—the receptors in our brain that match like a lock and key to the shape of the cannabis plant.

An easy definition of ECS? A system within the body that regulates others systems, kinda like a headquarters or something. What this means is that within the human body are receptors for the cannabinoids found in cannabis—interlocking puzzle pieces that seem to fascinate anyone who studies them.

ECS is an example of the type of information that is only now making its way into medical schools. I have a good friend who's been

practicing medicine since the late seventies, for example, who's never heard of it. Unlike a lot of systems and processes within our body, the scientific study of cannabis doesn't reach all the way back to the ancient Greeks or even to the European Renaissance of the 1600s. Heck, a lot of it doesn't even go back to the "peace and love sixties" for Pete's Sake. It's new. And that's why the collective outreach from people doing what I am doing is vital. As science plays catch-up, we have to learn by trying the stuff out and documenting how, why, when, and where it makes us feel.

Like any other medicine, experiences with cannabis vary from individual to individual, even from day to day for the same person: How tired you are, how healthy or ill you are, your diet, and even your particular hormonal balance at any given moment play roles in what will work best for you.

I've come to know what works best for me. And as I continue to grow my network with my tribe at Hi-Curious, we're moving in the right direction to track which products work best for which types of people are using them.

"But you never seem to be 'stoned,'" friends and followers often tell me.

That's because my preferred dosage is what many people know as "microdosing," where I take small quantities throughout the day. For me, and a lot of other people, that's the optimal method of consumption. Some people do it with LSD or psilocybin. I do it with THC because it's legal for me and because it works. On days where societal commitments force me to show up "a certain way" I do abstain—using mindfulness practices developed within my cannabis routine to keep me sane and still—but when I am free to my own schedule, microdosing is how I live much of my life. A little enhanced, the world is a little more colorful and alive.

Change can be scary—but without change the caterpillar would remain in its cocoon, never to become the butterfly it is so meant to be.

# Chapter the Last
## *The Journey Continues*

There's a picture on my Instagram of myself and a couple friends at Vail Mountain on a beautiful winter's day. The snow is fresh and the sun is shining. We're wearing silver ski suits, shiny as heck, with wraparound goggles and we're grinning widely. The photo captures a moment, a feeling—we are *present*.

And it looks like we're about to launch into space.

That's a good metaphor for how I feel right now. Launching, soaring, feeling light enough to fly.

I'm in a place of joy. I'm embracing my weird. I'm supported by like-minded friends in a community that works with cannabis—the plant that helped me awaken to this new beginning. The plant I'm working to make accessible, "normal" and out loud for people from all walks of this planet.

On my personal journey, I don't know exactly how I will get to the finish line, but I know I will get there. I know this because it's really not all about the finish line, not about the end goal, but the

process. I am journeying, and that is what it's all about. I am learning and loving and living and growing.

My heart is pointed in the right direction and my mind is strong.

I no longer feel like I have to control every little thing in my life. I no longer feel like I am living in a hamster wheel. I am free, like when I am out skiing, to make my own turns and feel the wind in my face, and simply *be*.

I feel comfortable in my own skin, I am present for my husband and my two sons. I am making choices that are motivated by excitement rather than fear. I am doing things for the feeling they give me on the inside rather than what "things" they can give me on the outside.

I have greater equanimity and healthier relationships. I feel good. And the wellness benefits of cannabis have helped me get here.

I came to Colorado with a vision, and that vision continues to grow clearer every single day. My business and community continue to grow. My passion to promote cannabis as a wellness supplement continues to grow. And the Hi-Curious community and the Hi-Curious empire continue to grow.

I used to think I'd help the world through fitness. Through workout routines and abdominal muscles. But, in this journey of perspective and an elevated interaction with the infinite, I have discovered that human beings are much more than our bodies. And so I wake up in the mornings with the aim to help humanity—our mindset, our soul, and our flow.

We are only just beginning to understand the ways cannabis can benefit humanity. We are living this grand experiment, and the time is now. The Cannabis Revolution is here. And you will continue to find me at its forefront.

I'm no guru or Buddha or priestess. I'm only Auntie Lauren, simply a thoughtful person who knows what cannabis can do if treated properly and applied wholistically.

I appreciate you. I appreciate the world and what it gives us. And I will leave you with this:

*Change can be scary—but without change the caterpillar would remain in its cocoon, never to become the butterfly it is so meant to be.*

XOXO *Auntie Lauren*

SEAMLESS
COMPATIBILITY
GIRO
Giro
tipsyelves

Before she discovered cannabis, Lauren Mundell was busy—busy glorifying productivity and trapped in the rat race culture of New York City. She was fighting pitch-room battles for a top PR agency and clawing her way to the top of the ladder to nowhere.

She was always wearing a mask, always hyper-aware of the opinions of others. Not even she could see that she had lost herself to the masks. She was a competitive, sharp and 'badass-bitch business woman' right down to the six-pack abs. She walked the walk (in stillettos). She made the money. She had all the things she'd once thought she wanted.

But it was never enough. And, the masks became all that were left. She forgot who she was in trying to become everything for everyone. Late-night emails, the 'working weekends,' that shooting pain in her leg, running late to everything that was important, mom guilt.

In trying to stay in control of everything, she completely lost herself.

Then, after Trump's election in 2016, Lauren's husband retired from the Navy and began using cannabis. Lauren was shocked. But, after seeing positive changes in him she became curious, High Curious.

What followed was a transformation, a reclamation of self and a wake-up call that this rat-race lifestyle she was living had turned her into a shell of herself she no longer recognized.

High Curious is the story of a woman who played by all the rules and by all accounts, was winning. But, winning was killing her. Call it burn-out or a mid-life crisis, but discovering cannabis at 43 upended Lauren's life and changed her, for the better.

Learning to use cannabis intentionally allowed Lauren to move past the un-addressed, crippling anxiety that was holding her back from enjoying the abundance of her life. This book tells the story of Lauren's seismic life-shift aided by cannabis and invites readers to open their minds to cannabis as a wellness supplement.

So get curious. Get High Curious.

# Bio

When Lauren Mundell discovered cannabis at 43, she couldn't believe that no one was talking about it as a wellness supplement. She turned to social media to find other people "like her" sharing how they used the plant. She quickly found out that unlike the passions she'd found before (fitness, healthy eating, knitting, running), there was no one openly sharing their healthy lifestyle with cannabis. Lauren left her high-powered NYC rat race life to build a business in the cannabis industry. Lauren's company, Hi-Curious helps aspiring cannabis entrepreneurs build successful e-commerce businesses.

Made in the USA
Columbia, SC
09 October 2021

46516848R10096

Printed in the USA
CPSIA information can be obtained
at www.ICGtesting.com
LVHW052149170924
791395LV00025B/239

9 798224 523191

## 标本的记录

缺乏详细采集地点记录的矿物和岩石标本毫无意义，不要相信自己的记忆，必须在现场，而不是回到家中才记下细节。在笔记本上详细笔记，画草图，用照相机拍下地层、岩石构造和地质状况。如果有便携式摄影机，更可保存详细的视听记录。

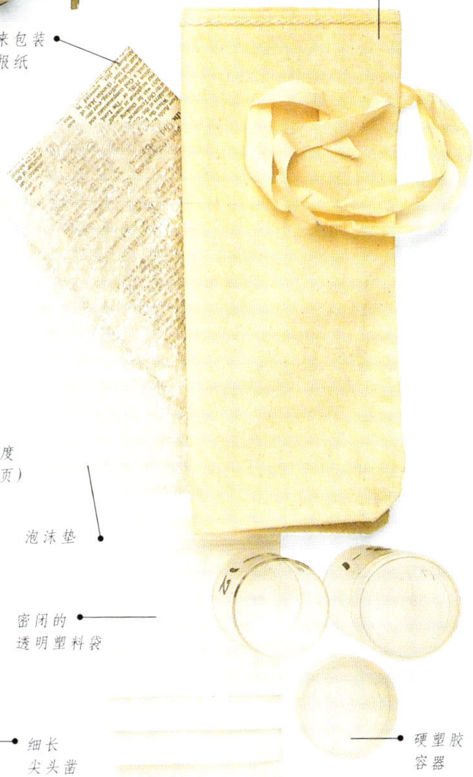


## 便携式放大镜

用一个十倍放大镜可以清楚地辨认岩石和矿物，并当场做出鉴定。

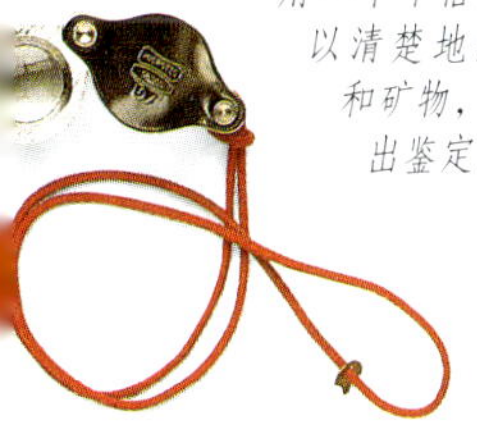

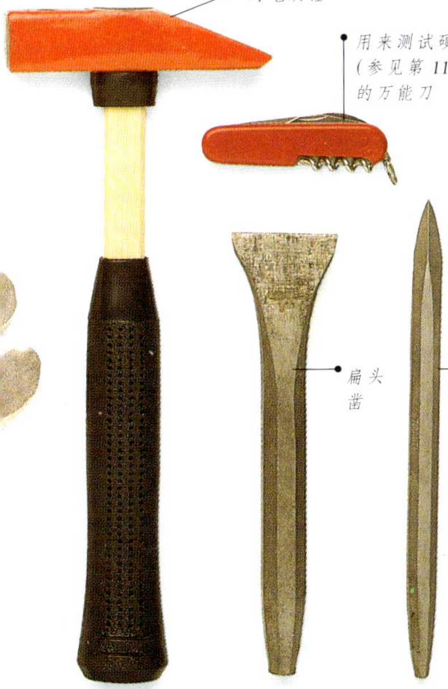


## 采集和包装

地质锤只用于敲打地表岩石，不用它挖掘露头。标本采集应有节制，采集后用报纸、布或“泡沫袋”将标本仔细包装，并清楚地标记。

# 室内工具

将采集的标本带回室内，必须细心地为鉴定做准备，然后予以陈放或贮藏。图示的工具是室内鉴定必备的。许多标本上粘有泥土或带岩石基质，必须先清除掉。可以用软毛刷除去松散的泥土和其他岩屑，避免用重或锐利的工具敲打或剔标本，除非你想使新鲜面显露出来。清除松散物质时，必用手握住标本，不要用老虎钳或金属夹，那样会损坏标本。如果标本是花岗岩或片麻岩等硬岩石，那么即使用相当粗的毛刷和自来水冲洗，也不会造成损伤。对于脆弱的标本，如方解石晶体，须用蒸馏水(其中不含活性化学添加剂)和非常细的毛刷。对于溶于水的矿物，须使用其他液体清洗，可以用酒精清洗硝酸盐、硫酸盐和硼酸盐矿物。稀盐酸是硅酸盐的良好清洗液，但溶解碳酸盐，把硅酸盐浸泡在酸液里过一夜，可清除其被覆的碳酸盐碎片。

**刮削和撬开的工具**

*用尖锐的金属工具可以剔除标本上的松散岩屑。小锥之类的尖头工具可撬开标本，不过得小心不要损伤内部的岩石，这是整理标本的第一步。*

**清洗用毛刷**

*根据标本的牢固程度，可选用不同尺寸的软毛刷乃至指甲刷清洗岩石和矿物，*

*软貂毛画笔是清除矿物上粘附的微粒的最佳工具，而指甲刷仅用于不会被损坏的硬岩石，如片麻岩、辉长岩。*

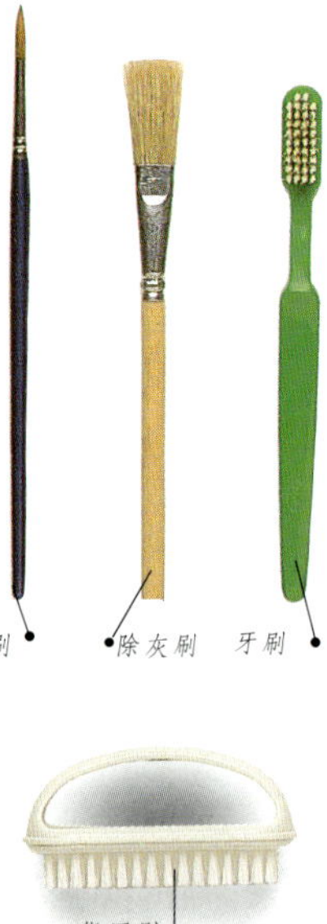

蒸馏水

## 清洗液

尽可能使用蒸馏水清洗标本，因为自来水中含有多种化学物质会与矿物起反应。稀盐酸可以溶解碳酸盐碎屑，这种酸很安全。

稀盐酸

## 矿物的测试

在室内，可用普通化学方法鉴定矿物。稀释的酸液能与特定的矿物发生持续反应，比如，碳酸盐在稀盐酸中发泡。也可用火焰进行测试，把标本放在木炭片上，用煤气火焰和吹管吹烧，这时，矿物火焰变色，显示出矿物的化学成分，或矿物熔化，产生小球珠状物，或散发出气味。

用来吸干清洗液的软纸

10倍的便携式放大镜用以鉴定矿物

可伸进裂缝里的棉花棒

瓷质条痕盘或条痕板

## 鉴定辅助工具

条痕盘、硬度测试工具和便携式放大镜是鉴定矿物不可缺少的辅助工具。硬度和条痕将在第25、26页分别介绍。

## 硬度测试工具

如果依次用日常物品刻划一个矿物，比如先用硬币，再用小刀、玻璃或石英，则可确定矿物的硬度。

玻璃的硬度6

石英硬度为7

泡沫包装袋上的标本

硬币硬度为3

小刀刃硬度为5.5

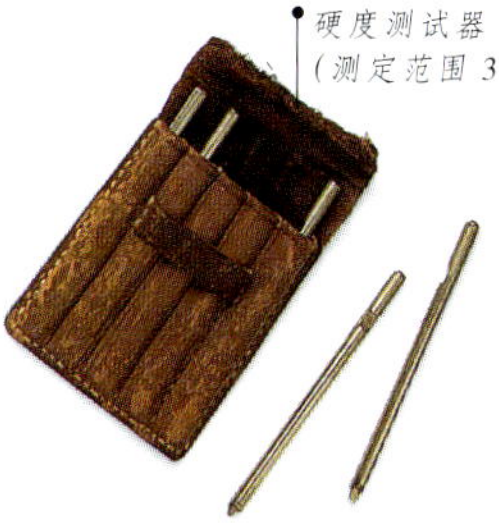

硬度测试器（测定范围3－10）

# 陈放标本

如果不能有条理地陈放岩石和矿物标本，则那些标本将失去科学价值。标本在采集并修理之后，即应陈放，为之编目、贴上标签，以便保存和展示。你也许想在家中陈列比较漂亮以及相当坚固的标本，那么不妨将之装在玻璃柜里，以免灰尘累积在小洞或缝隙里。把那些易碎的标本单独放入比它们稍大的厚纸匣或厚纸盒里，然后放入柜中。在每个标本匣底部放一张标本签，注明标本名称、产地、采集日期及编号。把每一件标本都编入你的目录中，为目录中的条目编号，与标本盒标签的编号一致。另外，应该在目录里留出备注栏以便填写更详细的资料。用笔填写或用电脑存入所有的地图参考资料、产地地质状况，如产地的其他岩石、矿物、构造情况，观察到的大范围相变和野外特征——矿脉和岩脉的延伸分布状况可能是关键的鉴定特征，此点可参照本书有关的矿物、岩石条目。

笔记本和圆珠笔

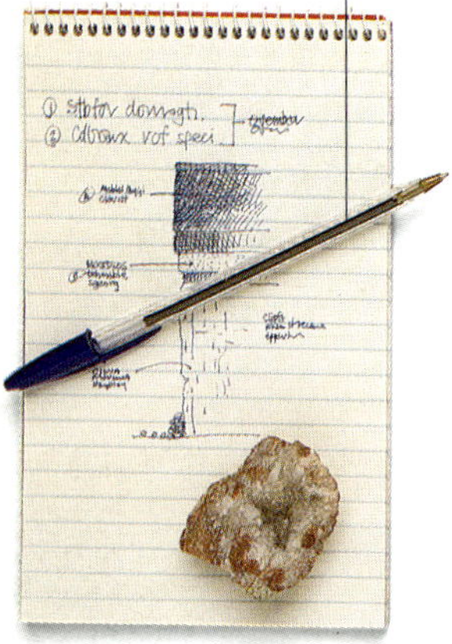

**笔记和记录**

*把你的野外笔记转抄到目录索引或存入电脑。在标本不重要的部位涂一小条修正液或白漆，然后写上标本编号。*

书写编号的衬底

修正液

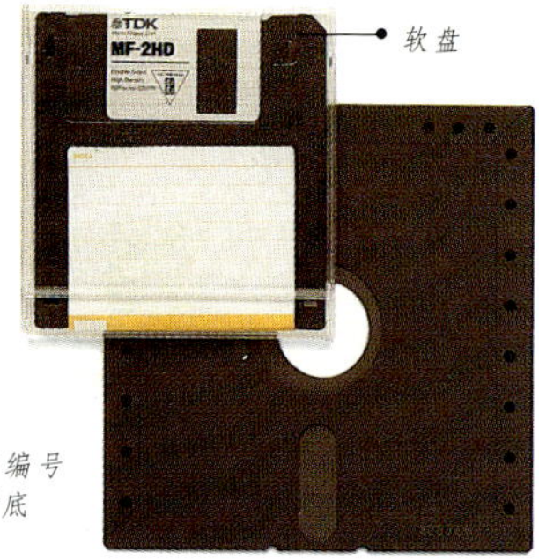


软盘

**电脑记录**

*电脑作业系统最为方便，可以贮存、添加和修正资料。*

**卡片索引**

*卡片索引目录既便宜、可靠，使用起来又快捷。可以按字母顺序编排标本。其空白处可以转录野外记录，甚至复制现场草图。*

卡片索引盒

用来编排目录的卡片

合理摆放标本的抽屉

标本签

衬有薄纸的纸盒

**贮存你的标本**

*把岩石和矿物放入厚纸盒，然后摆放到抽屉里。你可以在家里简单地做一些适于放在抽屉里及放标本的盒子，或者去专卖店购买。易碎的标本应用棉纸包起来，以防互相摩擦。另外，也可用盖子透明的小塑胶盒来存放标本。*

# 本书内容安排及其使用

本书分成两大部分：矿物和岩石。第46页至179页的矿物部分按矿物的化学组成分成八大类（参见第20至21页的说明）。化学成分最简单的矿物排在前面，随后是较复杂的种类。每个大类都先作一般介绍，然后一一介绍属于该类的代表性矿物，如下图所示的例解。第180页至249页的岩石部分系根据公认的三大岩石类别（参见第30至31页）安排的，典型的例解示如次页。

## 矿物

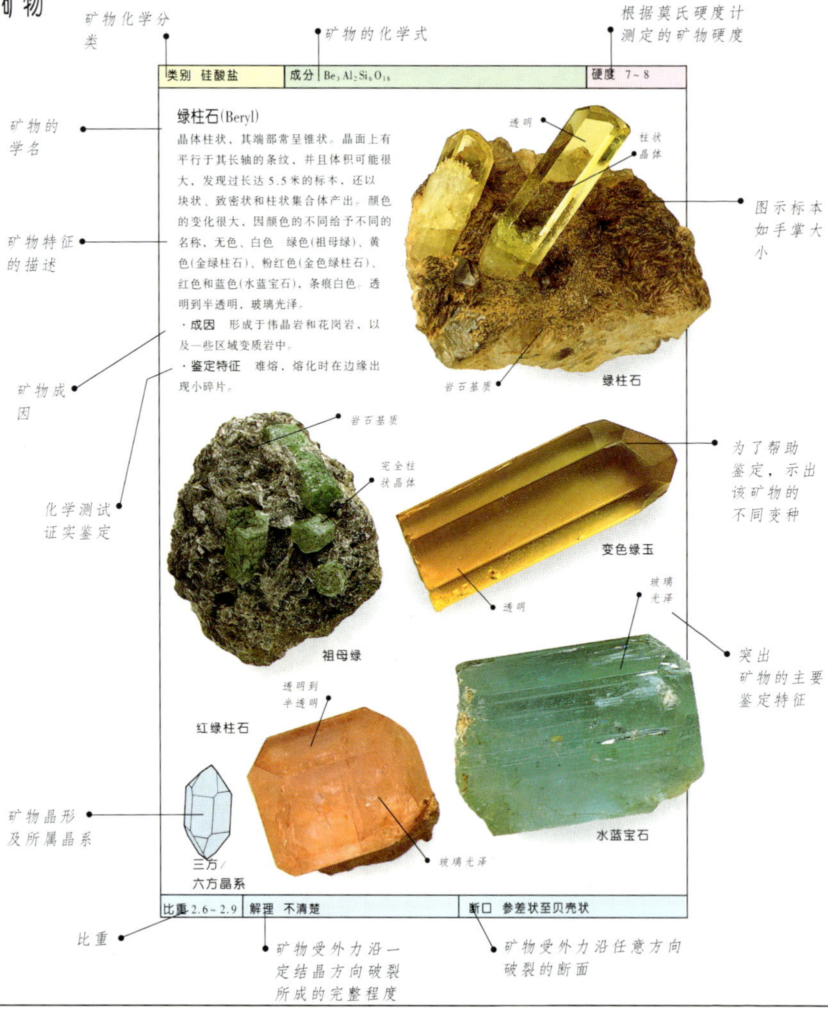

## 岩浆岩

岩石的种类

岩石成因类型

岩石颗粒大小

晶形：发育良好的为自形晶，发育不好的为他形晶

| 类别　火成岩 | 成因　喷出 | 粒度　细粒 | 晶形　他形、自形 |
|---|---|---|---|

岩石的矿物含量

颗粒描述

成岩环境

**细碧岩**(Spilite)

属基性岩，石英含量小于10%，硅含量平均45%－55%，以枕状熔岩产出。其斜长石常富含钠，辉石是构成细碧岩的主要矿物，常转化成绿泥石。

· **结构**　细粒，充满气孔。有时可见嵌入岩石基质中的杏仁子。

· **成因**　形成于海底，以水下熔岩流和枕状熔岩产出。

原标本大如手掌，足够鉴定用

| 分类　基性 | 产状　火山 | 颜色　暗色 |
|---|---|---|

化学成分：分为酸性、中性、基性和超基性

岩石形成时的岩浆活动环境

颜色的描述：分为浅色、中等、暗色

## 变质岩

| 类别　变质岩 | 成因　接触变质带 | 粒度　细粒 | 分类　接触变质 |
|---|---|---|---|

变质作用类型

**空晶石角页岩**(Chiastolite Hornfles)

灰色或浅棕色，矿物成分有石英、云母、红柱石和堇青石。基质上明显的薄刃片状晶体是空晶石，为红柱石的一种。

· **结构**　均匀细粒状，常含空晶石斑状变晶，一端呈斜方晶形，不规则排列。

· **成因**　紧靠火成侵入体，热接触变质作用。

| 压力　高 | 温度　适中至高 | 构造　结晶 |
|---|---|---|

成岩过程中的压力大小

变质作用中的温度条件

根据构造的有无概括细分

## 沉积岩

| 类别　沉积岩 | 成因　陆地 | 粒度　晶质 |
|---|---|---|

**琥珀**(Amber)

是已绝灭针叶树的树脂化石，质地柔软，并有松脂或半玻璃光泽，从透明到半透明不等。陷进粘稠的树脂中的昆虫和小脊椎动物，保存在琥珀里变成化石。虎珀常被用作珠宝。

· **结构**　断裂后呈贝壳状断口。

· **成因**　由针叶树的树脂形成，常见于沉积矿床。

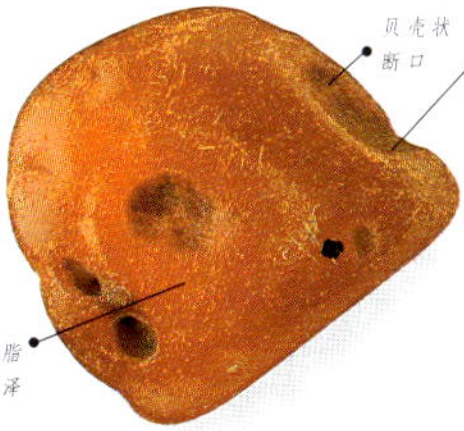


图中所示的标本和野外见到的一样，不同的是经过彻底清洗，显得更清楚

| 分类　生物岩 | 化石　脊椎动物、无脊椎动物 | 颗粒形态　无 |
|---|---|---|

根据材料来源的沉积岩分类

岩石中含有的化石

颗粒形状的描述

# 是矿物还是岩石？

岩石通常是几种矿物的集合体，不过有时只含一、两种矿物。同样，矿物或是游离而未化合的自然元素，或是元素化合物。金、银、铜为金属自然元素，长石、辉石、闪石和云母则是造岩的硅酸盐——一种金属元素与硅氧四面体($SiO_4$)化合而成的化合物。

## 什么是矿物？

除了少数例外(如水、水银、蛋白石)，矿物都是固体，是无机元素或元素化合物。它们有一定的原子结构，其化学成分无论是砂岩，还是在火山熔岩中的石英晶体，都有同样的化学和物理性质。

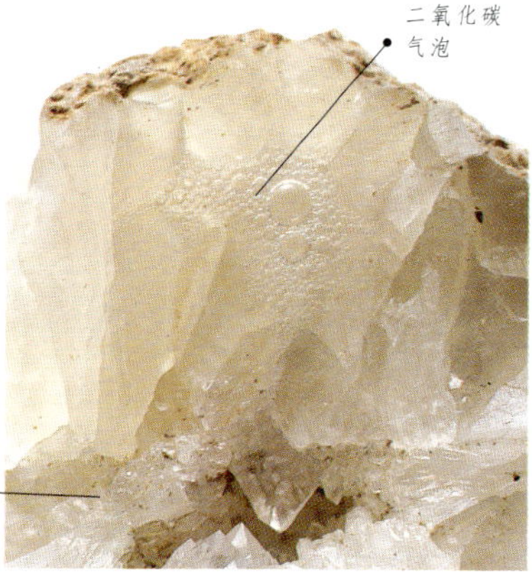


**物理性质**

*同一种矿物都有相同的原子结构。*

**化学性质**

*每种矿物都有一定的化学成分，且在固定范围内变化。*

**裂开的方解石菱形晶体**

**自然产状**

*矿物常从与岩浆岩伴生的热液中结晶生成(左图)。随着残余热液的消失，还可在火山口周围形成矿物皮壳。*

## 什么是岩石?

岩石是地壳的组成部分，根据成因可以分为三大类：岩浆岩、变质岩和沉积岩(参看第30至31页)。岩石是许多不同矿物颗粒的集合体，它们或融合、或胶结、或结合在一起。

**岩石：矿物的集合体**

*花岗岩主要是由三种矿物——石英、云母和长石组成的。在岩浆的冷却过程中，它们的晶体由于结晶作用而相互结合在一起。石英是灰色玻璃状，长石明亮，晶体柱状，云母则闪闪发光，为黑色或银白色。*

**石英**

*石英是花岗岩中常见的矿物，色淡，硬度大。*

**长石**

*花岗岩有两种长石，它们都发育成良好的晶体。*

**云母**

*在花岗岩中，云母呈小而发光的晶体，有深色的黑云母和浅色的白云母两种。*

**显微镜下的花岗岩**

*右图是放大了30倍的花岗岩。请注意组成岩石的晶体是如何连结的。*

# 矿物的形成

地球的地壳由岩石组成，岩石又是矿物的集合体。最佳矿物标本一般产于热液矿脉，是热液在地壳裂隙中循环流动的产物，热液中含有形成各种矿物的元素。矿物也形成于岩浆岩，由岩浆（地下熔化的岩石）或熔岩（喷出地表熔化的岩石）冷却直接结晶而成。先成岩再结晶时，一系列矿物会在变质岩中形成。某些沉积岩，如石灰岩、蒸发岩和氧化铁，会因接近地表的低温热液作用形成矿物结晶。

## 矿脉

下图示带状矿层切穿岩层，那里原是断层，即岩层发生错动和位移的断层带，或是地层未生错动和位移的破裂带，它们可被侵入矿脉完全填充，或围绕碎屑结晶（角砾岩）。

锡石

产于热液矿脉中的一种典型矿物

一种常见的脉状矿物，由地下的灼热化学溶液形成

乳石英

**石英脉**

左图是一条白色乳石英脉，穿过黑色板岩（最左图）。最初形成于地下深处，后来由于风化和侵蚀暴露于地表。

## 岩浆岩

岩浆冷凝时，矿物即在其中形成(参看第 32 页)。密度最大的铁镁硅酸盐矿物橄榄石、辉石形成于岩浆温度最高时，而密度较小的矿物，如长石和石英，则在岩浆后期形成。矿物在熔岩中可以充分的发展生长，从而生成完好的晶体。

**花岗岩露头**
从上图的岩浆岩——花岗岩露头上可见大的长石晶体嵌在岩石表面。

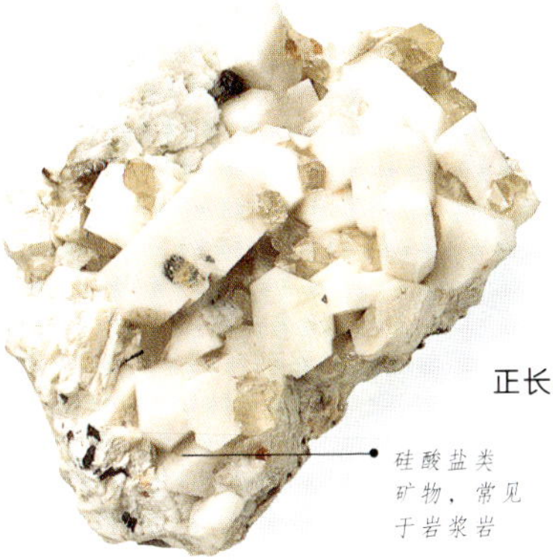

**正长石**

硅酸盐类矿物，常见于岩浆岩

**石榴子石**

贵榴石，一种常见于变质岩中的石榴子石

## 变质岩

石榴子石、云母和蓝晶石等系列矿物，都形成于变质岩(参看第 34 页)。温度和压力可以重组原岩中的化学组分，产生矿物，或者是具有化学活性的流体在岩石中循环流动增添了新成分。

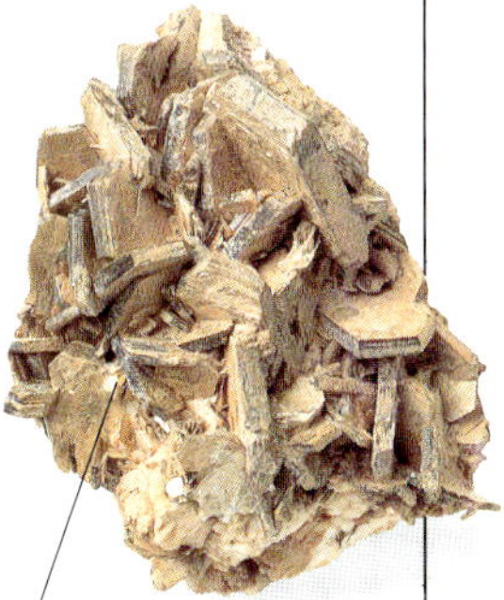

**白云母**

常见于许多变质岩(尤其是片岩)中的一种闪光矿物

**片岩露头**
地壳深处的岩石在高压下，褶皱形成片岩(左图)。

# 矿物的成分

矿物是游离而未结合的元素，或元素化合物，其成分可用化学式表示。萤石的化学式为$CaF_2$，表示钙原子(Ca)与氟原子(F)化合在一起，写在式子下方的数字2表示氟原子是钙原子的两倍。根据化学成分和晶体结构，对矿物进行分类。

## 自然元素

游离、未化合的元素，这类矿物较少，有50个左右，其中的一些(如金、银)具商业价值。

银

## 卤化物

所有这类矿物都含有卤素元素氟、氯、溴或碘。这些元素的原子与金属原子化合形成矿物，如石盐(钠和氯)或萤石(钙和氟)。卤化物也较少，约100种左右。

石盐

硫

赤铁矿

## 氧化物和氢氧化物

这类矿物有250多种。氧化物是由一至二种金属元素与氧化合而成的化合物，一种金属元素与水和羟基化合则形成氢氧化物。

## 硫化物

为常见的矿物，有300多种，为硫与金属、半金属元素的化合物，例如黄铁矿和雄黄。

黄铁矿

雄黄

蛋白石

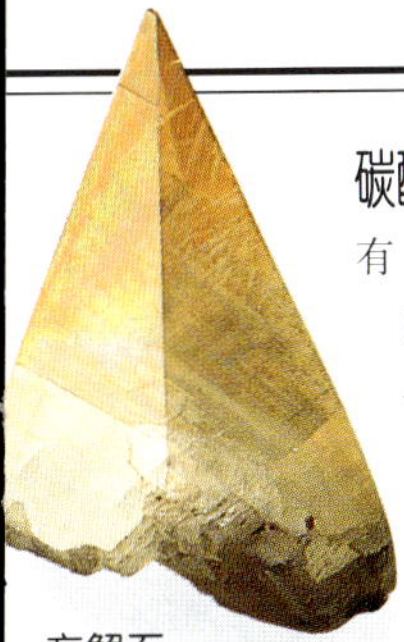

方解石

## 碳酸盐

有 200 种碳酸盐类矿物，由一种或多种金属元素与碳酸根$(CO_3)^{-2}$化合而成。方解石是最常见的碳酸盐，由钙与碳酸根化合形成。

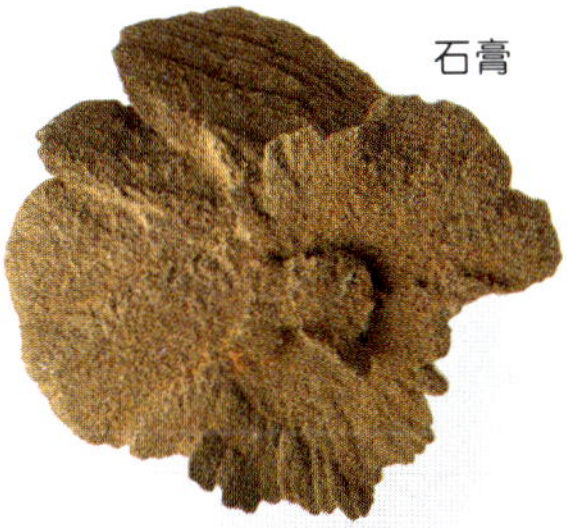

石膏

## 硫酸盐

是由一个或多个金属元素与硫酸根 $(SO_4)^{-2}$化合而成的化合物。

磷氯铅矿

## 磷酸盐

这类矿物色彩鲜艳，由一种或多种金属元素与磷酸根$(PO_4)^{-3}$化合而成。砷酸盐与钒酸盐与这类矿物伴生。

## 化学元素

| 符号 | 名称 | 符号 | 名称 | 符号 | 名称 |
|---|---|---|---|---|---|
| Ac | 锕 | Ge | 锗 | Po | 钋 |
| Ag | 银 | H | 氢 | Pr | 镨 |
| Al | 铝 | He | 氦 | Pt | 铂 |
| Am | 镅 | Hf | 铪 | Pu | 钸 |
| Ar | 氩 | Hg | 汞 | Ra | 镭 |
| As | 砷 | Ho | 钬 | Rb | 铷 |
| At | 砹 | I | 碘 | Re | 铼 |
| Au | 金 | In | 铟 | Rh | 铑 |
| B | 硼 | Ir | 铱 | Rn | 氡 |
| Ba | 钡 | K | 钾 | S | 硫 |
| Be | 铍 | Kr | 氪 | Sb | 锑 |
| Bi | 铋 | La | 镧 | Sc | 钪 |
| Bk | 锫 | Li | 锂 | Se | 硒 |
| Br | 溴 | Lu | 镥 | Si | 硅 |
| C | 碳 | Lw | 铹 | Sm | 钐 |
| Ca | 钙 | Md | 钔 | Sn | 锡 |
| Cd | 镉 | Mg | 镁 | Sr | 锶 |
| Ce | 铈 | Mn | 锰 | Ta | 钽 |
| Cf | 锎 | Mo | 钼 | Tb | 铽 |
| Cl | 氯 | N | 氮 | Tc | 锝 |
| Cm | 锔 | Na | 钠 | Te | 碲 |
| Co | 钴 | Nb | 铌 | Th | 钍 |
| Cr | 铬 | Nd | 钕 | Ti | 钛 |
| Cs | 铯 | Ne | 氖 | Tl | 铊 |
| Cu | 铜 | Ni | 镍 | Tu | 铥 |
| Dy | 镝 | No | 锘 | U | 铀 |
| Er | 铒 | Np | 镎 | V | 钒 |
| Es | 锿 | O | 氧 | W | 钨 |
| F | 氟 | Os | 锇 | Xe | 氙 |
| Fe | 铁 | P | 磷 | Y | 钇 |
| Fm | 镄 | Pa | 镤 | Yb | 镱 |
| Fr | 钫 | Pb | 铅 | Zn | 锌 |
| Ga | 镓 | Pd | 钯 | Zr | 锆 |
| Gd | 钆 | Pm | 钷 | | |

## 硅酸盐

这是一类重要而常见的矿物，有 500 多种。由金属元素与单个或连结的 Si－O(硅－氧)四面体 $Si_4$. 化合而成。硅酸盐又分成六个结构类型。

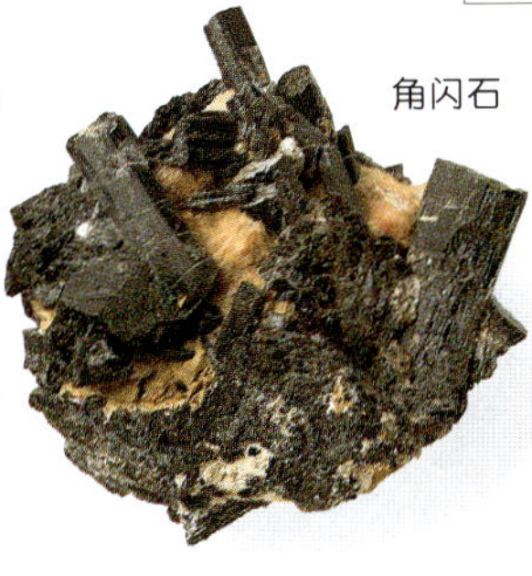

角闪石

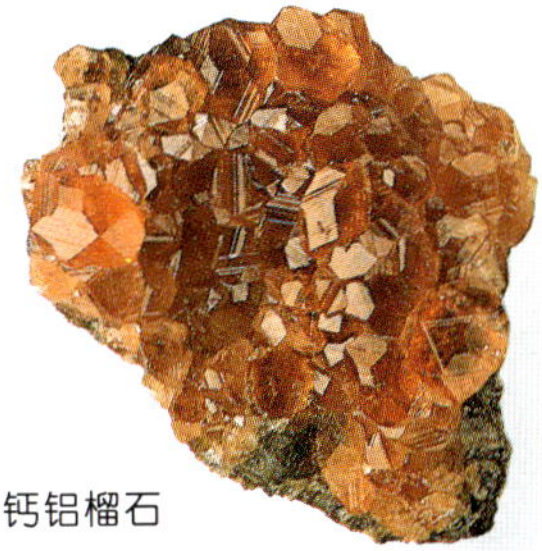

钙铝榴石

# 矿物的性质

矿物有许多可用以鉴定的特性。在测试一种矿物时，必须采取科学的方法，首先观察颜色(参见第26页)、光泽(参见第27页)、集合体形态(参见第23页)，然后测其硬度(参见第25页)、比重(参见第25页)和条痕(参见第26页)。有些矿物的断口和解理(参见第24页)很明显，有的须打碎矿物来观察。

## 晶系

根据矿物晶体的对称性，几何形状可分为六大晶系。每个晶系有多种不同的形态，不过，同一个晶系内的所有形态都与该晶系的对称性有关。研究矿物集合体，可得知矿物属于哪个晶系。标示在每种矿物侧旁的蓝色小图表示该矿物所属晶系。

透石膏

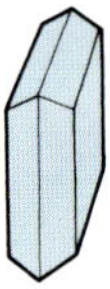

**单斜晶系**
*最常见的晶系之一，对称性低等轴晶系。*

黄铁矿

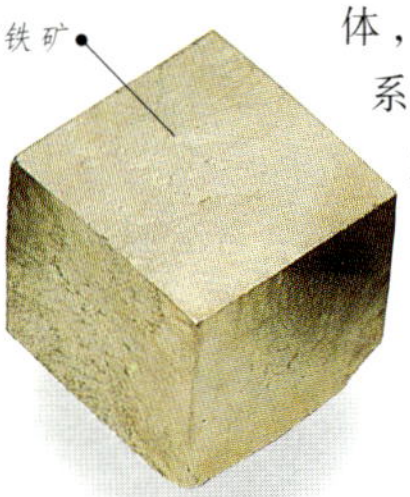

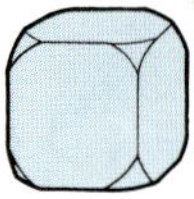

**等轴晶系**
*晶体主要呈立方体，不过也呈八面体和十二面体。*

重晶石

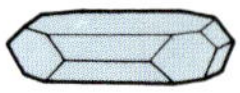

**斜方晶系**
*晶系的典型特征是晶体呈柱状和扁平板状。*

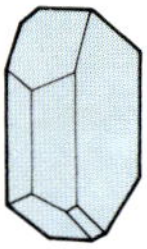

**三斜晶系**
*对称性最差的晶系。*

斧石

符山石

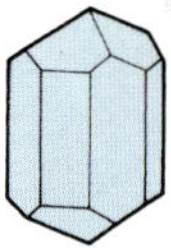

**正方晶系**
*晶体一般比等轴晶系的长。*

绿柱石

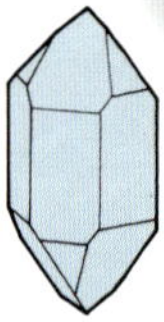

**六方晶系/三方晶系**
*本书将类似的这两个晶系归为一类，因二者有相似的对称性。*

## 集合体

集合体是晶体的外形特征，决定于其主要形态。下列为一些描述鉴定晶体集合体的术语。

**树枝状**

*状如树枝。*

**刃片状**

*看似刀刃。*

**柱状**

*呈相同断面。*

**针状**

*纤细针状块体。*

**柱状**

*柱状晶体集合。*

**块状**

*无定形。*

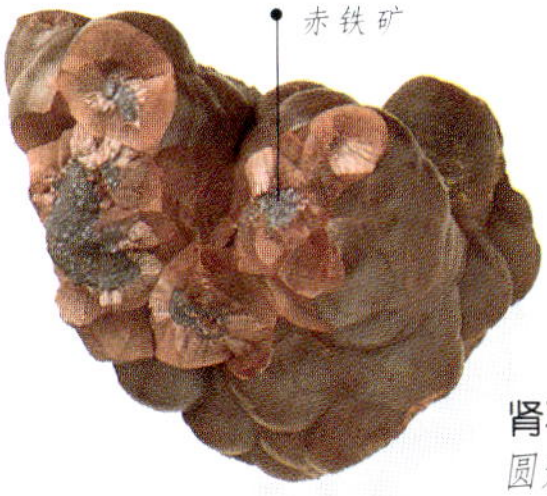


**肾状**

*圆形的肾状块体。*

## 双晶

同一种矿物的两个或多个晶体彼此有规律的连生在一起叫做双晶，接触双晶和穿插双晶两种，聚片双晶是两个以上的晶体彼此平行重复连生在一起的双晶。

**接触双晶**

*接触双晶的放射状块体。*

**穿插双晶**

*显示一个连生晶体的两部分。*

## 解理

解理是矿物沿一定的薄弱面裂开的方式，这些面一般处于原子层间或原子化学键力最弱的向。尽管解理面非常平整和均匀地反射光线，但不如晶面那样的光滑。本书将解理描述为完全、清楚、不清楚和无解理。

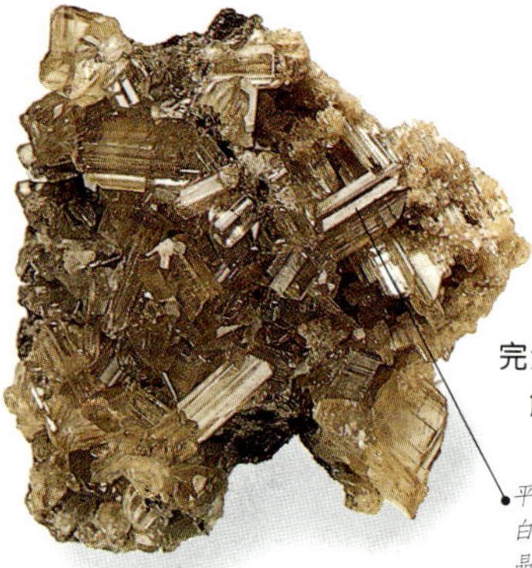


## 断口

用地质锤敲打矿物，它会断裂，并露出粗糙凹凸不平的表面，这就是断口（解理面一般很平整，用铁锤连续敲击产生完全相同的面）。大多数矿物能断裂或劈裂，不过有的只能断裂。本书使用的断口术语有：参差状、贝壳状、锯齿状和裂片状。

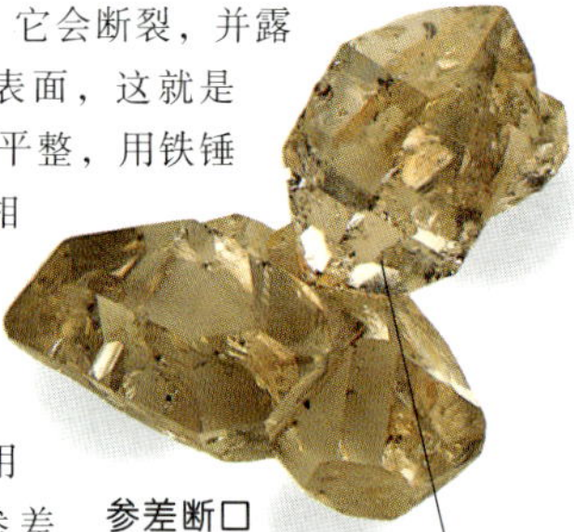

## 硬度

硬度测试可以有效地帮助我们鉴定矿物。硬度是指矿物抵抗外来刻划等的能力，莫斯(F.Mohs)发明了一套硬度标准，从硬度最小(1级)的滑石到硬度最大(10级)的金刚石。莫氏硬度计中等级高的矿物可以刻划等级低的矿物，如方解石能刻划石膏，但不能刻划萤石。矿物硬度也可以用日常用品来测定，如硬币能刻划硬度小于3.5的矿物。

手指甲：2.5

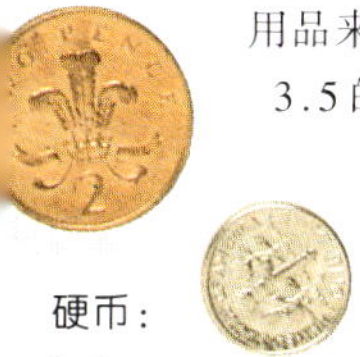

硬币：3.5

刀刃：5.5

玻璃：6

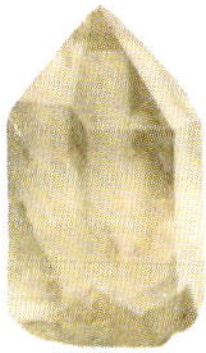

石英：7

## 莫氏硬度计

石 1　石膏 2　方解石 3　萤石 4　磷灰石 5　正长石 6　石英 7　黄玉 8　刚玉 9　金刚石 10

## 比重

矿物的比重是其重量与同体积的水重之比。比重可以用数字表示，如比重2.5表示该矿物比水重2.5倍。右图的石英标本比方铅矿大，但重量却较轻，因其比重小。

方铅矿比重：7.5

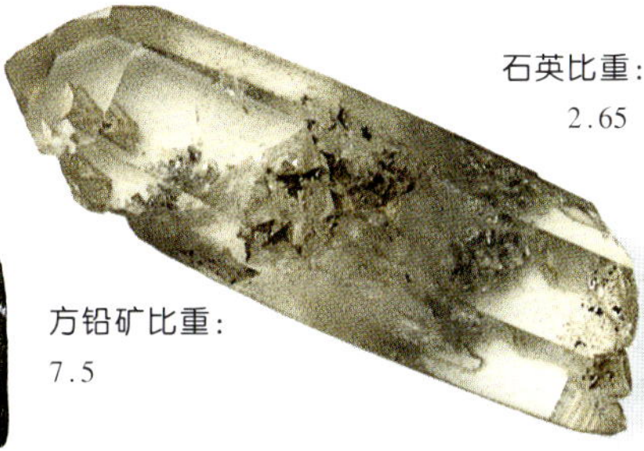

石英比重：2.65

## 颜色

矿物在自然光中呈现的颜色是一个显著而有用的鉴定特征。尽管颜色能帮助鉴定色彩鲜明的矿物，但是完全依靠这项特征也有不足，因为许多矿物，比如石英，会呈现多种颜色，况且不少矿物是白色或无色的图示的石英即呈现各种颜色。

玫瑰色

粉红色石英

乳石英

白色—灰白色

黄晶

黄色—黄棕色

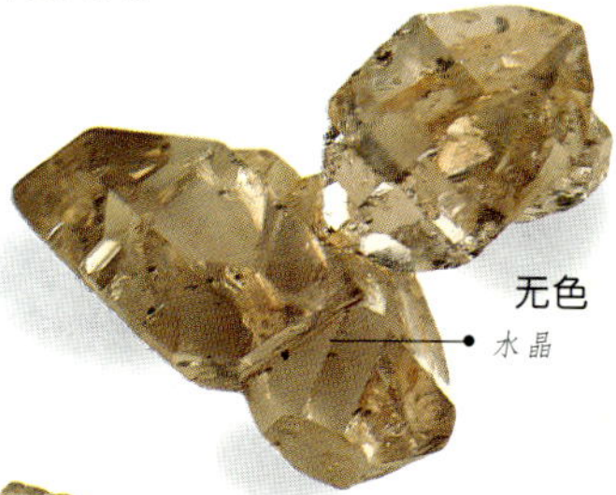

无色

水晶

烟晶

棕黑色

紫水晶

紫罗兰色

## 条痕

条痕是指矿物粉末的颜色。在白色无釉瓷板上刻划可以得到矿物的粉末颜色，即条痕。如果测试的是非常坚硬的矿物，则可以用地质锤敲碎一部分或用坚硬的表面与之摩擦。由于条痕色比矿物颜色稳定，所以是重要的鉴定特征。

铬铅矿

黄色

黄铜矿

黑色

雌黄

金黄色

辰砂

红色

赤铁矿

红棕色

辉钼矿

灰色

## 透明度

矿物能透过可见光的程度为矿物透明度，与矿物晶体结构原子的连接方式有关。矿物薄片(厚 0.03mm)能清晰透视其他物体的矿物为透明，能通过光线，但不能清晰透视其他物体者为半透明，光线完全不能通过者为不透明。

透明

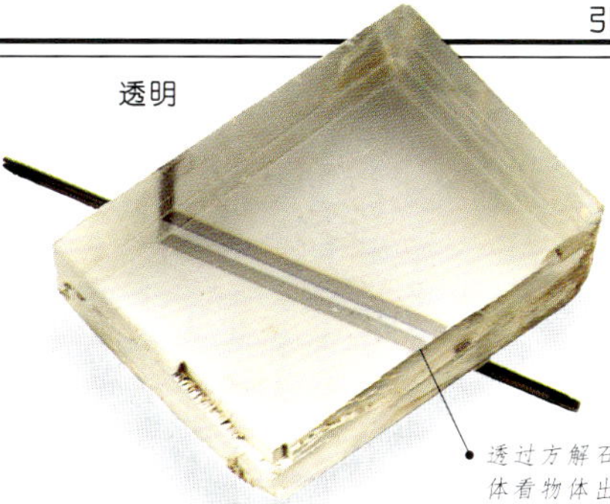

透过方解石菱面体看物体出现呈重影，因为光线折射两次

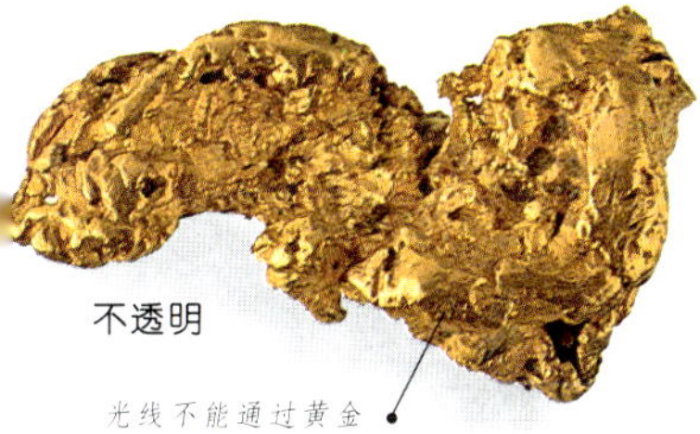

不透明

光线不能通过黄金

半透明

光线可以透过水蓝宝石

## 光泽

光泽是矿物表面对光的反射能力，决定于矿物的表面性质和反射率的大小。常用易于识别和感受的术语描述矿物光泽，有暗淡的、金属的、珍珠的、玻璃的、油脂的和丝绢的等等。

玻璃光泽

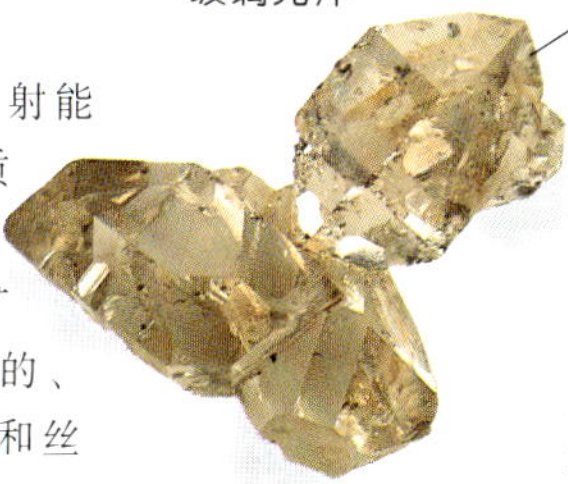

石英晶体的玻璃光泽

石盐表面的油脂光泽

油脂光泽

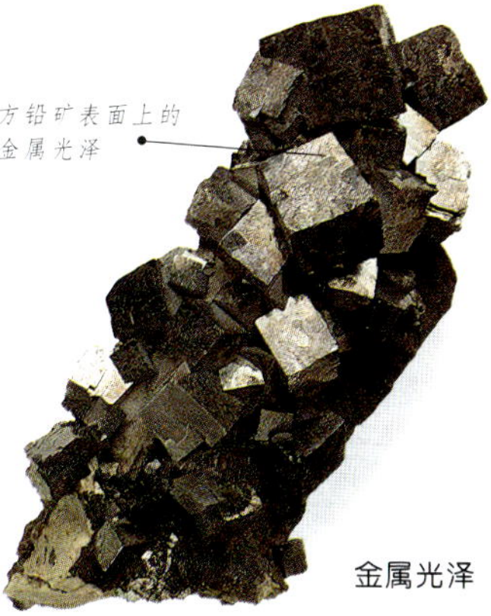

方铅矿表面上的金属光泽

金属光泽

丝绢光泽

“纤维石膏”表面的丝绢光泽

暗淡金属光泽

赤铁矿上的暗淡金属光泽

# 矿物的鉴定

为了帮助读者鉴定矿物，下列表格中将矿物按硬度大小排列，并附上其他一些明显、可靠的鉴定特征。

| 矿物 | 比重 | 解理 | 断口 |
|---|---|---|---|
| **硬度** < 2.5 | | | |
| 螺状硫银矿 | 很大 | 无 | 参差状 |
| 镍华 | 大 | 完全 | 参差状 |
| 水纤菱镁矿 | 中等 | 完全 | 参差状 |
| 绿铜锌矿 | 大 | 完全 | 参差状 |
| 钙铀云母 | 大 | 完全底面 | 参差状 |
| 铋华 | 很大 | 完全底面 | 参差状 |
| 辉铋矿 | 很大 | 完全 | 参差状 |
| 硼砂 | 很小 | 完全 | 贝壳状 |
| 水镁石 | 中等 | 完全 | 参差状 |
| 光卤石 | 很小 | 无 | 贝壳状 |
| 钒钾铀矿 | 大 | 完全底面 | 参差状 |
| 胆矾 | 中等 | 不完全 | 贝壳状 |
| 绿银矿 | 很大 | 无 | 参差至亚贝壳状 |
| 纤维蛇纹石 | 中等 | 无 | 参差状 |
| 辰砂 | 很大 | 完全柱面 | 贝壳至参差状 |
| 斜绿泥石 | 中等 | 完全 | 参差状 |
| 铜蓝 | 大 | 完全底面 | 参差状 |
| 冰晶石 | 中等 | 无 | 参差状 |
| 绒铜矿 | 中等 | 无 | 参差状 |
| 泻利盐 | 很小 | 完全 | 贝壳状 |
| 钴华 | 大 | 完全 | 参差状 |
| 方铅矿 | 很大 | 完全立方体 | 亚贝壳状 |
| 海绿石 | 中等 | 完全底面 | 参差状 |
| 石墨 | 中等 | 完全底面 | 参差状 |
| 石膏 | 中等 | 完全 | 多片状 |
| 石盐 | 中等 | 完全立方体 | 参差至亚贝壳状 |
| 水锌矿 | 大 | 完全 | 参差状 |
| 脆硫锑铅矿 | 很大 | 良好底面 | 参差至亚贝壳状 |
| 高岭石 | 中等 | 完全底面 | 参差状 |
| 青铅矿 | 中等 | 完全 | 贝壳状 |
| 辉钼矿 | 大 | 完全底面 | 参差状 |
| 白云母 | 中等 | 完全底面 | 参差状 |
| 钠硝石 | 中等 | 完全菱面体 | 贝壳状 |
| 雌黄 | 大 | 完全 | 参差状 |
| 金云母 | 中等 | 完全底面 | 参差状 |
| 淡红银矿 | 很大 | 清楚菱面体 | 贝壳至参差状 |
| 深红银矿 | 很大 | 清楚菱面体 | 贝壳至参差状 |
| 叶蜡石 | 中等 | 完全 | 参差状 |
| 雄黄 | 大 | 良好 | 贝壳状 |
| 海泡石 | 中等 | 未定 | 参差状 |
| 脆银矿 | 很大 | 不完全 | 参差至亚贝壳状 |
| 辉沸石锑矿 | 大 | 完全 | 参差至亚贝壳状 |
| 硫磺 | 中等 | 不完全底面 | 参差至贝壳状 |
| 针碲金银矿 | 很大 | 完全 | 参差状 |
| 钾盐 | 很小 | 完全立方体 | 参差状 |
| 滑石 | 中等 | 完全 | 参差状 |
| 铜铀云母 | 大 | 完全底面 | 参差状 |
| 钨华 | 很大 | 完全 | 参差状 |
| 钒钙铀矿 | 大 | 完全底面 | 参差状 |
| 硼钠钙石 | 很小 | 完全 | 参差状 |
| 蛭石 | 中等 | 完全 | 参差状 |
| 蓝铁矿 | 中等 | 完全 | 参差状 |
| 锰土 | 小 | 无 | 参差状 |
| **硬度** < 3.5 | | | |
| 水砷锌矿 | 大 | 良好 | 亚贝壳至参差状 |
| 硫酸铅矿 | 很大 | 良好底面 | 贝壳状 |
| 硬石膏 | 中等 | 完全 | 参差至多片状 |
| 叶状蛇纹石 | 中等 | 完全底面 | 贝壳至多片状 |
| 锑 | 很大 | 完全底面 | 参差状 |
| 星叶石 | 大 | 完全 | 参差状 |
| 氯铜矿 | 大 | 完全 | 贝壳状 |
| 重晶石 | 大 | 完全 | 参差状 |

| 矿物 | 比重 | 解理 | 断口 |
|---|---|---|---|
| 铝土矿 | 中等 | 无 | 参差状 |
| 黑云母 | 中/大 | 完全底面 | 参差状 |
| 方银铜氯铅矿 | 很大 | 完全 | 参差状 |
| 斑铜矿 | 很大 | 极不佳 | 参差至贝壳状 |
| 块硫锑铅矿 | 很大 | 良好 | 参差状 |
| 车轮矿 | 很大 | 不完全 | 亚贝壳至参差状 |
| 方解石 | 中等 | 完全 | 亚贝壳状 |
| 天青石 | 大 | 完全 | 参差状 |
| 白铅矿 | 很大 | 清楚柱面 | 贝壳状 |
| 辉铜矿 | 很大 | 不清楚 | 贝壳状 |
| 鲕状绿泥石 | 大 | 未定 | 参差状 |
| 光线矿 | 大 | 完全 | 参差状 |
| 叶绿矾 | 中等 | 完全 | 参差状 |
| 铜 | 很大 | 无 | 锯齿状 |
| 铬铅矿 | 很大 | 清楚柱面 | 贝壳至参差状 |
| 钒铅锌矿 | 很大 | 无 | 参差至贝壳状 |
| 硫砷铜矿 | 大 | 完全 | 参差状 |
| 三水铝石 | 中/大 | 完全 | 参差状 |
| 钙芒硝 | 中等 | 完全 | 贝壳状 |
| 金 | 很大 | 无 | 锯齿状 |
| 硫镉矿 | 大 | 清楚 | 贝壳状 |
| 黄钾铁矾 | 中/大 | 清楚 | 参差状 |
| 硫碳酸铅矿 | 很大 | 完全底面 | 贝壳状 |
| 锂云母 | 中/大 | 完全底面 | 参差状 |
| 针镍矿 | 很大 | 完全菱面体 | 参差状 |
| 橄榄铜矿 | 大 | 不清楚 | 参差至贝壳状 |
| 硫锑铜银矿 | 很大 | 不完全底面 | 参差状 |
| 杂卤石 | 中等 | 完全 | 参差状 |
| 银 | 很大 | 无 | 锯齿状 |
| 菱锶矿 | 大 | 完全柱面 | 参差状 |
| 无水芒硝 | 中等 | 完全 | 参差状 |
| 天然碱 | 中等 | 完全 | 参差状 |
| 钒铅矿 | 很大 | 无 | 贝壳至参差状 |
| 钡钒铜矿 | 大 | 完全底面 | 参差状 |
| 毒重石 | 大 | 清楚 | 参差状 |
| 钼铅矿 | 很大 | 清楚锥形 | 亚贝壳状 |
| **硬度** < 5.5 | | | |
| 明矾石 | 中等 | 清楚底面 | 贝壳状 |
| 方沸石 | 中等 | 极不佳 | 亚贝壳状 |
| 铁白云石 | 中等 | 完全菱面体 | 亚贝壳状 |
| 磷灰石 | 大 | 不佳 | 贝壳至参差状 |
| 鱼眼石 | 中等 | 完全 | 参差状 |
| 文石 | 中等 | 清楚轴面 | 亚贝壳状 |
| 蓝铜矿 | 大 | 完全 | 贝壳状 |
| 乳砷铅铜矿 | 很大 | 无 | 参差状 |
| 水胆矾 | 大 | 完全 | 贝壳至参差状 |
| 菱沸石 | 中等 | 不清楚 | 参差状 |
| 黄铜矿 | 大 | 不佳 | 参差至贝壳状 |
| 铬铁矿 | 大 | 无 | 参差状 |
| 辉砷钴矿 | 很大 | 完全 | 参差状 |
| 硬硼钙石 | 中等 | 完全 | 参差至贝壳状 |
| 硅孔雀石 | 中/大 | 无 | 参差至贝壳状 |
| 赤铜矿 | 很大 | 不佳八面体 | 贝壳至参差状 |
| 硅硼钙石 | 中等 | 无 | 参差至贝壳状 |
| 透视石 | 大 | 完全 | 参差至贝壳状 |
| 白云石 | 中等 | 完全菱面体 | 亚贝壳状 |
| 异性石 | 中等 | 不清楚 | 参差状 |
| 萤石 | 大 | 完全八面体 | 贝壳状 |
| 钴硫砷铁矿 | 很大 | 完全 | 参差状 |
| 针铁矿 | 大 | 完全 | 参差状 |
| 白钙沸石 | 中等 | 完全 | 参差状 |
| 交沸石 | 中等 | 清楚 | 参差至亚贝壳状 |
| 方硫锰矿 | 大 | 完全 | 亚贝壳至参差状 |

| 矿物 | 比重 | 解理 | 断口 |
|---|---|---|---|
| 黑锰矿 | 大 | 良好 | 参差状 |
| 异极矿 | 大 | 完全 | 参差至贝壳状 |
| 磷铍钙石 | 中/大 | 不佳 | 亚贝壳状 |
| 片沸石 | 中等 | 完全 | 参差状 |
| 蓝晶石 | 大/很大 | 完全 | 参差状 |
| 浊沸石 | 中等 | 完全 | 参差状 |
| 天蓝石 | 中等 | 不完全 | 参差状 |
| 纤铁矿 | 大 | 完全 | 参差状 |
| 褐铁矿 | 大 | 无 | 参差状 |
| 菱镁矿 | 大 | 完全菱面体 | 贝壳至参差状 |
| 孔雀石 | 大 | 完全 | 亚贝壳至参差状 |
| 水锰矿 | 大 | 完全 | 参差状 |
| 中沸石 | 中等 | 完全 | 参差状 |
| 砷铅矿 | 很大 | 无 | 亚贝壳至参差状 |
| 独居石 | 大/很大 | 清楚 | 贝壳至参差状 |
| 钠沸石 | 中等 | 完全 | 参差状 |
| 砷镍矿 | 很大 | 无 | 参差状 |
| 黝方石 | 中等 | 不清楚 | 参差至贝壳状 |
| 针钠钙石 | 中等 | 完全 | 参差状 |
| 镍黄铁矿 | 大 | 无 | 贝壳状 |
| 钙钛矿 | 大 | 不完全 | 亚贝壳至参差状 |
| 钙十字沸石石 | 中等 | 清楚 | 参差状 |
| 烧绿石 | 大 | 清楚 | 亚贝壳至参差状 |
| 磷氯铅矿 | 很大 | 极不佳柱面 | 参差至亚贝壳状 |
| 磁黄铁矿 | 大 | 无 | 亚贝壳状参差状 |
| 菱锰矿 | 大 | 完全菱面体 | 参差状 |
| 钠闪石 | 大 | 完全 | 参差状 |
| 白钨矿 | 很大 | 清楚 | 亚贝壳至参差状 |
| 钙沸石 | 中等 | 完全 | 参差状 |
| 臭葱石 | 大 | 不完全 | 亚贝壳状 |
| 菱铁矿 | 大 | 完全菱面体 | 参差状 |
| 菱锌矿 | 大 | 完全菱面体 | 亚贝壳至参差状 |
| 闪锌矿 | 大 | 完全 | 贝壳状 |
| 榍石 | 大 | 清楚 | 贝壳状 |
| 辉沸石 | 中等 | 完全 | 参差状 |
| 砷黝铜矿 | 大 | 无 | 参差至亚贝壳状 |
| 黝铜矿 | 大/很大 | 无 | 参差至亚贝壳状 |
| 杆沸石 | 中等 | 完全 | 参差至亚贝壳状 |
| 银星石 | 中等 | 完全 | 亚贝壳至参差状 |
| 硅锌矿 | 大 | 底面 | 参差状 |
| 黑钨矿 | 很大 | 完全 | 参差状 |
| 硅灰石 | 中/大 | 完全 | 多片状 |
| 磷钇矿 | 大/很大 | 完全柱面 | 参差状 |
| 红锌矿 | 很大 | 完全 | 贝壳状 |
| **硬度＜6** | | | |
| 阳起石 | 大 | 良好 | 参差至亚贝壳状 |
| 霓石 | 大 | 良好 | 参差状 |
| 镁黄长石 | 中等 | 清楚 | 参差至贝壳状 |
| 锂磷铝石 | 大 | 完全 | 参差状 |
| 锐钛矿 | 大 | 完全底面 | 亚贝壳状 |
| 直闪石 | 中/大 | 完全 | 参差状 |
| 钠铁闪石 | 大 | 完全 | 参差状 |
| 毒砂 | 很大 | 不清楚 | 参差状 |
| 辉石 | 大 | 良好 | 参差至贝壳状 |
| 板钛矿 | 大 | 不佳 | 亚贝壳至参差状 |
| 钙霞石 | 中等 | 完全 | 参差状 |
| 复砷镍矿 | 很大 | 清楚 | 参差状 |
| 顽火石 | 大 | 良好 | 参差状 |
| 钙铝黄长石 | 大 | 清楚 | 参差至贝壳状 |
| 蓝闪石 | 大 | 完全 | 参差至贝壳状 |
| 铁闪石 | 大 | 良好 | 参差状 |
| 蓝方石 | 中等 | 不清楚 | 参差至贝壳状 |
| 钙铁辉石 | 大 | 良好 | 参差至贝壳状 |
| 赤铁矿 | 很大 | 无 | 参差至亚贝壳状 |
| 角闪石 | 大 | 完全 | 参差状 |
| 硅镁石 | 大 | 不佳 | 参差状 |
| 紫苏辉石 | 大 | 良好 | 参差状 |
| 钛铁矿 | 大 | 无 | 贝壳至参差状 |
| 黑柱石 | 大 | 清楚 | 参差状 |
| 天蓝石 | 大 | 不清楚柱面 | 参差至多片状 |
| 白榴石 | 中等 | 极不佳 | 贝壳状 |
| 整柱石 | 中等 | 无 | 贝壳至参差状 |

| 矿物 | 比重 | 解理 | 断口 |
|---|---|---|---|
| 霞石 | 中等 | 不清楚 | 贝壳状 |
| 柱星叶石 | 大 | 完全 | 贝壳状 |
| 碱锰闪石 | 中/大 | 完全 | 参差状 |
| 杂硬锰矿 | 很大 | 未定 | 参差状 |
| 铌钇矿 | 很大 | 不清楚 | 贝壳状 |
| 方柱石 | 中等 | 清楚 | 参差至贝壳状 |
| 方钴矿 | 很大 | 清楚 | 参差状 |
| 砷钴矿 | 很大 | 清楚 | 参差状 |
| 方钠石 | 中等 | 不佳 | 参差至贝壳状 |
| 透闪石 | 中/大 | 良好 | 参差至亚贝壳状 |
| 绿松石 | 中等 | 良好 | 贝壳状 |
| **硬度＜7** | | | |
| 钠长石 | 中等 | 清楚 | 参差状 |
| 中长石 | 中等 | 完全 | 参差至贝壳状 |
| 钙长石 | 中等 | 完全 | 贝壳至参差状 |
| 歪长石 | 中等 | 完全 | 参差状 |
| 斧石 | 大 | 良好 | 参差至贝壳状 |
| 培斜倍长石 | 中等 | 完全 | 参差至贝壳状 |
| 锡石 | 很大 | 不佳 | 亚贝壳至参差状 |
| 硬绿泥石 | 大 | 完全 | 参差状 |
| 粒硅镁石 | 大 | 不佳 | 参差状 |
| 斜黝帘石 | 大 | 完全 | 参差状 |
| 铌铁矿 | 很大 | 清楚 | 亚贝壳至参差状 |
| 硬水铝石 | 大 | 完全 | 贝壳状 |
| 透辉石 | 大 | 良好 | 参差状 |
| 绿帘石 | 大 | 完全 | 参差状 |
| 锌铁尖晶石 | 很大 | 无 | 参差至亚贝壳状 |
| 硅铍钇矿 | 大 | 无 | 贝壳状 |
| 硬玉 | 大 | 良好 | 多片状 |
| 拉长石 | 中等 | 完全 | 参差至贝壳状 |
| 磁铁矿 | 很大 | 无 | 亚贝壳至参差状 |
| 白铁矿 | 大 | 清楚 | 参差状 |
| 微斜长石 | 中等 | 完全 | 参差状 |
| 钙钠奥长石 | 中等 | 完全 | 参差至贝壳状 |
| 蛋白石 | 中等 | 无 | 贝壳状 |
| 正长石 | 中等 | 完全 | 参差状至贝壳状 |
| 透锂长石 | 中等 | 完全 | 亚贝壳状 |
| 葡萄石 | 中等 | 清楚 | 参差状 |
| 黄铁矿 | 大 | 不清楚 | 贝壳至参差状 |
| 软锰矿 | 很大 | 完全 | 参差状 |
| 石英 | 中等 | 无 | 贝壳至参差状 |
| 蔷薇辉石 | 大 | 完全 | 贝壳至参差状 |
| 金红石 | 大 | 清楚 | 贝壳至参差状 |
| 透长石 | 清楚 | 完全 | 贝壳至参差状 |
| 黄锑矿 | 大/很大 | 未定 | 参差状 |
| 电气石 | 大 | 极不清楚 | 参差至贝壳状 |
| 符山石 | 大 | 不清楚 | 参差至贝壳状 |
| 黝帘石 | 大 | 完全 | 参差至贝壳状 |
| **硬度＞7** | | | |
| 红柱石 | 大 | 清楚柱面 | 参差至亚贝壳状 |
| 绿柱石 | 中等 | 不清楚 | 参差至贝壳状 |
| 玉髓 | 中等 | 无 | 贝壳状 |
| 金绿宝石 | 大 | 不清楚柱面 | 贝壳至参差状 |
| 堇青石 | 中等 | 清楚 | 贝壳状 |
| 刚玉 | 大 | 无 | 贝壳至参差状 |
| 金刚石 | 大 | 完全八面体 | 贝壳状 |
| 蓝线石 | 大 | 良好 | 参差状 |
| 蓝柱石 | 大 | 完全 | 贝壳状 |
| 石榴石 | 大 | 无 | 参差至贝壳状 |
| 橄榄石 | 大 | 不完全 | 贝壳状 |
| 硅铍石 | 中等 | 中等 | 贝壳状 |
| 红宝石 | 大 | 无 | 贝壳至参差状 |
| 夕线石 | 大 | 完全 | 参差状 |
| 尖晶石 | 大 | 无 | 贝壳至参差状 |
| 锂辉石 | 大 | 完全 | 参差状 |
| 十字石 | 大 | 清楚 | 参差至亚贝壳状 |
| 黄玉 | 大 | 完全 | 亚贝壳至参差状 |
| 锆石 | 大 | 不完全 | 参差至贝壳状 |

# 岩石的形成

岩石的形成循环往复。地壳深部的液态岩浆缓慢上升接近地表，形成巨大深成岩体(1)，较小的侵入岩，如岩脉(2)，熔岩流和火山。岩浆在冷凝过程中形成岩浆岩，如花岗岩。地球的运动使岩石上升到地表，受到风化、侵蚀而暴露，在冰川、流水和风

**岩石循环**

*下图所示的成岩循环一般要经历几百万年。*

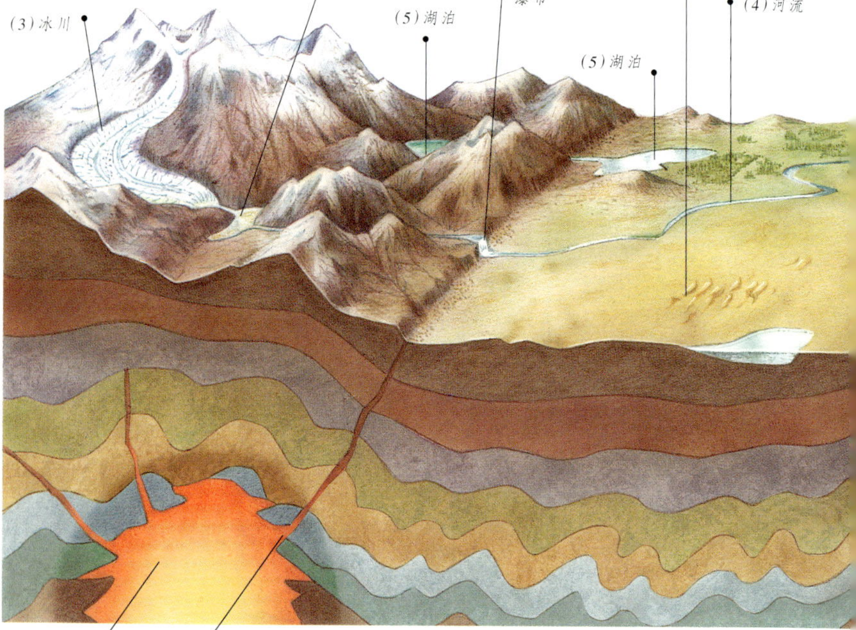

花岗岩

**岩浆作用**

*液态岩浆侵入岩层，在冷凝过程中形成花岗岩岩脉(左图)。*

片岩

**变质作用**

*造山运动中，温度和压力把沉积岩和岩浆岩变成变质岩。*

的风化侵蚀作用下，岩石破碎成颗粒，被冰川(3)、河流(4)和风搬运，逐渐在湖泊(5)、三角洲(6)和沙漠(7)沉积下来，形成沉积层，或在海洋形成沉积岩，如粘土岩和页岩(8)。大多数沉积物都堆积在大陆架(9)上，有些则被高密度水流通过海底峡谷(10)搬运沉积到更深的洋底。大规模的造山运动中，在高温高压作用下，沉积岩和岩浆岩变成变质岩，如片岩和片麻岩。温度和压力进一步升高，则岩石重新熔化，遂完成造岩的一个循环。

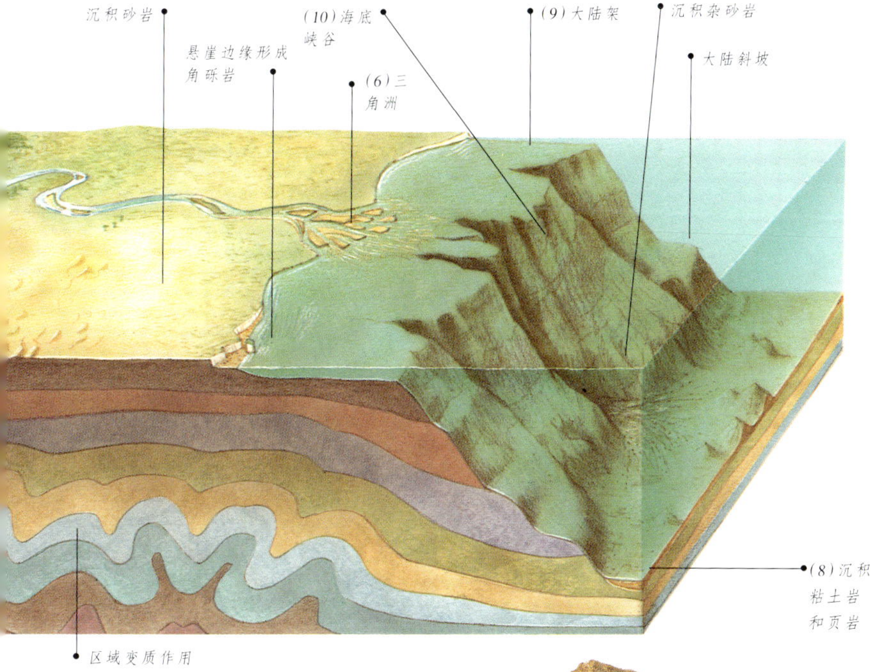

**沉积作用**

*砂岩主要由石英颗粒组成，石英从先成岩风化剥落下来，搬运到海洋或河流经沉积和压实形成砂岩。砂岩可能形成如左图所示海岸峭壁上的褶皱。*

# 岩浆岩的性质

岩浆岩是由液态岩浆或熔岩结晶而成。岩浆的原始成分、侵入地壳的方式及冷却速度，都会影响其组成成分和性质，如颗粒大小、晶体形状、矿物成分和整体颜色。

粗粒辉长岩是一种深成岩浆岩，其晶体颇大

## 成因

成因意指岩石属于侵入岩（岩浆于地下结晶）还是喷出岩（熔岩在地表结晶）。

**侵入基性岩脉**

*侵入到页岩中的岩浆岩粗粒玄武岩脉。*

辉石，一种铁镁矿物

## 产状

指熔岩冷却凝固形成的形态，如深成岩为大而埋深的侵入岩，可以长宽达数公里，岩脉为狭长、不规则的板状岩体，岩床则为整合的席状。

## 矿物成分

岩石是矿物的集合体，长石（右图）、云母、石英和铁镁矿物（上图）都是岩浆岩组成部分，矿物成分决定岩石的化学性质。

拉长石，长石的一种

## 颗粒大小

显示岩石属于深成岩(颗粒粗大)还是喷出岩(颗粒细小)。像辉长岩之类的粗粒岩浆岩具有直径超过5毫米的晶体，中粒的如粗粒玄武岩的晶体大小在0.5~5毫米之间，细粒的岩石，如玄武岩，其晶体直径小于0.5毫米。

1

2

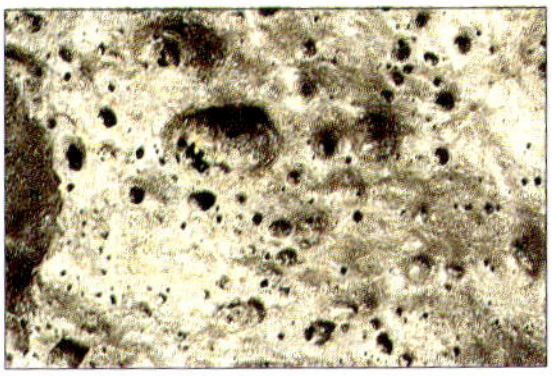
3

**观察颗粒**

*用肉眼就可以看出辉长岩(1)的单个颗粒，而要观察粗粒玄武岩(2)的单个颗粒须用便携式放大镜，细粒的玄武岩(3)的颗粒显微镜下才能辨认。*

## 晶体形状

缓慢的冷凝能使矿物晶体充分发育形成完好的自形晶，迅速的冷却则形成不佳的劣形晶。

## 结构

指颗粒或晶体的排列方式以及颗粒的大小相对。

**自形晶**

*左图是高倍放大的粗粒玄武岩切片，有完好的晶体。*

## 颜色

一般说来，颜色是化学性质的精确指标，反映出某种矿物的含量。酸性岩呈浅色，含65%以上的硅酸盐。基性岩呈深色，硅酸盐含量较低，且深色密度大的铁镁矿物，如普通辉石，占很大比例。

**浅色**

*流纹岩，属于酸性岩，含超过65%的硅酸盐和超过10%的石英。*

**颜色中等**

*安山岩，属于中性岩，含55~65%的硅酸盐。*

## 化学成分

根据化学成分，岩浆岩可分成以下大类：酸性岩，含65%以上的硅酸盐(包括10%以上的石英)；中性岩，硅酸盐含量为55~65%；基性岩，硅酸盐含量为45~55%(含10%以下的石英)；超基性岩，硅酸盐含量小于45%。

**深色**

*玄武岩，属于基性岩，含45~55%的硅酸盐。*

# 变质作用的类型

变质岩是岩浆岩、沉积岩及早已生成的变质岩的构造和成分产生相当大的变化形成的。先成岩在温度和压力的作用下(在造山带附近作用最强)形成变质岩。

## 区域变质作用

造山带的岩石因温度和压力作用而改变，形成区域变质岩，变质作用范围可达几千平方公里。下面依次说明岩石的性质怎样随着温度的升高、压力的增大而改变。

**变质岩地貌**
*片麻岩是强烈区域变质作用的产物，形成崎岖不平的地貌。*

页岩

**1. 无压力**
*含化石页岩是一种细粒的沉积岩，富含粘土矿物和石英，含腕足动物壳化石，未变质。*

板岩

**2. 低压**
*当含化石的页岩受到低压力作用时，化石扭曲或损坏，形成板岩。*

片岩

**3. 中压**
*板岩和其他许多岩石受到中温增压作用时，形成中粒片岩。*

片麻岩

**4. 高压**
*片麻岩这种粗粒的岩石形成于高压、高温热液活动强烈的地质环境，这种条件下，任何岩石都会发生变化。*

## 接触变质作用

变质带、岩浆侵入体周围或熔岩流附近的岩石会在温度的直接作用下变质，形成接触变质岩。温度可以使原岩中的矿物改变，引起重结晶，且使所含化石之类的特征消失。变质带的范围与岩浆或熔岩的温度及侵入体的大小有关。

岩浆的侵入

*在悬崖的底部可见深色的粗粒玄武岩侵入黑色页岩热流作用变质成较轻的角页岩。*

砂岩

*颗粒松散地胶结在一起*

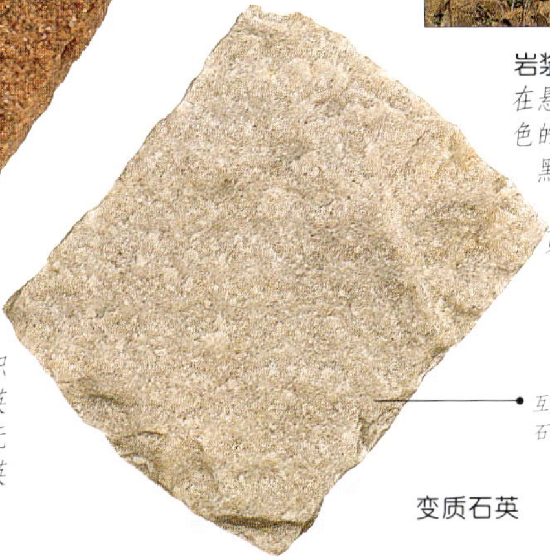

变质石英

*互相连结的石英晶体*

热接触变质

*上图的砂岩(一种多孔的沉积岩)受热变质后，变成变质石英岩(右图)，这是一种结晶、无孔的岩石，由相互连结的石英晶体镶嵌而成。*

## 动力变质作用

地壳内，尤其沿断层线，发生大规模运动时，出现动力变质作用。大块岩石被挤压在其他岩石之上，在它们相互接触的地方岩石被挤压研磨粉碎，形成糜棱岩。

岩石块体的运动

*上达悬崖中部的低角逆断层。*

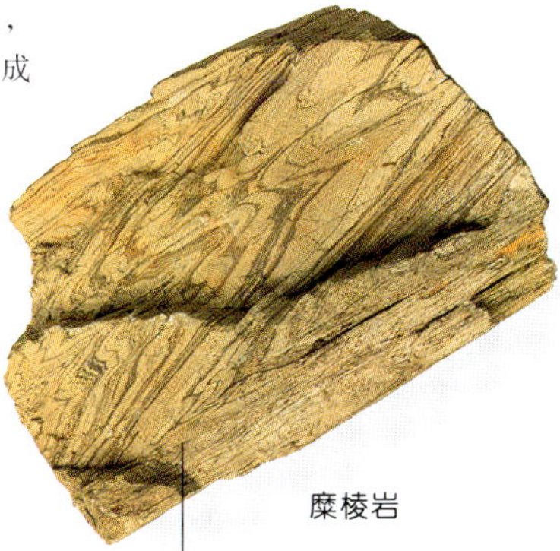

糜棱岩

*由于逆冲运动的力量，岩石受到极大的挤压和扭曲*

# 变质岩的性质

变质岩有一些特定的典型特征：组成的矿物常呈晶体出现，晶体的排列方向决定于温度、压力的共同作用，还是仅只温度的作用。晶体颗粒的大小反映它们所受温度和压力的程度，因此，仔细察看变质岩中的晶体有助于鉴定和确定其成因。

*片状片麻岩的深色黑云母带条*

片状

## 构造

矿物在岩石中排列和分布的特点。接触变质岩有着晶质构造，矿物通常不定向排列，不过，区域变质岩则呈片理构造，压力使某些矿物排成直线。

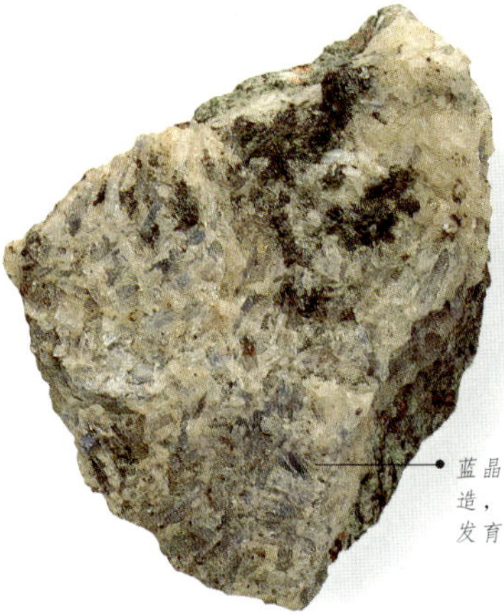

*蓝晶片岩有片理构造，但不如片麻岩发育*

结晶状

*在蓝色大理岩中，可见呈块状的不定向排列并融合一起的晶体*

## 颗粒大小

从颗粒的大小可以得知岩石所处的温度和压力条件。一般压力越大、温度越高，形成的矿物颗粒就越大，因此，低压下形成的板岩呈细粒，中压中温下形成的片岩呈中粒，高温高压下形成的片麻岩呈粗粒。

粗粒

片麻岩

片岩

中粒

黑板岩

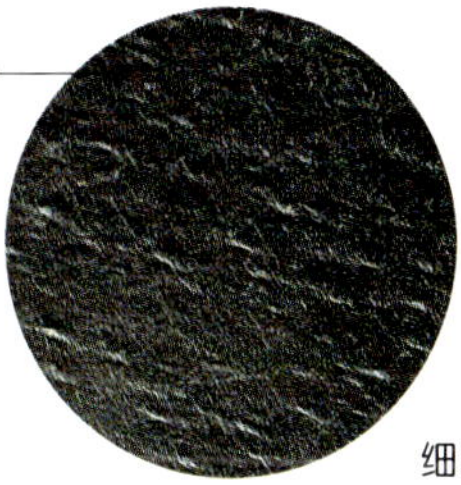

细粒

## 压力和温度

中、高级变质作用最低需要 250 ℃的温度(某些变质岩的生成温度可能低得多)，最高为 800 ℃，高于这个温度，岩石即熔化成岩浆或熔岩。压力从 2 000千巴至10 000千巴。

石英

云母

**片麻岩**

*显微镜显示的片麻岩中的石英和云母(左图)*

## 矿物含量

变质岩的特有矿物对鉴定很有帮助。石榴子石和蓝晶石存在于片岩和片麻岩，黄铁矿晶体常嵌生于板岩的劈理面，水镁石出现于大理岩。

**乳石英**

*见于变质石英和片麻岩*

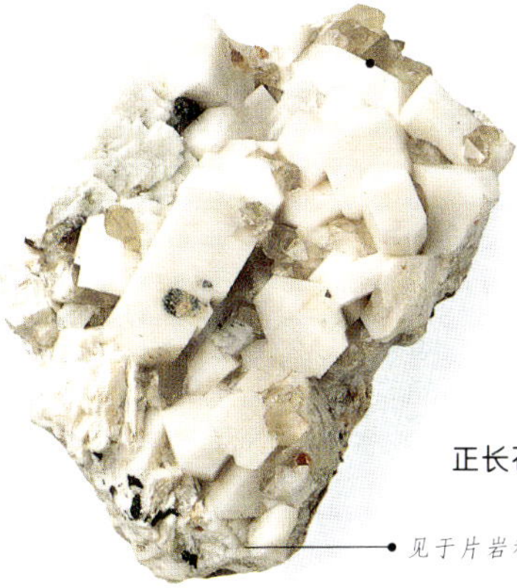

**正长石**

*见于片岩和片麻岩*

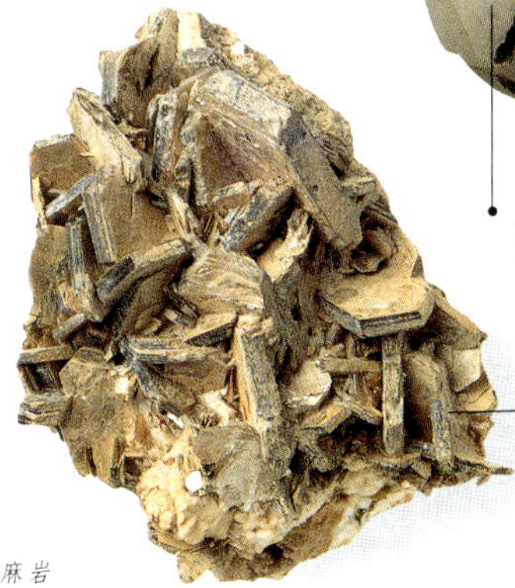

**白云母**

*见于片岩和片麻岩*

# 沉积岩的性质

由于沉积岩以层状产出，所以在野外很容易与岩浆岩与变质岩区别。通常沉积岩可以顺层剥离，另一重要特征是沉积岩一般含有生物化石，而岩浆岩从不含化石，变质岩中也很罕见。组成沉积岩的颗粒来源决定其形态，是鉴定的依据。

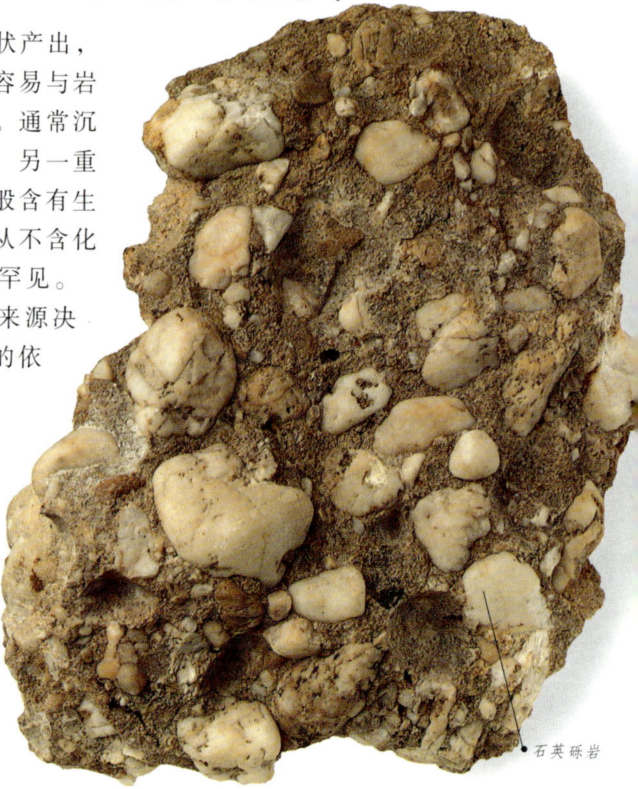


## 成因

沉积岩形成于地表或接近地表。岩石颗粒经过风、流水、冰川的搬运，然后沉积于陆地、河湖以及海洋环境如海滩、三角洲、海底等。

**沉积层**

*沙滩上的卵石和砂粒最终可能形成沉积岩。*

## 化石内容

化石主要产于沉积岩，它们是保存在沉积岩中的动植物遗体。岩石中所含化石指示岩石的形成环境，如海生生物化石说明岩石是在海洋环境下形成的。石灰岩是富含化石的沉积岩。

## 颗粒大小

尽管沉积岩颗粒的分类很复杂，但粗粒、中粒和细粒等术语仍经常使用。颗粒的大小从巨砾到粘土的微粒，组成粗粒岩石的碎屑肉眼可见，如砾岩、角砾岩和砂岩，中粒岩的颗粒用便携式放大镜可辨，如砂岩，细粒岩石包括页岩、粘土岩和泥岩。

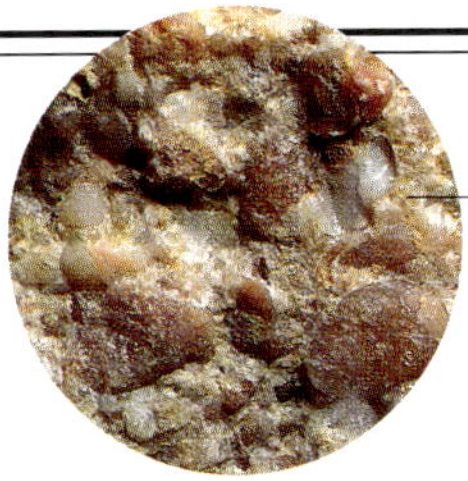

**放大的颗粒**

*高倍放大的岩石标本可见沉积物颗粒的形状，从圆形(左上图)到棱角状(右上图)不等。*

## 颗粒形状

沉积岩的颗粒形状决定于搬运方式。风蚀作用会形成圆形沙粒，带棱角的砾石，流水作用形成带棱角的砂粒状颗粒，而砾石成光滑的圆形卵石。

## 分类

分类表明岩石颗粒的来源，碎屑岩含有先成岩的颗粒，生物岩由壳或其他化石碎屑组成，化学岩是化学沉积的产物。

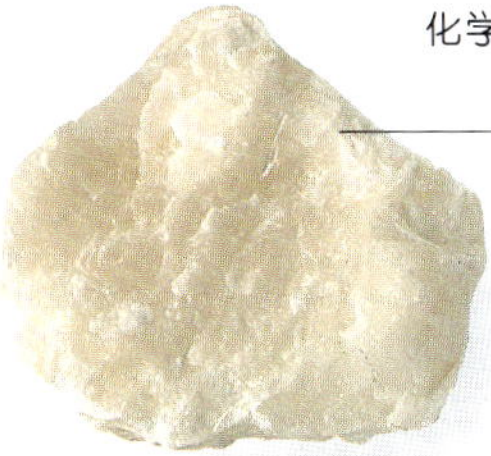

# 岩石鉴定检索

这个检索是为了帮助鉴定岩石标本而设计的。第一步，判断岩石是岩浆岩、变质岩还是沉积岩；第二步，确定颗粒的大小，按照检索，就能找到正确的分类位置，符号眼睛代表粗粒，放大镜代表中粒，显微镜代表细粒；第三步，必须考虑岩石的其他特征(颜色、构造、矿物组合)，以引导你参看本书有关岩石的条目。

## 第一步

### 岩浆岩?

岩浆岩呈晶质结构，是由矿物晶体互相连结聚集而成。岩石里的晶体或无规律聚集，或是显示出某种方向性。岩浆岩没有沉积岩的层理构造，也没有变质岩的片理构造。有些熔岩充满气孔。不含化石。

### 变质岩?

变质岩分为两大类，区域变质岩有独特的片理构造，常呈波浪状，不像沉积岩层理面那样平坦，接触变质岩晶体呈较不规则排列。

### 沉积岩?

沉积岩有明显的层理，颗粒连结松散，用手指可蹭下颗粒。石英是许多沉积岩的主要成分，方解石是石灰岩的重要组分，沉积岩含化石，依此可与岩浆岩和变质岩区别。

## 第二步

确定岩石成因类别之后，下一步就根据颗粒的大小进行划分。这里指的是组成岩石的颗粒的大小，而不是嵌生于其中的个别晶体的大小。

肉眼可见　需用放大镜　需用显微镜

### 岩浆岩

粗粒

中粒

细粒

### 变质岩

粗粒

中粒

细粒

### 沉积岩

粗粒

中粒

细粒

## 第三步

通过上两步你已确定手持标本属于岩浆岩、沉积岩还是变质岩，并已确定其颗粒的大小，如果是岩浆岩，那么下一步就是观察颜色，酸性岩富含密度小的淡色硅酸盐，颜色很浅，基性岩和超基性岩富含密度大的铁镁矿物，颜色深，中性岩恰如其

### 岩浆岩　粗粒

**浅色**
粉红色花岗岩 180，白色花岗岩 180，斑状花岗岩 181，文像花岗岩 181，石英二长岩 182，伟晶岩 185，白花岗闪长岩 187，正长岩 188，斜长岩 191

**中色**
角闪花岗岩 181，花岗闪长岩 187，闪长岩 187，正长岩 188，霞石正长岩 188，集块岩 204

**深色**
辉长岩 189，歪碱正长岩 189，橄榄辉长岩 190，角闪辉长岩 191，蛇纹岩 194，辉岩 194，角砾云橄岩 195，橄榄岩 195

### 中粒

### 变质岩　粗粒

**有片理**
片麻岩 213，褶皱片麻岩 213，眼状片麻岩 214，粒状片麻岩 214，混合岩 214，闪岩 215，榴辉岩 215

**无片理**
粒变岩 215，大理岩 216～217，夕卡岩 220

### 中粒

名，其矿物含量处于前两类之间，因此，颜色深浅也居中。如果是变质岩，那么应观察片理（某些矿物的定向排列）和无片理（结晶，无明显的构造），确定手持标本的所属，然后按表中提供的岩石名称和页码参阅，以获取进一步的鉴定资料。

| | 细粒 | |
| --- | --- | --- |
| **浅色**<br>微花岗岩 183，石英斑岩 184，文像斑岩 186，淡辉长岩 190 |  | **浅色**<br>流纹岩 196，熔结凝灰岩 206，火山弹 206 |
| **中色**<br>煌斑石 199，斜方斑岩 201 |  | **中色**<br>英安岩 197，煌斑岩 199，安山岩 199，粗面岩 201，浮石 205，凝灰岩 205，熔结凝灰岩 206 |
| **深色**<br>粗玄岩 192，苏长岩 192，橄长岩 193 |  | **深色**<br>捕获石 184，纯橄榄岩 193，黑曜岩 197，松脂岩 198，玄武岩 202，细碧岩 203，凝灰岩 204，火山弹 206，绳状熔岩 207 |

| | 细粒 | |
| --- | --- | --- |
| **有片理**<br>千枚岩 210，褶皱片岩 211，石榴石片岩 210，白云母片岩 211，黑云片岩 212，蓝晶片岩 212 |  | **有片理**<br>绿板岩 208，黑板岩 208，含黄铁矿板岩 209，含扭曲化石板岩 209，千枚岩 210 |
| **无片理**<br>大理岩 216～217，角页岩 218～219，空晶石角页岩 219，斑点板岩 219，变石英岩 220，夕卡岩 220 |  | **无片理**<br>大理岩 216～217，斑点板岩 219，夕卡岩 220，长英角岩 221，糜棱岩 221 |

## 第四步

对沉积岩，首先观察它的矿物成分，是由岩屑，即岩石碎屑组成的呢?还是主要由石英组成?石英通常呈灰色，且很坚硬，易于辨认。富含碳酸钙的石灰岩颜色浅

**沉积岩** **粗粒**

**主要含岩石碎屑**

复成砾岩 222，角砾岩 223

**主要含石英碎屑**

无此类岩石

**主要含碳酸钙**

角砾灰岩 223，豆状石灰岩 236，海百合石灰岩 238

**其他矿物**

无此类岩石

**中粒**

淡，与稀盐酸作用，起泡。手持标本如果主要是由碳酸钙和石英以外的其他矿物组成的，那么就要判断它属于下列四类中的哪一类，然后按照提供的岩石名称、页码查看进一步的鉴定资料。

| | 细粒 |
|---|---|
| **主要含岩石碎屑**<br>杂砂岩 229 | **主要含岩石碎屑**<br>无这类岩石 |
| **主要含石英碎屑**<br>砂岩 225，绿砂岩 225，粟砂岩 226，云母砂岩 227，褐铁矿砂岩 227，正石英岩（粉红色和灰色）228，长石砂岩 229 | <br>**主要含石英碎屑**<br>黄土 224，页岩 231，粉砂岩 232，泥岩 232，粘土 233 |
| **主要含碳酸钙**<br>鲕状石灰岩 236，贝壳石灰岩 239，泉华 241，钟乳石 242，石灰华 242 | <br>**主要含碳酸钙**<br>钙质泥岩 233，泥灰岩234，白垩 237，珊瑚石灰岩 238，苔藓虫石灰岩 239，贝壳石灰岩 239，货币虫石灰岩 240 |
| **其他矿物**<br>岩盐 235，石膏 235，钾岩 235，白云石 241，褐铁矿 243 | <br>**其他矿物**<br>泥砾 224，黄土 224，粘土 233，白云石 241，褐铁矿 243，无烟煤 244，煤 244，褐煤 244，泥炭 245，煤玉 245，琥珀 246，燧石 246， |

# 矿物

## 自然元素

自然元素是一种未与其他元素结合的单质矿物，可以分为三大类：第一类为金属元素，如金、银、铜；第二类为半金属元素，如砷、锑；第三类为非金属元素，如碳和硫。金属元素密度大、柔软、有延展性、可锻，不透明；常以不规则树枝状和纤维状产出；单个晶体稀有。与金属元素不同，半金属元素导电性能很差，一般呈状块状产出。非金属元素透明到半透明，均为绝缘体，常形成晶体。

| 类别 自然元素 | 成分 Au | 硬度 2.5～3 |
| --- | --- | --- |

### 自然金(Gold)

晶体呈立方体或八面体形等，但非常稀有。一般以颗粒状、片状、块状或树枝状集合体产出。颜色与条痕均为金黄色，含银则色变浅。不透明，金属光泽。

· **成因** 主要产于热液矿脉，常与石英和硫化物伴生；亦见于未固结的砂积矿床、砂岩和砾岩；也可在河床中找到颗粒状或块状的冲积砂金。用淘金盘淘洗沉积物，是寻找这种稀有而珍贵的矿物的古老方法。易把金与黄铁矿和黄铜矿混淆，不过，只需做几个试验就能鉴别出来。

· **鉴定特征** 不溶于任何单独一种酸液中，溶于王水。

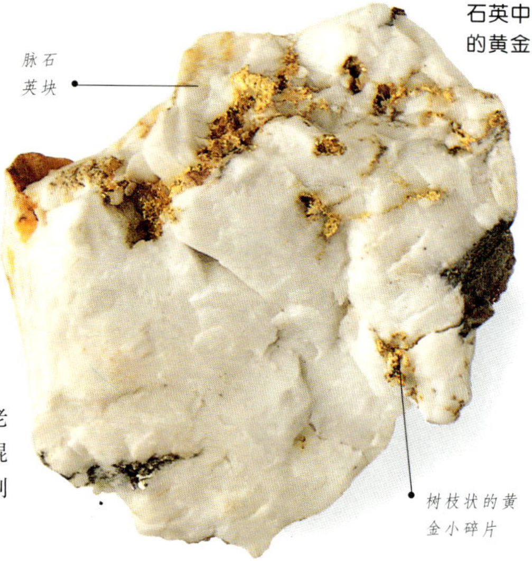

石英中的黄金

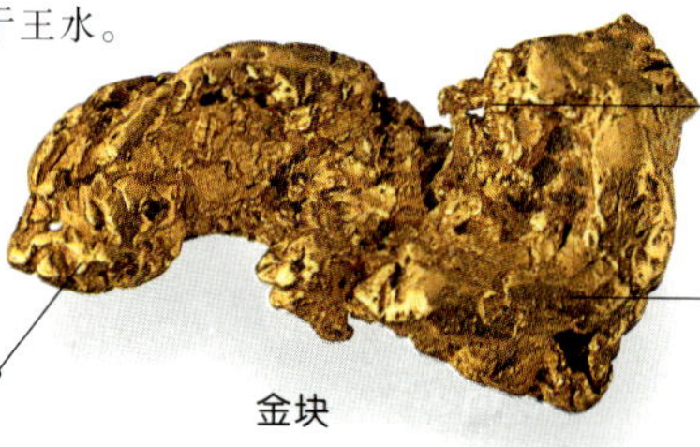

金块

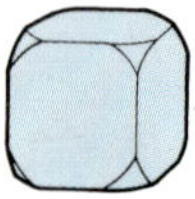
等轴晶系

| 比重 19.3 | 解理 无 | 断口 锯齿状 |
| --- | --- | --- |

| 类别 自然元素 | 成分 Ag | 硬度 2.5～3 |
| --- | --- | --- |

## 自然银(Silver)

晶体呈立方体或八面体罕见，有时呈平行带状。常见的有纤维状、鳞片状、树枝状和块状集合体。银白色，但暴露于空气中变色，条痕银白色。不透明，金属光泽。

· **成因** 形成于热液矿脉，也与金、其他含银矿物，以及金属硫化物伴生于矿床的氧化带。在一种称为银金矿的金银合金中，银占20～25%。

· **鉴定特征** 溶于硝酸，且熔点低，易熔。如果暴露于硫化氢蒸气中，银会失去光泽。为热和电的良导体。

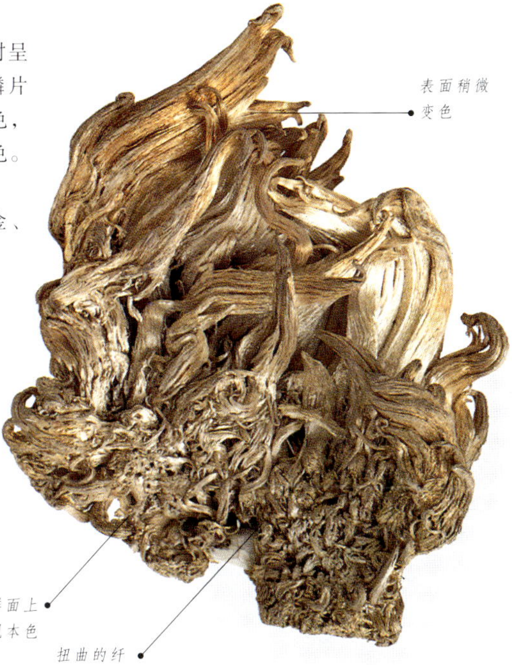


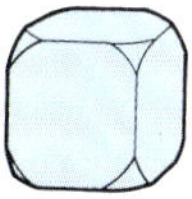


| 比重 10.5 | 解理 无 | 断口 锯齿状 |
| --- | --- | --- |

| 类别 自然元素 | 成分 Pt | 硬度 4～4.5 |
| --- | --- | --- |

## 自然铂(Platinum)

晶体呈立方体，但不常见。常以颗粒状、块状和鳞片状集合体产出。银灰至白色，条痕白色至银灰色。不透明，金属光泽。如果暴露于空气中，光泽不会褪失。

· **成因** 生成于原生基性和超基性岩，罕见于接触变质带。由于铂的比重很大，因此也会形成于砂积矿床中。

· **鉴定特征** 含有铁杂质时，铂会具有弱磁性。除了王水，不溶于任何酸中。

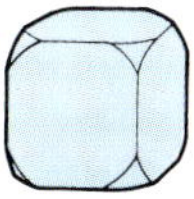


| 比重 21.4 | 解理 无 | 断口 锯齿状 |
| --- | --- | --- |

| 类别 自然元素 | 成分 Cu | 硬度 2.5～3 |
|---|---|---|

## 自然铜(Copper)

很少形成晶体，若形成晶体，则呈立方体、八面体或十二面体。常呈树枝状和块状集合体，也呈扭曲的铜丝状产出。颜色是鉴定的关键特征，铜的新鲜面呈铜红色或浅玫瑰色，氧化后出现棕黑色被膜，条痕铜红色。不透明，金属光泽。

· **成因** 主要产于硫化铜矿脉的转化。

· **鉴定特征** 溶于硝酸。

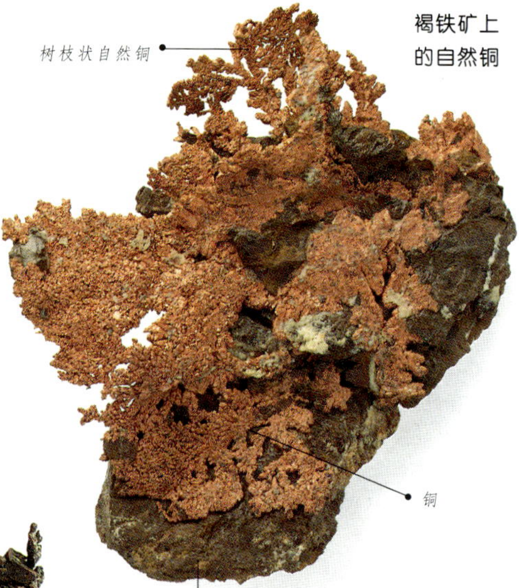


褐铁矿上的自然铜

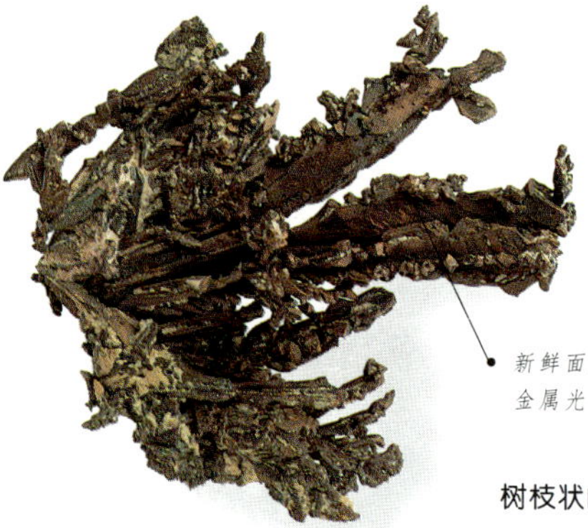


树枝状的铜

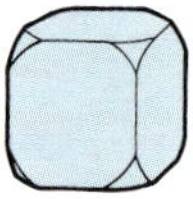

等轴晶系

| 比重 8.9 | 解理 无 | 断口 锯齿状 |
|---|---|---|

| 类别 自然元素 | 成分 Bi | 硬度 2～2.5 |
|---|---|---|

## 铋华(Bismuth)

形成不明显的晶体，常成双晶。一般为块状、叶片状、树枝状、网状、片状和粒状集合体。银白色，表面色微红或带晕彩，条痕银白色。不透明，金属光泽。

· **成因** 形成于热液矿脉和伟晶岩中。

· **鉴定特征** 低温下即熔化，易溶于硝酸。

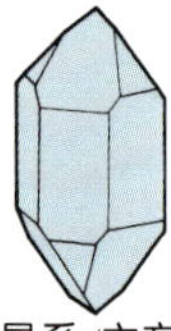

三方晶系/六方晶系

| 比重 9.7～9.8 | 解理 完全底面 | 断口 参差状 |
|---|---|---|

类别 自然元素 | 成分 As | 硬度 3.5

## 自然砷(Arsenic)

偶尔形成菱面体晶体，一般以粒状、葡萄状或钟乳状集合体产出。色浅灰，失去光泽后成深灰色，条痕灰色。不透明，金属光泽。

· **成因** 主要形成于热液矿脉。

· **鉴定特征** 受热后发出带蒜味的气体。

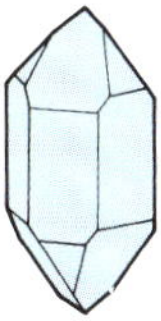

三方晶系/六方晶系

比重 5.7 | 解理 完全底面 | 断口 参差状

类别 自然元素 | 成分 Sb | 硬度 3～3.5

## 自然锑(Antimony)

晶体较少见，呈假立方体或板状，常成双晶。一般为块状、片状、粒状或针状集合体。浅银灰色，条痕灰色。不透明，亮丽的金属光泽。

· **成因** 与砷、银、方铅矿、闪锌矿、黄铁矿和辉锑矿共生于热液矿脉。

· **鉴定特征** 在空气中燃烧冒白烟；火焰蓝绿色。

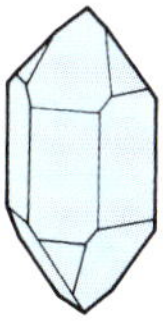

三方晶系/六方晶系

比重 6.6～6.7 | 解理 完全底面 | 断口 参差状

类别 自然元素 | 成分 S | 硬度 1.5～2.5

## 自然硫(Sulphur)

晶体板状、双锥状。硫也以块状、结壳状、粉状和钟乳状集合体产出。鲜艳的柠檬黄到棕黄色，条痕白色。透明到半透明，具松脂到脂肪光泽。

· **成因** 形成于火山口和温泉周围。

· **鉴定特征** 低温下即熔化，并释放出二氧化硫。

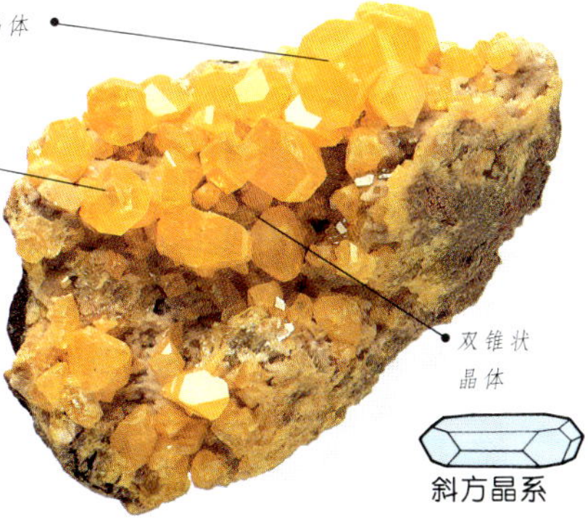


斜方晶系

比重 2.0～2.1 | 解理 不完全底面 | 断口 参差状至贝壳状

| 类别　自然元素 | 成分　Hg | 硬度　液体 |
|---|---|---|

## 自然汞(Mercury)

属于三方或六方晶系，不过仅在 39 ℃以下才呈菱面体晶体。常温下以液体状态存在，并形成小球珠。浅银白色，没有条痕色。不透明，有亮丽的金属光泽。

· **成因**　常与辰砂共生于火山口周围。

· **鉴定特征**　放入硝酸中会溶解。

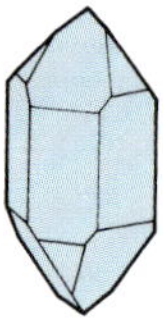

三方/六方晶系

放大的汞

| 比重　13.6~14.4 | 解理　无 | 断口　无 |
|---|---|---|

| 类别　自然元素 | 成分　Ni,Fe | 硬度　4~5 |
|---|---|---|

## 镍铁矿(Nickel－iron)

此矿物不常见，以块状和粒状集合体产出。铁灰色、深灰色或黑色，条痕铁灰色。不透明，新鲜面呈金属光泽。

· **成因**　形成于某些蚀变后的玄武岩，当玄武岩中富含铁的矿物产生化学还原作用时，就出现镍铁矿。有些种类也出现在因蛇纹岩化作用发生蚀变的超基性岩石中。常以铁纹石—镍纹石块体出现于陨石中。现代科学认为地核的大部分是由铁和镍组成的，但其在陆地上仍是稀有的材料。

· **鉴定特征**　镍铁矿具有强磁性。

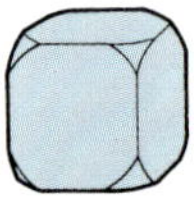

等轴晶系

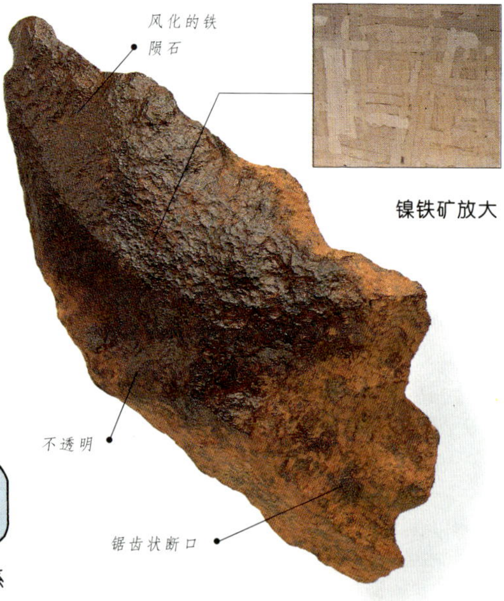


镍铁矿放大

| 比重　7.3~8.2 | 解理　不佳的立方体状 | 断口　参差状 |
|---|---|---|

| 类别 自然元素 | 成分 C | 硬度 10 |
|---|---|---|

## 金刚石(Diamond)

晶体呈八面体、立方体、十二面体和四面体，并有弯曲的晶面。金刚石也以带放射状结构的圆形块体(称为圆粒金刚石)还以及微晶块体产出(称为黑金刚石)。颜色丰富多彩：无色、白色、灰色、橙色、黄色、棕色、粉红色、红色、蓝色、绿色或黑色，条痕白色。透明到不透明，金刚光泽到油脂光泽。主要用作工业研磨材料，同时也是一种价值不菲、众所瞩目的宝石。

· **成因** 常产于超基性岩的金伯利岩(角砾云母橄榄岩)中，常呈岩管产出。

· **鉴定特征** 已知矿物中最硬的一种不能被任何其他矿物所擦划。

透明的金刚石

黄色金刚石

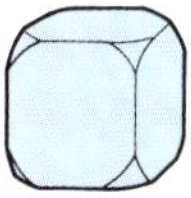
等轴晶系

| 比重 3.52 | 解理 完全八面体 | 断口 贝壳状 |
|---|---|---|

| 类别 自然元素 | 成分 C | 硬度 1～2 |
|---|---|---|

## 石墨(Graphite)

晶体呈扁平的六边形板状，也以块状、叶片状、粒状和土状集合体产出。深灰色到黑色，条痕深灰或黑色。不透明，有暗淡的金属光泽。

· **成因** 形成于板岩和片岩等变质岩中。

· **鉴定特征** 摸起来有滑腻感。在纸上摩擦，会留下灰色的痕迹。

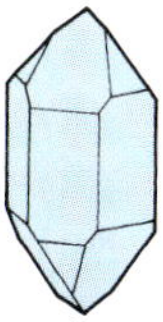
三方/六方晶系

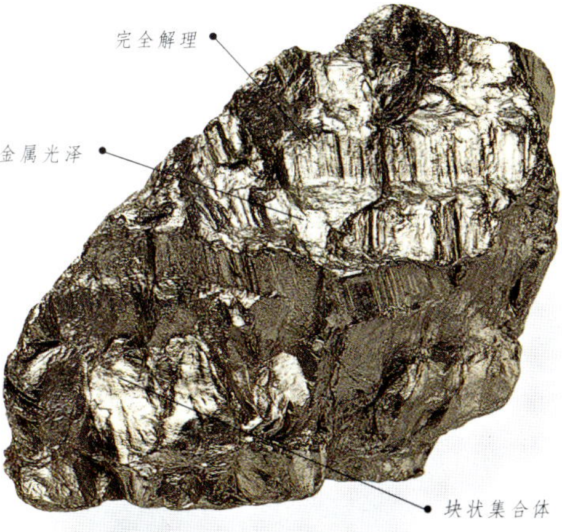


| 比重 2.1～2.3 | 解理 完全底面 | 断口 参差状 |
|---|---|---|

# 硫化物与硫盐矿物类

硫化物是硫与金属、半金属元素结合而成的天然化合物。当用硫化碲替代硫时，即产生碲化物；如果用砷替代硫，则产生砷化物。硫化物、碲化物和砷化物多有变体。许多硫化物都有金属光泽，并且柔软而致密(如方铅矿和辉钼矿)。有些则没有金属光泽(雌黄、雄黄)、或比较硬(白铁矿，辉砷钴矿)。通常晶体发育良好，并有高度的对称性。硫化物是非常重要的铅、锌、铁和铜矿石。由于它们易氧化成硫酸盐，所以形成于三千水位面以下的热液矿脉。硫盐矿物是金属元素与硫，以及半金属元素(如锑和砷)结合而成的天然化合物，其性质与硫化物相似。

| 类别 硫化物 | 成分 PbS | 硬度 2.5 |
|---|---|---|

## 方铅矿(Galena)

极常见的矿石矿物，呈立方体、八面体或立方八面体晶体，也以块状、粒状和纤维状集合体产出，颜色和条痕都是铅灰色。不透明，具有金属光泽。

· **成因** 热液上升到地壳上层形成方铅矿热液矿脉。与萤石、石英、方解石、闪锌矿和黄铁矿共生。

· **鉴定特征** 溶于盐酸，并产生带臭鸡蛋味的硫化氢。

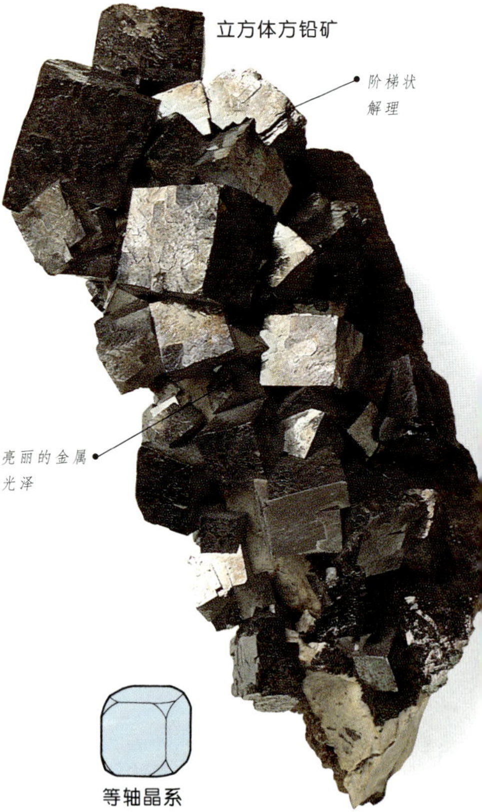


立方体方铅矿

方铅矿

等轴晶系

| 比重 7.58 | 解理 完全立方体 | 断口 亚贝壳状 |
|---|---|---|

| 类别 硫化物 | 成分 HgS | 硬度 2～2.5 |
| --- | --- | --- |

## 辰砂(Cinnabar)

晶体呈厚板状、菱面体和柱状，常成双晶。集合体以块状、皮壳状或粒状产出。颜色为典型的棕红色或猩红色，条痕猩红色。透明到不透明，金刚、半金属或暗淡光泽。

· **成因** 与雄黄和黄铁矿一起形成于火山道和温泉周围。其他共生矿物有自然汞、白铁矿、蛋白石、石英、辉锑矿和方解石。也可能产于与近期火山活动有关的矿脉或沉积岩中。

· **鉴定特征** 暴露于空气中稳定不变。

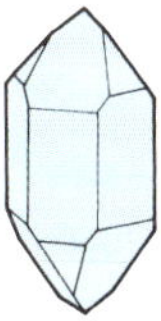

三方/六方晶系

| 比重 8.0～8.2 | 解理 完全 | 断口 贝壳状至参差状 |
| --- | --- | --- |

| 类别 硫化物 | 成分 CdS | 硬度 3～3.5 |
| --- | --- | --- |

## 硫镉矿(Greenockite)

晶体板状、锥状和柱状，不过更常呈土状覆于其他矿物表面。黄色、桔黄色、橙色或红色，条痕从桔黄色到砖红色。透明到半透明，松脂或金刚光泽。

· **成因** 当闪锌矿富含镉时，硫镉矿就会成为闪锌矿的交代和蚀变产物。尽管不常见，不过有时会与其他矿物，如葡萄石和沸石，一起形成微晶。

· **鉴定特征** 溶于盐酸，并产生带臭鸡蛋味的硫化氢。

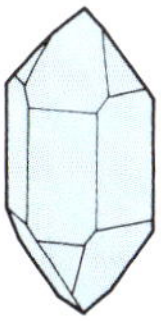

三方/六方晶系

| 比重 4.7～4.8 | 解理 清楚 | 断口 贝壳状 |
| --- | --- | --- |

| 类别 硫化物 | 成分 $Ag_2S$ | 硬度 2~2.5 |
|---|---|---|

## 螺状硫银矿(Acanthite)

晶体棱柱形。颜色为典型的灰色到铁黑色，条痕黑色。不透明，金属光泽。它与辉银矿为同质多象，也就是说，超过某个特定温度，螺状硫银矿会转变成另一种矿物，即辉银矿。

· **成因** 形成于热液矿脉，与自然银、淡红银矿、浓红银矿和其他硫化物伴生，如方铅矿。

· **鉴定特征** 螺状硫银矿溶于稀硝酸。易熔化，释放出含硫气体。

单斜晶系

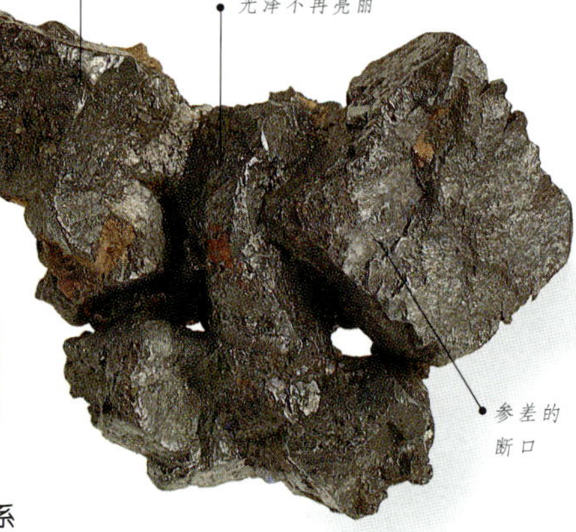


| 比重 7.22 | 解理 无 | 断口 参差状 |
|---|---|---|

| 类别 硫化物 | 成分 CoAsS | 硬度 5.5 |
|---|---|---|

## 辉砷钴矿(Cobaltite)

晶体呈八面体或假立方体，晶面常有条纹。一般呈块状、粒状和致密状集合体产出。灰黑色到银白色，做条痕测试时，会产生灰黑色的粉末。不透明；即使切成薄片，光线也不能透过。新鲜晶体呈金属光泽。

· **成因** 与其他砷化物和硫化物共生于热液矿脉(热液穿过地壳裂缝，冷却时生成矿物)和变质岩中。

· **鉴定特征** 易于熔化，并形成略带磁性的小珠粒，溶于硝酸。

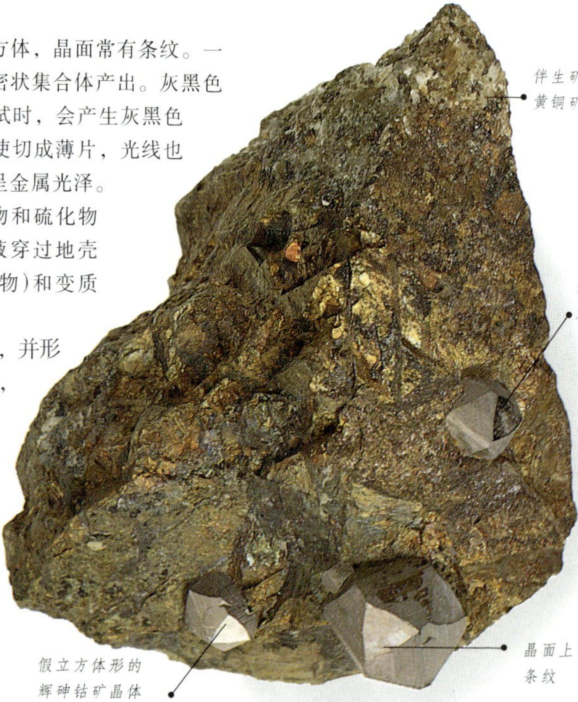


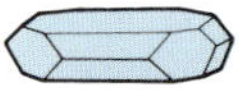

斜方晶系

| 比重 6.3 | 解理 完全 | 断口 参差状 |
|---|---|---|

| 类别 硫化物 | 成分 ZnS | 硬度 3.5～4 |
|---|---|---|

## 闪锌矿(Sphalerite)

晶体呈四面体和十二面体，并显出弯曲的晶面。一般呈块状、粒状、结核状和葡萄状集合体产出。颜色变化大从黑色、棕色、黄色和红色到绿色、灰色和白色，条痕从浅棕色到无色。半透明到透明不等，松脂到金刚光泽。英文又称作 blende 或 black jack。

· **成因** 常见于热液矿脉，并与白云石、石英、黄铁矿、方铅矿、萤石、重晶石和方解石共生。

· **鉴定特征** 加入稀盐酸会产生硫化氢，出现臭鸡蛋味，质纯的闪锌矿，不熔。不过，随着闪锌矿中铁含量的增加，熔点降低。

块状闪锌矿

结晶闪锌矿

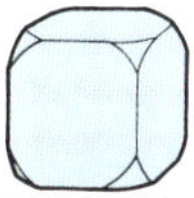
等轴晶系

| 比重 3.9～4.1 | 解理 完全 | 断口 贝壳状 |
|---|---|---|

| 类别 硫化物 | 成分 $Sb_2S_3$ | 硬度 2 |
|---|---|---|

## 辉锑矿(Stibnite)

晶体呈柱状，并常带有纵向条纹。一般呈柱状、粒状、致密状和刃状集合体产出，颜色和条痕都是铅灰色。不透明，金属光泽。

· **成因** 形成于热液矿脉，原岩全部或部分被热液携带的物质交代而成。

· **鉴定特征** 火柴火焰足以使辉锑矿熔化，溶于盐酸。

斜方晶系

| 比重 4.63～4.66 | 解理 完全 | 断口 参差状至亚贝壳状 |
|---|---|---|

| 类别　硫化物 | 成分　$Cu_5FeS_4$ | 硬度　3 |
|---|---|---|

## 斑铜矿(Bornite)

晶体呈立方体、八面体或十二面体，常有弯曲或不平坦的晶面。常呈致密块状或粒状。铜红色、棕铜色或青铜色，风化面呈蓝色；紫色和红色斑状锖色，因而有“孔雀石”的俗名。条痕灰黑色。不透明，金属光泽。

· **成因**　与石英、黄铜矿和方铅矿等矿物共生于热液矿脉，也形成于某些岩浆岩以及铜矿脉的氧化带。

· **鉴定特征**　溶于硝酸。

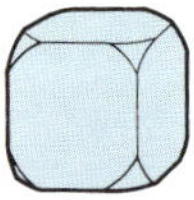

等轴晶系

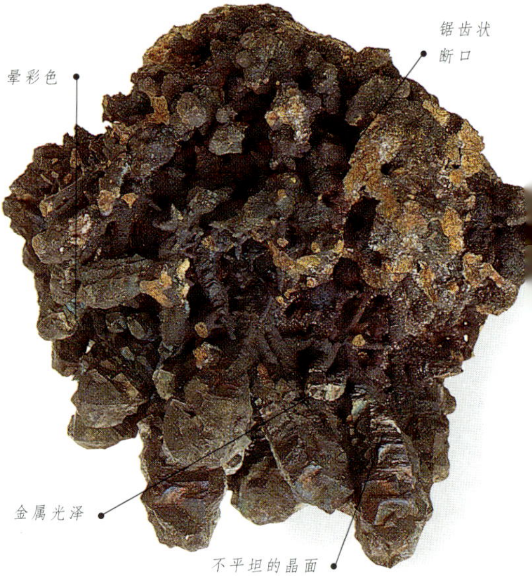


| 比重　5.0 ~ 5.1 | 解理　极不佳 | 断口　参差状至贝壳状 |
|---|---|---|

| 类别　硫化物 | 成分　$CuFeS_2$ | 硬度　3.5 ~ 4 |
|---|---|---|

## 黄铜矿(Chalcopyrite)

晶体呈假四面体，常呈双晶，晶面上有条纹。一般以致密块状、肾状或葡萄状集合体产出。黄铜色，表面带有蓝紫色晕彩，条痕绿黑色。不透明，金属光泽。

· **成因**　黄铜矿是最重要的铜矿石之一，形成于硫化物矿床，通常都是热液矿脉，并与磁黄铁矿、石英、方解石、黄铁矿、闪锌矿和方铅矿共生。此外，还铜矿床的蚀变。

· **鉴定特征**　溶于硝酸，燃烧时，火焰呈绿色。

正方晶系

| 比重　4.3 ~ 4.4 | 解理　不佳 | 断口　参差状至贝壳状 |
|---|---|---|

| 类别 硫化物 | 成分 $Cu_2S$ | 硬度 2.5～3 |
|---|---|---|

## 辉铜矿(Chalcosine)

晶体可呈假六方柱状双晶产出，但非常罕见，也以短柱状或板状产出，不过，最常见的是块状集合体。颜色和条痕都是深灰色。不透明，金属光泽。

· 成因　与其他矿物如斑铜矿、石英、方解石、蓝铜矿、黄铜矿、方铅矿和闪锌矿共生于热液矿脉。

· 鉴定特征　溶于硝酸，可熔。燃烧时火焰呈绿色，并释放出二氧化硫的气体。

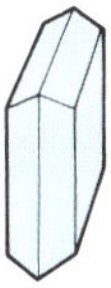

单斜晶系

| 比重 5.5～5.8 | 解理 不清楚 | 断口 贝壳状 |
|---|---|---|

| 类别 硫化物 | 成分 CuS | 硬度 1.5～2 |
|---|---|---|

## 铜蓝(Covellite)

晶体呈形态有六方薄板状，不过块状叶片状集合体更常见。颜色为靛蓝色，常带一些紫色晕彩，条痕从深灰色到黑色。不透明，半金属光泽到暗淡光泽。裂开之后，完全解理成柔软的薄片。

· 成因　形成于铜矿床氧化带——含铜硫物矿床的次生富集。

· 鉴定特征　极易熔化，火焰蓝色，溶解于盐酸。

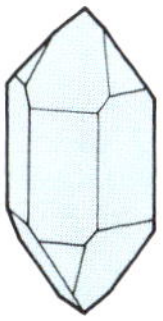

三方/六方晶系

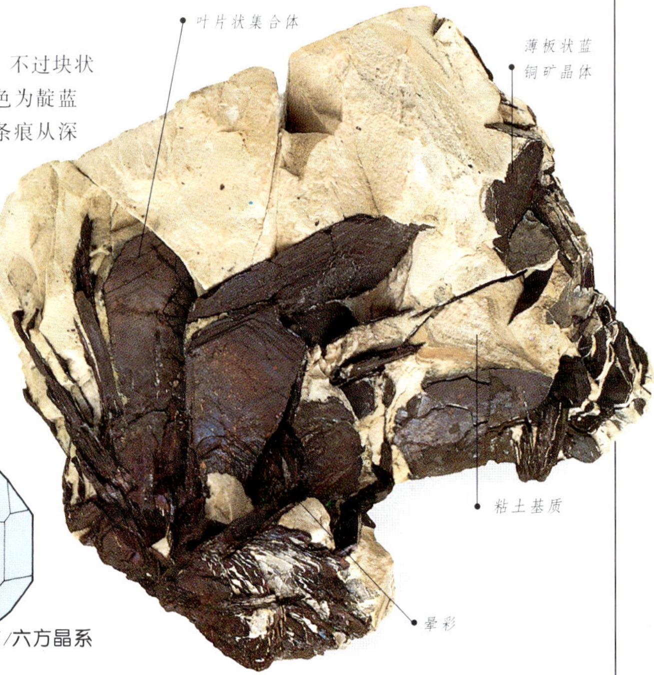


| 比重 4.6～4.8 | 解理 完全 | 断口 参差状 |
|---|---|---|

| 类别 硫化物 | 成分 $As_2S_3$ | 硬度 1.5～2 |
|---|---|---|

## 雌黄(Orpiment)

晶体罕见呈短柱状。常以薄叶片块体、块状或柱状集合体产出。常呈浓柠檬黄色，有时也呈棕黄色，条痕浅黄色。透明到半透明，新鲜面松脂光泽，解理面呈珍珠光泽。

· **成因** 见于低温热液矿脉，常与辉锑矿和雄黄共生，雌黄也形成于温泉周围沉积的皮壳内。

· **鉴定特征** 易于熔化。加热后会释放出强烈的大蒜味，是含砷矿物具有的典型气味。雌黄溶于硝酸，并在液体表面留下黄色的硫的痕迹。

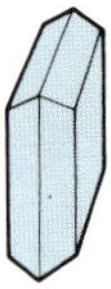


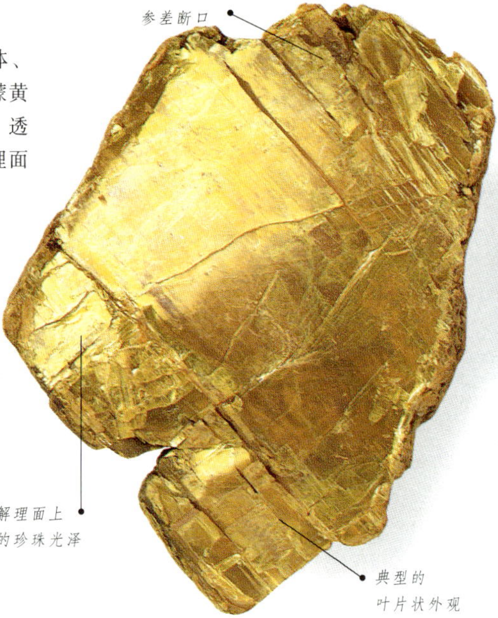


| 比重 3.4～3.5 | 解理 完全 | 断口 参差状 |
|---|---|---|

| 类别 硫化物 | 成分 AsS | 硬度 1.5～2 |
|---|---|---|

## 雄黄(Realgar)

短柱状、带条纹的晶体，常呈致密块状、和粒状集合体。鲜艳的红色到桔红色，条痕从桔黄色到桔红色。透明到半透明，松脂到油脂光泽。

· **成因** 形成于热液矿脉和温泉周围，并与辉锑矿、雌黄，以及铅、银和锑共生。

· **鉴定特征** 与其他砷矿物一样，加热后释放出浓烈的大蒜味。

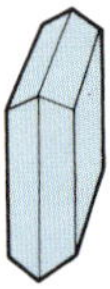

| 比重 3.56 | 解理 良好 | 断口 贝壳状 |
|---|---|---|

| | | |
|---|---|---|
| 别 硫化物 | 成分 $MoS_2$ | 硬度 1～1.5 |

## 辉钼矿(Molybdenite)

晶体常呈板状或桶状，也以叶片状块体、鳞片状或粒状集合体产出。灰色，条痕也是灰色。不透明，金属光泽。

· **成因** 形成于热液矿脉，也形成于花岗岩。

· **鉴定特征** 触摸有油脂感。

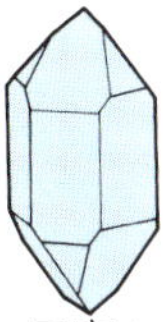

三方/六方晶系

| | | |
|---|---|---|
| 重 4.62～5.06 | 解理 完全底面 | 断口 参差状 |

| | | |
|---|---|---|
| 别 硫化物 | 成分 $MnS_2$ | 硬度 4 |

## 褐硫锰矿(Hauerite)

晶体呈八面体到立方八面体，也以块状或球状集合体产出。红棕色到棕色或黑色，条痕棕红色。不透明，金属光泽到暗淡光泽。

· **成因** 形成于蒸发岩，盐穹中。

· **鉴定特征** 溶于盐酸。

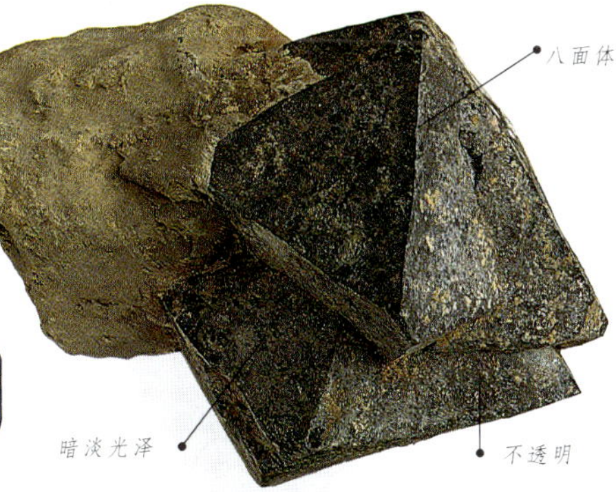


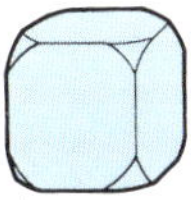

等轴晶系

| | | |
|---|---|---|
| 重 3.46 | 解理 完全 | 断口 亚贝壳状至参差状 |

| | | |
|---|---|---|
| 别 硫化物 | 成分 $Bi_2S_3$ | 硬度 2 |

## 辉铋矿(Bismuthinite)

晶体呈柱状或针状。辉铋矿也以块状、纤维状或叶片状集合体产出。铅灰色到银白色，条痕铅灰色。不透明，金属光泽。

· **成因** 形成于高温热液矿脉和花岗岩，与自然铋和多种硫化物共生。

· **鉴定特征** 溶于硝酸，并在表面上留下片状的硫颗粒。

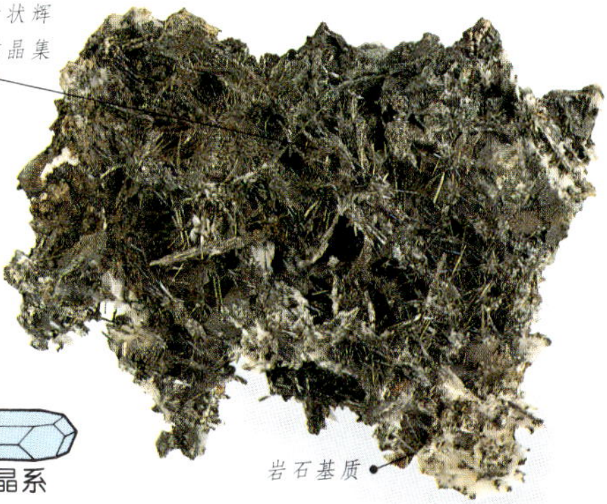


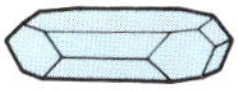

斜方晶系

| | | |
|---|---|---|
| 重 6.8 | 解理 完全 | 断口 参差状 |

| 类别 硫化物 | 成分 $FeS_2$ | 硬度 6~6.5 |
|---|---|---|

## 黄铁矿(Pyrite)

晶体呈立方体、五角十二面体或八面体，常见双晶现象，晶面通常有条纹。也以块状、粒状、肾状、钟乳状、葡萄状或结核状集合体产出。浅黄，因此有“愚人金”的别名，条痕绿黑色。不透明，金属光泽。

· **成因** 黄铁矿是岩浆岩、沉积岩和变质岩中一种常见的副矿物。

· **鉴定特征** 与硬金属物碰撞发出火花。易于熔化。

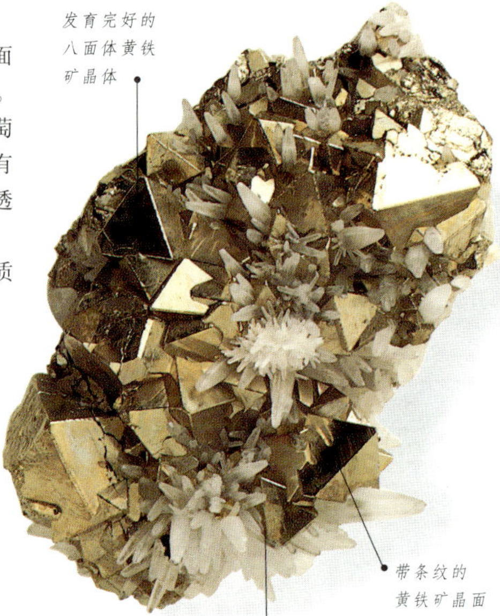

八面体黄铁矿

结核状黄铁矿

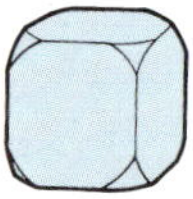
等轴晶系

| 比重 5.0 | 解理 不清楚 | 断口 贝壳状至参差状 |
|---|---|---|

| 类别 硫化物 | 成分 FeS | 硬度 3.5~4.5 |
|---|---|---|

## 磁黄铁矿(Pyrrhotite)

晶体呈板状或片状，常呈块状和粒状集合体。黄铜色到铜红色，脱色变成棕色，常带晕彩，条痕从深灰色到黑色。为不透明的矿物，金属光泽。

· **成因** 常形成于磁性岩浆矿床，尤其是基性和超基性岩。与黄铁矿、方铅矿、闪锌矿和其他硫化物共生。

· **鉴定特征** 具有磁性。

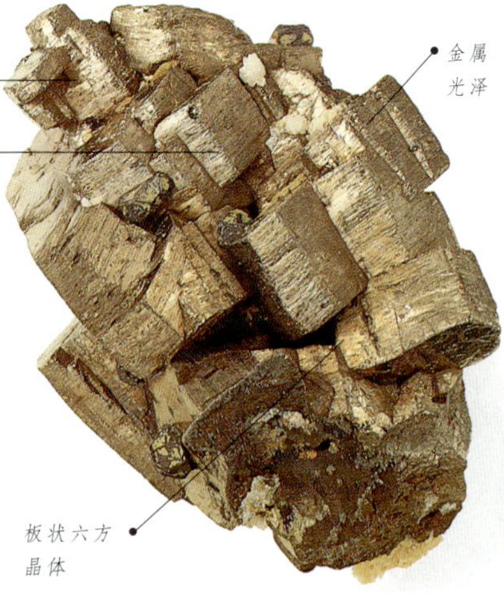

单斜晶系

| 比重 4.53~4.77 | 解理 无 | 断口 亚贝壳状至参差状 |
|---|---|---|

| 类别 硫化物 | 成分 FeAsS | 硬度 5.5~6 |
|---|---|---|

## 毒砂(Arsenopyrite)

晶体呈柱状，常见双晶。集合体块状、柱状和粒状。颜色为典型的银白色，脱色成粉红、棕色和铜色，并带有彩晕，条痕从黑色到灰色。不透明，金属光泽。

· **成因**　形成于热液矿脉、变质岩和基性岩中。

· **鉴定特征**　加热或与硬物碰撞释放出大蒜味。

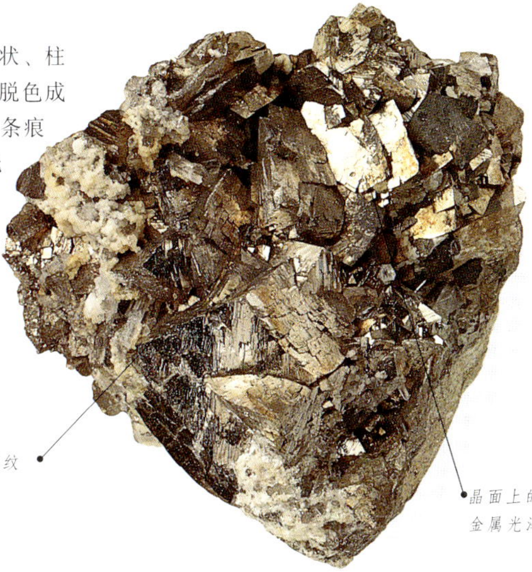


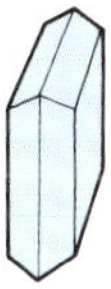

单斜晶系

| 比重 5.9~6.2 | 解理 不清楚 | 断口 锯齿状 |
|---|---|---|

| 类别 硫化物 | 成分 $FeS_2$ | 硬度 6.5 |
|---|---|---|

## 白铁矿(Marcasite)

晶体形态多样，包括板状和双锥体。由于成双晶的缘故，晶面常弯曲，并形成矛状或鸡冠状连生体。集合体块状、钟乳状或肾状。白铁矿结核具有放射状内部构造。其黄铜色稍浅于黄铁矿的颜色，暴露后变黑，条痕黑绿色。不透明，金属光泽。

· **形成**　常形成于页岩、粘土岩、石灰岩和白垩的酸性溶液渗透层。

· **鉴定特征**　暴露于空气中易分解，而与之化学成分相同的黄铁矿则不这么容易分解。溶于硝酸中，但于难溶解。

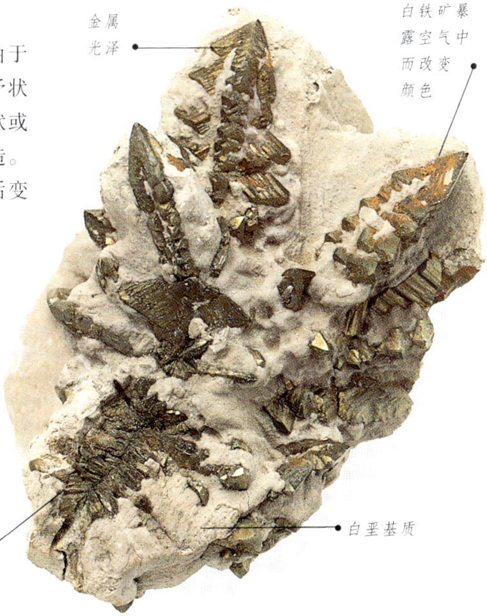


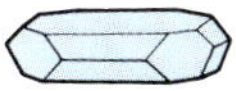

斜方晶系

| 比重 4.92 | 解理 清楚 | 断口 参差状 |
|---|---|---|

| 类别 硫化物 | 成分 NiS | 硬度 3~3.5 |
|---|---|---|

## 针镍矿(Millerite)

晶体通常细如毛发，呈放射簇状，也以块状集合体产出。黄铜色，条痕绿黑色。不透明，金属光泽。

· **成因** 常交代其他镍矿物，产于石灰岩、白云岩、蛇纹岩和碳酸盐矿脉中。

· **鉴定特征** 是电的良导体，容易熔化。

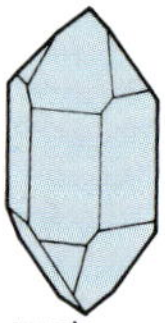

三方/六方晶系

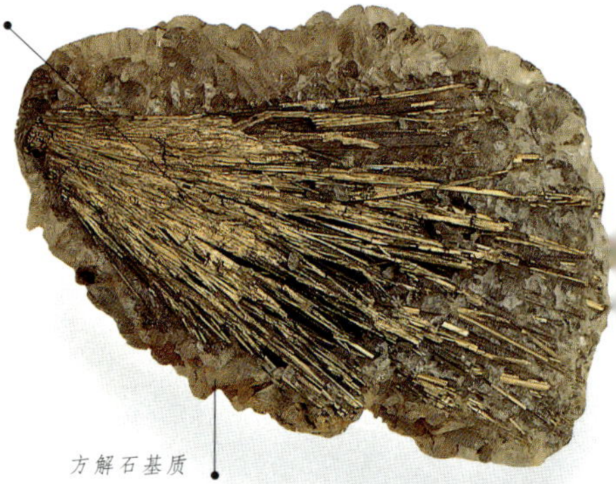


| 比重 5.3~5.6 | 解理 完全菱面体 | 断口 参差状 |
|---|---|---|

| 类别 硫化物 | 成分 (CO,Fe)AsS | 硬度 5 |
|---|---|---|

## 铁硫砷钴矿(Glaucodot)

晶体柱状、带条纹，可成双晶现象。以块状集合体产出。灰色到白色，条痕黑色。不透明，金属光泽。

· **成因** 与黄铁矿之类的矿物共生于热液矿脉。

· **鉴定特征** 溶于硝酸，加热后放出大蒜味。

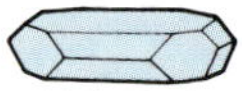

斜方晶系

| 比重 5.9~6.1 | 解理 完全 | 断口 参差状 |
|---|---|---|

| 类别 硫化物 | 成分 $(Fe,Ni)_9S_8$ | 硬度 3.5~4 |
|---|---|---|

## 镍黄铁矿(Pentlandite)

一般呈块状或粒状集合体产出。铜黄色，条痕棕色。不透明，金属光泽。

· **成因** 由于岩浆分凝而形成于基性岩，如苏长岩。常与黄铜矿、磁黄铁矿及镍的砷化物伴生。

· **鉴定特征** 极易熔化，并形成铅灰色的小珠。

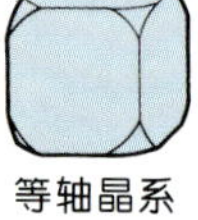

等轴晶系

| 比重 4.6~5.0 | 解理 无 | 断口 贝壳状 |
|---|---|---|

| 类别 碲化物 | 成分 $AuAgTe_4$ | 硬度 1.5～2 |
|---|---|---|

## 针碲金银矿(Sylvanite)

晶体短柱形，常成双晶。也以刃状、柱状和颗粒状块体产出。银白、灰色或黄色，条痕从银白色到铁灰色。不透明，金属光泽。

· **成因** 与萤石、其他碲化物、硫化物、碳酸盐、金、碲和石英共生于热液矿脉。经常发现1厘米长的纤细晶体与自然金共生。

· **鉴定特征** 溶于硝酸，留下金黄色残渣。在浓硫酸中加热后，溶液颜色变红。

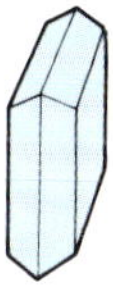

| 比重 8.1～8.2 | 解理 完全 | 断口 参差状 |
|---|---|---|

| 类别 砷化物 | 成分 NiAs | 硬度 5～5.5 |
|---|---|---|

## 砷镍矿(Nickeline)

砷镍矿很少形成晶体，偶尔生成小锥状晶体，常呈块状、肾状和柱状集合体。浅铜红色，渐渐变成黑色，做条痕测试时产生棕黑色粉末。不透明，金属光泽。

· **成因** 形成于热液矿脉和苏长岩，与银矿、镍矿和钴矿伴生。

· **鉴定特征** 砷镍矿溶于硝酸后溶液变成绿色。加热后股释放出大蒜味气体，极易熔化。

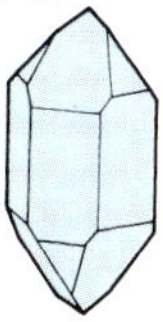

| 比重 7.7～7.8 | 解理 无 | 断口 参差状 |
|---|---|---|

| 类别 砷化物 | 成分 $(Co,Ni)As_{2-3}$ | 硬度 5.5～6 |
|---|---|---|

## 砷钴矿(Smaltite)

是方钴矿的缺砷变种。晶体呈立方体、八面体或立方八面体，也呈块状、粒状和网状集合体。锡白色，条痕黑色。不透明，金属光泽。

· **成因** 形成于热液矿脉。

· **鉴定特征** 加热后释放出大蒜气味。

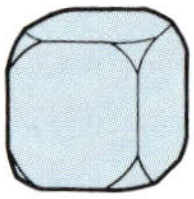

等轴晶系

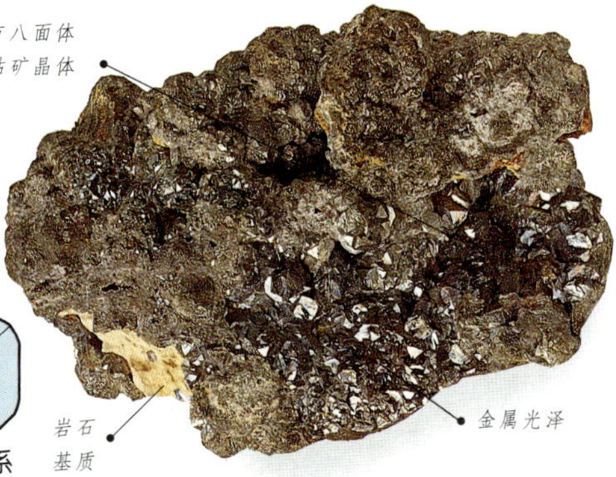


| 比重 6.1～6.9 | 解理 清楚 | 断口 参差状 |
|---|---|---|

| 类别 砷化物 | 成分 $(Ni,Co)As_{2-3}$ | 硬度 5.5～6 |
|---|---|---|

## 复砷镍矿(Chloanthite)

是镍方钴矿缺砷的变种。晶体呈立方体或八面体，也呈块状或粒状集合体。锡白色，条痕黑色。不透明，金属光泽。

· **成因** 形成于热液矿脉。

· **鉴定特征** 复砷镍矿富含镍，加热后，释放出浓烈的蒜味。

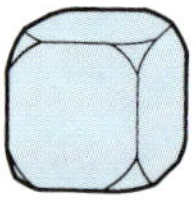

等轴晶系

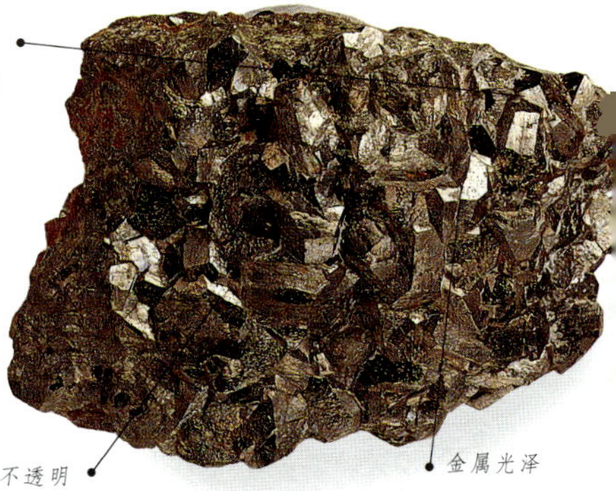


| 比重 6.1～6.9 | 解理 清楚 | 断口 参差状 |
|---|---|---|

| 类别 砷化物 | 成分 $CoAs_{2-3}$ | 硬度 5.5～6 |
|---|---|---|

## 方钴矿(Skutterudite)

是复砷镍矿—方钴矿—砷钴矿系列的中间成员。晶体形状主要为立方体，偶尔成八面体，也呈块状和粒状集合体，锡白色，条痕黑色。不透明，金属光泽。

· **成因** 形成于热液矿脉。

· **鉴定特征** 加热后释放出浓烈的大蒜味。

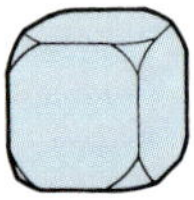

等轴晶系

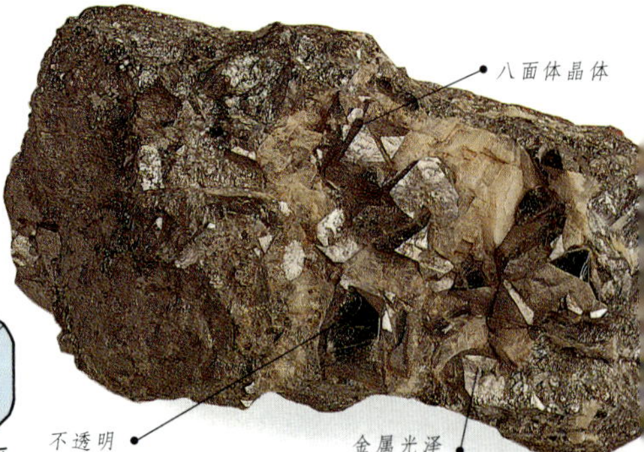


| 比重 6.1～6.9 | 解理 清楚 | 断口 参差状 |
|---|---|---|

| 类别 硫盐矿物 | 成分 $Cu_3AsS_4$ | 硬度 3 |
|---|---|---|

## 硫砷铜矿(Enargite)

晶体呈柱状或板状，常双晶，晶面上呈纵条纹。也以块状或粒状集合体产出。颜色和条痕一样，从深灰色到黑色。不透明，金属光泽。

· **成因** 产于热液矿脉或交代矿床中。热液上升时，其携带的矿物质沉淀形成矿脉。与许多矿物共生，如石英和硫化物，包括方铅矿、斑铜矿、闪锌矿、黄铁矿和黄铜矿。此外，也与硬石膏之类的矿物共生于盐穹。

· **鉴定特征** 加热后发出大蒜味。溶于硝酸。火柴火焰即能熔化此矿物。

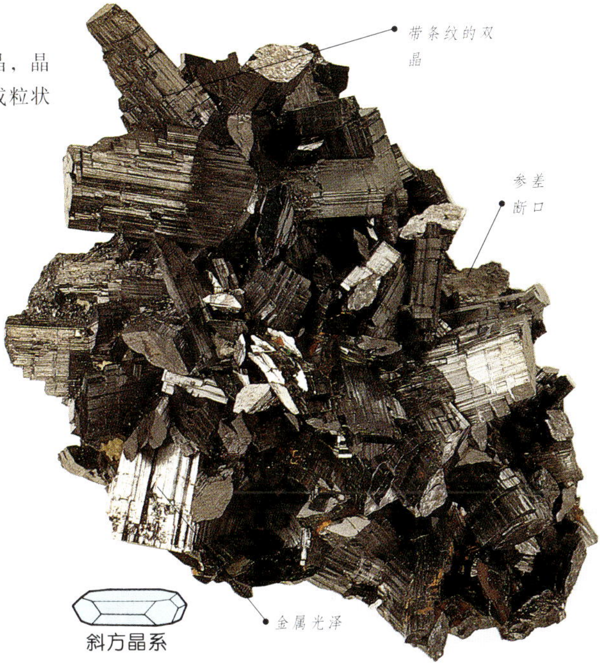

斜方晶系

| 比重 4.4～4.5 | 解理 完全 | 断口 参差状 |
|---|---|---|

| 类别 硫盐矿物 | 成分 $Pb_4FeSb_6S_{14}$ | 硬度 2.5 |
|---|---|---|

## 脆硫锑铅矿(羽毛矿)(Jamesonite)

晶体呈针状到纤维状，和以块状和羽毛状集合体产出，颜色和条痕都是深灰色。不透明，金属光泽。

· **成因** 形成于热液矿脉。灼热而富含化学物质的热液侵入节理和断层线冷却，形成矿物。脆硫锑铅矿与其他硫盐矿物共生，也与硫化物、碳酸盐岩以及常见的石英矿共生。

· **鉴定特征** 溶于盐酸。

单斜晶系

| 比重 5.63 | 解理 良好 | 断口 参差状至贝壳状 |
|---|---|---|

| 类别 硫盐矿物 | 成分 $Ag_5SbS_4$ | 硬度 2～2.5 |
|---|---|---|

## 脆银矿(Stephanite)

晶体短柱状或板状，有时成双晶，也呈块状集合体产出。颜色是典型的铁黑色，条痕黑色。不透明，金属光泽。

· **成因** 形成于矿脉，与自然银、硫化物和其他硫盐类，如螺状硫银矿、黝铜矿、硫锑铜银矿、淡红银矿和辉银矿共生。

· **鉴定特征** 溶于硝酸，同时产生砷和氧化硫。很易于熔化。

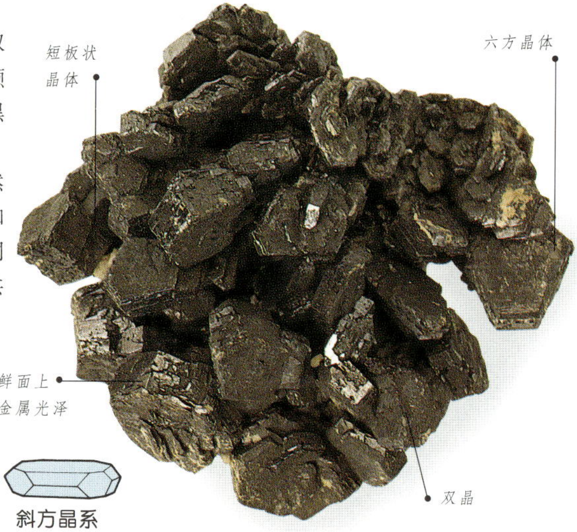


斜方晶系

| 比重 6.25 | 解理 不完全 | 断口 参差状至亚贝壳状 |
|---|---|---|

| 类别 硫盐矿物 | 成分 $Ag_3SbS_3$ | 硬度 2.5 |
|---|---|---|

## 深红银矿(Pyrargyrite)

晶体柱状或偏三角面体，有时成双晶，也呈块状、致密状集合体和浸染状颗粒产出。典型的暗红色到黑色，条痕暗红色。半透明，金刚光泽到半金属光泽。

· **成因** 与其他硫盐类，与银以及其他矿物，如黄铁矿、方铅矿、石英、白云石和方解石共生于热液矿脉。

· **鉴定特征** 溶于硝酸，易熔化。

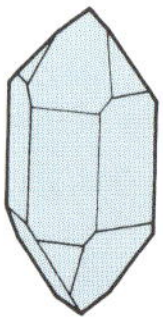
三方/六方晶系

| 比重 5.8～5.9 | 解理 清楚菱面体 | 断口 贝壳状至参差状 |
|---|---|---|

| | | |
|---|---|---|
| 别 硫盐矿物 | 成分 $(Ag)_{16}Sb_2S_{11}$ | 硬度 2~3 |

## 硫锑铜银矿(Polybasite)

晶体板状和假六方晶体，晶面常有三角形条纹，此外，也以块状集合体产出。铁黑色，条痕黑色，薄片可能呈暗红色。不透明，新鲜面呈金属光泽。

· **成因** 与自然银，以及其他硫盐矿物和硫化物，如方铅矿、辉银矿和其他银、铅矿物共生于热液矿脉。

· **鉴定特征** 在火焰中加热时，低温即熔化。

单斜晶系

| | | |
|---|---|---|
| 重 6.0~6.3 | 解理 不完全底面 | 断口 参差状 |

| | | |
|---|---|---|
| 别 硫盐矿物 | 成分 $PbCuSbS_3$ | 硬度 2.5~3 |

## 车轮矿(Bournonite)

晶体短柱状或板状，常成双晶并有条纹，，也以块状、粒状和致密状集合体产出。钢灰色到黑色，条痕灰色或黑色。不透明，金属光泽。

· **成因** 与黝铜矿、方铅矿、银、黄铜矿、菱铁矿、石英、闪锌矿和辉锑矿共生于热液矿脉。形成于含矿热液在地壳内的裂缝循环流动，冷却和分异。

· **鉴定特征** 在火焰中加热时，极易熔化。易溶于硝酸，并产生绿色的溶液，由此可知，车轮矿的化学成分中含有铜。

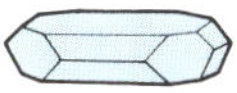

斜方晶系

| | | |
|---|---|---|
| 比重 5.7~5.9 | 解理 不完全 | 断口 亚贝壳状至锯齿状 |

| 类别 硫盐矿物 | 成分 $Cu_{12}Sb_4S_{13}$ | 硬度 3 ~ 4.5 |
|---|---|---|

## 黝铜矿(Tetrahedrite)

晶体形态为四面体，其英文名字即得自于此。常呈双晶，并有三角形晶面。还以粒状、块状和致密状集合体产出。灰色到黑色，条痕从黑色、棕色到红色不等。不透明，金属光泽。与下述的砷黝铜矿构成完全类质同象系列。

· **成因** 与硫化物、碳酸盐、石英、萤石和重晶石共生于热液矿脉。

· **鉴定特征** 溶于硝酸。

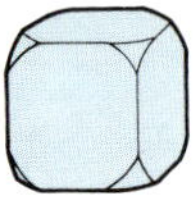

等轴晶系

| 比重 4.6 ~ 5.1 | 解理 无 | 断口 参差状至亚贝壳状 |
|---|---|---|

| 类别 硫盐矿物 | 成分 $(Cu,Fe)_{12}As_4S_{13}$ | 硬度 3 ~ 4.5 |
|---|---|---|

## 砷黝铜矿(Tennantite)

四面体晶体常被其他晶形代替常成双晶，也以块状、粒状和致密状集合体产出。深灰到黑色，条痕黑色、棕色或暗红色。不透明，金属光泽，有时光泽会非常明亮。

· **成因** 与多种矿物伴生于热液矿脉，如重晶石、萤石、石英、方铅矿、闪锌矿、黄铁矿、黄铜矿、方解石和白云石，也形成于高温热液和接触交代矿床。

· **鉴定特征** 溶于硝酸，且容易熔化。

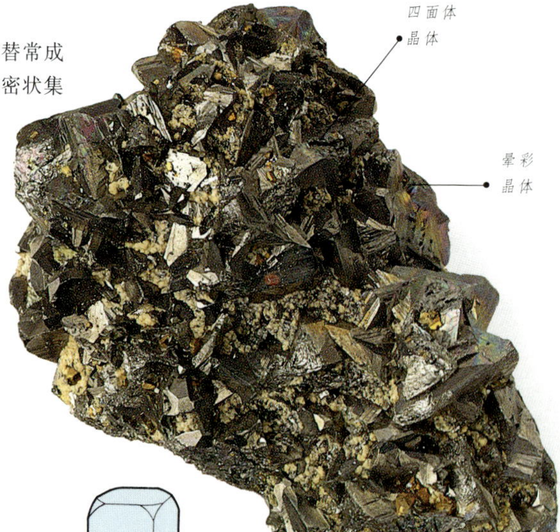



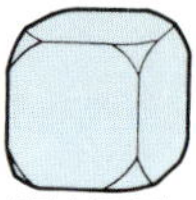

等轴晶系

| 比重 4.59 ~ 4.75 | 解理 无 | 断口 参差状至亚贝壳状 |
|---|---|---|

| 别　硫盐矿物 | 成分　$Pb_5Sb_4S_{11}$ | 硬度　2.5～3 |
|---|---|---|

## 硫锑铅矿(Boulangerite)

晶体呈长柱状，有时呈针状。也以块状、纤维状或羽毛状集合体产出。铅灰色到蓝灰色，条痕棕色。不透明，暗淡或金属光泽。

· 成因　与多种矿物共生于热液矿脉，包括方铅矿、黄铁矿、闪锌矿，硫盐矿物，如黝铜矿、砷黝铜矿和淡红银矿，以及石英和多种碳酸盐。

· 鉴定特征　在火焰中加热极易熔化。与冷的稀酸不发生反应，溶于热强酸。

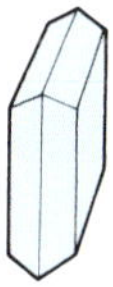

单斜晶系

| 重　5.8～6.2 | 解理　良好 | 断口　参差状 |
|---|---|---|

| 别　硫盐矿物 | 成分　$Ag_3AsS_3$ | 硬度　2～2.5 |
|---|---|---|

## 淡红银矿(硫砷银矿)(Proustite)

晶体柱状、菱面体和偏三角面体。也以块状或致密状集合体产出。鲜红色，条痕也是鲜红色，在光线下颜色变暗。半透明到透明，金刚光泽到半金属光泽。

· 成因　与多种矿物伴生于热液矿脉，如黝铜矿和砷黝铜矿，以及一些硫化物，如方铅矿，还有石英。

· 鉴定特征　溶于硝酸，易熔。

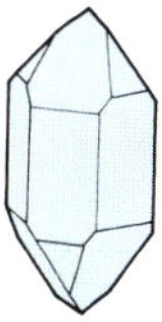

三方/六方晶系

| 重 5.55～5.64 | 解理　清楚菱面体 | 断口　贝壳状至参差状 |
|---|---|---|

# 卤化物

卤化物是金属元素与卤素元素（溴、氟和碘）结合而成的化合物。卤化物常形成于多种地质环境，有些卤化物，如石盐，常见于蒸发岩地层，这是一种交替沉积岩层，其中所含的蒸发岩矿物，如石膏、石盐和钾石盐按照严格的顺序沉积，并与泥灰岩、石灰岩构成互层。其他卤化物，如萤石，产于热液矿脉。卤化物矿物通常质软，多呈立方对称晶体，比重偏小。

| 类别 卤化物 | 成分 NaCl | 硬度 2 |
|---|---|---|

## 石盐(Halite)

晶体呈立方体，晶面常凹陷，称为漏斗状立方体骸晶。偶呈完好的八面体，常呈块状、粒状和致密状集合体产出，致密块状集合体称为岩盐。颜色多变，白色、无色、桔黄色、黄色、微红色、蓝色、紫色和黑色，然而条痕始终是白色。透明到半透明，玻璃光泽。

· **成因** 盐湖或泻湖里的水逐渐干涸沉积形成蒸发岩矿物。石盐与其他蒸发岩矿物，如钾盐、石膏、白云石和硬石膏共生。

· **鉴定特征** 有数种简单的方法可以用来检测石盐。味咸，易溶于冷水中，溶液干涸后会沉淀形成一些小漏斗状立方体晶骸。手摸石盐有油脂感。火焰黄色，由于可能含有杂质，因此产生绿色、桔黄色或微红色萤光。

漏斗状立方体晶骸

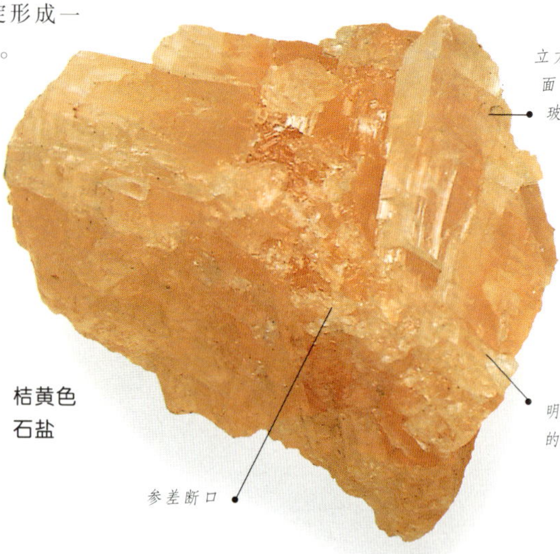


桔黄色石盐

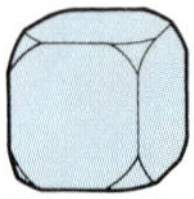

等轴晶系

| 比重 2.1~2.2 | 解理 完全立方体 | 断口 参差状至贝壳状 |
|---|---|---|

| 类别　卤化物 | 成分　KCl | 硬度　2 |
|---|---|---|

## 钾石盐(Sylvite)

晶体常呈立方体，偶尔呈八面体。还以皮壳状、块状或粒状集合体产出。颜色多变，无色、微白、灰色、微蓝色、黄色、紫色或红色，条痕白色。透明，玻璃光泽。

· **成因**　为一种蒸发岩矿物，由含盐溶液沉积而成。与石盐、石膏、杂卤石、光卤石和硬石膏共生。

· **鉴定特征**　像石盐一样溶于冷水。钾盐有股苦味。

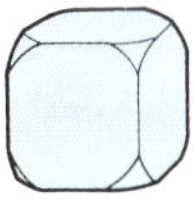

等轴晶系

| 比重　1.99 | 解理　完全立方体 | 断口　参差状 |
|---|---|---|

| 类别　卤化物 | 成分　AgCl | 硬度　2.5 |
|---|---|---|

## 氯银矿(Chlorargyrite)

晶体罕见，常以块状或薄片状，或皮壳状及蜡状层集合体产出。新鲜面无色，暴露后从灰色变为绿色或黄色，最后变成紫棕色。透明到几乎不透明，松脂到金刚光泽。

· **成因**　为银矿床氧化带的次生矿物。

· **鉴定特征**　常温下角银矿具可锻性；在蜡烛火焰下即可熔化。溶于氨水，却不溶于硝酸。

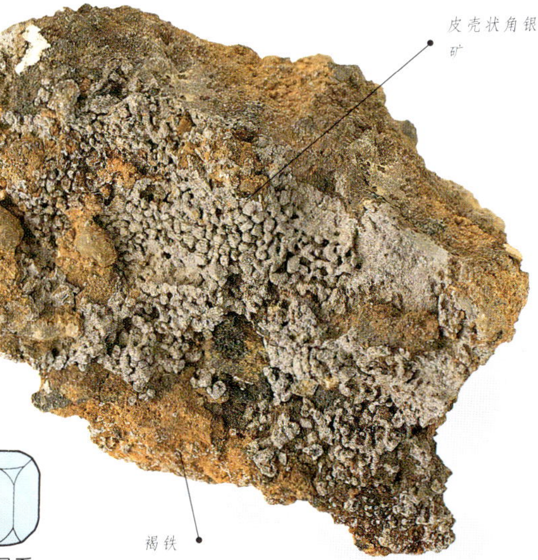


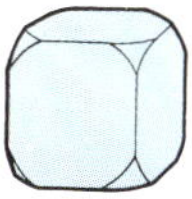

等轴晶系

| 比重　5~5.5 | 解理　无 | 断口　参差状至亚贝壳状 |
|---|---|---|

| 类别 卤化物 | 成分 $KMgCl_3 \cdot 6H_2O$ | 硬度 2 |
|---|---|---|

## 光卤石(Carnallite)

极少形成晶体。当以晶体产出时，形成假六方锥体，常呈粒状或致密状块体。光卤石为白色或无色，常因含细微氧化铁而呈红色。透明到半透明，具油脂光泽，表面闪光。

· **成因** 与沉积岩如泥灰岩、粘土岩、白云岩相关，形成于石膏、硬石膏、石盐(岩盐)和钾石盐连续沉积的蒸发岩地层中。

· **鉴定特征** 具苦味和咸味，并有潮解性。易熔化，火焰紫罗兰色，表明含钾。

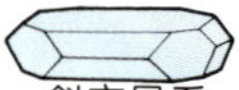

斜方晶系

| 比重 1.6 | 解理 无 | 断口 贝壳状 |
|---|---|---|

| 类别 卤化物 | 成分 $Na_3AlF_6$ | 硬度 2.5 |
|---|---|---|

## 冰晶石(Cryolite)

晶体呈假立方体和短柱状，常呈双晶，也以块状或粒状集合体产出。冰晶石无色、白色、浅黄色、棕色或浅红色，条痕白色。透明到半透明，玻璃或油脂光泽。

· **成因** 形成于岩浆岩，尤其是伟晶岩。

· **鉴定特征** 由于折射率与水相近，所以在水中几乎看不见。极易熔化，火焰黄色，表明含钠。熔化后形成的透明小球随温度的下降变得不透明。

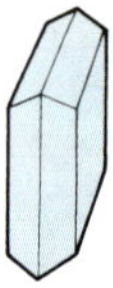

单斜晶系

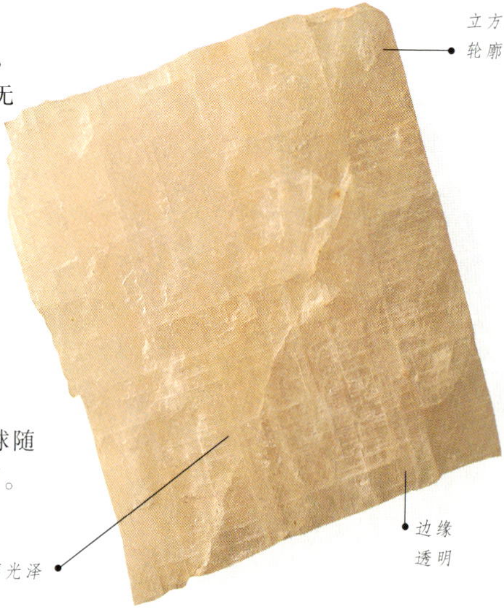


| 比重 2.97 | 解理 无 | 断口 参差状 |
|---|---|---|

| 类别 卤化物 | 成分 $Pb_{26}Ag_{10}Cu_{24}Cl_{62}(OH)_{48} \cdot 3H_2O$ | 硬度 3～3.5 |
|---|---|---|

## 方银铜氯铅矿(Boleite)

晶体呈立方体和八面体，属于等轴晶系(有些矿物学家把方银铜氯铅矿归入正方晶系)。暗靛蓝色，条痕呈略带绿色的蓝色。半透明的矿物，晶面显玻璃光泽，解理面呈珍珠光泽。

· **成因** 与数种其他次生铅矿物共生于铅矿床的淋溶带，包括方氯铜铅矿和水铜氯铅矿。

· **鉴定特征** 溶于硝酸，另一鉴定特征是易熔。

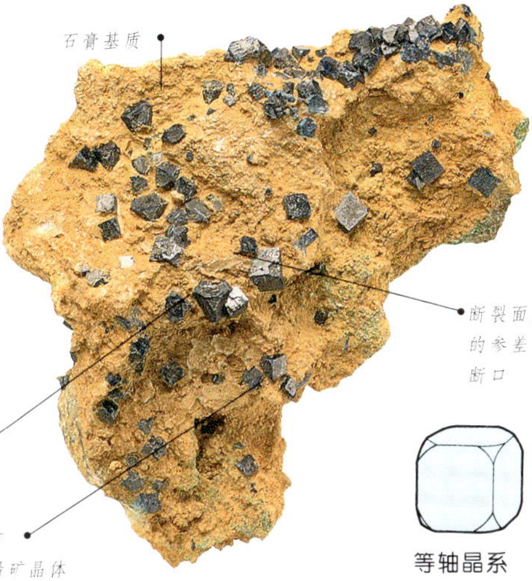


等轴晶系

| 比重 5.0～5.1 | 解理 完全 | 断口 参差状 |
|---|---|---|

| 类别 卤化物 | 成分 $Cu_2Cl(OH)_3$ | 硬度 3～3.5 |
|---|---|---|

## 氯铜矿(Atacamite)

晶体呈细长柱状或薄板状，常成双晶，晶面常有条纹。氯铜矿也以块状、纤维状和粒状集合体产出。鲜绿色到暗绿色，条痕苹果绿色。透明到半透明，玻璃到金刚光泽。

· **成因** 作为次生矿物与孔雀石、蓝铜矿和石英伴生于铜矿床的氧化带中，氯铜矿也形成于火山口周围。

· **鉴定特征** 溶于盐酸，但不起任何泡沫。易于火焰中即熔化，火焰呈蓝色。

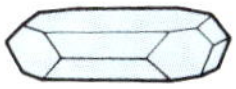

斜方晶系

| 比重 3.76 | 解理 完全 | 断口 贝壳状 |
|---|---|---|

| 类别 卤化物 | 成分 $CaF_2$ | 硬度 4 |
|---|---|---|

## 萤石(Fluorite)

晶体呈立方体和八面体，常成双晶，萤石也以块状、粒状和致密状集合体产出。颜色多变化，从紫色、绿色、无色、白色、黄色到粉红色、红色、蓝色和黑色等，条痕白色。透明到半透明，玻璃光泽。断开后，形成完全八面体解理，并在立方体晶体的各个角上形成三角面。

· **成因** 形成于热液矿脉中和温泉周围，是一种相当常见的矿物，与多种矿物伴生，如石英、方解石、白云石、方铅矿、黄铁矿、黄铜矿、闪锌矿、重晶石和多种其他热液矿脉矿物。

· **鉴定特征** 正如其名所示，在紫外光下发强烈萤光。

紫萤石

绿萤石

黄萤石

粉红萤石

蓝氟石

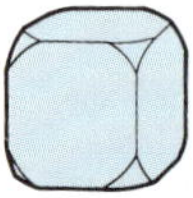

等轴晶系

| 比重 3.18 | 解理 完全八面体 | 断口 贝壳状 |
|---|---|---|

| 类别 卤化物 | 成分 $Pb_2CuCl_2(OH)_4$ | 硬度 2.5 |
|---|---|---|

## 羟铜铅盐(Diaboleite)

晶体板状，外形呈正方形，并且晶体通常很小，也以块状、粒状或薄板状集合体产出。颜色深蓝色，条痕浅蓝色。透明到半透明，新鲜面呈玻璃光泽。

· **成因** 形成于原矿的再次蚀变。可能是来自地表或地下的流体与原生岩石和矿物发生化学反应形成的，常与青铅矾、方银铜氯铅矿和白铅矿伴生。

· **鉴定特征** 在封闭试管内加热析出水分。

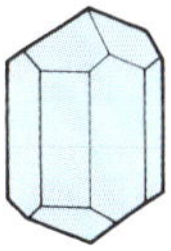

正方晶系

| 比重 5.42 | 解理 完全底面 | 断口 贝壳状 |
|---|---|---|

| 类别 卤化物 | 成分 $NaSr_3Al_3(F,OH)_{16}$ | 硬度 4～4.5 |
|---|---|---|

## 氟铝钠锶石(Jarlite)

有时形成极小的板状晶体，常见的为块状集合体。通常为白色，也可能呈棕色、灰色或无色，条痕白色。透明到半透明，晶面呈玻璃光泽。

· **成因** 较罕见的矿物，形成于两种主要的地质环境：与另一种卤化物冰晶石，产生于伟晶岩；也见于云母片岩。这些岩石形成于中变区域变质作用，并处于地壳下相当深的部位。在这种环境下，最可能与黄玉和萤石共生。

· **鉴定特征** 在封闭的试管内加热析出水分。

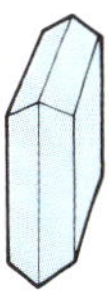

单斜晶系

| 比重 3.87 | 解理 未定 | 断口 参差状 |
|---|---|---|

# 氧化物和氢氧化物

元素与氧结合形成氧化物。最常见的例子是赤铁矿，一种氧化铁，即铁与氧(O)的化合物。氧化物形成多种矿物，产生于许多地质环境和大多数岩石类型中。赤铁矿、磁铁矿(另一种氧化铁)、锡石(氧化锡)和铬铁矿(氧化铬)都是重要的金属矿物。其他如刚玉(氧化铝)构成多种宝石，如红宝石和蓝宝石。氧化物的性质各不相同，各种宝石和金属矿石都很坚硬，比重也大。颜色变化不一，从红宝石的鲜红色，蓝宝石的蓝色，尖晶石(氧化铝镁)的红、绿、蓝色到磁铁矿的黑色。金属元素与水和羟基(OH)结合形成氢氧化物。较常见的例子是水镁石(氢氧化镁)。氢氧化物是氧化物与水经由化学反应而形成，通常硬度较低，如水镁石的硬度 2.5，三水铝石(氢氧化铝)的硬度 2.5~3.5。

| 类别 氧化物 | 成分 $MgAl_2O_4$ | 硬度 7.5~8 |
|---|---|---|

## 尖晶石(Spinel)

晶体呈八面体，有时呈立方体或十二面体，也成块状、粒状和致密状集合体。红色到绿色、蓝色、棕色和黑色，条痕白色。透明到不透明，玻璃光泽。

· **成因** 形成于各种变质岩，包括蛇纹岩、片麻岩和大理岩，也形成于基性岩。

· **鉴定特征** 特性之一是不熔。铬尖晶石是一种富含铬的变种；镁铁尖晶石是一种深色的，富含铁的尖晶石变种。

镁铁尖晶石

红宝石尖晶石

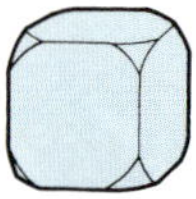
等轴晶系

| 比重 3.5~4.1 | 解理 无 | 断口 贝壳状至参差状 |
|---|---|---|

| 类别 氧化物 | 成分 ZnO | 硬度 4～4.5 |
|---|---|---|

## 红锌矿(Zincite)

晶体异极形锥状，不过很罕见，常以块状、粒状和叶片状集合体产出。暗红到桔黄色，条痕桔黄色。半透明到透明，半金刚光泽。

· **成因** 与方解石、硅锌矿、锌铁尖晶石、碱玄岩伴生于接触变质岩中。红锌矿是一种重要的锌矿，由于稀有而受到收藏家和矿物学家的珍爱。

· **鉴定特征** 溶于盐酸，不产生任何气泡。还具有萤光性，置于火焰中也不熔化。

三方/六方晶系

| 比重 5.68 | 解理 完全 | 断口 贝壳状 |
|---|---|---|

| 类别 氧化物 | 成分 $(Zn, Mn^{+2}, Fe^{+2})(Fe^{+3}, Mn^{+3})_2O_4$ | 硬度 5.5～6.5 |
|---|---|---|

## 锌铁尖晶石(Franklinite)

属于尖晶石类。晶体呈八面体，常具圆棱角。成粒状或块状集合体，颜色为黑色，条痕从红棕色到黑色。不透明，金属光泽。

· **成因** 形成于变质石灰岩和白云石的锌矿床中。与多种矿物如方解石、硅锌矿、红锌矿、蔷薇辉石和石榴子石伴生。

· **鉴定特征** 具弱磁性，在火焰中加热后变成强磁性，而且不熔。溶于盐酸，不生气泡。

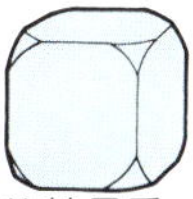

等轴晶系

| 比重 5.07～5.22 | 解理 无 | 断口 参差状至亚贝壳状 |
|---|---|---|

| 类别 氧化物 | 成分 $Cu_2O$ | 硬度 3.5～4 |
| --- | --- | --- |

## 赤铜矿(Cuprite)

晶体呈八面体、立方体和十二面体，双晶现象不常见。赤铜矿也以块状、致密状和粒状集合体产出。红色，条痕棕红色。半透明到透明，暴露于空气中变成半不透明。金刚光泽、半金属光泽或土状光泽。

**·成因** 分布广泛，形成于铜矿床的氧化带，与自然铜、孔雀石、蓝铜矿、辉铜矿和铁的氧化物伴生。

**·鉴定特征** 溶于硝酸和其他酸。可熔，火焰绿色。

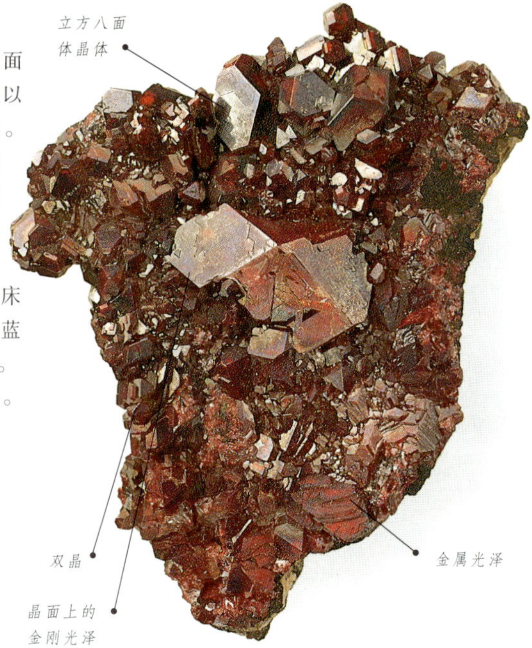


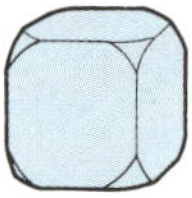

等轴晶系

| 比重 6.14 | 解理 不佳的八面体 | 断口 贝壳状至参差状 |
| --- | --- | --- |

| 类别 氧化物 | 成分 $FeCr_2O_4$ | 硬度 5.5 |
| --- | --- | --- |

## 铬铁矿(Chromite)

晶体呈八面体，不过较罕见。通常呈块状、粒状或结核状集合体。黑色到棕黑色，条痕深棕色。不透明，金属光泽。

**·成因** 形成于岩浆岩，尤其是超基性和基性岩；砂积矿床常含有铬铁矿。

**·鉴定特征** 不溶于任一种酸，具有弱磁性。置于火焰中不熔。

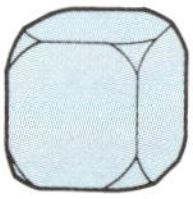

等轴晶系

| 比重 4.5～4.8 | 解理 无 | 断口 参差状 |
| --- | --- | --- |

| 别 氧化物 | 成分 $Fe_3O_4$ | 硬度 5.5～6.5 |
|---|---|---|

## 磁铁矿(Magnetite)

常见的氧化物矿物，晶体呈八面体和十二面体，也以块状和粒状集合体产出，颜色和条痕都是黑色。不透明，或呈金属光泽或暗淡光泽。

· **成因** 形成于岩浆岩中，也形成于矿脉和交代矿床。

· **鉴定特征** 正如其名所示，具有强磁性，能吸起铁屑，并使指南针偏转。

粒状磁铁矿

八面体晶体

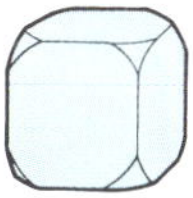
等轴晶系

| 比重 5.2 | 解理 无 | 断口 亚贝壳状至参差状 |
|---|---|---|

| 类别 氧化物 | 成分 $FeTiO_3$ | 硬度 5～6 |
|---|---|---|

## 钛铁矿(Ilmenite)

晶体常呈厚板状，有时成菱面体，常成双晶，也成片状、块状、致密状和粒状体。颜色黑或棕黑色，条痕从黑色至棕红色。不透明，金属光泽到暗淡光泽。

· **成因** 常以副矿物形成于许多岩浆岩，如伟晶岩，也形成于矿脉中。此外也见于黑砂中。

· **鉴定特征** 磨成粉末后溶于浓盐酸。冷却时具弱磁性。

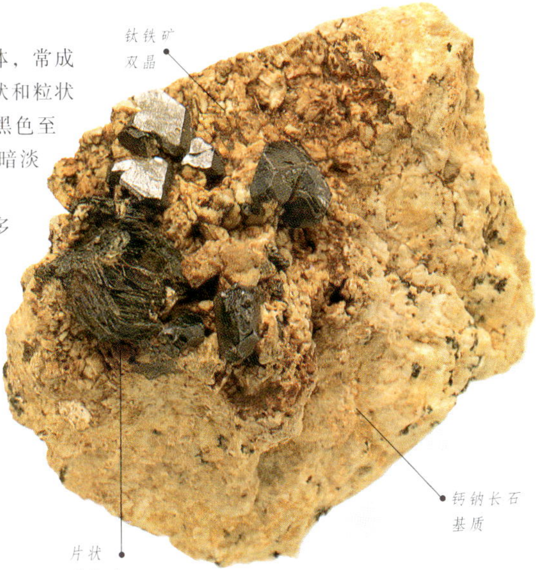


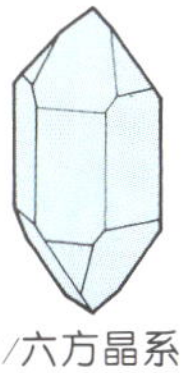
三方/六方晶系

| 比重 4.72 | 解理 无 | 断口 贝壳状至参差状 |
|---|---|---|

| 类别 氧化物 | 成分 $Fe_2O_3$ | 硬度 5～6 |
|---|---|---|

## 赤铁矿(Hematite)

晶体呈板状或菱面体，偶见柱状或锥状晶体。板状晶体形成玫瑰花式，称为铁玫瑰。多以块状、致密状、柱状、纤维状、肾状、葡萄状、钟乳状、叶片状和粒状集合体产生。赤铁矿形成肾状时，称为肾铁矿。颜色种类多，从浅棕色、鲜红色、血红色、棕红色到钢灰色和铁黑色，条痕棕红色。不透明，金属至暗淡光泽。

· **成因** 常形成于热液和交代矿床，也以副矿物形成于火成岩。

· **鉴定特征** 加热后变得有磁性。

六边形赤铁矿

肾铁矿

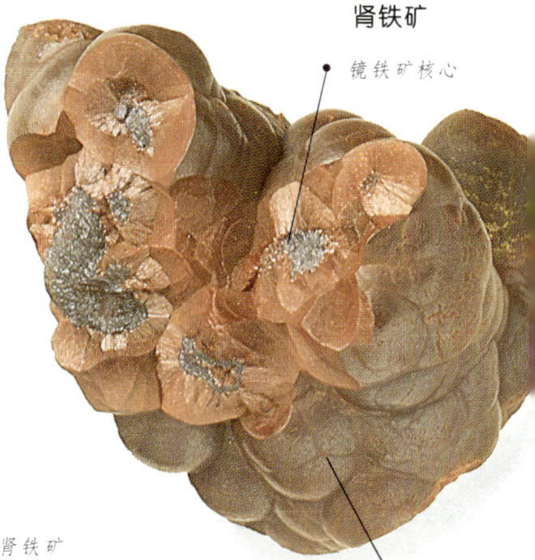


镜铁矿

块状赤铁矿

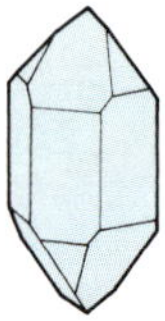

三方/六方晶系

| 比重 5.26 | 解理 无 | 断口 参差状至亚贝壳状 |
|---|---|---|

| 类别 氧化物 | 成分 $BeAl_2O_4$ | 硬度 8.5 |
|---|---|---|

## 金绿宝石(Chrysoberyl)

晶体呈板状或柱状，常成双晶，呈粒状和块状集合体。颜色变化很大，从绿色、黄色到浅棕色、灰色。其变种—变石在日光下呈绿色，在钨灯下呈红色。透明至半透明的矿物，玻璃光泽。

· 成因　形成于许多岩石中，如伟晶岩、片岩、片麻岩和大理岩。也产于冲积砂层中，因其有较强的硬度，能抵抗风化和侵蚀。

· 鉴定特征　不溶。

斜方晶系

| 比重 3.7～3.8 | 解理 清楚柱面 | 断口 贝壳状至参差状 |
|---|---|---|

| 类别 氧化物 | 成分 $SnO_2$ | 硬度 6～7 |
|---|---|---|

## 锡石(Cassiterite)

晶体呈短柱状、或细长柱状、或双锥状，及成块状、粒状、葡萄状和肾状集合体。典型的颜色从棕色到黑色，不过也可能呈浅黄色或无色，条痕白色、灰色或浅棕色。透明到几乎不透明。晶面上具有金刚光泽，断裂面呈油脂光泽。

· 成因　与石英、黄铜矿和电气石等矿物伴生于高温热液矿脉，也形成于某些接触变质岩中。

· 鉴定特征　不溶于任一种酸，不熔。

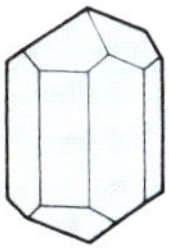

正方晶系

| 比重 7.0 | 解理 不佳 | 断口 亚贝壳状至参差状 |
|---|---|---|

| 类别 氧化物 | 成分 $Al_2O_3$ | 硬度 9 |
|---|---|---|

## 刚玉(Corundum)

晶体呈陡双锥状、柱状、板状或菱面体，也以块状和粒状集合体产出。颜色多变，但条痕仅呈白色。透明至半透明，玻璃光泽至金刚光泽。

· **成因** 形成于缺硅的岩浆岩和富含铝的变质岩中。

· **鉴定特征** 不溶。

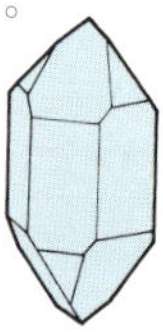

三方/六方晶系

| 比重 4.0～4.1 | 解理 无 | 断口 贝壳状至参差状 |
|---|---|---|

| 类别 氧化物 | 成分 $Al_2O_3$ | 硬度 9 |
|---|---|---|

## 红宝石(Ruby)

刚玉的变种之一，晶体呈双锥状、棱柱状、板状或菱面体状。红色，条痕白色。透明到半透明，玻璃至金刚光泽。

· **成因** 形成于岩浆岩与变质岩。由于硬度和密度较大，因此也产于河床砂砾层。

· **鉴定特征** 不溶于任何酸中。

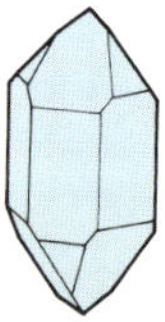

三方/六方晶系

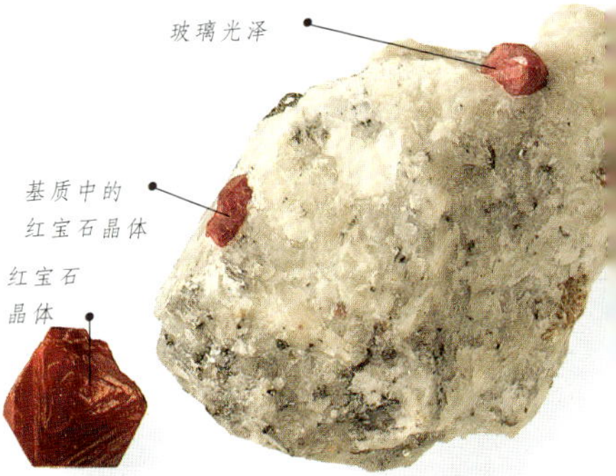


| 比重 4.0～4.1 | 解理 无 | 断口 贝壳状至参差状 |
|---|---|---|

| 类别 氧化物 | 成分 $Al_2O_3$ | 硬度 9 |
|---|---|---|

## 蓝宝石(Sapphire)

刚玉的蓝色变种。晶体呈双锥状、柱状、板状或菱面体。也成块状和粒状产出，条痕白色。透明至半透明，玻璃至金刚光泽。

· **成因** 形成于某些岩浆岩和变质岩中，也产于沉积冲积矿床。

· **鉴定特征** 不溶于任何酸，且不熔。

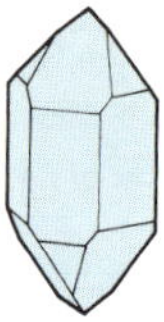

三方/六方晶系

| 比重 4.0～4.1 | 解理 无 | 断口 贝壳状至参差状 |
|---|---|---|

| 别 氧化物 | 成分 $MnO_2$ | 硬度 2~6.5 |
|---|---|---|

## 软锰矿(Pyrolusite)

晶体柱状，不过极罕见。常呈块状、致密状、柱状或纤维状集合体，树枝状皮壳也常见。黑色至深灰色，条痕黑色或蓝黑色。不透明，金属光泽至暗淡或土状光泽。

· 成因　在湖泊中和沼泽中形成沉积，也在深海底形成结核；是锰矿脉中的次生矿物。

· 鉴定特征　溶于盐酸。触摸后手上会留下烟色痕迹。

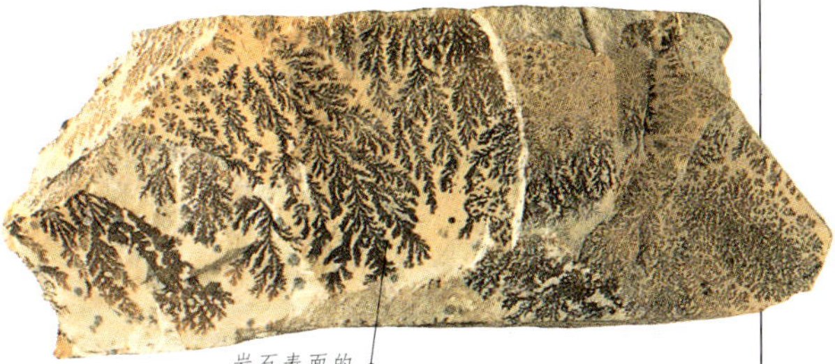

树枝状软锰矿

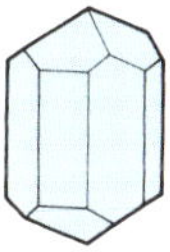
正方晶系

块状软锰矿

| 重 5.06 | 解理 完全 | 断口 参差状 |
|---|---|---|

| 别 氧化物 | 成分 $CaTiO_3$ | 硬度 5.5 |
|---|---|---|

## 钙钛矿(Perovskite)

晶体呈假立方体，并有平行于晶棱的条纹。也以肾状块体产出。黄色、琥珀色、深棕色或黑色，条痕从无色至浅灰色。透明到不透明，金属到金刚光泽。

· 成因　形成于某些基性和超基性岩、富含滑石和绿泥石的片岩以及一些大理岩中。钙钛矿也是某些岩石中的副矿物，副矿物不是主要的造岩矿物，其存在不影响岩石的基本化学性质或岩石的类别。

· 鉴定特征　只溶于热硫酸，并不熔。

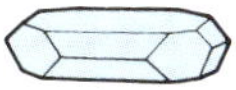
斜方晶系

| 重 4.01 | 解理 不完全 | 断口 亚贝壳状至参差状 |
|---|---|---|

| 类别 氧化物 | 成分 $TiO_2$ | 硬度 6~6.5 |
|---|---|---|

## 金红石(Rutile)

与板钛矿和锐钛矿一起形成三型系列。晶体柱状，常有条纹，也以纤细的针状晶体形成于石英中(网状金红石)，常成双晶。有时呈块状集合体。红棕色、红色、黄色或黑色，条痕从浅棕至浅黄色。透明到不透明，半金属至金刚光泽。

· **成因** 以副矿物的形式产于许多岩浆岩与片岩和片麻岩。有时会在石英、刚玉及其他透明主矿物中形成针状包裹体(“猫眼”和“星芒”)。

· **鉴定特征** 不溶于任何酸。

网状石英

块状金红石

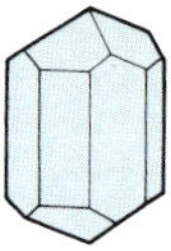
正方晶系

| 比重 4.23 | 解理 清楚 | 断口 贝壳状至参差状 |
|---|---|---|

| 类别 氧化物 | 成分 $TiO_2$ | 硬度 5.5~6 |
|---|---|---|

## 板钛矿(Brookite)

晶体呈板状，并有纵向条纹，也呈柱状晶体。棕色、红棕色或棕黑色，条痕白色、灰色或浅黄色。透明至不透明，金刚至半金属光泽。

· **成因** 产于多种地质环境。形成于某些变质岩中，尤其是穿过高度变质的片岩和片麻岩的岩脉。常与石英、金红石和长石伴生。原岩被侵蚀并重新沉积后，也以碎屑矿物的形式形成于沉积岩中。

· **鉴定特征** 不溶于任何酸，且不熔。

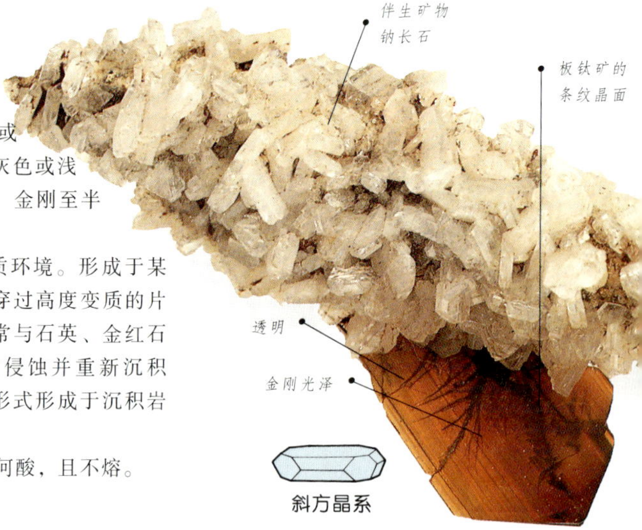


斜方晶系

| 比重 4.1~4.2 | 解理 不佳 | 断口 亚贝壳状至参差状 |
|---|---|---|

| 别 氧化物 | 成分 $TiO_2$ | 硬度 5.5～6 |
|---|---|---|

## 兑钛矿(Anatase)

晶体锥状，通常具条纹，深变变质的情况下晶体也可呈板状。棕色、深蓝色或黑色，条痕无色、白色或浅黄色。透明到几乎不透明，金刚到半金属光泽。

· 成因　这种二氧化钛特殊形态形成于某些变质岩，尤其是片岩和片麻岩。也以副矿物形成于某些岩浆岩，如闪长岩和花岗岩。当锐钛矿从原岩风化搬运并再沉积时，会出现于砂积矿床。

· 鉴定特征　不溶于任一种酸中。

斜方晶系

| 重 3.82～3.97 | 解理 完全底面 | 断口 亚贝壳状 |
|---|---|---|

| 别 氧化物 | 成分 $UO_2$ | 硬度 5～6 |
|---|---|---|

## 沥青铀矿(晶质铀矿)(Uraninite)

晶体呈立方体、立方八面体、八面体或十二面体，常以块状、葡萄状或粒状集合体产出。颜色和条痕从黑色到棕黑色，或者是灰黑色。不透明，半金属、油脂、暗淡或沥青光泽。

· 成因　形成于热液矿脉，也产于沉积岩，如砂岩和砾岩中，以及某些岩浆岩，如伟晶岩和花岗岩。

· 鉴定特征　具有强放射性。不熔。不溶于盐酸，但在硝酸中会慢慢溶解。

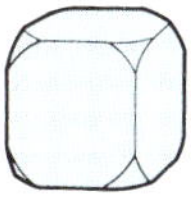

等轴晶系

| 重 6.5～10.0 | 解理 不清楚 | 断口 贝壳状至参差状 |
|---|---|---|

| 类别 氧化物 | 成分 $SiO_2$ | 硬度 7 |
|---|---|---|

## 石英(Quartz)

是最常见的矿物之一。晶体为端部呈菱面体的六方柱状，或为锥状，石英的晶面通常具有条纹，并且成双晶或歪晶。此外还以块状、粒状、结核状、钟乳状和隐晶质等集合体产出。颜色富于变化，白色、灰色、红色、紫色、粉红色、黄色、绿色、棕色和黑色，常无色透明。它还是一系次级宝石的来源，其中多种示如图，条痕白色。透明到半透明，新鲜呈面玻璃光泽。

**· 成因** 常形成于岩浆岩、变质岩和沉积岩，也常见于含金属矿物的矿脉之中。

**· 鉴定特征** 不溶，除非放入氢氟酸中。

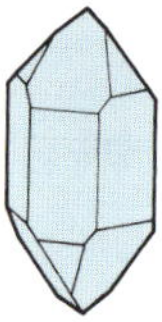

三方/六方晶系

烟石英

蔷薇石英

紫水晶

| 比重 2.65 | 解理 无 | 断口 贝壳状至参差状 |
|---|---|---|

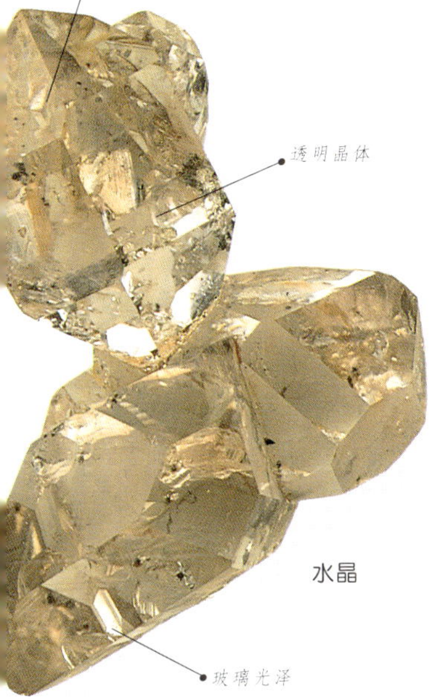


水晶

乳石英

黄晶

| 类别　氧化物 | 成分　$SiO_2$ | 硬度　7 |
|---|---|---|

## 玉髓(Chalcedony)

是石英的隐晶质异种，常以钟乳状或葡萄状块体产出。颜色多变化，白色、蓝色、红色、绿色、棕色或黑色。其变种包括不透明的碧玉，玛瑙，具有同心各色条带；苔纹玛瑙，带有深色树枝状花纹；绿玉髓，一种绿色变种；以及缟玛瑙，有着平行的条带。光玉髓为红色到红棕色；而肉红玉髓则从浅棕色到深棕色。玉髓条痕白色，透明到半透明或不透明，玻璃到蜡状光泽。

· **成因**　形成于多种岩石的裂隙中，尤其是熔岩。大多数玉髓是由富含硅的溶液，在较低的温度下沉积而成。此外，蛋白石脱水也可成。

· **鉴定特征**　以较高的比重可与蛋白石区分。

葡萄状玉髓

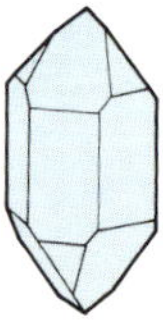
三方/六方晶系

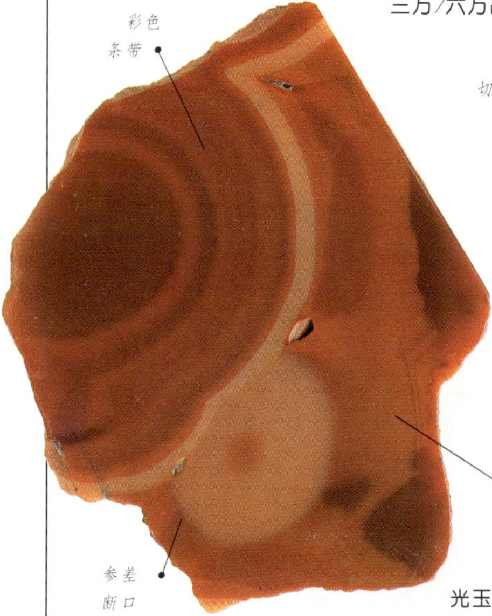

光玉髓

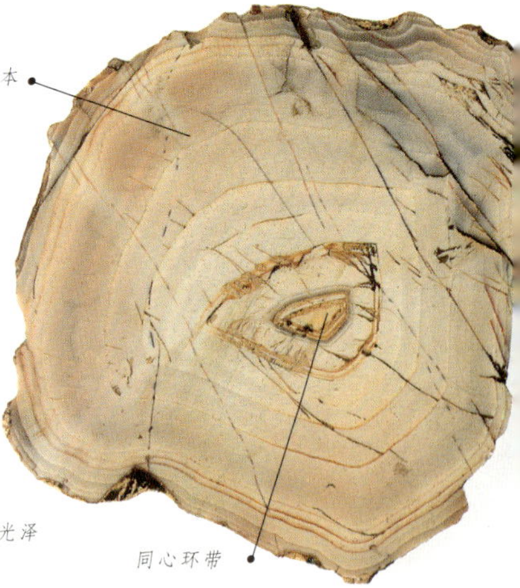

堡垒玛瑙

| 比重　2.65 | 解理　无 | 断口　贝壳状 |
|---|---|---|

绿玉髓

碧玉

缟玛瑙

| 类别 氧化物 | 成分 $(Fe,Mn)(Nb,Ta)_2O_6$ | 硬度 6～6.5 |
|---|---|---|

## 铌铁矿(Columbite)

与钽铁矿同族。晶体板状或棱柱状，常成双晶，也以块状集合体产出。灰黑到棕黑色，脱色后有彩晕，条痕暗红到黑色。该族矿物半透明到不透明，半金属到松脂光泽。

· **成因** 形成于花岗伟晶岩。

· **鉴定特征** 比重随钽含量而增大。

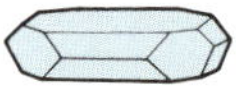
斜方晶系

| 比重 5.1～8.2 | 解理 清楚 | 断口 亚贝壳状至参差状 |
|---|---|---|

| 类别 氧化物 | 成分 $(Y,Ce,U,Fe)_3(Nb,Ta,Ti)_5O_{15}$ | 硬度 5～6 |
|---|---|---|

## 铌钇矿(Samarskite)

晶体呈柱状，横截面矩形，以块状或致密状集合体产出。黑色或浅棕色，条痕待定。半透明到不透明。新鲜面呈松脂、玻璃或半金属光泽。

· **成因** 形成于花岗伟晶岩。

· **鉴定特征** 溶于热酸，具有放射性。

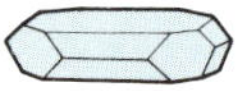
斜方晶系

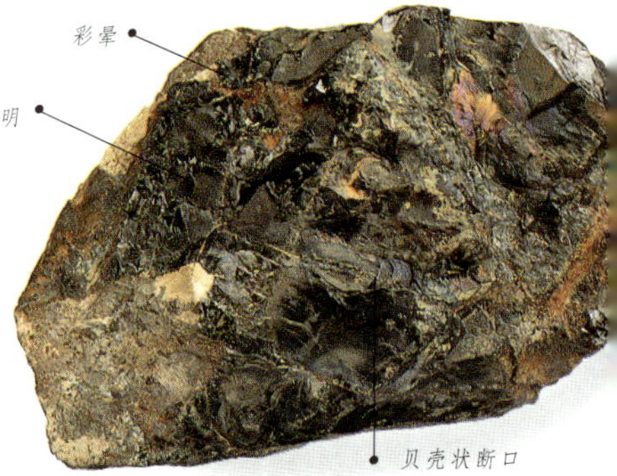


| 比重 5.15～5.69 | 解理 不清楚 | 断口 贝壳状 |
|---|---|---|

| 类别 氧化物 | 成分 $Mn_3O_4$ | 硬度 5.5 |
|---|---|---|

## 黑锰矿(Hausmannite)

晶体呈假八面体和锥状，常成双晶，另外也以粒状块体产出。棕黑色，条痕棕色。一般不透明，除非很薄的碎片才半透明。半金属光泽。

· **成因** 形成于接触变质岩石，也产于热液矿脉。

· **鉴定特征** 溶于浓盐酸。

正方晶系

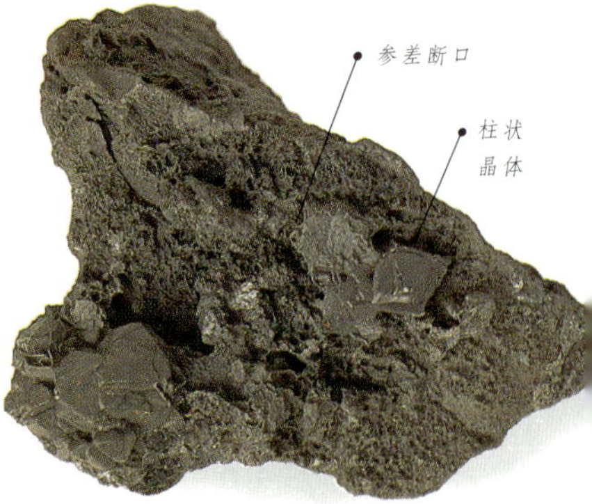


| 比重 4.84 | 解理 良好 | 断口 参差状 |
|---|---|---|

| 类别 氧化物 | 成分 氧化物和氢氧化物 | 硬度 软 |
|---|---|---|

## 锰土(Wad)

严格地说，锰土不是矿物，而是几种氧化物和氢氧化物，尤其是锰的混合物，一般含软锰矿和硬锰矿。非晶质，以肾脏状、树枝形、皮壳状或块状集合体产出。颜色通常为黯淡的黑色，也呈铅灰色、浅蓝色或棕黑色，条痕深棕色或棕黑色。不透明，暗淡或土状光泽。

· 成因　与锰矿形成于沉积环境中。

· 鉴定特征　在密封的试管内加热释出水分。

| 比重 2.8～4.4 | 解理 无 | 断口 参差状 |
|---|---|---|

| 类别 氢氧化物 | 成分 $(Ba,H_2O)(Mn^{+4},Mn^{+3})_5O_{10}$ | 硬度 5～6 |
|---|---|---|

## 杂硬锰矿(Romanechite)

过去，硬锰矿是单种矿物的名称，然而，最近的研究发现硬锰矿其实是杂硬锰矿的一种非晶质种类。以块状、葡萄状、肾状、钟乳状和土状集合体产出。黑色到深灰色，条痕黑色或棕黑色，并且闪闪发光。不透明，具半金属光泽。

· 成因　由其他矿物，尤其是富含锰的硅酸盐类和碳酸盐类的转化作用而形成。杂硬锰矿是一种常见的矿物，形成于石灰石被其他物质交代后的结核之中。

· 鉴定特征　溶于盐酸，并释放出氯气。在密封的试管内加热释放出水分。

块状杂硬锰矿

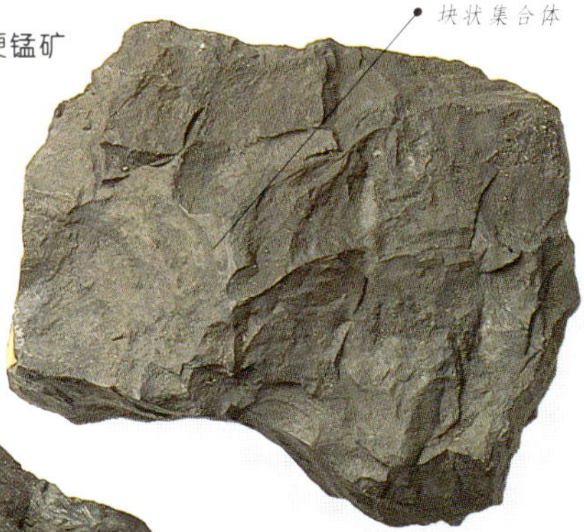

葡萄状杂硬锰矿

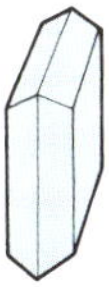

单斜晶系

| 比重 6.4 | 解理 未定 | 断口 参差状 |
|---|---|---|

| 类别 氧化物 | 成分 烧绿石$(Na,Ca,U)_2(Nb,Ta,Ti)_2O_6(OH,F)$ | 硬度 5~5.5 |
|---|---|---|

## 烧绿石—细晶石(Pyrochlore – Microlite)

此系列矿物的晶体为八面体，有时成双晶，也呈粒状和不规则块状集合体。棕色、红棕色或黑色，条痕从浅黄到棕色。半透明到不透明，玻璃到松脂光泽。

· **成因** 形成于伟晶岩与碳酸岩中。烧绿石—细晶石也以副矿物出现于霞石正长岩中。

· **鉴定特征** 细晶石不含铀(U)、铌(Nb)和钛(Ti)。此系列矿物具有不熔性。溶于盐酸，不过很难溶解。当钍和铀在化学结构上取代钙和钠时，该矿物即变得具有放射性。

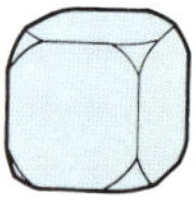
等轴晶系

| 比重 4.3~5.7 | 解理 清楚 | 断口 亚贝壳状至参差状 |
|---|---|---|

| 类别 氢氧化物 | 成分 $Al(OH)_3$ | 硬度 2.5~3.5 |
|---|---|---|

## 三水铝石(Gibbsite)

晶体呈假六方板状，也以块状、皮壳状产出。白色、灰色、浅绿色、浅粉红色或浅红色，条痕待定。透明到半透明，玻璃到珍珠光泽。

· **成因** 形成于热液矿脉，为铝矿物蚀变的产物。

· **鉴定特征** 贴近三水铝石时，会闻到湿粘土味。

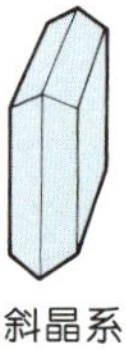
单斜晶系

| 比重 2.4 | 解理 完全 | 断口 参差状 |
|---|---|---|

| 类别 氧化物 | 成分 $SiO_2nH_2O$ | 硬度 5.5~6.5 |
| --- | --- | --- |

## 蛋白石(Opal)

非晶质矿物，集合体多变，呈块状、葡萄状、肾状、钟乳状、球状、瘤状及结核状。贵蛋白石呈乳白色或黑色，并带红、蓝、黄色的斑斓色彩。随着矿物中所含水温的增高，颜色发生变化，比如，用手温热贵蛋白石，会变得非常鲜艳。火蛋白石呈橙色或浅红色，斑斓色彩或有或无。普通蛋白石呈灰色、黑色或绿色，不具光彩。条痕白色。透明到不透明，玻璃到松脂、蜡状或珍珠光泽，但玻璃光泽最为常见。

· **成因** 形成于低温富含硅质的水中，尤其在温泉周围。不过，蛋白石几乎可以在任何一种地质环境下形成。

· **鉴定特征** 常在紫外光下发萤光，并且不溶于任何酸。加热后分解，并随水分子的脱离变成石英。不管蛋白石在空气中暴露的时间是长是短，矿物构造都会变得脆弱，这是水分的散失和断口被填充所致。

贵蛋白石

木蛋白石
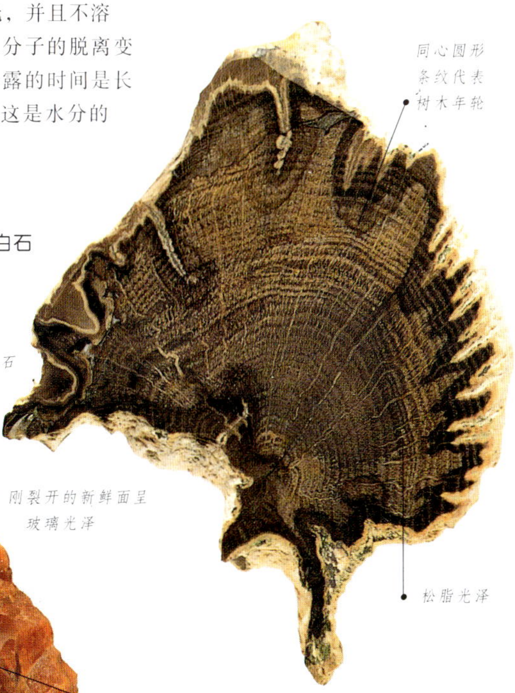

火蛋白石

| 比重 1.9~2.3 | 解理 无 | 断口 贝壳状 |
| --- | --- | --- |

| 类别 氢氧化物 | 成分 $Mg(OH)_2$ | 硬度 2.5 |
|---|---|---|

## 水镁石(Brucite)

晶体呈宽阔板状，常呈块状、叶片状、纤维状(纤水滑石)和粒状集合体。白色、淡绿色、灰色、浅蓝色，当含锰时，呈黄到棕色。水镁石透明，蜡状、玻璃或珍珠光泽(纤维状的变种呈丝绢光泽)。小心地剥开此矿物会从完全解理面得柔软、无弹性的薄片。

· **成因** 形成于变质石灰岩、片麻岩和蛇纹岩中。

· **鉴定特征** 溶于盐酸，不发泡，并不熔。

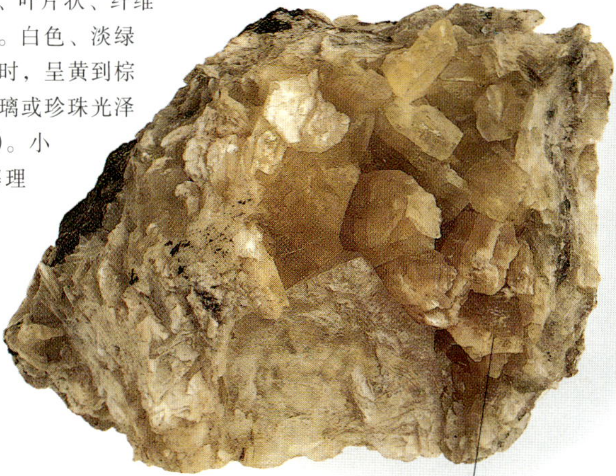


结晶水镁石

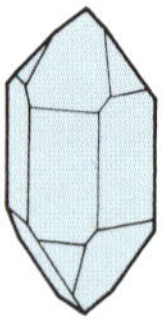

三方/
六方晶系

纤水滑石

| 比重 2.38～2.40 | 解理 完全 | 断口 参差状 |
|---|---|---|

| 类别 氢氧化物 | 成分 FeO(OH) | 硬度 5～5.5 |
|---|---|---|

## 针铁矿(Goethite)

有时会形成具纵向条纹的柱状晶体，常见的是块状、葡萄状、钟乳状和土状集合体。黑棕色，或从浅红色到黄棕色，条痕从橙色到浅棕色。不透明，晶面上呈金刚光泽，其他为暗淡光泽。

· **成因** 针铁矿形成于铁矿床氧化带。

· **测试** 加热后带磁性。

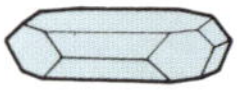

斜方晶系

| 比重 3.3～4.3 | 解理 完全 | 断口 参差状 |
|---|---|---|

| 类别 氢氧化物 | 成分 $FeO(OH) \cdot nH_2O$ | 硬度 5~5.5 |
| --- | --- | --- |

## 褐铁矿(Limonite)

不形成晶体，是一种非晶质物物，以土块状、结核状、乳头状和钟乳状集合体产出，并有放射状结构，常以黄铁矿和其他铁矿物的假像出现。黄色、棕黄色、棕色和浅黑色，条痕黄棕色。半透明或半不透明，玻璃、半金属、丝质或暗淡光泽。

· **成因** 在铁矿床的氧化带中以次生矿物的形式产出，也由沉积作用形成于海洋、淡水和沼泽中。

· **鉴定特征** 放在密封的试管内加热释放出水分，在酸中缓慢溶解。

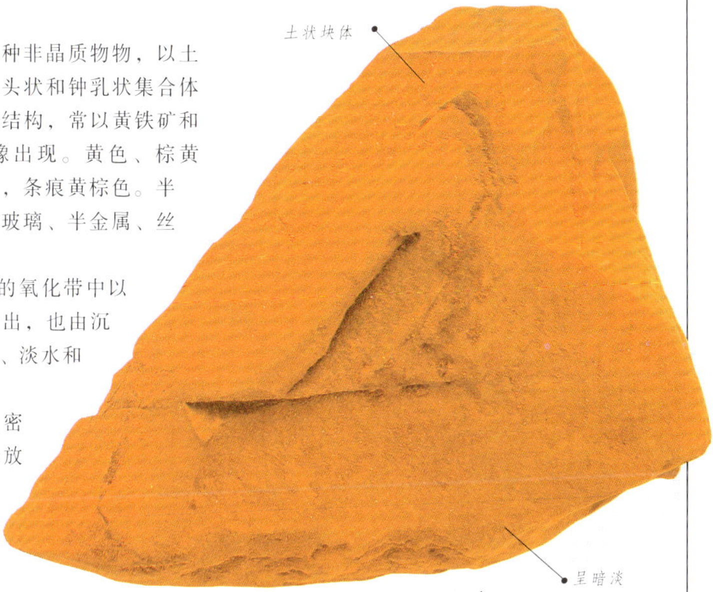


| 比重 2.7~4.3 | 解理 无 | 断口 参差状 |
| --- | --- | --- |

| 类别 氢氧化物 | 成分 $MnO(OH)$ | 硬度 4 |
| --- | --- | --- |

## 水锰矿(Manganite)

晶体呈柱面上具纵纹的柱状，并常聚集成束。常结为双晶，也以块状、纤维状、柱状、粒状、结核状和钟乳石状集合体产出。深灰色到黑色，条痕从红棕色到黑色。不透明，半金属光泽。

· **成因** 形成于低温热液矿脉，也形成于浅海堆积、湖泊和沼泽。有些水锰矿是天水在地下循环流动中沉积形成，也部分的在地表及地下流体循环中转变成软锰矿，而晶体形态不变。

· **鉴定特征** 溶于盐酸，并释放出氯。

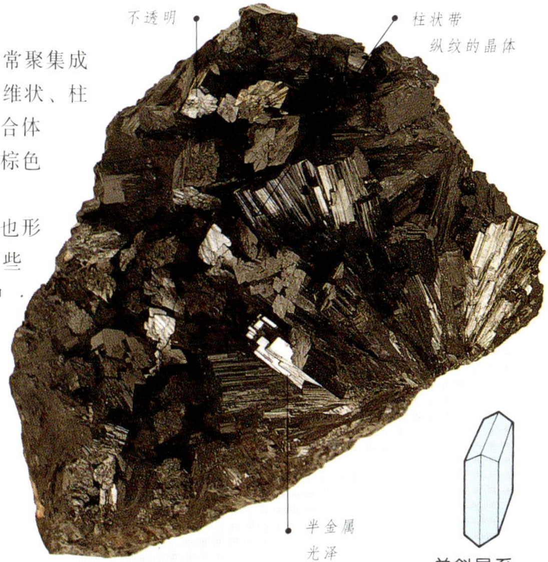


单斜晶系

| 比重 4.3 | 解理 完全 | 断口 参差状 |
| --- | --- | --- |

| 类别 氢氧化物 | 成分 FeO(OH)和 $Al_2O_3 2H_2O$ | 硬度 1～3 |
|---|---|---|

## 铝土(Bauxite)

是几种矿物的混合体，成分包括水合氧化铝、三水铝石、勃姆铝矿、硬水铝石和铁氧化物。严格地说，铝土为岩石，不过有时也划归矿物。其多变的成分使其性质多变。常呈块状、结核状、鲕状或豆石状产出。颜色变化也很大，从白色到浅黄色或红色、红棕色，正常情况下条痕白色。暗淡或土状光泽，不透明。

· **成因** 铝硅酸盐岩风化和变质后形成铝土矿，这种情况发生在热带气候条件下，当雨水将硅酸盐从岩石淋滤后，残留下铝矿物。

· **鉴定特征** 贴近铝土，会闻到一股湿粘土味。不熔，亦不溶。

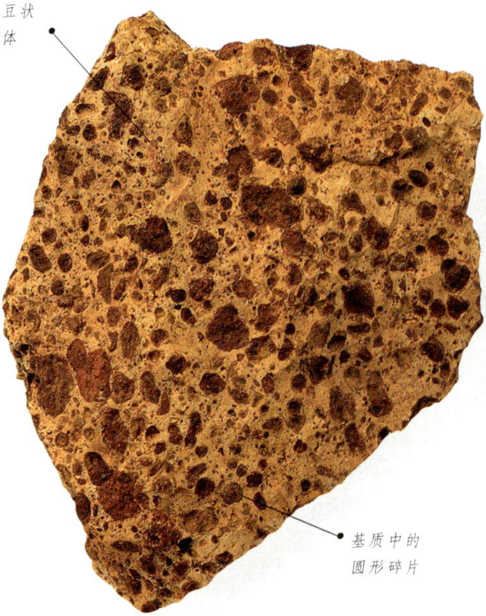


| 比重 2.3～2.7 | 解理 无 | 断口 参差状 |
|---|---|---|

| 类别 氢氧化物 | 成分 AlO(OH) | 硬度 6.5～7 |
|---|---|---|

## 硬水铝石(Diaspore)

晶体板状、针状或片状，也以块状、叶片状、鳞状或钟乳状集合体产出常呈浸染和粒状。白色、无色、浅灰色、浅黄色、浅绿色、棕色、紫色或粉红色，条痕白色。透明到半透明，玻璃光泽，不过在解理面上呈珍珠光泽。

· **成因** 形成于蚀变的岩浆岩和大理岩中。与磁铁矿、尖晶石、白云石、绿泥石和刚玉等多种矿物共生。当与铝土和含铝粘土矿物共生时，也见于粘土沉积。

· **鉴定特征** 不溶和不熔。

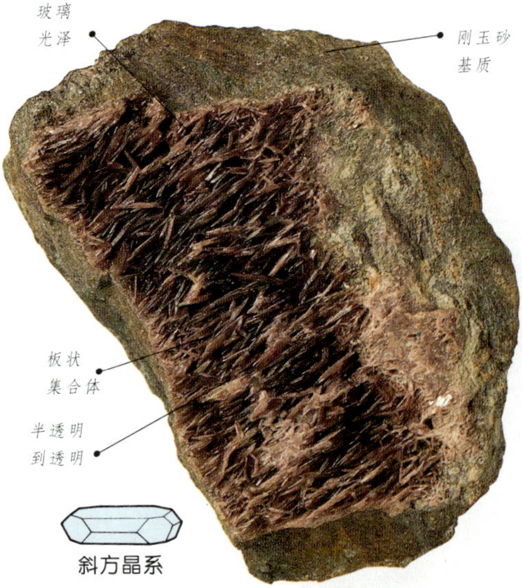


斜方晶系

| 比重 3.3～3.5 | 解理 完全 | 断口 贝壳状 |
|---|---|---|

| 别 氢氧化物 | 成分 $FeO(OH)$ | 硬度 5 |
| --- | --- | --- |

## 纤铁矿(Lepidocrocite)

晶体扁平板状，常见的为块状或纤维状集合体。深红色到红棕色，条痕桔黄色。是一种透明的矿物，半金属光泽。

· **成因** 常与针铁矿形成次生矿。

· **鉴定特征** 加热后具有强磁性。在盐酸中缓慢地溶解，在硝酸中快速溶解。

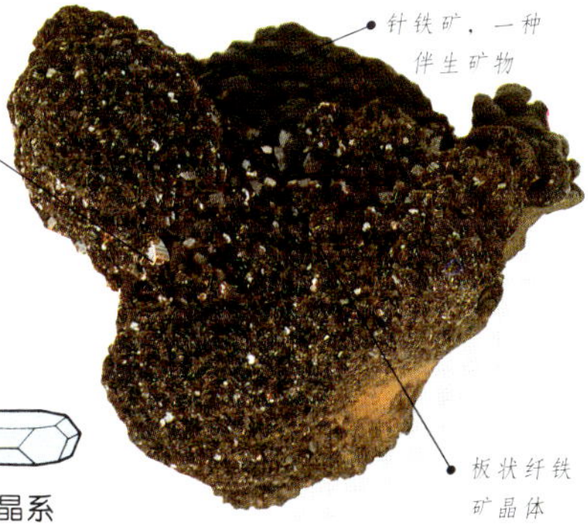


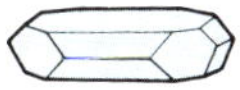

斜方晶系

| 重 3.9 | 解理 完全 | 断口 参差状 |
| --- | --- | --- |

| 别 氧化物 | 成分 $WO_3 \cdot H_2O$ | 硬度 1～2.5 |
| --- | --- | --- |

## 钨华(Tungstite)

晶体极小，板状，不过很罕见。常以块状、土状或粉状集合体产出。黄色或黄绿，条痕黄色。透明到半透明，土状或松脂光泽。

· **成因** 形成于原生钨矿风化。

· **鉴定特征** 溶于碱性溶液，但不溶酸。

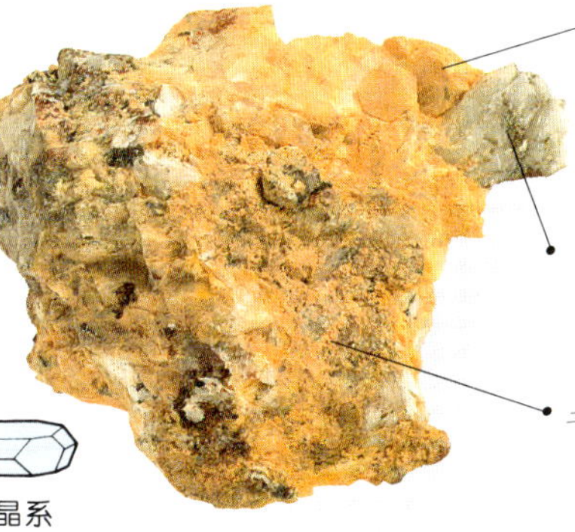


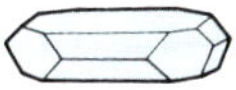

斜方晶系

| 重 5.5 | 解理 完全 | 断口 参差状 |
| --- | --- | --- |

| 别 氢氧化物 | 成分 $Sb^{+3}Sb_2^{+5}O_6(OH)$ | 硬度 4～5.5 |
| --- | --- | --- |

## 黄锑华(Stibiconite)

晶体会依照它所替代的原矿形态成为柱形。常见的集合体有块状、致密状或葡萄状，也以皮壳状产出。白色到浅黄色，因所含杂质的不同也呈橙色、棕色，灰色或黑色，透明到半透明，珍珠到土状光泽。

· **成因** 由辉锑矿风化而成。

· **鉴定特征** 在密封的试管内加热释放出水分。

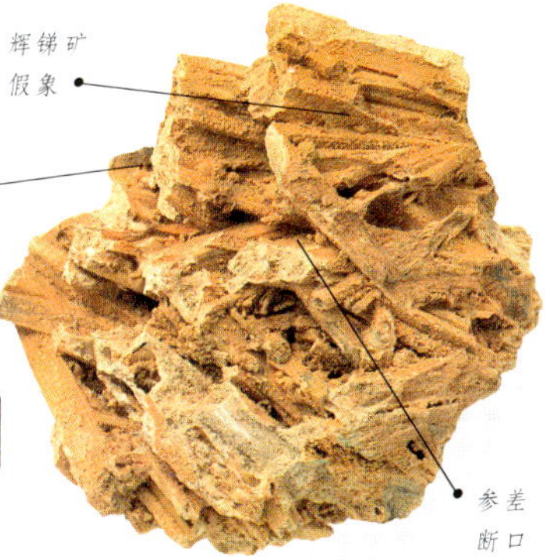


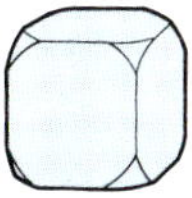

等轴晶系

| 重 3.3～5.5 | 解理 未定 | 断口 参差状 |
| --- | --- | --- |

# 碳酸盐、硝酸盐和硼酸盐

碳酸盐是由一种或多种金属或半金属元素与碳酸根$(CO_3)^{-2}$结合而成的化合物。方解石是最常见的碳酸盐，由钙与碳酸根化合而成。当钡替代钙时，形成毒重石，当锰替代钙时，形成菱锰矿。碳酸盐通常形成发育良好的菱面体晶形，并易溶于盐酸，颜色一般鲜明。硝酸盐是由一种或多种金属元素与硝酸根$(NO_2)^{-1}$结合而成的化合物(如钠硝石)。同属于这一系列的硼酸盐是由金属元素与硼酸根$(BO_3)^{-3}$结合而成的化合物(如钠钙解石、硬硼钙石)。

| 类别 碳酸盐 | 成分 $CaCO_3$ | 硬度 3.5～4 |
|---|---|---|

## 文石(Aragonite)

又称霰石，晶体呈柱状和细长柱状。常双晶，如果双晶交错生长，则形成假六方对称。集合体呈柱状、钟乳状、纤维状、放射状，珊瑚状，霰石华俗称“铁花”。文石呈白色、无色、灰色、浅黄色、绿色、蓝色、紫罗兰色、浅红色或棕色，条痕白色。透明到半透明，玻璃光泽。

· **成因**　广泛形成于变质岩和沉积岩中，也形成于石灰岩区域的洞穴、岩脉中，以及温泉周围。

· **鉴定特征**　溶于冷稀盐酸，并生气泡，紫外光下发萤光。

铁花文石

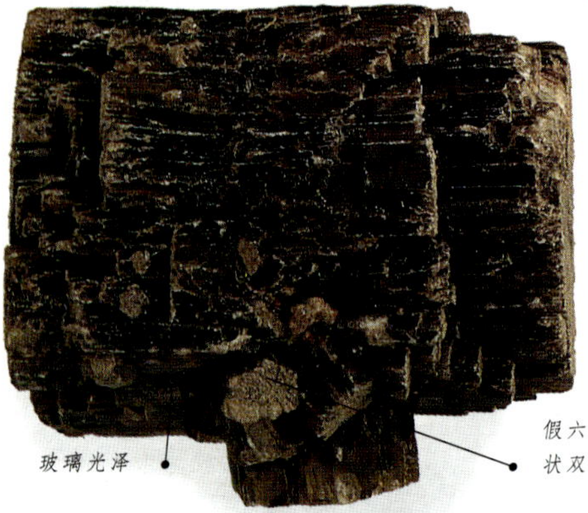


假六面体文石

斜方晶系

| 比重 2.94～2.95 | 解理 清楚轴面 | 断口 贝壳状 |
|---|---|---|

| 类别 碳酸盐 | 成分 $CaCO_3$ | 硬度 3 |
|---|---|---|

## 方解石(Calcite)

晶体呈菱面体和偏三角面体，其聚形呈钉头状和犬牙状。冰洲石的菱面体晶体具双折射性，常成双晶。方解石还以块状、粒状、纤维状和钟乳状集合体产出。白色、无色、灰色、红色、棕色、绿色和黑色，条痕白色到灰色。透明到半透明，玻璃到珍珠或黯淡光泽。

· **成因** 形成于许多岩石中，石灰岩和大理岩主要由方解石组成。

· **鉴定特征** 溶于冷的稀盐酸，发泡。

偏三角面体方解石

冰洲石

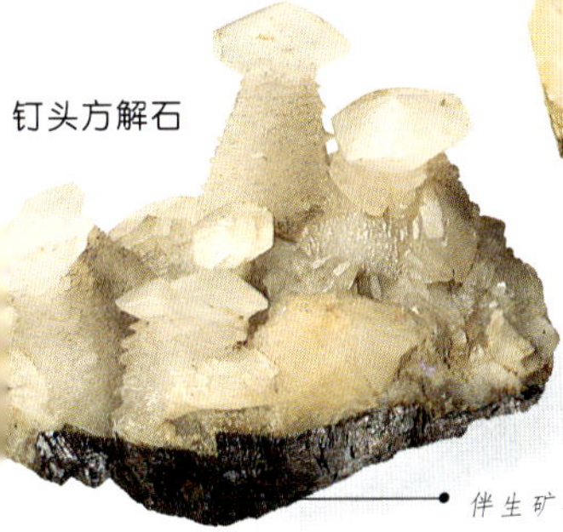


钉头方解石

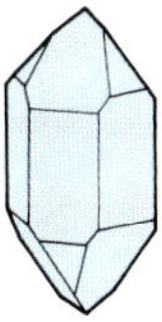

三方/六方晶系

| 比重 2.71 | 解理 完全 | 断口 亚贝壳状 |
|---|---|---|

| 类别 碳酸盐 | 成分 $BaCa(CO_3)_2$ | 硬度 4 |
|---|---|---|

## 斜钡钙石(Barytocalcite)

晶体呈具条纹的柱状，集合体块状。白色、浅黄色、灰色或浅绿色。透明到半透明，玻璃或松脂光泽。

· **成因** 形成于热液矿脉——即被具化学活性流体侵入的岩层断层或节理。这种岩脉可能源于与花岗岩浆和地下深处圈闭于海洋沉积中的卤水有关的热液，携带的化学元素即形成矿物。

· **鉴定特征** 与盐酸作用发生气泡。

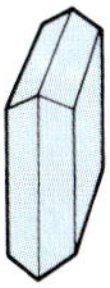

单斜晶系

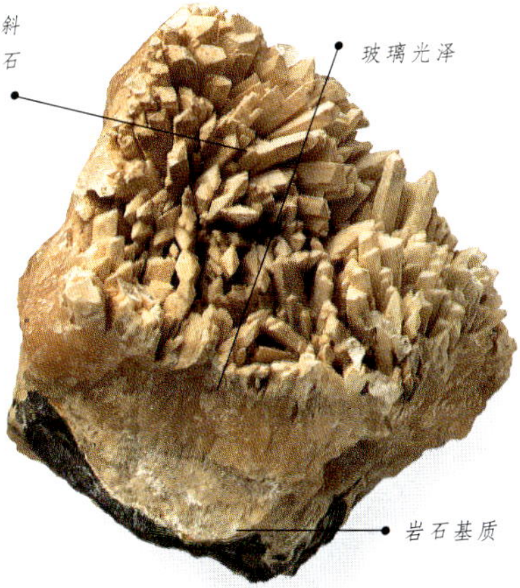


| 比重 3.66 ~ 3.71 | 解理 完全 | 断口 亚贝壳状至参差状 |
|---|---|---|

| 类别 碳酸盐 | 成分 $MnCO_3$ | 硬度 3.5～4 |
|---|---|---|

## 菱锰矿(Rhodochrosite)

有时形成菱面体、偏三角面体、柱状或板状晶体，不过菱锰矿常以块状、粒状、钟乳状、球状、结核状或葡萄状集合体产出。典型的颜色是粉红色至红色，但也呈棕色、桔黄色或浅黄色，条痕白色。透明到半透明，玻璃至珍珠光泽。

- **成因** 形成于热液矿脉和蚀变的锰矿床中。
- **鉴定特征** 溶于温盐酸，并发泡。

菱锰矿晶体

带状菱锰矿

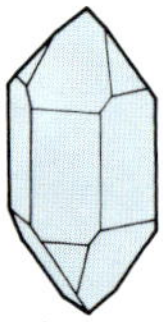

三方/六方晶体

| 比重 3.7 | 解理 完全菱面体 | 断口 参差状 |
|---|---|---|

| 类别 碳酸盐 | 成分 $CaMg(CO_3)_2$ | 硬度 3.5～4 |
|---|---|---|

## 白云石(Dolomite)

晶体呈菱面体，常有马鞍状的弯曲晶面，集合体常以块状和粒状产出。无色、白色、灰色、粉红色或棕色，条痕白色。透明到半透明，玻璃至珍珠光泽。

- **成因** 形成于热液矿脉和含镁石灰岩。
- **鉴定特征** 缓慢地溶于冷稀盐酸，依此可与方解石区分，后者在盐酸中反应剧烈，并发泡。

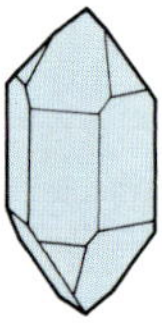

三方/六方晶系

| 比重 2.85 | 解理 完全菱面体 | 断口 亚贝壳状 |
|---|---|---|

| 别 碳酸盐 | 成分 $Ca(Fe,Mg,Mn)(CO_3)_2$ | 硬度 3.5～4 |
|---|---|---|

## 铁白云石(Ankerite)

是白云石类中的一种。晶体呈菱面体，集合体呈块状和粒状。白色、灰色、黄棕色或棕色，条痕白色。是半透明矿物，玻璃到珍珠光泽。

· 成因 形成于矿脉，有时与金和硫化物共生。

· 鉴定特征 溶于盐酸。

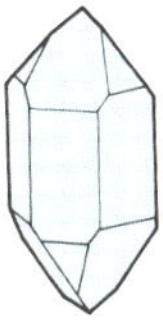

三方/六方晶系

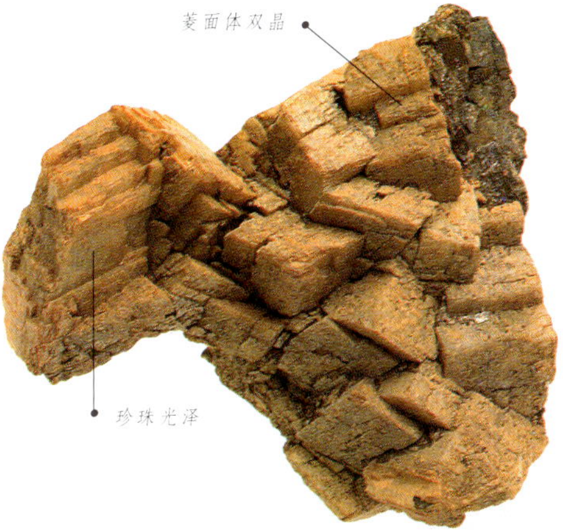


| 重 2.97 | 解理 完全菱形 | 断口 亚贝壳状 |
|---|---|---|

| 别 碳酸盐 | 成分 $ZnCO_3$ | 硬度 4～4.5 |
|---|---|---|

## 菱锌矿(Smithsonite)

晶体呈菱面体，常有弯曲的晶面，有时也形成偏三角面体的晶体。菱锌矿也以块状、葡萄状、肾状、粒状和钟乳状集合体产出。白色、灰色、黄色、绿色、蓝色、粉红色、紫色或棕色，条痕白色。半透明，玻璃或珍珠光泽。

· 成因 形成于铜锌矿床氧化带，与孔雀石、蓝铜矿、磷氯铅矿、白铅矿和异极矿伴生。

· 鉴定特征 溶于盐酸。

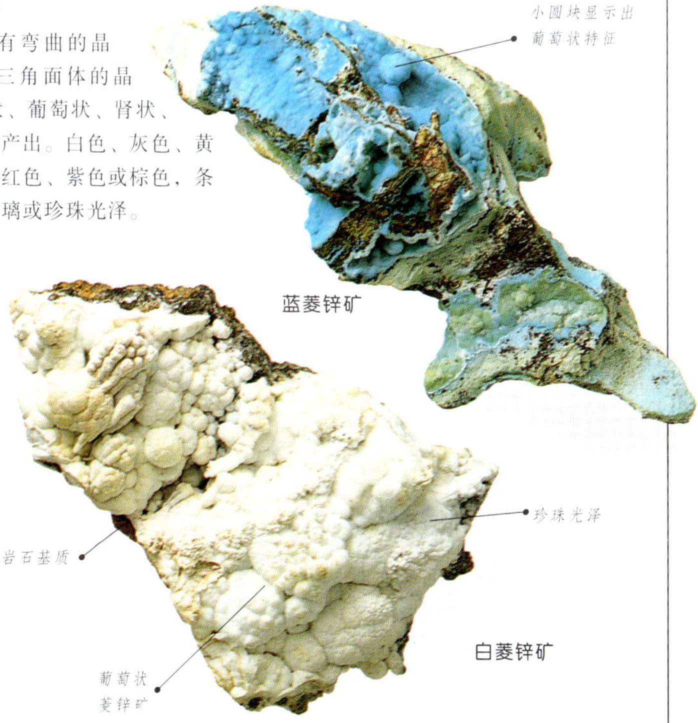


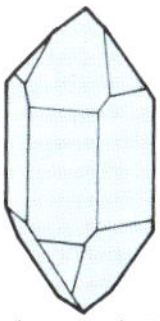

三方/六方晶系

| 重 4.3～4.45 | 解理 完全菱面体 | 断口 亚贝壳状至参差状 |
|---|---|---|

| 类别 碳酸盐 | 成分 $FeCO_3$ | 硬度 4 |
|---|---|---|

## 菱铁矿(Siderite)

晶体呈菱面体、板状、柱状和偏三角面体，晶面常弯曲，有时成双晶，也以块状、粒状、致密状、葡萄状和鲕状集合体产出。浅黄色、灰色、棕色、浅绿色、浅红色或几乎黑色，条痕白色。是半透明矿物，玻璃、珍珠或丝绢光泽。

· **成因** 形成于热液矿脉，也形成于沉积岩。

· **鉴定特征** 加热后具有磁性，并能在冷盐酸中缓慢溶解，当酸液加热时，发泡。

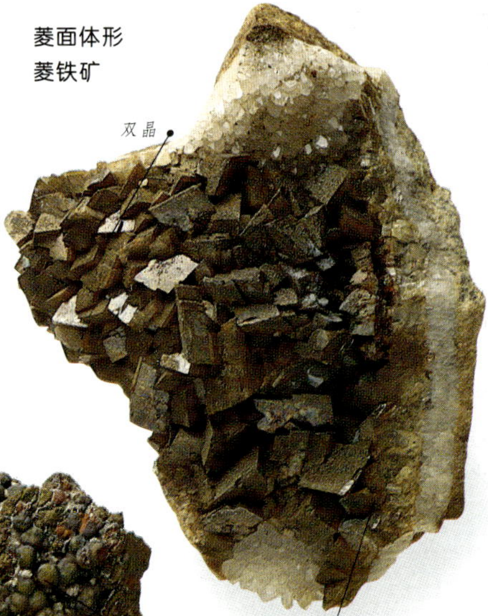


菱面体形菱铁矿

葡萄状菱铁矿

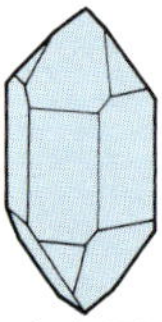

三方/六方晶系

| 比重 3.96 | 解理 完全菱面体形 | 断口 参差状 |
|---|---|---|

| 类别 碳酸盐 | 成分 $MgCO_3$ | 硬度 3~4 |
|---|---|---|

## 菱镁矿(Magnesite)

形成菱面体晶体，很少呈柱状、板状或偏三角面体形晶体。常以块状、片状、纤维状和粒状集合体产出。无色、白色、灰色、浅黄色或棕色，条痕白色。透明到半透明，玻璃或暗淡光泽。

· **成因** 形成于热液矿脉、变质岩和沉积岩。

· **鉴定特征** 溶于温盐酸中，并发泡。

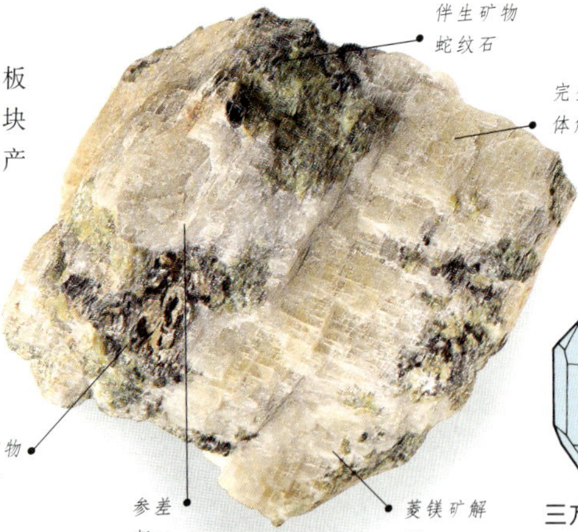


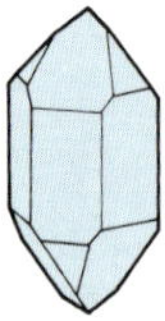

三方/六方晶系

| 比重 3.0~3.1 | 解理 完全菱面体 | 断口 贝壳状至参差状 |
|---|---|---|

| 别 碳酸盐 | 成分 $BaCO_3$ | 硬度 3～3.5 |
|---|---|---|

## 毒重石(Witherite)

晶体呈双锥状，常呈假六面体、双锥状，还以块状、粒状、纤维状和柱状集合体产出。无色、白色、灰色、黄色、绿色或棕色，条痕白色。透明到半透明，玻璃到松脂光泽。

· **成因** 与石英、方解石和重晶石共生于热液矿脉。

· **鉴定特征** 溶于稀盐酸，发泡。结构中的钡会增大其比重。粉状毒重石燃烧火焰呈苹果绿色。

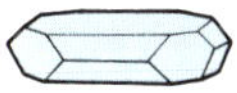

斜方晶系

| 重 4.29 | 解理 清楚 | 断口 参差状 |
|---|---|---|

| 别 碳酸盐 | 成分 $SrCO_3$ | 硬度 3.5 |
|---|---|---|

## 碳酸锶矿(Stromtainite)

呈柱状，或针状晶体，还以块状、粒状、纤维状和结核状集合体产出。白色、无色、灰色、浅黄色、浅棕色、浅绿色或浅红色，条痕始终是白色。透明到半透明，玻璃到松脂光泽。

· **成因** 形成于热液矿脉以及石灰岩和泥灰岩的空洞中。菱锶矿还与方铅矿、闪锌矿和黄铜矿伴生于含硫化物的矿脉中，也与碳酸盐，如方解石和白云石，以及石英伴生。

· **鉴定特征** 溶于稀盐酸，发泡。燃烧菱锶矿粉末火焰呈深红色。

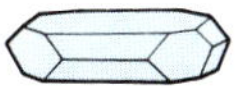

斜方晶系

| 比重 3.78 | 解理 完全柱面 | 断口 参差状 |
|---|---|---|

| 类别 碳酸盐 | 成分 $PbCO_3$ | 硬度 3~3.5 |
|---|---|---|

## 白铅矿(Cerussite)

晶体常呈板状，也可呈针状，常见双晶聚集，集合体块状、粒状、致密状和钟乳状。白色或无色，含铅的包裹体时也呈灰色、浅绿色或蓝色，条痕白色。透明到半透明，金刚、玻璃或松脂光泽。

· **成因** 形成于铅、铜和锌共生矿脉的氧化带。

· **鉴定特征** 溶于酸，尤其是稀硝酸，并生气泡，在紫外光下有时发萤光。

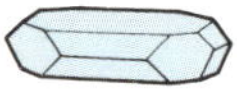

斜方晶系

| 比重 6.55 | 解理 清楚柱面 | 断口 贝壳状 |
|---|---|---|

| 类别 碳酸盐 | 成分 $Mg_2CO_3(OH)_2 \cdot 3H_2O$ | 硬度 2.5 |
|---|---|---|

## 水纤菱镁矿(Artinite)

针状晶体聚集成细枝状，也以纤维状集合体(常呈放射状)和球状块体产出。颜色和条痕都为白色。透明，晶体呈玻璃光泽，纤维集合体则呈丝绢光泽。

· **成因** 形成于超基性岩在蛇纹石化过程中的氧化，类似变质作用，由热液渗透岩石引起。

· **鉴定特征** 易溶于冷的稀释酸中，发泡。不熔，不过火烧时会释放出水分和二氧化碳。

单斜晶系

| 比重 2.0 | 解理 完全 | 断口 参差状 |
|---|---|---|

| 类别 碳酸盐 | 成分 $Cu_2CO_3(OH)_2$ | 硬度 3.5～4 |
|---|---|---|

## 孔雀石(Malachite)

晶体呈针状或柱状，常成双晶。常见的集合体有内部有同心层状或纤维状构造的钟乳状、葡萄状块体，及皮壳状。呈浓绿色，条痕淡绿色。半透明到透明。晶面上呈玻璃至金刚光泽，纤维状块体呈丝绢光泽。

· **成因** 形成于铜矿床的氧化带，常与次生矿物如蓝铜矿共生。

· **鉴定特征** 溶于稀盐酸。

带状孔雀石

葡萄状孔雀石

单斜晶系

| 比重 4.0 | 解理 完全 | 断口 亚贝壳状至参差状 |
|---|---|---|

| 类别 碳酸盐 | 成分 $Cu_3(CO_3)_2(OH)_2$ | 硬度 3.5～4 |
|---|---|---|

## 蓝铜矿(Azurite)

晶体板状和短柱状，可成双晶，还以块状、结核状、钟乳状和土状集合体产出。通常呈深蓝色，条痕浅蓝色。透明到不透明，玻璃或暗淡光泽。

· **成因** 形成于铜矿床的氧化带。

· **鉴定特征** 溶于盐酸，发泡。易熔，加热后变黑。

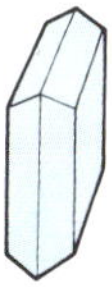

单斜晶系

| 比重 3.77～3.78 | 解理 完全 | 断口 贝壳状 |
|---|---|---|

| 类别 碳酸盐 | 成分 $(Zn,Cu)_5(CO_3)_2(OH)_6$ | 硬度 1～2 |
|---|---|---|

## 绿铜锌矿(Aurichalcite)

晶体呈针状或细长板状，绿铜锌矿还以簇状集合体和皮壳状产出，偶尔也呈粒状、柱状和片状集合体。颜色有淡绿色、绿蓝色或天蓝色，条痕浅蓝绿色。透明，丝绢或珍珠光泽。

· **成因** 与铜矿物，如蓝铜矿和孔雀石共生于铜和锌矿脉氧化带。

· **鉴定特征** 溶于稀盐酸，发泡。由于含铜，因此燃烧时火焰呈绿色，但不熔。

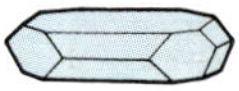

斜方晶系

| 比重 3.96 | 解理 完全 | 断口 参差状 |
|---|---|---|

| 类别 碳酸盐 | 成分 $Pb_4(SO_4)(CO_3)_2(OH)_2$ | 硬度 2.5～3 |
|---|---|---|

## 硫碳酸铅矿(Leadhillite)

晶体呈假六面体、板状或柱状，常成双晶，还以块状或粒状集合体产出。白色、无色、灰色、浅黄色、淡绿色或淡蓝色，条痕白色。透明到半透明，松脂光泽到金刚光泽。

· **成因** 形成于含铅矿脉的氧化带，与方铅矿、白铅矿、硫酸铅矿和青铅矿等矿物共生。

· **鉴定特征** 有时发出桔黄色萤光。

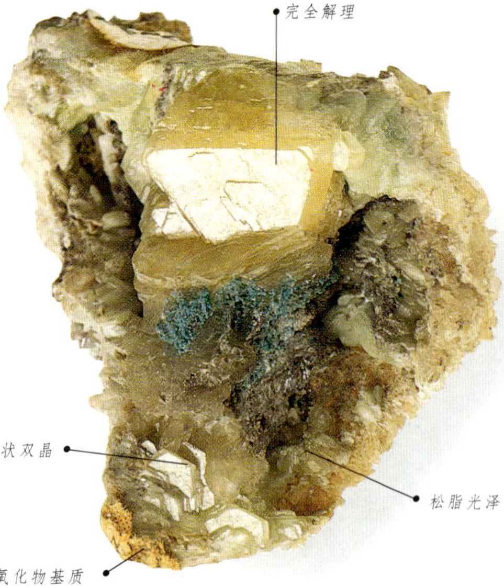

单斜晶系

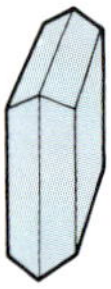


| 比重 6.55 | 解理 完全底面 | 断口 贝壳状 |
|---|---|---|

| 类别 碳酸盐 | 成分 $Zn_5(CO_3)_2(OH)_6$ | 硬度 2～2.5 |
|---|---|---|

## 水锌矿(Hydrozincite)

很少形成晶体，若形成晶体，则呈小而扁平或扁长板状，并且顶收束，常见的为块状、致密状、葡萄状、皮壳状和钟乳状集合体。白色或浅灰色，不过，也可呈黄色、粉红色或棕色，条痕白色。半透明，珍珠到丝绢光泽，有时呈暗淡光泽。

· **成因** 形成于含锌矿脉的氧化带。

· **鉴定特征** 溶于盐酸，加热后，会变成一团浅黄色的红锌矿。紫外光下有时发出蓝色萤光。

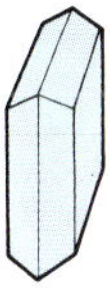

单斜晶系

| 比重 4 | 解理 完全 | 断口 参差状 |
|---|---|---|

| 类别 碳酸盐 | 成分 $Na_3(CO_3)(HCO_3)\cdot 2H_2O$ | 硬度 2.5～3 |
|---|---|---|

## 天然碱(Trona)

柱形或板状晶体，还以块状、纤维状和柱状集合体产出。灰白色、淡黄色或浅棕色，条痕白色。透明到半透明，具闪烁的玻璃光泽。

· **成因** 与硼砂、钙芒硝和其他盐类，以及蒸发岩矿物石盐、石膏、钾盐和白云石等共生于蒸发岩矿床，还会在干旱地区的土壤表层形成盐霜。

· **鉴定特征** 溶于盐酸，发泡。在密封的试管内加热释放出水分。

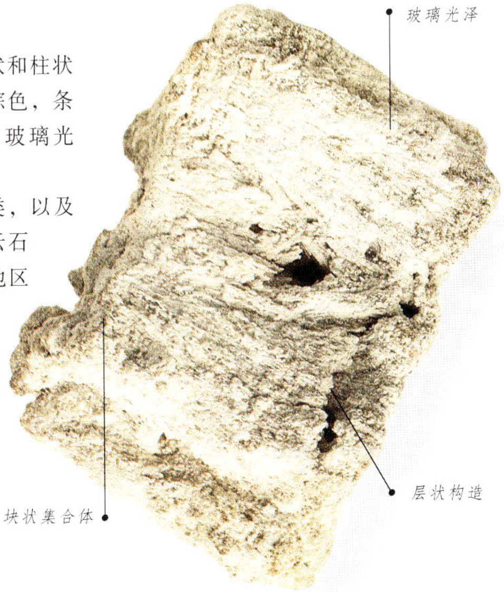


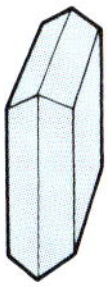

单斜晶系

| 比重 2.1 | 解理 完全 | 断口 参差状 |
|---|---|---|

| 类别 硝酸盐 | 成分 $NaNO_3$ | 硬度 1.5~2 |
|---|---|---|

## 钠硝石(Nitratine)

很少形成晶体，若成晶体，呈菱面体，并常成双晶，常以块状或粒状集合体产出，并成皮壳状。白色或无色，不过常因含杂质而变成灰色、黄色或棕色，条痕白色。透明，玻璃光泽。

· **成因** 在干旱地带的土壤表面形成盐霜，并与石膏伴生。钠硝石通常覆盖大片土地，在智利北部的沙漠中，巨大的钠硝石矿床延伸长达 724 公里，宽 16 到 80 公里。

· **鉴定特征** 易溶于水，地面上皮壳状的钠硝石溶于地表水。置入极易熔，火焰呈鲜黄色。会吸收空气中的湿气，具有潮解性。

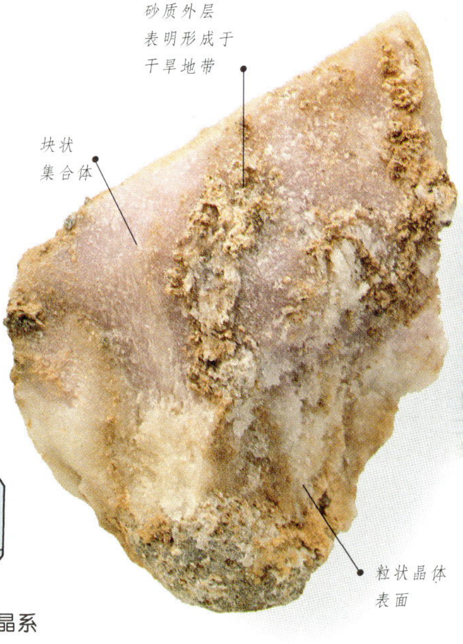


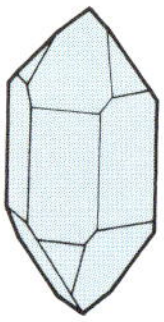

三方/六方晶系

| 比重 2.27 | 解理 完全菱面体 | 断口 贝壳状 |
|---|---|---|

| 类别 硼酸盐 | 成分 $Na_2B_4 \cdot O_5(OH)_4 8H_2O$ | 硬度 2~2.5 |
|---|---|---|

## 硼砂(Borax)

晶体短柱状，很少成双晶，集合体块状和皮壳状。白色、无色、灰色、浅绿色或浅蓝色，条痕白色。透明到不透明，玻璃或土状光泽。

· **成因** 形成于温泉周围和蒸发岩矿床。

· **鉴定特征** 溶于水，靠近火焰极易熔化，火焰黄色。经过一段时间，就开始脱水并变白，味苦是硼砂的特性。

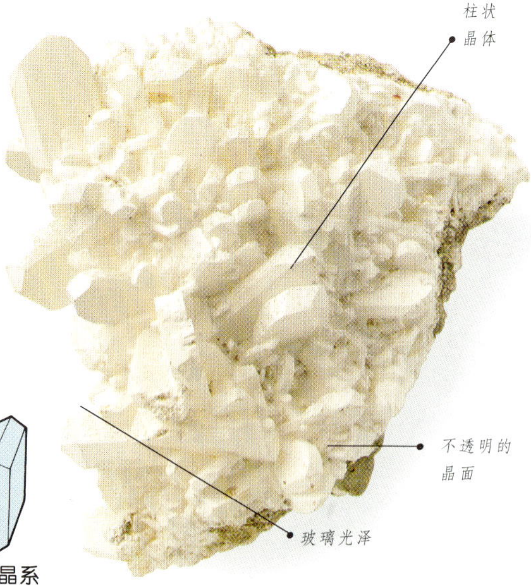


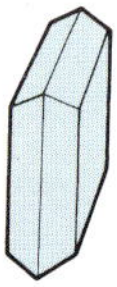

单斜晶系

| 比重 1.7 | 解理 完全 | 断口 贝壳状 |
|---|---|---|

| 类别　硼酸盐 | 成分　$Ca_2B_6O_{11} \cdot 5H_2O$ | 硬度　4.5 |
|---|---|---|

## 硬硼酸钙石(Colemanite)

晶体为短柱状，还以块状和粒状以及球状集合体产出。白色、黄色和灰色，条痕白色。透明到半透明不等，玻璃光泽。

· **成因**　形成于蒸发岩矿床。

· **鉴定特征**　溶于盐酸，易熔、易断裂。燃烧时火焰呈绿色。

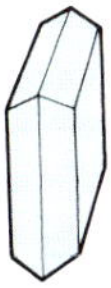

单斜晶系

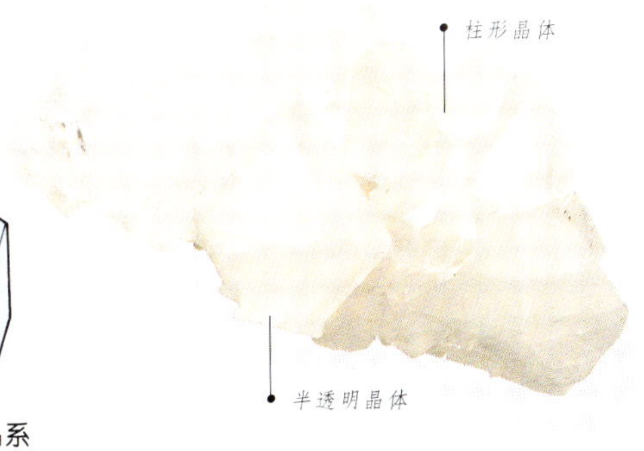


| 比重　2.42 | 解理　完全 | 断口　参差状至贝壳状 |
|---|---|---|

| 类别　硼酸盐 | 成分　$NaCaB_5O_6(OH)_6 \cdot 5H_2O$ | 硬度　2.5 |
|---|---|---|

## 钠硼解石(Ulexite)

晶体针状，常成球状集合体，以及纤维状或簇状块体。白色或无色，条痕白色。透明到半透明，玻璃或丝绢光泽。

· **成因**　形成于蒸发岩盆地。

· **鉴定特征**　不溶于冷水却溶于热水。易熔，膨胀。燃烧时火焰呈黄色。

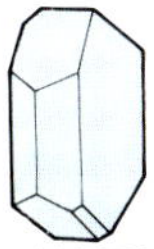

三斜晶系

| 比重　1.96 | 解理　完全 | 断口　参差状 |
|---|---|---|

| 类别　硼酸盐 | 成分　$Na_2B_4O_6(OH)_2 \cdot 3H_2O$ | 硬度　2.5～3 |
|---|---|---|

## 四水硼砂(Kernite)

晶体罕见，短柱形，不过，集合体通常是劈裂的纤维状块体。新鲜的斜方硼砂无色，除以呈白色，条痕白色。透明到不透明，玻璃、暗淡或丝绢光泽。

· **成因**　形成于蒸发岩矿床和矿脉。

· **鉴定特征**　溶于冷水。

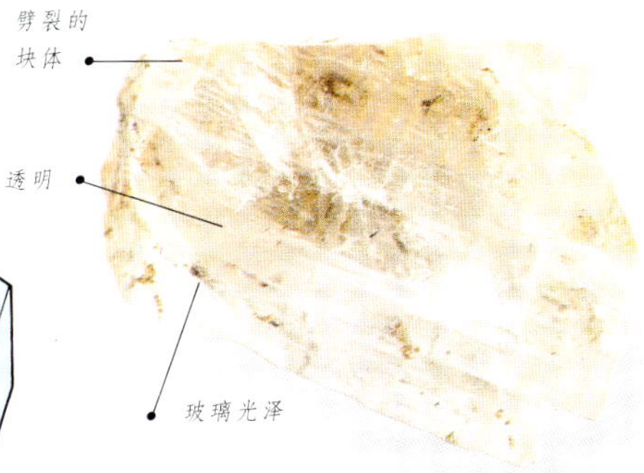


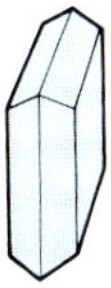

单斜晶系

| 比重　1.9 | 解理　完全 | 断口　多片状 |
|---|---|---|

# 硫酸盐、铬酸盐、钼酸盐和钨酸盐

硫酸盐是一种或多种金属元素与硫酸根（$SO_4$）$^{-2}$结合而成的化合物。石膏是数量最多的硫酸盐，产出于蒸发岩矿床，重晶石常形成于热液矿脉。大多数硫酸盐质软、色淡，往往密度小。铬酸盐是金属元素与铬酸根（$CrO_4$）$^{-2}$结合而成的化合物，铬酸盐少、罕见、颜色鲜艳（如铬铅矿）。钼酸盐由金属元素与钼酸根（$MoO_4$）$^{-2}$结合而成，钨酸盐由金属元素与钨酸根（$WO_4$）$^{-2}$化合而成，这两类矿物通常密度大、性脆，并有鲜艳的颜色（如钼铅矿、铅钼酸盐、白钨矿和钙钨酸盐）。

| 类别 硫酸盐 | 成分 $CaSO_4 \cdot 2H_2O$ | 硬度 2 |
|---|---|---|

## 石膏（Gypsum）

晶体呈板状和金刚石状，常见双晶，还以粒状块体（雪花石膏）和纤维状（纤维石膏）产出。玫瑰状块体称为沙漠玫瑰，呈放射状的称为雏菊石膏。颜色多变，从无色到白色、灰色、浅绿色、浅黄色、浅棕色和浅红色，条痕白色。

透明（如透明石膏）到不透明，玻璃光泽（解理面呈珍珠光泽），纤维状者呈丝绢光泽，而块状者常呈暗淡光泽。

· **成因** 以蒸发岩的形式形成于温泉周围和粘土层。

· **鉴定特征** 溶于酸。

沙漠玫瑰

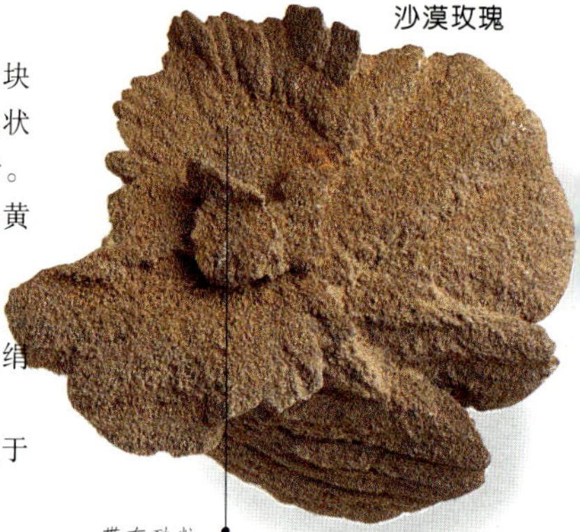


雏菊石膏

纤维石膏

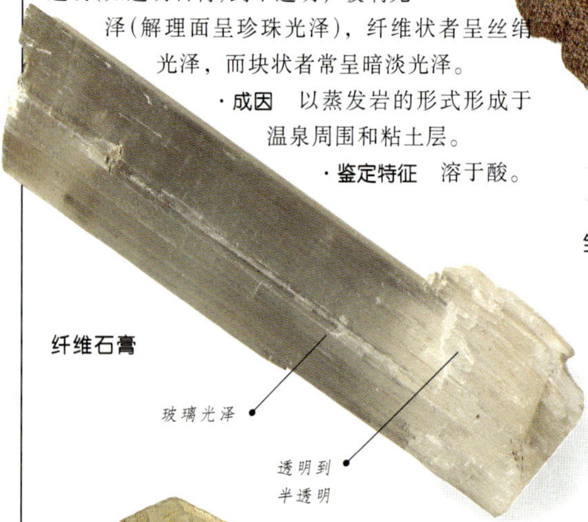

透明石膏

单斜晶系

| 比重 2.32 | 解理 完全 | 断口 多片状 |
|---|---|---|

| 类别 硫酸盐 | 成分 $SrSO_4$ | 硬度 3～3.5 |
| --- | --- | --- |

## 天青石(Celestine)

晶体板状和柱状，多为块状、纤维状、粒状或结核状集合体。无色、白色、灰色、蓝色、绿色、浅黄色、桔黄色、浅红色或棕色，条痕白色。透明到半透明，玻璃光泽(解理面呈珍珠光泽)。

· **成因**　与方解石和石英等矿物共生于热液矿脉，也形成于沉积岩(如石灰岩)，还生成于一些蒸发岩矿床和基性岩。

· **鉴定特征**　在紫外光下有时会发出萤光。不溶于酸，却微溶于水。加热后易熔化，并产生乳白色小球，燃烧时火焰呈深红色。

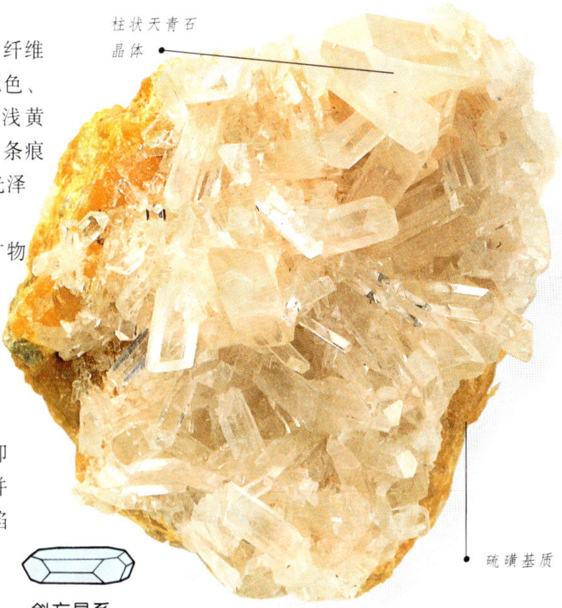


斜方晶系

| 比重 3.96～3.98 | 解理 完全 | 断口 参差状 |
| --- | --- | --- |

| 类别 硫酸盐 | 成分 $CaSO_4$ | 硬度 3～3.5 |
| --- | --- | --- |

## 硬石膏(Anhydrite)

晶体呈板状或柱状，不过常以块状、粒状和纤维状集合体产出。颜色从白色、灰色或浅蓝色到浅粉红色、浅红色或浅棕色，此外还有无色的，条痕白色。透明到半透明，玻璃、珍珠或油脂光泽。

· **成因**　常以蒸发岩的形式见于盐穹，与其他蒸发岩矿物，如白云石、石膏、石盐、钾盐和方解石共生，偶见与石英和方解石共生于热液矿脉。

· **鉴定特征**　加热后，易熔化，燃烧时火焰呈砖红色。

斜方晶系

| 比重 2.98 | 解理 完全 | 断口 参差状至多片状 |
| --- | --- | --- |

| 类别 硫酸盐 | 成分 $BaSO_4$ | 硬度 3～3.5 |
|---|---|---|

## 重晶石(Barite)

晶体板状和柱状，常成很大的晶体，还形成一种小而含沙的玫瑰状结核，称为沙漠玫瑰。集合体粒状、片状、纤维状、鸡冠状、土状或柱状。无色、白色、灰色、浅黄色、棕色、浅红色、浅蓝色或浅绿色，条痕白色。透明到半透明，玻璃、松脂或珍珠光泽。

· **成因** 与石英、方解石、萤石、方铅矿、黄铁矿、白云石、黄铜矿、闪锌矿等共生于热液矿脉，也形成于粘土结核、沉积岩层和温泉周围。

· **鉴定特征** 很难熔化，燃烧时火焰呈黄绿色，不溶于酸；有些变种具有萤光性，比重大极有助于识别。

结晶重晶石

鸡冠状重晶石

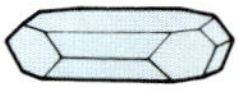

斜方晶系

| 比重 4.5 | 解理 完全 | 断口 参差状 |
|---|---|---|

| 类别 硫酸盐 | 成分 $PbSO_4$ | 硬度 2.5～3 |
|---|---|---|

## 硫酸铅矿(Anglesite)

晶体呈板状和短柱状，集合体块状、粒状、结核状和钟乳状。无色、白色、灰色、浅黄色、淡绿色或淡蓝色，条痕为白色。透明到不透明，玻璃、金刚或松脂光泽。

· **成因** 形成于铅矿脉的氧化带。

· **鉴定特征** 在紫外光下常显黄色萤光。

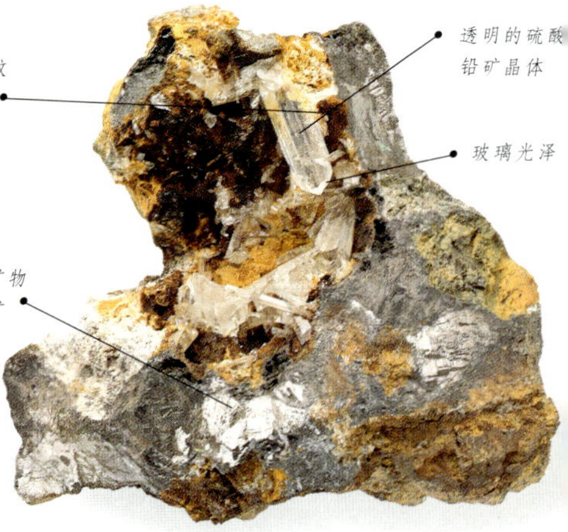


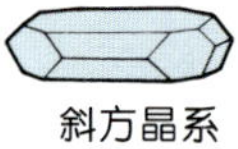

斜方晶系

| 比重 6.3～6.4 | 解理 中等底面 | 断口 贝壳状 |
|---|---|---|

| 类别 硫酸盐 | 成分 $CuSO_4 \cdot 5H_2O$ | 硬度 2.5 |
| --- | --- | --- |

## 胆矾(Chalcanthite)

晶体呈短柱状和厚板状，集合体钟乳状、纤维状、块状、粒状、致密状和皮壳状。颜色从天蓝色到深蓝色、蓝绿色或浅绿色，条痕无色。透明到半透明，玻璃到松脂光泽。

· **成因** 形成于硫化铜矿的氧化带，氧化作用通常由表层水循环引起，主要来源是雨水。热液来自地下深处，在压力作用下上升，也可能蚀变矿脉。当水在矿坑和矿井中渗出时，胆矾常在顶棚和支架上生成皮壳状和钟乳状胆矾，胆矾多形成于世界上气候干旱地区。

· **鉴定特征** 胆矾溶于水，在封密的试管内加热释放出水分。有一种独特的金属味道而有助于鉴定，另外胆矾有毒。

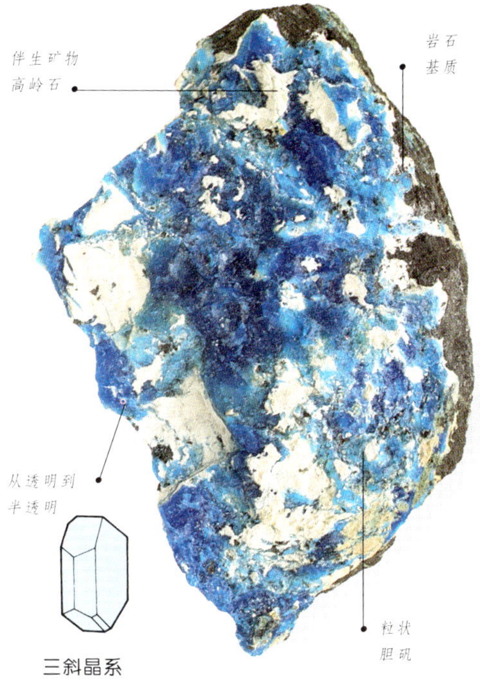


三斜晶系

| 比重 2.28 | 解理 不完全 | 断口 贝壳状 |
| --- | --- | --- |

| 类别 硫酸盐 | 成分 $MgSO_4 \cdot 7H_2O$ | 硬度 2~2.5 |
| --- | --- | --- |

## 泻利盐(Epsomite)

晶体较罕见，常呈块状、针形皮壳状或钟乳状集合体。白色、浅粉红色、无色或浅绿色，条痕白色。透明到半透明，玻璃到丝绢光泽。

· **成因** 形成于矿坑壁、石灰岩洞穴和岩石表面。泻利盐也见于世界上干旱地区，产于黄铁矿的氧化带。

· **鉴定特征** 极易溶于水，有一股苦咸味。在干燥的空气中易风化，在密封的试管内加热释放出水分。

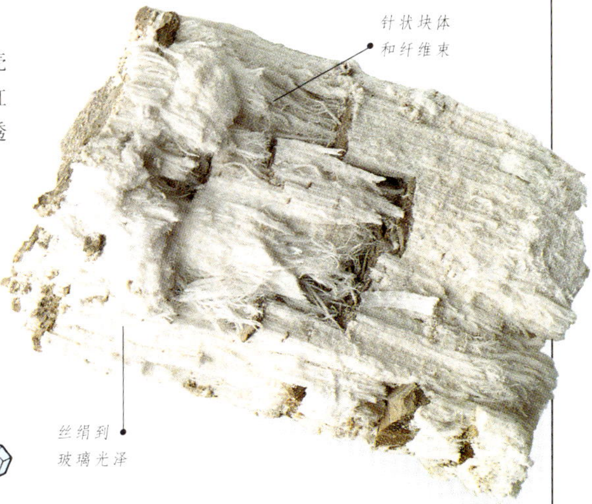


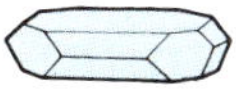
斜方晶系

| 比重 1.68 | 解理 完全 | 断口 贝壳状 |
| --- | --- | --- |

| | | |
|---|---|---|
| 类别 硫酸盐 | 成分 $KAl_3(SO_4)_2(OH)_6$ | 硬度 3.5～4 |

## 明矾石(Alunite)

晶体呈菱面体，常呈假立方体，常以块状、纤维状粒状和致密状集合体产出。白色，常带浅灰、浅红、浅黄或棕色色调，条痕白色。透明到几乎不透明，玻璃或珍珠光泽。

· **成因** 呈矿脉矿物的形式形成于火山岩。

· **鉴定特征** 在密封的试管内加热释放出水分。

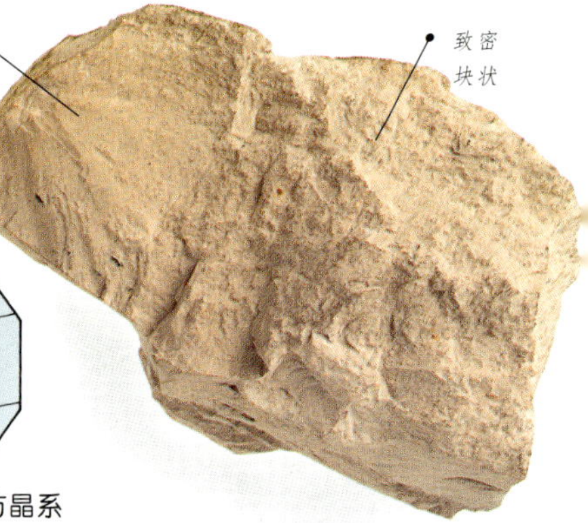


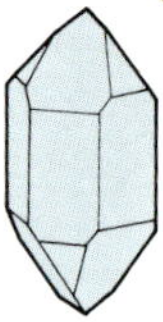

三方/六方晶系

| | | |
|---|---|---|
| 比重 2.6～2.9 | 解理 清楚底面 | 断口 贝壳状 |

| | | |
|---|---|---|
| 类别 硫酸盐 | 成分 $KFe_3^{+2}(SO_4)_2(OH)_6$ | 硬度 2.5～3.5 |

## 黄钾铁矾(Jarosite)

晶体细小，板状或假立方体，集合体块状、粒状、纤维状或土状。黄棕色到棕色，条痕浅黄色。半透明，黄钾铁矾的新鲜面呈玻璃或松脂光泽。

· **成因** 产于含铁矿床的裂隙和夹层中，富含铁的矿物氧化分解后形成黄钾铁矾，源于水及其他流体在地壳上部的循环。

· **鉴定特征** 独特的假立方体晶形有助于识别。

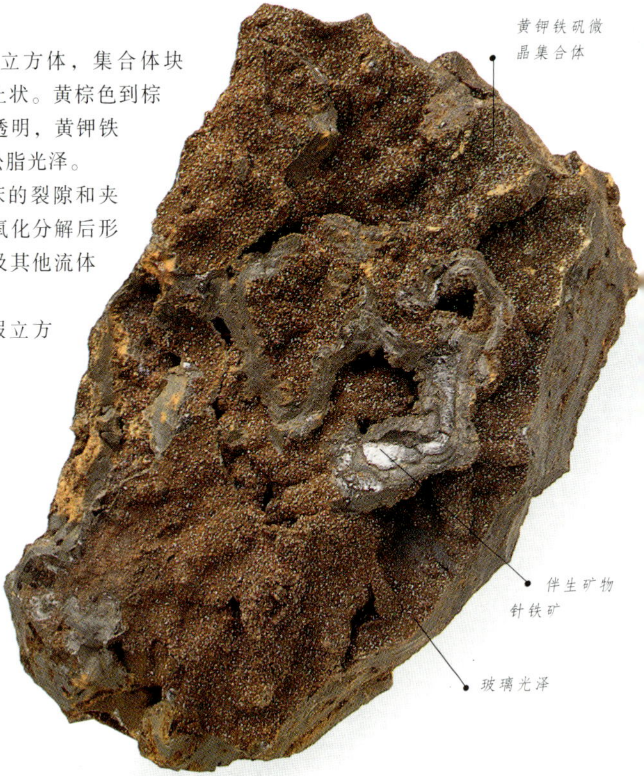


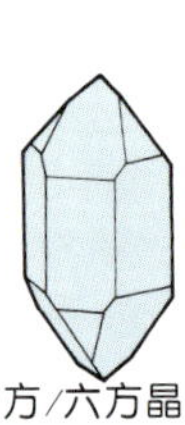

三方/六方晶系

| | | |
|---|---|---|
| 比重 2.90～3.26 | 解理 清楚 | 断口 参差状 |

| 类别 硫酸盐 | 成分 $Na_2Ca(SO_4)_2$ | 硬度 2.5～3 |
|---|---|---|

## 钙芒硝(Glauberite)

板状、柱状或双锥状晶体。无色、灰色或浅黄色，条痕白色。透明到半透明，具有玻璃光泽，解理面上呈珍珠光泽。

· **成因**　形成于蒸发岩矿床，当咸水、盐湖或海洋隔离的泻湖地区干涸后蒸发岩矿床。

· **鉴定特征**　部分溶于水，溶于盐酸。

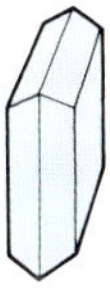

单斜晶系

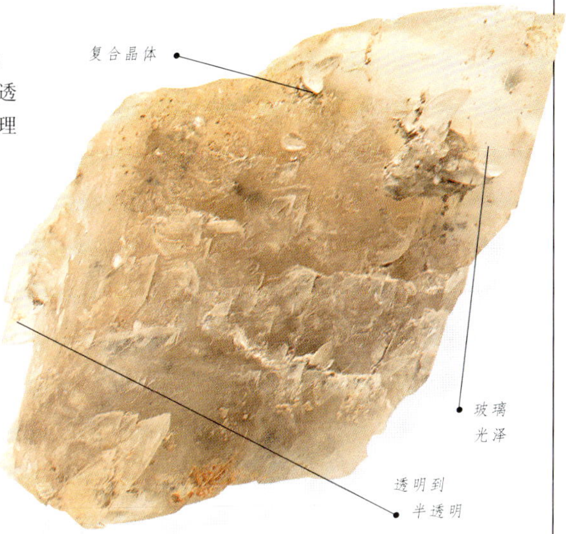


| 比重 2.8 | 解理 完全 | 断口 贝壳状 |
|---|---|---|

| 类别 硫酸盐 | 成分 $Na_2SO_4$ | 硬度 2.5～3 |
|---|---|---|

## 无水芒硝(Thenardite)

晶体呈板状、双锥状或柱状，常成双晶，还成皮壳状集合体。无色、灰白色、浅黄色、浅棕色或浅红色。透明到半透明，玻璃或松脂光泽。

· **成因**　形成于盐湖沉积和干旱地区的土壤表层。在盐湖中沉积时，与石膏、石盐、钾盐和钙芒硝共生。也形成于火山地区的硫质喷气孔周围一个壳状矿床。

· **鉴定特征**　冷水中极易溶，和石盐、钾石盐等相同，无水芒硝有咸味。

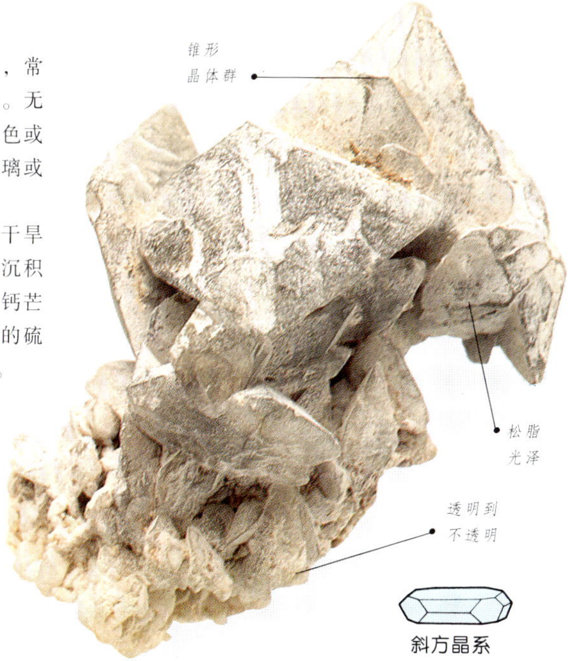


斜方晶系

| 比重 2.66 | 解理 完全 | 断口 参差状 |
|---|---|---|

| 类别 硫酸盐 | 成分 $K_2MgCa_2(SO_4)_4 \cdot 2H_2O$ | 硬度 3.5 |
|---|---|---|

## 杂卤石(Polyhalite)

很少形成晶体，形成时，则呈小扁长板状晶体，常成纤维状或叶片状块体集合体。由于含氧化铁包裹体，常呈肉粉红色到砖红色，不含杂质时，无色、白色或灰色，条痕白色。透明到半透明，松脂或丝绢光泽。

· **成因** 与石盐、石膏、钾盐、光卤石和硬石膏等矿物共生于蒸发岩沉积，很少形成于在火山活动。

· **鉴定特征** 味咸，但比石盐苦。

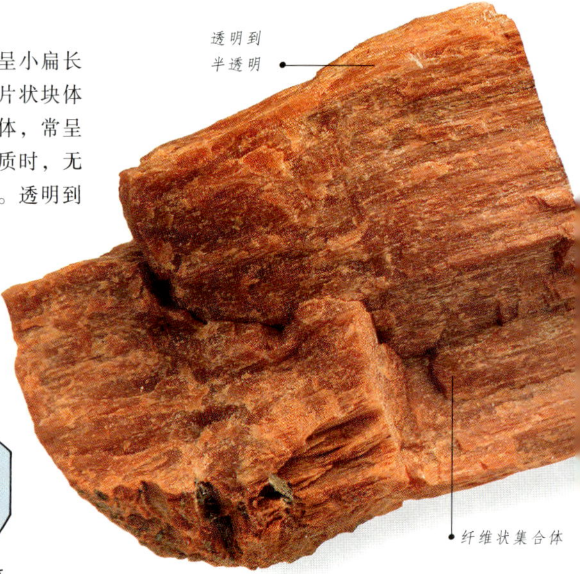


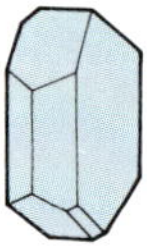

三斜晶系

| 比重 2.78 | 解理 完全 | 断口 参差状 |
|---|---|---|

| 类别 硫酸盐 | 成分 $PbCu(SO_4)(OH)_2$ | 硬度 2.5 |
|---|---|---|

## 青铅矿(Linarite)

薄板状或柱状晶体常分散在集合体中，常见双晶，青铅矿还形成皮壳状。深蓝色，条痕浅蓝色。半透明到透明，玻璃到半金刚光泽。

· **成因** 形成于铅矿和铜矿的氧化带，并与其他次生矿物水胆矾、硫酸铅矿和胆矾伴生。

· **鉴定特征** 青铅矿放入稀盐酸中生成一层白色，不发泡，不过，溶于稀硝酸。置于火焰中熔化，继续加热发出爆裂声并变黑。

单斜晶系

| 比重 5.3 | 解理 完全 | 断口 贝壳状 |
|---|---|---|

| 类别 硫酸盐 | 成分 $Fe^{+2}Fe_4^{+3}(SO_4)_6(OH)_2 \cdot 20H_2O$ | 硬度 2.5~3 |
|---|---|---|

## 叶绿矾(Copiapite)

晶体板状，常见皮壳状和鳞状或块状集合体。黄色、金黄色或桔黄色，也可黄绿色到橄榄绿。透明到半透明，珍珠光泽。

· **成因** 形成的硫化物如黄铁矿被氧化。

· **鉴定特征** 溶于水，溶液变浅黄色。较低温度下熔化。

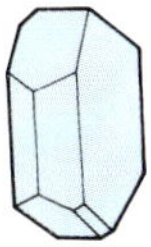

三斜晶系

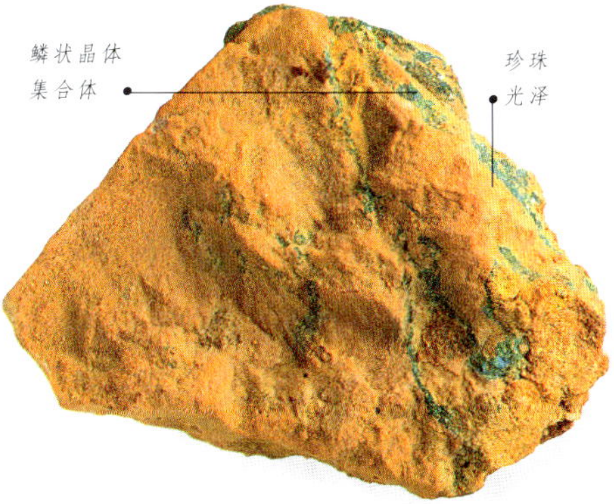


| 比重 2.08~2.17 | 解理 完全 | 断口 参差状 |
|---|---|---|

| 类别 硫酸盐 | 成分 $Cu_4Al_2(SO_4)(OH)_{12} \cdot 2H_2O$ | 硬度 3 |
|---|---|---|

## 绒铜矿(Cyanotrichite)

在簇状集合体中形成微小针状晶体，也呈皮壳状或纤维状细脉。浅蓝到深蓝色，条痕浅蓝色。半透明，丝绢光泽。

· **成因** 形成于矿石脉，尤其是铜矿的氧化带。

· **鉴定特征** 溶于酸，在火焰中熔化。

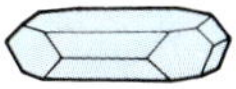

斜方晶系

| 比重 2.74~2.95 | 解理 无 | 断口 参差状 |
|---|---|---|

| 类别 硫酸盐 | 成分 $Cu_4SO_4(OH)_6$ | 硬度 3.5~4 |
|---|---|---|

## 水胆矾(Brochantite)

常呈粗壮的柱状、针状或板状晶体、集合体和晶簇壳产出，常见双晶。从祖母绿色到黑绿色，条痕浅绿色。透明到半透明，玻璃光泽。

· **成因** 形成于铜矿床的氧化带。

· **鉴定特征** 溶于盐酸和硝酸中。

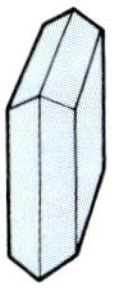

单斜晶系

| 比重 3.97 | 解理 完全 | 断口 贝壳状至参差状 |
|---|---|---|

| 类别 铬酸盐 | 成分 $PbCrO_4$ | 硬度 2.5～3 |
| --- | --- | --- |

## 铬铅矿(Crocoite)

晶体呈细长柱状，通常为集合体，也成块状。颜色通常呈鲜艳的桔红色，有时呈桔黄色、红色或黄色，条痕桔黄色。半透明，金刚到玻璃光泽。

· **成因** 形成于含铬及铅的矿脉和矿床的蚀变带和氧化带。其他铅矿物在热液的蚀变作用下，形成次生矿物铬酸铅矿成为一。与钼铅矿、白铅矿、磷氯铅矿和钒铅矿多种矿物共生。

· **鉴定特征** 易在火焰中熔化。溶于强酸，因此首先用强酸溶解从矿物分离铬。

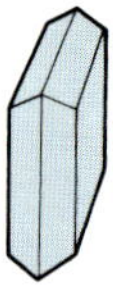

单斜晶系

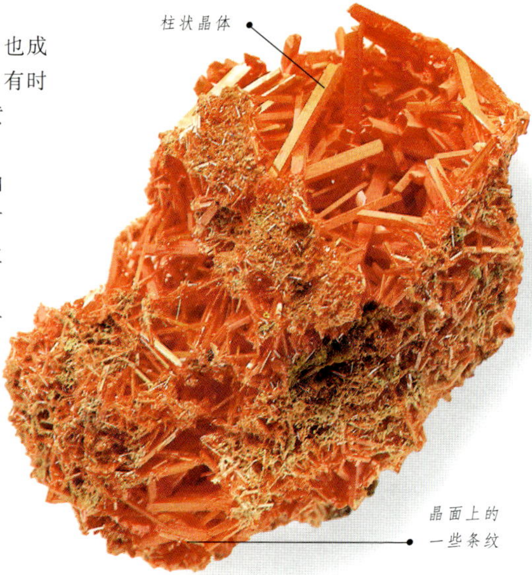


| 比重 6.0 | 解理 清楚柱面 | 断口 贝壳状至参差状 |
| --- | --- | --- |

| 类别 钼酸盐 | 成分 $PbMoO_4$ | 硬度 2.5～3 |
| --- | --- | --- |

## 钼铅矿(Wulfenite)

形成方形的板状和柱状晶体，集合体块状和粒状。典型颜色为橙色或黄色，也可呈棕色、灰色或绿棕色，而且颜色鲜艳，条痕白色。透明到半透明，松脂到金刚光泽。

· **成因** 形成于矿床循环流体(主要是水)作用的氧化带部，常与如白铅矿、褐铁矿、钒铅矿、方铅矿、磷氯铅矿、孔雀石和砷铅矿多种类的矿物共生。

· **鉴定特征** 易熔，溶于热盐酸中，在冷酸中溶解较缓慢。

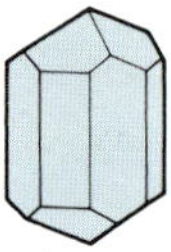

正方晶系

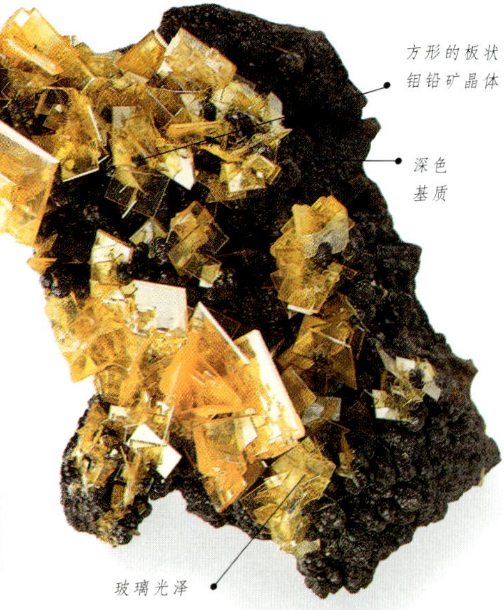


| 比重 6.5.～7.0 | 解理 清楚角锥形 | 断口 亚贝壳状 |
| --- | --- | --- |

| 类别 钨酸盐 | 成分 $(Fe,Mn)WO_4$ | 硬度 4～4.5 |
| --- | --- | --- |

## 黑钨矿(Wolframite)

钨铁矿——钨锰矿系列中的过渡矿物，晶体呈柱形或板状，常成双晶，集合体块状。黑钨矿呈棕黑色，条痕从红棕色到棕黑色。半透明到不透明，半金属光泽。

· **成因** 形成于花岗伟晶岩的石英脉中，常与锡石和毒砂伴生。

· **鉴定特征** 熔化缓慢。含钨铁矿时呈浅棕色，含钨锰矿则呈红棕色。

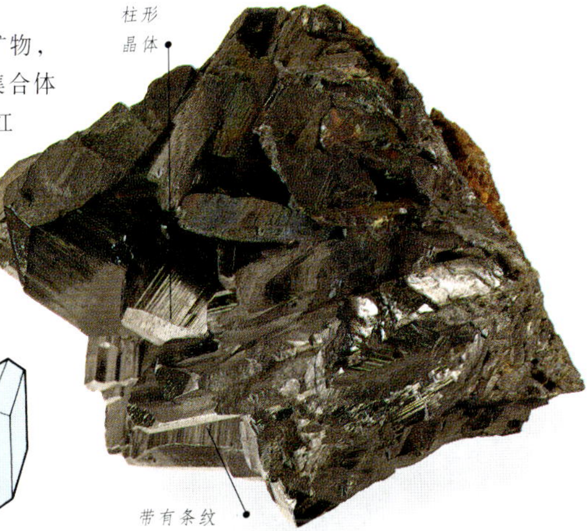


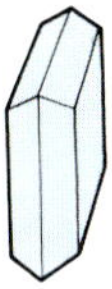

单斜晶系

| 比重 7.1～7.5 | 解理 完全 | 断口 参差状 |
| --- | --- | --- |

| 类别 钨酸盐 | 成分 $CaWO_4$ | 硬度 4.5～5 |
| --- | --- | --- |

## 白钨矿(Scheelite)

晶体假八面体状或双锥状，常成双晶，集合体块状、粒状或柱状。白色、无色、灰色、浅黄色、桔黄色、棕绿色、浅红色或紫色，条痕白色。透明到半透明，玻璃到金刚光泽。

· **成因** 形成于热液矿脉、接触变质岩和伟晶岩，也见于砂积矿床，并且常与黑钨矿共生，是重要的钨矿石。

· **鉴定特征** 在短波紫外光下此矿物发出鲜艳的蓝白萤光。溶于酸，可熔，但难熔。

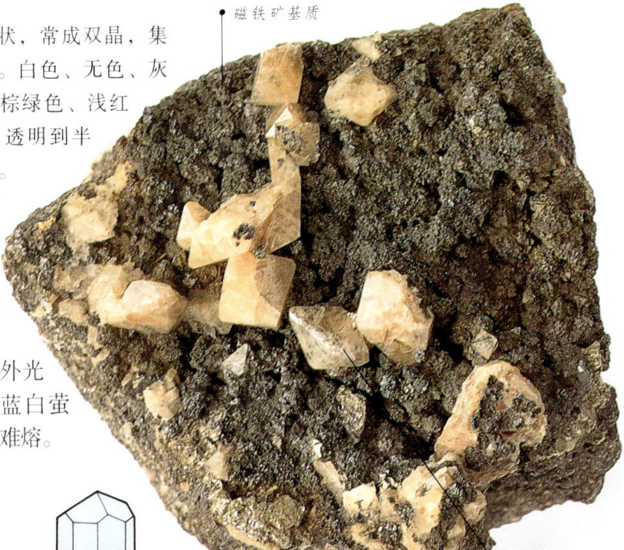


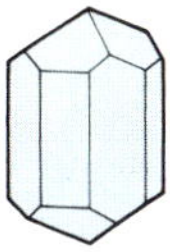

正方晶系

| 比重 5.9～6.1 | 解理 清楚 | 断口 亚贝壳状至参差状 |
| --- | --- | --- |

# 磷酸盐、砷酸盐和钒酸盐

磷酸盐、砷酸盐和钒酸盐为金属元素分别与磷酸根$(PO_4)^{-8}$、砷酸根$(ASO_4)^{-8}$、$(ASO_3)^{-1}$和钒酸根$(VO_4)^{-3}$、$(VO_3)^{-1}$结合而成的化合物。尽管已经发现几百种磷酸盐、砷酸盐和钒酸盐类矿物，但并不丰富。有些磷酸盐、砷酸盐属原生矿物，但这类矿物的大多数成员是从原生硫化物氧化形成的。它们的性质多样，不过都质软、易碎、多色，并且结晶完好。磷酸盐包括放射性矿物铜铀云母和钙铀云母、富铅的磷氯铅矿、天蓝色的天蓝石和绿松石（又名“蓝色幽灵”）。磷酸盐硬度多变化，从蓝铁矿的1.5到绿松石的5～6。许多砷酸盐矿物是收藏者追求的对象，尤其是结晶完好、颜色鲜艳的种类，如水砷锌矿、钴华、砷铅矿和乳砷铅铜矿。砷酸盐的比重通常在3～5之间，但砷铅矿含铅，比重达7.1～7.3。这类矿物的硬度常很低。钒铅矿可能是最有名且最常见的钒酸盐矿物，生成绚丽的红色和橙色六方晶体。

**类别** 磷酸盐 | **成分** $(Li,Na)AlPO_4(F,OH)$ | **硬度** 5.5～6

## 锂磷铝石(Amblygonite)

晶体短柱状，晶面常粗糙，常成双晶，常裂为块体。白色到灰白色，也可呈浅粉红色、无色、浅黄色、浅绿色或浅蓝色，条痕白色。透明到半透明，玻璃到油脂光泽。

· **成因** 形成于粗粒的花岗岩，包括伟晶岩。

· **鉴定特征** 属于含磷铝石——磷铝石系列中富含氟的端员成分。易熔，因为含锂，燃烧时火焰呈红色，溶酸，但很难溶。

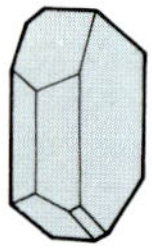

三斜晶系

**比重** 3.08 | **解理** 完全 | **断口** 参差状

| 类别 磷酸盐 | 成分 $(Mg,Fe)Al_2(PO_4)_2(OH)_2$ | 硬度 5.5～6 |
|---|---|---|

## 天蓝石(Lazulite)

晶体常呈假双锥状，也呈板状晶体，晶体可能相当大，常成双晶，集合体块状、粒状和致密状。蓝色，从浓的天蓝色到浅蓝色或蓝绿色，条痕白色。半透明到不透明，玻璃到暗淡光泽。

· **成因** 形成于多种地质环境，产于石英脉、花岗伟晶岩和变质岩，如变质石英。伟晶天蓝石常与红柱石和金红石共生。变质伴生矿物有石英、石榴子石、蓝晶石、白云母、叶蜡石、硅线石和刚玉。

· **鉴定特征** 在密封的试管内加热释放出水分。

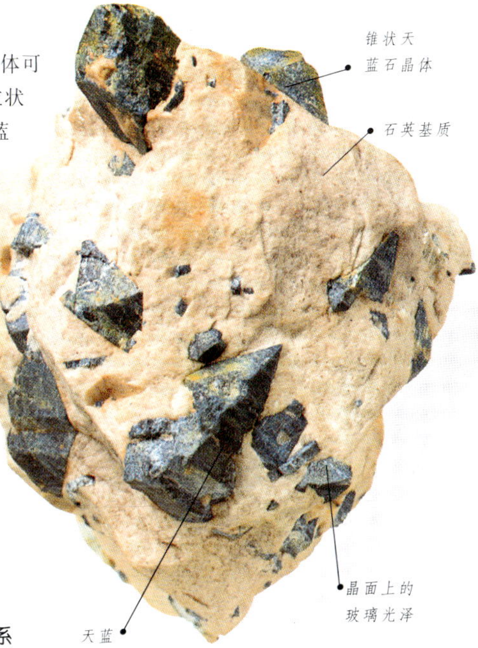


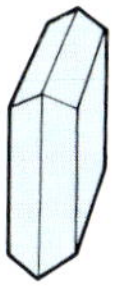

单斜晶系

| 比重 3.1 | 解理 不清楚至良好柱面 | 断口 参差状至多片状 |
|---|---|---|

| 类别 磷酸盐 | 成分 $Pb_5(PO_4)_3Cl$ | 硬度 3.5～4 |
|---|---|---|

## 磷氯铅矿(Pyromorphite)

晶体六方柱状，常呈圆桶状，集合体球状、肾状、粒状、土状、葡萄状和纤维状。绿色、橙色、灰色、棕色或黄色，条痕白色。透明到半透明，松脂到金刚光泽。

· **成因** 以次生矿物形成于铅矿脉的氧化带。

· **鉴定特征** 溶于某些酸。

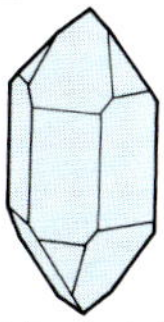

三方/六方晶系

| 比重 6.5～7.1 | 解理 极不佳的柱面 | 断口 参差状至贝壳状 |
|---|---|---|

| 类别　磷酸盐 | 成分　$Fe_3(PO_4)_2\cdot 8H_2O$ | 硬度　1.5～2 |
|---|---|---|

## 蓝铁矿(Vivianite)

晶体常呈长柱状或板状，集合体块状、刃片状或纤维状。新鲜蓝铁矿标本无色，条痕从无色到蓝白色。透明到半透明，玻璃或珍珠光泽。

· **成因**　形成于铁矿床和富锰矿床的氧化带。

· **鉴定特征**　溶于盐酸，易熔。

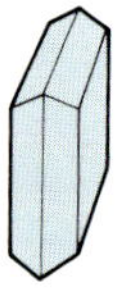

单斜晶系

| 比重　2.68 | 解理　完全 | 断口　参差状 |
|---|---|---|

| 类别　磷酸盐 | 成分　$Cu(UO_2)_2(PO_4)_2\cdot 8-12H_2O$ | 硬度　2～2.5 |
|---|---|---|

## 铜铀云母(Torbernite)

晶体呈板状，也呈鳞片状或片状集合体。绿色，条痕淡绿色。透明到半透明，玻璃到珍珠光泽。

· **成因**　沥青铀矿风化而成的次生铀矿物。

· **鉴定特征**　具有放射性，且化学性质不稳定，常变成准铜铀云母。

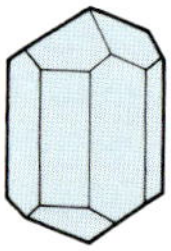

正方晶系

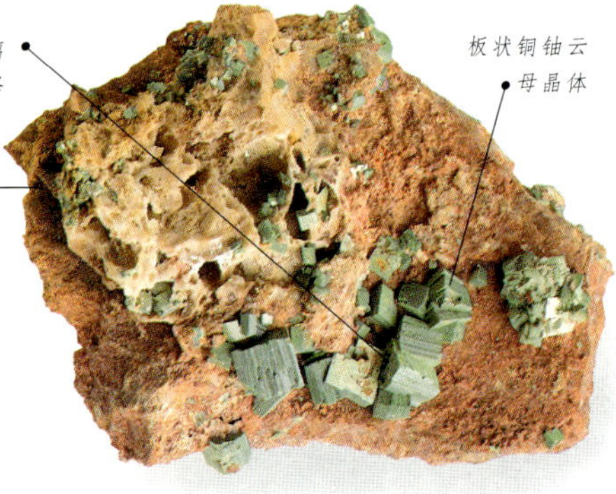


| 比重　3.22 | 解理　完全底面 | 断口　参差状 |
|---|---|---|

| 类别　磷酸盐 | 成分　$Ca(UO_2)_2(PO_4)_2\cdot 10-12H_2O$ | 硬度　2～2.5 |
|---|---|---|

## 钙铀云母(Autunite)

晶体呈板状，有时成双晶，还以皮壳状、粒状集合体产出。黄色到绿色，条痕黄色。透明到半透明，玻璃到珍珠光泽。

· **成因**　由原生铀矿风化而形成。

· **鉴定特征**　钙铀云母是一种放射性矿物。

正方晶系

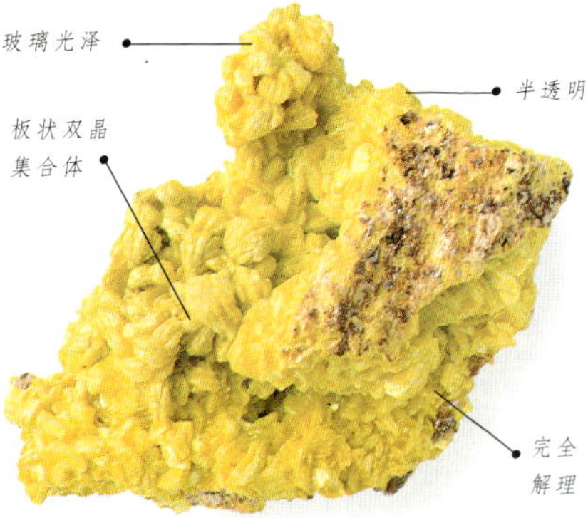


| 比重　3.05～3.2 | 解理　完全底面 | 断口　参差状 |
|---|---|---|

| 别 磷酸盐 | 成分 $YPO_4$ | 硬度 4~5 |
|---|---|---|

## 磷钇矿(Xenotime)

晶体呈柱柱锥，还呈等晶体。粗面晶体常以集合体产出，有时形成玫瑰形晶群，双晶罕见。黄棕色到红棕色，也呈灰色、浅黄色、淡绿色或淡红色，条痕浅棕色，也可呈黄棕色。半透明到不透明，玻璃光泽到松脂光泽。

· **成因** 形成于伟晶岩和多种酸性岩中，不过数量很少。此外，磷钇矿也形成于变质岩和阿尔卑斯式脉中，还以碎屑矿物见于沉积物中。

· **鉴定特征** 与锆石类似，不过锆石硬得多。

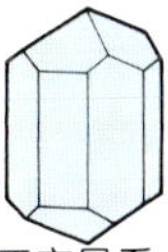

正方晶系

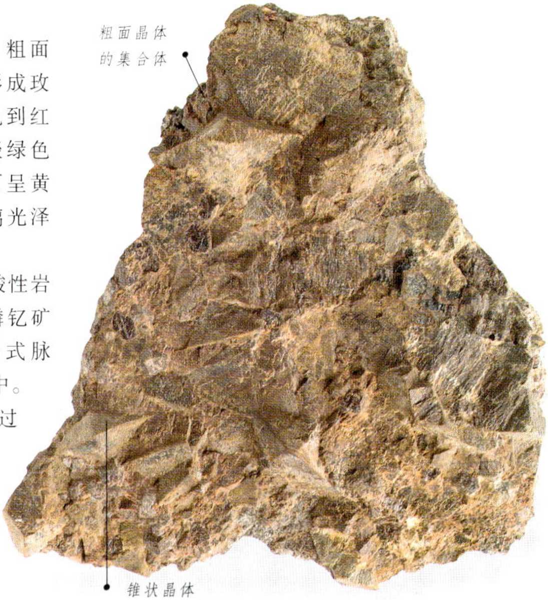


| 重 4.4~5.1 | 解理 完全柱面 | 断口 参差状 |
|---|---|---|

| 别 磷酸盐 | 成分 $(Ce,La,Nb,Th)PO_4$ | 硬度 5~5.5 |
|---|---|---|

## 独居石(Monazite)

组成独居石铈、独居石镏和独居石钕一矿物系列，晶体呈板状或柱状，不过常小，且成双晶，晶面通常粗糙或有条纹，也呈粒状块体。独居石棕色、红棕色、黄棕色、粉红色、黄色、浅绿色或近白色，条痕白色。透明到半透明，松脂、蜡状或玻璃光泽。

· **成因** 形成于伟晶岩、变质岩和矿脉，也见于砂积矿床，如河流和滩地的砂层。在伟晶岩中发现过重达几公斤的特大独居石晶体。

· **鉴定特征** 具轻度放射性的矿物。

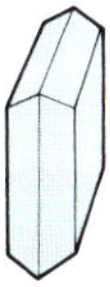

单斜晶系

| 比重 4.6~5.4 | 解理 清楚 | 断口 贝壳状至参差状 |
|---|---|---|

| 类别 磷酸盐 | 成分 $CuAl_6(PO_4)_4(OH)_8 \cdot 4H_2O$ | 硬度 5~6 |
| --- | --- | --- |

## 绿松石(Turguoise)

很少形成晶体，偶见短小柱状晶体。常成块状、粒状、隐晶质、钟乳状和结核状集合体，也成皮壳状和细脉状。绿松石的颜色从鲜艳的蓝色到浅蓝、绿蓝、绿色和灰色，条痕白色或浅绿色。晶体透明，玻璃光泽，块状的绿松石不透明，蜡状或暗淡光泽。

· **成因** 富含铝的岩浆岩和沉积岩风化淋滤生成绿松石。

· **鉴定特征** 溶于热盐酸。

三斜晶系

| 比重 2.6~2.8 | 解理 良好 | 断口 贝壳状 |
| --- | --- | --- |

| 类别 磷酸盐 | 成分 $Al_3(PO_4)_2(OH,F)_3 \cdot 5H_2O$ | 硬度 3.5~4 |
| --- | --- | --- |

## 银星石(Wavellite)

偶尔形成微小的柱状晶体，也见放射状针形球状集合体，还成皮壳。白色到绿白色、绿色，以及黄绿色到黄色、黄棕色，条痕白色。透明到半透明，玻璃、松脂或珍珠光泽。

· **成因** 作为次生矿物形成于岩石裂隙和节理面。

· **鉴定特征** 溶于多种酸，不熔。在密封的试管内加热释放出水分。

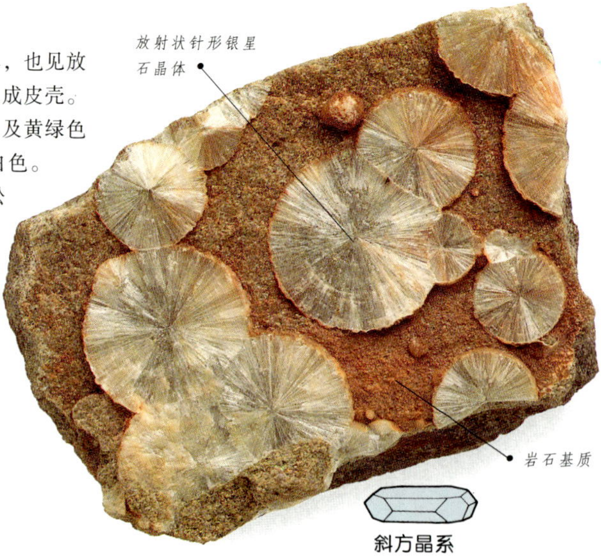


斜方晶系

| 比重 2.36 | 解理 完全 | 断口 亚贝壳状至参差状 |
| --- | --- | --- |

| | | |
|---|---|---|
| 类别 磷酸盐 | 成分 $Al(PO_4) \cdot 2H_2O$ | 硬度 3.5 ~ 4.5 |

## 磷铝石(Variscite)

晶体罕见，呈假八面体，常以块状和结核状集合体产出，也呈皮壳状或脉状。颜色为绿色。透明到半透明，玻璃到蜡状或暗淡光泽。

· 成因 形成于含水磷酸盐转化的含铝岩石。

· 鉴定特征 预热后放入酸中才会溶解，不熔。

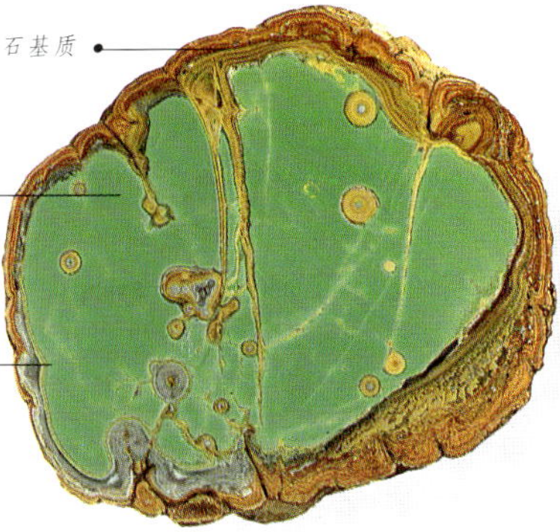


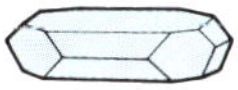

斜方晶系

| | | |
|---|---|---|
| 比重 2.6 ~ 2.9 | 解理 完全 | 断口 贝壳状或参差状至多片状 |

| | | |
|---|---|---|
| 类别 磷酸盐 | 成分 $Ca_5(PO_4)_3(F,Cl,OH)$ | 硬度 5 |

## 磷灰石(Apatite)

属于磷灰石族的一些矿物性质相近，晶体呈柱状或板状，并以块状、致密状和粒状集合体产出。通常呈绿色，也呈白色、无色、黄色、浅蓝色、浅红色、棕色、灰色或紫色，条痕白色。透明到半透明，玻璃到半松脂光泽。

· 成因 形成于岩浆岩和变质石灰岩。

· 鉴定特征 溶于盐酸。

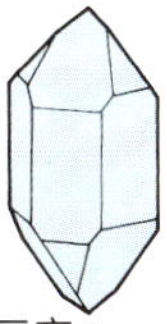

三方/六方晶系

| | | |
|---|---|---|
| 比重 3.1 ~ 3.2 | 解理 不佳 | 断口 贝壳状至参差状 |

| | | |
|---|---|---|
| 类别 磷酸盐 | 成分 $CaBe(PO_4)(F,OH)$ | 硬度 5 ~ 5.5 |

## 磷铍钙石(Herderite)

晶体呈柱状或板状，且常呈假斜方晶体，还以纤维状集合体产出。无色、浅黄色或绿白色。透明到半透明，玻璃光泽。

· 成因 形成于花岗伟晶岩。

· 鉴定特征 溶于大多数酸；有的标本在紫外光下发萤光。

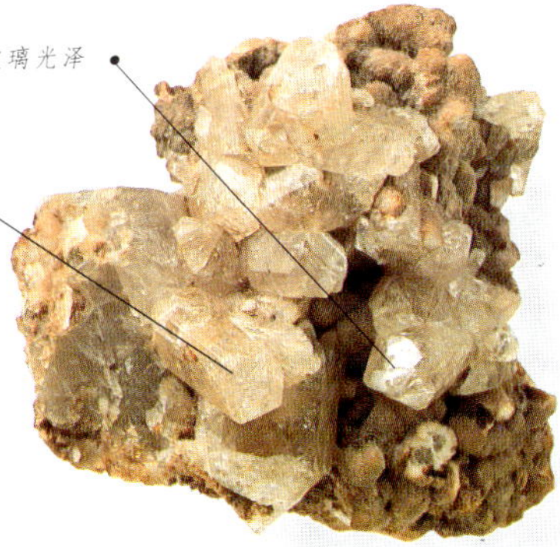


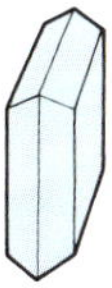

单斜晶系

| | | |
|---|---|---|
| 比重 2.95 ~ 3.01 | 解理 不佳 | 断口 亚贝壳状 |

| 类别 砷酸盐 | 成分 $Zn_2AsO_4(OH)$ | 硬度 3.5 |
| --- | --- | --- |

## 水砷锌矿(Adamite)

晶体呈长板状或等径形，也成双晶，以球状块体产出。通常呈鲜艳的黄绿色，条痕白色。透明到半透明，玻璃光泽。

**·成因** 形成于矿脉的氧化带。与方解石、褐铁矿、孔雀石，以及蓝铜矿、菱锌矿和异极矿等多种矿物伴生。

**·鉴定特征** 溶于稀释的酸中，有时在紫外光下发出萤光，火焰中熔化。

球状水砷锌矿

结晶水砷锌矿

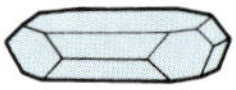

斜方晶系

| 比重 4.3~4.4 | 解理 良好 | 断口 亚贝壳状至参差状 |
| --- | --- | --- |

| 类别 砷酸盐 | 成分 $Ni_3(AsO_4)_2 \cdot 8H_2O$ | 硬度 1.5~2.5 |
| --- | --- | --- |

## 镍华(Annabergite)

晶体呈柱状晶面上带条纹；集合体呈皮壳状、土状或粉状块体。白色、灰色、淡绿色或黄绿色，条痕则比其颜色淡一些。透明到半透明，玻璃或珍珠光泽。

**·成因** 形成于镍矿的氧化带。

**·鉴定特征** 在封闭的试管内加热释放出水分。

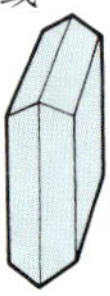

单斜晶系

| 比重 3.07 | 解理 完全 | 断口 参差状 |
| --- | --- | --- |

| 类别 砷酸盐 | 成分 $Cu_3(AsO_4)(OH)_3$ | 硬度 2.5～3 |
|---|---|---|

## 光线矿(Clinoclase)

晶体扁长或呈板状，常呈菱面体晶形，是为假菱面体。晶体或呈单晶，或呈蔷薇花状。暗绿蓝色到绿黑色，条痕蓝绿色。透明到半透明，晶面呈玻璃光泽，解理面呈珍珠光泽。

· 成因　以次生矿物形成于硫化铜矿床的地表和地下氧化带。常与橄榄铜矿伴生，属同族矿物。

· 鉴定特征　溶于酸，加热发出蒜味。

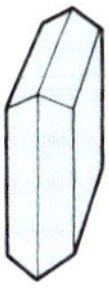

单斜晶系

| 比重 4.33 | 解理 完全 | 断口 参差状 |
|---|---|---|

| 类别 砷酸盐 | 成分 $Co_3(AsO_4)_2 \cdot 8H_2O$ | 硬度 1.5～2.5 |
|---|---|---|

## 钴华(Erythrite)

晶体呈柱状或针状，晶面有条纹，或呈刃片状集合体，还以土状块体产出。深紫色到淡粉红色，条痕比颜色稍淡。透明到半透明，金刚到玻璃或珍珠光泽。

· 成因　形成于钴矿脉的氧化带。

· 鉴定特征　溶于盐酸。

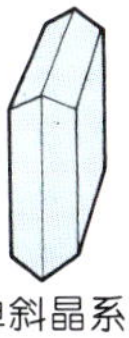

单斜晶系

| 比重 3.18 | 解理 完全 | 断口 参差状 |
|---|---|---|

| 类别 砷酸盐 | 成分 $Pb_5(AsO_4)_3Cl$ | 硬度 3.5～4 |
|---|---|---|

## 砷铅矿(Mimetite)

晶体呈针状到细长的柱状，有时呈圆桶状，这种情况下则称为磷砷铅矿晶体，也呈葡萄状、肾状和粒状集合体。黄色、橙色和棕色到白色、无色和浅绿色，条痕白色。透明到半透明，玻璃到松脂光泽。

**·成因** 形成于铅矿床氧化带，常与磷氯铅矿、钒铅矿、方铅矿、硫酸铅矿、异极矿和毒砂共生。

**·鉴定特征** 溶于盐酸。置于火焰中易熔，并释放出强烈的大蒜味。

柱状砷铅矿

磷砷酸铅矿

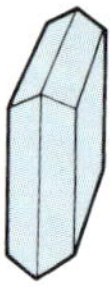

单斜晶系

| 比重 7.0～7.3 | 解理 无 | 断口 亚贝壳状至参差状 |
|---|---|---|

| 类别 砷酸盐 | 成分 $Cu_2(AsO_4)(OH)$ | 硬度 3 |
|---|---|---|

## 橄榄铜矿(Olivenite)

晶体呈柱状、针状和板状，也呈球状或肾状块体。橄榄绿、棕色、浅黄色、灰色或白色，条痕橄榄绿色，名称即源于此。半透明到不透明，玻璃到丝绢光泽。

**·成因** 形成于硫化铜矿床的氧化带，与孔雀石、蓝铜矿、方解石、针铁矿、透视石和臭葱石等矿物共生。

**·鉴定特征** 溶于酸，加热后发出蒜味。

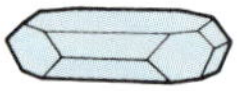

斜方晶系

| 比重 4.4 | 解理 不清楚 | 断口 参差状至贝壳状 |
|---|---|---|

| 别 砷酸盐 | 成分 $FeAsO_4 \cdot 2H_2O$ | 硬度 3.5～4 |
|---|---|---|

## 臭葱石(Scorodite)

晶体呈双锥状、柱状和板状，还以块状和土状集合体产出。浅绿色、灰绿色、蓝绿色、蓝色、浅棕色、无色、浅黄色或紫罗兰色，痕白色。透明到半透明，玻璃到松脂或暗淡光泽。

· **成因** 形成于砷矿床的氧化带。

· **鉴定特征** 溶于盐酸和硝酸，热后发出蒜味，密封的试管内加热释放出水分。

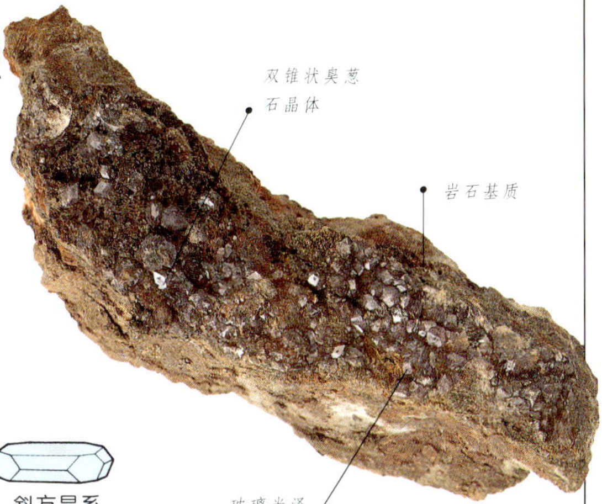


斜方晶系

| 重 3.28 | 解理 不完全 | 断口 亚贝壳状 |
|---|---|---|

| 别 砷酸盐 | 成分 $(Pb,Cu)_3(AsO_4)_2(OH)_2$ | 硬度 4.5 |
|---|---|---|

## 乳砷铅铜矿(Bayldonite)

常以块状产出，也呈粒状和粉状集合体。后二者常形成于岩石表面，除非高倍放大，很难察看出任何晶体。还以皮壳状、圆形结核状产出，并有纤维状、丝状内部构造。颜色常呈鲜艳的草绿色，也可为浅黄色或暗绿色，痕色待定。光线几乎不能透过结晶标本，所以乳砷铅铜矿被描述为亚半透明。松脂光泽，表面带粘性。

· **成因** 形成于铜矿床的氧化带，与橄榄铜矿、蓝铜矿、孔雀石和砷铅矿多种矿物伴生。

· **鉴定特征** 在封闭的试管内加热释放出水分。

单斜晶系

| 重 5.6～5.7 | 解理 无 | 断口 参差状 |
|---|---|---|

| 类别 钒酸盐 | 成分 $K_2(UO_2)_2V_2O_8 \cdot 3H_2O$ | 硬度 2 |
|---|---|---|

## 钒钾铀矿(Carnotite)

晶体极小而扁，以粉状、微晶状块体或皮壳状集合体产出。鲜黄色或绿黄色，痕黄色。半透明，晶体呈珍珠光泽，块体则呈暗淡光泽。

· **成因** 为次生矿物，地下水淋滤铀矿床而成。

· **鉴定特征** 具放射性，溶于酸。

单斜晶系

| 比重 4.75 | 解理 完全底面 | 断口 参差状 |
|---|---|---|

| 类别 钒酸盐 | 成分 $Ca(UO_2)_2V_2O_8 \cdot 58H_2O$ | 硬度 2 |
|---|---|---|

## 钒钙铀矿(Tyuyamunite)

呈微小的鳞片状和板状晶体，还呈块状、致密状和微晶状集合体。绿黄色到黄色，条痕黄色。半透明到不透明，蜡状、珍珠、金刚或暗淡光泽。

· **成因** 原生铀矿氧化带的产物。

· **鉴定特征** 具有放射性。

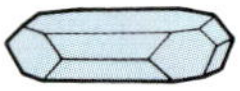

斜方晶系

| 比重 3.3~3.6 | 解理 完全底面 | 断口 参差状 |
|---|---|---|

| 类别 钒酸盐 | 成分 $Cu_3V_2O_7(OH)_2 \cdot 2H_2O$ | 硬度 3.5 |
|---|---|---|

## 钒铜矿(Volborthite)

呈皮壳鳞片状，常具三角或六边形的轮廓。常成片状双晶，还以玫瑰状或蜂窝状集合体产出。绿色、黄色或棕色，条痕待定。半透明，具有玻璃到珍珠光泽。

· **成因** 是其他钒矿物变化的产物。

· **鉴定特征** 溶于酸。

单斜晶系

| 比重 3.42 | 解理 完全底面 | 断口 参差状 |
|---|---|---|

| 类别 钒酸盐 | 成分 $Pb_5(VO_4)_3Cl$ | 硬度 3 |
|---|---|---|

## 钒铅矿(Vanadinite)

有时形成空心柱状晶体。鲜红色和桔红色到棕红色、棕色或黄色，条痕白色或浅黄色。透明到半透明，松脂到半金刚光泽。

· **成因** 形成于铅矿床的氧化带。

· **鉴定特征** 用酸加热检测钒铅矿，显示系列特征。在火焰中易熔，溶于硝酸。如果溶液蒸发，则出现红色残留物，由此可与其他相关矿物区分，后者留下的是白色沉淀物。

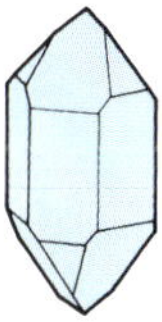

三方/六方晶系

| 比重 6.88 | 解理 无 | 断口 贝壳状至参差状 |
|---|---|---|

| 类别 钒酸盐 | 成分 $Pb(Zn,Cu)(VO_4)(OH)$ | 硬度 3~3.5 |
|---|---|---|

## 钒铅锌矿(Descloizite)

呈锥状、板状或柱状晶体，通常晶面粗糙，还以皮壳、羽毛状集合体和葡萄状块体产出。桔红色到红棕色或黑棕色，条痕黄橙色到红棕色。透明到半透明，玻璃到油脂光泽。

· **成因** 以次生矿物形成于矿脉和矿床的氧化带。

· **鉴定特征** 溶于盐酸和硝酸，在火焰中易熔。

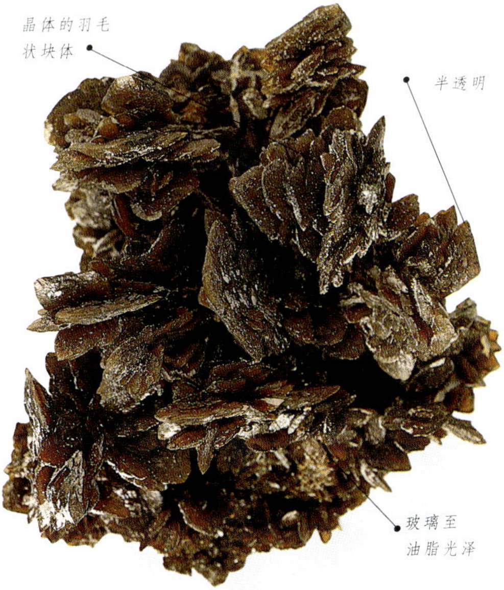


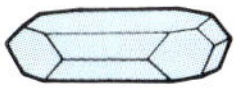

斜方晶系

| 比重 6.24~6.26 | 解理 无 | 断口 参差状至贝壳状 |
|---|---|---|

# 硅酸盐

硅酸盐是金属元素与单个或互相连接的硅氧四面体$(SiO_4)^{-4}$结合而成的化合物。按结构硅酸盐可分成六类：岛状硅酸盐，非硅阳离子与孤立的$(SiO_4)^{-4}$四面体结合；俦硅酸盐的特点是两个四面体连结在一起，并共有一个氧离子；环状硅酸盐，四面体联结成封闭的环；链状硅酸盐，其四面体连结成单链或双链；层状硅酸盐，具有薄薄层状构造，每个相邻四面体共有三个氧离子；架状硅酸盐，“框架”硅酸盐，每个硅原子与相邻的硅原子共用有个氧离子。硅酸盐是矿物中最大、数量最丰富的一类。原生硅酸盐是岩浆岩和变质岩的主要成分。硅酸盐都较硬，从透明到半透明，密度中等。

| 类别 硅酸盐 | 成分 $Fe_2SiO_4 - Mg_2SiO_4$ | 硬度 6.5～7 |
|---|---|---|

## 橄榄石(Olivine)

该系列矿物的晶体呈厚板状，且末端常呈楔形，一般呈块状、致密状和粒状集合体。绿色、绿黄色、黄棕色、棕色和白色，条痕无色。透明到半透明，玻璃光泽。橄榄石的宝石品种称为黄橄榄石。

· **成因** 作为橄榄石矿物系列代表的端员成分，镁橄榄石形成于基性和超基性岩，也见于大理岩，该矿物富含镁。另一端员成分代表矿物是铁橄榄石，富含铁，形成于快速冷却的酸性岩。

· **鉴定特征** 溶于盐酸，并出现凝胶。

贵橄榄石

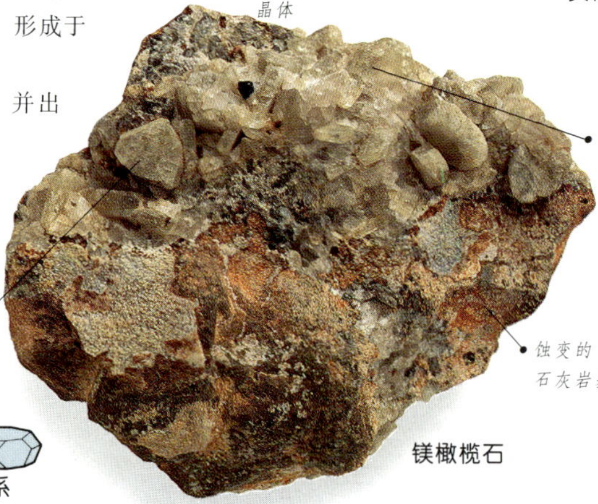

镁橄榄石

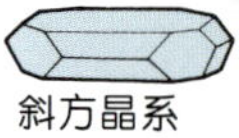
斜方晶系

| 比重 3.27～4.32 | 解理 不完全 | 断口 贝壳状 |
|---|---|---|

| | | |
|---|---|---|
| 类别 硅酸盐 | 成分 $Mg_3Al_2(SiO_4)_3$ | 硬度 7～7.5 |

## 镁铝石榴子石(Pyrope Garnet)

晶体呈十二面体或偏方三八面体，常以圆形颗粒集合体产出。浅粉红色或紫红色到深红色和近乎黑色，条痕白色。透明到半透明，玻璃光泽。

· **成因** 形成于各种超基性岩，包括橄榄岩，另外还形成于伴生蛇纹岩。

· **鉴定特征** 易熔，几乎不溶于酸。

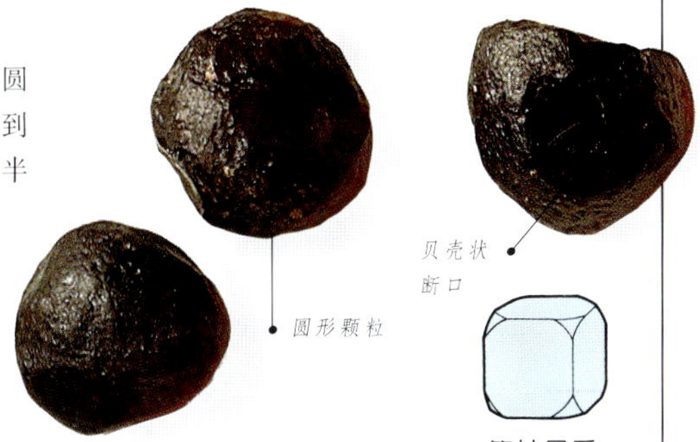


等轴晶系

| | | |
|---|---|---|
| 比重 3.5～3.8 | 解理 无 | 断口 贝壳状 |

| | | |
|---|---|---|
| 类别 硅酸盐 | 成分 $Ca_3Al_2(SiO_4)_3$ | 硬度 6.5～7 |

## 钙铝石榴子石(Grossular Garnet)

晶体呈十二面体或偏方三八面体，集合体呈块状、致密状或粒状。颜色变化大，绿色、黄绿色、黄色、棕色、红色、橙色、红棕色、白色、粉红色、灰色或黑色，条痕白色。透明到几乎不透明，玻璃或松脂光泽。

· **成因** 最常见于大理岩，不过也形成于多种变质岩。

· **鉴定特征** 不溶于酸。

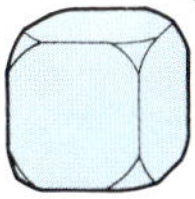

等轴晶系

| | | |
|---|---|---|
| 比重 3.4～3.6 | 解理 无 | 断口 参差状至贝壳状 |

| | | |
|---|---|---|
| 类别 硅酸盐 | 成分 $Fe_3Al_2(SiO_4)_3$ | 硬度 7～7.5 |

## 铁铝石榴子石(Almandine Garnet)

晶体呈十二面体、菱形十二面体或偏方三八面体，还以块状、粒状和致密状集合体产出。深红到红棕色和棕黑色，条痕白色。透明到半透明，玻璃或松脂光泽。

· **成因** 形成于区域变质岩，如片岩中。

· **鉴定特征** 不溶于酸，易熔。

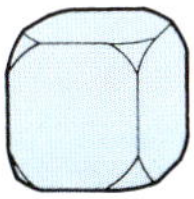

等轴晶系

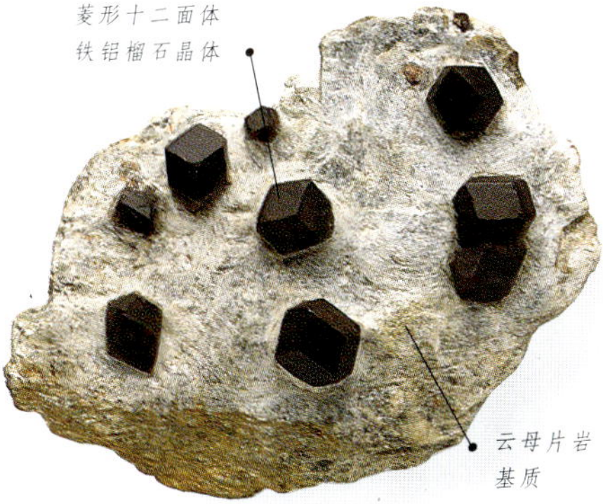


| | | |
|---|---|---|
| 比重 4.1～4.3 | 解理 无 | 断口 参差状至贝壳状 |

| 类别 硅酸盐 | 成分 $(Mg,Fe)_7(SiO_4)_3(F,OH)_2$ | 硬度 6 |
|---|---|---|

## 硅镁石(Humite)

晶体小而粗短，多变化，常呈多种集合体。白色、黄色、深橙色或棕色。透明到半透明，新鲜晶面呈玻璃光泽。

· **成因** 形成于接触变质石灰岩和某些矿脉中，与许多矿物伴生，包括方解石、石墨、尖晶石、透辉石、符山石、石榴子石和其他指示变质石灰岩的特征矿物。硅镁石类包括硅镁石、斜硅镁石、块硅镁石和粒硅镁石。

· **鉴定特征** 不需要进一步检测即可识别。

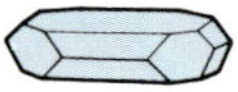

斜方晶系

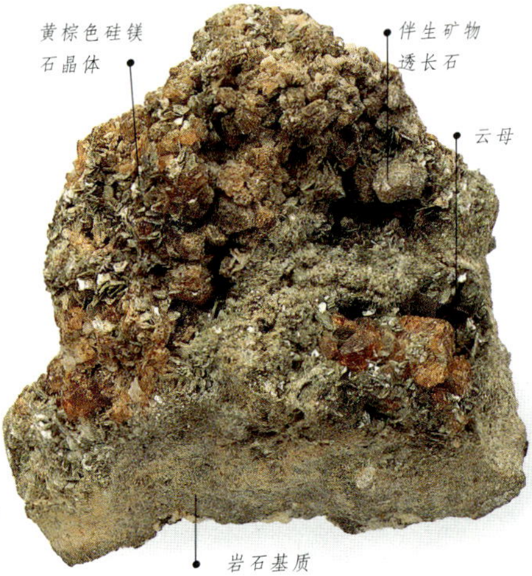


| 比重 3.24 | 解理 不佳 | 断口 参差状 |
|---|---|---|

| 类别 硅酸盐 | 成分 $(Mg,Fe)_5(SiO_4)_2(F,OH)_2$ | 硬度 6~6.5 |
|---|---|---|

## 粒硅镁石(Chondrodite)

硅镁石类成员之一，常呈多种集合体。常成片状双晶，也呈块状。黄色、红色或棕色。透明到半透明，玻璃光泽。

· **成因** 形成于接触变质石灰岩，有时也形成于碳酸岩，但罕见的，富含方解石的火成岩是为碳酸盐岩。

· **鉴定特征** 溶于热盐酸，且随溶液的冷却出现胶状沉淀物，不熔。

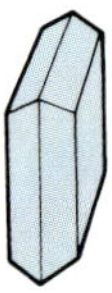

单斜晶系

| 比重 3.16~3.26 | 解理 不佳 | 断口 参差状 |
|---|---|---|

| 类别　硅酸盐 | 成分　$Al_2SiO_4(F,OH)_2$ | 硬度　8 |
|---|---|---|

## 黄玉(Topaz)

常成完好的柱状晶体，可成重量超过 100 公斤的巨晶，也呈块状、粒状和柱状集合体。颜色多变，白色、无色、灰色、黄色、橙色、棕色、浅蓝色、浅绿色、紫色或粉红色，条痕无色。透明到半透明，玻璃光泽。

· **成因**　常形成于伟晶岩，以及矿脉和花岗岩的裂隙中。与多种矿物共生，包括石英。

· **鉴定特征**　不溶于酸，火焰中不熔。

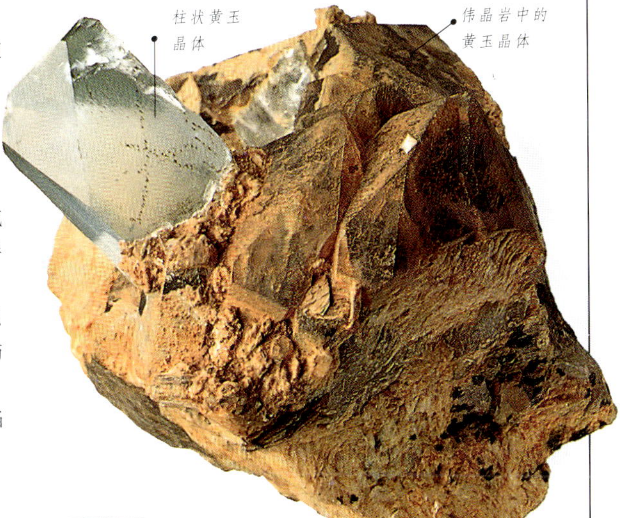


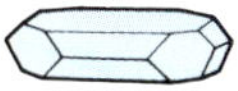
斜方晶系

| 比重 3.49～3.57 | 解理　完全 | 断口　亚贝壳状至参差状 |
|---|---|---|

| 类别　硅酸盐 | 成分　$Zn_2SiO_4$ | 硬度　5.5 |
|---|---|---|

## 硅锌矿(Willemite)

晶体呈六方柱状，端部常呈菱面体形，还以块状、纤维状、致密状和粒状集合体产出。白色、无色、灰色、绿色、黄色、棕色或浅红色。透明到半透明，玻璃或松脂光泽。

· **成因**　形成于锌矿床的氧化带和矿脉中，还经二次蚀变形成于变质石灰岩。

· **鉴定特征**　具强燐光，溶于盐酸，紫外光下呈鲜绿色萤光。

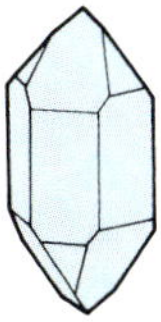
三方/六方晶系

| 比重 3.89～4.19 | 解理　底面 | 断口　参差状 |
|---|---|---|

| 类别 硅酸盐 | 成分 $(Fe,Mg,Zn)_2Al_9(Si,Al)_4O_{22}(OH)_2$ | 硬度 7～7.5 |
| --- | --- | --- |

## 十字石(Staurolite)

晶体呈短柱状，常成十字形双晶。深棕色、红棕色、黄棕色或棕黑色，条痕从无色到浅灰色。半透明到几乎不透明，玻璃到松脂光泽。

**·成因** 形成于地壳深处和区域变质岩，如高温和高压下生成的片麻岩和云母片岩。与蓝晶石、白云母、石榴子石和石英等变质矿物伴生。

**·鉴定特征** 某些变种含微量的锰，则易熔化。

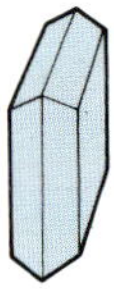

单斜晶系

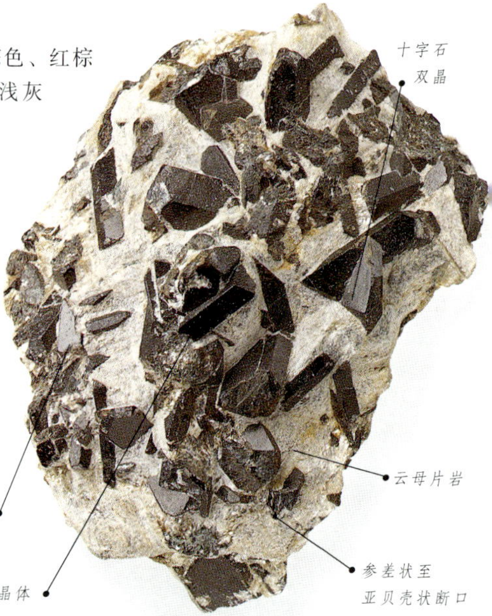


| 比重 3.65～3.83 | 解理 清楚 | 断口 参差状至亚贝壳状 |
| --- | --- | --- |

| 类别 硅酸盐 | 成分 $(Fe,Mg,Mn)_2Al_4Si_2O_{10}(OH)_4$ | 硬度 6.5 |
| --- | --- | --- |

## 硬绿泥石(Chloritoid)

晶体罕见，如果形成，则呈板状或假六方晶体，且常双晶，常以叶片状或块状，或者以鳞状或薄板状集合体产出。深灰色，或者从浅绿色到绿黑色，条痕色未定。半透明，解理面呈珍珠光泽。

**·成因** 形成于区域变质形成的岩石，如片岩和千枚岩，还形成于伟晶岩。伴生矿物有白云母、绿泥石、石榴子石、十字石(上例)和蓝晶石。

**·鉴定特征** 溶于浓硫酸，不溶于盐酸。具可熔，但难熔化。

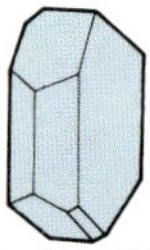

三斜/单斜晶系

| 比重 3.6 | 解理 完全 | 断口 参差状 |
| --- | --- | --- |

| 类别 硅酸盐 | 成分 $ZrSiO_4$ | 硬度 7.5 |
|---|---|---|

## 锆石(Zircon)

晶体呈柱状、四方双锥状，还呈放射状纤维集合体，常成双晶和不规则粒状。无色、红色、棕色、黄色、绿色或灰色。透明到不透明，玻璃、金刚或油脂光泽。

· **成因** 形成于岩浆岩如正长岩和某些变质岩。原生含锆石岩风化侵蚀后，形成含锆石碎屑沉积。

· **鉴定特征** 含少量的铀和钍，往往具有放射性。

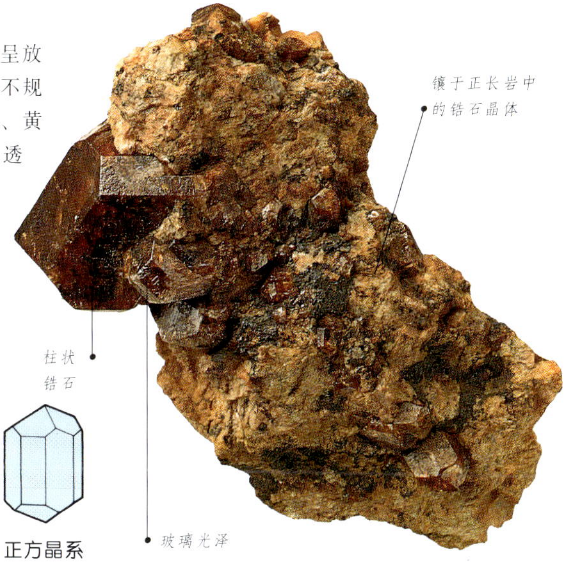


正方晶系

| 比重 4.6～4.7 | 解理 不完全 | 断口 参差状至贝壳状 |
|---|---|---|

| 类别 硅酸盐 | 成分 $Al_2SiO_5$ | 硬度 6.5～7.5 |
|---|---|---|

## 红柱石(Andalusite)

晶体柱状，横截面近正四边形(空晶石是红柱石的一种，具有十字形的横截面)，还以块状、纤维状或柱状集合体产出。粉红色、浅红色、浅棕色、浅白色、浅灰色或浅绿色，条痕无色。透明到几乎不透明，玻璃光泽。

· **成因** 形成于花岗岩、伟晶岩和多种变质岩中，与蓝晶石、堇青石、硅线石和刚玉等矿物共生。

· **鉴定特征** 不溶于任何酸，在火焰中加热也不熔化。

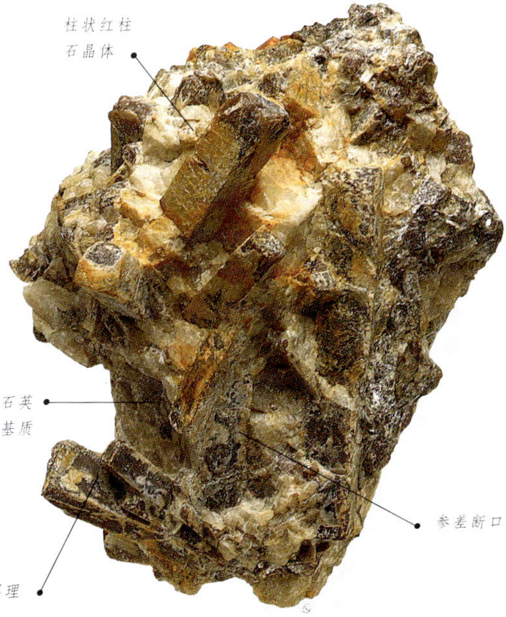


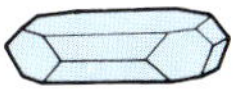

斜方晶系

| 比重 3.13～3.16 | 解理 清楚柱面 | 断口 参差状至亚贝壳状 |
|---|---|---|

| 类别 硅酸盐 | 成分 $Al_2SiO_5$ | 硬度 6.5 ~ 7.5 |
|---|---|---|

## 硅线石(Sillimanite)

晶体柱状，横截面近正四边形，还以纤维状块体产出。白色、无色、灰色、浅黄色、浅棕色、浅绿色或浅蓝色，条痕无色。透明到半透明，玻璃到丝绢光泽。

· 成因　形成于变质岩和一些岩浆岩中。

· 鉴定特征　不熔，也不溶于酸。

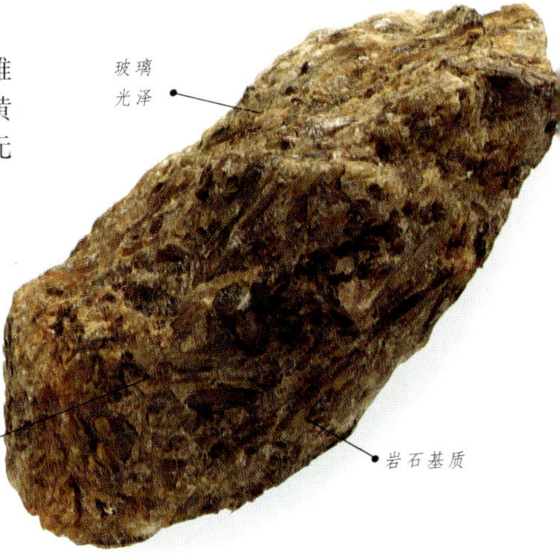

斜方晶系

| 比重 3.23 ~ 3.27 | 解理 完全 | 断口 参差状 |
|---|---|---|

| 类别 硅酸盐 | 成分 $Al_2SiO_5$ | 硬度 5.5 ~ 7 |
|---|---|---|

## 蓝晶石(Kyanite)

与夕线石和红柱石构成三同质多像变体型。蓝晶石常呈扁平柱状和片状晶体，且常呈扭曲或弯曲晶形，还以块状和纤维状集合体产出。蓝色、白色、灰色、绿色、黄色、粉红色或近乎黑色，并且单个晶体颜色多变化，条痕无色。透明到半透明，玻璃光泽，解理面上呈珍珠光泽。

· 成因　形成于许多变质岩，特别是片岩和片麻岩。因其存在于片岩中，地质学家得以推算它们形成时的温度压力条件。

· 鉴定特征　垂直解理面的硬度 6 ~ 7，平行解理面只有 4 ~ 5。

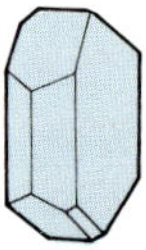

三斜晶系

| 比重 3.53 ~ 3.67 | 解理 完全 | 断口 参差状 |
|---|---|---|

| 类别 硅酸盐 | 成分 $CaTiSiO_5$ | 硬度 5~5.5 |
|---|---|---|

## 榍石(Sphene)

呈楔形或柱状晶体，常成双晶，还以块状、片状和致密状集合体产出。棕色、黄色、绿色、灰色、红色或黑色，单个晶体颜色多变化，也见无色者，条痕白色。透明到几乎不透明，金刚到松脂光泽。

· **成因** 以副矿物形式产于多岩浆岩。

· **鉴定特征** 溶于硫酸。

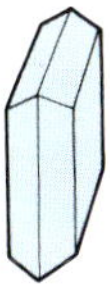

单斜晶系

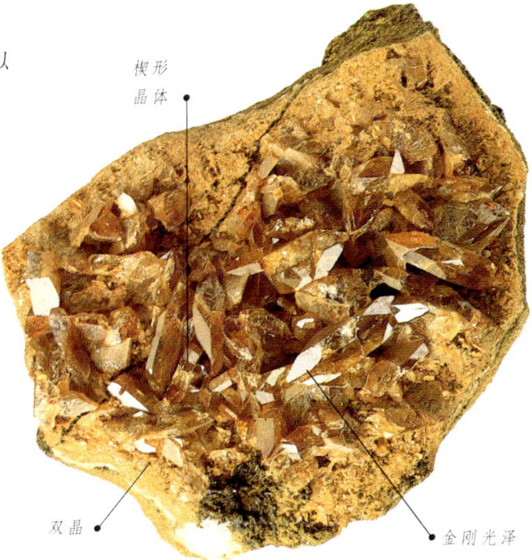


| 比重 3.45~3.55 | 解理 清楚 | 断口 贝壳状 |
|---|---|---|

| 类别 硅酸盐 | 成分 $Al_7(BO_3)(SiO_4)_3O_3$ | 硬度 8.5 |
|---|---|---|

## 蓝线石(Dumortierite)

偶尔形成柱状晶体，常见的为块状、纤维状、放射状和柱状集合体。蓝色、紫罗兰色、粉红色或棕色，条痕白色。透明到半透明，玻璃到暗淡光泽。

· **成因** 形成于粗粒酸性岩，包括伟晶岩。富含铝的岩石常含有蓝线石，尤其当这些岩石经过接触变质蚀变后。在地壳一定深变，化学物质丰富的环境里，岩浆缓慢冷却形成粗粒的伟晶岩。

· **鉴定特征** 不溶解于任何酸，即使置于火焰中也不熔化。

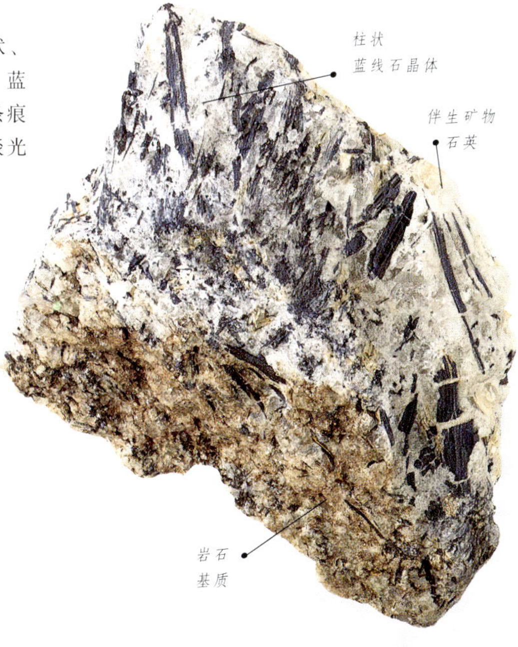


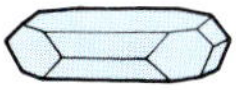

斜方晶系

| 比重 3.41 | 解理 良好 | 断口 参差状 |
|---|---|---|

类别 硅酸盐 | 成分 $BeAlSiO_4(OH)$ | 硬度 7.5

## 蓝柱石(Euclase)

晶体柱状。无色、浅白色、淡绿色、蓝色或淡蓝色，条痕白色。透明到半透明，晶面上呈玻璃光泽。

· **成因** 形成于花岗伟晶岩，还形成于冲积砂积矿床。

· **鉴定特征** 不溶于酸，难熔。

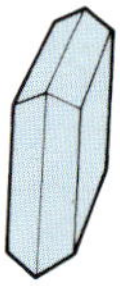

单斜晶系

比重 3.05～3.10 | 解理 完全 | 断口 贝壳状

类别 硅酸盐 | 成分 $K_2Ca_4Al_2Be_4Si_{24}O_{60}H_2O$ | 硬度 5.5～6

## 整柱石(Milarite)

晶体柱状。无色、浅棕色、淡绿色或黄绿色，条痕白色。透明到半透明，玻璃光泽。

· **成因** 形成于阿尔卑斯式脉和伟晶岩。

· **鉴定特征** 在密封的试管内加热释放出水分。

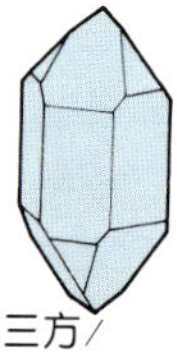

三方/六方晶系

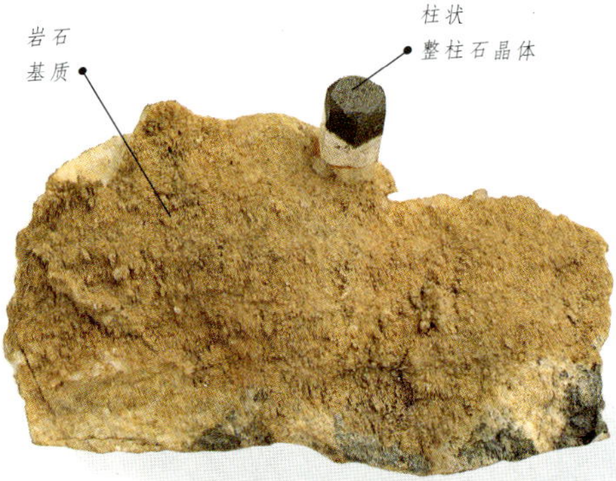


比重 2.46～2.61 | 解理 无 | 断口 贝壳状至参差状

类别 硅酸盐 | 成分 $Na_4(Ca,Ce)_2(Fe^{+2}Mn^{+2}, Y)ZrSi_8O_{22}(OH,Cl)_2$ | 硬度 5～5.5

## 异性石(Eudialyte)

晶体呈板状、菱面体或柱状。黄棕色到棕红色、红色或粉红色，条痕无色。半透明，玻璃到暗淡光泽。

· **成因** 形成于粗粒酸性和中性岩。

· **鉴定特征** 易溶于酸。

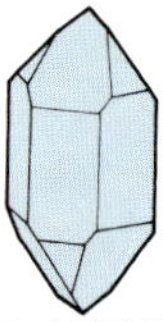

三方/六方晶系

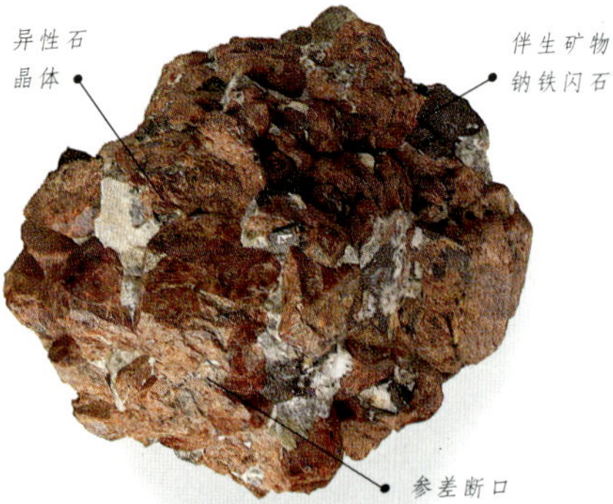


比重 2.74～2.98 | 解理 不清楚 | 断口 参差状

| | | |
|---|---|---|
| 别 硅酸盐 | 成分 $CaBSiO_4(OH)$ | 硬度 5~5.5 |

## 硅硼钙石(Datolite)

晶体呈柱状，多变化，还以粒状或致密状块体产出。由于存在杂质，颜色有无色、白色、淡黄色、淡绿色、浅粉红色、浅红色或棕色，条痕无色。透明到半透明，玻璃光泽。

· **成因** 形成于基性岩的岩脉和裂隙中，与方解石、石英以及某些沸石类矿物共生。

· **鉴定特征** 溶于酸，燃烧时火焰呈绿色。

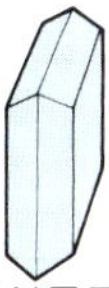

单斜晶系

| | | |
|---|---|---|
| 重 2.8~3.0 | 解理 无 | 断口 参差状至贝壳状 |

| | | |
|---|---|---|
| 别 硅酸盐 | 成分 $Y_2FeBe_2, Si_2O_{10}$ | 硬度 6.5~7 |

## 硅铍钇矿(Gadolinite)

晶体罕见，呈柱状，常以块状和致密状集合体产出。颜色的变化大，从黑色到绿黑色、棕色，有时呈浅绿色，条痕绿灰色。半透明到透明，玻璃到油脂光泽。

· **成因** 形成于粗粒中性岩，还形成于酸性岩，以及由侵入岩浆缓慢冷却形成的伟晶岩中。与褐帘石和萤石共生，也见于片岩和其他区域变质岩中。

· **鉴定特征** 是放射性矿物。溶于酸，并产生胶质沉淀物。加热后不熔，但裂为片状，并呈棕色。

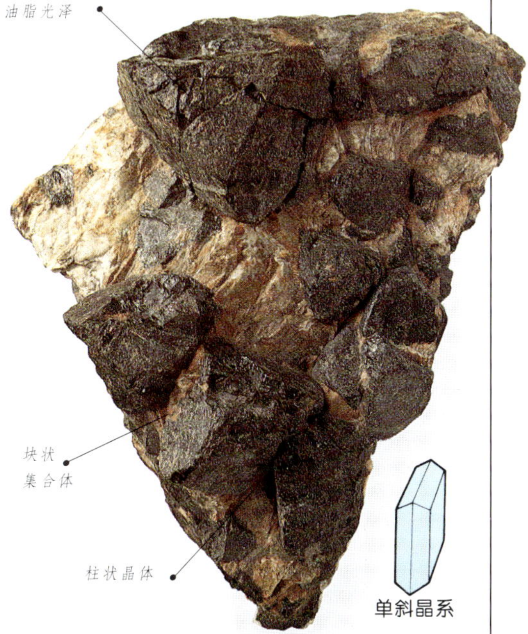


单斜晶系

| | | |
|---|---|---|
| 重 4.0~4.65 | 解理 无 | 断口 贝壳状 |

| | | |
|---|---|---|
| 类别 硅酸盐 | 成分 $Ca_2(Al,Fe)_3(SiO_4)_3(OH)$ | 硬度 6~7 |

## 绿帘石(Epidote)

晶体呈晶面带条纹的柱状，也呈厚板状和针状，通常呈块状、粒状和纤维状集合体。黄绿色到绿色、棕绿色到绿黑色或黑色，条痕无色或浅灰色。透明到几乎不透明，玻璃光泽。

· 成因　形成于变质岩或岩浆岩。

· 鉴定特征　不溶，但易熔。

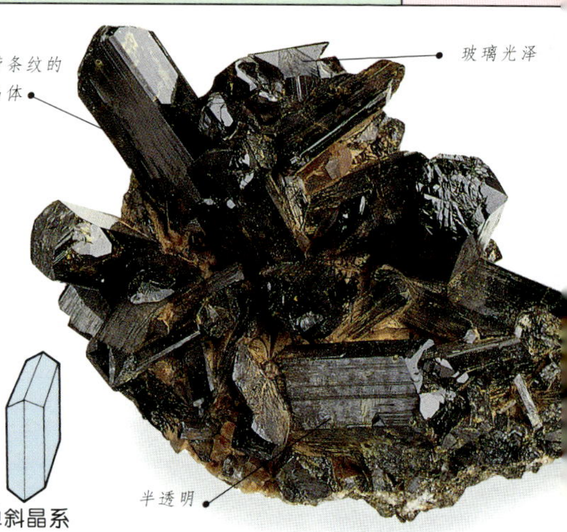


单斜晶系

| | | |
|---|---|---|
| 比重 3.35~3.50 | 解理 完全 | 断口 参差状 |

| | | |
|---|---|---|
| 类别 硅酸盐 | 成分 $Ca_2Al_3(SiO_4)_3(OH)$ | 硬度 6.5~7 |

## 黝帘石(Zoisite)

晶体呈柱状，通常有明显的纵条纹，还以块状、致密状和柱状集合体产出。白色、灰色、绿色、绿棕色、粉红色(锰黝帘石)、无色、蓝色或紫色(丹泉石)，条痕无色。透明到半透明，玻璃光泽。

· 成因　形成于多种岩石，包括变质岩、沉积岩和花岗岩。

· 鉴定特征　不溶于酸。

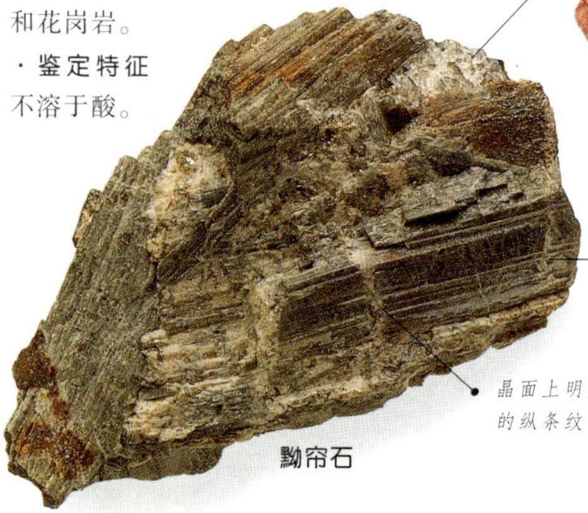


斜方晶系

| | | |
|---|---|---|
| 比重 3.55 | 解理 完全 | 断口 参差状至贝壳状 |

| | | |
|---|---|---|
| 别 硅酸盐 | 成分 $Ca_2Al_3(SiO_4)_3(OH)$ | 硬度 6.5 |

## 斜黝帘石(Clinozoisite)

晶体呈柱状，并带有明显的条纹，也呈成针状，并以块状、粒状或纤维状集合体产出。灰色、黄色、浅绿色、粉红色或无色，条痕无色或浅灰色。透明到半透明，玻璃光泽。

· **成因** 形成于接触变质石灰岩和区域变质岩。

· **鉴定特征** 不溶于酸。

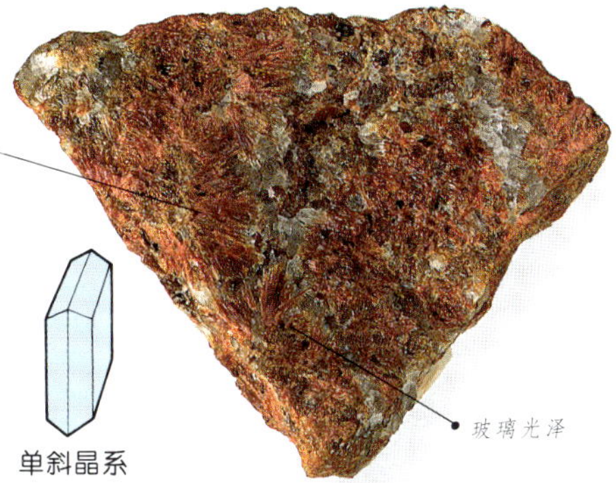


单斜晶系

| | | |
|---|---|---|
| 重 3.21~3.38 | 解理 完全 | 断口 参差状 |

| | | |
|---|---|---|
| 别 硅酸盐 | 成分 $Ca_2Al(Si,Al)O_7$ | 硬度 5~6 |

## 钙铝黄长石(Gehlenite)

属于黄长石类，晶体呈短柱状，还以块状和粒状集合体产出。灰绿色、棕色、黄色或无色，条痕未定。透明到半透明，玻璃到松脂光泽。

· **成因** 钙黄长石形成于玄武岩和接触变质石灰岩。

· **鉴定特征** 溶于强酸。

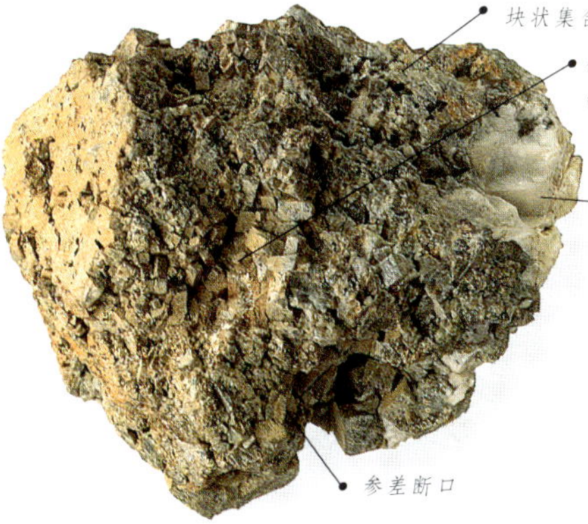


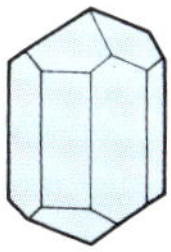

正方晶系

| | | |
|---|---|---|
| 重 3.04 | 解理 清楚 | 断口 参差状至贝壳状 |

| | | |
|---|---|---|
| 别 硅酸盐 | 成分 $Ca_2MgSi_2O_7$ | 硬度 5~6 |

## 镁黄长石(Akermanite)

晶体呈柱状，可成双晶，还以块状和粒状集合体产出。无色到灰色、棕色和绿色不等。透明到半透明，玻璃到松脂光泽。

· **成因** 形成于含杂质的变质石灰岩。

· **鉴定特征** 溶于强酸，并产生凝胶。

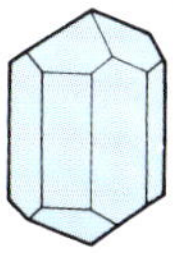

正方晶系

| | | |
|---|---|---|
| 重 2.94 | 解理 清楚 | 断口 参差状至贝壳状 |

| 类别 硅酸盐 | 成分 $Zn_4Si_2O_7(OH)_2 \cdot H_2O$ | 硬度 4.5～5 |
|---|---|---|

## 异极矿(Hemimorphite)

葡萄状异极矿

晶体薄板状，带有纵向条纹。由于晶体面端晶面发育不同，因此称为异极矿，还以块状、致密状、粒状、葡萄状、钟乳状、纤维状和皮壳状集合体产出。白色、无色、蓝色、浅绿色、灰色、浅黄色或棕色，条痕无色。透明到半透明，玻璃或丝绢光泽。

**·成因** 形成于锌矿脉氧化带，常与菱锌矿、方铅矿、方解石、硫酸铅矿、闪锌矿、白铅矿和绿铜锌矿共生。

**·鉴定特征** 在密闭的试管内加热释放出水分。溶于酸，并产生凝胶。难熔。

斜方晶系

结晶异极矿

绿色异极矿

| 比重 3.4～3.5 | 解理 完全 | 断口 参差状至贝壳状 |
|---|---|---|

| 别 硅酸盐 | 成分 $Ca_{10}Mg_2Al_4(SiO_4)_5(Si_2O_7)_2(OH)_4$ | 硬度 6～7 |
|---|---|---|

## 符山石(Vesuvianite)

晶体呈柱状和锥状，还以块状、粒状、柱状和致密状集合体产出。绿色、棕色、白色、黄色、红色或紫色。蓝色变种称为青符山石，白色或黄色的称为玉符山石。透明到半透明，玻璃到松脂光泽。透明的符山石为次等宝石，产于意大利的维苏威火山，符山石的英文名称 vesuvianite，亦名 idocrase。

· 成因　形成于接触蚀变的不纯石灰岩(矽卡岩)，以及某些岩浆岩中，如霞石正长岩。与透辉石、绿帘石、石榴子石、方解石、金云母和硅灰石共生。

· 鉴定特征　不溶于酸。

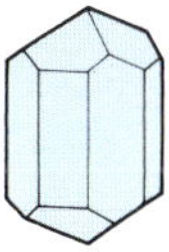

正方晶系

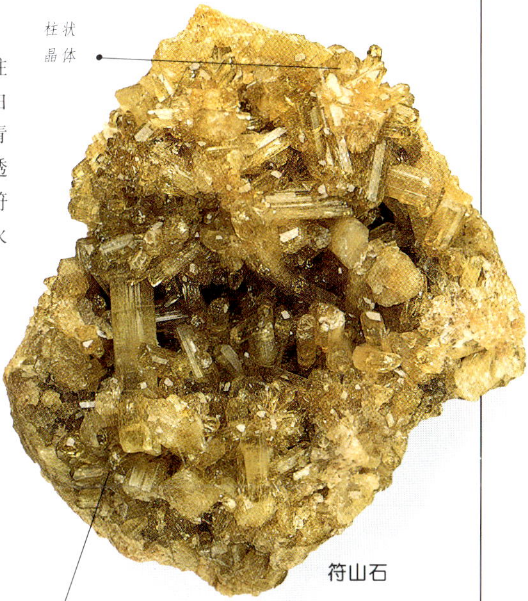


符山石

青符山石

玉符山石

| 比重 3.33～3.45 | 解理 不清楚 | 断口 参差状至贝壳状 |
|---|---|---|

| 类别 硅酸盐 | 成分 $Be_3Al_2Si_6O_{18}$ | 硬度 7~8 |
|---|---|---|

## 绿柱石(Beryl)

晶体柱状，端部常呈小锥状。晶体柱面常有明显的平行于长轴(纵向)的条纹，可生成巨大晶体，发现过长达5.5米的标本，此外还以块状、致密状和柱状集合体产出。颜色的变化很大，因此对不同色彩的绿柱给以不同的名称，无色、白色、绿色(祖母绿)、黄色(金绿玉)、粉红色(铯绿柱石)、红色和蓝色(海蓝宝石)，条痕白色。透明到半透明，玻璃光泽。

· **成因** 形成于伟晶岩和花岗岩，以及一些区域变质岩中。

· **鉴定特征** 很难熔化，熔化时会在边缘出现小碎片。

绿柱石

祖母绿

金绿玉

海蓝宝石

铯绿柱石

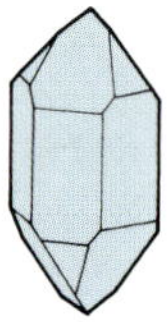
三方/六方晶系

| 比重 2.6~2.9 | 解理 不清楚 | 断口 参差状至贝壳状 |
|---|---|---|

| 类别 硅酸盐 | 成分 $Na(Mg,Fe,Li,Mn,Al)_3Al_6(BO_3)_3Si_6 \cdot O_{18}(OH,F)_4$ | 硬度 7~7.5 |
|---|---|---|

## 电气石(Tourmaline)

该族矿物的柱状晶体通常有纵向条纹，横截面呈球面三角形，还以块状和致密状集合体产出。电气石类共由七个不同的品种组成：锂电气石(多种色彩)、黑电气石(黑色)、钠铁电气石和镁电气石(棕色)、红电气石(粉红色)、铬镁电气石(绿色)和钙镁电气石(黑色、棕色、黄绿色)。晶体常一端呈粉红色而另一端为绿色，可生成相当大的晶体。条痕无色。透明到不透明，玻璃光泽。

**·成因** 形成于花岗岩和伟晶岩以及一些变质岩中，与很多矿物共生，如绿柱石、锆石、石英和长石。

**·鉴定特征** 该类矿物不溶于酸，颜色较深的品种比红色和绿色的品种难熔化。

红电气石

锂电气石

电气石

黑电气石

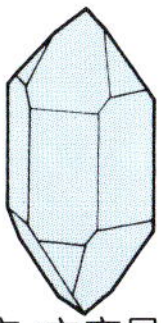
三方/六方晶系

| 比重 3.0~3.2 | 解理 极不清楚 | 断口 参差状至贝壳状 |
|---|---|---|

| 类别 硅酸盐 | 成分 $CaFe^{+2}_{2}Fe^{+3}(SiO_4)_2(OH)$ | 硬度 5.5～6 |
|---|---|---|

## 黑柱石(Ilvaite)

晶体呈密集柱状，并有金刚石形的横截面，晶面上呈纵向条纹，还以块状、柱状和致密状集合体产出。为深色矿物，黑色到灰棕色或棕黑色，条痕黑色，常微带绿色或棕色。不透明，黯淡的半金属光泽，有时显得光滑。

**·成因** 形成于岩浆或熔岩的接触变质带。也生成于岩浆岩正长岩中，但较不常见。

**·鉴定特征** 置于盐酸中，黑柱石会溶解，并有凝胶出现。在火焰中易熔化。

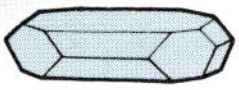
斜方晶系

| 比重 3.8～4.1 | 解理 清楚 | 断口 参差状 |
|---|---|---|

| 类别 硅酸盐 | 成分 $CuSiO_2(OH)_2$ | 硬度 5 |
|---|---|---|

## 透视石(Dioptase)

晶体柱状，常有菱面体形的端部，还以结晶集合体或块状产出。颜色从醒目的祖母绿色到深蓝绿色，条痕浅绿蓝色。透明到半透明，玻璃光泽。

**·成因** 形成于铜矿脉的氧化带，及其围岩的空洞和裂隙中。常与褐铁矿、硅孔雀石、白铅矿以及钼铅矿等矿物伴生。

**·鉴定特征** 溶于盐酸、硝酸和氨水，不熔。

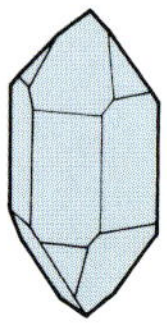
三方/六方晶系

| 比重 3.28～3.35 | 解理 完全 | 断口 参差状至贝壳状 |
|---|---|---|

| 类别　硅酸盐 | 成分　$Mg_2Al_4Si_5O_{18}$ | 硬度　7 ~ 7.5 |
| --- | --- | --- |

## 堇青石(Cordierite)

晶体呈短柱状，常成双晶，集合体块状和粒状。蓝色，浅绿色、浅黄色、灰色或棕色，常呈明显的不同色调，条痕无色。透明到半透明，玻璃光泽。

· **成因**　形成于岩浆岩和接触变质岩。

· **鉴定特征**　薄边在火焰中会熔化。

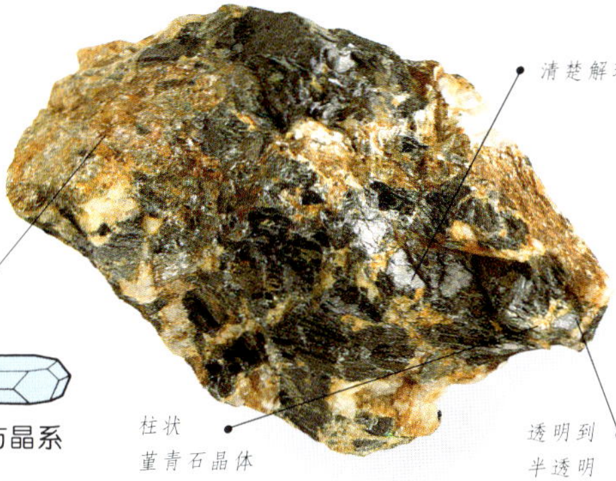


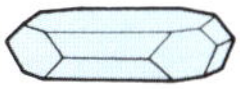

斜方晶系

| 比重 2.53 ~ 2.78 | 解理　清楚 | 断口　贝壳状 |
| --- | --- | --- |

| 类别　硅酸盐 | 成分　$Ca_2(Fe^{+2},Mn^{+2})Al_2BSi_4O_{15}(OH)$ | 硬度　6 ~ 7 |
| --- | --- | --- |

## 斧石(Axinite)

晶体呈板状和楔形，集合体块状和片状。红棕色、黄色、无色、蓝色、紫罗兰色或灰色，条痕无色。透明到半透明，玻璃光泽。

· **成因**　形成于接触变质蚀变的钙质岩石中。

· **鉴定特征**　易熔化。

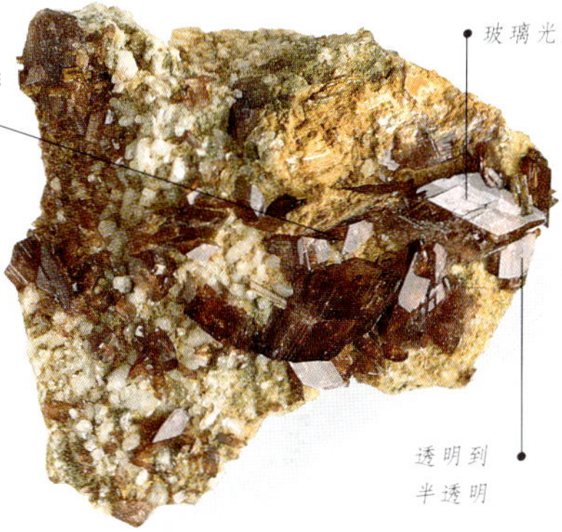


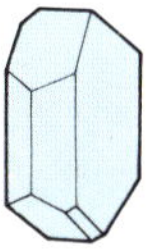

三斜晶系

| 比重 3.2 ~ 3.4 | 解理　良好 | 断口　参差状至贝壳状 |
| --- | --- | --- |

| 类别　硅酸盐 | 成分　$BaTiSi_3O_9$ | 硬度　6 ~ 6.5 |
| --- | --- | --- |

## 蓝锥矿(Benitoite)

晶体呈锥状或板状。蓝色、紫色、粉红色、白色或无色，且常呈多色，条痕无色。透明到半透明的矿物，玻璃光泽。

· **成因**　形成于蛇纹岩和片岩。

· **鉴定特征**　紫外光下发蓝色萤光。

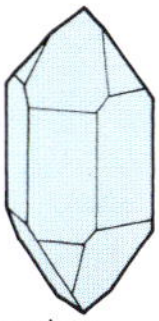

三方/六方晶系

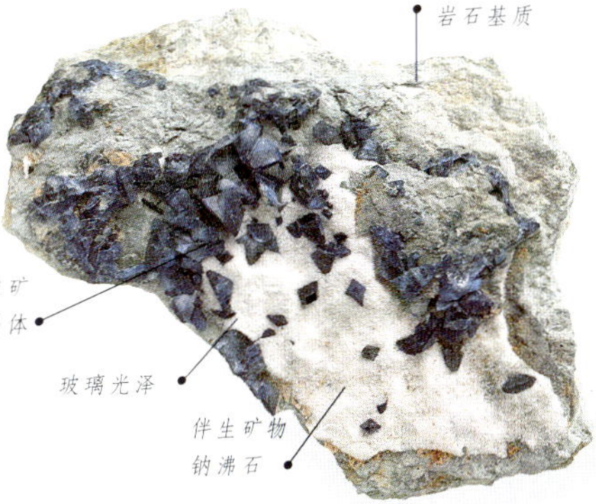


| 比重 3.64 ~ 3.68 | 解理　不清楚 | 断口　贝壳状至参差状 |
| --- | --- | --- |

| 类别 硅酸盐 | 成分 $Mg_2Si_2O_6$ | 硬度 5～6 |
|---|---|---|

## 顽火辉石(Enstatite)

辉石族成员之一，偶尔形成柱状晶体，常以块状、纤维状或片状集合体产出。无色、绿色、棕色或浅黄色，条痕无色或灰色。透明到几乎不透明，玻璃或珍珠光泽。

· **成因** 常形成于基性和超基性岩中，如辉长岩、粗粒玄武岩、苏长岩和橄榄岩。

· **鉴定特征** 不溶，也几乎不熔。

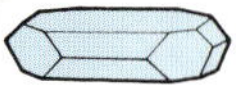
斜方晶系

| 比重 3.2～3.4 | 解理 良好 | 断口 参差状 |
|---|---|---|

| 类别 硅酸盐 | 成分 $(Mg,Fe)_2Si_2O_6$ | 硬度 5～6 |
|---|---|---|

## 紫苏辉石(Hypersthene)

属辉石族，偶尔形成柱状晶体，常以块状或片状集合体产出。棕绿色或黑色，条痕棕灰色。半透明到不透明的矿物，半金属光泽。

· **成因** 形成于超基性和基性岩。

· **鉴定特征** 可熔，发闪光。

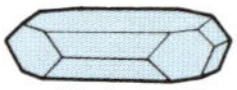
斜方晶系

| 比重 3.4～3.8 | 解理 良好 | 断口 参差状 |
|---|---|---|

| 类别 硅酸盐 | 成分 $CaMgSi_2O_6$ | 硬度 5.5～6.5 |
|---|---|---|

## 透辉石(Diopside)

属辉石族，晶体短柱状，常成双晶，集合体块状、片状、粒状和柱状。无色、白色、灰色、绿色、绿黑色、黄棕色或红棕色，条痕白色到灰色。透明到几乎不透明，玻璃光泽。

· **成因** 形成于许多变质岩和基性岩。

· **鉴定特征** 不溶于酸。

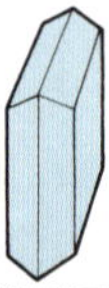
单斜晶系

| 比重 3.22～3.38 | 解理 良好 | 断口 参差状 |
|---|---|---|

| 类别 硅酸盐 | 成分 $CaFeSi_2O_6$ | 硬度 6 |
|---|---|---|

## 钙铁辉石(Hedenbergite)

晶体呈短柱状，且常成双晶，常见的是块状、刃状或片状集合体。棕绿色、灰绿色或暗绿色到灰黑色或黑色，条痕白色或灰色。半透明到几乎不透明，玻璃到松脂或暗淡光泽。

· 成因　形成于大理岩和多种岩浆岩中。

· 鉴定特征　不溶，但易于熔化。

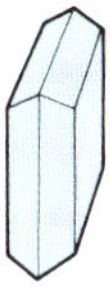
单斜晶系

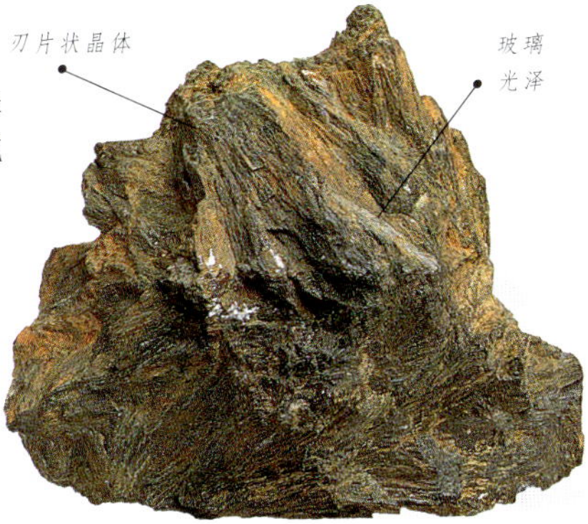


| 比重 3.50～3.56 | 解理 良好 | 断口 参差状至贝壳状 |
|---|---|---|

| 类别 硅酸盐 | 成分 $(Ca,Na)(Mg,Fe,Al,Ti)(Si,Al)_2O_6$ | 硬度 5.5～6 |
|---|---|---|

## 普通辉石(Augite)

属辉石族，呈短柱状晶体，常成双晶，还以块状、致密状和粒状集合体产出。棕色、浅绿色或黑色，条痕灰绿色。半透明到几乎不透明，玻璃到暗淡光泽。

· 成因　形成于多种基性和超基性岩和深变质岩。

· 鉴定特征　通常不溶于酸。

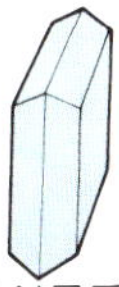
单斜晶系

| 比重 3.23～3.52 | 解理 良好 | 断口 参差状至贝壳状 |
|---|---|---|

| 类别 硅酸盐 | 成分 $NaFe_2Si_2O_6$ | 硬度 6 |
|---|---|---|

## 钝钠辉石(Aegirine)

属辉石族，长柱状晶体，晶面有纵纹，常成双晶，外还以纤维状集合体产出。

暗绿色、绿黑色、黑色或红棕色，条痕浅黄灰色。半透明到不透明，玻璃到松脂光泽。

· 成因　形成于中性岩和变质岩。

· 鉴定特征　易熔。

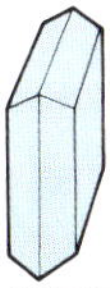
单斜晶系

| 比重 3.55～3.60 | 解理 良好 | 断口 参差状 |
|---|---|---|

| 类别 硅酸盐 | 成分 $LiAlSi_2O_6$ | 硬度 6.5~7.5 |
|---|---|---|

## 锂辉石(Spodumene)

晶体柱状，常扁平，成双晶，且柱面上有纵纹。有时晶体可能很大，还以可劈裂的块体产出。颜色变化大，无色、白色、灰色、浅黄色、浅绿色、祖母绿色(翠绿锂辉石)、粉红色或淡紫色(紫锂辉石)，条痕白色。透明到半透明，玻璃光泽。

· **成因** 形成于花岗伟晶岩，与其他伟晶岩矿物长石、白云母、黑云母和锂云母、石英、铌铁—钽铁矿、绿柱石、电气石和黄玉共生，锂辉石稳定，后生作用下部分或全部转变成粘土或云母。

· **鉴定特征** 不溶解，可熔化。由于含锂元素，火焰呈红色。

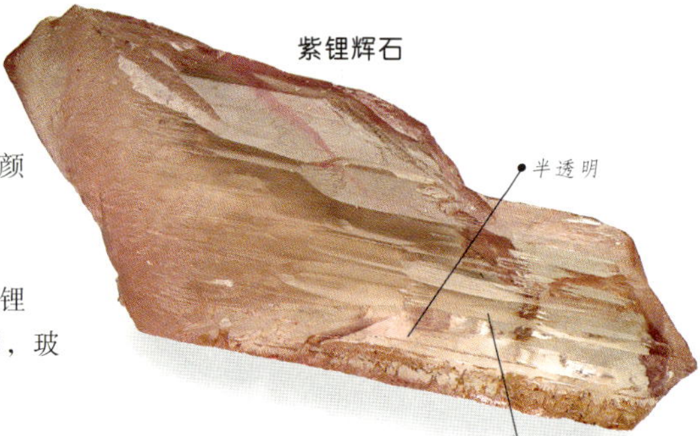


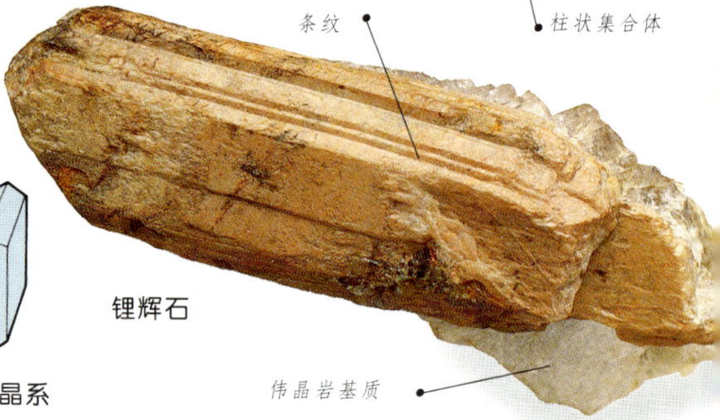


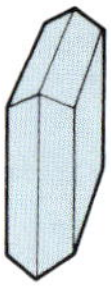
单斜晶系

| 比重 3.0~3.2 | 解理 完全 | 断口 参差状 |
|---|---|---|

| 类别 硅酸盐 | 成分 $Na(Al,Fe)Si_2O_6$ | 硬度 6~7 |
|---|---|---|

## 硬玉(Jadeite)

很少形成晶体，形成时，则呈细长的小柱状，晶面一般有条纹，且常成双晶。常见的是块状或粒状集合体产出。典型的颜色呈绿色，也有白色、灰色、紫红色，含氧化铁杂质时，则呈棕色或黄色，条痕无色。是贵重的装饰用宝石，半透明，具玻璃到油脂光泽。

· **成因** 形成于蛇纹岩化超基性岩和某些片岩，还见于小矿脉，以及燧石和杂砂岩透镜体。

· **鉴定特征** 不溶。

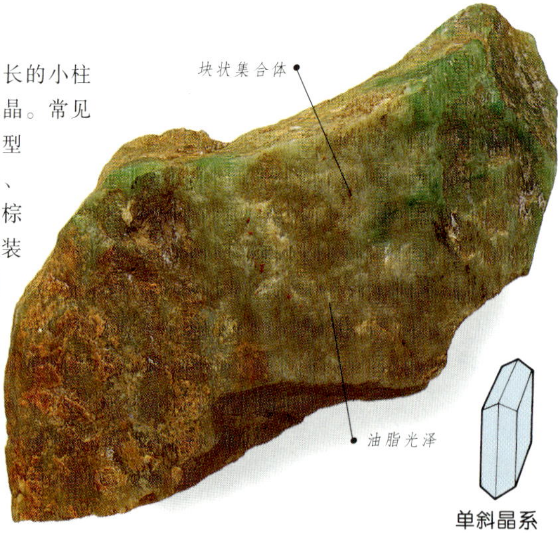


单斜晶系

| 比重 3.24 | 解理 良好 | 断口 多片状 |
|---|---|---|

| 类别 硅酸盐 | 成分 $Ca_2(Mg,Fe)_4Al(Si_7Al)O_{22}(OH,F)_2$ | 硬度 5~6 |
|---|---|---|

## 普通角闪石(Hornblende)

晶体柱状，横截面六边形，常成双晶，还以块状、致密状、粒状、柱状、刃片状和纤维状集合体产出。绿色、绿棕色或黑色，条痕白色或灰色。半透明到不透明，玻璃光泽。两组解理夹角 60° 或 120°。

· 成因　形成于岩浆岩，亦见于变质岩、角闪岩。

· 鉴定特征　不溶，难熔。

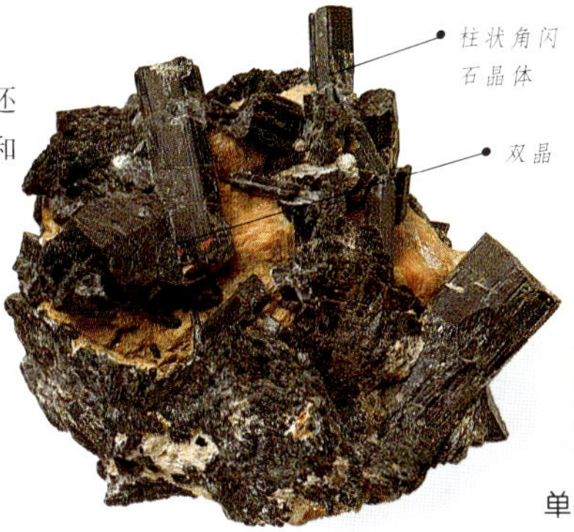


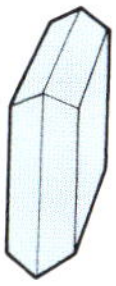

单斜晶系

| 比重 3.28~3.41 | 解理 完全 | 断口 参差状 |
|---|---|---|

| 类别 硅酸盐 | 成分 $(Mg,Fe)_7Si_8O_{22}(OH)_2$ | 硬度 5.5~6 |
|---|---|---|

## 斜方角闪石(Anthophyllite)

晶体柱状，少见，常以块状、纤维状或片状集合体产出。白色到灰色、浅绿色、棕绿色和棕色，条痕无色或灰色。透明到几乎不透明，玻璃光泽。

· 成因　形成于结晶片岩和片麻岩。

· 鉴定特征　不溶，也很难熔。

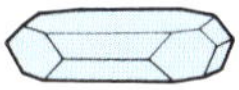

斜方晶系

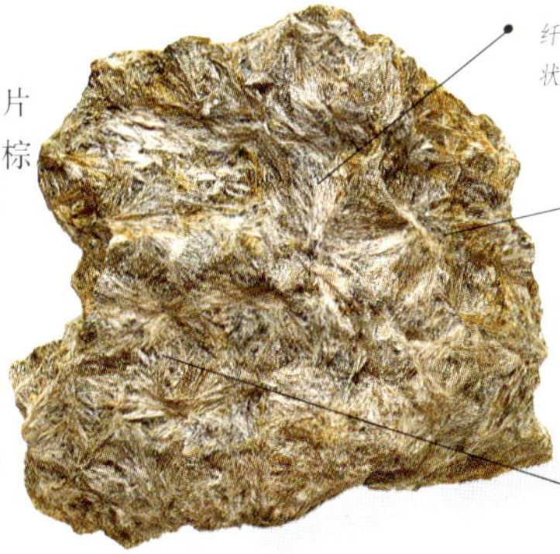


| 比重 2.85~3.57 | 解理 完全 | 断口 参差状 |
|---|---|---|

| 类别 硅酸盐 | 成分 $(Fe,Mg)_7Si_8O_{22}(OH)_2$ | 硬度 5~6 |
|---|---|---|

## 铁闪石(Grunerite)

是镁铁闪石——铁闪石闪石类的端员成分，晶体纤维状或片状，并常聚成放射状集合体，它们常成双晶。灰色、暗绿色或棕色。半透明到几乎不透明，丝绢光泽。

· 成因　形成于接触变质的岩石中。

· 鉴定特征　不溶。

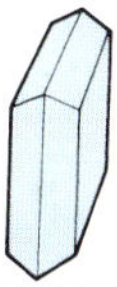

单斜晶系

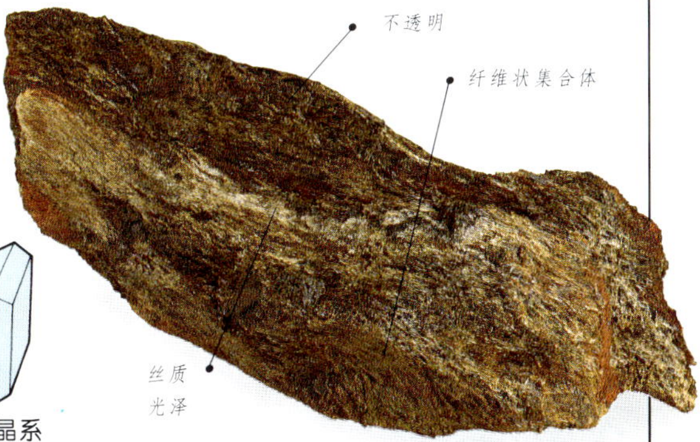


| 比重 3.44~3.60 | 解理 良好 | 断口 参差状 |
|---|---|---|

| 类别 硅酸盐 | 成分 $Na_2(Mg,Fe)_3Al_2Si_8O_{22}(OH)_2$ | 硬度 6 |
|---|---|---|

## 蓝闪石(Glaucophane)

属于角闪石族，晶体柱状，集合体块状、纤维状和粒状。灰色、蓝色、蓝黑色或紫蓝色，条痕灰蓝色。半透明，玻璃到暗淡或珍珠光泽。

· **成因**　形成于低温和高压下形成的变质岩。

· **鉴定特征**　溶于酸，易熔化，形成绿色玻璃。

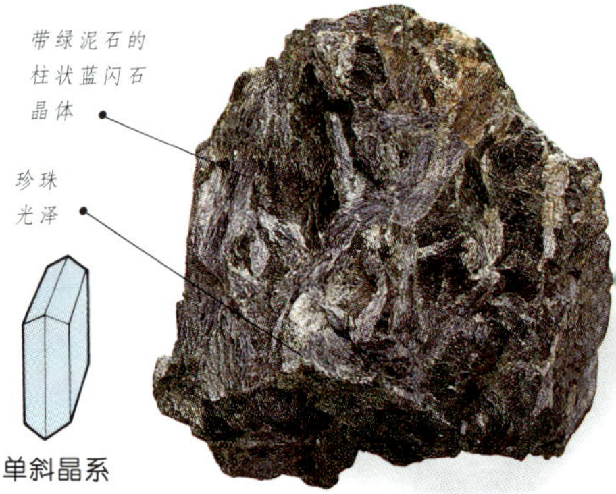


| 比重 3.08～3.15 | 解理 完全 | 断口 参差状至贝壳状 |
|---|---|---|

| 类别 硅酸盐 | 成分 $Na_3(Fe^{+2},Mg)_4Fe^{+3}Si_8O_{22}(OH)_2$ | 硬度 5 |
|---|---|---|

## 钠闪石(Riebeckite)

晶体柱状，晶面上有纵纹，还以块状、纤维状和石绵状(青石绵)集合体产出。深蓝到黑色，条痕未定。半透明，玻璃或丝绢光泽。

· **成因**　形成于许多岩浆岩和片岩中。

· **鉴定特征**　易熔。

| 比重 3.32～3.38 | 解理 完全 | 断口 参差状 |
|---|---|---|

| 类别 硅酸盐 | 成分 $Ca_2(Mg,Fe)_5Si_8O_{22}(OH)_2$ | 硬度 5～6 |
|---|---|---|

## 阳起石(Actinolite)

晶体呈长刃片状，常成双晶，也呈片状和柱状集合体，且呈放射状，还以块状、纤维状或粒状集合体产出。淡绿色到黑绿色，条痕白色。透明到几乎不透明，玻璃光泽。其致密的变种称为软玉，是玉的一种。

· **成因**　形成于片岩和角闪岩，源于变质基性岩的。

· **鉴定特征**　不溶于盐酸。

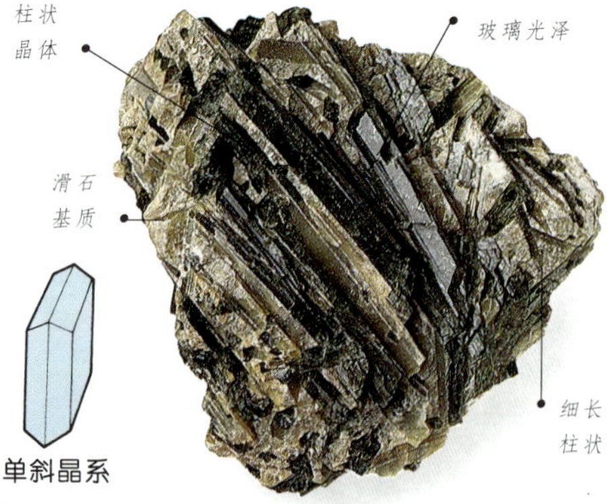


| 比重 3.0～3.44 | 解理 良好 | 断口 参差状至贝壳状 |
|---|---|---|

| 类别 硅酸盐 | 成分 $Ca_2(Mg,Fe)_5Si_8O_{22}(OH)_2$ | 硬度 5～6 |
|---|---|---|

## 透闪石(Tremolite)

晶体呈长刃片状，常成双晶，还以柱状、纤维状或羽毛状(呈放射状)，以及块状和粒状集合体产出。无色、白色、灰色、绿色、粉红色或棕色，条痕白色。透明到半透明，玻璃光泽。与阳起石属于同一亚族。

· **成因** 形成于接触变质白云岩及蛇纹岩。

· **鉴定特征** 不溶于酸。

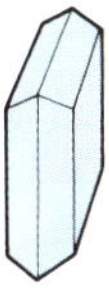
单斜晶系

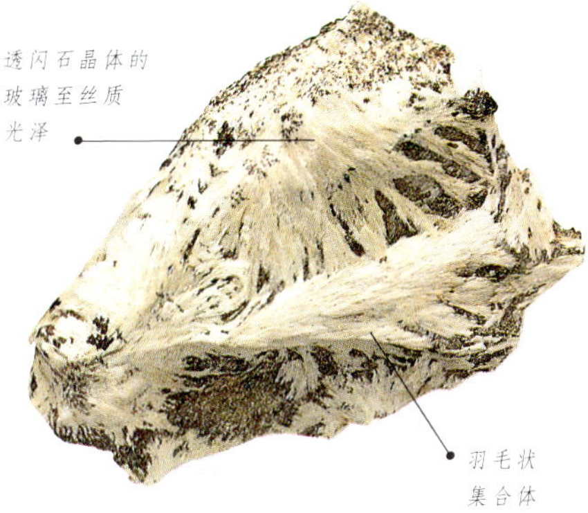


| 比重 2.9～3.2 解理 良好 | 断口 参差状至亚贝壳状 | |
|---|---|---|

| 类别 硅酸盐 | 成分 $Na_3(Fe,Mg)_4FeSi_8O_{22}(OH)_2$ | 硬度 5～6 |
|---|---|---|

## 钠铁闪石(Arfvedsonite)

晶体柱状和板状，通常呈集合体，常成双晶。绿黑色至黑色，条痕深蓝灰色。几乎不透明，玻璃光泽。

· **成因** 形成于岩浆岩，尤其是正长岩中，也见于一些区域变质岩中，如片岩。

· **鉴定特征** 不溶于酸。易熔，并形成具磁性的黑色玻璃。

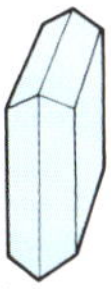
单斜晶系

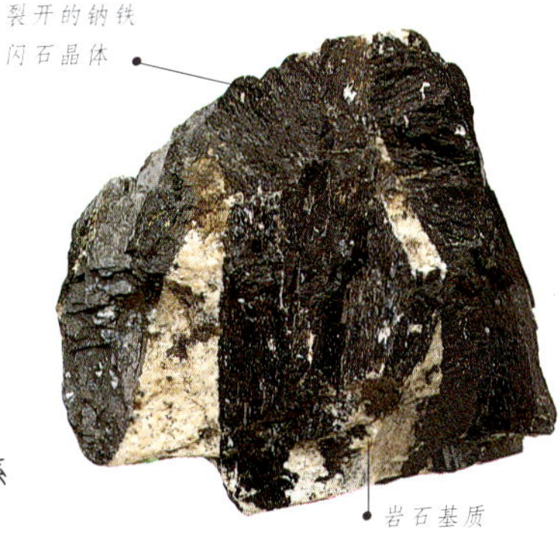


| 比重 3.37～3.50 解理 完全 | 断口 参差状 | |
|---|---|---|

| 类别 硅酸盐 | 成分 $Na_2Ca(Mg,Fe)_5Si_8O_{22}(OH)_2$ | 硬度 5～6 |
|---|---|---|

## 碱锰闪石(Richterite)

晶体呈长柱状。棕色、黄色、棕红色，或从淡绿到深绿色，条痕淡黄色。透明到半透明，新鲜面呈玻璃光泽。

· **成因** 形成于碱性岩以及接触变质石灰岩中。

· **鉴定特征** 在酸中几乎不溶，火焰中易熔化。

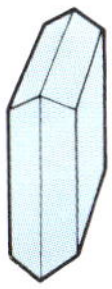
单斜晶系

| 比重 2.97～3.13 解理 完全 | 断口 参差状 | |
|---|---|---|

| 类别 硅酸盐 | 成分 $(Mn^{+2}, Fe^{+2}, Mg, Ca)SiO_3$ | 硬度 5.5 ~ 6.5 |
| --- | --- | --- |

## 蔷薇辉石(Rhodonite)

晶体板状，常带有圆润边缘，还以块状、致密状和粒状集合体产出。粉红到玫瑰红，也呈棕红色，常被黑色氢氧化锰被膜条痕白色。透明到半透明，晶面呈玻璃光泽，解理面则呈珍珠光泽。

· **成因** 形成于富含锰的变质岩，以及交代矿床，包括夕卡岩和大理岩，尤其是那些原先不纯的石灰岩。

· **鉴定特征** 相当易熔化，熔化时产生有色的玻璃状物质。

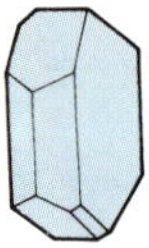

三斜晶系

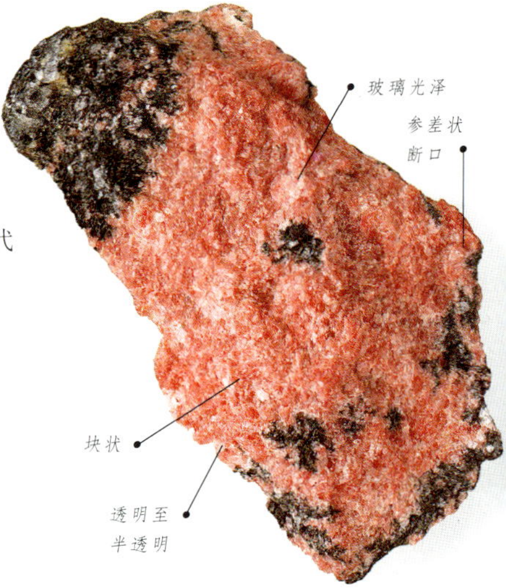


| 比重 3.57 ~ 3.76 | 解理 完全 | 断口 贝壳状至参差状 |
| --- | --- | --- |

| 类别 硅酸盐 | 成分 $NaCa_2Si_3O_8(OH)$ | 硬度 4.5 ~ 5 |
| --- | --- | --- |

## 针钠钙石(Pectolite)

形成针状晶体集合体，并常成球状块体，也呈板状晶体。白色、浅灰色或无色，条痕白色。半透明，新鲜面呈玻璃或丝绢光泽。

· **成因** 形成于玄武岩空洞中，并常与沸石类共生，如片沸石、钙十字沸石、方沸石、菱沸石和钠沸石。空洞是熔岩的气孔，当这些气孔被矿物充填后，称为杏仁子，这种结构的岩石称为杏仁状岩。

· **鉴定特征** 在盐酸中产生凝胶，在密闭的试管中加热析出水分。

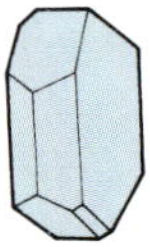

三斜晶系

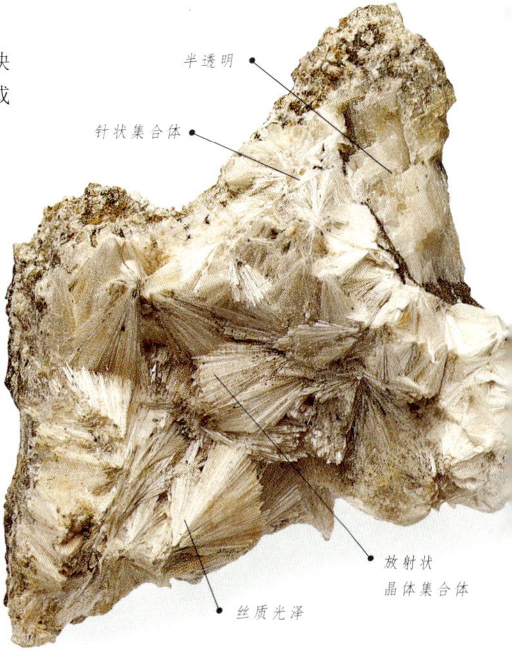


| 比重 2.74 ~ 2.88 | 解理 完全 | 断口 参差状 |
| --- | --- | --- |

| 类别 硅酸盐 | 成分 $CaSiO_3$ | 硬度 4.5～5 |
|---|---|---|

## 硅灰石(Wollastonite)

晶体呈板状，常成双晶。还以块状、纤维状、粒状和致密状集合体产出。白色到浅灰色，有时呈很淡的绿色或无色，条痕白色。透明到半透明，新鲜面上呈玻璃到珍珠光泽。

· **成因** 由不纯石灰岩变质而成，与水镁石和绿帘石伴生，这些矿物往往在大理岩上形成鲜艳的条纹。硅灰石还形成于某些岩浆岩，以及区域变质岩，如板岩、千枚岩和片岩。

· **鉴定特征** 溶于酸，并析出其所含的硅，也易熔。

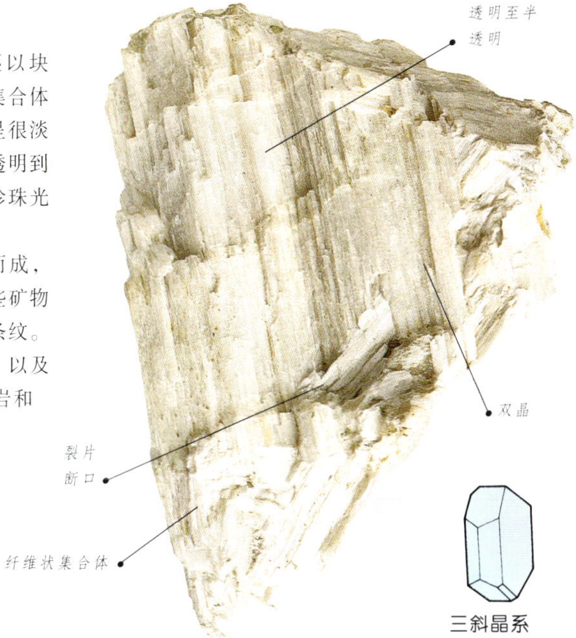


三斜晶系

| 比重 2.87～3.09 | 解理 完全 | 断口 多片状 |
|---|---|---|

| 类别 硅酸盐 | 成分 $KNa_2Li(Fe^{2+},Mn^{2+})_2Ti_2Si_8O_{24}$ | 硬度 5～6 |
|---|---|---|

## 柱星叶石(Neptunite)

晶体柱状，横截面呈正方形。尽管内反射呈深红棕色，但颜色为黑色条痕红棕色。几乎不透明，玻璃光泽。

· **成因** 作为副矿物形成于中性深成岩，如霞石正长岩以及有同样化学成分的伟晶岩中。还与蓝锥矿、钠沸石和硅钠钡钛石等矿物伴生于蛇纹岩。

· **鉴定特征** 置入盐酸中不溶解，在火焰中也不熔化。

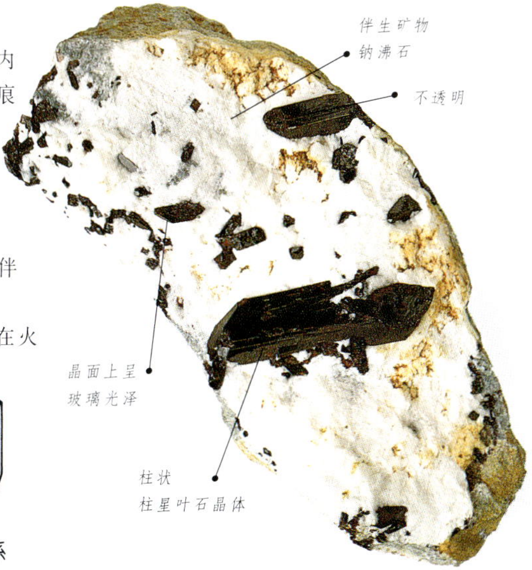

单斜晶系

| 比重 3.19～3.23 | 解理 完全 | 断口 贝壳状 |
|---|---|---|

| 类别 硅酸盐 | 成分 $(Mg,Fe)_3Si_2O_5(OH)_4$ | 硬度 2.5～3.5 |
|---|---|---|

## 叶蛇纹石(Antigorite)

晶体很小，呈薄片状或板状，还以块状、纤维状或叶片状集合体产出。白色、黄色、绿色或棕色，条痕白色。半透明到不透明，松脂或珍珠光泽。

· **成因** 形成于超基性岩蛇纹岩。

· **鉴定特征** 很难熔化。

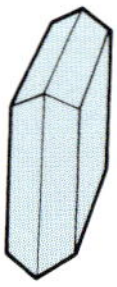

单斜晶系

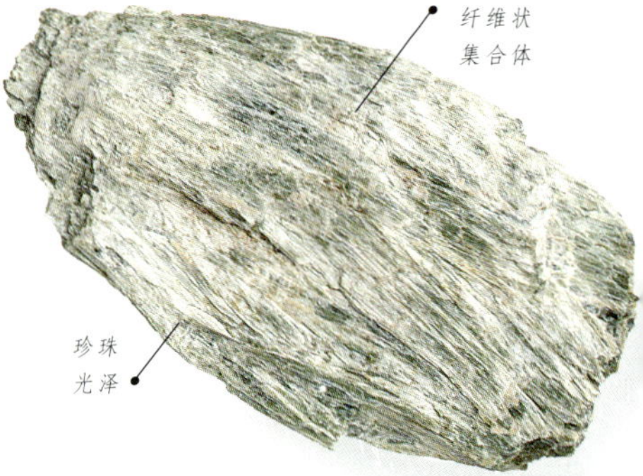


| 比重 2.61 | 解理 完全底面 | 断口 贝壳状至多片状 |
|---|---|---|

| 类别 硅酸盐 | 成分 $Mg_3Si_2O_5(OH)_4$ | 硬度 2.5 |
|---|---|---|

## 纤蛇纹石(Chrysotile)

集合体块状和纤维状，纤维状者(石绵的一种)可剥离成柔软的纤维。白色、灰色、绿色、黄色或棕色。半透明，丝质到油脂光泽。

· **成因** 形成于超基性岩蚀变生成的蛇纹岩。

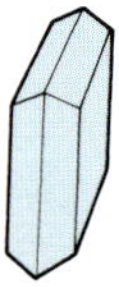

单斜晶系

| 比重 2.53 | 解理 无 | 断口 参差状 |
|---|---|---|

| 类别 硅酸盐 | 成分 $Mg_3Si_4O_{10}(OH)_2$ | 硬度 1 |
|---|---|---|

## 滑石(Talc)

晶体薄板状，还以块状、致密状、叶片状和纤维状集合体产出。浅绿到深绿、灰色、浅棕色或白色，条痕白色。半透明，暗淡到珍珠或油脂光泽。

· **成因** 形成于超基性岩和白云岩的蚀变。

· **鉴定特征** 极软，摸起来有油脂感。

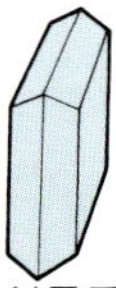

单斜晶系

| 比重 2.58～2.83 | 解理 完全 | 断口 参差状 |
|---|---|---|

| | | |
|---|---|---|
| 别 硅酸盐 | 成分 $(Cu,Al)_2H_2Si_2O_5(OH)_4 \cdot nH_2O$ | 硬度 2~4 |

## 硅孔雀石(Chrysocolla)

形成针状微小晶体，并呈放射状晶簇或紧密的集合体，还以块状、土状、隐晶质和葡萄状集合体产出。绿色、蓝色和蓝绿色，含杂质时，呈棕色到黑色，条痕白色。半透明到几乎不透明，玻璃到土状光泽。

· **成因** 形成于铜矿床的氧化带，与蓝铜矿、孔雀石和赤铜矿共生。是寻找铜矿的重要指示矿物。

· **鉴定特征** 在盐中分解。

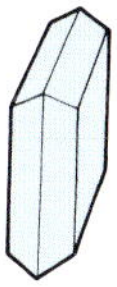

单斜晶系

| | | |
|---|---|---|
| 重 2.0~2.4 | 解理 无 | 断口 参差状至贝壳状 |

| | | |
|---|---|---|
| 别 硅酸盐 | 成分 $Be_2SiO_4$ | 硬度 7.5~8 |

## 硅铍石(Phenakite)

晶体呈柱状或菱面体，常成双晶，还以粒状和针状的集合体产出，以及呈放射状纤维质球粒。无色、黄色、粉红色或棕色，条痕白色。透明，玻璃光泽。

· **成因** 形成于热液矿脉和花岗岩，如伟晶岩和云英岩(蚀变花岗岩)。还形成于某些片岩，并与绿柱石、金绿宝石、黄玉、石英和磷灰石伴生。

· **鉴定特征** 不溶于酸，也不熔。

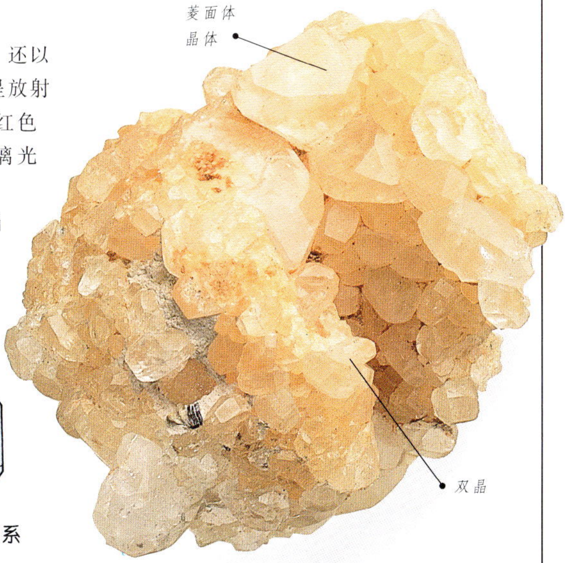


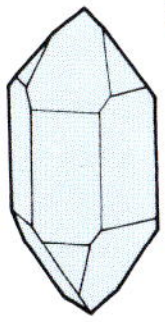

三方/六方晶系

| | | |
|---|---|---|
| 比重 2.93~3.00 | 解理 清楚 | 断口 贝壳状 |

| 类别 硅酸盐 | 成分 $KAl_2(Si_3Al)O_{10}(OH,F)_2$ | 硬度 2.5～4 |
|---|---|---|

## 白云母(Muscovite)

晶体呈板状，外形为假六边形，常成双晶，也呈片状和隐晶质。白云母还形成鳞片状和致密状块体，以及浸染状薄片。无色到白色或灰色，并可黄色、绿色、棕色、红色或蓝紫色，条痕无色。透明到半透明，玻璃到珍珠光泽。

**·成因** 形成于岩浆岩，尤其是花岗岩之类的酸性岩，还形成于变质岩，如片岩和片麻岩，云母片岩富含白云母。

**·鉴定特征** 不溶于酸。

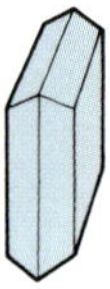

单斜晶系

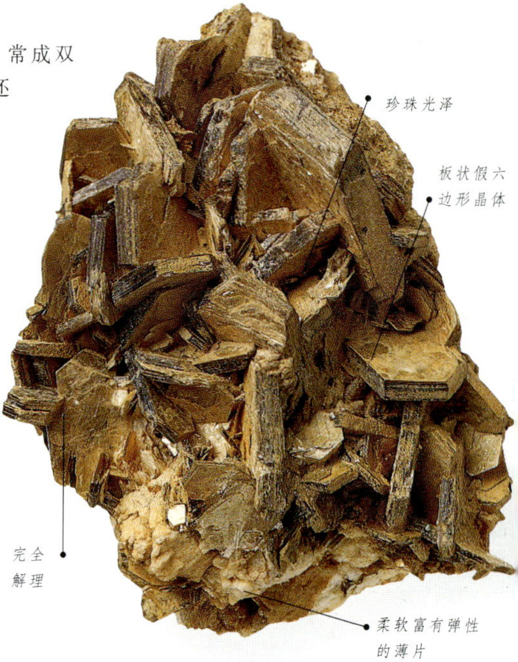


| 比重 2.77～2.88 | 解理 完全底面 | 断口 参差状 |
|---|---|---|

| 类别 硅酸盐 | 成分 $K(Li,Al)_3(Si,Al)_4O_{10}(F,OH)_2$ | 硬度 2.5～3 |
|---|---|---|

## 锂云母(Lepidolite)

晶体呈板状、外形假六边形，还以鳞状集合体和可劈裂块体产出。粉红色、紫色、浅灰色和白色，也可能无色，条痕也无色。透明到半透明，珍珠光泽。

**·成因** 形成于酸性岩，如花岗岩和伟晶岩。还常与电气石、锂磷铝石和锂辉石伴生，亦见于富含锡的矿脉中。

**·鉴定特征** 燃烧时火焰呈红色，不溶于酸。

单斜晶系

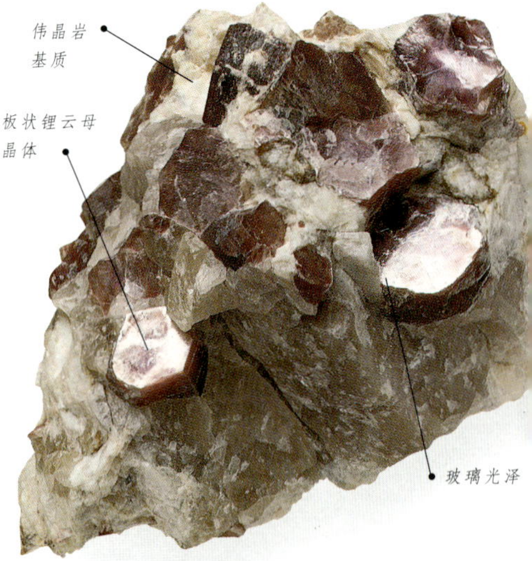


| 比重 2.8～3.3 | 解理 完全底面 | 断口 参差状 |
|---|---|---|

| | | |
|---|---|---|
| 别 硅酸盐 | 成分 $K(Mg,Fe^{+2})_3(Al,Fe^{+3})Si_3O_{10}(OH,F)_2$ | 硬度 2.5～3 |

## 黑云母(Biotite)

晶体板状或锥状短柱状，常呈假六方板状。黑色或深棕色到红棕色、绿色以及较少见的白色，条痕无色。透明到几乎不透明，灿光或玻璃光泽。

· **成因** 形成于岩浆岩和变质岩。

· **鉴定特征** 溶于浓硫酸中。

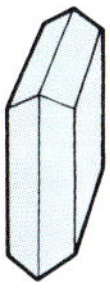

单斜晶系

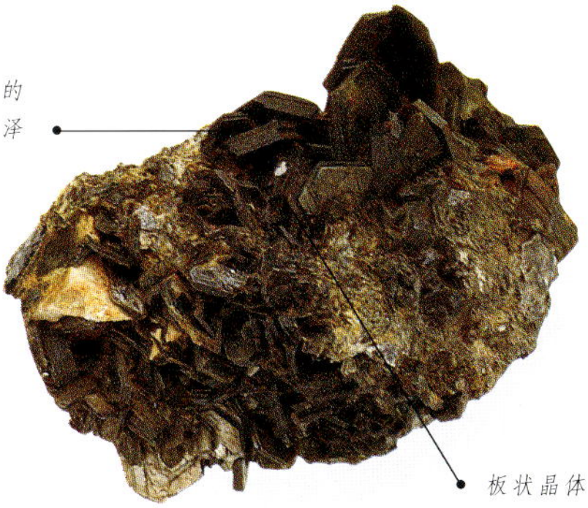


| | | |
|---|---|---|
| 重 2.7～3.4 | 解理 完全底面 | 断口 参差状 |

| | | |
|---|---|---|
| 别 硅酸盐 | 成分 $KMg_3Si_3Al_{10}(OH,F)_2$ | 硬度 2～2.5 |

## 金云母(Phlogopite)

晶体柱状和假六方板状，通常呈锥状，有时成双晶，还以板状和鳞状集合体产出。无色、黄棕色、棕红色、浅绿色或白色，条痕无色。透明到半透明，珍珠光泽。

· **成因** 形成于超基性岩和变质岩。

· **鉴定特征** 溶于浓硫酸。

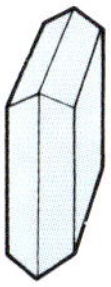

单斜晶系

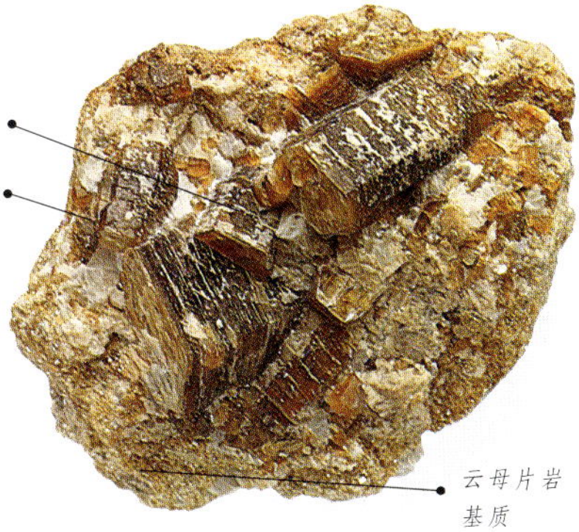


| | | |
|---|---|---|
| 重 2.76～2.90 | 解理 完全底面 | 断口 参差状 |

| | | |
|---|---|---|
| 别 硅酸盐 | 成分 $(K,Na)(Fe,Al,Mg)_2(Si,Al)_4O_{10}(OH)_2$ | 硬度 2 |

## 海绿石(Glauconite)

晶体微小，呈假六方外形，还以圆形、粒状集合体产出。常呈黯淡的绿色，也可呈黄绿色或蓝绿色。半透明到不透明的，暗淡或闪光光泽。

· **成因** 形成于海相沉积岩。

· **鉴定特征** 加热后释放出水分。

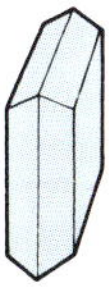

单斜晶系

| | | |
|---|---|---|
| 比重 2.4～2.95 | 解理 完全底面 | 断口 参差状 |

| 类别 硅酸盐 | 成分 $(Mg,Fe,Al)_3(Al,Si)_4O_{10}(OH)_2\cdot 4H_2O$ | 硬度 1.5 |
|---|---|---|

## 蛭石(Vermiculite)

系列矿物构成蛭石族，典型代表呈扁平板状晶体，并呈假六方体，属于单斜晶系。浅绿色至金黄色或棕色，条痕淡黄色。半透明，玻璃光泽。

· **成因** 黑云母和金云母转化而成。

· **鉴定特征** 加热后膨胀成扭曲的虫状。

| 比重 2.3 | 解理 完全 | 断口 参差状 |
|---|---|---|

| 类别 硅酸盐 | 成分 $(Fe^{+2},Mg,Fe^{3+})_5Al(Si_3Al)O_{10}(OH,O)_8$ | 硬度 2～2.5 |
|---|---|---|

## 斜绿泥石(Clinochlore)

晶体呈板状，横截面六边形，还以块状、叶状、鳞状、粒状或土状集合体产出。白色到浅黄色，或无色及绿色，条痕从无色到绿白色。透明到不透明，珍珠光泽。

· **成因** 形成于许多变质岩，尤其是片岩。

· **鉴定特征** 溶于强酸。

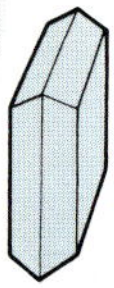

单斜晶系

| 比重 2.63～2.98 | 解理 完全 | 断口 参差状 |
|---|---|---|

| 类别 硅酸盐 | 成分 $(Mg,Fe)_3Fe_3(Al,Si_3)O_{10}(OH)_8$ | 硬度 3 |
|---|---|---|

## 鲕状绿泥石(Chamosite)

以致密状、块状和鲕状集合体产出。浅绿色到黑色，条痕白色或淡绿色。半透明，玻璃或土状光泽。

· **成因** 形成于多种沉积岩，如铁矿和粘土，并与菱铁矿(碳酸铁)共生。

· **鉴定特征** 加热后析出水分。

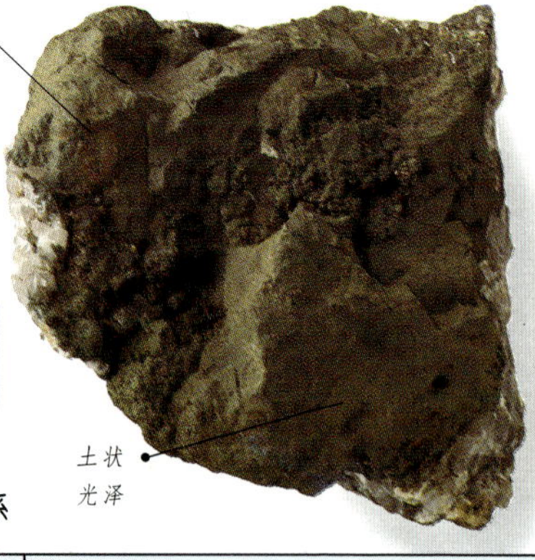


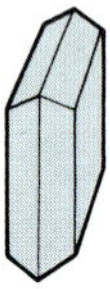

单斜晶系

| 比重 3～3.4 | 解理 未定 | 断口 参差状 |
|---|---|---|

| 类别 硅酸盐 | 成分 $Al_2Si_2O_5(OH)_4$ | 硬度 2~2.5 |
|---|---|---|

## 高岭石(Kaolinite)

该类矿物包括高岭石、珍珠陶土和埃洛石，形成很小的假六方板状或鳞片状晶体，还以块状、致密状集合体和土状或粘土状块体产出。白色和无色至浅黄色、浅棕色、浅红色或浅蓝色，条痕白色。透明到半透明，珍珠到暗淡或土状光泽。

· **成因** 由长石和其他富含铝的硅酸盐矿物风化而成，尤其在湿热地区。大量形成，于来自地下深处的热液穿过岩层，这种情况下，花岗岩转化成松散的石英和云母砂，同时伴生白色的高岭石粘土。

· **鉴定特征** 加水后有可塑性，在密闭的试管内加热后失去水分，如果要把高岭石族矿物区分开则需要特别的光学测试。

高岭石

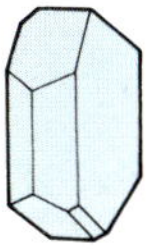
三斜晶系

珍珠陶土

叙永石

| 比重 2.6~2.63 | 解理 完全底面 | 断口 参差状 |
|---|---|---|

| 类别 硅酸盐 | 成分 $Ca_2Al_2Si_3O_{10}(OH)_2$ | 硬度 6~6.5 |
|---|---|---|

## 葡萄石(Prehnite)

晶体柱状、板状或锥状，常以葡萄状、肾状、钟乳状、粒状或致密状集合体产出。常呈绿色，也呈白色、无色、黄色或灰色，条痕无色。透明到半透明，玻璃至珍珠光泽。

· **成因** 形成于玄武岩的气孔。

· **鉴定特征** 加热后释放出水分。

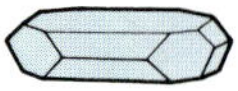

斜方晶系

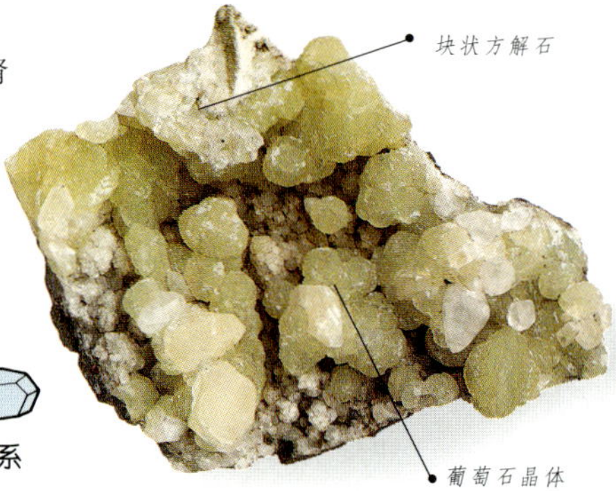


| 比重 2.90~2.95 | 解理 清楚 | 断口 参差状 |
|---|---|---|

| 类别 硅酸盐 | 成分 $(Ni,Mg)_6Si_4O_{10}(OH)_8$ | 硬度 2~4 |
|---|---|---|

## 硅镁镍矿(Garnierite)

晶体片状，也以微晶皮壳状和块状产出。鲜绿色为其所特有，也可呈白色，条痕浅绿色。透明到不透明，油脂状、蜡状或土状光泽。

· **成因** 岩浆岩中的硫化镍受热液蚀变形成硅镁镍矿。

· **鉴定特征** 不熔。

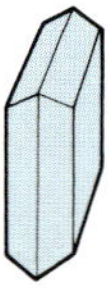

单斜晶系

| 比重 2.3~2.5 | 解理 无 | 断口 裂片状 |
|---|---|---|

| 类别 硅酸盐 | 成分 $Mg_4Si_6O_{15}(OH)_2 \cdot 6H_2O$ | 硬度 2~2.5 |
|---|---|---|

## 海泡石(Sepiolite)

以块状、纤维状、致密状、土状和结核状(英文称 Meershaum)集合体产出。白色、浅红色、浅黄色、浅灰色或蓝绿色，条痕浅白色。不透明，暗淡光泽。

· **成因** 形成于蛇纹岩风化壳。

· **鉴定特征** 通常呈干而多孔的块体，能浮在水面上。

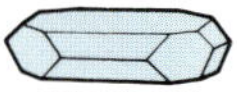

斜方晶系

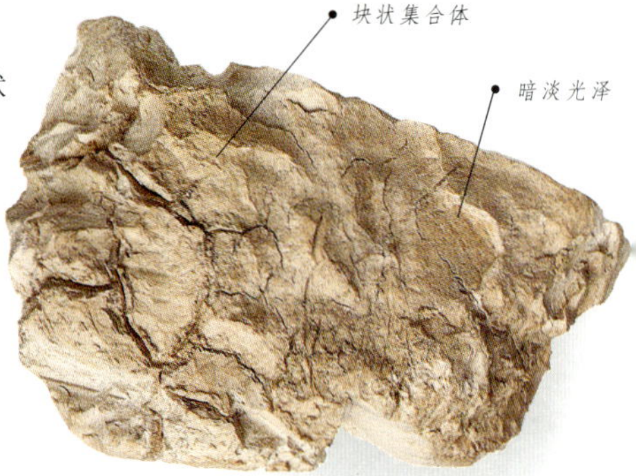


| 比重 2 | 解理 未定 | 断口 参差状 |
|---|---|---|

| 类别 硅酸盐 | 成分 $KCa_4Si_8O_{20}(F,OH)\cdot 8H_2O$ | 硬度 4.5～5 |
|---|---|---|

## 鱼眼石(Apophyllite)

晶体呈假立方体、锥状、板状或柱状，还以块状、叶片状或粒状集合体产出。白色、无色、黄色、粉红色或绿色，条痕白色。透明到半透明。新鲜面呈玻璃到珍珠光泽。

**·成因** 形成于热液矿脉以及玄武岩气孔与鱼眼石伴生的矿物有沸石、白硅钙石、方解石、石英、辉沸石、方沸石、葡萄石和钙沸石。

**·鉴定特征** 燃烧时火焰呈紫罗兰色，溶于盐酸，在密闭的试管内加热后释放出水分。

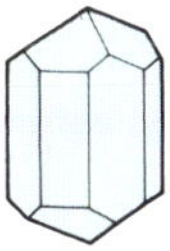

正方晶系

| 比重 2.3～2.5 | 解理 完全 | 断口 参差状 |
|---|---|---|

| 类别 硅酸盐 | 成分 $NaCa_{16}(Si_{23}Al)O_{60}(OH)_5\cdot 15H_2O$ | 硬度 3～4 |
|---|---|---|

## 白钙沸石(Gyrolite)

晶体呈放射片状，球粒状或结核状集合体产出。白色或无色；透明到半透明，玻璃光泽。

**·成因** 由硅酸钙矿物蚀变而成。作为一种次生矿物，白硅钙石与鱼眼石伴生，并产于岩石的空洞和裂隙中，尤其是玄武岩。发现过 5 厘米大的白钙沸石球粒和 30 厘米大的球粒集合体。

**·鉴定特征** 在密闭的试管内加热释放出水分。

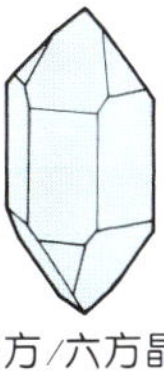

三方/六方晶系

| 比重 2.34～2.45 | 解理 完全 | 断口 参差状 |
|---|---|---|

| 类别 硅酸盐 | 成分 $Al_2Si_4O_{10}(OH)_2$ | 硬度 1～2 |
|---|---|---|

## 叶蜡石(Pyrophyllite)

晶体扁长板状，且常成歪晶，多以叶片状、纤维状、放射状和片状块体产出。白色、灰色、浅蓝色、浅黄色、浅绿色和绿棕色，条痕白色。透明到半透明，新鲜面上呈暗淡珍珠光泽。

**·成因** 与滑石、红柱石、硅线石和天蓝石共生于结晶片岩，还与云母和石英等矿物形成于热液矿脉。

**·鉴定特征** 与滑石类似，叶蜡石触摸有油脂感。加热成片剥落，且不溶于大多数酸。

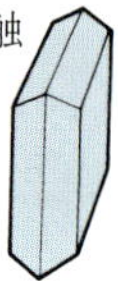

单斜晶系

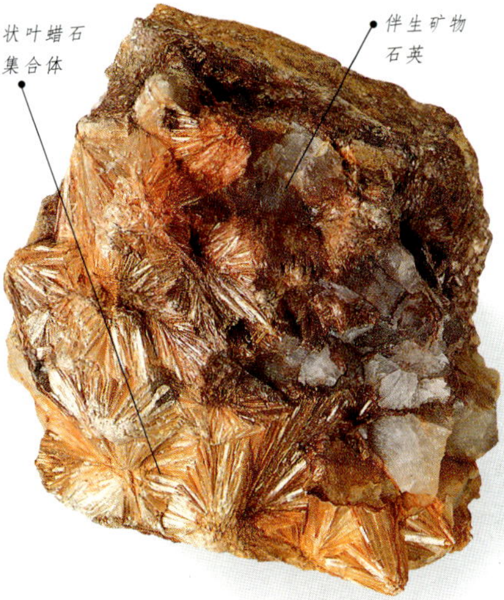


| 比重 2.65～2.90 | 解理 完全 | 断口 参差状 |
|---|---|---|

| 类别 硅酸盐 | 成分 $(K,Na)_3(Fe,Mn)_7Ti_2Si_8O_{24}(O,OH)_7$ | 硬度 3 |
|---|---|---|

## 星叶石(Astrophyllite)

晶体呈刃片状，常聚集成星射形状。黄铜色至金黄色，条痕浅绿棕色。薄片半透明，半金属至珍珠光泽。

**·成因** 形成于岩浆岩裂缝，尤其是正长岩这种含中性成分的粗粒岩浆岩，还产于其他深成岩。与石英、长石、锆石、钠闪石、榍石、云母和锥辉石等矿物伴生。

**·鉴定特征** 微溶于酸。在火焰中熔化成带弱磁性的深色玻璃状物质。极易碎裂，裂开后形成薄片。

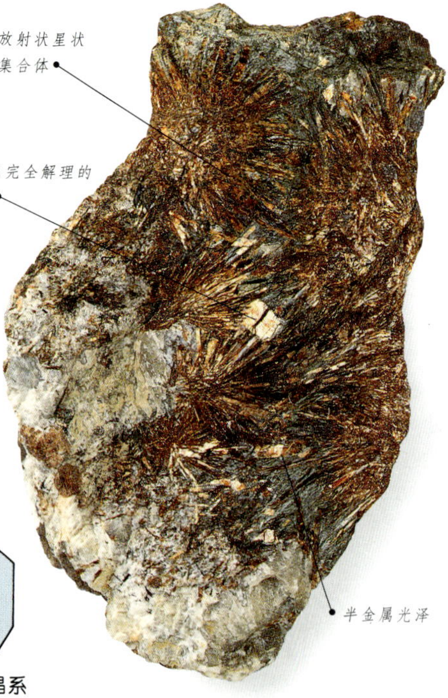


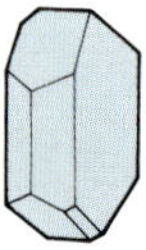

三斜晶系

| 比重 3.3～3.4 | 解理 完全 | 断口 参差状 |
|---|---|---|

| 类别 硅酸盐 | 成分 $(Na,K)AlSi_3O_8$ | 硬度 6～6.5 |
|---|---|---|

## 歪长石(Anorthoclase)

属于碱性长石类，短柱状或板状晶体，常成双晶，还以块状、片状、粒状或隐晶质集合体产出。浅黄色、无色、浅红色、白色、灰色或浅绿色，条痕白色。透明到半透明，玻璃光泽。

· **成因** 主要形成于火山岩。

· **鉴定特征** 不溶于酸。

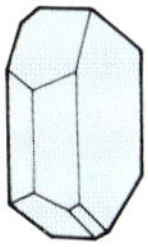

三斜晶系

| 比重 2.56～2.62 | 解理 完全 | 断口 参差状 |
|---|---|---|

| 类别 硅酸盐 | 成分 $KAlSi_3O_8$ | 硬度 6～6.5 |
|---|---|---|

## 微斜长石(Microcline)

是碱性长石，板状晶体，更常呈短柱状晶体，常成双晶，还以块状集合体产出。灰色、白色、浅黄色、浅红色或粉红色，绿色斜微长石称为天河石。透明到半透明，解理面呈玻璃或珍珠光泽。

· **成因** 形成于岩浆岩，尤其是花岗岩、伟晶岩和正长岩。还产于某些变质岩中，特别是片岩。此外，也见于热液矿脉和接触变质带。形成于伟晶岩的微斜长石，常与石英和钠长石伴生。

· **鉴定特征** 除了氢氟酸(务必小心使用)外，不溶于其他酸；在火焰中不熔。

天河石

斜微长石

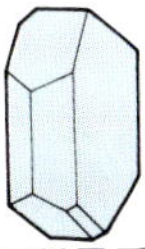

三斜晶系

| 比重 2.55～2.63 | 解理 完全 | 断口 参差状 |
|---|---|---|

| 类别 硅酸盐 | 成分 $KAlSi_3O_8$ | 硬度 6 |
|---|---|---|

## 透长石(Sanidine)

属于碱性长石类，晶体柱状或板状，常成为双晶。浅白或无色，条痕白色。半透明，晶面呈玻璃光泽。

· **成因** 形成于多种岩浆岩中，包括粗面岩和流纹岩，还见于某些接触变质岩。

· **鉴定特征** 不溶于大多数酸，完全溶解于氢氟酸，使用这种酸时，一定要特别小心。

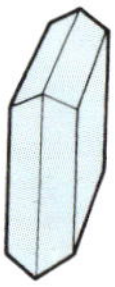

单斜晶系

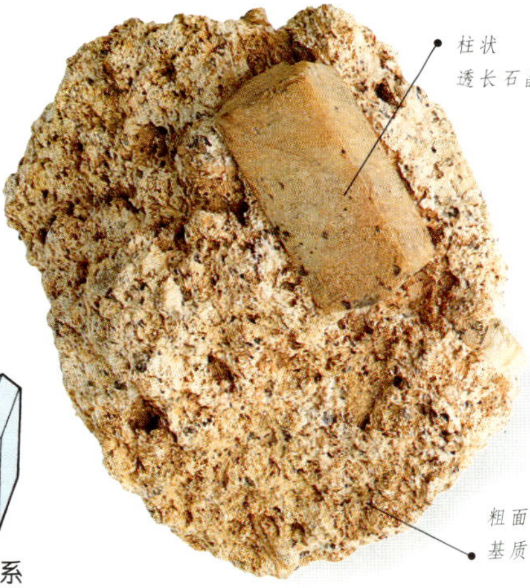


| 比重 2.56～2.62 | 解理 完全 | 断口 贝壳状至参差状 |
|---|---|---|

| 类别 硅酸盐 | 成分 $NaAlSi_3O_8$ | 硬度 6～6.5 |
|---|---|---|

## 钠长石(Albite)

是斜长石系列的端员成分，形成温度较低和富含钠。钠长石呈扁平板状晶体，常呈双晶，还以块状、粒状或片状集合体产出，薄片常弯曲。一般为白色或无色，也可呈浅蓝色、灰色、浅绿色或浅红色，条痕白色。透明到半透明，玻璃至珍珠光泽。

· **成因** 为许多岩浆岩的重要组成部分，如花岗岩、伟晶岩、流纹岩、安山岩和正长岩。钠长石还形成于某些变质岩如片岩和片麻岩以及沉积岩中，也见于热液矿脉。在某些情况下，会由其他长石如钠长石转化而成。

· **鉴定特征** 很难熔化，火焰呈黄色。

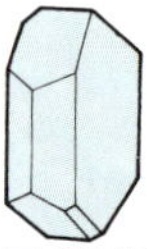

三斜晶系

| 比重 2.60～2.63 | 解理 清楚 | 断口 参差状 |
|---|---|---|

| | | |
|---|---|---|
| 类别 硅酸盐 | 成分 $(Na,Ca)Al_{1-2}Si_{3-2}O_8$ | 硬度 6~6.5 |

## 钙钠斜长石(Labradorite)

属斜长石类，很少形成晶体，如果形成，常成板状，且常成双晶，集合体块状、粒状和致密状。蓝色、灰色、白色或无色，且解理面上的色彩富于变化,条痕白色。半透明，玻璃光泽。

· **成因** 是某些岩浆岩和变质岩的重要组成部分，如玄武岩、辉长岩、闪长岩、安山岩、苏长岩和闪岩。常见于中性和基性岩，不过较少见于花岗岩。

· **鉴定特征** 裂开面上发闪光或闪烁是钙钠斜长石的重要特征，其粉末溶于酸。

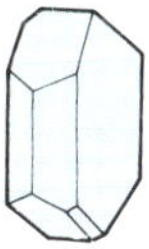
三斜晶系

| | | |
|---|---|---|
| 比重 2.69~2.72 | 解理 完全 | 断口 参差状至贝壳状 |

| | | |
|---|---|---|
| 类别 硅酸盐 | 成分 $CaAl_2Si_2O_8$ | 硬度 6~6.5 |

## 钙斜长石(Anorthite)

是斜长石类形成温度较高的端员成分。晶体短柱状，常成双晶，集合体片状或块状。灰色、白色、粉红色或无色，条痕白色。透明到半透明，玻璃光泽。

· **成因** 形成于许多岩浆岩，尤其是那些在高温下形成的基性岩，玄武岩、辉长岩、粗玄岩和橄榄岩。这种富含钙的斜长石会渐变为形成温度较低且富含钠的钠长石，还形成于一些变质岩中。

· **鉴定特征** 溶于盐酸。

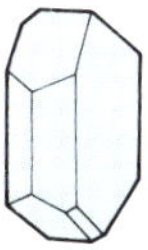
三斜晶系

| | | |
|---|---|---|
| 比重 2.74~2.76 | 解理 完全 | 断口 贝壳状至参差状 |

| 类别 硅酸盐 | 成分 $(Na,Ca)Al_{1-2}Si_{3-2}O_8$ | 硬度 6～6.5 |
|---|---|---|

## 中长石(Andesine)

斜长石系列成员之一。有时晶体板状，常成双晶，一般以块状、致密状和粒状集合体产出。灰色、白色或无色，条痕白色。透明到半透明，新鲜晶面呈玻璃光泽。

· **成因** 形成于中性岩和许多变质岩中，如安山岩和角闪岩。属于钙长石与钠长石之系列过渡类型。

· **鉴定特征** 钠焰呈黄色，钙焰呈砖红色，一定温度下，两种颜色都会出现。

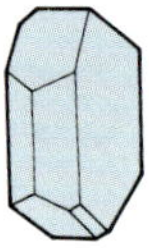
三斜晶系

| 比重 2.66～2.68 | 解理 完全 | 断口 参差状至贝壳状 |
|---|---|---|

| 类别 硅酸盐 | 成分 $(Na,Ca)Al_{1-2}Si_{3-2}O_8$ | 硬度 6～6.5 |
|---|---|---|

## 奥长石(Oligoclase)

斜长石系列成员之一。晶体板状，常成双晶，一般呈块状、粒状和致密集合体状。灰色、白色、线绿色、浅黄色、棕色、浅红色或无色，条痕白色。透明到半透明，玻璃光泽。

· **成因** 形成于许多喷发岩、变质岩以及深成岩，如花岗岩、伟晶岩、中性正长岩、粗面岩和安山岩、玄武岩。在变质环境中，奥长石形成于深变质的片麻岩和片岩。

· **鉴定特征** 包裹体呈现灿烂的反射光。

三斜晶系

| 比重 2.63～2.67 | 解理 完全 | 断口 参差状至贝壳状 |
|---|---|---|

| 类别 硅酸盐 | 成分 $KAlSi_3O_8$ | 硬度 6~6.5 |
|---|---|---|

## 正长石(Orthoclase)

是重要的造岩矿物。晶体柱状或板状，常成双晶，集合体块状、片状和粒状。白色、浅红色、无色、黄色、灰色或绿色，条痕白色。透明到半透明，玻璃到珍珠光泽。

· **成因** 形成于多种岩浆岩和变质岩，如花岗岩、伟晶岩、流纹岩、粗面岩、正长岩、麻岩和片岩，也形成于一些沉积岩。

· **鉴定特征** 不溶于酸，几乎不熔。

单斜晶系

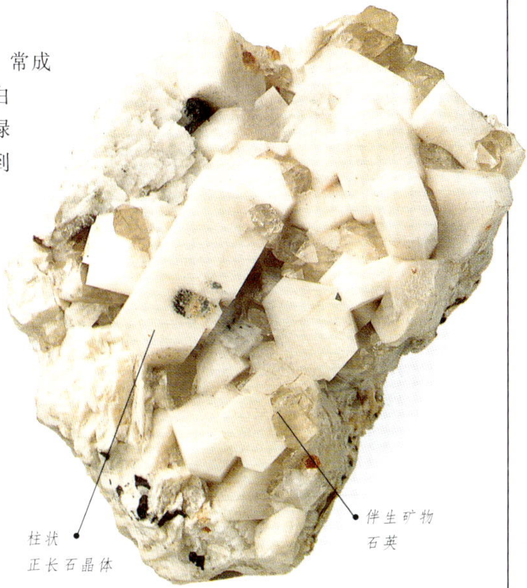


| 比重 2.55~2.63 | 解理 完全 | 断口 参差状至贝壳状 |
|---|---|---|

| 类别 硅酸盐 | 成分 $(Na,Ca)Al_{1-2}Si_{3-2}O_8$ | 硬度 6~6.5 |
|---|---|---|

## 培斜长石(Bytownite)

斜长石系列成员之一，晶体板状，常成双晶，一般以块状、致密状、粒状产出集合体。白色、灰色、浅棕色或无色，条痕白色。透明到半透明，玻璃光泽。

· **成因** 为许多岩浆岩的重要组成部分，如粗玄岩、玄武岩、辉长岩、苏长岩和斜长岩。也见于某些变质岩，如区域变质作用形成的片麻岩和片岩。

· **鉴定特征** 与其他斜长石类一样，显示出聚片双晶，据此可与正长石区分，后者为双晶单体。

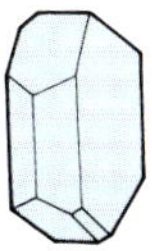

三斜晶系

| 比重 2.72~2.74 | 解理 完全 | 断口 参差状至贝壳状 |
|---|---|---|

| 类别 硅酸盐 | 成分 $(Na,Ca)_{4-8}Al_6Si_6(O,S)_{24}(SO_4Cl)_{1-2}$ | 硬度 5.5～6 |
|---|---|---|

## 蓝方石(Haüyne)

晶体呈十二面体或八面体，常成双晶，还以圆粒状集合体产出。蓝色到白色、绿色、黄色或红色，条痕浅蓝色或白色。透明到半透明，玻璃或油脂光泽。

· 成因　形成于贫硅的熔岩。

· 鉴定特征　溶于酸，并产生凝胶。

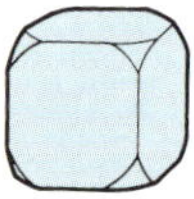

等轴晶系

| 比重 2.44～2.50 | 解理 不清楚 | 断口 参差状至贝壳状 |
|---|---|---|

| 类别 硅酸盐 | 成分 $(Na,Ca)_{7-8}(Al,Si)_{12}O_{24}[(SO_4),Cl_2(OH)_2]$ | 硬度 5～5.5 |
|---|---|---|

## 青金石(Lazurite)

晶体呈十二面体、八面体或立方体，不过非常少见，常呈块状或致密状集合体。深蓝色、天蓝色、紫罗兰色或绿蓝色，条痕鲜艳的蓝色。半透明，暗淡光泽。

· 成因　形成于高温变质石灰岩。

· 鉴定特征　溶于盐酸，并释放出一股“臭鸡蛋”味。

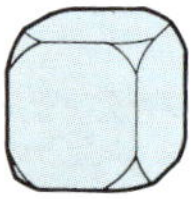

等轴晶系

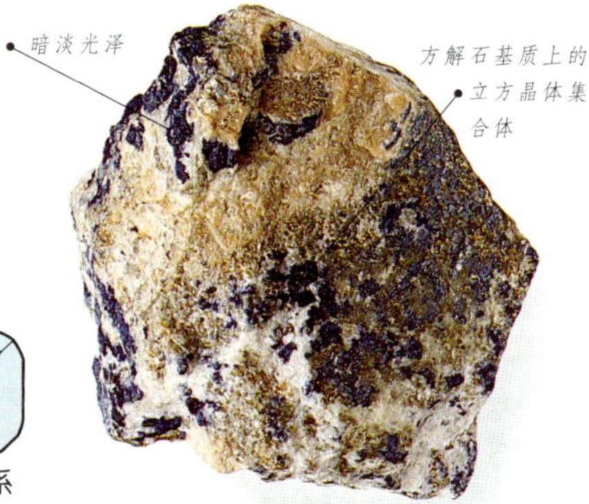


| 比重 2.4～2.5 | 解理 不完全 | 断口 参差状 |
|---|---|---|

| 类别 硅酸盐 | 成分 $Na_8Al_6Si_6O_{24}Cl_2$ | 硬度 5.5～6 |
|---|---|---|

## 方钠石(Sodalite)

晶体呈十二面体，常成双晶，还以块状或粒状集合体产出，并有同心构造。浅蓝到深蓝，也可呈白色、无色、浅黄色、浅绿色或浅红色，条痕无色。透明到半透明，玻璃到油脂光泽。

· 成因　形成于某些岩浆岩，正长岩。

· 鉴定特征　溶于盐酸和硝酸，并产生凝胶。

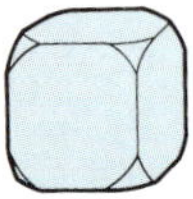

等轴晶系

| 比重 2.14～2.40 | 解理 差 | 断口 参差状至贝壳状 |
|---|---|---|

| 类别 硅酸盐 | 成分 $KAlSi_2O_6$ | 硬度 5.5～6 |
|---|---|---|

## 白榴石(Leucite)

晶体呈四方三八面体形，晶面上可见双晶条纹。常成双晶，还以块状和粒状。以及浸染颗粒状集合体产出。白色、灰色或无色，条痕无色。透明到半透明，玻璃光泽。

**· 成因** 形成于基性岩，尤其是富含钾的基性岩，如玄武岩和响岩。不稳定易变，所以很少在地质年代久远的岩石中发现。

**· 鉴定特征** 溶于盐酸。加热到 625 ℃以上时，晶体构造从正方晶系变为等轴晶系。

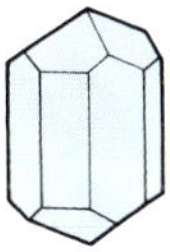

正方晶系

| 比重 2.5 | 解理 极不佳 | 断口 贝壳状 |
|---|---|---|

| 类别 硅酸盐 | 成分 $(Na,K)AlSiO_4$ | 硬度 5.5～6 |
|---|---|---|

## 霞石(Nepheline)

晶体常呈六方柱状，常以致密状、块状集合体产出。白色、无色和灰色到浅黄色、暗绿色和棕红色，条痕白色。透明到半透明，玻璃到油脂光泽。

**· 成因** 形成于许多含硅少的碱性岩，尤其是中性岩。还产于正长岩(霞石正长岩)和伟晶岩，偶见于片岩和片麻岩。

**· 鉴定特征** 溶于盐酸，并产生凝胶。燃烧时，火焰黄色，说明霞石含钠。

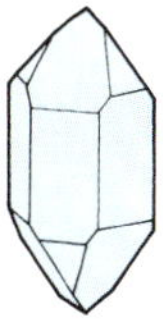

三方/六方晶系

| 比重 2.5～2.7 | 解理 不清楚 | 断口 贝壳状 |
|---|---|---|

| 类别 硅酸盐 | 成分 $Na_8Al_6Si_6O_{24}(SO_4)$ | 硬度 5.5～6 |
| --- | --- | --- |

## 黝方石(Nosean)

晶体呈十二面体，不过常以块状或粒状集合体产出。颜色多变化，从灰色、浅蓝色和棕色到无色和白色，条痕无色。透明到半透明，新鲜面呈玻璃光泽。

· **成因** 形成于含硅少的熔岩，如中性岩，响岩。黝方石这种方钠石类矿物常以大晶粒嵌入岩石基质，呈斑状结构，偶见于火山弹。

· **鉴定特征** 溶于酸，产生凝胶。

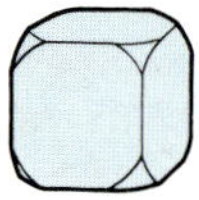

等轴晶系

| 比重 2.3～2.4 | 解理 不清楚 | 断口 参差状至贝壳状 |
| --- | --- | --- |

| 类别 硅酸盐 | 成分 $Na_6Ca_2Al_6Si_6O_{24}(CO_3)_2$ | 硬度 5～6 |
| --- | --- | --- |

## 钙霞石(Cancrinite)

晶体柱状，不过很少见，一般呈块状集合体。白色、黄色、橙色、粉红色、浅红色或浅蓝色，条痕无色。透明到半透明，玻璃、珍珠或油脂光泽。

· **成因** 形成于某些岩浆岩，包括碱性岩石，钙霞石在其中以原生矿物或霞石的蚀变产物产出。在正长岩中与方钠石伴生。还见于区域变质岩，如片麻岩。

· **鉴定特征** 溶于盐酸，发泡，并产生硅质凝胶。

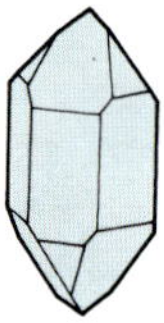

三方/六方晶系

| 比重 2.42～2.5 | 解理 完全 | 断口 参差状 |
| --- | --- | --- |

| 类别 硅酸盐 | 成分 $(Na,Ca,K)_4Al_3(Al,Si)_3Si_6O_{24}(Cl,F,OH,CO_3SO_4)$ | 硬度 5.5～6 |
|---|---|---|

## 方柱石(Scapolite)

富含钙的钙柱石和富含钠的钠柱石构成方柱石系列矿物。晶体柱状，还以粒状和块状集合体产出。无色、白色、灰色、浅蓝色、浅绿色、浅黄色、浅棕色、粉红色或紫罗兰色，条痕无色。透明到半透明，玻璃到珍珠或松脂光泽。

· **成因** 形成于原基性成分发生转化的岩浆岩，也形成于深变质岩，如片岩和片麻岩。

· **鉴定特征** 溶于盐酸。

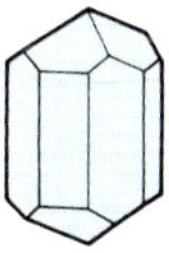

正方晶系

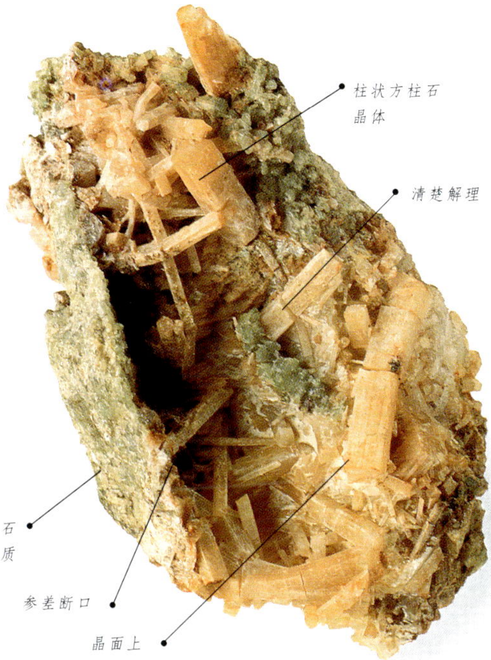


| 比重 2.50～2.78 | 解理 清楚 | 断口 参差状至贝壳状 |
|---|---|---|

| 类别 硅酸盐 | 成分 $LiAlSi_4O_{10}$ | 硬度 6～6.5 |
|---|---|---|

## 透锂长石(Petalite)

晶体小型，常成双晶，但罕见，常见的是大型劈裂块体。白色、灰色、浅粉红色、黄色或无色，条痕白色。透明到半透明，玻璃至珍珠光泽。

· **成因** 形成于粗粒酸性岩，与石英、锂云母、锂辉石和其他富含锂的矿物伴生。

· **鉴定特征** 燃烧时，火焰深红色，不溶。

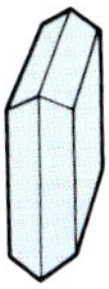

单斜晶系

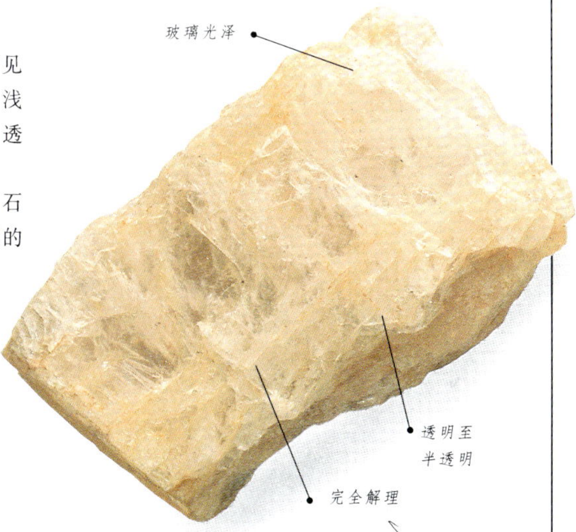


| 比重 2.3～2.5 | 解理 完全 | 断口 亚贝壳状 |
|---|---|---|

| 类别 硅酸盐 | 成分 $NaAlSi_2O_6 \cdot H_2O$ | 硬度 5～5.5 |
|---|---|---|

## 方沸石(Analcime)

沸石的一种，晶体呈偏方三八面体、二十四面体和变立方体，也以块状、粒状和致密状集合体产出。白色、无色、灰色、粉红色、浅黄色或浅绿色，条痕白色。透明到半透明，玻璃光泽。

· **成因** 形成于玄武质火山岩，由方钠石和霞石蚀变而成。还与其他沸石矿物和方解石产出于某些碎屑沉积岩。

· **鉴定特征** 加热熔化，火焰呈黄色，溶酸，在密闭的试管内加热有水分析出。

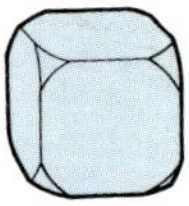

等轴晶系

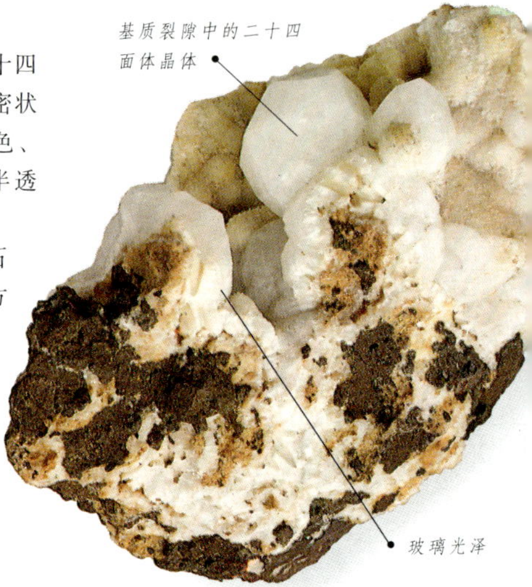


| 比重 2.22～2.29 | 解理 极不佳 | 断口 亚贝壳状 |
|---|---|---|

| 类别 硅酸盐 | 成分 $CaAl_2Si_4O_{12} \cdot 6H_2O$ | 硬度 4～5 |
|---|---|---|

## 菱沸石(Chabazite)

属于沸石族，晶体呈假立方体和菱面体，常成双晶。白色、浅黄色、浅粉红色、浅红色、浅绿色或无色，条痕无色。透明到半透明，玻璃光泽。

· **成因** 形成于玄武熔岩裂隙和某些石灰岩中。与其他沸石如交沸石、钙十字沸石、片沸石和钙沸石伴生，也与石英和方解石共生。还产于某些片岩；以及温泉周围热水沉积的矿物皮壳中。

· **鉴定特征** 在密闭的试管内加热析出水分。

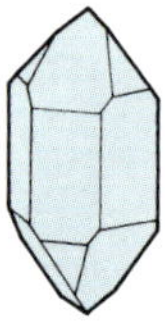

三方/六方晶系

| 比重 2.05～2.16 | 解理 不清楚 | 断口 参差状 |
|---|---|---|

| 类别 硅酸盐 | 成分 $(Ba,K)_{1-2}(Si,Al)_8O_{16} \cdot 6H_2O$ | 硬度 4.5 |
|---|---|---|

## 交沸石(Harmotome)

沸石的一种，晶体呈假正方双晶或假斜方形，以及放射状集合体产出。白色、灰色、粉红色、黄色、棕色或无色，条痕白色。透明到半透明，玻璃光泽。

· 成因　形成于玄武岩气孔中。

· 鉴定特征　熔化，溶于盐酸。

单斜晶系

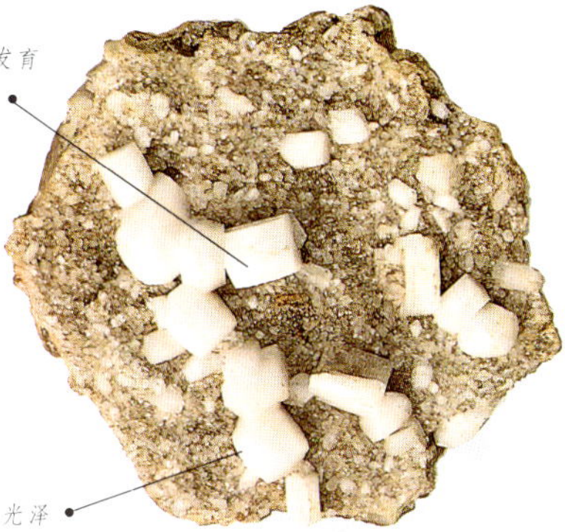


| 比重 2.41 ~ 2.50 | 解理 清楚 | 断口 参差状至亚贝壳状 |
|---|---|---|

| 类别 硅酸盐 | 成分 $(Na,Ca)_{2-3}Al_3(Al,Si)_2Si_{13}O_{36} \cdot 12H_2O$ | 硬度 3.5 ~ 4 |
|---|---|---|

## 片沸石(Heulandite)

沸石的一种，晶体板状和梯形，以块状和粒状集合体产出。有白色、灰色、黄色、粉红色、红色、橙色、无色和棕色，条痕无色。透明到半透明，玻璃至珍珠光泽。

· 成因　形成于玄武岩的气孔中。

· 鉴定特征　熔化，溶于盐酸。

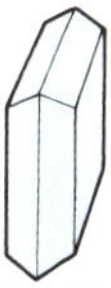

单斜晶系

| 比重 2.1 ~ 2.2 | 解理 完全 | 断口 参差状 |
|---|---|---|

| 类别 硅酸盐 | 成分 $CaAl_2Si_4O_{12} \cdot 4H_2O$ | 硬度 3 ~ 4 |
|---|---|---|

## 浊沸石(Laumontite)

晶体柱状，还以块状、纤维状、柱状和放射状集合体产出。白色、灰色、浅棕色、粉红色或浅黄色，条痕无色。玻璃至珍珠光泽，透明到不透明。

· 成因　形成于玄武岩裂隙中。

· 鉴定特征　溶于盐酸，并产生凝胶。

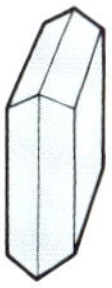

单斜晶系

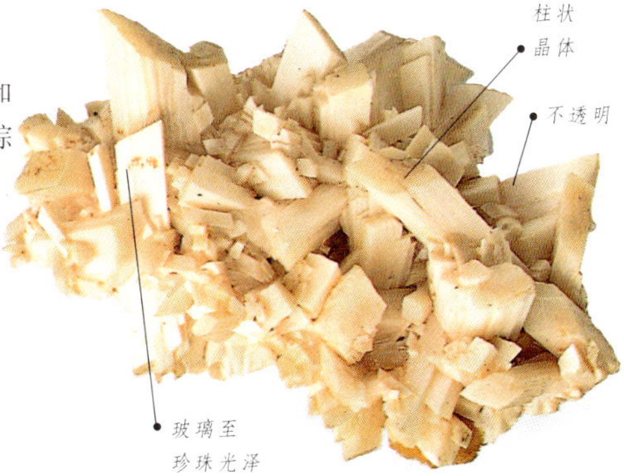


| 比重 2.2 ~ 2.4 | 解理 完全 | 断口 参差状 |
|---|---|---|

| 类别 硅酸盐 | 成分 $Na_2Al_2Si_3O_{10} \cdot 2H_2O$ | 硬度 5～5.5 |
|---|---|---|

## 钠沸石(Natrolite)

晶体呈细长柱状或针状，晶面上有纵条纹，还以纤维状、放射状、块状、致密状或粒状集合体产出。白色、灰色、浅黄色、浅红色或无色，条痕白色。透明到半透明，玻璃至珍珠光泽。

· **成因** 形成于玄武岩的气孔中。

· **鉴定特征** 溶于酸，产生凝胶。

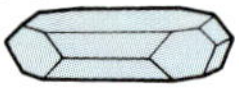

斜方晶系

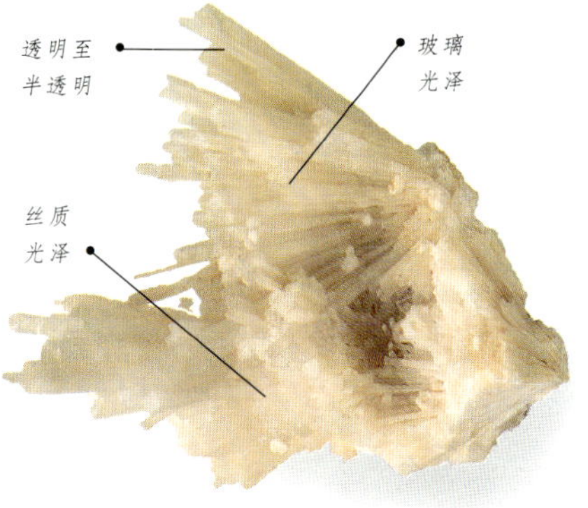


| 比重 2.20～2.26 | 解理 完全 | 断口 参差状 |
|---|---|---|

| 类别 硅酸盐 | 成分 $Na_2Ca_2Al_6Si_9O_{30} \cdot 8H_2O$ | 硬度 5 |
|---|---|---|

## 中沸石(Mesolite)

晶体呈纤维状或针状，聚为簇状或致密块状集合体，并常成双晶。白色或无色。透明，玻璃或丝绢光泽。

· **成因** 形成于玄武岩气孔中。

· **鉴定特征** 与溶于酸，产生凝胶，在密闭试管内加热析出水分。

单斜晶系

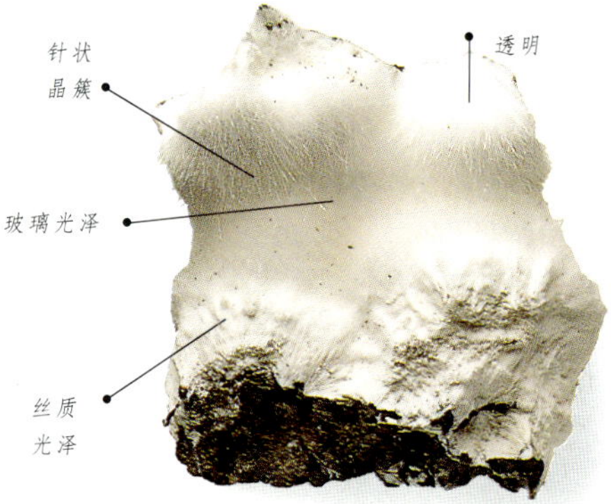


| 比重 2.2～2.3 | 解理 完全 | 断口 参差状 |
|---|---|---|

| 类别 硅酸盐 | 成分 $(K,Na,Ca)_{1-2}(Si,Al)_8O_{16} \cdot 6H_2O$ | 硬度 4～4.5 |
|---|---|---|

## 钙十字沸石(Phillpsite)

多以双晶产出。白色、无色、浅红色或浅黄色。透明到半透明，玻璃光泽。

· **成因** 形成于玄武岩的多孔状空洞、大洋底沉积以及温泉周围。

· **鉴定特征** 溶于酸中，并有两组清楚解理。

单斜晶系

| 比重 2.2 | 解理 清楚 | 断口 参差状 |
|---|---|---|

| | | |
|---|---|---|
| 类别 硅酸盐 | 成分 $CaAl_2Si_3O_{10} \cdot 3H_2O$ | 硬度 5 |

## 钙沸石(Scolecite)

呈带纵纹的纤细柱状晶体，还呈放射状纤维状块集合体。白色、浅黄色或无色。透明到半透明，玻璃至丝绢光泽。

· 成因　形成于玄武岩气孔。

· 鉴定特征　加热卷缩成虫状，且熔化。

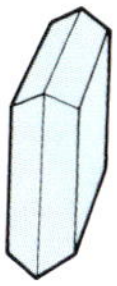

单斜晶系

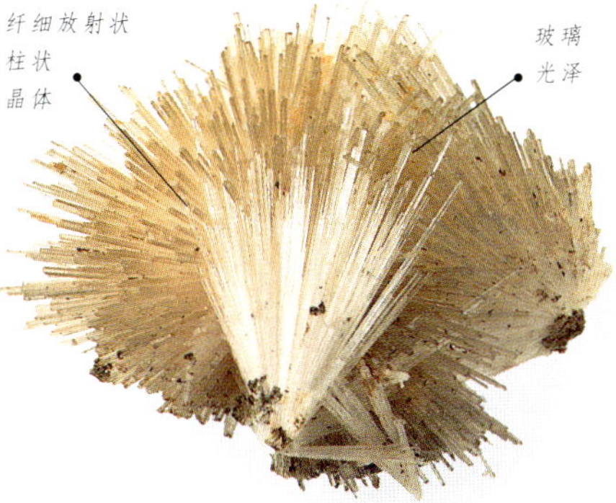


| | | |
|---|---|---|
| 比重 2.27　解理 完全 | 断口 参差状 | |

| | | |
|---|---|---|
| 类别 硅酸盐 | 成分 $NaCa_2Al_5Si_{13}O_{36} \cdot 14H_2O$ | 硬度 3.5～4 |

## 辉沸石(Stilbite)

晶体菱形，并呈十字形穿插双晶，集合体刃片状、球状和放射状块体。白色、灰色、浅黄色、粉红色、浅红色、橙色或棕色，条痕无色。透明到半透明，玻璃或珍珠光泽。

· 成因　形成于玄武岩空洞和其他熔岩。

· 鉴定特征　溶于盐酸。

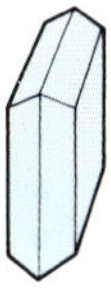

单斜晶系

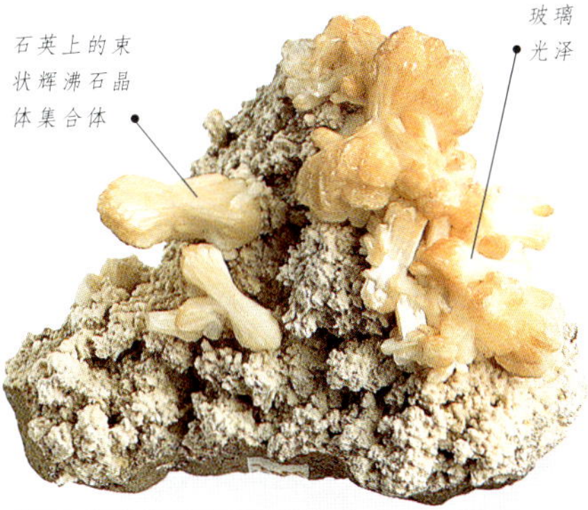


| | | |
|---|---|---|
| 比重 2.09～2.20　解理 完全 | 断口 参差状 | |

| | | |
|---|---|---|
| 类别 硅酸盐 | 成分 $NaCa_2Al_5Si_5O_{20} \cdot 6H_2O$ | 硬度 5～5.5 |

## 杆沸石(Thomsonite)

晶体针状、柱状，不过常以片状或放射状集合体产出。白色、无色、浅黄色、粉红色或浅绿色，条痕无色。透明到半透明，玻璃到珍珠光泽。

· 成因　形成于熔岩空洞。

· 鉴定特征　溶于盐酸，并产生凝胶。

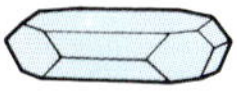

斜方晶系

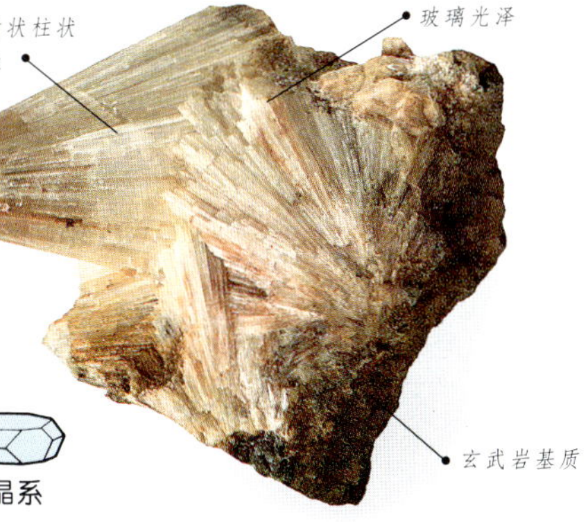


| | | |
|---|---|---|
| 比重 2.25～2.40　解理 完全 | 断口 参差状至亚贝壳状 | |

# 岩石

## 岩浆岩

岩浆岩是由熔融物质结晶而成。这种熔融的岩石称为岩浆。喷出地表的，称为熔岩。其主要成分为硅酸盐，含有硅、氧和其他元素，尤其是铝、铁、钙、钠、钾和镁。随着岩浆和熔岩的冷凝结晶，这些元素结合形成硅酸盐矿物，并构成成岩浆。

| 类别 岩浆岩 | 成因 侵入 | 粒度 粗粒 | 晶形 他形、自形 |
|---|---|---|---|

### 粉红花岗岩(Pink Granite)

花岗岩是最常见的侵入岩，酸性。硅含量超过 65%，最低石英含量 20%。钾长石(正长石、微斜长石)常比斜长石(富含钠)多，且呈粉红色。云母为深色的黑云母或银白色的白云母，可能含角闪石。

· **结构** 粗粒，晶体颗粒大于 5 毫米。

· **成因** 形成于地壳内部深处。

| 分类 酸性 | 产状 深成岩体 | 颜色 浅色 |
|---|---|---|

| 类别 岩浆岩 | 成因 侵入 | 粒度 粗粒 | 晶形 他形、自形 |
|---|---|---|---|

### 白色花岗岩(White Granite)

硅含量高，超过 65%，石英含量不少于 20%，因此归入酸性岩。钾长石(正长石和微斜长石)为主，颜色白色，常含钠斜长石。由于含黑云母和角闪石岩石表面呈斑点，也含色浅透明的白云母。

· **结构** 粗粒，长石和云母成自形晶，石英晶体他形。

· **成因** 形成于深成环境。

| 分类 酸性 | 产状 深成岩体 | 颜色 浅色 |
|---|---|---|

| 类别 岩浆岩 | 成因 侵入 | 粒度 粗粒 | 晶形 他形、自形 |
| --- | --- | --- | --- |

## 斑状花岗岩(Porphyritic Granite)

硅含量超过 65%，石英含量不少于 20%。含粉红色正长石和白色微斜长石或钠长石，黑云母晶体和石英颗粒清晰可见角闪石加重斑状外表。

· 结构　粒状或斑状结构，斑晶常是长石，可长达 6 厘米。

· 成因　岩浆在地壳一定深处通过两个阶段冷凝形成。

| 分类 酸性 | 产状 深成岩体 | 颜色 浅色 |
| --- | --- | --- |

| 类别 岩浆岩 | 成因 侵入 | 粒度 粗粒 | 晶形 他形、自形 |
| --- | --- | --- | --- |

## 文像花岗岩(Graphic Granite)

酸性岩，石英含量 20%，硅含量超过 65%。由钾长石(正长石、微斜长石)、钠斜长石、灰色石英和一些深色黑云母组成。

· 结构　粗粒，并有文像结构。

· 成因　由石英和钾长石同时结晶形成。

| 分类 酸性 | 产状 深成岩体 | 颜色 浅色 |
| --- | --- | --- |

| 类别 岩浆岩 | 成因 侵入 | 粒度 粗粒 | 晶形 他形、自形 |
| --- | --- | --- | --- |

## 角闪花岗岩(Hornblende Granite)

由 20% 以上的石英和 65% 以上的硅组成。钾长石(正长石和微斜长石)多于斜长石，角闪石以小块体和柱状晶体产出，含云母。

· 结构　粗粒，晶体等粒，使得其结构均匀。

· 成因　形成于地壳内部不同深处。

| 分类 酸性 | 产状 深成岩体 | 颜色 中等 |
| --- | --- | --- |

| 类别 岩浆岩 | 成因 侵入 | 粒度 粗粒 | 晶形 他形、自形 |
| --- | --- | --- | --- |

## 石英二长岩(Adamellite)

酸性岩，硅含量大于65%，石英含量超过20%。含有大量长石，其中钾长石(正长石和微斜长石)和斜长石含量相等。黑云母使石英二长石呈现出斑状外观，基质中有灰色石英小颗粒。

· **结构** 粗粒，虽呈斑状，但颗粒的大小通常相等。晶体很大，肉眼可见。虽然某些石英呈他形晶，但石英二长石中的大多数矿物晶体都是自形的。

· **成因** 伴随巨大深成岩体在岩浆中形成。

| 分类 酸性 | 产状 深成岩体 | 颜色 浅色 |
| --- | --- | --- |

| 类别 岩浆岩 | 成因 侵入 | 粒度 中粒 | 晶形 他形、自形 |
| --- | --- | --- | --- |

## 白色微花岗岩(White Microgranite)

酸性岩，硅含量超过65%，石英含量超过20%，其中钾长石(正长石和微斜长石)的含量多于斜长石。含深色黑云母或浅色白云母，聚集成块的黑云母使微花岗岩的颜色变深。

· **结构** 中粒，晶体小，5~0.5毫米之间，从而造成矿物鉴定的困难。颗粒大小通常均匀，不过很多晶体呈他形。由于快速冷却，有时呈斑状。

· **成因** 形成于伟晶岩外缘，也形成于在中等深变的小型岩浆侵入，形成岩床和岩脉。

| 分类 酸性 | 产状 岩脉、岩床 | 颜色 浅色、中等 |
| --- | --- | --- |

| 类别 岩浆岩 | 成因 侵入 | 粒度 中粒 | 晶形 他形、自形 |
| --- | --- | --- | --- |

## 粉红微花岗岩 (Pink Microgranite)

酸性岩，硅总含量大于 65%，石英含量超过 20%。如果占绝大多数的长石是粉红色正长石，则将影响岩石的颜色。含于微花岗岩中的黑云母呈深色斑点，基质中的灰色石英颗粒为他形晶。

· **结构**　中粒晶体颗粒 5～0.5 毫米之间，大小基本一致。

· **成因**　由岩浆浅成侵入形成于岩脉和岩床。

| 分类 酸性 | 产状 岩脉、岩床 | 颜色 浅色、中等 |
| --- | --- | --- |

| 类别 岩浆岩 | 成因 侵入 | 粒度 中粒 | 晶形 他形、自形 |
| --- | --- | --- | --- |

## 斑状微花岗岩 (Porphyritic Microgranite)

酸性岩，硅含量超过 65%，石英含量大于 20%。与其他几种花岗岩一样，钾长石(正长石和微斜长石)含量多于斜长石。具有嵌入基质的浅色长石斑晶，并含有深色黑云母。

· **结构**　中粒，晶体颗料大小 5～0.5 毫米。常见斑状结构，长石斑晶自形，常呈完好的晶体，并定向排列，从斑状构造可知岩浆的结晶过程。

· **成因**　形成于小侵入体，如岩床和岩脉。

| 分类 酸性 | 产状 岩脉、岩床 | 颜色 中等 |
| --- | --- | --- |

| 类别 岩浆/变质岩 | 成因 围岩 | 粒度 细粒 | 晶形 他形、自形 |
|---|---|---|---|

## 捕虏岩(Xenolith)

指被岩浆捕虏部分发生蚀变的岩块，它可能全部熔入岩浆消失。图示标本是包在粉红色花岗岩中的深色熔岩块，花岗岩中的长石、云母和石英与深色的捕获虏岩形成鲜明对比。

· **结构** 中粒到细粒，晶体颗粒大小0.5毫米，花岗岩是粗粒岩，晶体颗粒不小于5毫米。

· **成因** 形成于许多岩浆岩和侵入体环境。

| 分类 酸性至基性 | 产状 深成岩体、火山 | 颜色 深色 |
|---|---|---|

| 类别 岩浆岩 | 成因 侵入 | 粒度 中粒 | 晶形 他形、自形 |
|---|---|---|---|

## 石英斑岩(Quartz Porphyry)

酸性岩，硅含量超过65%，石英含量大于10%。微晶基质中含有石英和碱性长石(常是正长石)斑晶，石英斑岩中，正长石多于斜长石。这块标本中还含一些角闪石。

· **结构** 中粒，较小矿物颗粒包围各主要矿物的较大晶体(斑晶)，基质中这些较小颗粒大小一致。作为斑岩的石英斑岩形成于岩浆冷凝过程的两次结晶。

· **成因** 源于岩浆的侵入和冷凝，石英斑岩形成于小侵入体，如岩床和岩脉，一般形成于地壳浅部。

| 分类 酸性 | 产状 岩脉、岩床 | 颜色 浅色、中等 |
|---|---|---|

| 类别 岩浆岩 | 成因 侵入 | 粒度 极粗粒 | 晶形 自形 |
|---|---|---|---|

## 长石伟晶岩(Feldspar Pegmatite)

酸性岩，矿物成分与花岗岩一样，主要含有大量的长石(通常是粉红色或白色)、浅灰色石英和深色云母或闪石，硅含量远超过 65%。

· **结构** 由于冷凝过程缓慢，伟晶岩极粗粒，有时可成长达数米的晶体。图示标本中的白色长石晶体长变体超过 10 厘米，肉眼可轻易辨认。

· **成因** 形成于地壳深部，呈岩脉和矿脉，常分布在花岗侵入体边缘。

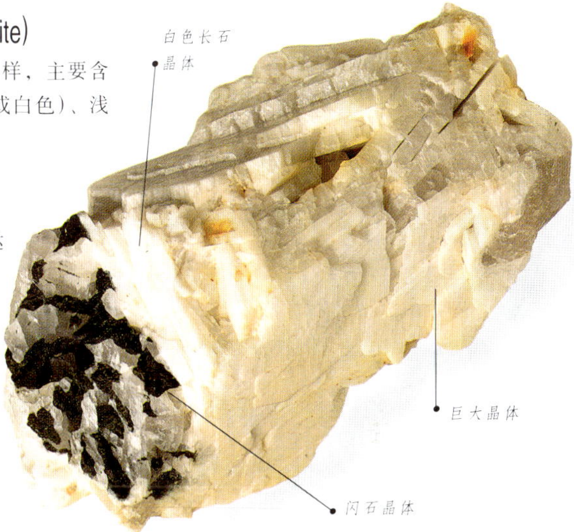


| 分类 酸性 | 产状 深成岩体、岩脉、岩床 | 颜色 浅色 |
|---|---|---|

| 类别 岩浆岩 | 成因 岩浆 | 粒度 极粗粒 | 晶形 自形 |
|---|---|---|---|

## 云母伟晶岩(Mica Pegmatite)

酸性岩，成分与花岗岩一样，硅含量大于 65%，石英含量超过 20%。岩石中的白云母能形成长超过 6 厘米的大薄片，此外含长石和黑云母。伟晶岩这个名称一般指成分酸性的岩石，但也用于形成极粗粒晶体的岩浆岩。

· **结构** 颗粒极粗是由于岩浆缓慢的冷凝，使其可能发育成达几英尺的巨大晶体。

· **成因** 形成于地表下深处的深成岩。岩浆冷却缓慢，常与后期热液伴生，它们带来稀有元素。

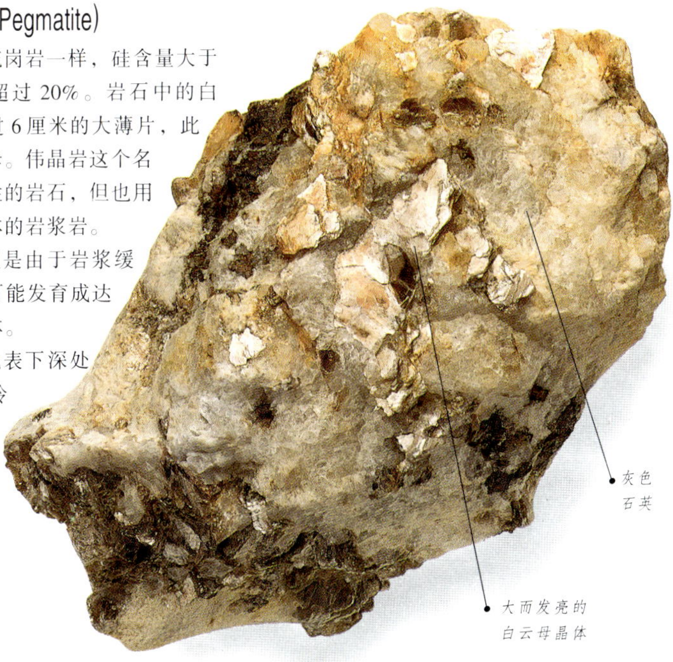


| 分类 酸性 | 产状 深成岩体、岩脉、岩床 | 颜色 浅色 |
|---|---|---|

| 类别 岩浆岩 | 成因 侵入 | 粒度 极粗粒 | 晶形 自形 |
|---|---|---|---|

## 电气石伟晶岩(Tourmaline Pegmatite)

与花岗岩相似，为酸性岩，石英含量大于20%，硅含量超过65%。灰色石英、粉红色钾长石和深色黑云母占矿物组分很大比例，岩石中深色柱状晶体为硼硅酸盐矿物电气石。

· **结构** 极粗粒，图示标本的较大晶体长5~6厘米，大多数为自形晶体(呈良好晶形)，电气石形成粗粒带条纹的柱状晶体。

· **成因** 形成于大侵入体，也见于岩脉和岩床中，是在地壳相当深处的岩浆缓慢冷却形成的。

| 分类 酸性 | 产状 深成岩体、岩脉、岩床 | 颜色 浅色 |
|---|---|---|

| 类别 岩浆岩 | 成因 侵入 | 粒度 中粒 | 晶形 他形、自形 |
|---|---|---|---|

## 文像斑岩(Granophyre)

酸性岩，石英含量大于20%，硅含量超过65%，含钾长石和斜长石、云母以及闪石。如果文像斑岩中含铁镁矿物，则呈较深的颜色。

· **结构** 中粒，呈斑状，文像斑状结构是长石和石英交互生长形成的，较小的文像结构也见于某些花岗岩。最好用放大镜或显微镜观察其结构。

· **成因** 产于深成大侵入体边缘，也见于半深成侵入岩。

| 分类 酸性 | 产状 深成岩体、岩脉 | 颜色 浅色、中等 |
|---|---|---|

| 类别 岩浆岩 | 成因 侵入 | 粒度 粗粒 | 晶形 他形、自形 |
|---|---|---|---|

## 粉红色花岗闪长岩(Pink Granodiorite)

属深成岩，主要由石英、斜长石和少量的碱性长石组成，次要成分有角闪石、黑云母和辉石。

· **结构** 中粒到粗粒，并有发育完好的晶体。

· **成因** 形成于多种侵入岩，是花岗岩族中最常见的一种岩石。

| 分类 中性 | 产状 深成岩体、岩脉 | 颜色 浅色、中等 |
|---|---|---|

| 类别 岩浆岩 | 成因 侵入 | 粒度 粗粒 | 晶形 他形、自形 |
|---|---|---|---|

## 白色花岗闪长岩(White Granodiorite)

硅含量少于花岗岩，为 55～65%。这种浅色花岗闪长岩含有占很大比例的灰色石英和白色长石，深色云母和角闪石使其呈现斑状。

· **结构** 粗粒，晶体发育完好，有些填隙石英呈他形晶体。

· **成因** 形成于多种岩浆侵入体中。

| 分类 中性 | 产状 深成岩体 | 颜色 浅色 |
|---|---|---|

| 类别 岩浆岩 | 成因 岩浆 | 粒度 粗粒 | 晶形 他形、自形 |
|---|---|---|---|

## 闪长岩(Diorite)

为中性岩，硅含量 55～65%。闪长岩主要由斜长石(奥长石或中长石)和角闪石组成，也含黑云母和辉石。

· **结构** 中粒到粗粒(有时呈伟晶型)，可为等粒结构，或由长石或角闪石斑晶构成斑状结构。

· **成因** 以独立侵入岩的形式，如岩脉形成，常是主要花岗岩石体的一部分。

| 分类 中性 | 产状 深成岩体、岩脉 | 颜色 中等、深色 |
|---|---|---|

| 类别 岩浆岩 | 成因 侵入 | 粒度 粗粒 | 晶形 自形 |
|---|---|---|---|

## 正长岩(Syenite)

粗粒深成岩，石英含量少最多10%，颜色浅淡，常与花岗岩混淆。为中性岩，硅含量55~65%，主要由碱性长石或钠斜长石组成，常与黑云母、闪石或辉石伴生。

· **结构** 粗粒，其中的所有矿物都可用肉眼辨认，并且颗粒大小相近。大粒晶体被细粒基质包围处有时呈现斑状，晶体他形到自形。

· **成因** 一般形成于小侵入体、岩脉和岩床中，并常与花岗岩伴生。

| 分类 中性 | 产状 深成岩体、岩脉 | 颜色 浅色、深色 |
|---|---|---|

| 类别 岩浆岩 | 成因 侵入 | 粒度 粗粒 | 晶形 自形 |
|---|---|---|---|

## 霞石正长岩(Nepheline Syenite)

为典型的中性岩，硅含量55~65%。含有较大比例的长石、闪石和云母，有时也含辉石，含似长石矿物——霞石，因而得名，不含石英。

· **结构** 粗粒，所含矿物肉眼可辨，晶体颗粒大小通常一致(等粒状)，有时也呈伟晶结构。

· **成因** 形成于与高碱性岩伴生的岩浆岩，这些岩石富含钠钾矿物。

| 分类 中性 | 产状 深成岩、岩脉 | 颜色 浅色、暗色 |
|---|---|---|

| 类别 岩浆岩 | 成因 侵入 | 粒度 粗粒 | 晶形 自形 |
|---|---|---|---|

## 辉长岩(Gabbro)

为基性岩，石英含量极少，含硅量比花岗岩少(约占总量的50%)，主要由钙斜长石、辉石(通常是普通辉石)、橄榄石和磁铁矿组成。

· 结构　为粗粒和等粒岩石。

· 成因　形成于深成侵入体，常呈层状产出。

| 分类 基性 | 产状 深成岩体 | 颜色 中等 |
|---|---|---|

| 类别 岩浆岩 | 成因 侵入 | 粒度 粗粒 | 晶形 自形 |
|---|---|---|---|

## 层辉长岩(Layered Gabbro)

与辉长岩一样为基性岩，主要矿物有富含钙的斜长石和辉石，还有橄榄石和磁铁矿。浅色和深色矿物交替聚集呈层状，层厚1米到数厘米不等，是重力沉降作用所致。

· 结构　粗粒，自形晶。

· 成因　形成于基性深成侵入体，有时产于主构造(岩盆)。

| 分类 基性 | 产状 深成岩体 | 颜色 中等 |
|---|---|---|

| 类别 岩浆岩 | 成因 侵入 | 粒度 粗粒 | 晶形 自形 |
|---|---|---|---|

## 歪碱正长岩(Larvikite)

辉石正长岩的变种，中性岩，含长石、辉石(通常是锑辉石)、云母和闪石，还含少量霞石和橄榄石。深灰色到浅灰色，长石常现特殊的光泽。

· 结构　粗粒，图示标本上可见呈块状的铁镁质矿物。

· 成因　形成于较小侵入体，如岩床。

| 分类 中性 | 产状 深成岩体 | 颜色 浅色、中等 |
|---|---|---|

| 类别 岩浆岩 | 成因 侵入 | 粒度 粗粒 | 晶形 他形、自形 |
| --- | --- | --- | --- |

## 橄榄辉长岩(Olivine Gabbro)

基性岩，硅含量小于55%，石英难得出现。铁镁矿物含量高，因此岩石呈暗色，密度大于花岗岩。含斜长石(一种富含钙的长石类)、辉石和橄榄石，常含少量磁铁矿。

· **结构** 粗粒，大多数为自形晶，颗粒大于5毫米，肉眼可见。颗粒大小均匀，可呈斑状结构——细粒的基质环绕较大的晶体。

· **成因** 形成于深成岩体，呈岩株、岩床和层状侵入体。

| 分类 基性 | 产状 深成岩体、岩脉、岩床 | 颜色 中等、深色 |
| --- | --- | --- |

| 类别 岩浆岩 | 成因 侵入 | 粒度 粗粒 | 晶形 他形、自形 |
| --- | --- | --- | --- |

## 淡辉长岩(Leucogabbro)

基性，硅含量小于55%。比其他辉长岩色浅，因斜长石含量较高。常与斜辉岩、辉岩伴生，有时含橄榄石和磁铁矿。

· **结构** 粗粒，晶体大于5毫米，肉眼可辨。

· **成因** 形成于深成岩体，常呈大侵入岩体。在结晶过程中由于重力作用，结晶体和残液分离，由残液形成系列岩石，这一过程叫做分离结晶作用。

| 分类 基性 | 产状 深成岩体 | 颜色 中等、浅色 |
| --- | --- | --- |

| | | | |
|---|---|---|---|
| 别 岩浆岩 | 成因 侵入 | 粒度 粗粒 | 晶形 他形、自形 |

## 角闪辉长岩(Bojite)

深成岩，含斜长石(拉长石)、棕色角闪石，以及少量辉石和黑云母，其中以棕色角闪石为主，氧化铁(磁铁矿)是常见的副矿物。角闪辉长岩呈斑点和条纹，以及含镁铁质矿物，十分醒目。

· **结构** 粗粒，晶体颗粒大于5毫米，大小均等，暗色矿物常成斑点和层状。

· **成因** 形成于地壳内部深处。

| | | |
|---|---|---|
| 分类 基性 | 产状 深成岩体 | 颜色 深色 |

| | | | |
|---|---|---|---|
| 类别 岩浆岩 | 成因 侵入 | 粒度 粗粒 | 晶形 他形、自形 |

## 钙长岩(Anorthosite)

基性岩成分，硅含量小于55%，几无石英。钙长岩至少含有90%的斜长石(拉长石——倍长石)，其他矿物有橄榄石、辉石和铁氧化物。有时石榴子围绕辉石形成反应边。

· **结构** 粗粒，色浅，深色矿物常平行排列。

· **成因** 形成于深成岩体，成岩株、岩脉和层状的侵入体。常在层状分异中与辉长岩伴生，也见于月球表面。

| | | |
|---|---|---|
| 分类 基性 | 产状 深成岩体 | 颜色 浅色 |

| 类别 岩浆岩 | 成因 侵入 | 粒度 中粒 | 晶形 他形、自形 |
| --- | --- | --- | --- |

## 粒玄岩(Dolerite)

基性岩，硅含量小于55%，石英含量少于10%。含富钙斜长石、辉石(普通辉石)及少量石英，有时含磁铁矿和橄榄石(如含橄榄石，则称为橄榄粒玄岩，如含石英，则为石英粒玄岩)。

· **结构**　中粒，晶体颗粒0.5~5毫米。斜长石的自形或半自形晶体嵌在辉石中。

· **成因**　常以岩脉和岩床产于玄武岩区，还以数以百计的岩脉或岩床与巨大侵入体伴生。

| 分类 基性 | 产状 岩脉、岩床 | 颜色 深色 |
| --- | --- | --- |

| 类别 岩浆岩 | 成因 侵入 | 粒度 中粒 | 晶形 他形、自形 |
| --- | --- | --- | --- |

## 苏长岩(Norite)

与辉长岩相似，属基性岩，硅的含量小于55%。苏长岩由斜长石和辉石组成，为辉长岩的变种，其中直辉石含量大于斜辉石。苏长岩的某些变种橄榄石，有时含黑云母、角闪石和堇青石。

· **结构**　粗粒，常呈层状构造。

· **成因**　由深成环境中的岩浆冷凝而成，与较大的基性岩体伴生，也常见于层状岩浆侵入。由于重力作用矿物成分分异，形成不同种类的岩石。

| 分类 基性 | 产状 深成岩体 | 颜色 深色 |
| --- | --- | --- |

| 类别 岩浆岩 | 成因 侵入 | 粒度 中粒 | 晶形 他形、自形 |
|---|---|---|---|

## 橄长岩(Troctolite)

属于辉长岩，硅含量小于55%。主要由富含钙斜长石和橄榄石组成，几乎不含辉石。橄榄石常蚀变成蛇纹石，橄长岩通常呈深灰色，并常呈斑驳状。

· **结构**　中粒到粗粒，多数晶体颗粒约5毫米左右，大小均匀。

· **成因**　形成于岩浆冷却缓慢的深成环境，常与辉长岩或钙长岩伴生，有时呈复杂层状。

| 分类 基性 | 产状 深成岩体 | 颜色 深色 |
|---|---|---|

| 类别 岩浆岩 | 成因 侵入 | 粒度 中粒 | 晶形 自形 |
|---|---|---|---|

## 纯橄榄岩(Dunite)

超基性岩，硅含量小于45%，不含石英。几乎全部由橄榄石组成，因此具有易辨认的浅绿色或浅棕色。纯橄榄岩英文又名“olivinite”，意为橄榄岩，由名称可知其矿物组成，铬铁矿以副矿物含于纯橄榄岩。

· **结构**　中粒，晶体颗粒0.5～5毫米，纯橄榄岩呈粒状和糖粒状结构。

· **成因**　形成于深成环境。在基性岩浆分异过程中，常形成小超基性岩体。由于地壳运动某些纯橄榄岩中的矿物常被压碎，成近固体状态，和其他基性岩浆形成超基性岩体。

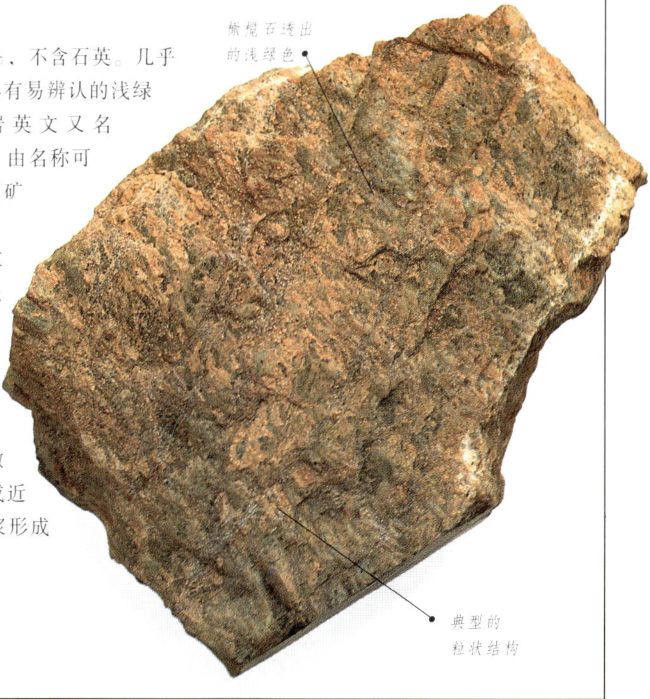


| 分类 超基性 | 产状 深成岩体 | 颜色 深色、中等 |
|---|---|---|

| 类别 岩浆岩 | 成因 侵入 | 粒度 粗粒 | 晶形 他形、自形 |
|---|---|---|---|

## 蛇纹岩(Serpentinite)

一种深成岩，属超基性岩，硅量小于45%。几乎全部由蛇纹岩矿物如叶蛇纹石和纤蛇纹石组成，常见残余橄榄石。其他有铁镁矿物石榴子石、辉石、角闪石，常含云母，此外有铬铁矿或铬尖晶石。色深，呈黑、绿、红色。

· **结构** 粗粒到中粒，大多数晶体肉眼可见。这是一种致密并常带有条纹的岩石，通常由纤维状蛇纹石形成纹脉。

· **成因** 以岩脉、岩株和透镜体产出。蛇纹岩是由其他岩石(主要为橄榄岩)蛇纹石化形成，常生成于褶皱变质岩中，可能由富含橄榄石侵入体的蚀变而成。

| 分类 超基性 | 产状 造山带 | 颜色 深色 |
|---|---|---|

| 类别 岩浆岩 | 成因 侵入 | 粒度 粗粒 | 晶形 他形、自形 |
|---|---|---|---|

## 辉岩(Pyroxenite)

是一种超镁铁质深成岩，硅的含量小于45%。正如其名所示，几乎全部由一种或多种辉石组成，含少量黑云母、角闪石、橄榄石和铁氧化物，辉石岩中闪亮的晶体为含量极少的长石。

· **结构** 粗粒到中粒，具有粒状结构，发育完好的晶体常成层排列，结构肉眼易于辨认。

· **成因** 形成于小型独立侵入体，常与辉长岩或其他超基性岩伴生。

| 分类 超基性 | 产状 深成岩体 | 颜色 深色 |
|---|---|---|

| 类别 岩浆岩 | 成因 侵入 | 粒度 粗粒 | 晶形 自形 |
|---|---|---|---|

## 角砾云橄岩（金伯利岩）(Kimberlite)

一种超基性岩，主要由蛇纹岩化橄榄石组成，与金云母、正或斜辉石、碳酸盐和铬铁矿伴生，也含镁铝榴石、金红石和钙钛矿，呈暗色。

・结构　粗粒，常呈斑状结构，角砾状。

・成因　形成于陡直的侵入岩岩管和其他岩浆岩体，岩管的直径一般小于一公里。角砾云橄岩管是金刚石的主要来源，其金刚石含量高，得以大规模开采，尤其在南非。

| 分类 超基性 | 产状 半深成、深成岩体 | 颜色 暗色 |
|---|---|---|

| 类别 岩浆岩 | 成因 侵入 | 粒度 粗粒 | 晶形 他形、自形 |
|---|---|---|---|

## 石榴子石橄榄岩(Garnet Peridotite)

硅含量小于45%，并且只由暗色矿物组成，几乎没有长石，主要是橄榄石和石榴子石，也常含辉石和或角闪石。

・结构　粗粒或中粒，石榴子石嵌生于粒状基质中，大小呈颗粒很小到大小超过5毫米的斑块。

・成因　形成于岩脉、岩床和岩株。有时与辉长岩、辉岩和钙长岩伴生，另外还见于玄武岩，或以捕虏体产于深变质岩中，石榴子石橄榄岩可能源于地幔。

| 分类 超基性 | 产状 深成岩体、岩脉、岩床 | 颜色 暗色 |
|---|---|---|

| 类别 岩浆岩 | 成因 喷出 | 粒度 细粒 | 晶形 他形 |
|---|---|---|---|

## 流纹岩(Phyolite)

是喷出岩，成分大体上与花岗岩相同。和花岗岩一样，常富含石英和碱性长石。与花岗岩不同的是，玻璃常是流纹岩的主要成分之一，常含黑云母。

· **结构** 是一种细粒酸性火山岩，常含斑晶呈斑状结构。基质晶体微小，肉眼难以辨认。由于熔岩的快速冷凝产生玻璃，具有气孔和杏仁子。

· **成因** 爆发从火山喷出，由粘稠的熔岩冷凝而成。熔岩常堵塞火山口，积聚气体，增大压力。

| 分类 酸性 | 产状 火山 | 颜色 浅色 |
|---|---|---|

| 类别 岩浆岩 | 成因 喷出 | 粒度 细粒 | 晶形 他形 |
|---|---|---|---|

## 带状流纹岩(Banded Rhyolite)

成分与花岗岩相似，石英、长石、云母以及玻璃是带状流纹岩的主要成分，也含角闪石。

· **结构** 细粒或极细粒，组成岩石的矿物微小，肉眼无法看清。流纹岩具流纹构造，即不同色彩和结构层状涡形的构造。球状结构，是由石英和长石的放射状针状集合体构成的。

· **成因** 由熔岩快速冷凝而成，因此形成微晶或玻璃，这种岩浆十分粘稠。

| 分类 酸性 | 产状 火山 | 颜色 浅色、中等 |
|---|---|---|

| 类别 岩浆岩 | 成因 喷出 | 粒度 细粒 | 晶形 他形、自形 |
| --- | --- | --- | --- |

## 英安岩(Dacite)

属中性岩，石英和斜长石是石英安山岩中的主要成分，含少量黑云母或角闪石或辉石。

· 结构　细粒，具斑状结构，晶体他形到自形。

· 成因　为喷出岩，也见于小侵入岩体。

| 分类 中性 | 产状 火山 | 颜色 浅色、中等 |
| --- | --- | --- |

| 类别 岩浆岩 | 成因 喷出 | 粒度 极细粒 | 晶形 他形 |
| --- | --- | --- | --- |

## 黑曜岩(Obsidian)

富含硅的火山岩，主要成分玻璃。黑曜岩又名玻璃火山岩，其含水量小于1%。

· 结构　玻璃质，偶见石英和长石斑晶。断裂后成贝壳状锐利断口，从旧石器时代起人类就利用此特性制作切割工具。

· 成因　喷出岩，由粘稠的酸性熔岩极快速地冷凝而形。

| 分类 酸性 | 产状 火山 | 颜色 暗色 |
| --- | --- | --- |

| 类别 岩浆岩 | 成因 喷出 | 粒度 极细粒 | 晶形 他形 |
| --- | --- | --- | --- |

## 雪花黑曜岩(Sonwflake Obsidian)

和黑曜岩一样，主要由玻璃而不是晶体组成，玻璃不透明时，会围绕各个中心在岩石表面形成独特的灰白色“雪花”。

· 结构　极细粒，还呈白色微晶斑。

· 成因　是一种，熔岩迅速冷凝形成的喷出岩。

| 分类 酸性 | 产状 火山 | 颜色 暗色 |
| --- | --- | --- |

| 类别 岩浆岩 | 成因 喷出 | 粒度 极细粒 | 晶形 他形 |
|---|---|---|---|

## 松脂岩(Pitchstone)

和其他许多喷出岩的成分相同，主要为火山玻璃，含一些斑晶。颜色很暗，光泽类似焦油或沥青。

· **结构** 尽管松脂岩中玻璃含量很高，不过所含结晶物质多于黑曜岩。可呈斑点或流纹，即使在显微镜下观察松脂岩，也不见发育完好的晶体。

· **成因** 由熔岩突然凝固而成，尤其在岩脉和流动体中，含有大量玻璃是熔岩快速冷凝的结果。

| 分类 酸性至基性 | 产状 火山、岩脉、岩床 | 颜色 暗色 |
|---|---|---|

| 类别 岩浆岩 | 成因 喷出 | 粒度 极细粒 | 晶形 他形 |
|---|---|---|---|

## 斑状松脂岩(Porphyritic Pitchstone)

色暗，玻璃状，尽管松脂岩的化学成分多变，但均属常酸性岩，某些松脂岩富含斑晶，常为石英、长石和辉石。某些岩石学家根据岩石的含水量区分松脂岩和黑曜石，松脂岩大于10%，黑曜岩则不到1%。

· **结构** 由于在快速冷凝过程中经历了两个阶段，因此形成长石斑晶，并嵌入细粒基质中。

· **成因** 形成于熔岩流和小岩床、岩脉中，并且靠近花岗岩块体。在上面两种情况下，熔岩迅速凝固，没有使晶体生长充分发育的时间，因此呈玻璃状。

| 分类 酸性至基性 | 产状 火山、岩脉、岩床 | 颜色 暗色 |
|---|---|---|

| 类别 岩浆岩 | 成因 喷出 | 粒度 中粒 | 晶形 他形、自形 |
| --- | --- | --- | --- |

## 煌斑岩(Lamprophyre)

成分多变，特点是铁镁质矿物呈明显的斑状，主要矿物黑云母、闪石和辉石以及长石(碱性长石或斜长石)都发育在基质中，副矿物有角闪石、方解石、榍石和磁铁矿。

· 结构　中粒，具有典型的斑状结构，黑云母和角闪石斑晶使岩石呈现独特的外观。

· 成因　形成于小侵入体、岩脉和岩床中，常呈热液蚀变，还与多种岩浆岩伴生，如花岗岩、正长岩或闪长岩。

| 分类 酸性至基性 | 产状 岩脉、岩床 | 颜色 中等 |
| --- | --- | --- |

| 类别 岩浆岩 | 成因 喷出 | 粒度 细粒 | 晶形 他形、自形 |
| --- | --- | --- | --- |

## 安山岩(Andesite)

中性岩，硅含量 55~65%，斜长石(中长石或奥长石)为其主要的成分，另外有辉石、闪石和黑云母。

· 结构　细粒，常呈斑状，嵌入基质的斑晶通常是白色板状长石晶体、黑云母、角闪石或辉石。

· 成因　以安山岩火山熔岩流的形式产出，分布之广仅次于玄武岩，形成于造山带，如南美安第斯山脉有大片安山岩分布。

| 分类 中性 | 产状 火山 | 颜色 中等 |
| --- | --- | --- |

| 类别 岩浆岩 | 成因 喷出 | 粒度 细粒 | 晶形 他形、自形 |
|---|---|---|---|

## 杏仁状安山岩(Amygdaloidal Andesite)

属中性岩，常呈斑状，含斜长石(一般为拉长石——奥长石)、辉石或黑云母。岩石基质呈深浅适中的灰色，而不是玄武岩的黑色。

· **结构** 细粒，常呈斑状。岩石表面可见很多小的圆形气孔，气体从熔岩中逃逸后留下气孔。被充填的气孔称为杏仁石，常为沸石类矿物充填，随着矿物的生长空洞逐渐变大。

· **成因** 火山喷出的熔岩快速冷凝形成杏仁状安山岩。

| 分类 中性 | 产状 火山 | 颜色 中等 |
|---|---|---|

| 类别 岩浆岩 | 成因 喷出 | 粒度 细粒 | 晶形 他形、自形 |
|---|---|---|---|

## 斑状安山岩(Porphyritic Andesite)

成分同安山岩，中性岩，硅含量55～65%，斜长石、辉石、闪石和黑云母都是主要成分。安山岩是一种颜色比流纹岩深的喷出岩，不过比玄武岩的颜色浅。

· **结构** 基质细粒，只有在显微镜下才能仔细地观察晶体，较大的长石和辉石斑晶嵌在基质中。从这种结构可知某些晶体是在地下岩浆未喷出前生长的，并表明火山喷发后，熔岩凝固极其迅速。

· **成因** 成熔岩流，常与安山岩火山伴生。

| 分类 中性 | 产状 火山 | 颜色 中等 |
|---|---|---|

| 类别 岩浆岩 | 成因 喷出 | 粒度 细粒 | 晶形 他形、自形 |
|---|---|---|---|

## 粗面岩(Trachyte)

硅含量 55～60%。粗面岩富含碱性长石，并含霞石或少量的石英(少于 10%)，也见少量暗色矿物，如辉石和霓石，不过粗面岩常呈浅色。

· 结构　细粒，常呈斑状，长石微晶呈流线构造。

· 成因　粗面岩以熔岩流，以及岩脉和岩床的形成产出。

| 分类 中性 | 产状 火山 | 颜色 中等 |
|---|---|---|

| 类别 岩浆岩 | 成因 喷出 | 粒度 细粒 | 晶形 他形、自形 |
|---|---|---|---|

## 斑状粗面岩(Porphyritic Trachyte)

与粗面岩成分相近，硅含量 55～65%，主要由碱性长石组成，还含一些石英、斜长石、辉石、角闪石和黑云母。

· 结构　细粒基质，常见自形斑晶，因而呈斑状结构。

· 成因　熔岩冷凝而成。

| 分类 中性 | 产状 火山 | 颜色 中等 |
|---|---|---|

| 类别 岩浆岩 | 成因 喷出 | 粒度 中粒 | 晶形 自形 |
|---|---|---|---|

## 斜方斑岩(Rhomb Porphyry)

中性岩，常被称为微正长岩。硅含量 55～65%，石英含量达 10%，主要矿物为碱性长石以及角闪石、辉石和黑云母。

· 结构　岩石中的长石斑晶的横截面呈菱形，因此得名。

· 成因　呈熔岩流和岩脉产出。

| 分类 中性 | 产状 岩脉、岩床 | 颜色 中等 |
|---|---|---|

| 类别 岩浆岩 | 成因 喷出 | 粒度 细粒 | 晶形 他形、自形 |
|---|---|---|---|

## 玄武岩(Basalt)

基性喷出岩，含钙斜长石和辉石，为所有熔岩中分布最广数量最多的一类岩石。磷灰石和磁铁矿几乎与之形影相随，有时含橄榄石。

· **结构** 细粒，晶体他形或自形，不过，即使放大镜下也难以看清。

· **成因** 由流动性强的玄武熔岩冷凝而成，因其强流动性，形成极厚的熔岩层，广泛分布于各大陆，且为构成洋底的主要岩石。著名的活玄武岩火山——冒纳罗亚火山喷出的玄武岩构造了夏威夷的大部分岛屿。

| 分类 基性 | 产状 火山 | 颜色 暗色 |
|---|---|---|

| 类别 岩浆岩 | 成因 喷出 | 粒度 细粒 | 晶形 他形、自形 |
|---|---|---|---|

## 斑状玄武岩(Porphyritic Basalt)

成分与玄武岩相似，硅含量45～55%，石英含量少于10%，斜长石(富钙)和辉石为其主要成分，也含橄榄石和磁铁矿。

· **结构** 细粒，具嵌入基质的斑晶，斑晶常为橄榄石(绿色)、辉石(黑色)或斜长石(石灰色)，由产出的斑状结构可知熔岩的冷凝曾经历两个阶段。

· **成因** 形成于洋底火山喷发，无气孔构造，能流动很长距离，熔岩流形成分布数千平方公里的熔岩高原。

| 分类 基性 | 产状 火山 | 颜色 暗色 |
|---|---|---|

| 别 岩浆岩 | 成因 喷出 | 粒度 细粒 | 晶形 他形 |
|---|---|---|---|

## 杏仁状玄武岩(Amygdaloidal Basalt)

基性岩，硅含量45~55%，钙斜长石和辉石为主要组成矿物，也有橄榄石和磁铁矿。

· 结构　具杏仁子结构(被矿物充填的气孔)为某些玄武岩的特征。充填矿物常为呈似玛瑙状的沸石和石英。

· 成因　由熔岩冷凝而成。

| 类 基性 | 产状 火山 | 颜色 暗色 |
|---|---|---|

| 别 岩浆岩 | 成因 喷出 | 粒度 细粒 | 晶形 他形、自形 |
|---|---|---|---|

## 多孔状玄武岩(Vesicular Basalt)

成分与玄武岩非常相似，钙斜长石和辉石是主要组成矿物，也含橄榄石和磁铁矿。

· 结构　充满空洞，称为气孔，基质细粒，常呈斑状。如果气孔充填了矿物，多孔状玄武岩就变成了杏仁状玄武岩。

· 成因　由玄武熔岩冷凝而成。

| 类 基性 | 产状 火山 | 颜色 暗色 |
|---|---|---|

| 别 岩浆岩 | 成因 喷出 | 粒度 细粒 | 晶形 他形、自形 |
|---|---|---|---|

## 细碧岩(Spilite)

基性岩硅含量平均40%左右，以枕状熔岩产出。其显著特点是斜长石为钠长石(富含钠)，细碧石中的辉石常蚀变成绿泥石，不过普通辉石不生蚀变。

· 结构　细粒，具充填矿物的气孔，时见嵌入岩石基质中的杏仁子。

· 成因　形成于海底，以水下熔岩流和枕状熔岩产出。

| 类 基性 | 产状 火山 | 颜色 暗色 |
|---|---|---|

| 类别 岩浆岩 | 成因 火成碎屑 | 粒度 粗粒 | 晶形 碎片 |
|---|---|---|---|

## 集块岩(Agglomerate)

是固结或非固结的粗粒火成碎屑岩，可能由完全混杂在一起的火山岩和围岩碎屑组成。

**·结构** 颗粒的大小变化相当大，岩石由棱角形至半圆形碎屑嵌入较细粒的基质组成。熔岩多孔，有时呈纺锤状。

**·成因** 通常堆积在火山口或火山周围。集块岩由熔岩碎屑和围岩碎块组成，在火山活动中，与熔岩一起喷出火山口，常与其他喷出沉积物如凝灰岩伴生。

| 分类 酸性至基性 | 产状 火山 | 颜色 中等 |
|---|---|---|

| 类别 岩浆岩 | 成因 火成碎屑 | 粒度 细粒 | 晶形 碎片 |
|---|---|---|---|

## 石质凝灰岩(Lithic Tuff)

属火成碎屑岩(凝灰岩)，其中岩屑的数量多于晶屑或玻璃质屑。

**·结构** 细粒，由固结的火山碎屑组成，碎屑通常小于2毫米。含许多结晶岩石碎片，如流纹岩、粗面岩或安山岩。

**·成因** 火山灰喷入大气沉积形成。石质凝灰岩有时形成于水下，成层理分明具有许多与沉积作用有关的构造，如层状构造和带状构造的岩石。在火山猛烈喷发时，火山灰被带到数公里高的大气，随风飘落到远离火山的地方，火山喷发带入高空的灰尘埃形成美丽的日落景色。

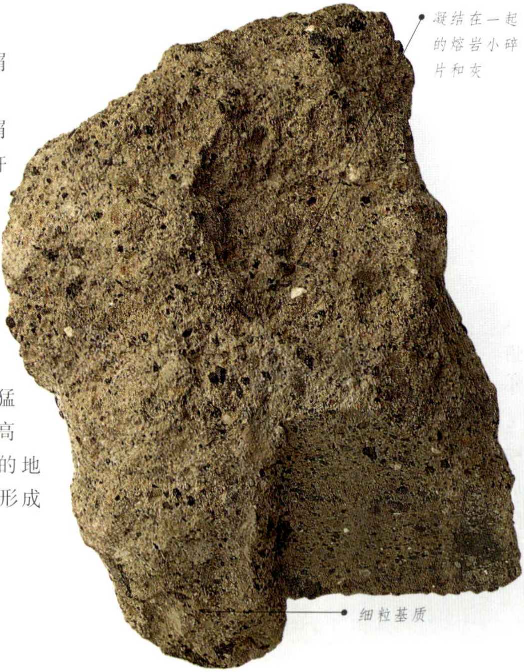


| 分类 酸性至基性 | 产状 火山 | 颜色 中等 |
|---|---|---|

| 类别 岩浆岩 | 成因 喷出 | 粒度 细粒 | 晶形 他形、自形 |
|---|---|---|---|

## 晶质凝灰岩(Crystal Tuff)

属凝灰岩，其中晶屑的数量多于岩屑或玻屑。大多数凝灰岩是岩屑、玻璃质屑或晶屑的混合物，组成晶质凝灰岩的矿物有长石、辉石和闪石。

· **结构** 细粒至中粒，晶体集合体嵌于火山灰基质中，晶体常自形。

· **成因** 由火山爆发喷出的火山灰形成。原形成的晶体与熔岩分离后，而可能积聚在沉降到陆地上或水下，如在水下沉积，则形成成层的具有沉积岩特征的凝灰岩。

| 分类 酸性至基性 | 产状 火山 | 颜色 中等 |
|---|---|---|

| 类别 岩浆岩 | 成因 喷出 | 粒度 细粒 | 晶形 他形 |
|---|---|---|---|

## 浮石(Pumice)

轻而多孔的岩石，其成分与流纹岩相同。其中含有许多硅酸盐矿物的微小晶体，如长石和铁镁矿物，此外还含有相当多的玻璃。

· **结构** 常被用作结构术语——描述像泡沫般的多气孔熔岩。具有高度的渣状结构，带有许多空洞和孔隙，这些气孔相互连接构成贯穿整个岩石的通道和管道，常被沸石填充。密度很小，可浮于水面。

· **成因** 伴随流纹岩火山喷发形成泡沫状熔岩，海底火山喷发产生的浮石会随海流漂流到远方，陆地火山爆发也形成浮石。

| 分类 酸性至基性 | 产状 火山 | 颜色 中等 |
|---|---|---|

| | | | |
|---|---|---|---|
| 类别 岩浆岩 | 成因 喷出 | 粒度 细粒 | 晶形 他形 |

## 熔结凝灰岩(Ignimbrite)

坚硬的火山凝灰岩，由晶体和岩石碎屑组成，嵌于熔结的玻璃质基质中，这种熔结方式常使玻璃原有的结构消失。成分与流纹岩相近。

**· 结构** 细粒，伴有带状构造。野外在露头上可见波浪状流纹。岩石中的玻璃质常在由火山灰、凝灰岩和熔岩微滴混杂时产生的气孔周围扭曲。

**· 成因** 由湍急翻滚，名为“火云”的熔结凝灰岩气体沉积而成，特别在火山猛烈爆发时能产生由气体和熔岩微滴构成的赤热气团，源于火山接近地表的快速喷发。

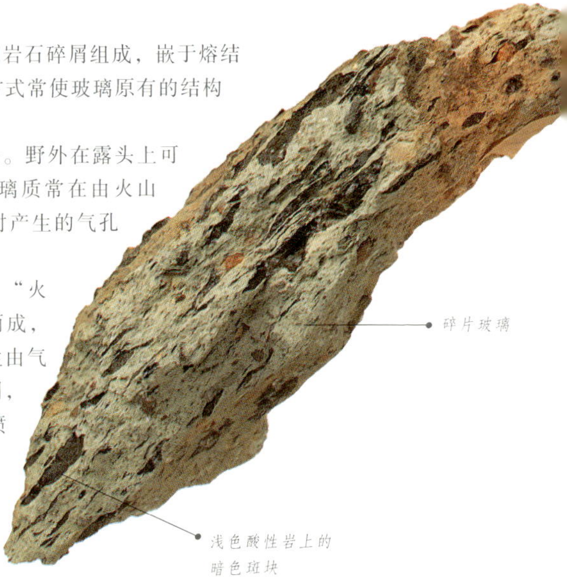


| | | |
|---|---|---|
| 分类 酸性 | 产状 火山 | 颜色 浅色、中等 |

| | | | |
|---|---|---|---|
| 类别 岩浆岩 | 成因 喷出 | 粒度 细粒 | 晶形 他形 |

## 面包皮火山弹(Breadcrust Volcanic Bomb)

火山弹的成分与某种火山喷发出的熔岩相同。凝固熔岩含硅量很高，则石英所占的比例也很高。凝固中性熔岩硅含量 55~65%，基性火山大多没有爆发性，所以很少形成火山弹。

**· 结构** 有着细粒的外壳，而内部的晶体则较粗。由于落地时的撞击，外壳留下疤痕和裂缝。火山弹中可能含有小围岩碎屑，是从火山管中撕扯带入的。

**· 成因** 火山弹是大小不等的熔融熔岩团，在剧烈的火山爆发时，从火山喷出并降落到地面形成的，这些熔岩团通常由多孔熔岩组成，在空中冷却时形成一层表皮，随后在着陆时裂开而产生面包皮状外表。火山弹直径有时长达一米，落在火山灰中形成弹坑。

| | | |
|---|---|---|
| 分类 酸性至基性 | 产状 火山 | 颜色 暗色 |

| | | | |
|---|---|---|---|
| 类别 岩浆岩 | 成因 喷出 | 粒度 细粒 | 晶形 他形 |

## 圆纺锤状火山弹(Rounded Spindle Bomb)

成分与某种火山喷发的熔岩相同，是安山岩或玄武岩火山，不过，也形成于酸性或其他中性熔岩火山。常富含硅，含石英、长石、云母等矿物，以及一些铁镁矿物，如角闪石。

· 结构　由细粒晶体组成，需在显微镜下观察。形状是由熔融熔岩团在空中飞行时扭曲而形成。

· 成因　熔融熔岩从火山中猛烈喷发形成圆纺锤状火山弹。

| | | |
|---|---|---|
| 分类 酸性至基性 | 产状 火山 | 颜色 中等 |

| | | | |
|---|---|---|---|
| 类别 岩浆岩 | 成因 喷出 | 粒度 细粒 | 晶形 他形 |

## 绳状熔岩(Ropy Lava)

形成于基性火山喷发，常为玄武岩，其中斜长石和普通辉石所占的比例很高，并含少量的铁氧化物，使之呈深色及高比重大。

· 结构　多孔，即其中含许多气孔，以后这些气孔会被许多矿物填充，包括石英、方解石和沸石气孔被填充后，称之为杏仁状岩。

· 成因　当熔岩从基性火山喷涌而出后，熔岩继续在凝结的相对坚硬、仍具塑性的外壳下流动时，形成绳状构造。硅含量低、气体含量高的玄武熔岩常具流动性，流动的熔岩使外壳伸长，因此造成褶皱和绳状外表。在夏威夷常见，绳状熔岩，当地称之为帕侯侯(Pahoehoe)，意为绳状成为地质学术语 Pahoehoe lava(绳状熔岩)。

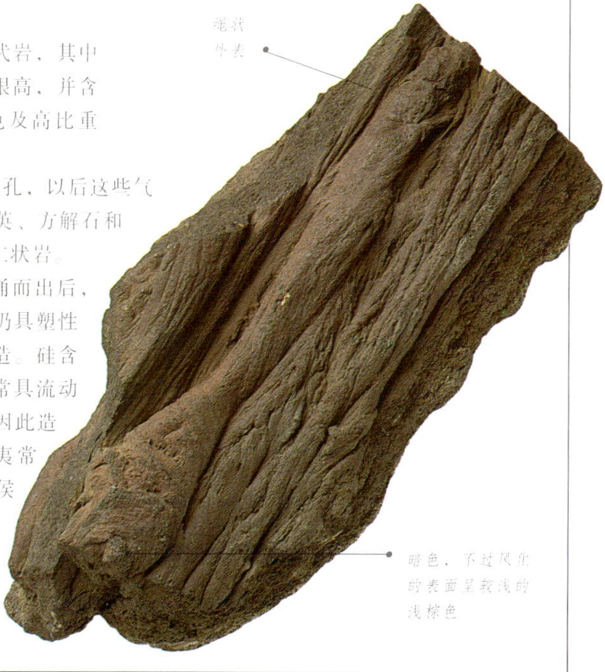


| | | |
|---|---|---|
| 分类 基性 | 产状 火山 | 颜色 暗色 |

# 变质岩

先成岩经过变质作用形成变质岩。接触变质作用是直接由高温而引起的，形成的岩石通常是结晶的。区域变质作用是由高温和压力引起的，产生片理或劈理，岩石中的矿物由于压力的影响呈定向排列和重结晶。动力变质作用主要是发生在逆冲断层带(断层面)的岩石变质。

| 类别 变质岩 | 成因 造山 | 粒度 细粒 | 分类 区域变质 |
| --- | --- | --- | --- |

## 绿板岩(Green Slate)

浅变质岩，源于粘土(页岩)泥质岩。由石英、长石和云母组成，含绿泥石，故呈绿色。

· **结构** 细粒，颗粒大小均匀，非常小，显微镜下方可见。

· **成因** 形成于细粒沉积物如粘土，火山灰的区域变质，云母和绿泥石均呈定向排列，形成完全板理。

| 压力 低 | 温度 低 | 构造 片理 |
| --- | --- | --- |

| 类别 变质岩 | 成因 造山 | 粒度 细粒 | 分类 区域变质 |
| --- | --- | --- | --- |

## 黑板岩(Black Slate)

由泥质沉物粘土、泥岩、页岩和细粒凝灰岩形成，含粘土矿物、石英、云母和长石，带有机成分的矿物石墨和黄铁矿使岩石呈黑色。

· **结构** 细粒，具有独特发育完全的板理，是由片状矿物如云母定向排列所致，使其容易裂成平行的板。

· **成因** 细粒泥质沉积物如泥石或页岩在低温低压下区域变质而成。

| 压力 低 | 温度 低 | 构造 片理 |
| --- | --- | --- |

| 类别　变质岩 | 成因　造山 | 粒度　细粒 | 分类　区域变质 |
|---|---|---|---|

## 黄铁矿板岩(Slate With Pyrite)

与其他板岩一样，由泥质沉积物形成，由石英、粘土矿物、绿泥石、云母和长石组成。正如其名所示，还含黄铁矿，黄铁矿或为细小分散的晶体，或为嵌入细粒基质的较大斑状变晶(不同的晶体)，常呈立方晶体。

· **结构**　细粒，只有黄铁矿的斑状变晶肉眼可辨，显微镜下才能仔细观察细粒基质。与其他板岩一样，具发育完全的板理，系片状矿物在压力下定向排列所致。

· **成因**　形成于低温和低压的条件，在这种区域变质条件下，生成完好的黄铁矿晶体。

| 压力　低 | 温度　低 | 构造　片理 |
|---|---|---|

| 类别　变质岩 | 成因　造山 | 粒度　细粒 | 分类　区域变质 |
|---|---|---|---|

## 含化石板岩(Slate With Distorted Fossil)

由泥质沉积物形成，含有构成原泥质沉积的矿物，石英、粘土矿物、云母长石，绿泥石是主要组成矿物，也含微小黄铁矿晶体。由于变质程度低，因此，含于原来页岩中的化石得以保存下来。

· **结构**　细粒，带少量黄铁矿斑状变晶。

· **成因**　页岩经浅变质形成含化石板岩，图示的腕足动物化石形态仍可辨，但由于形成板理时的剪切变质作用而变形。

| 压力　低 | 温度　低 | 构造　片理 |
|---|---|---|

| 类别 变质岩 | 成因 造山 | 粒度 中粒 | 分类 区域变质 |
| --- | --- | --- | --- |

## 千枚岩(Phyllite)

源于沉积物的低级变质，与板岩类似，但变质前的沉积物不限于粘土岩。其石英和长石的含量多于页岩，云母和绿泥石是主要成分，使其具有独特的丝绢光泽，呈灰色或绿色。

· **结构** 是一种片状岩石，细粒到中粒，明显的小石榴子石变晶嵌入波状片理中，低中压力下，云母和绿泥石定向排列，形成千枚状片理，呈显微鳞片状结构。

· **成因** 在较强压力和低温区域变质作用下，由泥质沉积物等形成。

| 压力 低、中 | 温度 低 | 构造 片理 |
| --- | --- | --- |

| 类别 变质岩 | 成因 造山 | 粒度 中粒 | 分类 区域变质 |
| --- | --- | --- | --- |

## 石榴子石片岩(Garnet Schist)

片岩的特征是，其中的片状和柱状矿物定向排列成明显的片状构造。富含云母(黑云母和白云母)，也含石英和长石。石榴子石常发育成完好的晶体，颗粒大小5毫米左右，形成于压力和温度的变化，常为红色变种贵榴石。

· **结构** 中粒至粗粒。由于云母定向平行排列，因此具发育完好的片理，并呈显微鳞片状结构。

· **成因** 形成于中级区域变质条件，深度大于千枚岩，压力适中，温度在改变岩石原有性质中起重要的作用。

| 压力 适中 | 温度 低至适中 | 构造 片理 |
| --- | --- | --- |

| | | | |
|---|---|---|---|
| 类别 变质岩 | 成因 造山 | 粒度 中粒 | 分类 区域变质 |

## 褶皱片岩(Folded Schist)

含石英、长石、黑云母和白云母，具为闪灼光亮的云母晶体增强的显微鳞片状构造为其特征。

· **结构** 中粒，所含矿物分隔成一条条带状。片理是沿岩石薄弱面劈裂的波状面，云母晶体使之更为发育。

· **成因** 形成于造山带的地下深处中压、中低温环境，是典型的造山带岩石。

| | | |
|---|---|---|
| 压力 适中 | 温度 低到适中 | 构造 片理 |

| | | | |
|---|---|---|---|
| 类别 变质岩 | 成因 造山 | 粒度 中粒 | 分类 区域变质 |

## 白云母片岩(Muscovite Schist)

富含银色的白云母，云母在岩石的波状片理面上定向排列。含石英、长石和一些黑云母，也含石榴子石和绿泥石。

· **结构** 中粒。云母晶体大小2~3毫米，云母条带的多少影响片理或波状片理的发育程度。

· **成因** 形成于中级区域变质，即中压、中低温条件下，由泥质岩变质而成，这种条件下常使泥质或粘土质原岩发生变质，其他岩石也常受到影响，片理不发育。

| | | |
|---|---|---|
| 压力 适中 | 温度 低至中 | 构造 片理 |

| 类别 变质岩 | 成因 造山 | 粒度 中粒 | 分类 区域 |
|---|---|---|---|

## 黑云母片岩(Biotite Schist)

含云母比例高，尤其富含黑云母，使其呈暗色，并含石英和长石。成分上，黑云母片岩与未经变质的泥质沉积物类似。

· **结构** 中粒，矿物晶体肉眼可辨，不过，最好用放大镜观察。图示标本上的暗色片状云母排列方向与片理一致。

· **成因** 泥质沉积物及其他岩石中级区域变质而成，否则不形成片理。

| 压力 适中 | 温度 低到适中 | 构造 片理 |
|---|---|---|

| 类别 变质岩 | 成因 造山 | 粒度 中粒 | 分类 区域变质 |
|---|---|---|---|

## 蓝晶片岩(Kyanite Schist)

主要由石英、长石和云母组成，其特点是含有蓝晶石，故名蓝晶石片岩。蓝晶石呈天蓝色的刃片状斑状变晶，并与片理平行，或呈晶体聚集，岩石常褶皱，其他矿物有石榴子石和十字石。整体呈浅灰色，或更深。

· **结构** 中粒至粗粒，肉眼可见矿物晶体，晶体常呈片状，也呈片麻状。

· **成因** 中高温压下，产于深变质带中心部，与夕线石和十字石片岩伴生。蓝晶石是地质学家用来确定变质程度的矿物之一，不同的温压条件形成不同的矿物，由此可判定不同的变质带。

| 压力 适中 | 温度 中至高 | 构造 片理 |
|---|---|---|

| | | | |
|---|---|---|---|
| 别 变质岩 | 成因 造山 | 粒度 粗粒 | 分类 区域 |

## 片麻岩(Gneiss)

变质岩，特点是具变质成因的片麻状构造。主要由长石和石英组成，含白云母、黑云母和角闪石及其他变质岩特征矿物辉石、石榴子石。

· **结构** 中粒到粗粒，特点是具不连续的明暗交替层，石英和长石形成浅色层，并呈粒状结构，铁镁矿物构成的深色层呈片麻状构造。

· **成因** 任何原岩经高度变质最终均形成片麻岩。由于高温高压的作用，矿物定向排列呈条带状。片麻岩常与变质沉积岩、或是变质岩浆岩、混合岩和花岗岩伴生。一般认为片麻岩组成了大部分深层大陆地壳。

| | | |
|---|---|---|
| 力 高 | 温度 高 | 构造 片麻、结晶 |

| | | | |
|---|---|---|---|
| 别 变质岩 | 成因 造山 | 粒度 粗大 | 分类 区域变质 |

## 褶皱片麻岩(Folded Gneiss)

与其他片麻岩一样，具深浅相间的片麻状条带，浅色条带富含石英和长石，深色条带由铁镁矿物如角闪石和黑云母组成。褶皱片麻岩中这些条带常十分明显，成分与花岗岩十分相近。

· **结构** 粗粒，所有矿物均肉眼可见。褶皱构造因矿物的分凝作用十分发育，并使部分岩石呈塑型。

· **成因** 形成于高度区域变质环境，在这种变质条件下，包括所有岩石、沉积岩、砂岩和页岩、岩浆岩(包括粗粒玄武岩)和花岗岩都会变成片麻岩。

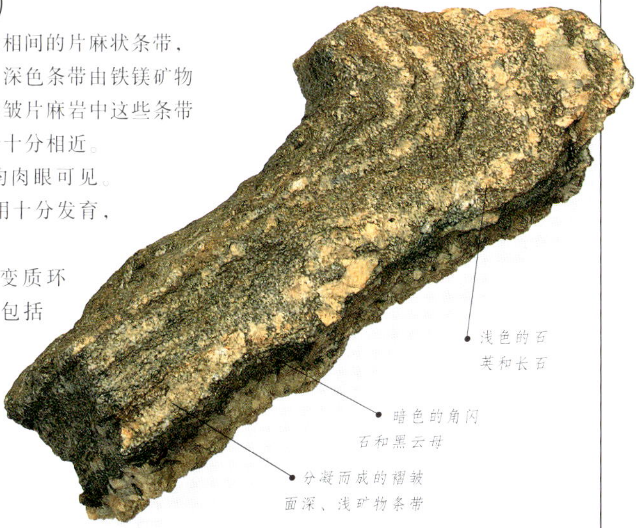


| | | |
|---|---|---|
| 力 高 | 温度 高 | 构造 片麻、结晶 |

| 类别 变质岩 | 成因 造山 | 粒度 粗粒 | 分类 区域变质 |
|---|---|---|---|

## 眼球状片麻岩(Augen Gneiss)

是一种花岗岩成分的变质岩，由石英、长石和云母组成的带状基质上含有大型的透镜状(眼或眼球状)长石晶体。

· 结构　粗粒，片麻状条带多少被眼状构造所替代。

· 成因　形成于高温高压的区域变质带。

| 压力 高 | 温度 高 | 构造 片麻、结晶 |
|---|---|---|

| 类别 变质岩 | 成因 造山 | 粒度 粗粒 | 分类 区域变质 |
|---|---|---|---|

## 粒状片麻岩(Granular Gneiss)

主要由浅灰色石英、白色和粉红色的长石以及深浅两种云母组成也含闪石和辉石，成分与花岗岩相同。

· 结构　晶体形成典型的明暗相间的片麻状条带，由于晶体互相结合形成粒状结构。

· 成因　在深变质环境下形成于地壳深处。

| 压力 高 | 温度 高 | 构造 片麻、结晶 |
|---|---|---|

| 类别 变质岩 | 成因 造山 | 粒度 粗粒 | 分类 区域变质 |
|---|---|---|---|

## 混合岩(Migmatite)

由片岩或片麻岩组成的混合变质岩，花岗岩成分呈层状或荚状，成分与花岗岩相近。

· 结构　粗粒，粒状结构。常像片麻岩那样呈条带状，不同的成分呈现片理。

· 成因　形成于深变质的区域变质。

| 压力 高 | 温度 高 | 构造 片麻、结晶 |
|---|---|---|

| 类别 变质岩 | 成因 地壳深部 | 粒度 粗粒 | 分类 区域变质 |
| --- | --- | --- | --- |

## 榴辉岩(Eclogite)

主要由辉石(绿色的绿辉石)、红色的石榴子石组成，有时含蓝晶石晶体。

· **结构** 中粒至粗粒，并可呈带状。

· **成因** 形成于地壳深处在最级高压高温环境，常与佩迪特岩和蛇纹岩伴生。

| 压力 高 | 温度 高 | 构造 片麻、结晶 |
| --- | --- | --- |

| 类别 变质岩 | 成因 地壳深部 | 粒度 粗粒 | 分类 区域变质 |
| --- | --- | --- | --- |

## 变粒岩(Granulite)

特点是辉石和透辉石或紫苏辉石的含量很高，也含石榴子石、蓝晶石、黑云母、石英和长石。

· **结构** 为坚硬块状粗粒岩，呈条带状，少呈片状。

· **成因** 一般认为形成于极高的温度和压力环境见于古代大陆地盾区域。

| 压力 高 | 温度 高 | 构造 结晶 |
| --- | --- | --- |

| 类别 变质岩 | 成因 造山 | 粒度 粗粒 | 分类 区域变质 |
| --- | --- | --- | --- |

## 闪岩(Amphibolite)

主要由闪石组成，常见的有角闪石，不过有时是阳起石或透闪石，也含长石、辉石、绿泥石、绿帘石和石榴子石。

· **结构** 粗粒，有时形成发育完好的叶理或片理。常见斑状变晶，尤其是石榴子石斑晶。

· **成因** 源于中、高级变质岩，主要由岩浆岩如粗粒玄武岩变质而成。

| 压力 高 | 温度 高 | 构造 片麻、结晶 |
| --- | --- | --- |

| 类别 变质岩 | 成因 接触变质带 | 粒度 细粒、粗粒 | 分类 接触变质 |
|---|---|---|---|

## 绿色大理岩(Green Marble)

主要由方解石组成，原岩为石灰岩，含有少量白云石。还含由石灰岩杂质形成的其他矿物如水镁石、橄榄石、透闪石和蛇纹石，它们使原本为白色的岩石呈浅绿色。

**·结构** 为结晶岩，用放大镜，尤其在显微镜下可见方解石晶体相互连接形成的镶嵌结构。原来石灰岩可能含有化石，但会在变质再结晶过程中消失。

**·成因** 形成于岩浆侵入引起的石灰岩热力变质。

| 压力 低 | 温度 高 | 构造 结晶 |
|---|---|---|

| 类别 变质岩 | 成因 接触变质带 | 粒度 细粒、粗粒 | 分类 接触变质 |
|---|---|---|---|

## 蓝色大理岩(Blue Marble)

主要由方解石组成，源于石灰岩，含少量白云石。石灰岩中含有的杂质在热力变质作用下重结晶时，形成新的矿物镁橄榄石、硅灰石、蛇纹石、水镁石、透辉石和透闪石。由于含透辉石，使蓝色大理岩发出诱人的蓝色。

**·结构** 为结晶岩，在放大镜下可见方解石晶体镶嵌结构，其他矿物则嵌入基质中。

**·成因** 石灰岩受岩浆侵入时形成，这时，方解石重结晶，使石灰岩的原有构造被破坏，并形成新的矿物。

| 压力 低 | 温度 高 | 构造 结晶 |
|---|---|---|

| 类别 变质岩 | 成因 接触变质带 | 粒度 细粒、粗粒 | 分类 接触变质 |
|---|---|---|---|

## 灰色大理岩(Grey Marble)

与其他大理岩石不同，灰色大理岩是由较纯石灰岩形成的，因此，钙硅质矿物含量少，富含方解石。显微镜下观察，可见少量的硅灰石、水镁石、透闪石、蛇纹石或透辉石。

· 结构　这种结晶岩的方解石晶体相互联结，从而形成浅色柔软的岩石，糖粒状的表面易于被刀刻划。大理岩放入盐酸中发泡，这是简便的测试方法。

· 成因　形成于接触变质带，尤其是在花岗岩侵入体附近，石灰岩受热并重结晶。

| 压力 低 | 温度 高 | 构造 结晶 |
|---|---|---|

| 类别 变质岩 | 成因 接触变质带 | 粒度 细粒、粗粒 | 分类 接触变质 |
|---|---|---|---|

## 橄榄大理岩(Olivine Marble)

主要含方解石，由石灰岩重结晶而成。在变质过程中还形成其他矿物，其中最重要的是橄榄石，绿棕色粒状晶体散布于大理岩中。

· 结构　具变晶结构，方解石晶体相互联结成块状橄榄大理岩。与原石灰岩不同的是，其中变质后的方解石颗粒间有间隙。因为方解石已经重结晶，所以，这种大理岩很少保存化石。橄榄石晶体呈粒状结构。

· 成因　由于岩浆岩侵入，石灰岩受热力变质作用而成。

| 压力 低 | 温度 高 | 构造 结晶 |
|---|---|---|

| 类别 变质岩 | 成因 接触变质带 | 粒度 细粒 | 分类 接触变质 |
|---|---|---|---|

## 堇青石角页岩(Cordierite Hornfels)

含有多种矿物，最终的矿物组合取决于原岩成分以及变质时的温度条件。常呈暗色，含石英、云母和堇青石，这些矿物是在变质时形成的。

· **结构** 细粒到中粒，含堇青石斑状变晶，大小数厘米。原岩沉积构造在变质重结晶过程中被破坏，所以无叶理等粒成分使其呈坚硬片状结构。

· **成因** 形成于接触变质带，产于靠近大侵入体(常是花岗岩)的围岩中。由接触变质带向低级变质岩如斑状板岩过渡。

| 压力 低 | 温度 高 | 构造 结晶 |
|---|---|---|

| 类别 变质岩 | 成因 接触变质带 | 粒度 细粒 | 分类 接触变质 |
|---|---|---|---|

## 辉石角页岩(Pyroxene Hornfels)

是坚硬、细粒、暗色的岩石，主要由石英、云母和辉石组成。角页岩中的辉石常以斑状变晶产出，由于所有的原生沉积构造在重结晶过程中被破坏，因此有些矿物肉眼是看不见的。角页岩没有成面构造，呈浅灰色、浅绿色或黑色。

· **结构** 细粒至中粒，颗粒大小均匀，经常形成辉石、堇青石或红柱石斑状变晶。高度重结晶作用使所有的原沉积构造消失。

· **成因** 形成于接触变质带温度最高的最内带，是花岗岩的侵入发生热力变质作用形成的。

| 压力 低 | 温度 高 | 构造 结晶 |
|---|---|---|

| 类别 变质岩 | 成因 接触变质带 | 粒度 细粒 | 分类 接触变质 |
|---|---|---|---|

## 石榴子石角页岩(Garnet Hornfels)

一般呈暗色，红色石榴子石斑块和晶体，嵌生于基质，还含石英、云母、长石和变质矿物堇青石和红柱石。

· 结构　细粒到中粒，具有坚硬、片状结构，清晰的石榴子石晶体呈斑状变晶结构。

· 成因　形成于大岩浆侵入体的接触变质带原岩为花岗岩、正长岩和辉长岩。

| 压力 低 | 温度 高 | 构造 结晶 |
|---|---|---|

| 类别 变质岩 | 成因 接触变质带 | 粒度 细粒 | 分类 接触变质 |
|---|---|---|---|

## 斑点板岩(Spotted Slate)

黑色、浅绿色或灰色，带有暗色斑点，这些斑点是变质矿物堇青石或红柱石构成的。还含大量未变质的原矿物，如石英和云母。

· 结构　与板岩的构造一样，劈理发育，特点是具有斑点，但常不太明显。

· 成因　形成于接触变质带边缘向角页岩过渡带。

| 压力 低 | 温度 高至适中 | 构造 结晶 |
|---|---|---|

| 类别 变质岩 | 成因 接触变质带 | 粒度 细粒 | 分类 接触变质 |
|---|---|---|---|

## 空晶石角页岩(Chiastolite Hornfles)

呈灰色或浅棕色，由石英、云母、红柱石和堇青石组成。基质上显著的刃片状晶体为空晶石，属于红柱石的一变种。

· 结构　由均匀的细粒晶体构成，其中常含红柱石斑状变晶，带有被细小的暗色颗粒包围的空晶石，其横截面呈十字形。

· 成因　紧靠岩浆侵入体形成，为变质提供了足够的温度。

| 压力 高 | 温度 适中至高 | 构造 结晶 |
|---|---|---|

| 类别 变质岩 | 成因 接触变质带 | 粒度 中粒 | 分类 接触变质 |
|---|---|---|---|

## 变质石英岩(Metaguartzite)

石英含量超过 90%，表面呈淡色、近乎糖粒状，由富含石英的砂岩变质而成。高倍放大可见云母、长石以及铁氧化物之类的矿物。

· **结构** 细粒到中粒，结构极均匀，石英晶体融合成坚硬的结晶岩石，因此其结构与原砂质沉积物完全不同，后者的颗粒之间具有孔隙。

· **成因** 形成于侵入体围岩的砂岩接触变质及区域变质。

| 压力 低 | 温度 高 | 构造 结晶 |
|---|---|---|

| 类别 变质岩 | 成因 接触变质带 | 粒度 细粒、粗粒 | 分类 接触变质 |
|---|---|---|---|

## 硅卡岩(Skarn)

含多种矿物，主要为方解石，另含橄榄石、方镁石、硅灰石、透辉石、石榴子石、蛇纹石、透闪石和其他变质石灰岩中典型的矿物，石榴子石常是钙铝榴石，还含矿石矿物黄铁矿、闪锌矿、方铅矿和黄铜矿。

· **结构** 细粒、中粒、粗粒俱有，某些矿物呈自形晶体，伴生矿物常在密集成斑块和结核状。

· **成因** 花岗岩或正长岩侵入体与石灰岩接触带接触变质形成夕卡岩，含有复杂的矿物集合体，石灰岩中的杂质与侵入体的热液交代产生各种矿物，常形成铜、锰和钼等矿床，储量丰富，具有经济价值。

| 压力 低 | 温度 高 | 构造 结晶 |
|---|---|---|

| 类别 变质岩 | 成因 接触变质带 | 粒度 细粒 | 分类 接触变质 |
|---|---|---|---|

## 长英角岩(Halleflinta)

由多种矿物组成，与其原岩——火山凝灰岩的原有成分有关，因此，长英角岩含石英，并且在变质过程中硅含量增加。常呈浅色，也呈棕色、粉红色、绿色、灰色或黄棕色。

· **结构** 细粒，显微镜下方可辨其矿物成分。结构均匀，呈燧石状、结晶质外观，断裂后产生锐利碎片状断口，也见层状构造，这与火山凝灰岩的原有层理有关，有时呈单独大粒晶体的斑状变晶结构。

· **成因** 由饱含次生氧化硅的凝灰岩接触变质而成，常与角页岩伴生。

| 压力 低 | 温度 高 | 构造 结晶 |
|---|---|---|

| 类别 变质岩 | 成因 逆冲带 | 粒度 细粒 | 分类 动力变质 |
|---|---|---|---|

## 糜棱岩(Mylonite)

矿物成分因变质的围岩性质而异，由两大类物质组成：一种是来自围岩的碎屑，称为“岩粉”，另一种是在变质过程中(或之后)形成的结晶矿物。颜色或暗或浅。

· **结构** 岩石变形作用而被破坏，颗粒形成小透镜状和块状斑纹。为细粒岩，但在某些粗粒标本上可见斑纹构造，并且表面上有线理。

· **成因** 形成于大规模逆冲断层，断层面两侧的岩石经受强大的剪应力，沿逆冲运动方向断裂并错动，这发生在与造山运动有关的地球运动中。

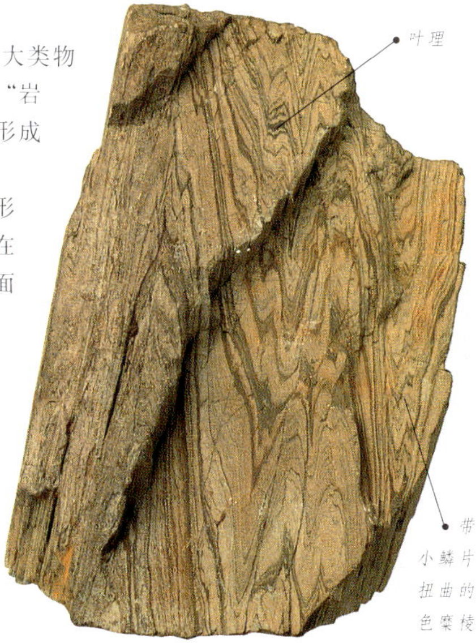


| 压力 剪应力 | 温度 低 | 构造 斑纹构造 |
|---|---|---|

# 沉积岩

沉积岩形成于地球表层，大多数形成于海洋，具有肉眼明显可辨认的层理。组成先成岩的颗粒经过风化、侵蚀和堆积形成碎屑沉积物。有机沉积物是由化石和来自一变生活过的有机体的物质形成的。化学沉积物如岩盐和方解石之类的物质是化学沉积的产物。

| 类别 沉积岩 | 成因 海水、淡水 | 粒度 极粗 |
| --- | --- | --- |

## 石英砾岩(Quartz Conglomerate)

由大量浅色石英碎屑构成细粒基质，基质含砂、粉砂、岩石碎屑和氧化铁，由氧化硅或方解石胶结在一起。

· **结构** 砾石圆形，基质带棱角或磨圆。由于其石英砾石粗粒，形成时处于动荡环境，因此很少含有化石。小块标本上难以见到层理构造。

· **成因** 形成于滨海、河流这种有足够的能量搬运大块物质碎块。

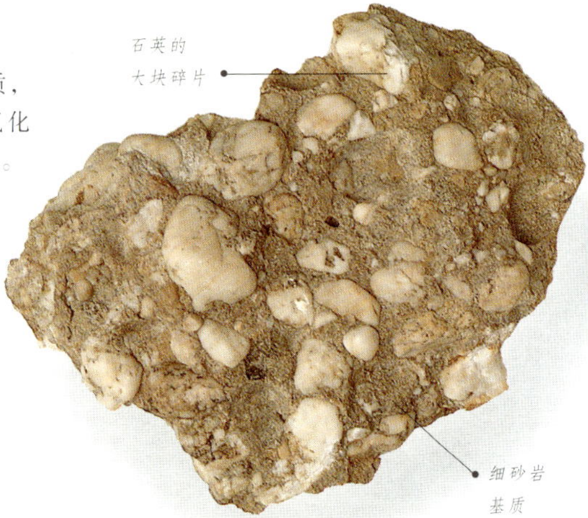


| 分类 碎屑岩 | 化石 很少 | 颗粒形态 ˙圆形 |
| --- | --- | --- |

| 类别 沉积岩 | 成因 海水、淡水 | 粒度 极粗 |
| --- | --- | --- |

## 复成砾岩(Polygenetic Conglomerate)

含有多种不同的物质，包括岩浆岩、变质岩、沉积岩碎块，以及单矿物颗粒。由多种矿物如石英、氧化铁和方解石胶结在一起。

· **结构** 复成砾岩中的颗粒呈圆形或半圆形，是流水作用的结果，基质的大颗粒之间常填充较小的棱角状碎屑。

· **成因** 形成于高能环境，如湍急的水流，可搬动巨大岩石碎块。

| 分类 碎屑岩 | 化石 很少见 | 颗粒形态 圆形 |
| --- | --- | --- |

| | | |
|---|---|---|
| 类别　沉积岩 | 成因　过渡带、水 | 粒度　极粗 |

## 石灰角砾岩(Limestone Breccia)

含有石灰岩碎块，并嵌入方解石胶结的细粒基质中也含其他矿物如石英以及其他岩石碎屑。

· **结构**　与砾岩的砾石明显不同，石灰角砾岩的呈棱角状，且个别砾石含有化石。

· **成因**　常见于大陆边缘的过渡环境中，在悬崖下方形成沉积，流水渗流悬崖和碎石堆时，沉积的钙质将碎屑胶结在一起。

| | | |
|---|---|---|
| 分类　碎屑岩 | 化石　无脊椎动物 | 颗粒形态　棱角状 |

| | | |
|---|---|---|
| 类别　沉积岩 | 成因　过渡带、水 | 粒度　极粗 |

## 角砾岩(Breccia)

砾石呈棱角状，成份可为任何一种岩石，角砾被细至中粒的矿物盐或砂胶结。

· **结构**　层理构造只能在野外的大范围看清，一般不含化石。其中的砾石和矿物碎屑呈棱角状，且包围的基质物质也呈棱角状。

· **成因**　其成因与石灰角砾岩类似，首先在悬崖底部形成岩屑堆，不过角砾岩中的粗碎屑不是钙质的。大型棱角状碎屑堆积可能形成于多种环境，尤其是机械风化作用活跃之处。

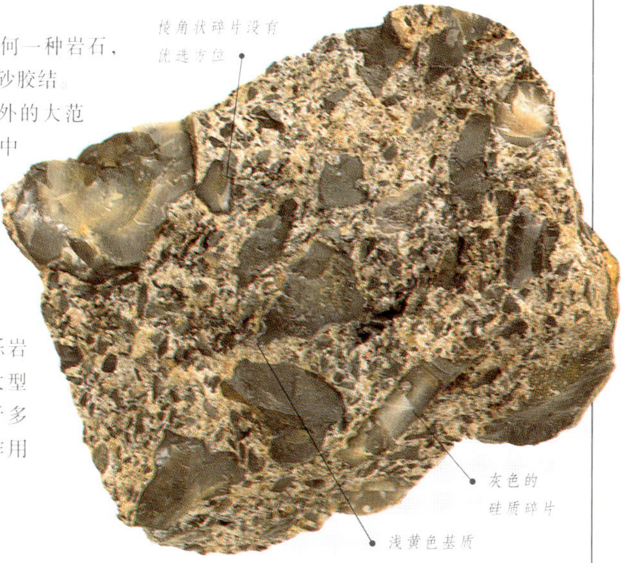


| | | |
|---|---|---|
| 分类　碎屑岩 | 化石　不常见 | 颗粒形态　棱角状 |

| 类别 沉积岩 | 成因 冰川、冰盖 | 粒度 细粒 |
| --- | --- | --- |

## 泥砾(Boulder Clay)

由大小不一的棱角状和一些圆形卵石组成，嵌入细粒未固结基质中。各种岩石不论大小，都一起嵌在粘土或砂质基质中。泥砾中的冰川碎屑称为冰漂石，它们被冰川搬离原产地，冰川碎屑可以帮助地质学家确定冰川总的运动方向。

· **结构** 碎屑主要呈棱角状，由各种未分选的物质组成，大小从粘土到漂砾不等。

· **成因** 冰川和冰盖消融中以残留堆积而成。

| 分类 碎屑岩 | 化石 罕见 | 颗粒形态 棱角状 |
| --- | --- | --- |

| 类别 沉积岩 | 成因 大陆 | 粒度 细粒 |
| --- | --- | --- |

## 黄土(Loess)

浅黄色或浅棕色土，由微小棱角状的石英、长石、方解石颗粒和其他矿物及岩石碎屑组成。

· **结构** 微粒风成土，呈多孔状和土状，胶结不佳，因此易碎。由于风的作用，其颗粒可能被磨圆，难以辨认层理。

· **成因** 风从冰川地区吹扬沉积物，由风搬运沉积而成，其物质可能来源于变质带区域。风成黄土形成厚层中，尤其在中国，不过也见于西欧。

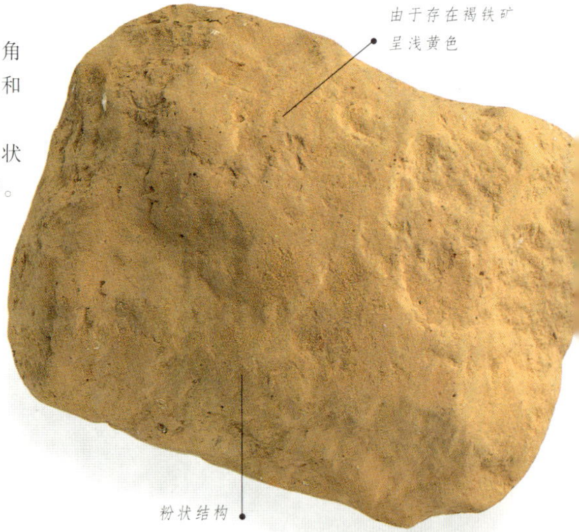


| 分类 碎屑岩 | 化石 罕见(中国常见) | 颗粒形态 圆形、棱角状 |
| --- | --- | --- |

| 类别 沉积岩 | 成因 海洋、淡水、大陆 | 粒度 中粒 |
|---|---|---|

## 砂岩(Sandstone)

主要由石英颗粒组成，也含长石、云母或其他矿物，被氧化硅、方解石或氧化铁胶结。

· **结构** 中粒，颗粒分选良好(大小均匀)，呈棱角状(粗砂岩)或圆形(砂岩)。

· **成因** 是极为常见的岩石，形成于多种地质环境，不过大多数砂岩都为水下沉积，尤其是海洋，或为风成沉积物，形成于干旱内陆。

| 分类 碎屑岩 | 化石 无脊椎动物、脊椎动物、植物 | 颗粒形态 棱角状、圆形 |
|---|---|---|

| 类别 沉积岩 | 成因 海洋 | 粒度 中粒 |
|---|---|---|

## 绿砂岩(Greensand)

属石英砂岩，含少量海绿石(一种只在海水条件下形成的绿色矿物)，少量云母、长石和岩石碎屑，被方解石胶结。海绿石来自原地(自生)，并以层状颗粒产出。

· **结构** 中粒，大多数颗粒呈棱角状，分选好。

· **成因** 形成于海洋，其组成矿物——海绿石是一种硅酸钾铁盐，用于放射性年代测定。

| 分类 碎屑岩 | 化石 无脊椎动物、脊椎动物、植物 | 颗粒形态 棱角状 |
|---|---|---|

| 类别 沉积岩 | 成因 大陆、海洋 | 粒度 中粒 |
|---|---|---|

## 红砂岩(Red Santstone)

主要由石英颗粒组成，也含云母和长石。红色是砂粒表面被覆赤铁矿所致，赤铁矿是一种氧化铁，由来自产地的富铁矿物氧化而成。

· **结构** 分选好，物颗粒棱角状或圆形，常见的沉积构造有交错层、波痕和干裂。

· **成因** 形成于大陆氧化环境，也常形成于浅海。

| 分类 碎屑岩 | 化石 无脊椎动物、脊椎动物、植物 | 颗粒形态 棱角状、圆形 |
|---|---|---|

| 类别 沉积岩 | 成因 陆地 | 粒度 中粒 |
|---|---|---|

## 粟状砂岩(Millet－seed Sandstone)

具明显的圆形颗粒，形似小米粒，因而呈粟米状结构。还含长石和岩石碎屑，常不含云母。颗粒外表常被覆薄层氧化铁。

· **结构** 分选极好，石英颗粒大小均匀。颗粒呈圆形，中等大小，化石非常罕见。

· **成因** 形成于干旱环境，石英砂粒在风的作用下磨成圆形。大砂丘层理构成粟状砂岩的特征，指示大陆沉积。

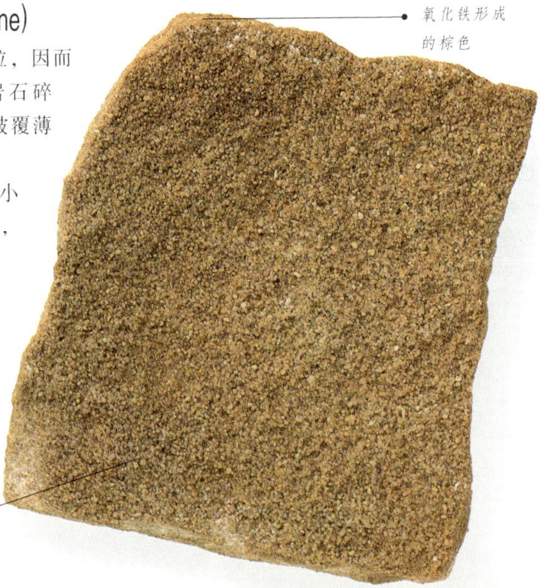


| 分类 碎屑岩 | 化石 罕见 | 颗粒形态 圆形 |
|---|---|---|

| | | |
|---|---|---|
| 类别 沉积岩 | 成因 海洋、淡水 | 粒度 中粒 |

## 云母砂岩(Micaceous Sandstone)

含丰富的石英及相当多的云母，还含长石碎屑和岩石碎片。在层理面，即砂岩表面，可见许多小而闪亮的云母薄片或是白云母、或黑云母，或是两者。

· **结构** 中粒，分选好，大多数颗粒呈棱角形，云母则呈薄片状。

· **成因** 云母在大陆风成沉积砂岩中罕见，因其薄片状集合体易被风破坏，含云母表明云母砂岩为水成，形成于湖泊、河流或海洋。

| | | |
|---|---|---|
| 分类 碎屑岩 | 化石 无脊椎动物、脊椎动物、植物 | 颗粒形态 棱角状、扁平状 |

| | | |
|---|---|---|
| 类别 沉积岩 | 成因 海洋、淡水 | 粒度 中粒 |

## 褐铁矿砂岩(Limonitic Sandstone)

富含石英，还含岩石碎屑以及长石、云母等。因含褐铁矿而得名，使其呈浅黄色或深棕色。

· **结构** 分选良好，大多数颗粒大小均一。碎屑呈棱角状，并被覆褐铁矿，褐铁矿也是胶结物质。与其他砂岩一样，层理发育，但单块标本上不明显。

· **成因** 形成于海水、淡水多种不同的环境。

| | | |
|---|---|---|
| 分类 碎屑岩 | 化石 无脊椎动物、脊椎动物、植物 | 颗粒形态 棱角状 |

| 类别 沉积岩 | 成因 海洋、淡水 | 粒度 中粒 |
|---|---|---|

## 粉红正石英岩(Pink Orthoquartzite)

与其他正石英岩一样，几乎全由石英组成，石英含量超过95%，硅质胶结。放大镜下可见某些其他矿物如长石以及岩石碎屑，化石罕见。

· **结构** 中粒，分选良好，优质粉红正石英岩具结晶外观。

· **成因** 长石含量很少，因此称为成熟岩，这是历经长期风化、侵蚀和沉积，几乎所有不稳定物质都从原岩中淘净，最后只剩下单一矿物石英的结果。

| 分类 碎屑岩 | 化石 罕见、无脊椎动物 | 颗粒形态 棱角状 |
|---|---|---|

| 类别 沉积岩 | 成因 海洋、淡水 | 粒度 中粒 |
|---|---|---|

## 灰色正石英岩(Grey Orthoquartzite)

成分与粉红正石英岩一样，石英颗粒使其呈灰色，含量超过95%。胶结物也是石英，将颗粒联结得非常牢固。偶尔含化石，有助于鉴别正石英岩和变质石英岩(变质石英砂岩)，但区分二者十分困难。正石英岩中可见层理和其他沉积构造，如交错层和粒级层，这些构造一般不见于变质石英岩。

· **结构** 中粒，分选性良好。

· **成因** 形成于海洋和淡水环境，并经历过完全的侵蚀和风化，与其他正石英岩一样，由于含大量石英，称为成熟沉积物。

| 分类 碎屑岩 | 化石 罕见、无脊椎动物 | 颗粒形态 棱角状 |
|---|---|---|

| 类别 沉积岩 | 成因 海洋 | 粒度 中粒、细粒 |
|---|---|---|

## 杂砂岩(Greywacke)

含有丰富的石英、长石和岩石碎屑，基质为粘土、绿泥石、石英和黄铁矿，不过矿物颗粒小得无法用肉眼辨认。

· **结构** 个别杂砂岩分选不佳，外观呈不同大小的颗粒，细粒基质中的大碎屑常含带棱角的颗粒。

· **成因** 海相沉积，形成于急速流动的深海浊流，岩石显呈多种沉积特征。

| 分类 碎屑岩 | 化石 罕见 | 颗粒形态 棱角状 |
|---|---|---|

| 类别 沉积岩 | 成因 海洋、淡水 | 粒度 中粒 |
|---|---|---|

## 长石砂岩(Arkose)

中粒至粗粒岩，颜色从浅粉红色至浅灰色。主要由石英组成，长石含量占1/3。颗粒分选良好，部分磨圆佳，呈圆形，与云母片一起被钙质或铁质胶结物胶结。

· **结构** 颗粒呈棱角状，一般分选良好。

· **成因** 形成于海洋和淡水环境，以及大陆。由于长石砂岩含有很多长石，因此称为未成熟岩。在干旱环境下，沉积物快速沉积，长石才能避免分解，长期的化学风化、侵蚀和沉积作用会使长石分解。大多数长石砂岩源于陆地上花岗岩崩解。

| 分类 碎屑岩 | 化石 罕见 | 颗粒形态 棱角状 |
|---|---|---|

| 类别 沉积岩 | 成因 海洋、淡水、陆地 | 粒度 粗粒、中粒 |
|---|---|---|

## 石英粗砂岩(Quartz Gritstone)

含超过 75% 的石英以及一些长石和云母，还含各种岩石碎屑，这取决于产生碎屑的母岩种类。胶结矿物常为石英，石英颗粒被覆的褐铁矿使之呈明显的浅黄色。

· **结构** 粗粒至中粒，颗粒分选良好，呈棱角状。粗砂岩有时胶结很差，用手指即可摩擦下颗粒。

· **成因** 形成于各种环境，海洋、淡水和陆地。大多数粗砂岩形成于淡水，如河流、三角洲，那里有足够搬运粗粒沉积的能量。

| 分类 碎屑岩 | 化石 无脊椎动物、脊椎动物、植物 | 颗粒形态 棱角状 |
|---|---|---|

| 类别 沉积岩 | 成因 海洋、陆地 | 粒度 粗粒、中粒 |
|---|---|---|

## 长石粗砂岩(Feldspathic Gritstone)

石英含量高，长石含量达 25%，还含云母以及岩石碎屑。成分与长石砂岩相近，具有大小相等的颗粒。颜色呈浅棕色，含粉红正长石时，则带粉红色调。胶结物石英或氧化铁。

· **结构** 粗粒至中粒，颗粒棱角状，尽管当长石沿解理面裂开时呈现扁平面。分选良好，大多数颗粒大小一致。

· **成因** 在过渡带快速沉积而成，长石在长期风化中分解。

| 分类 碎屑岩 | 化石 无脊椎动物、脊椎动物、植物 | 颗粒形态 棱角状 |
|---|---|---|

| 类别 沉积岩 | 成因 海洋 | 粒度 细粒 |
|---|---|---|

## 黑色页岩(Black Shale)

与其他页岩一样，由粘土矿物的混合物以及石英、长石和云母碎屑组成。富含碳质，也含黄铁矿和石膏，黄铁矿形成于静水深处缺氧还原条件下，在层面上常呈立方体晶体产出，黑色页岩中的化石常被黄铁矿化。

· **结构** 极细粒，矿物晶体在显微镜下可见。细层理，沿层面易于剥离，常含压扁的化石。

· **成因** 粘土物质沉积形成于海洋，黑色页岩常含海洋生物化石，如软体动物。

| 分类 碎屑岩 | 化石 无脊椎动物、脊椎动物、植物 | 颗粒形态 棱角状 |
|---|---|---|

| 类别 沉积岩 | 成因 海洋、淡水 | 粒度 细粒 |
|---|---|---|

## 化石页岩(Fossiliferous Shale)

成分与其他页岩相近，方解石含量高，源于所含化石，除完整化石外，还含化石碎片。

· **结构** 由于颗粒微，因此含有多种保存微细构造的化石，如腕足动物化石。页岩中常保存软体动物，如菊石、双壳类和腹足类化石，此外也见节肢动物、三叶虫和笔石，它们的微细构造在黑色页岩中得以保存，还含植物和脊椎动物化石。

· **成因** 形成于浅海，也形成于淡水环境由所含化石可推测其沉积条件。

| 分类 碎屑岩 | 化石 无脊椎动物、脊椎动物、植物 | 颗粒形态 棱角状 |
|---|---|---|

| 类别 沉积岩 | 成因 海洋、淡水 | 粒度 细粒 |
|---|---|---|

## 粉砂岩(Siltstone)

石英含量多于泥岩或页岩，常呈纹层状，这是由于颗粒大小以及有机成分或碳酸钙的含量的变化所致。

· **结构** 细粒，粉砂岩中的个别岩屑和矿物颗粒非常小，无法用肉眼辨认。

· **成因** 属于粉砂粒级的沉积物在压缩作用下形成粉砂岩，形成于多种环境，包括海洋和淡水水域，由所含化石可推知其沉积环境。由于含长石以及除石英之外的其他矿物，粉砂岩为成熟岩。长期的风化分解长石和其他矿物，最后只留下石英颗粒。

| 分类 碎屑岩 | 化石 无脊椎动物、脊椎动物、植物 | 颗粒形态 棱角状 |
|---|---|---|

| 类别 沉积岩 | 成因 海洋、淡水 | 粒度 细粒 |
|---|---|---|

## 泥岩(Mudstone)

由粘土矿物以及石英、长石碎屑和云母混合组成，常含氧化铁。

· **结构** 极细粒，肉眼无法辨认颗粒。其许多特征与页岩相同，可能含有化石，但层理不如页岩发育。

· **成因** 形成于多种沉积环境，由混浊的泥质沉积物在海洋和湖泊中沉积而成。仔细研究泥岩所含的化石，并与之近缘的现生生物生活方式进行对比，有助于确定岩石的生成环境。

| 分类 碎屑岩 | 化石 无脊椎动物、植物 | 颗粒形态 棱角状 |
|---|---|---|

| | | |
|---|---|---|
| 类别 沉积岩 | 成因 海洋、淡水 | 粒度 细粒 |

## 钙质泥岩(Calcareous Mudstone)

正如其名所示，与泥岩相似，不过方解石含量很高，也含石英、长石碎屑，含化石，色浅。

· **结构**　粘土，肉眼不能辨认颗粒。颗粒大小均匀，由于不过重结晶常改变颗粒原有形态。以独特的方式裂开，呈亚贝壳状断口。由于方解石含量高，因此置于冷盐酸中起泡。

· **成因**　形成于海洋和淡水环境。由于颗粒极细，因此易被水搬运至海洋和湖泊，与砂、粉砂和钙质有机物共同堆积。

| | | |
|---|---|---|
| 分类 碎屑岩 | 化石 无脊椎动物、植物 | 颗粒形态 棱角状 |

| | | |
|---|---|---|
| 类别 沉积岩 | 成因 海洋、淡水、陆地 | 粒度 细粒 |

## 粘土(Clay)

富含粘土矿物，由此得名，也含石英、云母和长石碎屑。

· **结构**　粘土，甚至在显微镜下也不能辨认个别矿物。粘土有一种独特的味道，颗粒吸水后膨胀变得柔软。

· **成因**　形成于多种环境，深海、浅海(粘土中的牡蛎化石显然来自海洋)和湖泊，也形成于陆相沉积，冰川粘土是岩石在冰川作用下粉化的产物。在化学风化下，某些硅酸盐矿物，如长石，在原地风化残积形成粘土矿物。由于其颗粒极细，因此粘土中的化石都保存得很好。

| | | |
|---|---|---|
| 分类 碎屑岩 | 化石 无脊椎动物、脊椎动物、植物 | 颗粒形态 棱角状 |

| 类别 沉积岩 | 成因 海洋、淡水 | 粒度 细粒 |
|---|---|---|

## 红色泥灰岩(Red Marl)

是介于粘土和石灰岩之间的一种沉积物，包括钙质粘土和泥质石灰岩之间的分粒作用。钙质占40～60%左右，还含石英碎屑和淤泥颗粒，其红色系由氧化铁造成的。

· **结构** 由于泥灰岩细密，因此只有在显微镜下才能观察，颗粒发育完好，被方解石胶结。

· **成因** 常见于浅湖沉积，含植物化石。也形成于蒸发岩盆地与石膏和石盐形成互层。

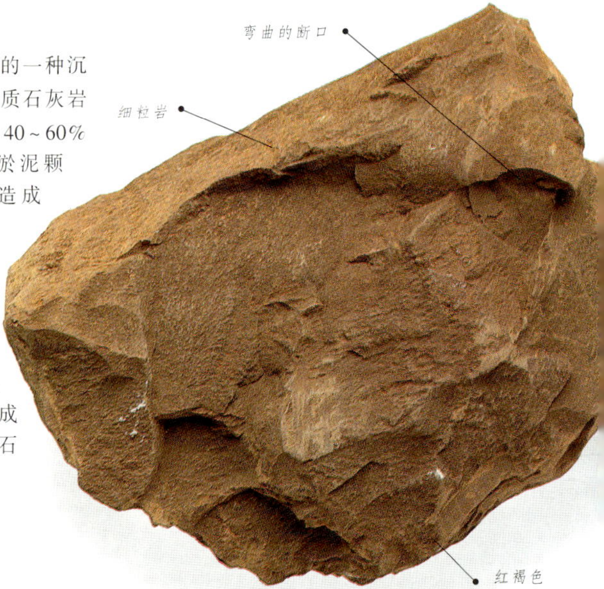


| 分类 碎屑岩 | 化石 无脊椎动物、脊椎动物、植物 | 颗粒形态 棱角状 |
|---|---|---|

| 类别 沉积岩 | 成因 海洋、淡水 | 粒度 细粒 |
|---|---|---|

## 绿色泥灰岩(Green Marl)

与红色泥灰岩一样，介于粘土和石灰岩之间，只不过颜色不同，由于含海绿石和绿泥石等矿物，因此呈浅绿色。绿色泥灰岩中方解石的含量也很高。

· **结构** 微粒，只有在显微镜下才能看清个别颗粒。由于含有方解石，因此置于冷稀盐酸中起泡。

· **成因** 形成于海洋和淡水环境，绿色泥灰岩含海绿石，海绿石是海相沉积的指相矿物。

| 分类 碎屑岩 | 化石 无脊椎动物、脊椎动物、植物 | 颗粒形态 棱角状 |
|---|---|---|

| 类别 沉积岩 | 成因 海洋、盐湖 | 粒度 晶质 |
|---|---|---|

## 岩盐(Rock Salt)

主要由石盐组成，含粘土矿物和氧化铁杂质，含氧化铁时，常呈红棕色。

· 结构　块状，粗晶质，有时成发育完全的立方晶体。在压力作用下，岩盐变得有塑性，形成盐栓而侵入其他岩层。

· 成因　形成于咸水中，如盐湖，并依沉积顺序生成其他蒸发岩，与白云岩和石膏等共生。

| 分类 化学岩 | 化石 无 | 颗粒形态 结晶 |
|---|---|---|

| 类别 沉积岩 | 成因 海洋、盐湖 | 粒度 晶质 |
|---|---|---|

## 石膏(Rock Gypsum)

常以块状石膏(含水合硫酸钙)产出。

· 结构　粗粒到细粒，呈纤维状集合体，常强烈扭曲，也成层状，常与砂岩、泥灰岩和石灰岩成互层产出。质地柔软，用指甲可轻易地刻划。

· 成因　与白云岩、泥灰岩以及硬石膏、石盐和方解石等矿物伴生于蒸发岩中。

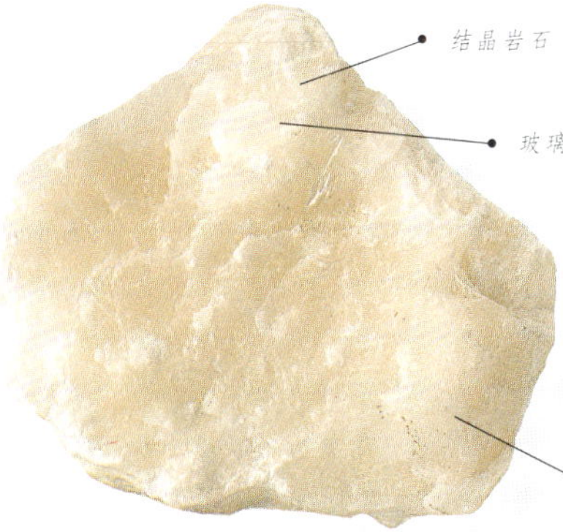


| 分类 化学岩 | 化石 无 | 颗粒形态 结晶 |
|---|---|---|

| 类别 沉积岩 | 成因 海洋、盐湖 | 粒度 晶质 |
|---|---|---|

## 钾岩(Potash Rock)

主要是钾盐和石盐的混合物。质纯的钾盐结晶呈浅灰色，含氧化铁时则呈桔红色。

· 结构　在岩层中与岩盐、石膏和白云岩共生。

· 成因　由咸水按一定沉积顺序形成，产于包括白云岩、泥灰岩和泥岩等的蒸发岩。

| 分类 化学岩 | 化石 无 | 颗粒形态 结晶 |
|---|---|---|

| | | |
|---|---|---|
| 类别 沉积岩 | 成因 海洋 | 粒度 粗粒 |

## 豆状石灰岩(Pisolitic Limestone)

与鲕状石灰岩相似，不过所含构造较大，较不规则，如豌豆般大小，称为豆石。方解石围绕沙粒或贝壳碎屑沉积形成豆石，胶结物为方解石。

· **结构** 粗粒，豆石大小均匀，常呈扁平状，与球状的鲕粒不同。，富含各种无脊椎动物化石。

· **成因** 与鲕状石灰岩相似，形成于浅海，这种环境有利于方解石的沉淀。古代，尤其是中生代浅海常出现这种环境。

| | | |
|---|---|---|
| 分类 化学岩 | 化石 无脊椎动物 | 颗粒形态 圆形 |

| | | |
|---|---|---|
| 类别 沉积岩 | 成因 海洋 | 粒度 中粒 |

## 鲕状石灰岩(Oolitic Limestone)

碳酸钙含量高，还含少量石英和其他矿物碎屑，常含化石碎片。

· **结构** 主要由紧密堆积在一起的鲕粒组成，称为鲕状岩。鲕粒是由同心层组成的球状或椭圆形构造，由方解石组成，在典型的浅色岩石基质上肉眼清楚可见圆形的鲕粒。

· **成因** 形成于温暖扰动的浅海，潮汐、急流和海浪使碳酸钙围绕石英微粒沉积。

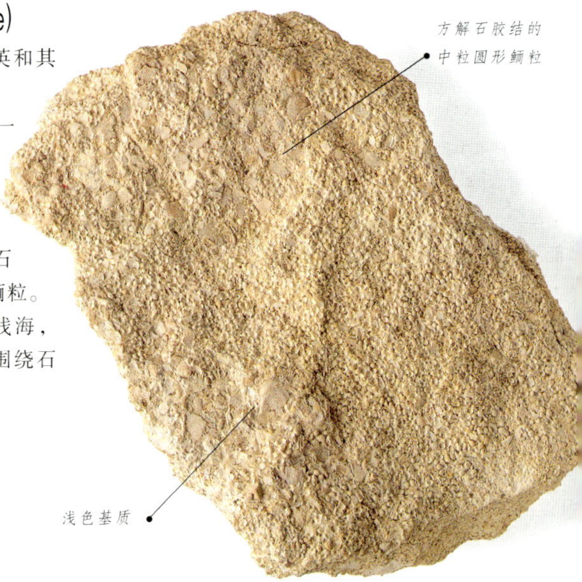


| | | |
|---|---|---|
| 分类 化学岩 | 化石 无脊椎动物 | 颗粒形态 圆形 |

| | | |
|---|---|---|
| 类别 沉积岩 | 成因 海洋 | 粒度 细粒 |

## 白垩(Chalk)

是由方解石组成的纯石灰岩，只含少量粉砂或泥质。主要由微生物遗骸组成，如颗石藻类和有孔虫，只有借助显微镜方可见。常含肉眼可见的大化石，如软体动物如菊石、双壳类、腕足类和棘皮类动物化石。白垩也含碎屑物质，主要是石英，以及其他矿物碎屑。

**· 结构** 是微粒、粉状、柔软的岩石，遇冷稀盐酸强烈起泡。

**· 成因** 形成于白垩纪海洋，当时沉积白垩的大陆架所处深变比现在要大，其中所含的少量碎屑物质表明周围的陆地地势低洼而干旱。

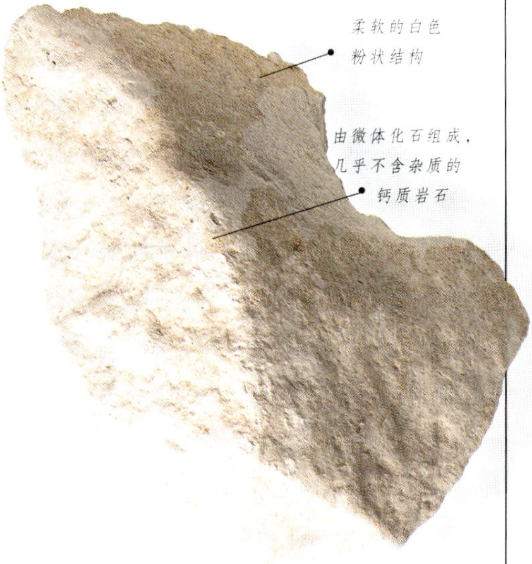


| | | |
|---|---|---|
| 分类 化学岩 | 化石 无脊椎动物、脊椎动物 | 颗粒形态 圆形、棱角状 |

| | | |
|---|---|---|
| 类别 沉积岩 | 成因 海洋 | 粒度 细粒 |

## 红色白垩(Red Chalk)

为细粒石灰岩，由于含氧化铁(赤铁矿)碎屑，因此呈红色，还含杂乱分布的石英砾石。红色白垩中的大多数微粒是微体化石，如颗石藻类，常见的大化石有箭石、菊石、双壳类和棘皮类动物。

**· 结构** 颗粒微小，只有用显微镜才能看见单个颗粒。

**· 成因** 一般认为在海洋缓慢沉积而成，红色的赤铁矿可能来自附近的红土表层。研究红色白垩中的化石可以更详细地了解其沉积环境。

| | | |
|---|---|---|
| 分类 化学岩 | 化石 无脊椎动物 | 颗粒形态 圆形 |

| | | |
|---|---|---|
| 类别 沉积岩 | 成因 海洋 | 粒度 粗粒 |

## 海百合石灰岩(Crinoidal Limestone)

主要由细粒或较大的方解石晶体组成，它们自动物骨骼，如海百合骨板，主要由海百合茎组成。

· **结构** 岩石中的大块碎片都是断裂的海百合茎，呈长圆柱形，或为单独的圆形骨片，方解石胶结，它们被紧密的胶结在块状方解石基质上。

· **成因** 形成于海洋环境，因由海百合组成而得名。海百合类属海洋生物，与海星和海胆近缘，海百合出现在珊瑚石灰岩中，显示它们栖息于浅海环境，海百合不是海百合石灰岩中唯一常见的化石，还可富含腕足类动物、软体动物和珊瑚。

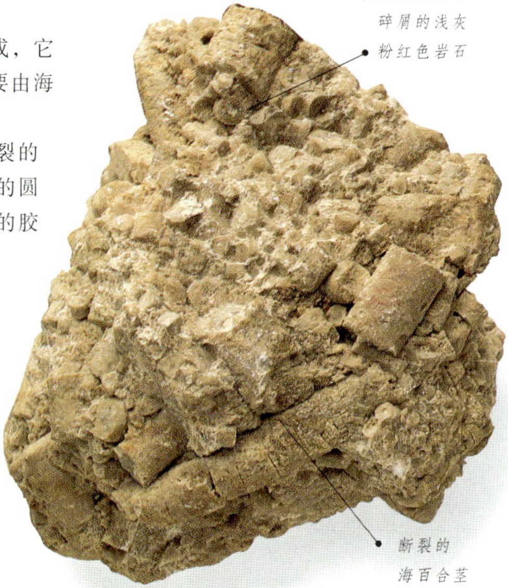


| | | |
|---|---|---|
| 分类 有机岩 | 化石 无脊椎动物 | 颗粒形态 棱角状、圆形 |

| | | |
|---|---|---|
| 类别 沉积岩 | 成因 海洋 | 粒度 细粒 |

## 珊瑚石灰岩(Coral Limestone)

几乎全部由珊瑚化石的钙质残骸组成。其单独的构造称为珊瑚体，被包含在富含钙的泥质基质中。除高含量的方解石外，石灰岩泥质含少量碎屑物质，如粘土和石英。

· **结构** 结构取决于保存在岩石中的珊瑚种类。基质细粒。

· **成因** 形成于海洋环境，研究个别珊瑚可更详细的了解成岩环境。大多数珊瑚石灰岩形成于大陆架，除富含珊瑚化石外，也含其他浅海无脊椎动物化石，如腕足类、头足类、腹足类和苔藓虫化石。

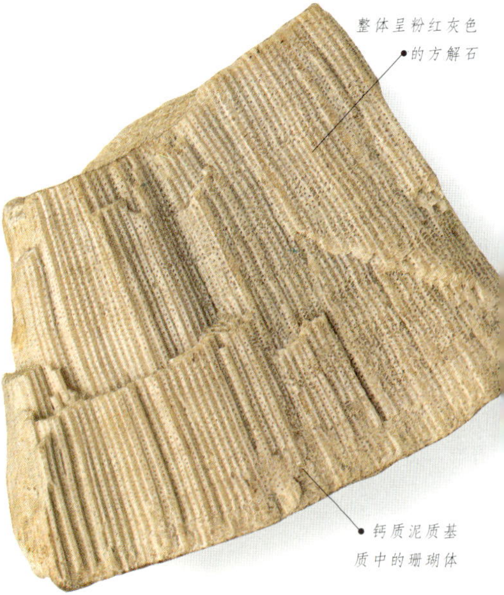


| | | |
|---|---|---|
| 分类 化学岩 | 化石 无脊椎动物 | 颗粒形态 棱角状 |

| 类别 沉积岩 | 成因 海洋、淡水 | 粒度 中粒、细粒 |
| --- | --- | --- |

## 贝壳石灰岩(Shelly Limestone)

对含大量化石贝壳石灰岩的总称，含有多种腕足动物和双壳类壳化石。方解石胶结，含矿物碎屑和氧化铁，岩石呈浅棕色。

· **结构** 基质中粒到细粒，棱角状碎。

· **成因** 主要形成于海洋，极少数形成于淡水环境。与其他许多含化石的岩石一样，仔细研究其中的化石可以了解成岩环境。

| 分类 化学岩 | 化石 无脊椎动物 | 颗粒形态 棱角状 |
| --- | --- | --- |

| 类别 沉积岩 | 成因 海洋 | 粒度 细粒 |
| --- | --- | --- |

## 苔藓虫石灰岩(Bryozoan Limestone)

方解石所占的比例很高，另外还含有极少量的碎屑物质，如石英和粘土，它们使岩石颜色变深。苔藓虫石灰岩主要为灰泥质，含网状的苔藓虫化石为其特征。

· **结构** 形成基质的灰泥质细粒，结构均匀。

· **成因** 形成于海洋环境，一般源于钙礁沉积，苔藓动物如网格苔藓虫(Fenestella)有助生物礁的巩固与生成。除苔藓动物外，生物礁还养育有丰富的生物，因此这种石灰岩富含软体动物、腕足动物和其他海生无脊椎动物化石。

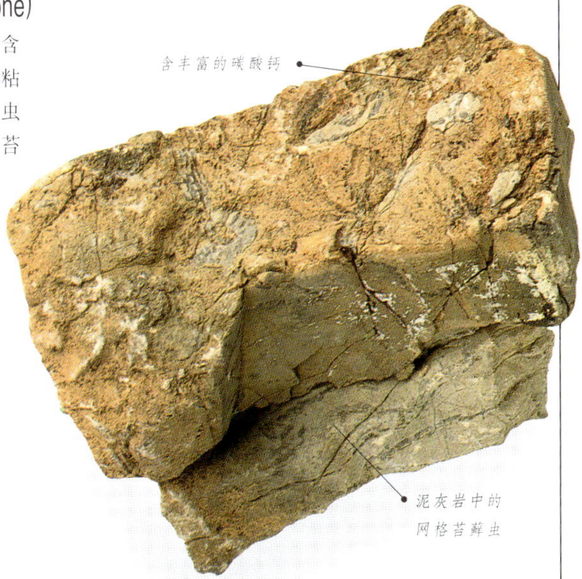


| 分类 化学岩 | 化石 无脊椎动物 | 颗粒形态 棱角状 |
| --- | --- | --- |

| 类别 沉积岩 | 成因 淡水 | 粒度 中粒、细粒 |
| --- | --- | --- |

## 淡水石灰岩(Freshwater Limestone)

分布不如海相石灰岩普遍，以含淡水生物化石为特征。与其他石灰岩一样，碳酸钙含量很高，并含石英碎屑和粘土。

**· 结构** 基质为钙质结晶，紧密胶结。主要由泥灰质，以及腹足类外壳组成，由化石可判定石灰岩属于海相或淡水相。方解石含量高，遇冷稀盐酸发泡。

**· 成因** 形成于钙含量高的淡水湖，地层记录中稀有。

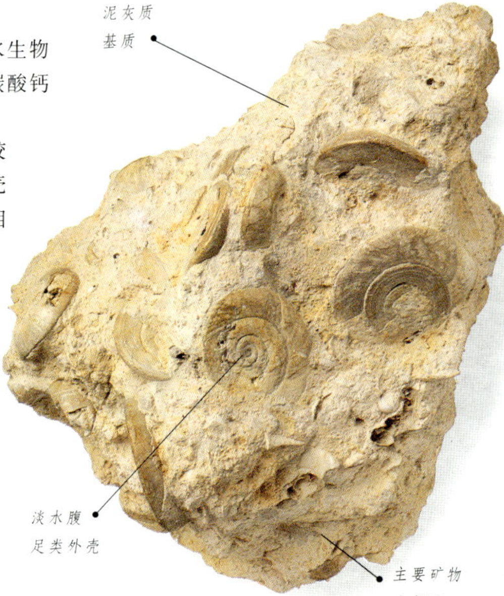


| 分类 化学岩 | 化石 无脊椎动物、植物 | 颗粒形态 棱角状 |
| --- | --- | --- |

| 类别 沉积岩 | 成因 海洋 | 粒度 细粒 |
| --- | --- | --- |

## 货币虫石灰岩(Nummulitic Limestone)

含有大量的碳酸钙，主要由完整的或破碎的圆形有孔虫货币虫化石组成，方解石胶结。与其他主要由单一生物化石组成的石灰岩相同，货币虫石灰岩也含其他化石，还含少量碎屑物质，一般为石英。

**· 结构** 基质细粒，化石大小不一，最大的货币虫直径达 2 厘米，

**· 成因** 形成于海洋环境，见于局部地区，埃及金字塔就是用这种特别的石灰岩建造的。

| 分类 化学岩 | 化石 无脊椎动物 | 颗粒形态 结晶 |
| --- | --- | --- |

| 类别 沉积岩 | 成因 海洋 | 粒度 中粒、细粒 |
| --- | --- | --- |

## 白云岩(Dolomite)

英文岩石与矿物同名，白云石含量很高的缘故，此外含矿物碎屑和次生氧化硅(燧石)。白云石是碳酸镁矿物，因此白云岩常较其他石灰岩颜色深(一般呈奶油棕色)。白云岩的化石含量少于其他石灰岩，这是由于成岩过程中的重结晶作用使化石受到破坏。

· **结构** 等粒结构，白云岩块体通常呈致密状和土状。

· **成因** 形成于海洋环境，一般认为大多数白云岩是交代原石灰岩二次形成的。

| 分类 化学岩 | 化石 无脊椎动物 | 颗粒形态 结晶 |
| --- | --- | --- |

| 类别 沉积岩 | 成因 陆地 | 粒度 细粒 |
| --- | --- | --- |

## 泉华(Tufa)

主要由方解石(碳酸钙)组成，其中所含的氧化铁杂质使泉华呈现出独特的黄色和红色。多砾的泉华称为石质结砾岩，这是一种多孔、常无层理的沉积物。石灰华是一种更致密、呈带状的泉华。

· **结构** 为结晶物质，可含砾和呈沉积纹理。

· **成因** 碳酸钙由富含钙的水沉积而成，见于悬崖、洞穴和采石场的岩石表面，尤其是石灰岩地区。植物与苔藓经常被泉华覆盖，保存成为皮壳状、富含钙的化石。这种保存非常迅速，在有利的条件下，现生生物在几个月内即被生皮壳。

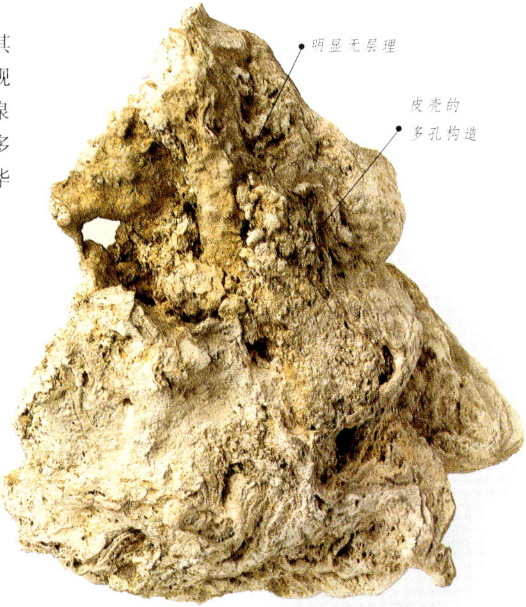


| 分类 化学岩 | 化石 植物、无脊椎动物 | 颗粒形态 结晶 |
| --- | --- | --- |

| 类别 沉积岩 | 成因 陆地 | 粒度 晶质 |
|---|---|---|

## 石灰华(Travertine)

主要由纯碳酸钙组成，还含一些石英碎屑和粘土，几乎不含化石。石灰华是一种颜色很淡的岩石，除非含有铁化合物或其他会使岩石呈现颜色的杂质。沉积物呈圆形、葡萄状，常具有带状构造。

· **结构** 由方解石的微小晶体组成，并将其他沉积颗粒胶结。在很多情况下，石灰华产于岩层中，常成层产出。

· **成因** 常与深源喷出的泉水有关，许多温泉，尤其是火山地区的温泉，固体碳酸钙沉积形成石灰华。

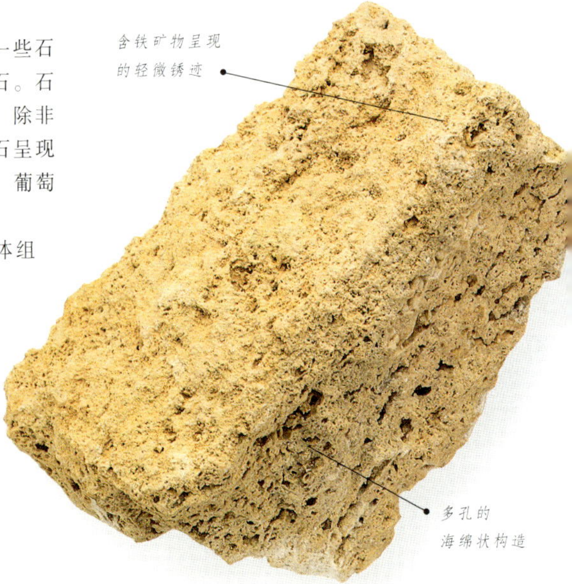


| 分类 化学岩 | 化石 罕见 | 颗粒形态 结晶 |
|---|---|---|

| 类别 沉积岩 | 成因 陆地 | 粒度 晶质 |
|---|---|---|

## 钟乳石(Stalactite)

是由碳酸钙组成的沉积构造，有时因含杂质如氧化铁而带色。

· **结构** 在石灰岩地区钟乳石常悬生于洞穴顶部，细长。与之对应的是生长于洞穴底部的粗短的石笋，有时钟乳石和石笋连接成石柱。

· **成因** 由从洞穴顶部裂隙渗出的含钙的水沉积而成。当富含钙的水与空气接触时，释放出二氧化碳即形成硅酸钙沉积，水分的蒸发加快了这个过程。富含钙的水从钟乳石底部下滴，形成石笋。

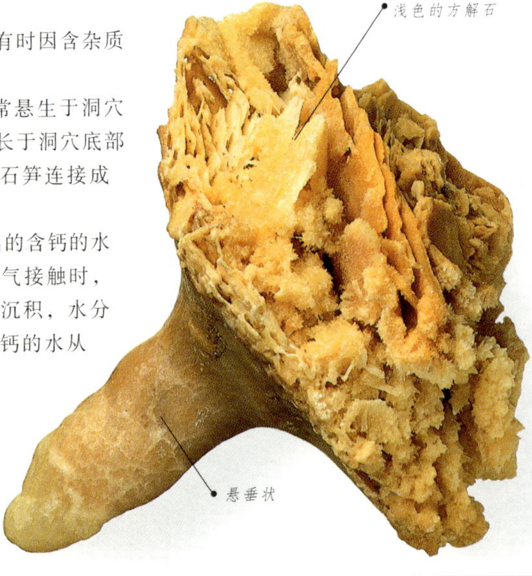


| 分类 化学岩 | 化石 无 | 颗粒形态 结晶 |
|---|---|---|

| | | |
|---|---|---|
| 类别 沉积岩 | 成因 陆地 | 粒度 中粒、细粒 |

## 带状铁质岩(Banded Ironstone)

为铁质燧石，呈显著的带状构造，带状是由燧石和层状菱铁矿或赤铁矿交替组成，并产生相当程度的重结晶。磁铁矿和黄铁矿也见于岩石的层状含铁矿物条带中。

· **结构** 细至中粒。

· **成因** 大多数带状铁质岩形成于20~30亿年前的前寒武纪。带状铁质岩可能形成于封闭的湖盆或内陆盆地，但尚无定论，不过，它确实出现在许多沉积环境中，从浅水和潮间带至深水环境，有些地区的证据显示它形成于沼泽和海滨泥地。有些地质学家认为，生物活动对于碳酸盐和硫化物结合沉积起重要作用，这一观点十分有趣，因为带状铁质岩形成时，地球上只有一些非常原始的生物。

| | | |
|---|---|---|
| 分类 化学岩 | 化石 无 | 颗粒形态 结晶 |

| | | |
|---|---|---|
| 类别 沉积岩 | 成因 海洋 | 粒度 中粒 |

## 鲕状赤铁矿(Oolitic Ironstone)

由紧密胶结在一起的鲕粒组成，易被菱铁矿和其他含铁矿物替代，也含石英、长石和其他矿物碎屑。原岩可能富含钙，后来被含铁矿物交替。与鲕状石灰岩中的鲕粒一样，小而圆。

· **结构** 岩石中的碎屑颗粒呈棱角状，方解石是鲕粒间常见的胶结物。

· **成因** 形成于海洋环境，鲕状赤铁矿可能沉积后不久即发生变化，或者在沉积时就已富含铁。

| | | |
|---|---|---|
| 分类 化学岩 | 化石 无脊椎动物 | 颗粒形态 圆形、棱角状 |

| 类别 沉积岩 | 成因 陆地 | 粒度 中粒、细粒 |
| --- | --- | --- |

## 烟煤(Bituminous Coal)

褐煤层在压力作用下形成烟煤或“家用煤”。质硬而脆，含炭量高。具有交替的闪光层和暗淡层，含可辨别的植物物质。触摸污手。

· **结构** 结构均匀，外观似熔合物质。呈两组节理以直角相交的构造，因此烟煤断裂后成似立方体。

· **成因** 在压力和埋藏热——水分挥发作用下，由泥炭的聚积和后成变化而成。

| 分类 化学岩 | 化石 植物 | 颗粒形态 无 |
| --- | --- | --- |

| 类别 沉积岩 | 成因 陆地 | 粒度 中粒、细粒 |
| --- | --- | --- |

## 无烟煤(Anthracite)

与其他煤不同，含炭量极高，挥发分含量低，一般不呈带状。

· **结构** 与烟煤相比更具玻璃质感，无烟煤燃点远高于其他煤。

· **成因** 由泥炭聚积而成。一般认为，由于压力，特别是温度的增加，导致挥发物质的挥发，因此形成等级较高的煤。

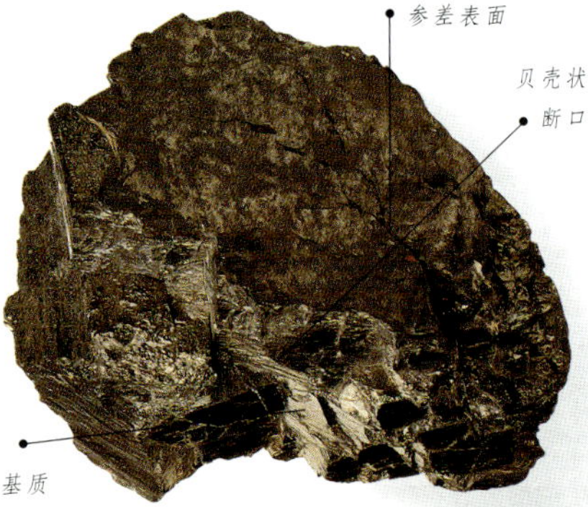


| 分类 化学岩 | 化石 植物 | 颗粒形态 无 |
| --- | --- | --- |

| 类别 沉积岩 | 成因 陆地 | 粒度 中粒、细粒 |
| --- | --- | --- |

## 褐煤(Lignite)

棕色的煤，碳含量在烟煤和泥炭之间，褐煤仍含大量杂乱堆积的植物碎片。

· **结构** 不如其他煤致密，含水量高，易碎，还含较多的挥发分和杂质。

· **成因** 是低级煤，最常见于第三纪和中生代岩层，其中的植物物质没有发生变化。偶尔也由浅层泥炭形成。

| 分类 有机岩 | 化石 植物 | 颗粒形态 无 |
| --- | --- | --- |

| 类别 沉积岩 | 成因 陆地性 | 粒度 中粒、细粒 |
| --- | --- | --- |

## 泥炭(Peat)

是植物转变成褐煤和烟煤的初始阶段，颜色从深棕色至黑色，含炭量与挥发分各占50%。质地松脆，用手即可弄碎。

· **结构** 可见大量植物碎片，时见植物根部。含水量很高，干燥后不均匀开裂，性柔软。

· **成因** 植物残骸在森林底部、沼泽或高沼地沉积形成泥炭，现在用作燃料的大多数煤矿床源于森林泥炭。现代泥炭堆积主要由苔藓、灯心草和芦苇构成的，厚可达数米。经由腐烂和再组合，泥炭堆积的底层变得致密，颜色加深，质地变硬，同时含炭量增高。

| 分类 化学岩 | 化石 植物、无脊椎动物 | 颗粒形态 无 |
| --- | --- | --- |

| 类别 沉积岩 | 成因 海洋 | 粒度 中粒、细粒 |
| --- | --- | --- |

## 煤玉(Jet)

含炭量高，因此被归为煤的一类，是一种致密物质，常见于沥青页岩。条痕棕色，具贝壳状断口，坚硬得足以磨光。很少见于地理分布广的地层中。

· **结构** 仔细观察，可见木质组织构造。具有玻璃光泽，因此煤玉常被用来制作饰品和珠宝。

· **成因** 其成因尚无定论，一般认为，这种黑色、像煤一样的岩石是在海洋形成的，木块和其他漂浮植物浸泡吸水，沉入海底泥质沉积中形成的，常见于海相岩层，其他煤则形成于陆地。

| 分类 化学岩 | 化石 植物 | 颗粒形态 无 |
| --- | --- | --- |

| 类别 沉积岩 | 成因 海洋 | 粒度 细粒 |
|---|---|---|

## 燧石(Chert)

以硅质结核或片状产出，尤其是在石灰岩之类的沉积岩和熔岩中。燧石通常呈浅灰色。

· **结构** 由隐晶质氧化硅组成，显微镜下方可辨其成分。断裂后具有参差状至亚贝壳状断口，质地坚硬，小刀不能刻划。

· **成因** 由氧化硅沉积而成，可能以胶体状态存在于海底，氧化硅源于生物遗骸。

| 分类 化学岩 | 化石 无脊椎动物、植物 | 颗粒形态 结晶 |
|---|---|---|

| 类别 沉积岩 | 成因 海洋 | 粒度 细粒 |
|---|---|---|

## 燧石(Flint)

主要指产于西欧白垩中的硅质结核，坚硬、致密，质地均匀，断裂成贝壳状断口，其薄片被原始人用作工具。

· **结构** 完全由氧化硅组成。燧石中的隐晶质氧化硅来自含海绵针骨的有机蛋白石。

· **成因** 以带状和结核状产于石灰岩，尤其是白垩，常含化石。

| 分类 化学岩 | 化石 无脊椎动物 | 颗粒形态 结晶 |
|---|---|---|

| 类别 沉积岩 | 成因 陆地 | 粒度 晶质 |
|---|---|---|

## 琥珀(Amber)

是已绝灭针叶树树脂化石，质软，具松脂或半玻璃光泽，透明到半透明。陷入粘稠树脂中的昆虫和小脊椎动物被保存在琥珀中成为化石，经常被用来制作珠宝。

· **结构** 断裂后具贝壳状断口。

· **成因** 由针叶树的树脂形成，常见于沉积矿床。

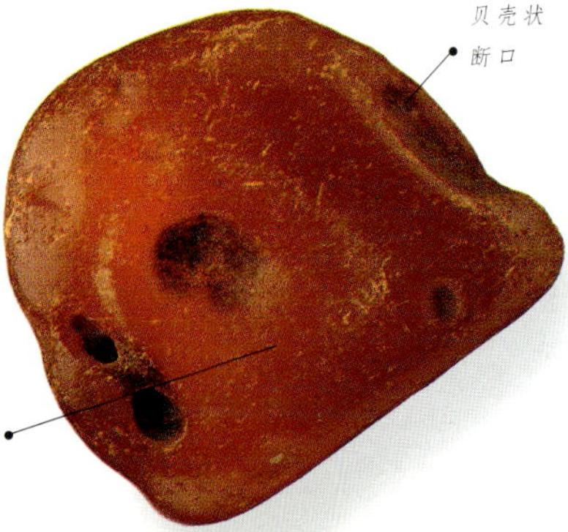


| 分类 生物岩 | 化石 脊椎动物、无脊椎动物 | 颗粒形态 无 |
|---|---|---|

| 类别 沉积岩 | 成因 后沉积作用 | 粒度 晶质 |
|---|---|---|

## 龟甲状结核(Spetarian Concretion)

与母岩物质组成相同，由氧化硅、碳酸盐矿物或氧化铁胶结。龟甲结核具有放射状和多边形内部脉状图案——由方解石组成。

· **结构** 坚硬外壳状上具有放射状和同心状的裂隙构造打开结核后，可见内部脉状构造。

· **成因** 成岩作用(柔软的泥质物质变成岩石的过程)中，由矿物的分凝作用使物质围绕一个核聚集而成，这个核可能是一个沉积颗粒或一个化石。结核形成后，收缩中形成称为隔壁的裂隙。

| 分类 化学岩 | 化石 无脊椎动物 | 颗粒形态 结晶 |
|---|---|---|

| 类别 沉积岩 | 成因 后沉积作用的 | 粒度 晶质 |
|---|---|---|

## 黄铁矿结核(Pyrite Nodule)

以圆形、葡萄状或圆柱状结核产出，由黄铜色黄铁矿组成。风化面常呈黄—黑色，变成黑色或棕黄色，常见于页岩和泥岩。

· **结构** 这种圆形结核的内部构造呈针状晶体从中心向四周放射。结核形状多变化，板状或蛋形，甚至呈几近有机体的外表。

· **成因** 形成于富含黄铁矿的页岩、粘土和其他泥质岩中，也常见于白垩。形成机理还不十分清楚，可能是黄铁矿围绕一个核心沉积而成。

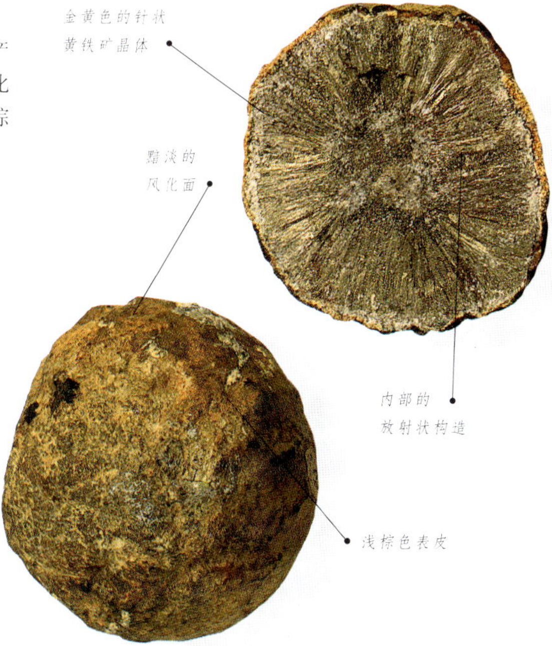


| 分类 化学岩 | 化石 罕见 | 颗粒形态 结晶 |
|---|---|---|

| 类别 陨石 | 成因 外星 | 粒度/结晶 结晶 |
| --- | --- | --- |

## 铁陨石(Stony Iron)

由各占50%左右的金属和硅酸盐物质组成，金属成分为镍铁合金，硅酸盐成分为见于地球上许多岩石中的矿物，如橄榄石、辉石和斜长石。

· **结构** 岩石般的表面呈现多种组分，包括晶体，橄榄石之类的硅酸盐矿物常因风化而剥落，使其表面产生麻点。

· **成因** 相当罕见，只占已知陨石4%。地质学家通过铁陨石可以了解某些元素在熔融和矿脉形成过程中如何与铁或硅结合，同时可了解具有铁核心和硅酸盐外壳的其他行星。

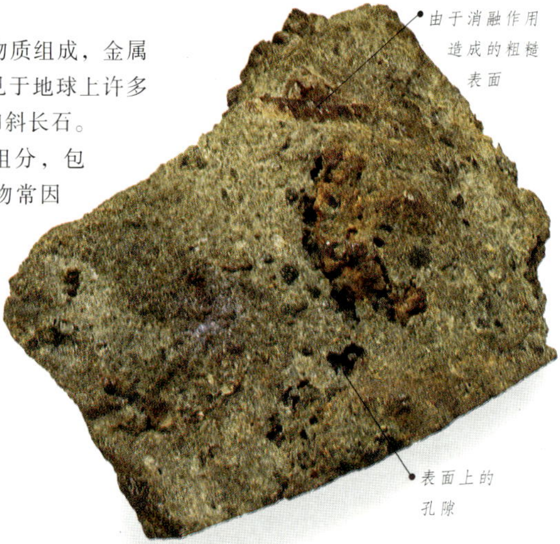


| 分类 铁石 | 形状 棱角形、圆形 | 成分 硅酸盐、金属 |
| --- | --- | --- |

| 类别 陨石 | 成因 地球 | 粒度/结晶 玻璃 |
| --- | --- | --- |

## 熔融石(Tektite)

这种富含氧化硅的玻璃物质曾被认为是陨石，现在根据它们在地球上的分布和化学性质，科学家认为熔融石可能不是来自外星，其成分与某些岩浆岩的成分相似。熔融石氧化硅含量高，且富含氧化钾、氧化钙和氧化铝。

· **结构** 小，重约200~300克，呈薄饼状或椭圆形，表面光滑或粗糙。

· **成因** 成因尚无定论，可能是陨石撞击地表岩石熔化而成，人们过去认为的熔融岩，是月球火山喷发溅落到地球上的观点并不正确。

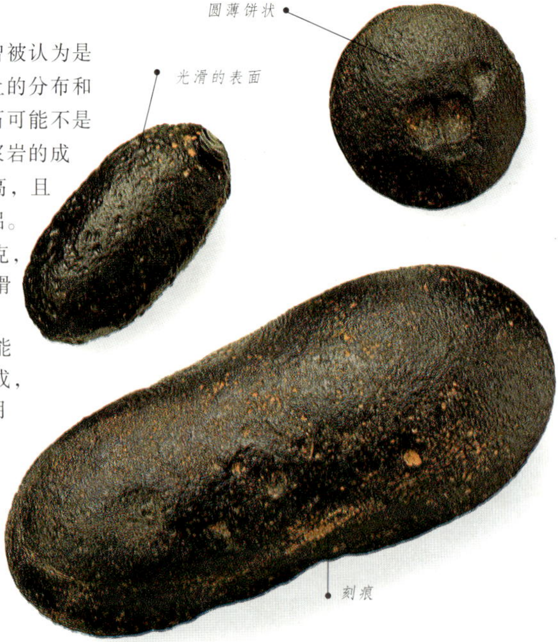


| 分类 似曜岩类 | 形状 圆形 | 成分 硅酸盐 |
| --- | --- | --- |

| 类别 陨石 | 成因 外星 | 粒度/结晶 结晶 |
| --- | --- | --- |

## 球粒陨石(Chondrite)

是陨石中最大的类，含硅酸盐矿物，主要是辉石和橄榄石，以及少量斜长石和镍铁。

· **结构** 具有一种由球粒陨石小圆颗粒组成的构造。整体无定形，不过许多呈圆形或圆顶状图示棱角状的标本是陨石下落冲击破裂的碎片。

· **成因** 成因尚无定论，不过其化学性质类似代表地幔物质及构成行星的微行星。这种陨石的放射性年代测定结果为46亿年，是迄今地球上最古老的岩石，一般认为这是太阳系形成的时期。

| 分类 球粒陨石 | 形状 圆形 | 成分 硅酸盐、金属 |
| --- | --- | --- |

| 类别 陨石 | 成因 外星 | 粒度/结晶 结晶 |
| --- | --- | --- |

## 无球粒陨石(Achondrite)

构造和成分与球粒陨石不同，无球粒，陨石硅酸盐含量高，与见于地球的岩石类似，含辉石、橄榄石和斜长石等矿物。不过，无球粒陨石成分比球粒陨石多变，且常含极少金属铁。

· **结构** 颗粒大于球粒陨石，缺乏陨石球粒。

· **成因** 由于与地球地幔物质和玄武质基底的岩石相似，因此可能来源于火山，也可能来自造行星的微行星。

| 分类 无粒陨石 | 形状 棱角状、圆形 | 成分 硅酸盐 |
| --- | --- | --- |

# 名词解释

本书尽量避免使用专有名词，不过此类书籍多少使用一些也是必要的，以下对经常出现的矿物和岩石术语一一做出简要的说明。此外，为避免出现生僻词句，将某些定义做了简化和概括，例举从略。下面黑体字起始的词条是对术语的说明，许多关键用语在本书序言部分的彩色图片中已做了解释。

- **刃状** 矿物晶体呈刀刃状。
- **土状** 不反射光的矿物光泽。
- **小骨片** 指海百合的骨板，海百合属于棘皮动物门。
- **不整合** 岩层间的沉积间断。
- **中性岩** 硅含量55~65%的岩浆岩。
- **贝壳状** 许多矿物和岩石的弯曲或贝壳状断口。
- **化石** 保存于地层中的生命的记录，化石可以是骨骼和贝壳，也可以是足印、排泄物或钻孔。
- **风成的** 指风成沉积物，一些沉积岩的特点，如沙丘层理，就是风成构造。
- **气泡** 熔岩固结后留在熔岩中的空洞。
- **叶片状** 微层或鳞片构成的薄板状或薄层状。
- **片理** 形成于中粒和粗粒岩石中的叶理，通常是由片状矿物颗粒形成。
- **文像结构** 石英和长石规律的交生形成的岩石结构。
- **火山渣状** 充满空洞和空隙的熔岩或其他火山物质。
- **火山管** 熔岩流动的裂缝。
- **火成碎屑** 从火山口中喷出的火山碎屑物质。
- **双晶** 指连生在一起，共有一个晶面的两个晶体。
- **叶片状** 不同矿物的页状平行定向排列或分凝作用。
- **包体** 包在晶体或岩石中的另一种物质的晶体或碎片。
- **主要矿物** 用来作岩石分类及命名的矿物成分。
- **闪石类** 一类常见的成岩矿物，通常成分复杂，不过大多数都含有铁镁硅。
- **闪光化** 某些矿物由像氧化铁这样的微小似杆状侵入造成的闪亮色彩。
- **半深成的** 在地壳相对较浅处形成的侵入体。
- **劣形的** 结晶很差的晶体。
- **网状** 网格状的结构。
- **似长石矿物** 化学性质和结构与长石相似的一类矿物，不过硅含量很少。
- **自形的** 有良好晶面的晶体。
- **交代的** 通过添加或交代化学物质而改变岩石或矿物成分的过程。
- **次生矿物** 由于次生作用形成于岩石中的矿物。
- **异极** 晶体两端晶面发育不同。
- **块状** 无定形的矿物集合体。
- **豆石** 像豆大小，具有同心内部构造的沉积颗粒。
- **杏仁子** 喷出岩气泡被矿物填充而成常见的填充矿物包括石英、方解石和沸石类。
- **围岩** 围绕岩浆侵入体或熔岩岩浆的岩石。
- **针状** 针状矿物集合体。
- **层理** 沉积岩的构造，依层理面分层。
- **副矿物** 岩石中含量微少，从大小及化学成分上可忽略不计。
- **板岩劈理** 见于某些区域变质岩的构造，将岩石顺劈理分裂成薄片。
- **松脂光泽** 松脂般的反射。
- **枕状熔岩** 形成于海底，状如圆枕头状熔岩块。
- **矿脉** 层状矿物块体，常切穿岩层。
- **岩床** 整合于岩层的层状岩浆侵入体。
- **岩脉** 层状岩浆侵入体，并从切穿原岩石构造。
- **岩粉** 指细粒粉末状岩石碎屑，是冰川作用的产物。
- **碎屑的** 由原岩碎屑和颗粒组成的沉积物。
- **岩屑堆** 风化作用形成的未固结岩屑堆积，常见于山麓和悬崖下。
- **结构** 岩石颗粒或晶体的大小、形状及其相互之间的关系。
- **岩基** 巨大、形状不规则的岩浆岩体，由地下深处岩浆侵入而成。
- **岩盖** 有圆形顶部的岩浆侵入体，常有平坦的底部。
- **金刚光泽** 与金刚石光泽非常接近的明亮的矿物光泽。

**·金属光泽** 像新鲜金属一样的光泽。

**·放射性测年** 通过各种方法求得放射性元素与其蜕变产物之比之确定矿物和岩石的绝对年龄。

**·底面解理** 与矿物晶体底面平行的解理。

**·泥质的** 由泥或粘土形成的沉积物。

**·沸石** 为含水硅酸铝化物，其特点是易失水，又具可逆性。

**·玻璃光泽** 具有玻璃般的光泽。

**·玻璃质结构** 岩浆岩快速冷却形成玻璃。

**·树枝状** 树枝形矿物习性。

**·砂质** 沉积岩源于砂，也包括砂岩。

**·砂砾矿床** 常在冲积层或海滩形成的矿床，主要由比重大或耐风化的矿物构成。

**·重结晶** 在固体状态下，岩石中新矿物颗粒的形成。

**·侵入** 岩浆岩体侵入先成岩，常以强行侵入或岩浆顶蚀作用发生。

**·冲断层** 一种断层（地壳岩石的断裂），老岩层俯冲到新岩层上，形成低角度断层面。

**·结核** 一般为分散。单独的圆形结核状石块，常见于页岩或粘土层。

**·盐丘、盐穹** 大的侵入盐块体。

**·热液矿脉** 形成于岩石裂隙，矿物从富含水分的岩浆热液沉积而成。

**·造山带** 地壳正在或曾经活动，正在形成或曾经形成山脉的区域。

**·基质** 英语中也称 matrix，嵌有大粒晶体的岩石块体。

**·基性岩** 硅含量 45～55% 的岩浆岩，石英含量小于 10%，富含铁镁矿物。

**·接触变质带** 围绕岩浆侵入的地区，围岩发生接触变质作用。

**·假晶** 呈另一种矿物晶形的晶体。

**·分选良好** 组成沉积岩的颗粒大小均匀。

**·深成岩体** 由岩浆固结形成于地下深处的岩浆岩块体。

**·粘土矿物** 是一类铝硅酸盐矿物，常见于沉积岩。

**·粒状** 含颗粒或呈颗粒状。

**·粒级层、序粒层** 指沉积构造，意为岩层的颗粒从下到上逐渐由粗变细。

**·隐晶质的** 晶质，但颗粒非常微小，只有在显微镜才能看清单个晶体。

**·斑状** 岩浆岩结构，相对大的晶体嵌入岩石基质中。

**·斑状变晶** 变质岩的结构，相对大的晶体嵌入岩石基质中，如石榴石子嵌入片岩中。

**·斑晶** 嵌于岩浆岩基质中的相对大的晶体，并使岩石呈斑状结构。

**·超基性岩** 硅含量小于 45% 的岩浆岩。

**·蒸发岩** 咸水蒸发后形成的矿物或岩石。

**·暗淡光泽** 仅有微弱反射的光泽。

**·锯齿状** 矿物断口，其表面粗糙，有小突起，像铸铁断裂面。

**·微晶质** 显微镜下才能观察到的微小晶体。

**·解理** 某些矿物沿着与内部原子构造相关的层面断裂的方式。

**·酸性岩** 含 65% 以上的硅和 20% 以上石英的岩浆岩。

**·鲕粒** 组成鲕状岩的单个球状颗粒，通常为钙质，并有结核状或放射状结构。

**·漏斗晶** 一些石盐的晶面呈空洞、阶梯状的晶体。

**·整合** 岩石层序无间断的构造。

# 索 引

## 二 画



## 三 画



## 四 画



## 五 画



## 六 画

## 七　画



## 八　画

## 九　画

## 十　画



## 十一画

## 十二画

## 十三画



## 十四画



## 十五画



## 十六画



## 十七画